MW01147597

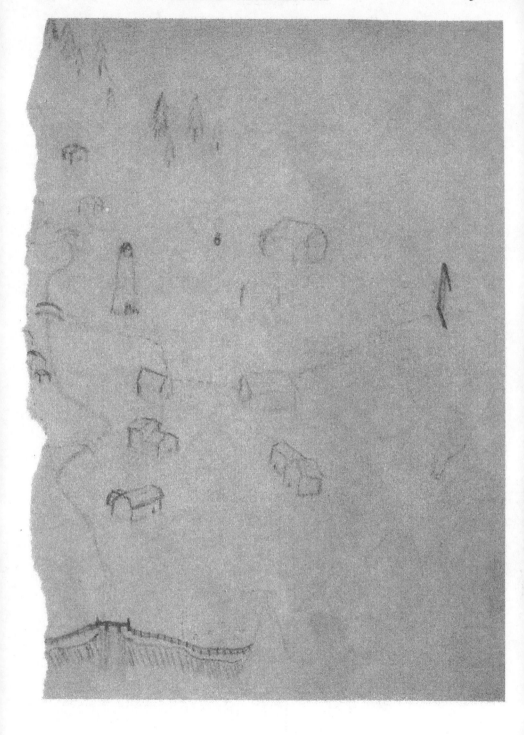

Copyright © 2012 by Mike Jack Stoumbos.

All rights reserved. No part of this book may be reproduced or transmitted in any form or by any means, electronic or mechanical, including photocopying, recording, or by any information storage and retrieval system, without permission in writing from the copyright owner.

This is a work of fiction. Names, characters, places and incidents either are the product of the author's imagination or are used fictitiously, and any resemblance to any actual persons, living or dead, events, or locales is entirely coincidental.

This book was printed in the United States of America.

ISBN-13: 978-1475123319

The Baron
Would Be Proud

a storyteller's story

Mike Jack Stoumbos

The People Will Be Acknowledged

As a first-time novelist, I was very fortunate to have the support of friends and family throughout the writing and publishing process. I am forever grateful to those who assisted me in putting this book together, from technological help, to beta-reading, and even general encouragement. As I work towards each new creative endeavor, I continue to benefit from the guidance of my wife, Morrigen.

In addition, I would like to show my appreciation for those who contributed to my fundraiser and pre-ordered copies of my book before there was a book to be had.

Tommy Yacoe, Michelle Cooper, Sarah Shay, Bobby Stoumbos, Sara and Alex Charney Cohen, Chris and Heidi (Dad and Mum) Stoumbos, Ian Bone, Joseph DeLong, Robin Rose, Ali Mitchell, Toni Rose, Tad Cook, Kari Jacobs, Sohroosh Hashemi, Hootan Esfahani, John Detherage, Tracy Hartford, Zachary Stoumbos, Thea Hamar, Beau Dupuis, Aaron Perlmutter, Joyce Kilmer, Jonathan H. Keith, Zack Demopoulos, Garth McMurtrey, Darkersun, Zoey Stoumbos, Tony Dozier, and Patrick Kelly

Thank you all—this book is dedicated to you.

"Humility is a virtue all preach, none practice,
and yet everyone is content to hear."

> ~ *John Selden (a 16th century English gentleman and juror who recorded so very many of his claims about the shoulds and should-nots of human interaction that we can only conclude he hadn't a thimbleful of that same virtue to his well-dressed name)*

In this hypocrisy, we storytellers are the worst of all.

Prologue – A Long Scroll and a Long Feather Quill

An old man sat upon an older rock.

The rock welcomed the man who sat upon him, and the man appreciated the rock upon which he sat. For some decades longer than either the man or the rock could remember, they had held this appointment every morning under the first traces of twilight, and as far as either of them knew, this particular grey and breezy day was entirely indistinguishable from any other.

Not unlike the man upon the rock, the rock sat upon a hill, and the two of them had had a similar standing date for a fair shot longer, and the man was quite content to climb the hill to commune with his rock. From there, upon his rock upon the hill, the man could see the whole of the town, just before it woke.

Every morning, he took with him a long scroll and a long feather quill. The quill and the scroll seemed about as perfect a match as the man and his rock, and could be easily carted around in the rope about his waist, resting just beside a second pen which probably hadn't carried ink in decades. Since he only ever used the feather quill, hardly anyone apart from the rock glimpsed or paid mind to the nib-pen, and never for long enough to notice or comment on the letters *JT* etched into the side and stamped with gold.

He never brought an inkwell with him, but somehow he never ran out of ink while upon the rock. The rock had been quite curious about this during their first few encounters but had resolved that the matter could be explained away simply with two brief acknowledgments. The first, the man was only ever with the rock for a short time, and hardly wrote anything of notable length. The second, the rock had concluded that the man probably had an inkwell at home.

The rock had never seen the man's home, but he could discern that it lay in the direction from which the man came each day. The hill was entirely aware of the old man's small abode and gladly let the rock know exactly where it sat.

The house was on a far corner of the village, farther away from the town square than most others, but that was just as well. The man, as we have noted, was getting on in years. Like most elderly men, he did not appreciate much in the way of loud noise and disturbance, but even in the center of their village, there was not much noise or disturbance to go around. Given its small size, the whole populace was largely quiet and calm, so volume was likely not the primary reason for the old man's withdrawal.

The man recognized that he was quite different from his neighbors, and, to be fair, so did they. Many of them accounted for this deviation by concluding that at his age he was most apart from his wits. A fair conjecture, seeing as this particular old man happened to be the oldest man in the entire village, and had been for twelve years by the time our story begins.

He did show some signs that he was in a less stable state than his younger fellows, for he had a very peculiar way of looking at people, as if he were hoping to find something, but grew quite disappointed when he discovered that it was not there. Many would add that he hardly listened to a word of any conversation, but would somehow know everything that had been said. Most could not recognize the more subtle points, but one aspect was acknowledged throughout the village: he hardly ever spoke a word but to make it a rhyme or a riddle.

Though they frequently whispered on his curious quotations, no one begrudged the old man his little quirks and eccentricities. It was a luxury well-afforded by his long life. Still, it did mean that he should be more inclined than the rest to keep to himself, and the villagers were more than happy to leave him be.

Regardless of rumors and assumptions, it hardly mattered to the rock whether the old man had in fact gone batty, and perhaps that is one reason that the old man and the rock got on so well.

So he sat, and the rock sat, and the hill sat, and the three watched as the sky above slowly began to brighten even though the sun was still buried beneath the jagged horizon. And as he sat, he took quill to scroll and began to scratch as he spoke, muttering an odd little poem which fortunately sets the stage for our story:

"There is a pass between the mountains,
Amidst the caves and rocks and snow,
And in that pass there lies a village,
Where trav'lers never seem to go.

No one can say how long they've been there—
Their numbers never seem to grow—
And yet not one will ever leave there,
And so it's all that they will know.

They have no cares, concerns, or questions
Except which way the wind should blow,
But you'll find they are truly happy;
And I suppose that goes to show…"

But then the old man stopped. He looked up and saw that the sun was creeping over the distant mountains and that its first true rays were shining upon his face. He stood, nodded toward the rock, and, with quill and scroll in hand, began down the hill once more.

The rock let out a relaxed sort of sigh, both in greeting of the coming sun and in thanks for the old man's simple words, for the rock and hill had watched over this village for more generations than they bothered to count. And the rock and hill—like every person living there—loved the little village.

But, even for all their years and wisdom, neither the rock nor its hill could have ever imagined what the coming winter would bring to their home.

This is of course the story of that little village, the town and community called Adleship Isle. But before I can tell *that* story, I have to tell *this* story.

Part I – An Inconvenient Winter Storm

There once was a god called Hephaestus...

I – A Bottle of Chianti

There was once a god called Hephaestus.

Bearing more power in his little finger than the whole of Greece, Hephaestus ruled the forge with absolute power and is hailed for having crafted Hermes' sandals, Helios' chariot, and even Achilles' armor. He was so successful that the Romans likewise adopted Hephaestus as a god, and—after a very strange bastardization of the once powerful name—rechristened him Vulcan. In remembrance of this lord of blacksmiths, sculptures of his likeness have been erected across the lands throughout history, several which represent him holding a hammer over an anvil and others in which he wields a pair of tongs over a barbecue grill. Some even glorify him enough to place an axe at his belt or in his third hand.

And yet, almost ironically, he never received quite the acclaim that one particular human seemed to have gathered quite easily.

In fact, the only way Hephaestus-the-god could even begin to compare to this man was that they coincidentally shared the same name. And rather than believing Hephaestus-the-man had been named for the god, several historians have popularized the notion that perhaps the Greek lord of blacksmiths (in his wisdom) foresaw the coming of the individual represented in our story and masterfully chose to name *himself* for the wonderful man who was then unborn.

But really, such was so very long ago that any argument on the plausible possibilities would serve no purpose other than to split hairs which are often better left unsplit.

But enough about the Greek Hephaestus! The man which this story regards happens to be an English Hephaestus, who, according to popular belief, was actually a bit taller than his Greek predecessor. To be fair though, even the English Hephaestus was only English by blood and birth. And even for all the honor and prestige of merry old England, the nation to which Hephaestus *truly* belonged was far more exclusive, far more elite, and—in almost every way possible—far superior.

Hephaestus had been ordained into an order of men who bore no country, yet somehow owned a piece of them all. He was a traveling merchant, and one of the select few men who could deservedly call himself by this enviable title. Now, perhaps some centuries later, with the advent of new means for mass-transportation, this particular career path might have become more commonplace and less special, but in the days of Hephaestus, very few men ever acquired the wealth or the wisdom to advance to those glorious ranks.

For Hephaestus, wealth and wisdom seemed to come quite easily. Of course there are hardly records of the revenues of persons within this profession, but even in the days long after they have gone, we can still manage a guess. How successful a merchant has been depends wholly on his reputation; if a man is known five hundred miles in any direction from his home town, he has made quite a dent in the unwritten annals of the traveling merchants; if a man is known five *thousand* miles in any direction, he is nothing short of legend.

In his day, and probably in many beyond, Hephaestus trumped all legends. At any rate, he must have; how many other merchants of that day do you know by name?

But even for his charms and good graces and genuinely honed skills, there is one factor of Hephaestus' fame which can only be attributed to luck: his long life.

By a certain age and after a certain number of years of traveling, most merchants would meet an unfortunate and occasionally humorous end while abroad. It might happen that—due to a mistranslation—a merchant would accidentally insult a godhead in a small indigenous village and thereafter find his very own *un*godhead promptly removed from his neck and replaced on a pike. Perhaps he would be converted by an emphatic blizzard into a sturdy block of ice while in the Himalayas, or he might volunteer to be a foundation of a newly-forming island when he slips into the mouth of a budding volcano somewhere in Polynesia.

To this end, most merchants would try not to venture too far from their native lands, or retire early enough to not suffer one of the terrible fates listed above. 'Go out while you're ahead,' so they say. If nothing else, most traveling merchants had the good sense to follow established travel routes, thereby increasing their chances of surviving to return home.

But Hephaestus, a pioneer in his trade, had not only traveled through every continent multiple times but usually managed to forge his own trail. So, against all odds, by the time we meet him in our story, Hephaestus had reached the noble age of sixty-five, by which most would have seen fit to retire. In fact, after so many years, Hephaestus' happy notoriety compelled all of his rivals to anxiously await his withdrawal so that they would no longer fall under his exemplary shadow.

The place where you will first meet this giant of the merchandise world happens to be a merchants' square, characteristic of an English market, and based in a port on the northern coast of France.

Hephaestus' servants were put up in lodgings for the night and his pack animals were in their stalls, being groomed and fed to prepare for the next day's departure. Hephaestus himself had a small matter of business to take care of before he could permit himself to relax like the rest, and for that, he would pay a visit to a local colleague[1].

See the man at the stall with the sign RARE HATS AND BOOTS OF THE ANCIENT ORIENT? See how this little man grows green with envy when Hephaestus enters the square, how his brows crinkle into one another, making lines in that dome of a forehead? This man is called Chefield—a curious name, seeing as he's neither a chef nor a field. Nonetheless, he is a traveling merchant. You might be wondering why his stand looks so permanent a structure when he, like Hephaestus, travels the world. Well, it happens that *this* day is the sixteenth of December, which would prompt many travelers in the northern hemisphere to take long and much-deserved hiatuses from their journeys.

All merchants at some time or other would break down their carts to set up shop and live like most stationary folk, at least for a month or so before going on again. Some stopped for Christmas, some for their home-nation's Independence Day. For Chefield, like most *a*religious, *a*political persons, the period that governed his longest vacation was that during which it was least practical to travel.

He knew—or at least assumed—that Hephaestus did the same at some point or another, even though neither he nor any other in their line of work had the slightest notion of where Hephaestus stayed.

---

[1] This term is—of course—a misnomer. No other in Hephaestus' domain would even be able to compare to, much less eclipse, this lord of merchants. I only use the term because that's what Hephaestus, in his mercy, would call this other gentleman.

Chefield was one individual who frequently tried to pry this information out of Hephaestus—as you will soon see for yourself.

"Good evening, Chefield!" Hephaestus called as he crossed to the stand, a smart cherrywood cane crooked underarm.

"Oh good lord!" exclaimed Chefield, who—as I noted—is not religious. "My dear friend Hephaestus! Can it be that our prodigious brother has finally returned?"

Hephaestus neglected to answer the inane rhetorical question, but contributed some non sequitur smalltalk of his own, "And you are looking in very good health as well, Mister Chefield."

"You're too kind," Chefield replied through a smile that was too big for his cheeks. "Have you just arrived in town?"

"And soon to leave as well, it seems."

"Always on the move, Hephaestus," returned Chefield, wagging a finger, "I've always admired that." (This was how his mouth translated jealousy.) "When do you leave?"

"Tomorrow morning. And my haste," he explained, "is precisely why I would beg a favor of you. Forgive me for so quickly segueing to such mercenary matters."

"Oh, no, no, no, *no!*" insisted Chefield, promptly placing a CLOSED sign in front of his little stand and stepping out from behind it to converse with a man who stood at least a head taller than him, and whose beard measured another two heads on its own.

Chefield was quite eager to help Hephaestus, (even more eager to inform rivals that their chief competitor had come to him first). Though he did not yet know the favor, he was quite tickled by the prospect. "I must say that I'm charmed by the very notion that you'd come to me," he said, paraphrasing less eloquently what I said only moments before. "Whatever can I do for you?"

"Well, sadly, I need to replace one of my servants."

"Oh dear. Anyone I know?"

"I'm afraid so," Hephaestus said, nodding, "My Mister Thurgood, who's been in this almost as long as I have, it seems has found it necessary to retire."

"That's terrible!" exclaimed Chefield with the kind of sincerity that only comes from salesmen.

"Well, it's understandable, really. The man is near-seventy, and the last time we went through Greece, he decided to settle down in a home in Zakinthos, where—as it turns out—he already has three illegitimate children."

Hinting, but trying not to sound pressuring, Chefield noted, "Well, you're not too far behind him then, are you, Hephaestus? You just had your sixty-fifth, if I'm not mistaken."

"You are," lied Hephaestus, knowing that he meant age and not number of children, "but, in any case, I need yet another man, to fill Mister Thurgood's shoes and complete my seven for my next tour."

"And I'm touched that you came to me."

"Oh, I'm not necessarily looking to relieve *you* of one of your men," Hephaestus hurriedly clarified, "but you know this town, and I'm in need of one now, before I cross back into England."

"You're looking into some tough terrain then?" asked Chefield.

"Very. Now, if I'm not mistaken Chefield, you're here every winter, so I'm sure you know someone who—"

But Chefield, having noticed an opportunity, interrupted his 'friend' mid-sentence, to say, "Yes, every year. I must say, I adore this port; I'd wager it's one of the best places on earth."

And Hephaestus, graciously accepting the bait, returned, "Maybe *one of*."

"O-oh?" Chefield serpented closer beside Hephaestus. "I hear a challenge in your tone, old friend. Where is it that *you'll* be spending your next holiday?"

Many men would have skirted the issue, played the game for a little longer, but Hephaestus, lord of formidable constancy replied, "You know very well that I don't discuss it." Before Chefield could say anything further, Hephaestus went on: "Now you can ask all you like, but from one colleague to another, I respect you enough to let you know that I will never tell you where it is I settle."

Graciously taking the rejection, Chefield stepped back from Hephaestus, allowing him his victory. "You have to excuse us our curiosity. When the most known man for hundreds of miles disappears every year for most of two months, people start to show suspicion."

Chefield waited for Hephaestus to reply, but since he conceded nothing, Chefield eventually said, "It must be paradise."

"Yes. Chiefly because people like you don't know it exists." Because Chefield looked severely offended (an expression that hadn't a touch of authenticity), Hephaestus said, "Our people trade information by the fistful, Mister Chefield. Now, I think my home-away-from-road is the most serene bit of civilization I've ever touched, and if a whole bunch of merchants were to discover it, they would ruin it."

Thankfully, Hephaestus didn't go into exactly how or why, or it might make some of this story appear redundant.

"Now I've lost my train of thought," said Hephaestus, clearly just changing the subject as he scratched his grey head. "What were we on about before?"

"Your servant," supplied Chefield.

"Oh yes!" came Hephaestus, who had remembered all along. "So do you happen to know any available young men that I might enlist in my employ? And remember that I don't go under fourteen, no matter how desperate the parents are to ship them off."

"Yes, actually, come to think of it," said Chefield, just coming to think of it, "a barrowman's son by the name of Lance: strong, strapping, nineteen I believe, and not burdened by an abundance of brains."

"And he's available?"

"Well, not exactly: he's due to ship out on Sly Finnigan's Tour due south in mid-February if memory serves, but I'm sure if you offered Sly a bottle of that lovely Chianti you carry, you could take the boy of his hands."

"Oh, and which Chianti would that be?" Hephaestus asked, only somewhat innocently, tapping his cane lightly on the stone ground.

Chefield's saliva glands worked overtime at the memory of that beautiful exotic taste, and the muscles in his face strained to keep him from drooling. His eyes widened in hopeful anticipation, and he replied, "The same one you let us try last year."

"Well, I see rumors of my Tuscany tour precede me," Hephaestus said. "I suppose I could part with a bottle in exchange for his finding a new deckhand."

"You know, I can tell him for you when he sets up shop tomorrow morning."

"That would be wonderful! I do however need to find the boy tonight. You see I'm looking to take a boat up as soon as possible, as I have a rather pressing appointment in our northern motherland on the eighteenth."

Chefield whistled. "Cutting it a little close, aren't you?"

"Terribly, yes, but I've a favor to call in from a captain with a very fast vessel, and frankly this appointment cannot wait." Swiftly sidestepping any potential questions, Hephaestus changed the subject with, "Out of curiosity, do you know the boy's shoulder-span?"

"Not off the top of my head," said Chefield, who'd begun to scrawl Lance's address on a scrap of paper. "Why?" he asked with a smirk, "Are you having him fitted for a uniform?"

"Hardly," said Hephaestus, whose servants did in fact wear matching uniforms. "Just curious on how stout he is."

"Well, he's built tough," Chefield assured him. "Here," handing Hephaestus the paper, "this is where you can find the boy. Give me two bottles, and I can get one to Sly."

"Capital!" declared Hephaestus. "I can have those for you first thing in the morning. Oh! And do you happen to know if he understands Greek?"

"Who, the boy?" Chefield resumed his place behind his stand and downturned the CLOSED sign. "No, I would imagine not. Probably has English, French, and a wink of Spanish."

"Oh, I was afraid of that," said Hephaestus. "With the absence of Mister Thurgood, I no longer have Greek covered among my languages." It was common for the longer-range merchants to carry translators as their servants for every major language they should come across. As Hephaestus annually circumnavigated the globe, he was far from an exception.

"Well, with any luck you won't need it for quite a time," offered Chefield.

"Yes, but it makes it so much harder to sell ancient plays and documents when I can't even make out the phonetics." Hephaestus probably would have kept griping if not for two things: the first, it was unbecoming on a man of his reputation, and the second, he really was in a hurry and hoped to retire by sunset in order to rest for the long journey. "Oh well," he resolved.

"Hephaestus," came Chefield once more, his brow this time arched quizzically, "if your paradise is so special a secret, what do you do to ensure that your servants will never lead anyone there?"

"Honestly, I don't have to do anything. My retired servants would never let on such a precious secret, but even if they wanted to, they'd be held back by two insurmountables. No one they told would ever be able to find it, and no one they told would be willing to believe that such a place still exists."

And with a small, somewhat smug smile, Hephaestus left his colleague to his hat-stand and set off to complete the rest of his evening's affairs.

II – Eggs

This is Julian. He will be playing this story's hero, if that's alright with you. Now, I know at first glance he may not *look* like a hero. Perhaps he's a little on the scrawny side, and his nose may stick out a bit, but take one good look into those big brown eyes and tell me that's not the truest soul you've ever seen.

Really, I dare you.

Look, if you're not quite satisfied, firm up his physique in your imagination and assume that he has the hands of a master sculptor who still seeks his medium.

Julian was seventeen at the time, and he lived alone.

He just so happened to be the youngest person in the whole of the village to have his own house, which had brought him some prestige and some speculation. It was the house that his father had built, and that his mother had tended to, but neither one of them built nor tended any longer. When they had first passed—one right after the other, without hesitation—the whole village mourned collectively, and everyone sympathized with the then fifteen-year-old orphaned boy.

Sympathy turned to curiosity when Julian elected himself too old to be taken in by adoptive parents, and some still did wonder why the boy never married or opted to live with another family. However, after two years had passed, only those closest to him still thought much on his somewhat anomalous lifestyle.

His existence would have been considered far more peculiar had he not taken up his father's work soon after the man's death. Once again, his age and autonomy were peculiar, but his work did serve to fill the void of a carpenter in Adleship Isle and allowed for the small populace to move on all the more rapidly from the tragedy.

So by the time he began this fateful winter, Julian was known by the collective town as merely "that carpenter, who seemed to get things done in a timely and sensible manner." To those who regularly employed his services, he was "the pleasant young lad, who had taken a near mastery of his humble trade." To those who considered themselves close friends of his, he was "a dreamy-eyed boy, who—despite the tragedy in his life—was a delightful and interesting individual to have around."

In his own eyes, Julian felt out of place.

It was not that he did not like his home town. In truth, he had never known anything else with which to compare it, and neither had anyone else who lived there. Even so, Julian was convinced that he was missing something—or that something was missing him—and that it had very much to do with the place he called home.

Piers, the town shepherd, and his wife, Lilli, the girl with the beautiful voice, often surmised that it was because Julian had not found himself a wife. But of course, as the town's newlyweds they would naturally view life in terms of love.

Clemens, a grocer, would often tell his wife, Rosa, that the boy's mannerisms could be attributed to the fact that he did not have enough to keep himself occupied, that the trick to finding belonging was staying busy. Of course, "busy" was probably the defining factor of Clemens and Rosa's whole existence. While Clemens raised the finest potatoes anyone had ever seen and managed the town's food storage and distribution, Rosa was quite engaged in raising their five children as well as a leading member of the seamstress circle.

Sherman, the tailor below the falls, assured his wife, Hannah, that Julian's oddities were merely part of a phase of life, and that it only showed because he had neither parents nor siblings with whom he could discuss these emotions, thereby purging them from his mind and making him the clearer for their absence. Hannah, a schoolteacher, could hardly argue, having dispatched two 'fine examples' of her own into homes, lives, and trades of their own.

Though neither Dietrich nor Elke could agree on the particular phrasing, they both seemed to feel that Julian's oddness could be explained by his 'higher mental aptitude.' Dietrich, a stargazer and astrologer, was pleased to find himself slightly peculiar as well and took it as a sign of intelligence. His wife, who spent most of her time testing the boundaries of the science of pastry-baking, felt that Julian possessed that rare, instinctual gift of higher perception, which she had accredited to herself. Keep in mind that townsfolk were inclined to take this couple's opinions with a fistful or so of salt, which was fair because neither spouse thought its counterpart had a jot of wisdom. They had been married for over forty years and both seemed to prefer Julian's company to each other's. Perhaps this was why they had never had any children.

Of course, there was more to the boy's predicament that had not yet been told, but that's another day and another chapter. The morning in this chapter has very little significance, other than that it occurs just two days before the most momentous holiday in the town's calendar. Coincidentally on that day, Julian woke up precisely as Hephaestus' voyage to England was being launched.

His nose responded to the sun before his eyes and ears. He groaned once and turned over onto his left shoulder, trying to shake off his obligation to rise. Nonetheless, a fierce call of nature prompted his feet over the side of the bed and groggily out the front door of his cottage. He was greeted by a not-quite-pleasant blast of light reflected from the snow of the distant peaks. The cold began to creep up his ankles, so in haste, Julian undid his trousers and put a hole in the dirt.

He went back inside, trying to remember which day it was. He splashed cool water against his face, scrubbed at his teeth with a dry rag, and lifted his bangs to feel for how many new bumps had emerged on his forehead overnight.

He pulled on boots that were a little too short about the ankles, but nonetheless fit his soles. Then, taking his coat from the hook on the wall, Julian exited his front door yet again and took the path down the hill.

The hill and the rock watched him and found themselves thinking, *Ah, there goes Julian again.* The rock on the hill sat just above Julian's house, which sat just above the dwelling of the old man, who lived with his daughter, her husband, and their little girl, Miriam.

Miriam was six. She had blue eyes and blonde hair and looked to be the picture-perfect fairy-tale daughter, a comparison that her father had never thought on, having never read a fairy-tale—or anything else for that matter which came from outside their town. Miriam slept in the loft in their small house, against a partition beyond which slept her grandfather.

Her parents, Manuel and Meredith, shared a room on the ground floor, which was adjacent to a lively little kitchen, with a nice table and a strong stone oven. When Julian came in through the front door, Meredith was already at the stove, her hands busied with a breakfast befitting folks soon to put in a hard day's work.

"Mornin' Meredith," said Julian. He put a hand about the woman's shoulder, kissed her cheek, then plucked up two boiled eggs which he took to the table.

"Julian? Oh, Julian!" she said, whirling about, "Dietrich asked Manny if you'd be by today."

"For the roof?" Julian asked, juggling a hot boiled egg between his palms. "Yes, I'm actually on my way, just have a—uh—breakfast issue first," indicating the egg.

Shoeless feet padded rapidly down the ladder, and with them came a small voice, calling, "Julian!"

"Miriam!" Julian returned. "My little snap-pea, how are you doing this morning?"

But Miriam gave no answer. As excited as she was to see the closest thing to a sibling she had ever known, Miriam merely threw her arms about Julian's neck in greeting.

"Honey," said her mother, "why don't you go wash your face, and I'll put out some eggs for you."

Miriam nodded and left the room.

"Julian," sang Meredith—as she did whenever she called a name, "did you see my father on your way down?"

"Hmm?" asked a muffled Julian, toast crumbs slipping from his lips. "No, no'm," came the answer, "Pops is likely on his rock again riddling his verse."

"Oh, I wish he wouldn't this time of year," replied a worried Meredith, wringing well-pruned hands on a pristinely white apron. "It's getting colder every day, and he seldom remembers to wear shoes anymore."

"And it's starting to rub off on Miriam," said Julian with a smirk.

Heavier feet, with markedly leathery soles, clopped through the kitchen behind Julian and arrived beside Meredith. Beneath the bush of his mutton chops and bearing breath of similar odor, Manuel's lips made contact with his wife's cheek, eliciting from her a charming giggle.

"Morning, Julian," he bid in a rough but warm voice.

"Mornin', Manuel," Julian returned.

Manuel sat beside Julian on the wooden bench with yet another hard clop, and asked after the eggs, which Meredith merrily served.

"Have you got Dietrich's roof today, then?" asked Manuel, before shoveling a forkful of egg into his already round cheeks.

"Yessir, and Rosa's place and Sherman the tailor's," replied Julian. "Everyone's got some last-minute request before the traveler gets here. You'd think he'd never seen the village before."

Manuel nodded in earnest, "Hear, hear."

"And—with all the stuff he brings—I *know* he's been to much more elegant places than here," he went on. As Meredith set a steaming plate before him, Julian exclaimed, "Mm'boy! What's on these today, Mum[2]?"

"Same's yesterday," replied a bustling Meredith, whose right hand turned the eggs on the skillet while her left generously buttered the toast. Her kitchen was always its busiest in the morning, but it knew that it would get a rest the moment the majority of the household left.

Miriam came running back into the kitchen, almost tripping twice on her skirts. "Julian! Julian!" she squeaked as she made her way to the table. "Did Momma te—"

"Oh, honey, that's Grandpa's seat," said Meredith, before Miriam had even pulled herself onto the bench.

Miriam quickly scooted aside. "Julian, did Momma tell you she found a mouse living in a cabbage?"

"Oh, my goodness, it was dreadful!" exclaimed Meredith without turning away from her stove.

Leaning across the table to his daughter, Manuel gently took her hand and said, "Mayhap best not to talk on that while we're eating, dear."

"Just lying there, right inside the head!" Meredith went on, clearly having missed Manuel's comment. "Burrowed in like it was a house, of all things, and then I go to peel away a leaf and out it jumps!"

"You know," said Julian, pointing with his fork, "They say Franz knows how to deal with rodent issues in gardens. If you want me to talk to him, I could—"

"Momma!" called Miriam, just over Julian's voice, "Are my eggs done, Momma?"

"Almost, honey," sang back Meredith.

"But don't put 'em all in one basket."

This last comment caused both men to look at their plates and grin, biting back the chuckles that tried to emerge whenever the grandfather entered a conversation. Meredith and Miriam turned their

---

[2] I should point out that 'mum' was merely a term of endearment with no motherly connotations, seeing as Meredith was less than a decade older than her orphaned friend.

attention to the barefooted figure in the doorway. Not a one of them knew the expression Jonas had just used.

Jonas would be the name of the old man that we met earlier in our story. However, because there are multiple old men in this narrative, and one of them is soon to adopt that very same pet name, we shall call Jonas 'Jonas' hereafter, and sometimes 'Pops' as granted by Julian, Manuel, and even Meredith sometimes.

Jonas only managed to get a few steps into the room before Meredith rushed to his side to escort him to the table. Though he tried to grunt her off his arm, his daughter was too persistent to let him go until he was securely installed beside Miriam on the bench.

"Dad, what did I say about wearing shoes outside?" asked a worried Meredith as she rushed yet another plate to her petite daughter.

"He says, 'Wear the sole, heal the soul,'" Miriam chimed, as though she'd given that rationale before.

Exasperated, Meredith put her fists on her hips and sighed toward the ceiling. The ceiling didn't mind. "Honey, I don't even know what that means."

"Oh, it's a pun," explained Julian. Indicating his foot with his fork, he said, "See if you wear down the sole of your foot, then you're actually refreshing your—"

"Yes, *thank you*, Julian."

The boy shut his mouth and resumed chewing. He looked to Manuel, who shrugged then looked to Miriam, who smiled.

"Dad," said Meredith, placing one hand on his shoulder, "look, I don't want you going outside without your shoes or else you'll get sick."

Jonas looked at the hand on his shoulder, then at Meredith's concerned expression, which he only aggravated further when he returned, "Hey-ho, nobody's home."

Meredith shook her head and returned to the sizzling skillet on the stove.

To change the potentially somber subject, Julian turned to Manuel and asked, "Are you going to be working the food stores today?"

"Mm-hmm!" hummed an affirmative through a pocket of eggs. After a swallow, Manuel said, "Yes, well, store sorting. We're rationing for when Hephaestus comes."

"Gotta plan for parties," said Julian.

"Starting with tomorrow's," continued Meredith.

"Assuming he's on schedule," remarked Manuel.

"Well, he has been every year," said Meredith, rushing a plate of eggs to her father.

"You're forgetting?" returned Manuel. "Think it was twelve years ago, a wheel on his cart broke, set him back four days. I'll tell you what, scared the folks half to death." He nodded to Julian, whose wide eyes indicated his intrigue. "See, as long as I can remember, he'd never been late before, and who knows what could have happened to him in that wide old world outside."

"Manny," hissed Meredith, sitting down with a plate of her own, "you'll frighten Miriam, all that talk of the Big Out There."

"He will not!" protested Miriam, sputtering flecks of egg across the table. Miriam was careful not to catch Julian's eye, afraid that he would catch her lie.

To be fair, Julian was quite anxious at the idea himself; everyone living in the Isle carried a fascinated fear when it came to the 'Big Out There,' which made them all the more titillated over their imminent visitor.

And why shouldn't they have been impressed? So far as they knew no one had ever successfully entered or left their town, save for the legendary Hephaestus and his servants, and how Hephaestus found it in the first place was anyone's guess. But this story is not about the wonder-merchant's discovery of Adleship Isle; it's about Julian, the town, and—at this moment—the little family that he liked to think of as his own.

The characters, you've met: obviously there's Manuel, called Manny by his loving wife Meredith; Miriam, their six-year-old snap-pea of a daughter; and finally Jonas, the oldest man in the village and Meredith's father, who, in the last decade or so, had drifted from his senses almost altogether.

To be fair, Jonas had hardly been a normal individual in any of the Isleans' recollections. Everyone in the town knew that he liked his riddles and puns and rhymes, and even into his sixties could be heard singing from the roof of the bell-tower just off the town square.

But after his wife had passed, the old man began to appear even older and had to be taken in by his daughter. By this time, he would no longer sing amiably, but merely mutter little expressions, sometimes bitter-sounding, to himself and anyone within earshot.

On this particular morning, after staring at his steaming eggs on a plate, Jonas interrupted the Hephaestus talk with, "If'n I ever saw a chicken, whose ticker wasn't tickin', it would cause my blood to thicken, and my tummy too would sicken."

The others stopped talking and looked up at the loony old man. There was a moment of silence, but not long enough to kill the lively breakfast conversation.

It was Julian who picked up the conversation once more with, "Is 'sicken' the best? I would think 'stricken.'"

"And I'm sure you could use 'pickin'' in there," offered Manuel, nodding at his own genius of an idea.

"What about 'quicken'?" asked Meredith and was immediately met with murmurs of approval.

"There's always 'clicking' and 'flicking,'" Julian suggested.

"Licking?" squeaked an excited Miriam, drawing laughter from the others, who went on then to playfully argue over 'sticking,' 'pricking,' and 'tricking.'

Now, I don't want you to think of this breakfast's affairs as an anomaly; this was the routine that followed Julian and his assumed family every day, excepting illness and holidays. In fact, the only thing that could mark this particular day was its near proximity to Hephaestus' arrival, and even that was an expected, annual occurrence.

In the opinion of your narrator, the people of this town called Adleship Isle had gotten a little too used to 'expected.' Fate—in the form of a mountain blizzard—must have found it high time to rattle them.

III – A Treatment Called Liverpool Silver

The Baron Pan Bordolo always waxed his mustache. He used a treatment called Liverpool Silver, which smelled a little like dried clams stewed in musket grease, and he diligently applied it every morning. He would curl the ends into perfect ringlets which would close around either side of his nose when he smiled.

The Baron was not nearly old nor stuffy enough for such a fashion to look becoming on him. He claimed to wear the curled stache for two reasons: first, that it made his eyes twinkle, and second, that no matter how harsh the wind, his mustache would never freeze.

This may seem a somewhat irrelevant function, given the Baron's eyebrows and lashes were already caked in ice and snow. But because his Liverpudlian Anti-Freeze kept the frost off his upper lip, the Baron remained happy, even when his companions were not. Understandably, morale is difficult to preserve after a few days lost in the mountains.

The five walked steadily eastward in single file, as they had since their transatlantic voyage had safely docked in the Baron's dear homeland. The Baron took second in line. In front of him walked a thin man; behind him followed an old man, a short man, and a giant man, who, with the help of two noble beasts of burden, towed a roofed wooden cart.

In a clarion voice that rang out with the grandeur of churchbells, the Baron called over the wind, "Fletcher! Any sign of the road?"

The thin man called Fletcher had long, golden-brown hair, which was always tethered behind his head. He had large eyes that magnified his every expression and emphasized the childlike fascination he had with just about everything. (Everything, that is, except snails; Fletcher despised snails.)

"Nothing, boss!" he called back, "If there's a path anywhere 'round here, we've already lost it."

The short man who walked behind the old man was holding a sharp black cane, which he thrust through the snow. Upon impacting ground, he tore the skewer from the earth and authoritatively declared, "No one's walked on this spot for a hundred years."

"Thank you, Geru!" the Baron shouted. "Oswald, can you see any lights ahead?"

The old man called Oswald squinted against the pelting snow and demanded, "What, what, what?"

Geru, a short, square face to match his short, square body, reached up to grab hold of Oswald's elbow. The old man startled, issuing another pair of shivering "What"s.

Geru yelled up to him, his high, clanging voice breaking against the cold air, "He asked if you see any lights ahead!"

"Oh! Oh, lights! Yes, lights!" the old man muttered—or was possibly yelling; we cannot be certain. Oswald proceeded to rummage through a long faded coat, fishing about for a telescope which turned out to be over his shoulder. Putting the telescope up to his eye, he announced, "It's white, Sir Baron. White, white all around."

"Well, this is no good," said the Baron, and his mustache bobbed in agreement. "Pigby!" he called to the last in their line, "How are the yaks looking?"

The giant man called Pigby had a thick leather belt about his chest. The belt was tethered to the wagon tongue which was tethered to the yaks. Were you to see the size and strength of this individual, you might indeed believe that Pigby was pulling more weight than either of the beasts beside him. The giant man had no hair and no hat to match, and was darker of skin than any single person in the United Kingdom[3].

Pigby bellowed up to the Baron, "They'll be needing a rest soon, boss!"

"We might need to make camp for the night," said the Baron.

"'Night'?" repeated the irritated Geru. "It might as well be midafternoon for all we can see through the clouds!"

Indeed, they had walked into a doozie of a blizzard during a doozie of a winter, and the sky looked to be night above anyway.

The Baron stopped walking. The old man, the short man, and finally the giant man with the two beasts also stopped. The thin man

---

[3] A term which was then just two years old.

walked only a few paces farther before turning back to face his leader for instructions.

Baron Pan Bordolo sighed.

"Alright," he said to Pigby, "ask Ten ha if she'll be ready to make camp."

Pigby was about to call her name when the door of the wagon opened, issuing jets of steam into the snowy air. Behind the steam appeared the face of a girl, but indeed not just any girl. Ten ha, by far the youngest in the Baron's troupe, happened to appear exceedingly more bizarre than any of her terribly extreme companions could ever hope to.

The intense steam from her indoor mobile kitchen made it so the crew (and the audience of this book) had to receive her gradually, which I actually find fortunate for our purposes. After all, gossip and rumors indicate that the mere sight of Ten ha's face had forced several men across the lands to vow lifelong silence and reverence believing that they had accidentally seen god.

Her eyes were always the first to be noticed, seeing as they were actually purple bordering on magenta, excepting when the light would glance against them just so, creating an unmistakable gold sheen before resuming their violet hue.

Next people had to try to suss out her hair. Now, even I cannot quite discern how red and silver managed to mix without looking the least bit pink, but apparently whatever agent mixed Ten ha's genetic material did, rendering a hue that was nearly as shocking as her eyes and even more lustrous.

The following features: her lips, her nose, those curious cheekbones were often noted as 'possibly foreign' or some other indistinct distinction, such commentary characteristic of persons who could hardly grasp proportional anatomy and instead took their chances with straws.

Curiously, no one really noticed her skin tone. It's hard to say exactly what shade it took, but the color somehow compelled people to reassess other skin tones with some scrutiny, wondering why this person was so pale or dark or yellow, red, brown, pink compared to what they suddenly saw as the perfection of Ten ha.

The Baron's explanation for Ten ha's appearance was simple; mine will not be. When asked as to the reason for the young woman's eclectic sort of beauty, he'd simply say, "Breathtaking, isn't she?"

Of course, as foster parent, Baron knew the long version as well, but didn't find it necessary to let on the details of Ten ha's origins.

The cliff-notes version goes like so: Ten ha's father was a half-Negro, half-Cuban, native-American-raised sugar slave[4] who spoke fluent French, Spanish, Portuguese, and a certain Dutch dialect that very few Austrians had ever heard of. He was hired—(yes, as a free man)—into the trade—('the trade' being the service of traveling merchants)—when he was seventeen. Per request of his master, he converted to Judaism, (though never entirely abandoning his mother's instructions of "The-Good-Lord-God-and-Savior-Jesus-Christ-young-man!"),   and traveled along this way until he met Ten ha's mother at age twenty-two.

Ten ha's mother was the daughter of a traveling merchant, a Chinese-Indian-Indonesian man, who spawned her through a French-Russian Buddhist whore who stewed opium in the Saudi State of Nejd. Growing up, Ten ha's mother worked as a scullery maid and heard complaints between Arabs and Hindus so often that soon she had acquired Arabic and Hindi (obviously) as well as her mother's Russian, her father's Mandarin, and a kind of Egyptian sign language that most modern historians are convinced never existed.

The end result is fairly commonplace: Ten ha's mother and father met one night, and when their respective employers were sleeping, proceeded to produce Ten ha. How she came to be with the Baron is a story that might not be appearing in this text.

All that you need to know is that Ten ha, a girl of only sixteen acted as the Baron's translator and his limitlessly international cook, and that she was sticking her head out of the surprisingly warm wagon to ask, "Yes, sir?"

"Are we ready to make camp, my dear?" the Baron shouted back.

"The stove's keeping nice and hot!"

Whether or not we see this as an answer, Pigby determined that it was good enough and let down his load, indicating that the panting pack animals could do the same.

---

[4] Yes, slavery finds mention in this text. As it turns out, the events I will describe occur just after the turn of the 19th century, so slavery would still be a running institution in the new nation of the United States as well as a handful of European countries. That being said, there is none and never has been in the little village of Adleship Isle, so you need not worry there. However, if this first mention offends you terribly, I can only apologize and inform you that you are not obligated to finish this text if you do not wish to.
As a footnote to the footnote, if this text were assigned by your 9th grade English teacher, you should probably disregard the previous sentence.

"Finally," grumbled Geru as he trudged toward the cart. (I must admit, I find it difficult not to giggle at the image of a man as short as Geru, who stood four-foot-seven-and-five-eighths, trying to wade through snow which probably passed his knees.) He entered the bright yellow warmth of their cart, bidding Ten ha to quick shut the door behind him.

The Baron tried to find a patch of snow that was stiffer than the others around, as if standing higher might permit him to see farther in a blizzard. From the highest available mound, he peered out through the wind and glimpsed a great whopping nothing.

The thin man approached him, asking in a dialect that tried to blend Sydney with Dublin, "Boss, should I scout ahead a ways?"

"No, Fletcher, we'd best set for the night, hope the whole thing blows over." Fletcher gave a nod and retreated to the cart, and the Baron resumed with, "Pigby—"

The giant man could tell by his employer's tone that a negative bidding was about to be conveyed. "Yes, sir," he replied without sign of sway.

"Pigby, the weight of the cart may be too much to brave the storm. We might need—" At this the Baron hesitated, for he dared not say 'dispose' before his companions. "To re...think—*rearrange*, Pigby, the merchandise that's slowing the yaks."

Pigby's jaw trembled in apprehension, for this unmentioned suggestion was a ghastly affront to all of their sensibilities. The artifacts they carried had been gathered from every corner of the world—(keep in mind that some persons still thought that the world was a cube in those days)—and Pigby, the master of accounts and inventory, could not bear to rate value for weight and dispose of the least necessary objects.

"The-the merchandise, sir?" repeated Pigby, with such a poignant stammer that it begs a second mention. And whether or not he agreed with the Baron, he found himself saying, "I think—I believe, sir, that the yaks can manage. And I'm not falling short yet, sir—am I?"

This attempt to save their hard-earned goods was met with a sympathetic smile and a command that was worded as a request. "Please take a final inventory for me and when next we advance we'll determine... how best to allocate resources."

Pigby's head visibly drooped into his shoulders and, like a scolded pup, he made his way back to the cart with a loyal, "Yessir."

The Baron watched as the door was opened and reshut, leaving him to stand in darkness once more. He looked to the final party, the old man who—bless his persistence—still stood with his spyglass, scanning the invisible horizon for any trace of light.

"Oswald," said the Baron, drawing nearer to the old man. "Oswald, we can't go any farther today. They're all exhausted—as are you."

The old man did not withdraw the spyglass from his eye until the Baron placed a hand on his shoulder, causing him to startle. "Oswald?" asked the Baron, a concerned smile beneath his mustache. "Time to go back inside, old friend."

Oswald looked as though he should protest, then acquiesced by slinging the old telescope over his shoulder. He started to speak, found his voice too cold to emerge, swallowed to warm his throat, then tried again: "Sir," he began, "should we—what I mean, sir—should we think to-to turn around and make our way back?"

The Baron raised a questioning eyebrow; this was a suggestion that very few of his friends had dared ever venture. The Baron Pan Bordolo never turned back. This was not his cool-guy catch-phrase—the Baron didn't believe that catch-phrases were cool. He was simply very persistent, persistent enough to arbitrarily decide to cross a series of mountains in December when there were at least a dozen easily-available alternatives. Some might see this as a fault, but we shall determine it to be an endearing quirk if you don't mind.

His sense of determination was as firm as the rings of his mustache, and so he replied to Oswald, "England's not a very wide island, Oswald. We're bound to reach the other side eventually."

"I see, sir," said Oswald with a nod.

"Get some rest," urged the Baron, knowing Oswald would take the friendly nudge as an order from a superior.

To that end, the old man straightened with military rigor and saluted his Baron. He probably would have turned sharply on a heel to make his exit, but for the ankle-deep snow which would have persuaded him to career over. But as he began towards the cart, Oswald came to notice—as did this narrator—that the Baron did not follow him. Turning back over one shoulder, he asked, "I say, are you coming, sir?"

The Baron appeared not to hear. He tried to squint, to lean forward, to poise on his tip-toes, but to no avail; nothing would grant him farther sight through the whipping and winding snow.

The Baron Pan Bordolo reached into his jacket and withdrew from the breast-pocket a small leather-bound book, whose spine he creased over itself once he had flipped to the right page. Whether or not he could actually make out the faded text in the dim light, he seemed to smirk with satisfaction while he ran his index finger along the margin. He closed and repocketed it, content turn back to his man to say, "Yes, Oswald; I'm coming."

Oswald waited for his Baron to arrive at his side before proceeding back to their cozy cart, where the thin man, the short man, the giant man, and the girl had set down for supper. Once they had closed the door behind them, there was hardly a fleck of light outside. But no matter how cold, harsh, or lifeless the terrain ahead, the Baron had made his decision—and a good thing too, or else this story would never have occurred, would never have been recorded for posterity, and you would not be excitedly reading it right now.

Against any of their best suspicions, the town of Adleship Isle lay in wait hardly ten miles from where they had stood.

IV – A Bowtie

Let us turn for a moment to the household of a man named Sebastian. Presently, Sebastian himself is being strapped into a bowtie. His youngest daughter, Samantha, is knocking at her sister's door. And her sister, Sabrina, having heard the knock, is urging a lover from her bed and soon thereafter out the window. As these characters are individually important on their own merit, I shall spend a moment on each.

We will begin with Sebastian. He is the town's Libburus. For all of you who live in the twenty-first century, that best translates to 'Mayor.' For all of you who once occupied the twelfth century region of Saxony, it best translates to a very sturdy veal shank. Sebastian may have been both.

Now I know what you're thinking: Sebastian is probably a large man dressed in unnecessarily fancy robes, who treats his servants poorly, his wife worse, who is bigoted, narrow-minded, and averse to change, and therefore will end up playing this story's villain.

However, you would be wrong concerning all of the details, excluding that of his short-sightedness and his comfort with his unvarying lifestyle. The simple fact of the matter is that there is not a true 'villain' in this story—leastways not in the manner of Disney or John Hughes. Though Sebastian will have his issues in the latter part of this piece, he will never outright antagonize Julian. In fact, for the majority of the novel, he shall scarcely realize our hero even exists.

You will probably find the Libburus of Adleship Isle to be a rather lovable, if somewhat portly and thick-headed, gentleman. His servants happened to feel that way—albeit, there weren't many of them and both were at least partially family, through marriage or otherwise. One such servant will be fitting Sebastian into his evening-wear when you meet him.

The man in the mirror seemed confused with the bowtie about his opposite's neck, but the servant—a short, wigged personality with a bulbous nose but elegant lips called Cletus[5]—was quite confident with the apparatus.

Sebastian eyed the little bulge in the skin beneath his chin with suspicion, such as a gardener eyes an errant rodent whom he notices eyeing the ripening radishes. He had wondered whether Cletus could manage the little bow around his stout neck, but—as is customary among perfectly poised manservants—Cletus assuaged his lord's insecurities.

"There you are, sir," he said, with a stiffly maintained lower lip. After one final fluffing of the bowtie's wings, Cletus released his grip and let the Libburus admire the fine handiwork on his fine neck.

"Yes, but do you think that His Magnificence will like it?" asked Sebastian.

"He says that it is the very latest in fashion, sir," replied the good Cletus.

"Yes, but he said that last year," fussed Sebastian, "Suppose it's no longer the latest fashion—suppose they've come up with something even later. They are a very progressive people I should think."

"Impossible," replied Cletus with proud resolve, but much more pride than resolve, "If they have indeed progressed so far, why have they never managed to reach us?"

Sebastian found this proof enough and assumed a satisfied smile as he continued to admire his reflection. What he did not consider at that moment was that every article of clothing he had on came from some nation or township beyond his own. In fact, near every formal article in the wardrobes east of the river had been a gift from the only external vendor the Isle had ever known, but I am getting ahead of myself and must introduce you to the Libburus' dwelling.

Sebastian's house had a total of twelve rooms—making it the largest house in the town—and comprised his bedroom, his closet, his kitchen, his dining room, his two servants' quarters, his guest room, his company room, his trophy room, the bedrooms of his two daughters, and finally the cellar.

If you're wondering about the washrooms, take a moment to consider the time-period of this story, and the fact that Adleship Isle did

---

[5] In case I've confused you, the *man* is called Cletus; the nose and lips are Algernon and Ferdinand respectively.

not have enough inhabitants to warrant a sophisticated sewage-control system.

If—on the other hand—you are *not* hung up on tedious details and anachronisms, you might be wondering about the two daughters, neither of which has been properly introduced.

Sebastian loved his daughters. He loved them so much that he often lied about the elder's age, so as to make her appear less 'ripe for marriage' as it were. But, as the Isle was small and could be likened to a beehive, secrets were difficult to keep from those who wished to learn of them.

If I don't mention the wife and mother, it is because she does not exist when our story begins. Sadly, she fell ill to a particular condition (which the people of Adleship had never heard of) almost ten years prior, leaving the daughters in the care of the father and the servants.

Now let us turn to Sabrina. Seeing as she was both nineteen and the eldest daughter, it would ordinarily be incumbent upon her to marry by the time we first meet her, but as neither she nor her father was interested in such an arrangement, the issue needed not often be raised.

Knowing that her father was like to be much occupied with his own reflected image, Sabrina had taken the opportunity to have one of her more frequent dalliancers over to engage in activities which are best not described in detail. Having concluded their dealings, and feeling satisfied enough to not complain, Sabrina was urging her visitor to leave, when she was interrupted by her younger sister's knock. Sabrina, a most resourceful creature, was thankful for this signal.

Upon hearing the knock, she appeared flustered, (which she was very good at), and then moved her fluster towards panic, (which she could not fake quite as well).

Luckily, Junkin[6] took her sincerely. He quickly moved to put on her clothes, then, realizing they were not his own, took them off, and started over again.

Sabrina, doing her best to produce a yawn, called to the other side of the door, "Who is it?"

"It's me," replied the sweet and innocent voice of her sister.

Through a harsh whisper, Junkin began, "Miss Sabrina, I—"

---

[6] It was a well-known fact that 'Junkin' was not his real name, but as no alternative appears in any records, none shall appear in this text either and you shall have to accept Junkin, pronounced, to the best of my knowledge, *Yoon-Kin*.

Sabrina shushed him with a swift kick to the shin, which Junkin was forced to nurse in silence. "Oh—well, I'm just waking up from a nap; just a moment."

"Alright," came the soft reply.

The more accustomed to haste, Sabrina was fastened into her nightgown before Junkin had even finished his trousers.

Because he was farther from her feet, Junkin ventured again, "Miss Sabrina, when can I see you again?"

"Hush!" hissed the other, with a glance back at the door, "And away with you! Out! Out!"

As Junkin went toward the window, he offered, "Maybe-maybe tomorrow?"

"Idiot: Hephaestus arrives tomorrow—now get out!"

"Well, maybe to celebrate his safe arrival—"

"Out!" she said again, abandoning her whisper, which Junkin took to its intent and dove through her window, tumbling over the gabled shingles on the other side.

Sabrina breathed, her hands pressed into her abdomen, and recollected her poise—poise befitting of a lady.

"Sabrina?" sounded with another knock.

"Yes, yes, sister, I'm coming."

She opened the door to reveal Samantha—who was exactly the character you'd expect her to be.

Samantha was only sixteen—incidentally the same age as Ten ha, but don't expect anything to play from that coincidence—and she looked to be the stock ingénue. She was a small-featured strawberry-blonde with pale eyes and a timid, close-lipped smile which she had been wearing until she'd gotten a look at her sister.

"Sabrina!" she exclaimed, "Are you alright? You're all flushed and perspiring—"

"Yes, yes, I'm—" Sabrina cleared her throat with confidence, "I was having a nightmare when you woke me.'

"Oh, dear, I'm sorry."

"No, no, I should be thanking you; had you not knocked I might never have gotten free."

"Oh." Samantha shifted, as if to try to see past her sister into the recently sullied bedchamber, but Sabrina shifted with her, blocking her view.

"Was there something you wanted?"

"Hmm? Yes! Oh, yes," said the younger, "I'm going to the well, and you have my washbasin."

"Of course!" Sabrina quickly collected and returned it to the doorway without giving Samantha much time to peek. "Here you are."

They each waited for the other to speak, but Sabrina managed to be more stubborn than Samantha, who said, "Oh, well... thank you."

Sabrina nodded her sister away, and was about to close the door when she heard, "Oh, and father should be calling us for supper. Within the hour."

"Yes," replied Sabrina, "thank you." She closed the door, deciding that her sister was simply being friendly, rather than issuing a warning. Even so, Sabrina went to her mirror, agreed that she was indeed very red-faced, and began brushing her hair so as to be presentable.

Julian lay on his back near the cart that held his tools. Between himself and the cart lay Miriam, pointing one small digit up to the sky and saying, "That one looks like Miss Condamine's hair!"

Julian, issuing an amused laugh, regarded the cloud and admitted, "Well, yes; it does."

Miriam turned over onto her stomach. She picked at the grass, most of it near frozen, with mittened fingers until she found a dandelion that had been pressed into the chilled earth. "Is it gonna snow today, Julian?"

"Not sure if we'll get any today," Julian replied, without looking at her. Instead, he continued to face the sky, looking for a cloud that looked like a girl. Or if not the whole girl, a face, a hand, maybe some trace as fair as her skin.

Then some ruckus invaded his thoughts, and he was forced to turn and look excitedly at the house, where he saw a young man tumble out a window and across the old shingles, which—very craftily, I might add—caught his shirt and pulled it from his body, making the snow drift that cushioned his landing a great nuisance indeed.

"Sod it!" came the exclamation when he collided, and quickly after, "Great Fred[7]!"

---

[7] There had never been a man named 'Scott' in the written history of the Isle, so 'Great Fred' evolved into the common turn of phrase.

Up a hill from the fallen gentleman and intrigued at the scene, Julian propped himself onto his elbows to watch. Miriam arrived beside him and asked, tugging at his sleeve, "Julian, what's that man doing?"

Julian, aware of the window from which he had fallen, deftly explained, "He's testing the softness of the snow."

When the man stood, brushing off flakes which quickly turned to chilled water, Julian recognized him as Junkin. Junkin didn't recognize anything other than his own discomfort, shrieking, "Bloody Jessop!" as he looked for his shirt. He spotted it on the roof and for a moment considered fetching it before wrapping his arms decidedly about his midsection and trudging up the hill, to where Julian and his miniature charge lay.

"Why hasn't he got his shirt?" asked Miriam.

"Oh, that was just an accident. See?" he said pointing, "The roof took it." Then, as Junkin grew closer, Julian stood to greet him. "You okay?"

"I'm-ub ch-chilled to th-the bone," chattered Junkin.

"Is the snow soft enough?" asked Miriam, scrambling to her feet.

Without letting Junkin qualify that comment, Julian quickly removed his coat. "Here, take this. You can get it back to me later."

"Thanks," muttered Junkin, wrapping himself in Julian's somewhat smallish overcoat. "I've g-got to get, b-but I'll see you."

"At the Hephaestus Feast-us, yes," Julian finished.

"Right." Junkin nodded to Julian, glanced at Miriam, then trudged off in unlaced shoes.

Julian watched him go, smirking in amusement. He heard Miriam begin to ask another question, but paid no attention to it, for at that moment, the sound of an opening front door bid him turn back to the house.

I'll ask you to kindly pause for a moment, for—you see—this character's entrance demands a little more grandeur than I can establish on the page in the short time we have. Were this a motion picture or even a stage play, this introduction would call for musical scoring, so if I may, I kindly suggest you find the appropriate accompanying melody, something lofty, wafty, and sweet. Personally, I go straight to my Broadway selection: usually "Some Enchanted Evening," which is playing as I write these words.

Once you have the proper ambience, you may see Julian seeing Samantha. The moment she stepped outside her door, it began to snow:

not an icy, uproarious blizzard, but a soft, comforting trickle of snowflakes, which caught her eyelashes and peppered her hair.

One clever little snowflake tried to skirt past the lashes and into her open eye, causing Samantha to laugh, and if that doesn't make all of the little hairs on the back of your neck stand on end, you're clearly not listening to the right song.

Either way, it gave Julian goosebumps, and he found himself laughing with her, even though he was over fifty feet away and she could neither hear nor see him. He watched her as she proceeded along the house, keeping upon the laid stones and out of the snowdrifts still shaped from the week before. Once she reached the well, she drew her hair away from her face to see her reflection in the water, water which never froze in the town of Adleship Isle.

Samantha set down the basin at the well, dipped her fingers into the water, and resisted the urge to shiver. After filling the basin, she wrang out her hands, pushed up the sleeves of the heavy gown, and drew the water across her porcelain skin, one arm at a time, and then on to her neck and finally her face.

Julian savored every moment of it, as he had every day for—well, no one exactly knows how long, but we can assume it's somewhere between days and years. The story behind Julian's infatuation with Samantha goes like so: One day Julian saw Samantha and fell promptly in love.

And at this moment in our story, knowing nothing of her distant admirer, Samantha looked up and saw Julian. Julian was met by an irrational panic and strongly considered ducking out of sight. But, either because he was aware that she had already seen him or because he could not bear to look away, he remained, staring back at her.

And she conveyed 'hello' by way of a smile. And Julian smiled as well, because he had nothing else to do. And Miriam could not manage to coax the snowflake from her nose onto her tongue. And the narrator resolved to stop starting sentences with 'and.'

At some point during Julian's staring, Samantha indicated the basin and appeared to call something to them. Julian either could not quite understand or was totally oblivious that he had even been spoken to, but as Miriam tugged at his sleeve, he was compelled to ask, "How's that?"

"Would you like some water?" she repeated, holding out the basin.

"Oh," said Julian, and after another affirmative tug from Miriam, answered, "Why, yes, please."

He and the little girl made their way along the hill, down to the well where Samantha stood waiting.

"Here you go," she said, handing the basin to Miriam, who had to take it in both hands to steady it enough to drink. "You're Manuel's girl, aren't you?"

"Yes'm," came the little reply.

Then Samantha looked up at Julian and as she registered his face, had to put both hands up to her mouth in embarrassment. "Oh, I'm sorry. Remind me your name."

"Uh—It's—um—it's Julian."

"Julian," she repeated, as if trying to seal the face in her mind. "Well, Julian, are you excited?"

Julian startled. "No. Why-why should I be excited? Wha'did I—I didn't—"

"Well, for the arrival of His Well-Traveledness. Surely you haven't forgotten."

"No!" exclaimed Julian once again, with a laugh that may or may not have been forced, "No, no. Of course, how silly of me."

She giggled. Amiably, not mockingly. "Yes, well... Were you going to take a drink, Julian?"

Julian was about to ask 'How's that' before he noticed that the basin was already in his hands. "Yes," and then as an afterthought, just before touching his lips to the water, "thank you."

"You're welcome." She nodded with a smile, and Julian felt compelled to grin as well.

When he straightened and returned her basin, Samantha glanced back at her house, the large Libburus house which indicated her standing, the walls that—to Julian—kept her away. "Well... It was nice seeing you both; and I'm sure I'll see you tomorrow."

"Can't wait," replied Julian, and with another nod, his goddess left his side and reentered her home, closing the door behind her with a tragic thud.

Miriam tugged once more at Julian's sleeve, and Julian, tearing his eyes away from the door, sighed, "Alright then, snap-pea, let's go home."

They went back up the hill, Julian collected his wheelbarrow, and Miriam—who had obviously been puzzling over this issue for quite some time—ventured, "Julian, why did the roof take his shirt?"

Julian would have laughed, but his mood did not allow him. "Sometimes funny things happen, Miriam," was his eventual reply.

Miriam pursed her lips, puzzling at what Julian might have meant. Little did she know that his justification would the best adage from preserving sanity over the winter weeks to come.

Julian had no expression to make, for—at the moment—none would console him.

You probably want to feel bad for our hero: to be rejected so, but technically Julian had never been rejected. It might surprise you to know that—as Julian had been gazing[8] on her for quite some time—Samantha noticed Julian's presence once every few weeks, and never seemed to find it odd or sinister or romantic in the least. The truth was that she would be very unlikely to even consider a prospect from the other side of the river.

This, to Julian, was the real tragedy, and here's why: As the daughter of the standing Libburus, Samantha was not eligible for marriage to a commoner.

Adleship Isle, as you will soon learn, had only two classes: noble and not. This was not questioned; it had never failed, so why should it need to be changed? The commoners lived to the west, and the noblemen dwelt in the east[9], as they always had for as long as anyone in the Isle could remember.

The nobles of course were those persons eligible to be named Libburus. Beyond that single distinction, there was very little that actually gave them standing over the more common consorts. Presently, the nobility belonged to four families, but it is believed by this narrator that they all stem back to an original Libburus of Adleship Isle, whenever that was.

(Please note that this theory is not a proven fact, though I would much like it to be. However, seeing as very few historians have ever ventured theories on the origins of the higher class in the Isle, you will be hard-pressed to find any research to the contrary.)

In either case, in the noble ranks stood four families, each entitled to submit one party for election of Libburus once every seven

---

[8] We say gazing instead of spying here, because it inspires a much less hostile connotation.

[9] Consult the map near the cover of this manuscript; you will find a series of smallish houses to the west of the town square, and to the immediate southeast there will be a few (noticeably larger) plots. That which lies just north of the town square would be that of the standing Libburus.

years, (unless of course one family had held the post for three straight terms, and was mandated to step down for the three to follow.) And to ensure that only noble-blood attained the state of Libbur-hood, only nobles were entitled to marry into the family of the acting Libburus over the years that he presided.

This becomes Julian's problem, and—if you are a sympathetic reader—yours by extension.

Now, Samantha's nobility would still raise issue were she not the daughter of the current administration. In most cases, to marry outside of the noble line—especially for a noble lady—was to lose the noble line, so it was a rarity indeed.

But Julian could not quell his love, so he continued to watch, to wish, and to dream, fearing that Samantha would never notice his tenders, his attentions. You may find yourself asking, "Why," you will say, "if he is so enamored with her, does he not proclaim himself and hope to whisk her away?"

Well, I can assure you that you will soon observe one of the most courageous pursuits of love ever to have occurred in the known world. And for those of you who are impatient, you haven't very long to wait to see Julian spurred into such action as the Isle had never known.

V – Seven Sturdy Servants
(Eight Able Oxen, and One Well-Worn Wagon)

December the eighteenth brought a cold wind from the north, which the recently-returned troupe of travelers was eager to meet.

Hephaestus checked his watch and frowned at the short hand, willing it to reverse a few ticks; he was nearly an hour late for his appointment.

He stood, flanked by two men, all facing up a long hill, which was most drowned by snow. Behind them followed the cart: a monstrous creature not dissimilar to a captain's quarters on a transatlantic vessel towed by eight able oxen. Four other men were situated about the leviathan, fixed to certain handles, so that they too could help push. And the last party, whom you shall not see for quite some time, was inside re-salting the leftover dinner items.

And so we feature the glory of his high-honored Hephaestus, accompanied by seven sturdy servants, eight able oxen and one well-worn wagon.

They had paused at the end of a road, the last road they would see for miles, which—as was English tradition in those days—was marked by a sign reading: HERE ENDS THE ROAD.

The hill was daunting, the weather was frigid, but Hephaestus was prepared. He turned back to the lot, stretched one arm toward the blizzarding sky ahead and shouted, "This is it, boys! Marshal your strength; we won't be sleeping tonight."

A long staff—both to support and to probe the ground for sturdiness—was given him by the man on his left in trade for the cherrywood cane, and Hephaestus began.

Part II – An Unprecedented Arrival

After one final fluffing of the bowtie's wings, Cletus released his grip and let the Libburus admire the fine handiwork on his fine neck.

VI – The Great Bronze Bell

The old man named Jonas watched the sunrise from his rock that had no name. He saw the sparkles in the river that parted the village. He saw that the shadow of the bell-tower stretched over the whole town and even past the west gate. He saw the swirling flurries in distant skies which seemed to avoid their nestled mountain pass. And just as he made to stand, Jonas heard the peppered rooster issue its triumphant greeting to the sun, signaling the people of the Isle that their year-long wait was over.

Manuel awoke with a ready grin. He stayed only long enough to kiss the sleeping Meredith, then was immediately up out of bed. He quickly fastened his boots, wrestled the sleep from his eyes, and bounded out the door.

Manuel took each step eagerly, gratefully along the cobblestone pathways, across the bridge and to the bell-tower. The bell-tower joined no church, needed no support other than its foundation stones and stretched only three or four stories into the air. And yet it was both the highest and the grandest building in the village. Manuel did not stop to catch his breath as he pulled himself up the stairs, spiraling about in cylindrical stone walls.

He reached the top: the slotted room with the great bronze bell, on which the new sun shone, illuminating the word 'Lucky' cast into its side. And Manuel rang the bell.

From the house overlooking the sheep fields, Piers sat up, dressed himself, and pulled the blanket once again over Lilli. He kissed her once on each cheek and twice on the lips, and took his jacket from the hook.

Up the road, near the mid-bridge beside the watermill, Clemens the grocer shot right out of bed—his Rosa already up to bustle about her wardrobe—and said a quick, "Bye, love" before likewise barreling into the cool morning.

To the far north, just below the waterfall, Sherman the tailor donned his glasses, accepted the scarf that Hannah wrapped about his neck, and was still buttoning his jacket when he reached the road.

And Manuel, having come down from the tower, was met by Piers and Clemens and Sherman, and the four—without a word—hustled to the woodshed, that stout little building by the big barn. They each took a corner, with Piers and Manuel on the heavier end and maneuvered the banner's frame from the shed and out into the open town square.

There were two holes, recessions bored into the stony patio that showed evidence of years and years and years of wear, and the four men met them precisely. With a firm thrust, they set the posts into the holes and raised the frame until it stood proudly vertical. Wooden supports were wedged into place, and at the feet of these supports each man took a metal stake and hammered their wooden arch into sturdy perfection.

They straightened once more and went to the base of the bell-tower, where they retrieved the well-preserved banner.

By this point, the families had begun to fill the square—little children barely awake and bundled with their rosy-cheeked mothers and fathers. Little by little, they filtered out their doors and into that grand huddle which only happened a few times each year.

Careful not to let it touch the ground, the four men, unrolled the twelve-foot banner and swung it over the apex of its frame. As they fastened it into place, it billowed out to read, "Welcome Hephaestus."

The men and women all around them cheered, including the Libburus and the noble folk, the children, and even Julian, who you're sure to spot in the crowd if you look for him. And Julian turned from the sign to spot Samantha, who was embraced by her father. This of course was no surprise, but you'll pay mind to Samantha looking back at Julian and paying him a friendly nod.

The only one who did not whoop and roar at the festivities continued to sit upon his rock. He could hear it all below but did not rush to join. Jonas watched what he could see of them, and found himself muttering, "Same time, same place."

He made to get up, but then, as a quick afterthought, found himself whispering, "New rhyme, new face," and quickly scrawled it down before he could forget. After reading and rereading it to satisfaction, Jonas stood and patted the rock 'goodbye.' We, so many years later, cannot know how or why he was inspired to write such, but I think you'll agree that it was quite a coincidence.

The rock was amazed by this foresight as well.

VII – Ice

After long debate, the Baron and his crew resolved a fair strategy of distributing the load without abandoning any items. In fact, this suggestion was not even raised, as the Baron knew the very mention would damage morale.

With some creative engineering, Geru and Pigby managed to outfit every member of their little troupe with riggings and satchels to carry portions of their merchandise so as to relieve the fatigued pack animals (Pigby included) enough that they could navigate the uneven rocks and snow.

Fletcher, still at the helm, was strapped to some forty pounds of fancy china, pottery, pannery, cutlery, and crockery. Oswald wore some muskets, pistols, and the oddest-looking blunderbuss ever to be banned from production in Western Spain. Geru held bizarre jars and bags filled with spices and medicine and what-else-have-you, culminating in a shrunken head over his right shoulder which faced squarely toward the Baron.

Now the Baron Pan Bordolo did not exempt himself in the least from carrying duty. He was packed from bow to stern with an assortment of rugs, blankets, and quilts—some of which were woven from the most sadistically-heavy threads in six continents[10]. In fact, aside from Pigby who helped shoulder the cart, the Baron assumed more weight than any of his fellows.

Ten ha no longer rode in the cart, but she was asked to carry only herself. (The Baron was a gentleman and in those days, it was uncouth to

---

[10] Antarctica notwithstanding.

ask a lady to haul much of anything, especially a lady so small as Ten ha[11].)

Though the snow had not stopped in the least, the wind had slowed enough to offer them some relief from the biting cold. Though Oswald's compass was acting amiss, Geru claimed that he could decipher the refraction of the sun's rays through the overcast skies and keep their course due east. And though they were all a little bit chilled, and a little bit soggy, and more than a little tired, the Baron's mustache never came uncurled.

And so all may have been well—the party and the yaks and that merry little cart—had Oswald not swayed.

The Baron saw the old man make one misstep, then sway rather heavily to his right. It was one of those occasions where gravity was resisted—if only for a moment—by sheer force of will. Geru and Pigby, too terrified to move, watched the old man hang in the air. Even Fletcher's suspicions must have prickled, because he had begun to turn about by the time gravity had won the day, and the old man fell.

The snow, despite its chill, was not wholly unpleasant; rather it was a simple stone wedging Oswald's shoe as he collapsed that twisted the ankle.

With a quick, "Ooh!" the old man toppled, followed closely by a clack of gun barrels, followed shortly thereafter by the clatter of the clutter being dropped from the party's shoulders as they rushed to help him.

"Oswald, are you alright?" squeaked an excited Geru.

"I say 'my foot!'" announced Oswald, by way of an answer, and all looked down to see a submerged shoe.

Pigby, ever the problem-solver reached down to un-wedge the captive appendage, which caused a yelp of "Ah! You're hurting me—" But so strong was the giant of a man that the old man was freed before he could finish his protest.

"Oswald," came the Baron, genuine concern in those twinkling eyes, "can you stand?"

Oswald strained to move the foot, and found that his ankle most refused to pivot. "Sir!" exclaimed Oswald, "It hurts, sir!"

"Geru?" asked the Baron, and Geru served his verdict.

---

[11] With any luck, it will escape the reader's notice that Ten ha was in fact taller than Geru.

"The swelling's coming up," said Geru, without needing to pull up the pant-leg for inspection.

"Well, pack it in ice." This last came from Fletcher, who was entirely aware that they were surrounded on all sides by snow, for which he received glares. (At other points in our little drama, we'll see the group take to Fletcher's humor much more amiably, but not here.)

Geru, his professionalism barring the thin man's distraction, continued to squint. "I can look on it more, but I think we'll conclude it's a sprain."

"A sprain, sir!" protested the unfortunate Oswald.

"Which means he can't walk," the Baron finished.

The Baron and his Geru regarded one another. They both knew that they did not know how far they were from civilization, and as they likely didn't have enough to burn to make it through the night *and* keep traveling the next day, stopping was not an option.

However, before they could even look at the cart, Pigby's deep dark voice cut in. "The cart can't take one more. Not to mention, the rifles and muskets. Sir, the yaks are near shut out by the cold, and we've not seen a road in three days. I've never shouldered harder terrain since you had us climb that damned volcano—"

"Language, Pigby," said the Baron, seeing as the lady—whether or not she cared a wink—was present.

"We'll use the fireworks!" suggested Geru, "We'll signal someone—"

"Who?" Fletcher asked, for even though the cart carried some of the finest and brightest in oriental pyrotechnics, the snow and ground-level clouds would shroud the blast even to an audience direct beneath them. "Besides, we're saving those for the New Year I thought."

"We won't make it to the New Year if we don't think of something!" exclaimed the short man.

"Sir, we've a problem," repeated the giant man, "We're lost, winter's set in, and we've a man who can't walk."

While these were all fair points and the crew required an answer of him, no solution would present itself to the Baron Pan Bordolo. His saving grace came in the form of Ten ha's hand, planted on his shoulder and accompanied by a simple question in his ear: "What would your godfather do?"

The Baron pursed his lips, which he did not like to do, as it took emphasis from his curled stache. He looked at the old man, looked at the cart, then tasted the air.

The Baron finally turned to Fletcher. When the thin man met his gaze, it was with undeniable conviction: a promise that he would follow the Baron's any request, even—if need be—to his very grave.

The Baron issued a nod. "Run, Fletcher. Don't stop 'til you've found a man, a town, or a road."

And Fletcher was gone.

VIII – Coco

Klaus was making coco. Unfortunately, as Adleship Isle was not the least bit tropical, there was not a single cocoa bean to be found. Coco, like many other modern or international facets of the Isle, had been brought by Hephaestus in years prior.

The villagers took it to mean not 'hot chocolate' as you might, but rather a milk-based drink that was somewhat bitter, somewhat sweet, and served hot. The milk was easy enough to gather from any of the cow-herders; both the bitter and the sweet were extracted from trees on the ridge of the falls by Klaus himself[12]. He had whipped up a batch for the occasion and set it over a fire in the square, so as to warm the stomachs of the bundled people waiting for Hephaestus' arrival.

At a stand to his left, Simeon, one of the wheat tenders, had brewed a barrel of ale, which was served cold but had certain warming properties of its own.

Everyone brought his own mug, goblet, or ladle, and each went in turn to have his drop of one or both—including the children, whose parents took it upon themselves to finish whatever the little ones couldn't.

Julian, one of Meredith's scarves around his neck, approached the stands with three mugs to ask for two cocos and one ale. Simeon, like most men of the village probably assumed that the ale was for Manuel, who could hardly let on that his wife had a stronger stomach than he; luckily, it wasn't such a hard thing to hide, as both beverages smelled mostly the same.

---

[12] The pine-bark extract Klaus used was actually quite commonplace in Europe in those days, particularly among transatlantic traders who had determined that it acted as a mild euphoric. Ergo, even those who did not like the taste of Klaus' coco still liked Klaus' coco.

The servers said their courtesies, wishing good tidings for Hephaestus' Day, which Julian returned generously. He bid thanks, and was about to leave when he discovered that he did not know how to hold all three mugs and guarantee the safety of the liquids inside.

His rescue came in the form of a young man called Raul, who arrived fortuitously at Julian's shoulder—just in time for the readers to meet him. He asked Simeon to "Please, fill'er up," then greeted his friend with, "Morning, Julian! Happy Hey-Day."

"Happy Hey-Day to you, Raul."

Raul took his goblet back from Simeon and sipped before giving Simeon his nod of approval on yet another incomparable batch. "Can I carry one of those for you?"

"Oh, yeah—thanks."

"Gladly." So Raul took up Manny's mug and followed Julian's weave through the crowd back to the family.

Raul was maybe only an inch taller than Julian, but he seemed to see over Julian's head by virtue of posture alone. He was also a little bit sharper of feature—aside from the broken nose that he earned falling out of a tree at eleven—with dark hair but blue eyes. To you, he might look a more fitting hero of the piece than the boy in front of him. And it would be fair to compare the two in most respects, seeing as Julian and Raul were hardly four months apart in age, which leads us to Raul's next comment.

"Will I see you at my birthday?"

"Of course!" Julian replied. "You know, I feel like I haven't seen you in days."

"Yeah, well you can blame my dad for that one: he's got me practicing reading and writing and all so's I can start teaching once I'm an adult, right." Julian was certain without needing to see that Raul was rolling his eyes, especially as the older boy added, "He says wood-chopping isn't suitable for people on our side of the river."

Julian decided not to qualify the comment, as he did not want to inadvertently stir the son into a tiff against his father, Eugene—whose comments on Raul's responsibility to position were frequent indeed.

When the boys arrived, Meredith was urging her father to sit down, while he recited some nonsensical adage back to her: "Tedious waste of time, to sit and hear so many hollow compliments and lies."

Raul issued a greeting to the man of the house, which was returned with a "Happy Hey-Day to you too, m'boy!"

Raul, without really thinking on it, made to offer the coco to Manuel, and Manuel—clearly the quicker on his feet—protested, "Oh, *no*. No, this is Meredith's coco. I had the ale; the ale's for me; thank you Julian." He reached hurriedly forward and took one mug from Julian, drank, and then grimaced, forcing an embarrassing, "Mmm*mmm*. That's good, that is."

"Here you go, Miss'm," said Raul, handing the coco to Meredith, which she took politely enough for him not to notice her annoyance. From there, he went on to exchange the *how-are-you*s, *hope-all-is-well*s, and *what-about-this-weather-we've-been-having*s, so as to cover all the bases of polite conversation. Seeing as most everyone in the Isle knew each other and needed not worry on any foreign anomalies of speech pattern or turns-of-phrase, small-talk could be passed at lightning speed. So after hardly a moment's more pleasantries, Raul paid a quick nod to Julian and left, .

Julian was calling, "Cheers, Raul," after his friend, while Meredith sent a scowl over to her husband.

"Honestly!" said Meredith, once Manuel had gotten the drinks to their respective owners, "Why can't you just admit you don't like Simeon's ale?"

"Sorry, love," he repeated, "but all my friends drink beer and none of their wives do, so what should they think?"

"They should think," said Meredith, turning back to her father, "that your wife is from good stock. I mean just look at this one here."

The comment toward Jonas was mostly sarcastic, and spoken in exasperation, but Jonas seemed to take it to heart. Squinting one eye and crooking his finger, Jonas advised his son-in-law, "Look to your health— for health is the second blessing that we mortals are capable of!" before finally sitting.

"Finally," sighed Meredith, sitting beside him. Then, to Miriam, who was pulling grains one-by-one from a stalk of wheat, asked, "Are you sure you don't want some coco, sweetie?"

And Miriam, lying on her stomach, propped on her little elbows, did not look up from the stalk to say, "Not thirsty."

Meredith, her motherly demeanor chiming away, looked up to Julian to ask, "Anything else for you?"

"Honestly, I'd like to know what the first blessing is," replied Julian, gesturing to Jonas who seemed to have forgotten that he'd said anything at all.

And so, sitting on rolled blankets, they waited: Julian with his extended household, nestled among dozens of others, all staring into the cloud-covered sun for the arrival of their Hephaestus. As the minutes became hours, they grew even quieter, even more attentive, such that by noon every Adleship Islean was totally silent and fixated on the east gate.

In retrospect, Sebastian noted that maybe he should have kept someone looking westwardly as well.

IX – Little Cottages

Fletcher carried a horn, a pitted black number taken off a ram that Pigby had killed for supper some years ago. The thin man would blow it to call ahead to other travelers, to signal back to the Baron, and—seeing as he'd memorized military calls for seventeen nations, thirteen tribes, and one very confused East-Asian sentry—to clear out potential danger ahead.

Once they'd hit snow, however, Geru had given Fletcher yet another horn—once more for signaling, but this time with fire. It was filled with magnesium-heavy gunpowder, which could provide both a loud bang and a bright orange flash. Pigby had dubbed it a 'flash-bang'; Oswald contrarily called it 'that bloody blinding thing' or 'I say—what—What!?'

To keep out moisture, both were provided wax seals once they hit temperate or sopping-wet geographies. Merry-Old-England constituted.

The blow-horn was black and the bang-horn was white, which made them distinguishable, excepting in blizzards, in which both looked dark to black and misted in white flurries.

So when Fletcher plucked the wax off of one and tried to blow, he was not surprised to taste bitter saltpeter, which he quickly spat out.

Fletcher slung the white horn back on his shoulder, grasped the second, bit off the wax and blew.

He heard his own voice echo back three times, through mountains and wind, but, however long he stood, panting into the gale, Fletcher's call received no reply. So he kept running.

And running.

Fletcher leaned over to pant for (the fourth? No!) the fifth time. The air was too cold; the wind was too dry; and his lungs were too tired to blow.

Even so, fortitude, loyalty, and—to be entirely honest—force-of-habit bid him place his lips once more on the horn and...

Wheeze.

His voice and breath rasped, audible to his own ears even through the wind, but the horn did not sing.

So he tried a second time, as persons tend to do, but had not taken enough of a breath and so had to abort, gasping.

Fletcher let himself breathe and tried to assemble enough saliva to swallow. Then, mustering as much air and strength as his skinny frame would allow, Fletcher issued a blast—or at least the start of a blast—which quickly fettered away again, leaving Fletcher most defeated and hopeless.

Until he heard a reply.

He thought he might be imagining it at first, or maybe his ear was distancing an echo. But Fletcher, a master of his trade, had perfect pitch and could not support such a ridiculous notion for more than a second seeing as the disparity of its note was apparent.

He *knew* the sound was real, that it was not an echo of his own horn—in fact, not any horn—but a very distant bell. Fletcher could not see its owner; were it a clear day, he *might* have seen the town, but only just. With no more than his ears to direct his heading, Fletcher started running again as the third chime sounded.

So, with a new spur to make him move, the thin man bolted across the snow, following the *Bong!*—silence—*Bong!*—silence, and willing it, all the while, not to cease.

Fletcher did not know what he had expected to find, but as he ran he was most surprised to discover the cloud-break. The road's sudden emergence—appearing underfoot as if a geological afterthought—was jarring, yes, and the massive wooden archway, with the sign reading ADLESHIP ISLE seemed so new and alien to Fletcher that it may as well have been in Eskimo—but nothing compared to the light, to nearly-clear sky above.

He found himself half-staring at it as he passed under the bizarre sign and into the town, glancing down to see where he was going from time to time, but unable to shake his wonderment: the snowfall had lessened, the wind had softened, and—though it was still winter—the air had grown considerably warmer.

Fletcher was flanked by little cottages and went to the first one he found, beating the door and yelling, "Hello!" The lack of an answer hardly slowed him down, for there was quickly another, on which he bestowed the same courtesies.

By the third and fourth houses, "Hello," came instead as a question. In particular, "Hello? Is anyone there? Hello?"

After a short time, the thin man grew flustered, which quickly turned to concern, which even more quickly turned to panic. By the sixth house he was yelling, "In the name of the lord, open the door!"

By this point, all of the elasticity had been worn from his legs, and his voice had been all but murdered by the horn and the blizzard and—due to the empty streets—the despair. So when I say 'he staggered out into the middle of the road'—I really do mean staggered. "Is anybody there?" he cried, "Anyone?"

His shoulders sagging under the weight of his task, Fletcher was near to collapse when he saw, silhouetted against the thinly veiled sun, a tower. *The* tower. There was—after all—only one in the Isle. And Fletcher *knew* it was the same bell-tower.

There wasn't a living soul in sight, but Fletcher, whether or not he concluded so consciously, understood that a bell needed someone to ring it in order to make a sound. So he limped toward that beacon on the horizon.

When Fletcher came to the bridge, he was so surprised to find running water—that is, water that had not frozen over—that he nearly fell over one side, and overcompensated so much when catching himself that he almost toppled over the other.

Only after he had crossed, stumbling back down onto solid ground and into the square, he saw the people. And not just a few—not two or three weary, frozen travelers like himself—but a whole town. He even had to rub his eyes before he bothered to believe it.

They were all seated—under blankets and wraps and each other's arms, clustered in what he only assumed were families, households—and each and every one of them was facing away from him.

Afraid that they should disappear were he to blink, Fletcher approached the nearest cluster, tapped one man on the shoulder, and started to speak. But hardly had he managed to rasp, "Sir," before the man spat a quick "Shh!" back at him.

Fletcher then went to the woman off his shoulder, and she—likewise without looking at him—hissed a harsh, "Quiet!"

Fletcher was taken aback. He shook his head—rattled is probably more the word—and hustled over to yet another family. He only got as far as "Excuse me—" when he was silenced by a swift, "Keep it down!"

Fletcher was not a man of exceeding faith, but he was quite certain that if he believed in hell, he had found it. His fears were only bolstered by the assortment of "Hush yourself!" "Pipe down!" and "Silence, boy!"

Fletcher did not understand. He didn't even know what precisely he did not understand, but as his joints alone were not going to hold him aloft, he knew that he had to reach someone quickly. So he took hold of one woman's shoulder, and—with something of a prayer—started to say, "Mum, I need to—"

But Rosa, the wife of Clemens who knew every face in their little village perfectly, did not let him finish. When she saw him, she knew that his face should not exist. And so she screamed.

Fletcher started, Clemens stared, each family turned to look, and though their eyes willed themselves to wander back to east gate for His Highest's arrival, they could no longer ignore this thin man who was very much not a resident of their village.

And the town erupted.

X – The Big Wooden Arch

Lance, the barrowman's son, had never considered himself a particularly brave man, but he wouldn't think himself a coward either.

His reaction to their environment was most understandable, considering that every other man there had completed the tour at least four times previously and that Lance had only been pressed into Hephaestus' service two days before. Sometime during their ascent Lance realized that he could see neither a town, a road, nor even the sky, and received a prompt panic attack.

He addressed this setback masterfully by managing not to collapse and by quickly assuring the others, "I'm alright."

Hephaestus, ever a stalwart leader of men, relocated Lance to the rear of the wagon, so that its hull could block the view ahead. Though Lance complied simply to follow orders, he was soon greatly surprised to find that he was greatly relieved by what he could not see. Some hundred years later, behavioral psychiatrists would perform similar experiments on rats and come to the same conclusions. I imagine they'd be kicking themselves over wasted time if they ever came across Hephaestus' travel diaries.

I would talk about the snow to further describe the scene, but I think you've already an idea of just how frightful the weather had been and how relieved they would all be once they were rid of it. Ordinarily, Lance would not have believed so bizarre a conjecture that the weather would 'clear up' once they'd reached their destination, but with how eager the others pushed to get there, he could hardly discount the notion.

And even though every hill and pass appeared identical to him, Lance was assured by the self-assurance of his leader that soon there would not only be some peace from the wind, but food, lots of it, and the company of the most delightful people ever known.

Hephaestus was the most excited of all: due to a comparatively speedy ascent, this year he would arrive just after noon, which he understood to mean that every eye would be turned in his direction as he strode gallantly into the square. Unfortunately, he would start this Christmas season with disappointment.

When the snow started to clear and—squinting—he spotted the big wooden arch, Hephaestus called back to the crew, "Here we go, boys; march proudly and smile."

So smile they did, all the way through the arch and onto the road, which popped them into the square. They smiled right up until they met the screeching hubbub of multitudes of terrified citizens of the Isle.

Mothers kept their children behind them, the men kept their wives behind them, and the children, unshakably curious, kept trying to get around both parents to get a better few. And not one of them had noticed the severely put out lord of merchants.

It took only seconds for Hephaestus to locate the subject from which they recoiled. The thin man about the middle of the clearing, for some reason clutching two horns to his chest, looked just as frightened and bewildered as they.

The merchant did not look back at his fellows, did not hesitate; Hephaestus threw open his arms, and, striding into the square, announced, with a voice befitting of the power in his name, "People! Ladies and gentlemen of Adleship Isle, this man means you no harm!"

They may not have understood, the provincial civilians, precisely what this meant, but every single one of them—please pay this the emphasis it deserves: *every single one of them* turned to him with a perfect trust. Fletcher thought for a moment that he had never seen this kind of trust, without acknowledging that he and most of his fellows frequently showed such for their Baron.

When this grand man approached the thin man, it did not surprise Fletcher that the people made a path for him, reverently, as citizens would a priest or prince. To Fletcher, who was no longer certain that he was in England, or even Europe for that matter, this cloaked, hooded, and bearded gentleman who must have stood a head taller than him was most likely a wizard.

"This man," Hephaestus went on, with the same volume and grandeur, "is just a weary traveler, lost his way, who is coming to you for help." He placed a hand on Fletcher's shoulder and asked, "Isn't that right, son?"

Fletcher considered fainting. And he may have, had he not been so intrigued. Never before had he seen a man so old with eyes still so bright. He had difficulty explaining why—after having arrived at precisely the wrong moment in precisely the right town—the detail of Hephaestus' eyes struck him so. For whatever reason, they brought him calm, they dissipated the momentary horror, and somehow they bid him nod and say, "Yes, sir."

Hephaestus did not know how true his own assumption was, but he was relieved that the young man was not stupid enough to say 'no.' Hephaestus addressed the town once again, "Now, who among you will help him?"

The town collectively remained silent; it seemed to be the most viable option in their present circumstances. Manuel eyed Sherman, and Piers eyed Clemens, and each set, without being able to come up with a reason to speak, looked to the next and gained nothing from that exchange or the one after. Questioning gazes without answers were on and on through the crowd and between families until they had reached and settled on—much to his chagrin—the Libburus.

Sebastian probably would have stood and stared perplexedly back had Cletus not realized that his Libburus was expected to respond, and the man-servant cleared his throat loudly to alert his charge. And when Sebastian did not notice this, Cletus took the liberty to nudge him (hard) in the ribs.

"Wh-wh-wh—" sputtered Sebastian, took a steadying breath and started again: "What would you have us do?"

Hephaestus surveyed the crowd. He was tempted to survey the young man who was on his knees beside him, but didn't feel he was in a place to hesitate. "He needs something to drink. Someone fetch him tea, or— Or something." Turning back to Fletcher, he asked, "Would that be alright, son?"

Fletcher tried to say thank you, but—probably because it was just mentioned—found his mouth quite removed of moisture and so nodded.

Hephaestus straightened again, knowing that he needed to delay his own resentment for the strange arrival that had overshadowed his own. He could see from half a glance how disappointed his fellows looked, having not been received with the warmth and total abandon that he had promised them—except for Lance who was merely confused. He could also see that not a single member of that little town had moved.

Raul happened to notice this at the same time. He may not have had the courage to move on his own just at that moment, but he spied Julian not far to his right and so said, "Julian."

Our young hero turned to hear: "Come on, let's go get'm some coco."

Julian wasn't sure if he'd found the strength to move, but his legs were carrying him nonetheless into the clearing followed by Raul, his hands clutching his mug, which he hadn't thought on taking with him but was lucky to have.

When they got to Klaus' stand, Julian found himself whispering over his shoulder, "What are we doing?"

"I don'know—I dunno, just shuddup." Raul did not seem angry, just a little scared, more-than-a-little confused, and unwilling to talk.

They each filled their glasses; Julian couldn't see why they needed two for one man, unless alien people needed to drink more than they did. Julian shouldered his way back through the crowd, by now aware that Raul was purposefully letting him go first, and realizing that, for the thirty seconds or so that they had gone, not one else had spoken or moved any closer to the stranger.

Julian looked to Hephaestus before he offered the drink to the alien, as a child might look to a fireman before he tries to pet the relatively large Dalmatian. At a nod from Hephaestus, Julian reached out with two hands to give his mug to Fletcher, who took it with a scratchy, "Thank you."

Julian felt compelled to smile as he stepped back, as if to say, 'I was happy to do so, kind sir, and, no, I'm not afraid of you.' He justified his inability to speak by noting that he wasn't sure the alien could understand him anyway.

Hephaestus kindly commended Julian with a "Good lad." Once Julian had reached a safe distance, Raul too patted his shoulder in congratulation.

I suppose it shouldn't surprise that after so harrowing an experience, Julian should want to look for Samantha. Maybe she wasn't really proud of him; maybe he was just projecting the expression because he needed to see it so. Either way, when he saw her face, Julian blushed and dared to feel proud of himself as well.

XI – A *Tuhnk* and a *Fwhahff*

All five were seated cross-legged in their wagon, save for Oswald who lay along the back wall, so as to keep his leg a little more elevated. Though its base could more than support the strain of their weight, its wooden walls continued to creak against the wind. One sad solitary candle stood in the center of them, surrounded by a circle of ruddy old playing cards, on which the corners were so torn and frayed that every card should have been distinguishable from its neighbor—that is if anyone besides Fletcher had bothered to memorize them.

Ten ha wiggled her nose, the Baron thumbed his stache, Geru clicked his tongue, and Pigby bent his brow.

"Geru, sir," said the Baron, as shiftily as he could manage, "Have you any twos?"

"Go fish."

And the Baron drew. Had he followed Fletcher's admirable lead, he should have known to select the card three to the left of the one he chose, but as they were not gambling today, he cared little.

Pigby grumbled something unintelligible. Because he appeared unpleasantly disgruntled and had double the weight advantage of every person there, no one bothered to ask after the statement. But as Pigby's irritability wanted an audience, he said, "Why 'Go fish' at a time like this? There's three feet of snow out there!"

Without making eye contact, Geru asked, "Have you ever heard of ice fishing?"

And to match his irony, Pigby replied, "No, I haven't, Geru; how's it done[13]?"

---

[13] You may not have known Pigby had actually spent a fairly lengthy tour in Quebec and the south-eastern portion of the Northwest Territories years prior.

Geru clicked his tongue yet again, but did not respond.

Apparently unconcerned with poking the proverbial bear, and having poked a great number of bears in his travels, the Baron said, "It's your go, Pigby."

Pigby considered not playing for bitterness' sake, but as he observed that he held three kings and may yet make a stab at pulling ahead, asked the Baron, "Have you got any kings, sir?"

"Go fish," he replied, which was followed quickly thereafter by a grunted 'Bullocks.'

So when Ten ha, without so much as a blink, asked Pigby for his kings, the giant of a man understandably rippled with:

"Dammit all to—"

"Language," interrupted the Baron.

Pigby pursed his lips for a moment before settling on, "—Helsinki."

He gave his cards to the girl, who set out her fifth set, a whole four more than any other competitor.

At that moment—while Oswald was straining to see the very suspenseful game and Geru was calculating his next move—the candle blew out with an airy *fwhahff*. Not so many can take an airy *fwhahff* when stranded about a mountain top, which might never have been successfully navigated, leastways not in December, in England, in a century some before your own.

Fletcher had been gone for hours. They probably would have known precisely how long, had Oswald been mobile enough to reach and flip the hourglass when was needed or had Pigby remembered to wind his timepiece. So, with no knowledge of where he was (or even if he still was), they were forced to wait, knowing without saying that they should have to wait out the night, and—if he should not return—swing back in the other direction and hope to god for sunlight.

The Baron knew Pigby was only a few errant remarks away from announcing that they would all die. This would ordinarily not serve so harsh a verdict, for, over his years of service with the Baron Pan Bordolo, Pigby had made such an announcement on four occasions. (He would have made a fifth as well, eighteen months prior in the Philippines, had he not been underwater at the time.)

Geru of course knew this, but he had a particular sense of sarcasm that bid him probe at Pigby when afforded the opportunity—but I won't take any more time on this for the moment, as you're clearly anxious to get back to the story.

For now, Pigby would only mutter, "Bullocks."

"I'll find the light," offered Geru, making to stand, but at the same time, so did Ten ha, and their foreheads collided with a *tuhnk*. Now some people can handle a *tuhnk*, but a *tuhnk* and a *fwhahff*—well, that's a strain that no group can very well take.

Clutching at his forehead, Geru grunted once, and tried to convince himself to strike the candle back up. He even ventured an, "Okay, so—" but couldn't manage to finish the thought.

Pigby stayed seated, clenching and unclenching his fists, refusing to speak until one more person said something hopeful; one statement of false optimism, and he'd make the proclamation once more.

Now, the Baron knew not to say reassuring words, but he also knew that the old man with the propped ankle had only a few seconds more before he asked a question, a question which would mandate the Baron's cheery disposition, a disposition which was only held up by the Liverpool Silver about his upper lip.

And that's when they heard the horn. It burbled slightly against the wind and the wood of the wagon, but it still made its way to their ears.

"By George," whispered the Baron, only hardly daring to be hopeful, "that's Fletcher's horn!"

And then he held his breath, for if Pigby hadn't heard it as well, he should surely say, 'We're all going to die.' And yet the giant stayed silent.

When it sounded a second time, the Baron laughed triumphantly.

"I hear it!" affirmed a squeaking Geru.

"Could it be just an hallucination?" asked Oswald, unable to believe their own good fortune.

"It may have," said the Baron, "except that all of us heard it, which can only mean two things: that either we have developed brilliant synergy, or—" and having finally found the latch, flung open the door, "—Fletcher's come back for us."

XII – A Tapestry

Hephaestus did not take disappointment well. That is not to say that he would be outwardly bitter, impolite, or unpleasant; no, his actions were—as always—that of a perfect gentleman, but on the inside, a violent storm raged on[14]. There was commotion and fear in the Isle, and general hullabaloo pervaded his paradise, on account of some man who reputedly called himself a Baron.

When that odd thin man first looked up from the mug—Well, not first; the *first* thing he said was, "Good god: it's syrup," but soon after, "My employer and four others are out in the snow still; I was sent for help."

'Help' Hephaestus could understand. He had rescued stranded sailors, returned lost children to their parents, personally cauterized open wounds, and even played midwife to a giant panda some years before. So—even though he was miffed on being upstaged, irked that he had to quell an eruption, and frankly pissed that he was not collectively cheered as he sipped his inaugural coco—Hephaestus would not turn down a very valid plea for assistance.

But when Hephaestus replied, politely repeating the point, "Your master sent you for help?" the young man very flippantly corrected him.

"My *employer*," he said, "the Baron Pan Bordolo, sir, keeps employees not servants."

Why did this upset Hephaestus? Was it because he had seven men in tow that he only ever referred to as servants, even those who were his oldest closest friends, and that they might get ideas of entitlement?

---

[14] To avoid cliché statements, the editor has suggested that I change 'storm' to 'tornado' and 'raged on' to 'twirled tirelessly.' The narrator would like to note that the editor's suggestion provides wonderful alliteration.

Well, only a little. But really it was the sheer impoliteness with which this unmannered boy, whom—as far as Hephaestus was concerned—he had just single-handedly saved, spat back in his face. (Not literally of course.)

What pestered him further was that—once he had demonstrated to the town that the thin man was most likely human and should not mean to frighten[15] them—they all seemed more interested in him than they did their old friend. Even though all questions were still addressed directly to Hephaestus, most of them regarded the thin man, for whom Hephaestus felt like something between a translator and a parrot.

"I'm so terribly, terribly sorry, Your Grandestness," spoke the Libburus the moment he'd gotten Hephaestus inside and away from the town square. "We were so awaiting your arrival— All of the preparations have been made; nothing is spoiled; we'll still be having the Hephaestus High-Feast-us!" Sebastian sputtered. He continued to wring his hands, though there was no water on them.

Hephaestus held his mouth securely closed. Had he opened it at that moment, he probably would have screamed, and he was certain that Sebastian had never been screamed at, nor would be able to handle it. Sebastian was not a thin man and had a bowtie restricting the hang of his second chin, and Hephaestus felt that if he was startled enough his neck might explode in protest, like a giant Indian Show-Balloon. He hoped that refraining from speech until they were inside the Libburus' house would give him proper time to cool down. About this, Hephaestus was wrong.

While railing about how his entrance had been overshadowed by another man—(he should have said 'lesser' but did not feel like sounding too superior to be likable)—Hephaestus exclaimed, "It's a travesty, Sebastian!"

Sebastian knew not how this occurrence was anything like a tapestry, but nodded nonetheless. (The bowtie ventured to nod as well.)

Sometime soon after, as if implying that this 'Fletcher' knew whose presence he had interrupted, Hephaestus noted his intentions as "Egregious, Sebastian!"

Sebastian could not quite discern just what made the thin man so gregarious, but he accepted the claim without question. (The bowtie knew what egregious meant.)

---

[15] Note that it's 'frighten'; the citizens of the Isle were, for the most, unfamiliar with the term 'kill.'

Hephaestus should have been hungry. He was actually very hungry, but annoyed stubbornness would bid him refuse food, just in case it would make him feel better. When his veteran servant, (whose name you will later learn is Trenton), asked if they could go eat, Hephaestus almost refused his men that happiness as well, but of course could not be thought of as mean and begrudgingly consented.

So he sent Trenton and the others to their midday meal—that is, those whom he had not sent out with the thin man to find this 'Baron'— four of his own seven servants, seeing as none of the townspeople were willing to brave the weather. Hephaestus felt most helpless when Lance, the new-blood, insisted that he should leave as well: that this young man had been lucky enough to be invited into this paradise, and yet was so startled that he should wish to escape within five minutes of his arrival was utterly unacceptable!

The people of Adleship Isle had welcomed their old friend, but with fluster, not ardor. His own servants seemed to have lost some measure of confidence—perhaps not confidence in Hephaestus himself, but for a man with so much responsibility, you can imagine that any such loss would be unnerving at best, crippling at worst.

What made matters worse is he couldn't figure out how-in-the-world someone else had managed to find his own personal mountain pass, especially from the west, when Hephaestus himself had only ever successfully navigated an east-borne entrance.

According to this Fletcher character, it had been an accident. (Point of fact, this Fletcher character was a hell-of-a-lot more confused about his present circumstances and location than the great merchant could ever be.) However, Hephaestus did not know what Fletcher thought; so this peculiar interloper may have arrived in the Isle on this day on this time just to steal the thunder of a more deserving man.

And Hephaestus stood, accompanied by his own brooding and the apologies of the Libburus. He pressed his forehead against the glass of the upper story window and watched the now-empty town square, where the people would reconvene for the evening's celebration. And this sight brought him further offense because he *knew* that the next time the citizens congregated, it would be for the arrival of another traveler, a man with whom Hephaestus should need to share center stage.

XIII – Matching Uniform

Perhaps it would have irked him even more had he known who precisely this Baron was. And maybe if the Baron Pan Bordolo had been informed of Hephaestus' profession, he should have been more prepared for their initial meeting.

This narrator finds it ironic, however, that Fletcher never managed to glean Hephaestus was a traveling merchant, especially when the older man wished to radiate this fact with every fiber of his being. Assuming that both Fletcher and his 'employer' should know the masterful reputation at the mere utterance of their master's name, Hephaestus' servants never bothered to explain it either.

They were professional, ever professional, and silent, mostly silent. When Fletcher successfully navigated them back to the cart, they stopped well short of it, hands clasped behind their backs like a regimented military outfit, while the thin man spoke with his Baron.

Every experienced man in Hephaestus' charge knew better than to eavesdrop. Only Lance tried to pick out the conversation that followed and, given the wind, happened to miss most of it.

Fletcher, expecting eavesdropping, maintained a whisper as he told the Baron about the little town that he stumbled upon, the people gathered silently in something of a town square, their reaction to him, and the…well, he wasn't certain of who or what the older gentleman was.

"But, see, boss, that's just it!" Fletcher went on. "He came out of nowhere, and they all believed him, every word of it and followed him like—like a herd animal that works even better than sheep!"

"Nice," came Geru in reply.

"I'm sorry," said the Baron, who—with his little entourage about his shoulders—was far more interested in the prospect of possibly surviving the night, "but you're saying that he saved you from—from what?—a horde of angry villagers?"

"No, no, no, no, no, no." It's entirely possible that Fletcher went on, but for the sake of flow, we shall continue. "They weren't—Just scared, or-or-or confused, or—either way, he-he—This man, he—"

"He stopped them," finished the Baron.

"Calmed them," Fletcher corrected.

"Right…" The Baron Pan Bordolo looked to Geru, then to Oswald, and lastly to Pigby, who still stood between the two yaks, straddling the wagon tongue. "And we're being recovered on his orders."

Fletcher nodded. "On his suggestion."

"And they call him 'Hephaestus.'" This detail both intrigued and disturbed the Baron far more than any other; the only thing worse than encountering a real-life demigod was encountering a man who believed he was—especially if the general masses supported his delusion. Wanting to establish that this man was not in fact *the* Hephaestus, the Baron went on to say, "So he's sort of their shaman—"

"Or high priest," suggested Geru.

"A chief cleric," offered Pigby.

"The celebrant," concluded Ten ha[16].

Fletcher shrugged. "I would have said 'wizard.'"

Though the Baron turned away, he was heard to mutter, "Bloody hell, we've wandered into *The Tempest*." He did not approve of their circumstances; so long as we're on the subject, they had faced worse, but the Baron tended to bristle a little more fervently against worrisome literary references than real-life peril.

Then again, he carried his own book to combat them.

After scouring over the maps, Oswald had apologetically informed them that he could find no town reachable with their present heading. Of course Geru could not even determine at what altitude or coordinates they stood, so even Oswald's cartographic conclusion was inconclusive. So the Baron—with nothing else to do—had no choice but to obey the four militant strangers[17], not to *trust*, mind you, but to follow them, graciously and politely.

Surely, had his mustache not been firmly fixed in perfect ringlets, the Baron should not have been so confident in this decision.

---

[16] Oswald would have contributed were he not in the cart with his leg elevated.

[17] To be fair, only three of the strangers were truly militant. The fourth was named Lance.

As a group, not one in the Baron's employ could take much of an issue with their new destination as none muster more suspicion than he had desperation. Most of their attitudes translated to relief, other than Fletcher who was anxious in anticipation for his colleagues' reactions.

Prone to flights of fancy and a frequent reader of escapist fairy tales, Fletcher was terrified that no one else in the Baron's troupe would find the town in the same state that he had, and that maybe it had taken the opportunity of his leaving to collapse once again into dust. He decided to take solace in the four broad-shouldered servants in matching uniform, each evidence that there was indeed a place called Adleship Isle.

Ten ha took the four men as objects of intrigue. The crew had been rescued before—and captured, and kidnapped, hauled into villages on a series of poles to be offered up to a god, interrogated about their invasive or malicious intent as spies, and even been thrown surprise birthday parties by peoples that they had never before seen, but never before had they been received apathetically.

So curious was this reaction that Ten ha decided to step out of the cart to walk among them, pulling back her overlarge winter hood to better inspect the specimens. She was fascinated and frustrated that she could hardly manage eye contact with any of them, as they seemed conditioned straight ahead as they marched the Baron's cart across the snow.

When she found the one that appeared just organic enough to possibly carry a dialogue, Ten ha felt compelled to initiate an unsolicited conversation. Unconvinced that the others were in fact humans and not animated clay soldiers from childhood ghost stories, Ten ha approached him warily, but he, in his own anxious manner, seemed like he should be more frightened of her than she of him.

And indeed he was.

Upon first sight of Ten ha with her hood back and face visible[18] Lance startled and near dropped his hold.

"Hi," she said.

Lance was too busy wondering after the color of her eyes to notice that she'd said anything.

So Ten ha tried again, with, "Bonjour."

This time Lance was pretty sure she was speaking to him, but couldn't respond for awe of her hair.

---

[18] Keep in mind that it was still snowing, but there were two lanterns about the front of the cart which lit up Ten ha's curious contours and Lance's baffled expression.

So Ten ha tried again, with, "Hola…"

Still trying to digest the remainder of her appearance, Lance could only manage, "Huh?"

And Ten ha, not certain on where else to go, asked, "Konnichiwa?"

"Oh, I'm—I'm sorry—I don't—"

"Oh! So you do speak English!" she exclaimed, quite happy on this turn—not because she was uproariously fond of English; the universal linguist was simply keen on speech.

"Oh, yes, yes," came Lance in reply, "Yes, I'm—um—English, yes. What-what-what are you?"

Had Lance had more time to react, he may yet have been more tactful, but as it were, Ten ha paid no nevermind to it herself. "I'm a cook. I work for the Baron Pan Bordolo."

Lance found a laugh emerging from the smirking side of his mouth. He tried to retract it, but it had already reached the girl. "Yes, but where are you from?"

Ten ha had to walk just a little quicker to follow this man, picking up her knees to stay out of the snow. "Straight from the Americas, most recently Boston—"

But she should only get so far before he would correct her, saying, "No: you. Who are you? Where did you come from?"

Ten ha felt her brow furrow in question, unsure of exactly what was being asked or how to answer it. She may have sampled a guess, had one of the men, another servant to a stranger, not called back:

"Oy! Save your breath for carryin', lad!" And then this gentleman turned back to shoulder into the Baron's cart, his scowl practically visible through the back of his head.

Ten ha couldn't help but notice that Lance, when he braced himself against his handle, had far more impressive shoulders than the man who had just reprimanded him. Ten ha sped her step to get closer to one of those shoulders and whispered, "My name is Ten ha."

And he, smiling for a reason he could not discern whispered back, "I'm Lance."

Had the Baron ever met Freud, his ears would have perked at the name, but when Ten ha later mentioned it, all that the Baron concluded was that the boy's title was likely sharper than his wit.

Of course, when Ten ha joined him behind the cart, the Baron was primarily pondering the steaming cup of tea he should make himself once they reached this specter town. Geru, walking just beside his Baron was consumed with a much grimmer thought.

"They're going to eat us."

The Baron stifled a laugh. "Geru, I assure you that no one ever got eaten by being stranded on a mountain[19]."

"Maybe none that you know of," he grumbled in reply, "I mean, how should you have ever heard of it, if none of them survived?"

The Baron would have smirked at this as well, but he did not wish for the lady to see that he took such things lightly.

"Perhaps," ventured she, "that's why we never heard of the town in the first place, this Adleman, Adleston... What was it again?"

Luckily, our little group wasn't held in suspense, for not long after Ten ha's inquiry, Fletcher could be heard calling from the front of the pack, "There it is! Ha! I told you it was there; I told you, I did!"

And sure enough, some fifty feet before them stood the sign, reading ADLESHIP ISLE.

---

[19] We apologize for the Donner Party reference.

XIV – Boots

Sebastian elected to be excited. Yes, he was a little bit scared, but—to be fair—he was only scared a few days out of the year, so it was quite a thrill for him. Besides, he had Hephaestus, who, may I remind you, *was* an outsider to help advise him on the new outsider. And because the thin stranger was (to his memory) both two feet shorter than Hephaestus and looked like 'people didn't eat where he came from,' Sebastian's minor anxieties would not eclipse his fascination.

His daughters did what daughters do: that is they redid their dresses and makeup, Samantha because she saw her older sister doing so and thought it polite. Sabrina dipped into the most exotic of her imported wares[20] to paint herself in what she only assumed was the latest and greatest fashion of the Big Out There. All the while she faced her mirror, she wore a determined little lopsided smirk, the likes of which history would never rival.

Clemens, Sherman, Piers, and of course Manuel, after a brief huddle, called the new arrival "Amazing," "Unbearable," "Unbelievable," and "A Danger to the Food Storage"—the last of which was patently untrue. Piers wondered—only for a moment, mind—if they should perchance change the banner to welcome the new stranger as well, which brought a series of reprimands from Sherman and Clemens. They each eventually resolved to quickly go home to comfort their wives, who 'might be in shock[21].'

---

[20] *All* of Sabrina's wares—makeup and otherwise—had come from Hephaestus, so to call it imported is a little unnecessary.
[21] The wives were not the least in shock.

Mothers took their children home, intending to get them re-cleaned-up, before resolving that they should probably just wear whatever it was they already had on for Hephaestus.

Raul told Julian to quick, run back home, then meet up again to watch the new arrivals. Julian didn't have long enough to consider his mood, but in retrospect, he would note that he had never been more intrigued about any single happening in his life. He hardly said a word to Meredith or Miriam as he took another boiled egg for the road. And going out the door, he very nearly ran over Jonas.

He issued a quick "Sorry" before continuing on.

Jonas paid him no mind, as he—for the first time in some time without his daughter's insistence—was lacing his boots.

XV – Persian Rugs, Chilean Flutes, and Chinese China

Pigby noticed that the roads were paved as they entered the city. Sure, it wasn't stellar groundwork, but cobblestones in any form far beat out snow and ice and mountains.

Oswald, poking his head out of the little latching window, noticed the architecture the trimwork on the buildings, the brickwork and woodwork. He wondered on the Germanic construction long before he wondered just how such a remote location had afforded such a wealth of materials.

Geru, ever the scientist, noticed as many of you meteorologically-minded readers already have, how the snow, wind, and for that matter cloud-cover virtually ceased upon their western gate[22]. It was almost as if the words "Adleship Isle" acted as a threshold against any inclement weather.

And Ten ha—with all of her knowledge of language, translation, *mis*translation, and general typos—marveled at the missense of the term 'Isle.' She could see no oceans, no sand, not a single palm tree, and yet, branded into a sign far older than her, stood a word that spoke otherwise.

The Baron Pan Bordolo's attentions would be aimed at the people. After all, he had received no evidence that these citizens wouldn't try to eat them, wouldn't stone them for some artifact they carried, wouldn't craftily poison them for traveling with person of color. He had no way of knowing that they wouldn't congenially and politely sacrifice them to whatever god it was they served who may or may not have been named Hephaestus.

---

[22] Note: there was in fact some snow falling as they entered the Isle, but it— pardon the phrase—paled against the blizzard of the mountains all around.

Considering how they spied at the Baron and his crew, it was difficult to confirm or deny any of these notions. In what flashes and glimpses he caught of the coyly spying villagers, the Baron concluded that they all looked somewhat frightened, somewhat fascinated, and somewhat hungry. After years and years of traveling about the third, fourth and even fifth-world settlements, the Baron had seen all sides of poverty, famine and general starvation and could, by now, read even the minutest hunger in a glance.

Their hunger was not desperate, nor encompassing, but it seemed to stand out above all other intentions. (To be fair, the Baron Pan Bordolo may have been projecting on account of his own hunger; to be even more fair, the people of the Isle were hungry, long awaiting the afternoon's festivities and particularly their annual and ridiculously-titled 'Hephaestus High-Feast-us.')

As he scanned face after partially-hidden face, the Baron was actually surprised to find that any individual should stand out to him, much less a teenage boy. But the Baron took one look into this boy's eyes and indeed glimpsed the truest soul he had ever seen[23].

Looking back from his hiding place on the hill above the road, Julian tried to hold the Baron's eye as long as he could, and assumed the Baron's stare to be more commanding than his own. There was an intensity, an excitement, a sense of experience and moreover a stubbornness in this man's gaze that assured Julian he had stared down more people more often and for far longer than Julian could ever hope to.

Julian also concluded that this man was the leader of the strange little group, perhaps like Hephaestus and his servants. Except the Baron's servants weren't uniform: they were each more diverse than any two men living in the Isle, and somehow the Baron still stood out.

Julian did not equate him to the Libburus; Libburi don't travel. He had never before heard of a Baron—or Duke, Knight, or Count, or any nobler class or aristocracy, apart than their two-tiered 'upper' and 'lower.' Though he would eventually call him "Sir Baron" and even more eventually invoke the name "Pan," Julian first knew the Baron Pan Bordolo as the "Mustache Man."

And to Julian's surprise, the Mustache Man turned his gaze first. (The Baron only looked away because Geru was once again at his ear, likely whispering on how hungry the villagers looked, but Julian did not know this.)

---

[23] Not to brag, but "Told you so."

Raul, who had ducked out of sight by Julian's side, asked, "Did he see you?" (Raul was not a coward, merely cautious; after all, there was no evidence that his head should not pop of his shoulders if looked at by this stranger with the loopy mustache.)

Julian, not wanting to squeak if he tried to speak, merely nodded and watched as the Mustache Man continued down the road toward the bridge and the town square.

A little more bold and a little more impatient[24], Raul scrambled back to his feet, grabbed Julian's arm and asked again, "Did he see you?"

"Yes. *Yes*," he said again, wrenching his eyes from the large covered cart to look back at Raul. "He looked right at me."

"Well, c'mon!"

And they ran toward the river, keeping to the frosted grass, along the banks and the ditches. Julian followed Raul, darting from stone to stone across the river where it ran shallow, where they had played as children, to beat the Baron to the square.

The people had gathered once more, a neat cluster of bodies donuted around the square, opening only for the bridge, all holding their breath. Julian and Raul shouldered their way into clear view just as the Baron managed his way across the bridge.

Hephaestus stood about the center of the square. The Libburus was placed on his right. In his wisdom, Hephaestus saw fit to tell Sebastian that this was for his benefit, because it would feature his best side.

Really, it was because he knew that most people—reading left to right—would probably prefer to see Sebastian first because, for one, his height lent to a nice upsloping photographic effect. For another, Hephaestus considered the possibility that his image and reputation may be so imposing that any unsuspecting stranger would go into shock from seeing His Grandeur unless they were to warm up to someone of Sebastian's stature beforehand.

But it was Hephaestus who was shocked, for he had never seen an assortment of persons such as these. Of course, having traveled all four corners of the globe—and by rumor having discovered the fifth— Hephaestus had seen all kinds of people and within them all extremities, deformities, or abnormalities. Never had he seen so separate and diverse

---

[24] It's always amazing how much they go hand-in-hand, and mark it: I will show you evidence of such.

kinds collected together—literally combined into one in the case of Ten ha.

This shock—courtesy of his grace under pressure—did not show. Hephaestus stood firmly, arms open, with a good and comforting smile for the wayward traveler, while he surveyed the tallest black man, the shortest Oriental[25], and the shiniest Chinese[26] possibly ever to exist. Perhaps had Oswald—an all-English-blood New-Englander—not been slung up in the cart, Hephaestus would have felt more assured, but that is neither here nor there.

Hephaestus too picked out the 'Mustache Man' as the leader, and hoped, when he caught the whiff of his Liverpool Silver treatment, that as an Englishman, he might be acquainted with legend of Hephaestus and thus make mutual trust a much easier thing to manage. So when he declared, "Welcome, sirs!" it was directly to the Baron Pan Bordolo.

"Welcome," he repeated, "to Adleship Isle!"

The Baron's crew, having been welcomed several dozen times to several-dozen places, knew to nod in unison, and the crowd, though still somewhat frightened, applauded.

Fletcher, feeling that he knew these people better than the Baron, looked up at them, waved, and issued a "Thank you," which settled the applause.

"Sir," replied the Baron, "I am clearly indebted to you and your men for the rescue of me and mine."

Hephaestus, loving the flattery only almost as much as he loved playing humility, said, "Oh, Tut! Sir—think nothing on it, for I am sure you would have done the same in my place."

This brought a smile to the lips of our Baron, who—until that last—was unsure of how to react to such a people. This politeness was indicative of only one thing: the Baron had dealt with people like Hephaestus all his life, for the Baron knew Englishmen.

Hephaestus was simply relieved that this man understood English, meaning that he could personally handle negotiations. He cleared his throat, put out his right hand, and said, "My name is Hephaestus."

The Baron—not certain if he should cower or smirk at this name—proceeded forward from the protection of his group and took the

---

[25] Oriental meant in those days what you would call 'Arab' which pertained to the Persian-perceived personage of the company, Geru.

[26] Oversimplified to mean Ten ha, if you were wondering.

hand. "Mister Hephaestus: the lord of blacksmiths, lord of all men who call themselves 'Black' or 'Smith'—that must be quite a large demographic in our little England, mustn't it?"

Hephaestus, still shaking the hand, said through somewhat gritted teeth, "I'll take your jest as benign, sir."

"I appreciate the kindness," the Baron returned. "I am the Baron Pan Bordolo."

"A Baron," Hephaestus repeated.

"*Yes*, a Baron." The Baron cleared his throat, as if to confirm his presence. "And I *am* thankful to your men. We could not have gotten here without them."

"Yes, well, seven sturdy servants, sir; that's what gets it done."

It was not wholly funny, but for whatever reason, the Baron clamped his jaw shut to keep from laughing. Once he was certain he could speak without so much as a giggle, the Baron said, "Come again?"

"Eight able oxen," Hephaestus declared, "and seven sturdy servants, sir, to pull one well-worn wagon. And that's how I get up the mountain."

The Baron surely would have quipped against the use of such campy alliteration, but—seeing as the man calling himself Hephaestus was responsible for his safety—held back. Instead, he only said, "I see. Very good, sir."

Hephaestus probably would have asked after the title once more, had his thoughts not been interrupted by Sebastian who asked, "Does this mean they're not going to eat us?"

Hephaestus assured him, "No, they're not going to eat you."

"Are-Are you sure?" insisted Sebastian, "They look very hungry."

The Baron, less than arms-reach away, placed a hand on Sebastian's shoulder and said, "They are within earshot."

Sebastian, not knowing what a faux pas was, understood that he had committed one and retreated a step or two.

"Mister Bordolo," said Hephaestus, assuming that the Baron would not correct him, "might I introduce the Libburus, or, as you might say, mayor, of Adleship Isle: Sebastian."

"A pleasure," returned the Baron, recognizing how Hephaestus had 'missed' his title. He offered Sebastian a hand, which the Libburus tentatively took, and informed him, "You know there is a man in my company whom you would get along with famously." And he made to point out Geru.

As he had been concentrating so severely on the Baron, it wasn't until this moment that Hephaestus truly saw the cart: this large, thatch-roofed cabin-on-wheels, that needed four of his servants to be towed across the bridge. Hephaestus' eyebrows arched, his nostrils flared, but he put them away again before anyone could see. "What is that, sir?"

"Oh that! Yes, my cart, sirs. Let me tell you, it was pretty difficult getting it all the way up the mountain; I do not envy your boys right now—"

Hephaestus took a stride forward, which effectively placed himself between the Baron and the imposing cart. "Yes, what are you carrying?" he asked, a little more shakily than he had intended.

The Baron tried to assuage the other's foreboding by casually responding, "Oh, knickknacks, odds and ends, items of worth, mirth, and dearth," which his fellows qualified in chorus:

"Persian rugs," said Pigby.

"Chilean flutes," said Fletcher.

"Chinese china," said Geru.

"You know," concluded the Baron, "the works."

"So you are," began Hephaestus, beginning to lose his breath in something that verged on what normal people might equate to a panic attack, "you just happen to be carrying pieces from all over the world through England?"

"Yes. They're for trade," the Baron explained modestly.

Hephaestus needed no further explanation; his dread was confirmed. Hephaestus knew of no fur trapper or arms dealer that sold authentic Persian rugs, Chilean flutes, and Chinese china alongside. Hephaestus suddenly—for the first time in his travels through Adleship Isle—felt the eerie sensation that the village was a bit too small for him. Keeping down the lump in his throat, which barely permitted him speak, Hephaestus dared utter the question: "You're a traveling merchant?"

"Yes—" the Baron began to say but was cut off when Geru, Fletcher, and Pigby interjected practically simultaneously:

"Not *just* a traveling merchant."

Hephaestus visibly bristled at this claim.

The Baron looked back to his fellows and, with a nod, bid them both his thanks and to stand down. Returning to the merchant opposite, the Baron Pan Bordolo responded in as polite a manner as he could, "I am an adventurer."

"But a traveling merchant."

"Well…" The Baron surveyed the crowd, trying to determine what news this should effect. "Yes."

The people of the Isle stared in silent wonder; they knew that Hephaestus called himself this, but otherwise had no idea what it meant, so it was not the crowd that reacted, but the lord of merchants who had his own wagon, his own set of servants, and his own reputation to protect. Though he justified his next for the sake of the town, the reader will plainly see that it was for his own pride.

Hephaestus lowered his voice, abandoned any trace of a smile, and said in a harsh whisper to the man calling himself 'Baron,' "I think you should be ashamed of yourself."

The Baron was not fully taken aback, but he did move in the reverse. "Beg pardon?"

"To take advantage with that façade: parading yourself as a Baron among persons who know no better so they will receive you as nobility. For all I know, you're just a commoner with a keen forge hand."

"Forge hand—" began the Baron, about to make a derisive remark on the misplaced 'Hephaestus' before he was interrupted by Geru, who—having impeccable hearing—had caught the last.

"How dare you!" he announced, striding forward. "I demand you take that back, sir, for the sake of your head!"

"Geru—Please." And upon eye-contact with his Baron, the short man took grumbling back to his rank. The Baron refaced Hephaestus, and said, with a somewhat pained smile, "Mister *Hephaestus*, sir. I am sorry if my presence has affronted you in any way, but that is my name."

"Which I refuse to believe," returned Hephaestus. As if to demonstrate his resolve in this matter, he crossed his arms about his chest.

Most of the townsfolk were unable to hear this exchange, and even if they could, the argument would probably just confuse them, but they could feel the tension in the words and the two men. Each man in the Baron's crew wondered whether he should retrieve a weapon from their well-stocked wares. Hephaestus' men, split between the Baron's cart and flanking their leader, held still, awaiting new orders. Except for Trenton, who proceeded a few readying paces forward just in case.

The Baron himself, for however offended he may have been, attempted to laugh off the situation and so returned, "Well, I pray you enlighten me as to why I should be so hard to believe."

"Quite simply because I have never heard of a 'Baron Pan Bordolo,'" returned Hephaestus.

"Oh!" The Baron gave one sharp guffaw to this last and said, "And that's reason enough to reject my existence, is it?"

"Boy," began Hephaestus, "I have traveled all over the world, and never have I seen or heard rumor of a—"

"And this lends you the lens of absolute truth, does it?" returned the Baron, and—before Hephaestus could speak again— "You know everything there is to know, so anything you *don't* know simply cannot be? Well, that's rich! And I tell you, I *have* heard of Hephaestus, but—*hmm*—you don't sound Greek to me, and I don't see a hammer anywhere on your person, and—apart from your Merlin's beard—I can't quite imagine how you'll have lived for three thousand years!"

Hephaestus beat one fist against his chest and declared, "My *mother* named me 'Hephaestus,' Mister Bordolo!"

"And shortly after her virgin birth, proceeded to dip you by the heel into the river Styx, no doubt?"

"You go too far!"

Perhaps they would have fought. This seemed likely, even to a populace that was little acquainted to the concept of fighting. Had it actually come to blows, Pigby could have torn the men from one another, but luckily, it was Trenton, Hephaestus' right-hand man, who strode into the square, hands out to the whole of the donut, yelling, "Hephaestus! Stand down."

And stand down he did. Still feeling that his haven of Adleship Isle could be torn out from under him by the presence of another merchant, Hephaestus stood down.

The Baron took his cue from the man opposite. Stepping back, he said, "Sir."

"Sir," nodded Hephaestus. "Well, that settles…" He eyed the cart. "…introductions."

"Yes," replied the Baron, "I suppose it does."

"Sir Baron!" came Trenton, taking the Baron's attention before he could about-face. "Certainly, you will join us in the town feast tonight."

The Baron, caught quite off-guard, knew no appropriate reaction besides the trite: "Oh, I wouldn't impose—"

"But-but I insist!" came Sebastian, for—no matter how frightened he should be by the foreigner—he would never refuse an opportunity to feed a guest, however guestly the Baron may have been.

The Baron was somewhat confused about the nature of his welcome. Torn between Hephaestus' insistence against his title and

Sebastian's warm smile, (but knowing that his crew would never forgive him if he refused them a meal after some of the longest days of their lives), the Baron consented.

"Then I appreciate and shall not refuse your invitation," said the Baron, "Thank you, Sebastian."

Sebastian puffed up like a pigeon, beamed, and realized that he could not speak for he had swallowed his tongue.

"Very good, sir," said Trenton. He raised an eyebrow to Hephaestus, telling him to—for Christ's sake—behave himself, then spun on a heel and removed himself from the situation.

"This is excellent!" exclaimed Sebastian, having once again found his tongue. And then he inadvertently said the worst thing he possibly could have: "Now we can celebrate the arrival of two—*two* travelers!" this last to the village, not His (rather perturbed) Granditude.

The town appeared uneasy, but intrigued. The Baron's crew appeared tickled.

The Baron himself had a moment of realization, and saw fit to ask Hephaestus, "The feast is for you?"

"To hail his visit," explained Sebastian.

"A feast for your *visit*?" the Baron repeated.

Hephaestus cleared his throat. "For my safe arrival."

"Oh, then you're not from here, either," concluded the Baron, unsure of why no one had brought this up earlier.

At this, Hephaestus laughed, and only most of it was forced. "Well, I should think not." And with some sweeping gestures, said, "I am Hephaestus."

"Yes," returned the unsuspecting Baron, "so you've said."

This flustered Hephaestus some more, and he found himself slowly stating, "No, you see, I, sir, *am Hephaestus*."

"Yes," repeated the Baron, "the 'god of the forge.'"

"*No*, the merchant!"

Fletcher was heard saying, in genuine surprise and intrigue, "There's a Hephaestus, God of Merchants?"

But the Baron, paying him no mind, was amazed at the coincidence: "You mean to say, sir, you are a merchant as well?"

"Yes!" exclaimed Hephaestus, getting a little too excited for his own good. "Of course I'm a traveling merchant—Mister Bordolo, I don't mean to boast, but I am *the* traveling merchant, and surely—*surely*, if you called yourself a merchant you would have heard of me, especially if you are—as you sound—an Englishman."

The Baron, more interested than offended presently, said, "I am an Englishman. But I've never heard of you."

The townsfolk gasped; not only was the Out There already *Big*, it was suddenly big enough for someone to not know who the Master Fascinator was.

Hephaestus too was trying to keep hold on his reality. His crew, particularly Trenton, could tell that he was reeling, but none felt it their place to venture forward and interject. Eventually, he managed to wheeze out, "How is that possible?"

The Baron grinned. He did not know why this was such an issue to Hephaestus, but he managed to find it amusing. "Well, you're only meeting me for the first time, but you'll soon learn that I tend to keep away from 'mainstream' areas."

"As do I!"

"Alright, alright—" The Baron, wanting to keep from exploding this particular issue, turned back to the cart and shouted, "Oswald?"

From behind the cart's closed door came a somewhat muffled, "What-what?"

So Pigby opened the door.

"Say, Oswald," continued the Baron, "are you familiar with a Hephaestus?"

"Yes, sir," came the old man's voice once again.

"Not the Greek god, Oswald."

"Yes, sir."

"The *merchant*, Oswald."

"Yes, sir."

"Ah, well there you go then," said the Baron, refacing Hephaestus, a smile across his lips, and over his shoulder, yelled, "Thank you, Oswald; that'll be all!"

"Thank you, sir," were the last words heard from Oswald before Pigby once again closed the door on him.

"Oswald," explained the Baron, "my literaturist and historian."

Hephaestus tried not to react to 'historian' as a remark against his age.

The Libburus was more concerned by the cart and the voice that had come out of it. Assuming—*hoping*, rather—that there was a man inside, to whom it belonged, Sebastian cocked his head for a better view and asked, "Why is he…"

"In the cart?" asked the Baron, "Oh, he's been hammocked— twisted his ankle on the mountain, which is—in some part—why we needed to come here, and why—if it is not too much to ask—we should need to stay until it heals."

"Oh! B-b-but of course!" stammered the Libburus, without knowing what else to say.

This request to stay may not have raised such hell had it not been for the next set of comments. See, the Baron, being polite—at least to Sebastian—assured him that they would 'be off again' the moment Oswald was better, (which may have taken over a week as was, but the length of invasion from this foreigner didn't spark a fire until one of Hephaestus' servants had spoken up).

From where he stood beside the Baron's cart, trying not to stare too obviously at Ten ha, Lance felt a sudden spur of chivalry, to which he straightened, strode forward, and declared, "Not in this weather, you won't! No man should dare travel 'til after the winter's over."

And Hephaestus, caught up by his own offense and some sort of bizarre competition, saw his first chance to show up the so-called Baron who claimed to not know who he was. "Yes!" he began—and mark this, for it is quite clever, "It is preposterous that you should think to travel any-time before the winds turn 'round, which puts you here through January. No, don't think on it—don't think for a second—you *must* stay here. But—oh..." as if just realizing for the first time, "You can't really fit six people in that little cart for a whole month, now, can you?"

Now, the town had already decided, as they did every year, that their Hephaestus, (as well as his seven sturdy servants), would be put up in the Libburus' home. No one had planned to take in this new invader; no one had even considered the possibility of his arrival.

The Baron—not knowing precisely what Hephaestus had done, but smelling some foul play—raised an eyebrow and glanced across the crowd, between the heads of households. "Well," he said, daring to anticipate the response to his comment, "I'll be needing a place to stay then, I should think."

The Baron Pan Bordolo wondered if there would be an awkward silence, or thought that maybe the people might look to their 'mayor' who would deliver a polite excuse, but he had not considered that the people of Adleship Isle had never dealt with real outsiders before. He quickly learned this, for—all at once—the ruckus and babble of the citizens very nearly threw him from his feet.

Before the Baron could alleviate the tension or assuage some fears with a joke, Clemens the grocer had declared—quite assuredly— that there was simply not enough food in their house for six guests. Piers was convinced that his wife, Lilli, had contracted some terrible illness which they should not wish to pass on to their guests. All that Sherman could manage was a sputtered "Well, I—But I—See I—"

"I say," said the Baron, but if he ever did mention what it was he said, it was lost in the din of the townspeople, all of whom were discovering some reason why they couldn't host the Baron for the winter.

The Baron took a few steps back, nearly running into Pigby, who—to be fair—was a large target.

"Admirable hospitality," muttered Geru.

Oswald, already hard of hearing and unable to see a single thing through the walls of the cart, was shouting, "What-what-what?"

Amid the commotion of a whole village—half of whom were discussing the sure threat of plague—even the mayor could be seen marking in his head the space of his house to justify that he too could not take the stranger's men, "Yes, yes—I-I'm afraid that counts out the last of my rooms!"

The Baron turned to see Hephaestus, who wore a wry sort of smirk, which put dimples in his cheeks. And Hephaestus caught his eye as well; had the older merchant known then the rivalry that this little bit of contact would spark, he would have had the good sense to look away.

The Baron Pan Bordolo, his forehead furrowed in concentration, his gaze lost in the other merchant's, had stopped rightly listening to the sounds around him. So when the silence erupted out of the middle of the commotion, it shocked him.

Here is what happened:

Julian was not certain what it was that he felt but was certain he did not want it to go away. He was also confident that this peculiar new sensation had something to with the Mustache Man. So when he heard everyone—including Manny and Meredith—saying that they couldn't put up the visitor, he wondered if his stomach might fall through his heels.

"Raul!" he said, taking his friend's shoulder, "Why don't you offer to take him? Your house has plenty of room."

"Are you crazy?" Raul hissed in return. "My dad would ship me out for that."

Julian could see the Baron scanning the crowd, and so Julian too surveyed the shaking heads. Somewhere in his search, his eye just sort of caught Samantha—the way that young children sort of catch colds, and editors of *The New Yorker* catch subtle nuance—and it stayed fixed.

He perceived her to be frightened. Of course, this may have been a projection again; after all, why shouldn't he want to protect the love of his life, and how better to protect her than to invent something that should frighten her? But Julian could only see that she was turned amiss by this commotion, by the confusion and uncertainty. Julian, a boy of seventeen and limited education, did not exactly formulate a plan, but he knew that present anxieties revolved around the Baron's not having a place to stay.

So Julian attempted to straighten. His posture pulled itself up—or perhaps it was forward: one can never be too sure.

And he spoke. He must have. He wasn't immediately certain of this, but for some reason most of the heads were turning toward him and most of the hubbub had stopped.

Raul, Manuel, and a very fussy Meredith had clearly heard Julian announce—quite stoutly, I might add—"I'll take him."

So when the town quieted, Julian, blood pounding in his ears, still staring at Samantha, went to speak again. This time even the Baron could hear the lad whom he would learn to call Julian saying, "I can take them. I'll keep the traveler and his men for the winter."

The Baron looked from Geru, to Fletcher, to Ten ha, and lastly to Pigby. With some irony in his tone, he noted, "Boys, I think we've found our savior."

The Baron Pan Bordolo then surveyed Julian, whose chest heaved up and down from the adrenaline of the boldest gesture of his life, and whose gaze he followed until it landed on the oblivious young woman in the crowd. "Hmm," he observed, "there's good news in this."

"How's that?" asked Geru.

"If I am to be in a boy's debt, I'd much rather he be a lover than a lawyer."

There was a moment of whispering, then a longer moment of craning necks to better see Julian. Of course, most everyone knew who Julian was, but—for some reason—they needed to see what he looked like again, as if it might shed some light as to why he had spoken up. However, as Samantha was one of the first to pick him out of the crowd, Julian was forced to blush and look away, leaving all following glancers unable to see the direction of his infatuated gaze.

The Libburus was not a supremely confident man. As you may have noticed, he had difficulty not sounding nervous in new situations. But he was—against whatever adversity—able to carry out his necessary duties. This included cutting the ribbons on new buildings, taking the first bite at a feast, patting the heads of youngsters, and—when there was quiet around a pending decision—to forwarding the conversation.

He stepped toward Julian—only two paces, so not close enough to scare the boy, if indeed the boy should be scared. "This is a generous offer, young man. Can you show these travelers comfort and hospitality through the winter?"

"Well…" Julian had not planned on justifying himself. In fact, he had not planned on anything. He did not know what would happen over the next few weeks; at the time, all he knew was that Raul, Manuel, and Meredith, and probably half the people in the village were looking at him and thinking, *You can still refuse.*

But he couldn't. Not really. Not anymore. So he said, "My house is intended for four, and it's only me, so I can make room for them."

The Libburus surveyed the crowd one last time. As there appeared no objectors, he announced, "Then it is settled! The visitors shall live with the boy Julian[27] for the duration of their stay here in Adleship Isle." And as Julian stepped forward, out of the donut and into the clearing, the Libburus took it upon himself to introduce the Baron to Julian. But because he remembered neither the Baron's title nor name, said, "Sir…Visitor, might I introduce to you Julian."

"I am honored to make your acquaintance, Julian," to which Julian could only nod.

While the Baron sent Julian to meet his crew—the members of which were stranger than Julian could tell from farther away, particularly the dark man whose hands looked like shovels—the Libburus dismissed the curious Isleans back to their homes and the donut gradually unraveled.

After thanking Sebastian, whose name he had already forgotten, the Baron was about to leave as well, but was stopped briefly by Hephaestus, and his solemn expression. Hephaestus pulled the Baron close to his own shoulder and whispered something which even Geru couldn't hear. Then, with a firm and at least partially respectful nod, the Baron excused himself.

---

[27] It is widely believed that Sebastian only knew Julian's name on account of Cletus whispering it behind him, for such was not beyond the realm of possibilities.

XVI – Bedding

Though they grumbled at the obligation, Hephaestus' same servants about-faced the cart and crew to the far northwest corner of the town to where Julian's house lay.

Hephaestus' servants, once they'd parked the cart just beside the cottage, (which looked only slightly larger than the cart itself), nodded politely, and asked Julian directions back and left. Julian, the observant type neglected to notice that Lance attempted to linger.

It took him hardly five minutes to arrange the house for guests. He stopped—for only a moment, mind—to consider the master bedroom, which had been most untouched since his parents had left it. The loft space, where he had slept as a child, was almost entirely bed anyway, and the main room, in which he *now* slept had floor-space enough for the giant man once the couch was tucked into the corner. In any case, it was large enough for all of them to fit conceivably, provided that no man slept alone.

However, there remained a more pressing problem, seeing as one of their members was *not*, in fact, a man. The Baron—being a gentleman—insisted that Ten ha take the master suite while himself, Julian, and Pigby shared the main room, but there simply wasn't enough floor to contain anyone else along with Pigby.

So Julian, against Ten ha's protest that she could just sleep in the cart, threw on his boots again and ran down the path to Meredith's.

"Well, of course she's welcome!" assured the mother, trying to sound far more excited than she really was. "Yes, yes, of *course*—if you've got the lot of them up there, we can certainly help by squeezing one in down here."

"Well, just the girl, Mum," explained Julian. "The Baron-man thinks it's impolite to have her stay in a room with a man."

"Which is why she'll bunk with Miriam."

"And Jonas?" asked Julian, reminding Meredith and the readers that the grandfather chap happened to share the loft.

"And Jonas…" Meredith turned away to busy her hands, so as to make her stalling appear activity-oriented rather than solution-missing. "Jonas will go up and stay with you, yes? I mean, the whole reason you needed a space was for—"

"That's great, Mum," said Julian, "I'll collect his things; you can send him on up when he gets back."

"Julian," she began, the concern in her voice concerning the boy, "are you sure about leaving them up there by themselves? They do seem like a rather peculiar group."

Julian elected not to imagine what they were doing to his home.

Of course, the guests, when left alone, were chiefly concerned with talking over Hephaestus, the man who had been happy, then appeared scared, then self-righteous, then angry, put off, vengeful, secretive, and so on and so forth—all the while standing off the left shoulder of the man who was *actually* the leader of this little place.

He apparently had a role, a duty in this tiny mountain pass, even though it had been confirmed that he did not actually live there. "Did you notice," he entreated the lot of them, "that his one and only concern was saving face in front of them?"

"Which he hardly has to do—" squeaked the short man, whilst carrying a large trunk across the main room. "They'd eagerly eat out of the palm of his hand if he gave them permission."

Taking the trunk from Geru, Pigby hoisted it up onto the loft, and added, "They worship the stones he walks on."

"And would kill a score of sheep for his arrival," finished Ten ha, taking the trunk from Pigby and opening it to withdraw the bedding inside.

Fletcher, who had the old man slung about his shoulder in order to escort him and his ankle to a place to sit, asked, "Okay, so, that being said, have we any evidence that he's not the god 'Hephaestus' himself?"

There was a significant pause, the kind which might follow a grand realization or precede a descent into giggles. But alas, for the Baron's crew, who—in traveling both the known and unknown world—had experienced such pauses thousands of times, there was very little need to react.

Instead, the Baron just shook his head and said, "Oh, Fletcher, I'm so glad you're the one who said that. If not, I should have to lose some faith in mankind."

Oswald, upon being set quite un-gently on Julian's couch, inquired in earnest, "Then what exactly is he, sir?"

The Baron, from where he leaned against the wall, took this opportunity to straighten up and stride into the center of the space, saying, "Well, he's an Englishman, whatever else he is, and Englishmen, I know how to handle. Englishmen, I know how to read."

"How do you figure, sir?" came Pigby, "I couldn't place an accent anywhere on him."

"Because of his stubbornness; because of all the pride there was to hurt. I know Englishmen, boys, and I can tell you even gods were never so proud." The Baron smirked at his fun little quip. "No, he is a gentleman, and must be dealt with like one."

"You want him torn down from his pedestal, boss?" asked Fletcher.

"Preferably," replied the Baron.

"Your book have any insight on how to do that?" Pigby asked.

Having flipped through the little leather binding hardly thirty minutes before, the Baron replied, "Not exactly."

"A word on that," came Geru, having retrieved another suitcase from the cart and seeming to have heard the whole of the conversation while outside, "Why didn't you just show it to him? Would've shut him up and saved us all some trouble."

"Don't ever tell me what to do with my book, Geru. There are things I will not tolerate, and there are things for which you will walk back down the mountain by yourself, blizzard or no blizzard." Once Geru had resignedly lowered his head, the Baron resumed, "That overstuffed popinjay can criticize and scrutinize me, but he will never touch this book." Only after the Baron had made secure eye contact with each of his fellows did he finally release the protective palm from his breast pocket, assured that they would not bring it up for quite some time.

It was Ten ha then who remarked, "You know, he didn't seem all that bad to me."

Had Geru a pin on hand, he would have dropped it to see if it was audible.

"Not that bad?" returned the incredulous Fletcher, his brow rising even more than his voice. "I have never met a man more pretentious, and I hardly know the chap!"

"He did belittle the Baron, dear," said Geru.

"Which was rather unfounded," came Pigby.

"I say, yes, I say," finished Oswald, without really contributing anything at all.

"Oh, and that's just the beginning!" Fletcher found a chair and leapt on top of it for the sake of his speech, which he was like to do. "I mean, what was with the names—Dear God! I would die before I'd ever let anyone call me anything like 'His High-Honored Hephaestus,' no, sirree[28]!"

Careful to over-enunciate every word, he added, "Did you not see how he was hailed by the whole of that Himalayan Hermitage, who hocked at his heavenly hair—Bah!" after which Fletcher appeared to spit so as to get the taste out of his mouth. "That hat-hoisting, hosiery-hemming, hippo-haggling Hephaestus, him and his seven sturdy servants—Great gravy, boss, it's all just too much."

"But didn't you just say that he saved your life?" countered the Baron, silencing the thin man and bidding him return to the floor.

"Let's be perfectly fair," said the Baron, "while I admit that I was not cordially impressed by his manners, I don't think the old fool means ill for us[29]. As much as you may find him unreasonable, rude, overbearing, arrogant, tedious, boring, difficult, unmannered, provincial, stupid..." The Baron went on quite some time, but I'll skip to the end: "...we must all take note that it is essentially he who is running the show here."

"Which leaves a question, sir," said Geru, glancing at the door to make certain that Julian had not yet returned. "There was something he whispered to you back there and took great care not to let any of us hear it."

"Or any of the other villagers," came Ten ha.

"Oh, that, yes, well..." The Baron too made certain the front door was shut. "He told me that I wasn't to sell or trade a single thing until I had spoken with him this evening."

"Bullocks!" announced Fletcher. In a show of manly patriotism, he sprang back to his feet and declared almost mightily, "Well, we'll

---

[28] It took him near twenty minutes, but Pigby eventually concluded that the thin man's equivalent title would be the Fast Flight-Footed Fletcher, the cadence for which most definitely inspired 'Fine Four-Fendered Friend' in *Chitty Chitty Bang Bang*.

[29] Hephaestus considered himself neither old, nor a fool, and would gladly engender ill-will if he had heard such a remark.

show him, won't we, lads. Hell, we'll sell off twice the loot at twice the value. That's four times—back me up, Pigby!"

"Maybe it's not the best time to piss off the establishment, as it were," the giant man said, forcing Fletcher to check the arithmetic on his own.

"No, see, it wasn't a warning," clarified the Baron. "There was no protection of territory or anything like that. It was a simple fact. Eerie almost. That—under no circumstances—are we to try to sell anything among these people."

There was a moment of silence, during which none of the Baron's crew made eye contact in order to contemplate the strangeness of this mandate. It was as if they should set off some ancient curse if they broke the rule, as if Pandora herself had craftily laid a trap for them.

Naturally, every one of them was tempted to break the rule, if only to find out what lay on the far end of the chain reaction, to see whether a bullet or a flower should emerge from the barrel, so to speak. I should imagine that you, like the Baron's men (and woman) are curious as well, but sadly, your thoughts on this matter will be interrupted, for at that moment, Julian appeared through the front door. The crew immediately resumed unpacking, their gossip circle effectively dispersed by the time Julian had entered the cottage. (Truth be told, Julian would likely have thought nothing of it had he caught them mid-discussion.)

"Alright," he began, "so I've talked with Meredith just down the way, and they'll have the...um—" Julian pointed to the girl.

"Ten ha," she supplied.

"*Ten ha*, thanks—um—" Julian was forced to stop and recollect for a moment, once again coming to grips with the shapes and colors of the travelers. "Yes, so if-if no one minds, she'll stay down there in a room with Meredith's daughter, and we'll take her father up here."

"What, *my* father?" asked Ten ha, those purply eyes growing even wider. "No, no, no, see—*he's* not my father."

But as Ten ha did not indicate any individual, Julian was made confused by her correction. Of course, Julian knew that *he* had meant Jonas, and not Ten ha's father at all, but he was curious as to who she assumed Julian would assume toward. So he asked, "Wait—I—Which one's *not* your dad, then?"

Fletcher, Pigby, Geru, and Oswald each raised a hand and spoke (in only-slightly-staggered unison), "I am."

The Baron cleared his throat. "He means Miss Meredith's father." Then turning to Julian, "That is what you meant, lad, yes?"

"Yes. Right." Julian looked over the travelers, whose names he had not entirely memorized, to see if he could glean some acknowledgment from any of them that they had heard what he said. No one spoke in the affirmative, but no one objected either. So Julian went on to distribute sleeping arrangements, putting Oswald—on account of his ankle—on the daybed; Pigby on the floor; Fletcher, Geru, and the Baron sharing the loft; and himself and Jonas in the master bed.

The men and woman continued to stare at him. Of course they were perfectly innocently studying him—as they had been trained to do—but Julian had never been studied before. He felt a little awkward, but could not discern whether or not they could tell.

They could tell.

It was the Baron who decided to spare the boy by saying, "Well, we owe you our thanks then, son."

"Right." Julian pulsed on his heels.

"Do you mind if I ask you something, boy?"

It took Julian longer than he would have liked to admit to determine that 'boy' referred to him. To be fair, he had been called lad, son, and boy all over the last minute. To be less fair, the Baron did not know whether the young man was called Julian, Julius, or Julliard, so his ability to *not* confuse him was slim to nil.

As Julian didn't answer otherwise, the Baron proceeded. He first took a deep breath, which rolled his mustache up around his nose, as if coiling before the pounce, then asked, "Might I inquire—" for which he had already assumed permission "—as to who Mister Hephaestus is?"

"His Great Mysteriousness?" asked Julian—which met nods from the Baron's crew. "Well, he's a traveler." After a moment's consideration, "He's *the* traveler. He comes every year. He always has."

The Baron shook his head, trying to make sense of the affair. "So he's just a visitor then?"

Julian shifted on his soles, not quite knowing how to venture a response. He could tell that this was something of an issue for the Baron's men, but he didn't know how to satisfy them with an answer. The answer that he chose was his best bet at satisfying himself, whether or not it should mean anything to the foreigners: "Hephaestus is the *only* visitor who's ever been to Adleship Isle."

Pigby, Fletcher, Geru, and Oswald leaned forward. "Ever?"

"The only one in a hundred years."

Julian, unfamiliar with life in the Big Out There, did not realize what a miraculous notion this was, but he could see that it had reached the strangers.

They seemed to want to ask on this. As it turned out, not a one of the Baron's crew had ever heard of a city, village, or town which was literally unreachable by any other; even the remotest of Tibetan encampments would commune with a neighbor, who would in turn commune with his neighbors and so on and so forth, until one of them had reached a major port. And finally, that major port would have been reached at one time or other by a traveling merchant.

Having never known such a freak occurrence as Adleship Isle, the Baron's men (and woman) hardly knew what to ask. So Ten ha looked to Fletcher, who looked to Oswald, who looked to Pigby, who looked to Geru, who looked to their Baron on what to do. The Baron shook his head, 'no,' having concluded that it would be best to wait on any ventures until he had talked to Hephaestus that evening. The crew resolved to wait for word from their boss.

Pigby must have felt amiss in just standing there and so said, "Geru, why don't let's grab another load from the cart."

"Oh, yes!" chimed Geru, "Yes, of course; can't very well relax if you haven't unpacked."

And with that, the giant man and the short man exited. (If they had been worried about startling Julian with their extreme natures, then they should have taken Ten ha with them as well.)

Fletcher took it upon himself to alleviate the awkwardness. Once he'd crossed the room to Julian, he threw an arm over his shoulders and said, "Julian, m'boy—that is your name, yes?"

Julian would have responded in the affirmative, but he had trouble answering when being escorted by the thin man who smelled curiously like apple-smoked bacon.

"Here, have a seat," Fletcher went on, sitting Julian down on his own daybed beside the old man. "Now, Julian, you're probably wondering what the hell kind of name Geru is anyway."

The Baron smirked.

Julian found himself wondering what-the-hell-kind-of-name *Fletcher* was. "Um…"

"See, he's from India, and not the American kind either." Fletcher tried to illustrate in the air in front of them what and where India was. "His parents are actually from England—London, but he…"

And that was all Julian was able to understand. To the best he could figure, every single person that travelled with the Baron Pan Bordolo was from a new and excitingly different location, across things called oceans and continents. Julian had heard of foreign lands before in snippets from Hephaestus' servants, but these explanations—probably because they were told directly to him—were even more fascinating and bewildering.

While Pigby, Geru, and Ten ha unloaded the cart, the Baron took it upon himself to sit back and listen to Fletcher and watch the young man who had indeed been their savior that day.

As Fletcher told his tales, Julian, still unsure of what exactly he'd committed to, grew more and more excited about the confusion he could hope to find in the weeks to come.

XVII – A Single Dinner Roll

You have never been to a feast.

You might object to this statement, but I think you will find that that what *you* call a feast is not really a feast at all.

You have been to gatherings, to dinner parties, to company-catered buffets, and you may have thought they were feasts, but the sad truth stands that the practice of feasting hardly exists in your world. (It is all the more sad because—seeing as I am writing this and you happen to be reading it—your world *is* my world, and I have never been to a feast either.)

Now, if you are highly religious or retain strict cultural roots to a people that is not entirely globalized[30], you may yet be exempt from my claim, but bear with me a paragraph or two before you skip ahead to the next section of dialogue. You may have celebrated a feast day of a particular saint or god, but you have likely not known total abandon to food the way the people of Adleship Isle did when Hephaestus arrived.

A true fest celebrates the food, and uses the food to celebrate the occasion or honor the individual. A true feast does not concern itself with calories, cholesterol, or fat content: only taste. There is no concern for cost or responsible allocation of resources. There will be more than enough food for every attendee, and there will be leftovers for them to take home.

It is not a deliberate binge either—guzzling up as much as possible for one day to make up for a meager or lousy year. This is a modern thought. Understand that a true feast pays no regard for

---

[30] By 'globalized,' I mean 'averaged,' 'integrated,' or 'muted,' 'amalgamated,' and 'assimilated' into an assumed norm. The non-globalized cultures of which I speak are those that do not hold themselves accountable to the world-stage.

yesterday, tomorrow, last week, or next year; it celebrates a here-and-now.

The Baron and his crew had—thankfully—been to feasts before. At feasts, visitors are not strangers; they are family. Guests would not be alienated or made to feel distant or even separate. Though the people of the Isle might be wary toward the strange men the by the following morning, the night of the Hephaestus High-Feast-us was celebrated precisely how it should have been—with all parties eating alongside as equals.

However, equal or not, hardly a citizen knew what to say to the crew, and so could only smile and nod, then quickly turn to his or her spouse or parent to whisper about the man who called himself a 'Baron.' The notion of 'Baron,' was incredibly difficult for the children, who—if they had ever heard the word—understood it to mean 'barren.' 'Barren'—considering the cart, the people, the clothing, and the visible knickknacks he carried—could not accurately sum up the stranger. Some parents informed their children that it was likened to their own Libburus and that this Baron effectively Libbured over the four men and a woman that went with him. Others yet assumed that it was just a name, perhaps a surname or foreign-sounding first name. (Even though the people of the Isle never *used* surnames, historians are quite certain that they must have had them.)

So—where previous years' conversations were festooned with remarks on His Eminent Presenceness—today's talk turned to the traveler. The *new* traveler, that is, this distinction put the *old* traveler amiss. And yet, when the Baron and his crew arrived, Hephaestus was playing the part of the polite gentleman.

Yes indeed, the older merchant wore an expression best reserved for he who is trying to swallow his own left foot but still pretending to enjoy it.

In some countries, feet are a delicacy. In some still, *human* feet are a delicacy. But this was England, and though Hephaestus had travelled all over the world and sampled all forms of cuisine in his journeys, the thought still made him gag, as it did all good Englishmen.

Luckily for Hephaestus, he was good at disguising his disgust. Even more luckily for the Baron, he knew Englishmen, and could detect the faint note of gag on his face.

The Baron walked into the square in a fine evening suit. His crew was dressed in odd assortments of formal and (for lack of a better term) *ethnic* garb.

Fletcher was in tan tails, tweeds, and tights which made him look strikingly like Disney's cartoon rendition of Ichabod Crane. Geru, with a near-Maharajah motif, looked a little bit over-bejeweled; of course, the moment anyone thought such, he had to immediately feel guilty for the indirect commentary on Geru's stature, (even though Geru likely wore more fake gems per square inch than anyone they had ever heard of). Oswald, though casted and crutched, was ornamented in a heavy, ruffled number, which produced plumes about his chest and wrists that would rival a peacock. Ten ha wore an elegant silk gown, which boasted a slit that ran the long length of her left leg, and was most likely intended to catch the eye of a certain young man, but that's another part of the story.

Pigby took the rear, and looked a little like a matador for the colors and the shapes created by his clothes. That being said, he somehow managed to leave his chest largely bare, and had something of a headdress strapped to his shiny dome of a forehead. A giant in his own right, Pigby (unintentionally) amplified every image that he projected, and so warranted the most gossip and head-turning.

Hephaestus, from his seat at the head table, was most excited, intrigued, annoyed *and* terrified by the presence of the Mustache Man himself, and so watched him all the while the group was escorted to their table—(which had unfortunately been set for only six, the setters having forgotten Julian, leading to apologetic bustle thereafter to find the additional chair). And when Pigby first sat down and—to the great surprise of the villagers—broke the chair, which likewise had to be replaced. And when Geru, apparently too small for the table, but still too proud to say so, was given a wooden block, (which was previously being used as a chair as well), to prop him to a proper level.

Even after the three replacement chairs were replaced for their original sitters, Hephaestus *still* could not take his eyes off of the Baron, who—perhaps just to grate on him—persisted in smiling through his ringletted mustache. Though he could ordinarily pride himself on impeccable hearing and even better active listening skills, Hephaestus missed the whole first two sentences that Trenton said off his shoulder. The third followed:

"He'd like to know how he should address the stranger."

"How's that?" Hephaestus returned, to which Trenton rolled his eyes, but not so much to show disrespect.

"Sir, Sebastian would like to address the stranger, but he would like your council," said Trenton, most likely repeating what he had said before, with the utmost patience. "He's been trying to wave you over for quite some time."

So Hephaestus stood and made his way along the table toward the Libburus, who indeed kept waving until Hephaestus was literally touching him.

"Yes, yes, so," Sebastian began, "I'd like to say a few words to the Mustache Man, to welcome him you see, to say that we are *not* afraid of him and-and that he should enjoy his stay and the food." Sebastian paused to think. "Or the food and his stay; which do you think is better?"

"I'm certain you will know what to say when the time comes."

Sebastian nodded, "Quite right, quite right. And yet, Your Multiknowingness," he went on, drumming his fingers against one another, "I don't quite know what to call him, see."

Hephaestus hesitated. He may have been considering misinforming his old friend that he should simply stick with 'Mustache Man'—but don't fault him for that temptation. I know *I* would have been tempted, simply because the title amuses me so, even if I wasn't the least bit miffed by the credit-stealing Baron. But Hephaestus, whatever his thoughts on the matter, took a deep breath in and said, "I think 'Sir Baron' should be fine."

"Right. Yes, well." He seemed to think on this for time before concluding once again, "Right."

From over at their table, the Baron's crew had noticed Hephaestus' stare and that their Baron did not give him the satisfaction returning his gaze.

"He's doing it again," muttered Geru after turning back to the center of the table. "He's staring at us."

"Well, so is everyone else," remarked Ten ha, who—like the Baron—did her best to look totally oblivious to their attention. *Un*like the Baron, she failed.

"With good reason," said Fletcher, straightening the tie about his neck. "We look pristine."

"But of course," added Pigby, hunched over the table, his massive shoulders shadowing out Oswald, who in turn tugged proudly at his cuff, saying:

"I should say so!"

"And why shouldn't they," added Geru. "They're planning to eat us."

This comment elicited groans from everyone at the table but for the Baron, who smirked. "Geru, they're not going to eat us."

"How can you possibly know that?" he protested, and validly too.

"Can't be," Fletcher responded, "we'd hardly feed half of them."

"We could if we were just the main course," remarked Ten ha. "Then they could satisfy the rest with side dishes. Appetizers, salads, hors d'oeuvres, what you will."

"Can you please stop talking about food?" requested Pigby, though it sounded more like a grumble or low growl. "You're making me hungry."

"Yeah, when do they serve, anyway?" came Fletcher.

"Just as soon as they've cooked us," replied a fidgeting Geru.

And at that precise moment, a hand was clapped on Geru's shoulder which produced a manly squeal. The hand turned out to belong to Julian, who was just returning to their table. (Yes, it seems I forgot to mention—silly of me, really—that Julian, after setting them at the table, had gone for whatever reason, and was just getting back.)

With only a moment's hesitation on account of Geru's outburst, Julian proceeded with, "They're just about ready to serve, but wanted me to ask if any of you have any special rituals before the serving of food."

The Baron's crew looked between one another with some confusion. They hadn't the slightest idea as to whether Julian meant joining hands and saying grace, or sacrificing a lucky virgin to a begging fire. Fletcher wanted to ask, but the Baron replied before he could manage.

"I am quite certain that any traditions of your fair people shall suffice for us," he graciously explained, "and we are glad to participate in any events in which we would be welcome."

To which Geru added, "Provided we get to keep our limbs."

This comment raised sniggers from the Baron's crew, as well as the eyebrows of Julian, who clearly did not understand why Geru should have anything to fear.

Now, do you remember what I said about feasts? Well, *that* is precisely what came out of that big storehouse right beside the town square, hauled out on some-dozen trays, with several carts, and a few whole tables, completely stacked, carried by stout gentlemen, like Manuel and Clemens. From what they observed, the spread had every single item that the Baron's crew could possibly want. Perhaps they would have desired something more glamorous on an ordinary day, but after so recently cheating certain death, their tastes seemed somewhat simpler and hence exceedingly satisfied.

Now, I will not describe every item on the tables—I am neither J. R. R. Tolkien nor Brian Jacques—but I will say this: any negative rumors or remarks regarding British cooking describe methods and persons that have never reached Adleship Isle.

According to Pigby, the plates literally materialized in front of them, and with that resonating hum of glass and ceramics, sang a song to beckon each member of the Baron's crew to the newly-erected buffet table. Oswald kept his head on a swivel, but even he managed to miss most of how that bustling little village got the food set up so quickly.

It was the edge of winter, and even though hardly a snowflake touched soil on the Isle, the air was quite deliciously chilled. But, as they approached the buffet, in the mob that formed around either side of the long serving stretch, the crew had to gasp at the warmth of the food. Geru gasped a second time when Pigby took a surprised step back and nearly landed on the man who was half his size.

The platters were about the size of wagon wheels, and Oswald was quite certain that the serving spoons were in fact shovels, which stacked their plates with the fullest portions of bread and meat and savory and sweet that they could possibly eat and then some. The Baron checked his coat pocket—not the one with the book, but that which held his emergency tin of Liverpool Silver, which the food might melt away.

So, after they had been served by smiling villagers, the crew went and sat down, led by their ambassador, Julian, who was busy once again scanning the crowd for Samantha. While he had been away previously, our hero had been speaking with Raul, who sat at a table adjacent to the head table, with his father Eugene, his mother, two younger sisters, three aunts, four uncles, and five cousins. He and Raul were friends of course, but Julian's primary reason for stealing away was to go toward the young lady's table, and though he saw the Libburus and his man-servant Cletus, (as well as our Algernon and Ferdinand[31]), Julian could not place his lady anywhere. After stalling with Raul for quite a time, he eventually had no choice but to return to his charges, whom—to the best he could figure—he had only adopted so as to impress the young lady who was presently absent.

And this is why: you see, when the Baron, his crew, and our story's hero crossed the bridge that evening, Samantha had been crouched neatly out of view, so that she could peer just over the ridge without being noticed. More accurately, she was crouched off her older

---

[31] If you have forgotten, these were Cletus' prestigious nose and lips.

sister's shoulder, having followed Sabrina up to their hiding place in the first place. The older sister wore a determined sort of grin on her face as she watched them, and said—to no audience aside from the lucky readers, "He's mine."

Of course you may take ill to this, assuming that Sabrina means Julian and that a farce of love-triangles fit for a Shakespearean comedy is about to take place. Thankfully (as we all breathe a sigh of relief) that is not the case. Sabrina might strike you as one who conquests. However, given the slim population of the Isle, and that it was somewhat uncouth to pursue persons in the first-cousin bracket, there were indeed very few quests for her to take.

But when she saw the Baron, that dear little lady seemed to take him as the most perfect opportunity for adventure to ever arrive in her homeland. Perhaps it was the curled stache, or the consequentially twinkling eyes, or even just the proper timbre of his voice, but in any case, she was most-determined to have him, and so painted herself for the occasion, with the aid of her younger sister, of course.

It was Samantha who strung Sabrina into her corset, Samantha who held the mirror, fastened the hair, and helped to make Sabrina blossom into the most brilliant flower ever to bloom in the deep winter. She did not begrudge Sabrina these obligations, so neither should we; as a kind, loving sister, she was happy to help. This meant that Samantha herself did not have nearly the same detail work put into her evening attire, but she did look fitting of the lady she was.

However, if we take rumor to be correct, the moment Samantha saw Julian, she ducked out of sight. For reasons she could not discern, Samantha felt suddenly self-conscious beside her radiant sister, and— even more troubling—was the fact that she was troubled at all. Her hands rushed to her blushing cheeks, and she instantly regretted not painting her face more thoroughly.

"Look at the way those tights pull," observed Sabrina, "Just imagine what a man could do with legs like that!" This comment bid Samantha to look back over the ridge once again to examine the Mustache Man's calves, which were indeed quite strong, probably on account of carrying him around the world some several times over.

If you, good reader, happen to be a teenager at the time you digest these words, you might feel your gorge rise as you consider the probable age gap faced by Sabrina in courting the Baron. But let us acknowledge that these happen to be different people in a different time-period and culture than yourself, and that your own brand of modern vampire fiction allows for age-gaps of two-hundred years. Besides, Sabrina placed the Baron's age at thirty at most.

In any case, due to their spying, Julian had missed running into Samantha, and by the time the sisters had returned to their father's table, everyone was already up and self-serving.

In handfuls of twelve at a time, the townsfolk finished at the buffet and sat back down with their piled plates, dutifully and hungrily waiting to eat until after the address to the people.

The Baron took his cue from Julian, and the crew followed their Baron. (Pigby would have begun without prompt had Geru not taken care to repeatedly jab him in the ribs every time he started for the food.) Hands were poised, ready to draw silverware from the table and begin eating on a moment's notice—silverware which too seemed to have materialized[32].

When the last of the servers had collected their own dinners and sat down, an expectant silence fell over the town.

The Baron raised those twinkling eyes of his up to the head table and politely held his lips closed while the Libburus stood to give the address. The Libburus was probably shorter than every other man at the table, but as he was the only person standing—mind you, the *single only person* standing in the entire populace—he managed to look like a giant. Not only that, but his presence, his demeanor, and his voice were larger than life as well. Take note, for this is quite a speech; here is how it went:

"Fellow families of Adleship Isle, ladies and gentlemen, children and ancients, friends and strangers from here and abroad, welcome! Welcome one and all to the Annual Hephaestus High-Feast-us, our celebration to honor His White-Beardedness, the traveler from the Big Out There!"

This was met with cheers to which the Libburus put up a hand, silencing the townsfolk. "I know many of you have put in many hours in preparation for his arrival, and for that work and this meal, I would like to extend my thanks to a few of our citizens."

And, without use of a scroll, book, or even a single notecard, Sebastian rifled off some four or five dozen names, paying a smiling nod to each group or family there. During this list, Pigby took the opportunity to grumble about the food getting cold, and Geru once again popped him in the ribs. Oswald and Fletcher tried to follow the direction of the

---

[32] The silverware had actually been placed for them while they each gathered their food.

Libburus' proclamations so that they may get to know the people, but quickly lost themselves in the sheer quantity of acknowledgements. (The only name that they retained happened to be 'Manuel,' which was only because Julian whooped when it was given.) Ten ha had her gaze fixed on a strapping young man by the name of Lance, and therefore paid very little attention to the speech.

The Baron, smiling broadly beneath brunette ringlets could only admire how tightly knit the whole town was. Whether the Libburus had actually gone and memorized the names for the speech or simply knew everyone well enough, the very nature of the acknowledgements complimented the Baron's sentimental side.

"...Additionally," Sebastian went on, addressing the whole of the town, "I would like to thank the Mister Baron Sir—who *is* a stranger— but still granted us the honor of attending our feast. Sir Baron," he said, nodding very directly to our own Baron Pan Bordolo, "we hope you will enjoy your time here and that you return to the Big Out There with fond memories."

The Baron raised his glass in commendation, a gesture which made the Libburus feel quite fluttery inside.

"And lastly," he cleared his throat, and as if conditioned to do so, the entire town held its collective breath, "I would like to commemorate our neighbor and friend, Julian. Come now, boy, stand up!"

Julian, who had been holding his breath with the rest of them, suddenly forgot how to exhale and so stood up looking somewhat unnerved.

"I want to personally thank Julian for offering to host the Mister Baron Sir, and his disciples, and-and-and for demonstrating, young Julian, that hospitality that we all should imbibe here in Adleship Isle."

This was—point of fact—the first time that he had stood up in front of the town since his parents had died, and likely would not have been so pleased with the comparison, but that this time, everyone— without any kind of cue—began applauding.

The Baron leaned over to Oswald and muttered, "But for his misuse of 'imbibe,' I'd say he's quite a speaker."

"Quite, yes," replied the old man.

Adleship Isle's very own old man, (whose daughter kept one hand on his forearm), beamed proudly, as if he felt he too could take credit for Julian's stellar upbringing. To be fair, the rest of Jonas' household felt somewhat smug about their relation to the suddenly-very-recognized young man, especially Manuel, (who felt he had been recognized twice.)

"And now," said Sebastian, once the clapping had mostly subsided, "for the breaking of the bread!"

Even though the townspeople again fell silent, a sudden wave of excitement swept through the crowd, which stopped when it collided with Pigby, whose hunger must have had a lot more inertia. Of course, Julian had explained this tradition to the Baron and his crew, but the instruction could never fully prepare them for this particular ritual.

"May I have the heads of the noble families please?" said Sebastian, "and our friend, His Prominence. And, Sir Baron, I would be honored if you would join us as well."

The Baron stood, and proceeded into the center of the square along with the noblemen, where they gathered around a small square table, on which was set a huge platter with a single dinner roll.

Don't worry: no miracle will be taking place here; this is not a modern rendition of 'Jesus Feeds Five Thousand' with an inexplicably small amount of food. For one, we have already established that there are obscene amounts of other foods prepared for this feast. For another, this particular roll had an approximate diameter of three generous feet.

The one Libburus, the two merchants, and the three noble gentlemen each seized a section and pulled. To the narrator's astonishment, the roll came apart in six nearly-even sections. The clever Baron was not so surprised, as he assumed (rightly) that the leavened leviathan had been deeply scored about the underside to anticipate such pulling. And each of the six gentleman proceeded in his own separate direction to distribute the contents of his hands.

Soon, every single person in the town, including the Baron's crew, had a small tuft of the bread pinched between his fingers. I say 'tuft' because it was just that sort of consistency, with raised feathers of dough that were so neatly undercooked that they had no room to crumble or fall, which was good, because falling bits of bread tended to bounce participants out of the competition.

'Participants' included every man, woman, and child who held a piece of the bread; the game was last-one-standing. It was played like so: at the word from the Libburus, everyone split his tuft in two, ate one portion and proceeded to press the other into his right palm, so that it would stick.

Now, the Baron's crew—upon tasting the bread—would note that it was somewhat sticky and doughy. Ten ha, given her experience in world cuisine could likely tell all of the ingredients from the first nibble, but they all supposed that the bread was engineered specifically for such a tradition.

"Cheers!" exclaimed Julian, and clapped his hand against Fletcher's, withdrew and found that Fletcher's lump had added itself to his hand. Oswald lost his piece to the Baron, and Geru to Pigby. Ten ha, for the odd number at the table, had turned to the table adjacent—because everyone was clapping palms and exchanging bread by means of adhesion—and gave her piece away to Piers.

As you read and reread this description, you may find yourself wondering why anyone would participate in such a tradition. The easy answer is for good luck. If you clap hands with the whole town and you are the last person to hold dough in your palm, you will obviously have a good year.

If it still seems strange to you, ask yourself why people rip dried chicken bones and make wishes. Why, in Greece, a variation of this game is played for Easter, in which friends bonk their eggs together, and the winner is he whose does not break. If you have ever blown out the candles on a birthday cake, looked for the coin baked into the New Year's bread, or flashed your breasts at Mardi Gras, you have no room to protest the bread-slapping game of Adleship Isle.

The sounds of a thousand slap-splats intermingled with the laughter and cheers very rhythmically, and the optimistic philosopher would find it necessary to point out how the bread game managed to connect everyone in the town. Julian's piece went to the Baron, then to Manuel, Lilli, Dietrich, and finally Marta (the rather-rotund butcher's daughter), who had received hers from her father (the butcher), Elke (the baker), and Norbert (the candlestick-maker), Eugene, Cletus, and finally Samantha.

The Baron's crew, knowing that they were to wait until this game was done before they began eating, had been worried that they should not be able to contain themselves, but it managed to capture all of their attention and enthusiasm enough to postpone their hunger for the couple of minutes it took. The only one who might have started eating during was (thankfully) the only member of the Baron's crew who remained in the game until the end.

Amidst cheers and exclamations, Clemens, his right hand almost completely enclosed in smashed bread, strode into the clearing at the center of the square to face off against Pigby. Clemens the grocer was a big man, not nearly so big as Pigby, but he sported a walrusy mustache which made up for any disparity of size—also he had bigger hands than anyone in the history of the Isle, (as concluded by the astrologist and palm-reader, Dietrich). Such a palm was ready to meet Pigby's with a huge helping of bread.

The suspense might make you hold your breath, but take comfort in the sea of smiles surrounding the competitors. Even Hephaestus, who had been admittedly grumpy before, was as relaxed and entertained as he should have been.

When the glorious finalists clasped hands, he gasped with the rest of the town in that second before they pulled away. The great ball of greasy bread, tinted from the many hands that had held it, stretched between the two palms, before deciding to reside in Pigby's.

Applause raised about them; sticky, doughy applause, while the citizens scraped at their hands to push the dough to the ground. Even Clemens, who had very nearly succeeded himself, stepped back to clap for the winner.

Pigby just looked stunned.

So, while Fletcher whistled and Geru bid a "Well done, old chap!" Julian stepped forward and took Pigby's arm, shouting through the din:

"Now throw it on the ground!" Which Pigby did. "Now step on it!" Which Pigby also did.

Then like some great prize-fighter who had just survived a grizzly bear, the giant of a man raised his arms in triumph, balling them into fists for all the Isle to see. And when he grinned, Julian was impressed by how white his teeth looked against his black skin.

The Libburus was laughing in joy and satisfaction. His town seemed quite happy, so why should not the Libburus be? The strangers had participated in their ritual, and fortune had bestowed them good luck in their victory. Good luck was not a thing to resent in the Isle. Good luck meant acceptance; good luck helped disperse the fears of the populace such that they did not cower away from Pigby but surrounded him.

Sebastian cleared his throat. He did not even look to Hephaestus for approval when he declared, "Eat up and enjoy, my friends! Happy Hey-Day!"

Which was followed by an equally enthusiastic refrain of "Happy Hey-Day!" and soon after, the entirety of Adleship Isle plunged headlong into their full plates and delightful conversations.

Over at Manuel's table, Meredith was glittering with excitement over the giant man, whose huge hand had managed to hold more bread than any she had ever seen. This made Manuel—who had won just two years prior—grumble against the subtle and probably unintended jab against his virility. Manuel's insecurities caused Julian—as they may have caused you—to smirk.

Julian was then met with a pat on the back from Raul, congratulating our hero for the acquisition of his giant. In fact all of the nobles were now charmed by the man who had recently terrified them, which must have opened them to second impressions of the rest of this strange group of travelers, in whom they suddenly saw the potential for new knowledge and—at the risk of sounding exploitive—entertainment.

The Libburus excitedly retold the events of Pigby's victory as though they were from an epic tale of one hundred years prior rather than three minutes. Cletus, happily to listen to his bubbling employer, continued to contentedly consume his feast, chewing with his mouth politely closed. Even Trenton, who had likely seen even more amazing competitions, had eagerly enveloped himself in the fascinating tale that the Libburus spun.

And Hephaestus, poor Hephaestus, was sipping his inaugural coco without a single soul watching. Where were the cheering hordes that had come to hail his safe arrival? Looking on at someone else's, for the first time in memory.

When he felt the hand on his arm, when he heard its owner clear his throat, and when he looked back to see the proud Hephaestus standing off his shoulder, the Baron was not the least bit surprised. His companions on the other hand seemed to forget how to breathe.

"Good evening, Mister Hephaestus!" exclaimed the Baron, as barons tend to do, especially among rivals or enemies.

"Yes—er—" Hephaestus began, for only true Englishmen say 'er' when they really mean 'um.' "Sir Baron, won't you join me on a walk? I'm sure we have some things to discuss."

The Baron surveyed his men (and woman) who—though recently guzzling like drought-starved vultures—had frozen mid-forkful to stare at their boss. He clicked his tongue twice, possibly in irritation, or possibly just to clear his palette of gravy, then, against the hopes of his crew, did not slap Hephaestus across the face with a white glove and instead stood.

The Baron's Adam's-apple bobbed before it said, "Very well. Fletcher, make certain that they keep well-behaved." With that, he turned and followed the other merchant out of the square.

The crew ventured a collective swallow once their leader was out of sight. Fletcher didn't even have to conduct it.

Let me explain: now, I know the bulk of you that have been paying any attention whatsoever to the group dynamics of the travelers will be scratching your heads over Fletcher's appointment as conduct captain. After several years of playing the stalwart leader, the Baron learned that the best way to keep Fletcher from acting out was to instill in him the illusion of responsibility. If any of the others sported antics, Geru might hit them, or Pigby might scold them, or Oswald might get confused; unfortunately Fletcher had already developed an immunity to hittings, scoldings, and confusion.

On the other end of the square, the Libburus was scratching his head as to the whereabouts of Hephaestus.

XVIII – A Certain Kind of Moment

"I'm sorry to have pulled you away, but I do believe we should get some key items sorted if we are both to stay in this town."

"Fair enough," replied the Baron.

They had come to a small dirt hillside, just on the other side of the river. Because the town square was a fair distance from them, they were almost completely consumed by shadow and silhouette, which gave the whole rendezvous a sort of cloak-and-dagger motif which made the Baron feel quite tingly. He would have been worried that Hephaestus might stab him, except that the Baron didn't like to be distracted by such trivial concerns.

To make matters easier, Hephaestus struck up a candle which was located in a free-standing lamp that the Baron had not before noticed. "To begin," began Hephaestus, for the second time mind, "I hope you will excuse my manner. Earlier this afternoon, that is."

This did not surprise the Baron. He was well-familiared with men flattering so as to elicit desired responses from persons they hardly respected and liked even less. So, to that end he replied, "Well, I must admit, I am surprised by your candor, Mister Hephaestus."

"Oh, please, just 'Hephaestus'—You see, my friend, I am not what you would call a humble man. I have come to a certain level in my career and notoriety for which I expect a certain comparable degree of recognition." He took a deep breath. Just one, of course, for he could not lose momentum. "Additionally, I have a certain…history with this town. It is not my home; I am not a native, but I do consider myself a long-time friend of these people, and after touring the world for near eleven months, every year, I find myself here, for five weeks or so to rest in the comfort of this lovely village called Adleship Isle."

"That was quite a sentence," mused the Baron, realizing—as barons also tend to do—that Hephaestus spoke for four whole lines without reaching a period.

"Yes, well, you see, the people of Adleship Isle, because they are so hard to locate, receive no other annual visitors—or visitors at all. So when I arrive," Hephaestus explained, "they celebrate; they actually raise a holiday in my honor, which is something that over the years I have come to love and accept as a blessing for me alone. So, when I felt threatened—" the great merchant caught himself, aware that 'threatened' might not be the best way to effect a civil dialogue. "When I learned that I would be sharing this day with someone else, I reacted impolitely and immaturely, and for that I apologize."

The Baron attempted to survey the eyes of the man opposite, but could see no sign of insincerity. Perhaps, thought the Baron, this was because Hephaestus' apology was in fact the genuine article. I say '*the* genuine article,' because there surely has never been another genuine apology between two men in power in the history of the world.

"Well, thank you." The Baron made certain to keep his arms folded across his chest so he would not yet be expected to shake Hephaestus' hand over their understanding.

"Which leads me," the other went on, "to the real reason I asked you to meet me here. My rudeness, intolerable as it may be, is not nearly so pivotal nor so touchy a subject as the precious state of this town itself."

The Baron was tempted to thumb his mustache. To be fair, you would probably be as well, if you are in fact the type to wear a mustache, and for good reason. This is the scene which—if this were a film—would segue into a montage of the pastime of our happy little town which reveals *why* in fact this town is so happy, a part of the reason for which is that it is so small—but then again, I am getting ahead of myself, and should just let you listen to Hephaestus' explanation, which the Baron fortunately prompts.

"You mean that it is so isolated?" inquired the Baron. "Are you worried that when I leave I should tell others of its location?"

"Yes, as a matter of fact, but that is assuredly not the primary issue. May I ask, sir, did you find yourself wondering why no one has mentioned the price for the food? Why no one—even the ones who would not host you—made no mention of the cost for rooming?"

"Well, I assumed that the idea of hotels would be of little use in a town with no visitors."

"Did you notice," the older merchant went on, practically interrupting the Baron, "a single person asking for your wares, to see your stock, requesting the opportunity to shop?"

"It seems we startled them out of any such—"

"They didn't ask because they are completely unaware that any such thing is possible."

The Baron was taken aback. To the untrained eye, he might have appeared shocked, but we know that he was merely moderately perplexed, to which end he said, "How's that?"

"The reason—the *only* reason why the people in this town don't ask after a merchant's goods and trade is because not one of them has ever assigned worth or value to a single item, meaning they have no currency, and no standard of trade. This whole entire village is one cooperative community," he finished, punctuating the last by driving his cane against the dirt with force that was quite impressive for a man of his age.

During the silence of revelation, the sound of singing wafted over from the blazing festivities, barely a quarter of a mile away. Hephaestus took very secure hold of the cane, as if he were afraid that the joyous music should whisk him away if he did not keep an anchor to the ground.

"So no sense of money."

"None whatsoever," Hephaestus affirmed. "You'll stay here, Sir Baron, for the winter weeks, and you will learn that this place is the closest to paradise left on this earth, and I fear that that should all crumble if anyone tried to introduce something like money."

"But they're so modern," protested the Baron. He of course had not seen much of their operations, but he had gathered that the men and women of the Isle, who lived in modern-looking houses, and spoke modern English should function in a modern society, which included such things as money and commerce. "You'd think that it would be a part of their society."

"You would," agreed Hephaestus, "but somehow, alas, it is not." Turning away from the lights and sounds, Hephaestus began to pace around the Baron, tapping at the dirt in front of him with the cane. "Which is why I asked you not to sell anything, not to try to buy or to trade anything."

We cannot be certain whether the Baron actually believed Hephaestus, but he certainly seemed very intrigued at the prospect. And as Hephaestus went on to say that none of their companions were even allowed to mention money to the people, the Baron continued to listen intently, all the while wondering if this absence of currency was indeed the sole reason for this people's overwhelming contentment. As we have mentioned, the Baron had been to a feast before, but he couldn't help but be enthralled by this particular town's abandon and whimsy which rang a shot or two above the common threshold.

"Then the boy," said the Baron, "the boy Julian; why would he bother to put us up? Why if there is nothing to gain from it?"

And, not knowing Julian enough to accurately assess and comment on the situation, Hephaestus replied as honestly as he could manage, "The difference between the people of the Isle and people like you...or me is that they don't see life in terms of loss or gain. They do things for each other because they don't know any different."

"So that boy stuck up for me as a favor?"

"Perhaps." Hephaestus shrugged and moved closer to the Baron until he was standing off his shoulder, while they looked upon the glow of the festivities. "I suppose we, in the modern world, lost sight of *favors* the moment someone attached the word *owe*."

"Touché," remarked the Baron with a nod. The Baron licked his lips to dust off the crumbs of the humble pie they had just shared. "Well, though I can't say that I was impressed with your manners earlier, I can respect why you felt uneasy. And now that I know, and my crew will know, I can promise only our best to keep this place happy."

The Baron shook his right hand from his sleeve, and was about to reach forward to shake on their agreement, when Hephaestus interrupted him.

"And I can trust you to keep the rules?"

The Baron stopped short. He raised a quizzical eyebrow. "About the money?"

"No, the-the rules, Mister Bordolo. The rules for us."

The Baron attempted to raise his brow farther but found that put a strain on his forehead, and so repeated, "About the money."

"No, the rules, Mister Bordolo! The Rules!"

In detecting the hint of capitalization in his tone, the Baron changed tact to ask, "What 'Rules'?"

Hephaestus placed a palm against his forehead, undoubtedly to check whether or not his skull had exploded upon the utterance of this last. Now, even though his blood did not legitimately reach a boiling point, it is very possible that steam would have been visible through his ears, just because the Baron asked 'What Rules?'

The older merchant bit his lip to refrain from saying what first impulse bade him. He felt personally affronted by the Baron's confusion, as—some would say—well he should. The Rules were a given to him, and—one would imagine—to all those who had been inducted into the order of traveling merchants. I have said that he was a part of a special society—a nation, yes?—well, do nations not have laws? (All but Adleship Isle perhaps, but once again I am getting ahead of myself.)

You see, you in your modern days and modern nations, bolstered by modern police and modern religion, may not know all of the minor, piddly bylaws and miniscule, petty clauses, but you are familiar—I dare assume—with at least a few primary tenets of your state. I should think that everyone is aware of laws against murder, theft, or parking too close to a fire hydrant, and if they are not, I should be inclined to wonder if they are in fact American citizens as they claim[33].

Hephaestus, as you might imagine, had the same near-reaction against our dear Baron. He was most tempted to exclaim, 'Aha! I knew it; you are not a traveling merchant; I doubt you to be even a Baron; I have seen through your spell!' At which point the Baron, having been successfully proven false would promptly transform back into a raven and crankily flit away.

But, seeing as the Baron was not in fact a wizard—(to the best we can determine wizards and the practice of wizardry do not exist)—and such a series of comments would only cause further conflict, Hephaestus refrained.

Keeping his pride behind his teeth, Hephaestus said, "Seven Rules, Mister Bordolo. Seven Cardinal Rules for the ranks of traveling merchants, which we all must obey without question."

"Cardinal Rules of Traveling Merchants, you say?" asked the Baron, as if he assumed that the other man might yet be spinning an elaborate yarn.

"I'll assume that you are new to the game, Mister Bordolo, and that your last master was not as keen to acquaint you with them," to which the Baron stiffened, but Hephaestus went on anyway with, "but I assure you: if you ask any traveler of a professional bearing, he will tell you the very same." Hephaestus strode past the Baron to the lamp, where he quite promptly extracted the candle to plant in the ground before them, which focused its little halo of light on the dirt rather than their faces.

---

[33] Point of honesty, my friends, regardless of my heritage and parents' ancestry, I *do* happen to be an American citizen.

The Baron looked about to speak, to protest as it were—the edges of his stache coiled in anticipation, but he was silenced by the warm song of cool steel.

Hephaestus swiftly drew his sword from his cane. It was a magnificent specimen—so magnificent in fact that the Baron had not even noticed that the smooth cherrywood had concealed a blade. With the pinpoint precision of a brain surgeon—an occupation which did not even exist at that time—Hephaestus scrawled the quick heading *RULES* in the dirt, saying as he did, "These—are—the seven rules—of traveling—merchants." And as a final added flourish, deftly underlined the letters in his heading.

"Number one," he said, writing the numeral in the dirt. "You may not—upon entering a new town, territory, province, or principality —claim any untrue purpose for your arrival." And beneath *RULES* he had written the paraphrase *NO FALSE PRETENSE*.

The Baron made to speak. He probably had a point, some rational objection, or even just an amusing joke to quip, but before he could say "I—" the other merchant cut him off with:

"No, my friend: there are seven rules in full, and I should scarcely get through any of them if we have interruptions."

The Baron thought that '*we*' was not the correct term, as only Hephaestus felt interrupted, but said nothing.

"Now, number two," Hephaestus continued, writing ahead of himself as he went: "You may not lie about the functionality or value of items for sale to primitive or modern persons." And once he had finished scribing the paraphrase, added, "No implying either.

"Three!" he announced, clearly on the proverbial roll, "You may not kill any native inhabitants," to which the Baron would have objected had Hephaestus not followed with, "unless first attacked."

And then, as if leaping upon the Baron's next thought, said, "Number four: you may not purposefully provoke native inhabitants to attack so you may kill them, and thus comply with the self-defense caveat of rule three. Number five: you may not sleep with influential men or women."

"Any special circumstance on that one?" inquired the playful Baron, properly treating the 'Pan' in his title.

Hephaestus, apart from rolling his eyes, ignored that last, and continued with number six: "You may not rearrange the political or social structure of any nation or community."

This was shortly followed by, "Is that even possible?" which was ornamented in chuckles.

"It's easier than you think," Hephaestus informed him, then refaced his list and wrote a very bold numeral 7. Speaking in a harsher voice than he had for any of the previous six, Hephaestus declared, "Finally, *you may not*— having acquired a greater knowledge of science and superstition—take advantage of any people by pretending to be a god. In other words—" he said, indicating his writing in the dirt, "*DON'T—PLAY—GOD!* You see?"

And following the direction of the merchant's blade-point, our Baron read and re-read Hephaestus' list, which—printed into soil as if in stone—followed:

RULES
1 - NO FALSE PRETENSE
2 - NO MISLEADING SALES
3 - NO KILLING
4 - NO INSTIGATING
5 - DON'T DATE THE DUCHESS
6 - DON'T CROWN KINGS
7 - DON'T PLAY GOD!

And with this last, Hephaestus re-sheathed his blade, which this narrator happens to find profound for some reason he cannot aptly describe. Perhaps we could focus on the putting away of the sword that writes the laws, or even the mere fact that it was the sword that wrote the laws, or leave that consideration for another day.

The sword's song hung loosely in the air between the two men. The Baron was the first to interrupt it, asking, "And they all know it?"

"Every one of them," repeated the older. "Every merchant who came before you, and every single one that will follow. And whoever you inherited your mantle from: they followed too."

"Hmm," replied the Baron, which—to the best Hephaestus could figure—was a response in the affirmative. Even so, the Baron made no comment on this nature of inheritance and kept his book in his pocket.

Hephaestus squinted. Unfortunately, it was already quite dark out, so if Hephaestus had been watching for the Baron to blink or in some other way show his hand, he was sorely disappointed. He grew hopeful when the Baron next began, but—as you might expect—our Baron skipped the subject entirely.

"And these are enforced by…what?" asked the Baron, craning his neck to better read the rules. "Some 'roaming police force' perhaps?"

And before Hephaestus could venture a 'Beg pardon' the Baron elaborated: "You know—a group of traveling palace guards, armed to the finger-nails, who fix on locations needing justice. Excluding, of course, places like this which cannot be found."

"Now, Mister Bordolo—"

"Or maybe a universal checkpoint, whereat all of the merchants are required to stop every few months and confess under aid of truth serum—which I happen to carry—"

"*No*, Mister Bordolo!"

"Ooh!" the Baron exclaimed, having apparently not understood Hephaestus' protest, "Is there a curse perhaps? Some ancient magic to send woe upon the transgressor? I happen to be rather fond of those fairy tales."

"Mister Bordolo!" announced Hephaestus, as would a school head-master upon admonishing an errant student, "If you have respect whatsoever for the trade to which you *profess* to belong, you will kindly shut up and listen." After which he paused, so as to confirm that his words had had some effect. Then, speaking softly so as to effect an 'eerie warning' motif—ineffective to our Baron of course, but nonetheless— said, "Nobody sends the consequences, but they will always happen."

"Like karma?"

"Like cause-and-effect," corrected Hephaestus. "The proof is— as they say—in the pudding[34]. The rules were not designed to weigh on our consciences; we do not care about punishment, only prevention; there is no final judgment, sir, but if you break them," Hephaestus said, pointing toward the happy little lights and sounds, "you will witness the decay of society."

"All of society, then?"

"Any society in which you upset their way of life by breaking these rules, Mister Bordolo; do you understand?"

The Baron ventured a smile as he said, "I understand that you have a vested interest in preserving this town," well-aware that he had not quite answered Hephaestus' question.

---

[34] As it turns out, this particular turn of phrase was not 'as they say' in Hephaestus' day. As Don Quixote might have informed them, 'the proof of the pudding is *in the eating*.'

"Can I trust you—and your crew—to keep these codes, in your best, Mister Bordolo?"

Mister Bordolo toed at the dirt, as if threatening to 'accidentally' scuff the list. He took one deep breath, and only one mind you, before saying, "Why not address me by my proper title?"

Hephaestus, most distracted by the toe of this ruffian's shoe, was stupored into asking, "Excuse me?"

And the Baron, slowly, pointedly, emphasizing each—individual—word... "Call me by my proper title, and I'll keep your codes, Your Grandestness."

Hephaestus may have waited a full minute—waiting no doubt for the Baron to crack a smile or burst into laughter upon saying 'Your Grandestness'—before he consented. "Sir Baron," he said, "can I count on you?"

It was actually impressive to the lord of merchants how quickly color and warmth came to the Baron's cheeks. His mustache curling up over a smile, the Baron thrust out a hand, proclaiming, "Splendid, sir, this should be just splendid!"

And Hephaestus, after a moment examining the hand, took it in agreement. One firm shake was all they needed, and though the townsfolk were too distracted by their celebration to notice, the reverberation of this single motion could be felt by our friend the rock on his older friend the hill.

This narrator would like to postulate that when Hephaestus and the Baron shook hands, they likely connected the longest chain of consecutive handshakes ever in existence[35].

The Baron, too focused on the immediate agreement to fully realize the universal ramifications, felt a chill run from the small of his back up his spine and onto his neck. This of course made him cock his head roughly to one side, to which Hephaestus asked, "Is there something wrong, Sir Baron."

"Hmm?" The Baron looked up to the other man, well-aware of how much taller he happened to be. "No. No, I just—Well, it's curious, but I have a feeling that this thing was quite a thing. You know?"

If you have been following Hephaestus' character, you might assume that he would find such a mode of speech incredibly base or in the least inarticulate, but strangely, at that moment, he felt just as struck

---

[35] Six-degrees-of-separation enthusiasts and people who play 'Kevin Bacon' are probably just riveted over the possibilities created by this meeting.

as the Baron, as evidenced by his sudden need to lean on his cane. And he said, the nerves in his hips quivering, "In fact, yes. Yes, I think... This is a certain kind of moment."

The Baron and Hephaestus regarded one another earnestly, as if to say, 'Hmm, I don't know what to say,' and that was all.

No matter what had led them to this point, and no matter what this simple conversation and agreement would lead to, I offer my strict assurance that you will never hear these two men speak so ineloquently again.

XIX – Pudding

Were this a television series, you would just be coming back from a commercial break, or maybe this would be the start of a new episode, assuming that the previous ended with *to be continued...* And so, after some riveting advertisements, we shall resume: you've made your popcorn, or had your bathroom break, or even possibly a good night's sleep. And it would have been *very* good, because frankly, our last chapter ended on such a delightfully high note that every tenor in the audience felt compelled to cross his legs.

You see, while the two merchants were away, the whole rest of the town and their seasonal visitors had plowed on through six or seven courses which included five different selections of meats with dozens of sides, and were concluded by twenty-one kinds of dessert, each baked in bulk, which represented every family containing at least one party who believed she (or he) could bake. To be more accurate, there were really only twenty—seeing as both Hannah and Rosa used the same recipe for bread-pudding, but both women were so convinced that her own was so wildly different and much better than the other's that no one was willing to contest this. However, if there ever was any 'contest' the winner would far-and-away be Elke, the oldest woman in the village and the wife of the stargazer Dietrich.

Among the desserts sat a flat dozen raspberry pies, which thoroughly excited Pigby. So, after their little bout with the bread, Clemens decided to challenge the same giant man to a pie-eating contest—in good nature of course, which led to the two men laughing wildly once they realized that (mostly due to them) the entire village had run out of raspberry pie. This did not distress any of the townsfolk, who still had access to other pies, and cakes, and puddings, and some sorts of sweet pastes made mostly with fruit and what you will.

And as the men and women and a few of the children began to grow full, a small wooden stage was set up, whereon the citizens who could play instruments, or sing songs, or juggle, or even stand in an interesting way for a prolonged period would perform. Yes, this town and its people were without money; granted, they didn't know trade, but whatever happened to cut them off from the world must have happened after the invent of string and wind instruments because—good god!—could the fiddlers strike a mean ditty!

Fletcher would be the first to point out—as an international music-man—that all of their songs resided within two keys, and could only follow one of four structures—(every one of which can be located in the poetry of Robert Burns)—but all parties were contented enough by food, relaxed enough from alcohol, and just plain joyful enough for the sake of the occasion, that not a one paid any ill mind to this happenstance.

As Hephaestus and the Baron were walking back toward the town square, their smug smiles radiating evidence of their compromise—which given the pride of the men involved was nothing to scoff at—they could hear Lilli's beautiful voice striding along the smells of decadent desserts. And, filled with warmth at that moment, Hephaestus couldn't help but feel gratitude for not only the festivities, but the reassurance that practically nothing had changed; he had arrived there safely, and the town was still happy.

Sure, this arrival did not have the same stand-alone sensation of years previous, but in fairness, he couldn't feel slighted. Not really. The fact remained that the feast was in his honor and would not have occurred if not for his arrival, which afforded satisfaction enough.

The Baron too could sense the softening of Hephaestus, which greatly relieved him, and in turn greatly relieved the onlooking Geru and Trenton, their mutual feelings trickling down through Sebastian, the nobles, and gradually the whole town. Even those who had not even considered that something might be amiss must have felt a load lift from their chests.

The audience applauded when the young lad named Hans concluded his limerick set, took a bow and stepped down from the stage. No one even bothered to bristle when Fletcher, the alien, mounted the stage, holding a fiddle at his waist and sporting Pan Pipes about his neck.

"Well, then," he began, in that near-Australian dialect, "I don't know if I can top the verse of this fine gentleman—serious chops, kid—but I humbly offer to you this song which I hope will tickle your sensibilities. I call it 'A Subtle Tribute to...'" and with a pause for emphasis, Fletcher shot a glance at Hephaestus and said, "'...Alliteration.'"

The Baron took this opportunity to raise his eyebrows, for beneath them, in his twinkly little irises was located fear. Perhaps the gods of irony themselves had conspired to bring the Baron and Hephaestus back to the feast at precisely this moment, because the Baron—even though he had never before heard it—had a pretty good idea of the song his minstrel would deliver.

And maybe you, dear reader, too remember the Baron Pan Bordolo himself telling Fletcher this about Hephaestus: "'He is a gentleman, and must be dealt with like one.'

'You want him torn down from his pedestal, boss?' Fletcher had asked.

To which the Baron regretfully replied, 'Preferably.'"

At that moment, in the instant before the cigarette butt ignites the forest, or the last cable of the suspension bridge snaps, or the beautiful white dove relieves herself on the wedding cake—unable to move, unable to stop Fletcher from saying whatever it was he would say—all that rang in the Baron's mind was his thin man's testimony, 'Dear God! I would die before I'd ever let anyone call me anything like 'His High-Honored Hephaestus,' no, sirree!'

As a final remark, in a voice that was not confined to the Baron's memory, Fletcher said, "I'm sure my lord Hephaestus will appreciate it." And though the Baron knew it was not possible, he would have sworn that a spotlight had settled upon Hephaestus at the first strum of Fletcher's fiddle. His song went like this...

> "A pox upon a pair of pawns
> Who held to hate and harm
> Do death so dark to make its mark
> Lie ling'ring in alarm
>
> Far from the finds of foolish fun
> Of silent slumber's sleep
> Part passing prayer from lions' lairs
> Where wrath and ruin will reap
>
> Have heathens hoist their heavens high
> To testify to truth

Can't take the cold of echo's old
Yawn, yearning for its youth

A mix of many mingling mice
Knit nettles near high noon
Still setting sun says day is done
And marks the midnight moon[36]

Shift shells to shy the shot of shame
From every evil eye
Such scathing scowls and guarded growls
And demons too will die

To boast above the beck'ning beast
(Whose soul the saints can't save)
May make man more than will or war
And grant the ghoul his grave

I vie this vast and varying verse
'Gainst gents and jesters' gall
But buffoon's braided beards will bark
For foppish folderol!"

Which Fletcher punctuated by throwing his head back and arms into the
air with triumph, like a gladiator whose opponent lay beheaded at his
feet.

The Baron was afraid to look at Hephaestus, but he could feel the
man seething. Hephaestus's face, still contorted into a polite smile,
seemed to crack against the strain. And—as salt in all of those freshly
opened wounds—the town erupted in applause. Even a few of
Hephaestus' servants, without realizing that this piece was in mockery of
their master, were clapping heartily alongside the Libburus and his
daughters and Cletus.

Trenton said nothing.

---

[36] It was at this point that Fletcher broke for a flute solo, which was actually
quite impressive, impressive enough that—according to Dame Rumor—the
Baron attempted to slip away while Hephaestus would not notice. Rumor also
persists that Hephaestus held him back with the word, "Stay."

And as Fletcher took his bows, Pigby, Geru, Oswald, and Ten ha kept glancing furtively between one another, not knowing how to comment. Oswald, without the luxury of his own motor skills was silently willing Ten ha to run to their Baron to ask what they should do. Geru wanted to blame Pigby for not stopping Fletcher and hauling him off the stage mid-song.

In fact, even the Baron couldn't say at the time why he didn't call Fletcher down. He would later tell Oswald that he couldn't have raised his voice against the song because it would have created more suspicion of foul play than just letting Fletcher have his fun. In fact, hardly a soul was aware that the piece was meant to mock the merchant anyway. Perhaps that struck Hephaestus more, or perhaps he would have claimed it did even if he would have been more hurt the other way around. In either case, the older merchant knew that he had been snubbed, knew that he had been insulted, and knew that that poor excuse for a singer[37] had directed that unfortunate blindside at his pride.

So, while Fletcher continued to take curtain calls, Hephaestus offered one last, "*Sir Baron*," through gritted teeth rounded to proudly walk away..

"Wait—" was the first that came out of the Baron's mouth, but he was abruptly interrupted.

"You will not stop me; you will not delay me; you have insulted me, and have no call to retain me."

This time, when Hephaestus made to leave, the Baron reached out and took hold of his arm. Hephaestus stopped, but only for a moment. The Baron did not have a chance to speak, or simply didn't have the words: for the older man swiftly brought round his cane and struck the Baron hard on the shin.

The Baron issued a sharp "Ow!" before unhanding Hephaestus and hopping to relieve himself.

Hephaestus let out a scoff, or perhaps it was a grunt. The Baron couldn't be too sure from his vantage point. Either way, when he looked up, all he could see was the steady swish of the older man's cape as he passed swiftly through the crowd.

The head table was unfortunately close to the stage, such that as Hephaestus brushed by, he could hear Fletcher heartily call out, "Did you enjoy that, my good man?"

---

[37] In Hephaestus' defense, Fletcher was fighting off a cold; in Fletcher's, Hephaestus was being unfairly cruel.

In his best to ignore, Hephaestus continued straight to Trenton, who was blocked by the Libburus, who fluttered about in asking, "Wasn't that wonderful?"

As Hephaestus responded with only a scowl, and brushed passed his old friend with a less-than gentle shove, Trenton, in immitigable professionalism, planted himself squarely before his master. "Milord," he began, but did not get to finish.

"Don't! Don't, Trenton!" Hephaestus, his lower lip protruding to indicate his mood, shifted his eyes between his servants, a few of which had recently wiped smiles from their faces. Snorting from his nose like some enraged boar, the lord of merchants grumbled, "I'm going back to the house."

Trenton—whatever his reasons; mayhap he thought his master reacting too harshly, or perhaps he had an idea of how to amend the situation—tried again with "Milord—"

Hephaestus bellowed, "Let me *be*, Trenton!" loud enough that the noble-folk nearby actually paused their merriment to look over and see what was wrong. Unfortunately, it also alerted Fletcher, who, having come down from the stage had arrived behind Hephaestus.

"Oh, don't take it so hard, old man; it was all in good fun."

Hephaestus turned. His head down, his shoulders curled forward, he looked as if he should try to charge the young man. "You will show the proper respect for a man of my—"

"Oh, of course, of course! Let it be known that I shall never make fun of his hard-headed ham-heaving Hephaestus ever again."

"I'll teach you to—" began Hephaestus and would have likely taught Fletcher something, but that Trenton cut him off.

"Milord, stand down. Remember no violence in the Isle." He put a hand on his master's shoulder, taking care of his charge as one might an ailing uncle. "Let's get you to the house," to which Hephaestus actually relinquished his balled fists and turned around.

"Yes, Trenton," he said, more defeat in his tone than Napoleon should experience in Russia. And—though the night's events would not glorify him—let the record show that he did his very best not to look back or even listen to Fletcher, but alas.

"Yes, goodnight, Hephaestus!" called Fletcher, "Oh, he who has the hat-hair of helmeted hired Hessians!"

And Hephaestus' last nerve snapped: "That does it!"

Trenton put up his arms, and the Libburus squealed in fear, but Hephaestus did not notice. He did the first thing that occurred to him and scooped a handful of that starchy white foam from the mashed potato vat at the table beside him and hurled it as hard as he was able in Fletcher's direction.

I say 'Fletcher's direction' because the thin man ducked smoothly out of the potato projectile's path, giving it a clear line to Hannah, the wife of Sherman, the tailor.

Hannah, who had worn her best dress for the occasion, shrieked—which is understandable: how should she ever get white off of her off-white clothing? Sherman, who had not noticed the argument, was appalled, and in looking up, saw Clemens, the grocer, laughing amiably at what had just transpired.

Sherman, mistaken, picked up a bowl and flung its contents—which were pudding—in Clemens' direction, globbing the man, his facial hair, and his immediates in dollops of creamy custard.

Though their father was too stunned to speak, Clemens' children were far too tickled by the happenstance and each began throwing food at all of the people surrounding.

Were this a Saturday-morning cartoon, someone wearing a baseball cap would surely appear from the lower right corner of the screen to shout 'Food Fight!' but as this was Adleship Isle, a town that had never known fighting, no such cry was heard. The result however was the same.

Soon the children were throwing at their peers, and—once their mothers were trying to stop them—their parents. One or two stained nobles quickly took vengeance upon nearby families, and the commoners, largely unaware of the gap in class, defended their own families' honor with every dish and dessert that they could find. Cakes catapulted about the tables, fruits flew through the air, and steady streams of ale strode between the cobblestones.

Hephaestus' servants gathered about him like a human umbrella, and with a series of hardy "This way sir!"'s escorted him from the square. Those men who attended the Libburus, though they were few, took their cue from Cletus, (who took his cue from Trenton), and escorted their lord and master away as well, while being pelleted by potatoes.

When the Baron, dipping and dodging as he wove through the maelstrom, came upon Fletcher, his minstrel was happily hopping over puddles of soup, and exclaiming, "Great gravy, boss! This is incredible!"

The Baron took this opportunity to slap Fletcher (hard) on the arm, to stop his skipping. "Fletcher, you numbskull! I had that affair settled before you sang your song."

"What in God's name is this about?" exclaimed a high-pitched voice, which emanated from some two feet below their heads. Geru, his cane walking a few paces ahead of him, led the pack as they intercepted the Baron.

"Blame the nitwit!" came the Baron.

"Boss!" called Pigby, trudging along the short man's wake, "Boss, we need to get out of here!" Ten ha quickly arrived at his side and nodded her agreement, which forced the Baron to make a quick head count.

"Well, blast it! Where's Oswald?"

A hand shot up from behind Pigby's back, and—to explain his slight stoop—Oswald's voice proclaimed, "Up here, sir!"

"It's madness out there!" said Ten ha from beneath one of the larger serving platters, which—though it functioned as a shield—was not at all becoming on her figure. "We have to get out of here!"

"Yes, yes, of course," said the Baron, his head swiveling about as he scanned the crowds and began to call, "Julian! Julian, boy, where are you?"

Now, Julian was where any young man might be, any young man who is most in love that is. This was the most violent an event as young Julian had ever observed, and—even though he did not have the austere examples of John Wayne's motion pictures—he had the undeniable sensation that this would indeed be the perfect opportunity to rescue his lady and prove his love for her.

Unfortunately, as they lived on opposite sides of the town, they sat on opposite ends of the square, and the young Julian was forced to zigzag about the crowds looking for her. He hardly avoided a sturdy pound cake and only barely ducked a chicken breast, tossed from assailants unknown, and managed to slip and fall just the once when he stepped on a glob of butter. He had arrived at the head table and was about to start calling her name when he heard the Baron yell his, and Julian stopped.

He could see Samantha, and she saw him; he was sure of it this time. She was on the edge of the road back to her own house, calling her sister's name, but for some reason, when she saw Julian, she stopped too. To our young hero, it was as if she knew that he was looking for her, and she was indeed left breathless by the thought. But the spell of this moment, possibly not even long enough to be called such, broke utterly when the Baron called again.

Though the Libburus' lovely daughter seemed almost entirely out of the fray, Julian still felt a sense of duty to her. However, he felt in his heart that he could not abandon his previous charge, which consisted of six aliens who were likely in far more peril than she.

Julian probably would have remained to struggle with this issue for as long as he could, but for the saving grace of one of Hephaestus' servants, the man named Lance. He, upon the worried exclamations of her father, had run back to the square to retrieve the two (presumably) defenseless daughters. Lance took Samantha's shoulders, startling her slightly, saying, "Miss, I need to get you'n your sister back now."

And as Samantha quickly related that she had no idea of where Sabrina had gone, Lance caught sight of Julian and nodded. It was a nod to say, 'Don't worry; she'll be alright; I know what she means to you, and I will deliver her securely back to her father's care. And by the way, good on you for hosting the visitors when no one else would.' This— even though he didn't speak a word—was quite possibly the longest thing Lance ever said, and Julian was grateful for the assurance.

Julian was tempted to linger, but the call of the Baron Pan Bordolo bid him save his love for another day. And he tore his gaze away from Samantha just in time to be splattered in a shepherd's pie, wielded by Junkin. The older boy began to laugh at his own jibe and was just as suddenly doused in ale, which—given the weather—left him quite cold and speechless as when we first met him.

Following the arm that held the pitcher, Julian spotted Raul who—with the broadest of grins—shouted, "Gotta keep alert, Julian!" and went right back to his battle.

Julian gave Raul a thankful wave and scurried away, flecks of gravy slipping off his cheeks as he ran.

Samantha watched him go, for as long as she could, that is, before she was interrupted by an angry sister, who—without a proper segue—demanded of her sibling, "Where did the Baron go? Did you see him?"

Samantha spun to see Sabrina, looking quite upset. And why shouldn't she be? One of the teenage boys from another noble family had dumped a plate of cheese into her décolletage, which completely ruined the sensual appeal of the dress. Or enhanced it, if you'd prefer.

"I don't know," said Samantha, "I think he escaped."

"So you're telling me that that gorgeous man was probably covered in pudding and he got away?"

Samantha probably would have tried to reply—without any sarcasm, mind—but for the dutiful Lance, who said, "Ladies, I'll take you back now, then."

Sabrina, with a grumble, consented. Allowing, like Julian, to let her conquest rest for the night, but vowing that she would shortly try again.

As it turns out, the Baron was still calling the boy's name as Julian reached the aliens. He would have liked to calm them down, to tell them that this sort of thing happened all the time, but the fact of the matter stood that he had never seen anything like this and was just as—if not more—surprised than they.

Luckily for him, Geru spoke first, saving Julian the duty explanation. "You have to get us out of here!" yelled the short man.

"Alright," said Julian, "I'll take you all straight back. Are all of you— Wait! Where's Oswald?"

At that perfectly-timed juncture, a splat was heard and Oswald sputtered from Pigby's back, "What ho! I say, who threw that? Who-who threw that? Have you no respect for an old man, I say?" (This of course went on for quite some time.)

Julian waved an arm to get their attention, and then, sure to keep his head low, started toward the west side of the square, calling, "Follow me!"

They passed families in little clusters and huddles, many of whom were fleeing from food as it if were a sign of the apocalypse. At least, the parents were; most of the children were desperately trying to escape their own mothers so they could throw at least one more thing before being hauled off to the tub and then to bed. When Miriam, a delightful ball of well-frothed cream in her palm, escaped her mother, Fletcher very nearly ran her over.

Instead, he scooped her up, placing the little snap-pea against his shoulder, hardly dropping a moment of momentum. "Hey there, dolly," he said.

"Manny! Meredith!"

"Julian?" came the reply, and Manuel popped his head out from behind an overturned table.

Meredith arrived a moment later, her feet shuffling quickly along to keep up with her hips, trying counter-effectively to clean off her sullied dress with her even dirtier apron. And when she saw Miriam and the state she was in, announced, "We will have quite a talk when we get home, young lady!"

Miriam, looking backward over Fletcher's shoulder, tried to crane her neck around to whine, "Momma!" but descended into giggles when she saw that her momma looked far dirtier than she.

Meredith put a pout on her face and her hands on her hips and would have likely increased the shallow threat of punishment had the Baron not spoke next.

"Oh, don't be so hard on the little lamb, Mirabel!" he said, doing his best not to sound out of breath. "After all, this whole mess is in fact Fletcher's fault."

"But it was a good song!" Fletcher protested. "Wasn't it a good song?"

"Well," came Manuel, hiding beneath his own hands, "mayhap we should get back home and *then* sort this out."

To which Julian nodded, asking, "Yeah, where's Jonas?"

"Oh, bless my soul..." muttered a most-rattled Meredith, then in her full voice, "Father? Father, where'd you go?"

It was Oswald, with a vantage similar to Miriam's who said, "There he is!" and pointed out our nearly forgotten old man, Jonas.

Jonas, his boots unlaced, was walking without aid of a stick or cane. And though all the others were crouched or trying to hide themselves, Jonas stood upright. And though everyone else was covered near head to toe in something sweet, savory, or sticky, Jonas looked remarkably clean.

Meredith, ever the protective daughter ran up and took Jonas by the shoulders and shook him once, demanding, "Father!" and after no response, "Jonas?"

Jonas looked up, the smile on his face apparent to all onlookers, and said, "The food that to him now is as luscious as locusts, shall be to him shortly as acerb as the coloquintida."

And then from the Baron, then Geru, and finally Oswald, they heard:

"How's that?"

"What did he say?"

"What-what—I say—?"

Now, while the reader might wish to dwell on this for a moment—perhaps you even recognized Jonas' quotation—the narrator regretfully reminds you that there was still food whizzing about through the air and that our characters were in near-certain peril and had no time to lose.

This is evidenced by Pigby's comment, "We've no time to lose!" after which he, even with the wounded Oswald on his back, took off like a bull, letting the Baron's crew and the rest of the family follow the path that he was sure to clear.

Fletcher, still somewhat confused and lingering behind them ventured one last defense. "*I* thought it was a good song."

And to be fair, for a day's composition, I'm certain it was. But then again, this story has been passed down so many hands that it's impossible to tell whether we have actually managed the real text of the 'Tribute' as it were. In any case, record indicates that plenty of the warring townsfolk found themselves humming it long after the Baron and his crew had departed.

The food fight eventually dissipated, and—even though several parties had irrevocably spoiled some of their best outfits—most of the Isleans would forget their grudges by the following morning and embrace as brothers once again. However, one grudge stuck more fiercely than any bread pudding ever could, and I'm quite certain you all know to whom I refer—and to think that Hephaestus and the Baron had very nearly patched things up. Then again, if they had, it would have meant the end of our story.

Thankfully, much to the contrary, there are several more events to follow, because that—my eager readers—was only the first day.

Part III – An Intriguing Little Town

...he would have sworn that a spotlight had settled upon Hephaestus at the first strum of Fletcher's fiddle.

XX – Too Much to Drink

The rock had trouble waking up the next morning.

Whereas men experience hangovers when they have had too much to drink, large rocks, lofty land masses, even great mountains can grow quite wearied by repeated stimulation—especially when they are trying to sleep. And of course *anything* in excess will produce some degree of negative consequence, so any ripple in the earth, any quakes, tornadoes, avalanches, while initially pleasurable to the geologic formations, will eventually begin to take their toll. In example, an overly energetic party will start by tickling the rock; its rhythmic vibrations will soothe the rock's old sores, grievances, and complaints so thoroughly that soon the rock is begging for more, more, more, until—Whoops!—it's taken in too much, and would surely suffer for it the following morning.

Some say that hangovers are nature's way of teaching lessons to the recipients, so that they may live their lives better and know never to consume in such excess again. But no matter the knowledge acquired, people—and apparently rocks—still return to their drunkenness and inevitably their hangovers.

The old man voiced a sympathetic groan as he slid his last stride up the hill, once again in bare feet. His boots were of course left by the bed, where they had been tossed the night before, a bed which he recognized upon waking as not his own. Perhaps the confusion of this switcheroo prompted the book-leaving, or maybe he—knowing that his doting daughter was not under the same roof—decided to take advantage of his new found freedom. In either case, his feet were far too callused to notice the minimal snow beneath them anyway.

The rock, sensing that Jonas felt similar to it and its hill, did not bother to ask how he was feeling. (As it turns out, the hill got to bed so late that it was still very much asleep, and the rock wisely chose not to disturb it.)

Now, the rock was very perceptive, especially as far as rocks go, but might I note that without the hill, the rock had very little means of communicating or receiving what went on in the village. The rock did not have eyes after all; if it did, it most definitely would have warned Jonas before the old man sat down.

To be fair, Jonas might not have even noticed. It was anyone's guess as to whether our soon-to-be completely senile chap would simply take his seat, write his lines, and be off on his merry way never-the-wiser.

But, alas-alack, as Jonas drew up his paper and quill, poising the tip against his palm and preparing for the inspiration to flow down through his wrist and onto the page, he caught sight of two figures that caused him to relinquish his jaw—for as the sun peeked over the peaks, it illuminated Geru and Pigby, wearing nothing more than sandals to protect them against the elements and 'grasping the bird's tail' as they warmed up with their morning yoga routine.

XXI – The Coloquintida

The farther Pigby stretched, the more his burdened muscles protested, protests which the giant was sure to vocalize.

"Yes, my dear Pigby," said Geru, who—though far more flexible—admittedly had a much shorter distance to reach, "*That* is the sound of progress. That, m'boy, is the sound of five—ten—*twenty* more years of mobility. Now, open your palms, let the tension out your belly and reach yourself gently into urdhva dhanurasana[38]!"

It took every last nerve for Pigby to arc himself about and mirror the short man—a very creative funhouse mirror mind—but once he'd arrived, his body refused to hold steady. His forearms trembled, his knees quivered, and the giant man began lowering himself gently down to the frosted grass that would ease his aching back.

Geru's eyes were closed, so he could not see Pigby's giving up, but still he called out, his voice unencumbered by his taxing posture, "Straighten the arms, Pigby. Don't you dare give in." And as he heard Pigby grunt his way back to position, the shorter smugly added, "If I can do it you can."

As if a running jackhammer were resting on his chest Pigby gritted back, "You didn't carry a cart up a mountain yesterdauurghh!"

"Which—if you don't properly stretch—you might never be able to do again."

Were Pigby in a position to smack Geru for his unwanted chipperness, he likely would have. The last time he did so, rumor

---

[38] *Urddhva dhanurasana*, also called *upward bow*, *wheel*, and occasionally *the bridge*, is a yoga pose which arcs a man backwards so that he is held up by only his hands and feet with his abdomen positioned higher than the rest of his body. The editor, who practices yoga, winced when he saw the name. The narrator would like to confide that he chose it largely because it sounds like a dinosaur.

indicates, Geru landed the next town over. This time, he resigned to grumble, "Sod off!"

"Don't tell me; tell it to the pain, Pigby!"

"Sod off!" came the full-throated bellow, which echoed all around, likely waking the town better than the roosters had[39].

Geru grinned and even through his closed lids caught the light of the rising sun across the clear skies. This was going to be a good day.

And why shouldn't it be? For once in their travels, the Baron's prestigious crew had landed in a town where they were under no obligation whatsoever to try to sell, study, or inventory a thing. Now this is not to say that they disliked their jobs; quite the contrary, but even the man who most adores his work looks kindly on rare opportunities that completely relieve him of it.

I'm sure you're all wondering how the Baron's men (and woman) took to the verdict that the Isle was a no-sell town. I'll apologize seeing as this story is not all that interesting. See, after the sticky conclusion of the feast, the crew reconvened in Julian's little house while Julian rushed down to Meredith's to help Jonas relocate for the coming weeks. During that window of solitude, the Baron told his crew exactly what Hephaestus had said.

The Baron had a stellar memory (not quite as photographic as Oswald's) and was a thrilling storyteller (not nearly as energetic as Fletcher) and so conveyed the details in as vivid and accurate a manner as he could. Biases aside, the crew soon got the gist of the absence of money. Their reactions went like so:

Oswald was stunned; Ten ha was quizzical; Pigby was skeptical; Geru took the opportunity to announce, "You're jiggered!"

But Fletcher, his long fingers prodding anxiously at his chin, mused in awe, "Of course! It all makes sense now."

Of course, it didn't *all* make sense, but no one would dare say otherwise after Fletcher's epiphany. Point of fact, had they all banded together, the rest of the Baron's crew could have shot down the thin man, giving way to further discussion on the subject, which, frankly, were all keen to discuss. Unfortunately, as none knew what the others were thinking, and so too put hands to *their* chins, cocked their heads to one

---

[39] The rock was indeed grateful that they were located in neither avalanche territory nor conditions.

side[40] and gave a collective "Hmm" as they pretended to grasp this concept without question.

Once Fletcher, the resident dumbbell had spoken, neither Pigby (the higher in mathematics) nor Geru (the higher in science) nor Oswald (the higher in philosophy) nor Ten ha (the most soft-spoken) would say the next word on the matter.

This meant that no one spoke for quite some time. It is assumed that Geru and Pigby tried to relate telepathically, but they had not yet perfected this technique—(one is advised to check their progress about five years after this story takes place.)

In any event, the Baron took their silence as understanding, and—having expected a much harsher reaction—was quite relieved.

You see, even though the majority of their time was spent swapping food and stories with whatever locals they encountered, the Baron's crew was never 'not working.' Regardless of harrowing and bizarre circumstances, they were always eagerly trying to sell or trade with nearby folks to increase the range even if not the value of their goods.

As the lot bedded for the night, (with Oswald on the couch, Pigby on the floor, Ten ha down the road, and the other three in the loft), the band of adventurers found not anxiety but excitement. Yes, they loved their jobs, but more than that, the Baron's crew—and this made him both grateful and proud—loved new challenges.

The challenge: to do one's business without engaging in any business; the method: truly whatever they desired. Why, even though 'work' was completely cut off by the condition of the Isle's trade and currency—both of which were zero—every man had his own set of intrigues to tackle in the coming weeks.

We'll start with Pigby; he *is* the largest and likely most noticeable party, and his objective was probably the simplest, but not the least noble. Pigby had rather taken to Clemens the night before, probably because he sensed a kind of raw machismo which struck his approval, and had resolved to 'commune with the people.' We can call this assimilation, but as that term has gained a negative connotation in your time, we shall say integration, as in an early Dian Fossey.

Oswald, the resident historian, was convinced that—even though he had never heard of the place—*some*where *some* record must have

---

[40] To the left, if you must know.

survived, possibly in fragments, that might reveal the fascinating origins of the place called Adleship Isle.

Similarly, Geru, who had noticed the abrupt change in the weather, had a phenomenon of climate to study. As to the blizzard's inability to enter the town, he had some theories of course; Geru was uniquely able to form a theory from less than half a glance, and if he never managed another, he should still defend this first impression with his dying breath. At least this time he *knew* that there was a geological, meteorological, climatological (if that is in fact a word) explanation for not just the weather but how the people on the Isle had survived as a self-contained ecosystem, and he was determined to collect it.

Fletcher's aim was—to him—the only logical course of action seeing as none of the aforementioned others had any bearing on necessity. Assimilation was merely a matter of acting; the town was far more interesting if one did not know its history; and the climate could simply be the result of magic! No, Fletcher meant to engage in grifting—not in any manner harmful mind. So he couldn't directly sell or trade? Fine! Fletcher would spend the next few weeks acquiring little artifacts from the residents, while discreetly unloading a great bulk of the crew's expendable wares as 'gifts.' He still intended to make good on the promise to "sell off twice the loot for twice the value."

Ten ha's project was named Lance.

And finally, we reach the Baron, needed to find a use for his time as well, and assumed the most honorable undertaking of all. Even though you may not be wholly impressed with the way our Baron handles Mister Hephaestus, you should know that he had never breached a contract, never broken a clause, and had absolutely never missed payment on a debt. The Baron Pan Bordolo had decided that he would find a way to pay the lad Julian properly for his troubles.

Now, as you might imagine, this was not only the most gallant but probably the most difficult task, given that the term 'pay' did not exist in the Isle excepting as an antecedent to 'heed.' But it was more complicated still, for you see[41], Julian's house was not a common inn; it was his own space and his own home that he gave up in kindness for others; it was—if it did function as an inn—the only one of its kind in the

---

[41] The editor has informed me that I have become far too liberal with the phrase "You see" and assures me that, yes, the readers can see, lest they would not be reading this text. I asked him if the publisher could reach the brail book market. (Pending.)

whole of the Isle, (which obviously increased the value); and it was gifted at the risk of Julian's reputation in so communal a town that to be ostracized would mean certain death[42].

So—even if monetary value is eliminated from the equation—the Baron could understand the immense cost that this imposed on the lad, and the Baron meant to pay this cost in full. But how? How do you pay off a great debt when you may not give the recipient the slightest indication that he is being paid? (No, I'm honestly asking. Perhaps you can come up with an answer because—to be perfectly honest—I couldn't.)

As for Hephaestus' seven rules, everyone in the Baron's employ found them laughable, but each agreed to comply, and so, the lot was released to their sleep, and they all went to bed dreaming of what wonders they could accomplish over the few short weeks.

Because such musing is exhausting work, the Baron did not wake up until after the sun had already risen. This was an anomaly for him; usually he liked to scope out the new market for the day before dawn and return after the giant man and the short man had concluded their ye-olde-yoga-in-the-nude. But this morning, with no market to speak on, he found himself slithering down from the loft, after the sun had already completely filled the small abode through the single window. His bare toes touched floorboards just as the grandfather of our story, Jonas[43], opened the front door and entered Julian's household, clutching a small scroll and quill with white knuckles, obviously tensed from what he had just seen.

"Good morning, old chap," said the Baron, and happily Oswald was not present to confuse the title.

The grandfather did not pause, did not look up at the man with the magnificently curled mustache, and instead said only, "Two of far nobler shape, with native honor clad in naked majesty." By the time he had finished this little blurb, he had most made his way back toward the only separated room, and soon after closed the door behind him.

---

[42] I would like to point out that, thankfully, there are no recorded cases of this ever occurring in Adleship Isle, but I imagine that the fear of this unknown—whether or not they could rationalize it—kept the townsfolk from venturing too far out of line.

[43] Yes, how about 'the grandfather'? I am having quite a time not calling him 'the old man' on account of the competitor, Oswald, and he is the only grandfather in our story... I shall refer to him as 'the grandfather' from here on out.

"Extraordinary," mused the Baron.

He was so impressed by this that he turned to pass the comment along to one of his fellows, but was surprised that they were all somewhat elsewhere. Let me explain: even for his whimsy and spontaneity, the Baron was still in many ways a creature of habit. He liked to wake up bright and early, bathe were there a bath to be had, apply his Liverpool Silver, and read a page or two of his little book before any of his friends were ready to begin their business. That being said, he was often the first one awake, and never the last.

He took some solace in the hope that Ten ha was still asleep down the road and that he had not entirely been left in a lurch. (She was already out and about, but let us afford him his fantasy.)

Luckily, he did not have to muse on his own sluggishness for long, for the front door opened yet again, producing not only his old friend with the spectacles, but the lad Julian underarm being used as a crutch.

The Baron was about to speak, but discovered that he would have been interrupting a story, for Julian was saying, "So they were going to eat you?"

"Oh, they would have, m'boy," laughed Oswald, as they hobbled toward the couch, "had Fletcher not sung a note so high and so shrill that they were actually convinced their stomachs should split open while they digested him." And the two laughed in such unison that the Baron was forced to reassess how long he'd been hibernating.

"Oh, Oswald!" began the Baron.

"Not now, sir!" said the old man, "I've something very important, sir, see?"

The Baron of course did not see, but probably gained some inkling when Fletcher entered just behind them, his arms loaded with books.

And he tried again, with, "I say, Fletcher—"

"Right, boss, in a moment though," said the thin man, brushing by him and proceeding toward Oswald. He set down the bulk of the books, the majority of which were impressively thick tomes set into hard, textured bindings which looked somewhere between tree-bark and tortoise skin, and took one for himself: a pocket-sized manual which from the outside resembled the Baron's. Leaving the old man to the lad's care, the thin man popped open this book, rounded his shoulders forward, and had mostly disappeared by the third paragraph.

"Here, here, let me have it, then," said Oswald, beckoning the largest volume into his lap once Julian had him sitting. "There we are."

As Oswald began to flip pages, each requiring a whole arm's length to turn, the Baron tried to speak again, but was cut off by Geru and Pigby, clad in large grey robes, carrying sopping bedrolls, and in the middle of an argument, entering the front door.

"Not when there's bloody snow on the bloody ground!" protested Pigby, slamming the door behind him. The Baron winced, worried that the house might collapse, and Julian, assured of its sturdy frame and his own construction, smiled with satisfaction.

"Don't be such a baby; you were on a blanket," said Geru, shoving the same rolled blankets up against the wall.

"Fat lot of good it does when it soaks through."

"Look, if you're going to *be the cobra*, you have to withstand the elements."

"*Cobras* don't live in the snow!"

Well, seeing as zoology was *his* field, and not the giant's, Geru puffed up about the chest, planted his hands on his hips, and declared, "You couldn't possibly know that."

"Oh for God's sakes, Geru!" announced the Baron, catching wind of the robes and what they usually meant.

"What?" returned the short man, more defensively than innocently, which led the Baron to believe that he didn't know the spur for his employer's reprimand.

"Geru—Pigby!—you can't go out there like that. Not here!"

Pigby and Geru looked to one another, before the larger observed, "But you've never said we couldn't do our exercises."

"Even when we were at the nunnery," chimed Geru.

"Yes, well at the nunnery, you at least stayed out of sight."

"Oh, not entirely," came the peanut gallery. His nose still in the book, and his eyes only periodically flitting up to meet them, Fletcher explained, "See, there was a bell-tower, saw right into the little glade they went to—a bunch of the nuns'd gather up up there every morning. I mean, one time, I followed them just to see what they were looking at, and lucky me, I got a big eyeful of—"

"Besides," said Geru, who courteously timed the interruption so all audiences (including yourselves) could stop holding their breaths, "I don't think anyone was up early enough to see us."

"Oh!" Oswald raised a finger and—without raising his head from his book either—took the floor, "we were. Myself, Fletcher and the boy here."

"And Mum often gets the house up with the sun so as to intercept Jonas," said Julian.

"And Jonas!" exclaimed the Baron, striking his palm so firmly against his own forehead that his mustache nearly rattled out its rings. "The old man, came in before you, said—Well, now I know what he was talking about." All that was left for the Baron to decide was whether the grandfather's comment had been ironic or in earnest.

"See, boss," began Pigby, doing his best to sound non-confrontational, which—strictly due to the size of his frame and pitch of his voice—was fairly self-defeating, "We looked for a place where no one would see us, but it's snowing right outside the gate." And then to Fletcher, excitedly, as though the thin man should not believe this fantastic account, "I swear: an inch out the town and you're blind."

"So we set on the hill tucked behind Julian's; there's a dip of flat ground blocks us from everyone but overhead onlookers," Geru finished. "I can't see why we need to walk on eggshells just because another merchant was here first."

"A god of merchants," noted Fletcher, without looking up from his text.

"He's not a god, Fletcher; he's just—" then, Geru, finding himself frustrated at the thin man's lack of attention, suddenly demanded, "What in the hell are you reading?"

Fletcher stopped. When he looked up his eyes certainly seemed the largest feature on his face, with the brows squeezed up, like a pitiful hound pleading with its master. In Fletcher's case, usually the more innocent he looked, the more likely it was that he had committed some crime, but this time, he merely raised the book enough for the others to see the front cover, which read, *The Prince*. "It's Machiavelli," he said, sounding so hurt by the harsh accusation that Geru felt compelled to say:

"Oh, I'm sorry, Fletcher; I didn't mean to..." But the thin man had already gone back to the book.

It was at that moment—during a lull of no more than a second, which grew out of Geru's guilt—that Julian, a very confused third party to this charming exchange, was preparing to form a question. As to what he would ask, the Baron was not certain, but he was quite sure that anything about the argument, the giant and short men's exercises, or even Fletcher's text—sociopolitical dynamite in handbook form—would set off a possibly unwanted vein of conversation which he could not easily field, knowing so very little of their town. So our dear Baron took it upon himself to speak before Julian could fully form the words which he appeared so keen on saying.

"Look," he said to Geru, sounding quite conclusive, "If we're to survive the winter without startling the pants off of these people, then you've got to keep yours on."

Geru looked as though he should protest, but the Baron raised an eyebrow vey pointedly in Julian's direction. Pigby opened his mouth too, but before he could say a word, the Baron twitched his mustache in conjunction with the aforementioned brow, and the giant man too was silenced. You might be scratching your heads at this description of directed eyebrow pointing, but know that in the Baron's line of work, where he mingled every day with strange new cultures, being able to signal with the tiniest gesture was essential[44].

And to continue his steamroll, the Baron said, "Lad, I think I find myself quite hungry."

"Oh, Mum's got the eggs downways," said Julian, his thoughts too interrupted to voice curiosities.

"Here, you know what," came the Baron, putting an arm about the young man's shoulders, "how about you bring up about a dozen raw eggs and you let us cook for you. We've got quite an assortment in the wagon."

Julian grinned at this thought—a touch of exoticism, no doubt, but perfectly good-natured. "Yeah, I'll do that," he said, and started toward the door.

"Oh!" squeaked Geru, commanding his attention once more, "Fetch Ten ha will you. She is the chef after all."

Julian gave a nod, his eyes flitting somewhat anxiously to the still strange assortment of houseguests, and pulled the door closed behind him as he left.

"Well, that went well," muttered the Baron.

"If by that you mean myself and Pigby, I don't think a soul even saw us," said Geru, ascending the loft to retrieve his clothes.

"Besides," boomed Pigby, "how do you even know anyone would find it odd?"

---

[44] The editor suggested I remove this point, due the difficulty of finding an actor who could make this gesture—when this story is released in television or on film, that is.

"Well, because someone did—the grandfather chap, in fact," said the Baron, checking to see that the door was still closed, "he said—" And the Baron stopped. Confound it all, after the protests and hullaballoo from the others, he couldn't well remember what Jonas had said, and so fumbled, "Well, I don't—alright, I can't recall what it was he said, but I'm certain it was a quotation, or-or—"

"Oh, you mean last night?" came Fletcher.

"I caught that too," said Pigby.

"And me," chimed Geru.

"Already on it!" announced Oswald, and punctuated this last with a brusquely turned page of his ancient tome.

"You know what he said?" asked the Baron, and had started toward Oswald's text, when once more interjected an opening door.

The Baron instantly straightened, turning back around to face Jonas, and in his wake followed every other member of his crew. They watched as the grandfather, unaccompanied by shoes, shuffled from the bedroom to the front door, none speaking in case he might say something.

With a little glint in those beady eyes, Jonas looked up at the Baron, smiling as if to say, 'Hello.' He then wrapped his leathery claw about the door handle, tugged it open and escaped, leaving the lot with no new comment to sort through.

"You think it was a quotation then, boss?" asked Pigby, after everyone had stopped holding his breath. The giant man had by this point pulled on clothes, and actually looked like he took up more space in the house than he had wearing the robe. He folded the thick dark forearms across his chest and chewed at the side of his cheek before saying, "If it's from literature, where would he get it in this place?"

"Well, how do we even know it was from outside? Maybe the man's just peculiar," offered Geru.

"No, I'd doubt that." Fletcher kept his finger on his present paragraph, but let his book fall closed and straightened to engage the others. "I mean, I don't remember the line, but I'm certain the terminology he employed was not germane to the colloquial lexicon."

"Yes, well," the Baron went on, careful not to show that he actually needed to process Fletcher's comment, "is it then possible that he too is from outside this town."

"What? Like Hephaestus?" asked Geru. "I don't think His Foppishness even acknowledged Jonas. Besides everyone treats that grandfather like he's been here a thousand years."

"Thank you, doctor hyperbole," muttered Pigby, to which Geru bristled.

"I suppose it's possible that he arrived so long ago that not a soul remembers a time when he was not present." The Baron teased at his mustache and noted with lament that he had not applied any of his treatment that morning. "*Or*," he went on, pointedly italicizing the transition to draw attention away from his unmannered stache, "perhaps this town's not so isolated as our dear friend Hephaestus claims."

Now even though nothing would thrill them more than to find out that the rival merchant was lying to them, you, the reader, know that no matter what other deceit Hephaestus might spin, the isolation of the Isle was an unequivocal fact. Even so, the Baron's crew was keen equivocate it some more.

Their explanations for how it might be reached or how the whole town was just a conspiracy were absurd at best, and all fell flat when put against the question of why not a one of them had ever heard of this town before. It took a few bogus theories and a good deal of ceiling-staring for the crew to regretfully resolve that they couldn't shake Hephaestus' authority on the matter.

"So..." trailed the Baron, "We're in agreement then? Adleship Isle is actually the most foreign spot on the globe. But if it's so remote, how did he find it?"

"Our illustrious Hephaestus?" Pigby scoffed, "Well, he knows everything, so it shouldn't be too much trouble, now should it?"

Fletcher once again suggested that they could not rule out that Hephaestus was in fact a god, for which Geru rapped him hard on the arm.

"You know," Geru said, while the thin man rubbed at the new bruise, "he could have stumbled into it unawares. After all, *you* did just that, sir."

"I did at that," admitted the Baron, "It's a terrible coincidence, our both arriving here accidentally, but I suppose it could be possible."

"Well, why not?" came Fletcher, striding to the center of the room, "It's the stuff that fairy tales are made of—yes?—but all the fairy tales start somewhere. You know, the Dutch have this saying—"

But we should never find out which particular saying the Dutch had, seeing as Oswald's voice suddenly erupted with, "Aha! I say I've found it! I found it!"

The others turned to see the old man where they'd left him, sitting on the couch with his foot propped up and a thick volume laid out across his lap, and before they could rightly suss out just what was going on, he continued to sputter, "I found it—I knew I would! I say, I knew I would" And so fervent was his excitement, that no one bothered stop his momentum and instead gathered around to hear, "Right here, it says 'The food that to him now is as luscious as locusts, shall be to him shortly as acerb as the coloquintida: Shakespeare's *Othello*; Act one; Scene three; so there!" And with that he shut the massive book, a rather dramatic gesture, fitting of such a dramatic revelation.

Now, as the Baron's crew was just arriving at his side by the time Oswald had closed the tome, Geru had to ask, "How's that?"

"Act one, scene three; he quoted *Othello*—*Othello* exactly."

"Who did?" asked Fletcher.

"What's this, then?" came Pigby.

"The old man[45]!" announced Oswald, possibly confusing the reader, "That old man from last night—the-the ancient fellow, when they took him with them, he said just that!" Oswald grinned, feeling most satisfied with the point he had just raised.

However, as no one else had been present at the start of Oswald's train of thought, none had accurately followed it to the end. The Baron placed himself just off the old man's shoulder and asked, "Now, what was it that man had said?"

Oswald was about to laugh—After that explanation, why on earth should his Baron ask so silly a question?—but upon scanning the rest of the curious crew, resigned to groan and reopen the book, saying, "I'll find it again."

"Well, there's a start," said the Baron, while Oswald rummaged through the pages again, "it's Shakespeare."

Fletcher nodded. "First prints wouldn't be until a decade or so into the seventeenth century."

"Do you think the town was founded after that?" asked Pigby.

"I don't think they'd have such a strong isolation mentality after less than two centuries," said the Baron authoritatively, as if he'd had the misfortune of living that long.

"Here it is!" the old man said again, his finger once again on the pivotal line: "'The food that to him now is as luscious as locusts, shall be

---

[45] The editor has suggested that I change this to 'the grandfather' keeping with my earlier comment, but—unfortunately—I have no control over what Oswald says. I should add that Jonas was older than Oswald.

to him shortly as acerb as the coloquintida.'" This time, after reading it, he waited for permission before closing the book.

"Well, what does that gobbledygook mean?" demanded Geru, the resident philistine.

Fletcher, making a face, followed with, "Locusts are *luscious*?"

"You're forgetting our tour in Egypt," said Pigby.

Fletcher shut his eyes tight and shook his head. "No, I'm not."

"Coloquintida," asked the Baron, "it's bitter, isn't it?"

"Ten ha would know," offered Pigby.

"Of course! Where the devil is she?" their leader asked, looking around as if he thought Ten ha should appear right behind him.

"Well," Geru went on, "assuming it is, bitter that is, food that was good is now bad, as in rotting?"

"No, no, he said it during the food fight!" announced Fletcher, to which Pigby arrived in agreement:

"Yes, what was good food became projectiles."

"No-no-no—you don't get it at all!" Oswald shook his head so fiercely that his glasses may well have shot off his face and shattered on the wall. Once he was certain he had everyone's attention, the old man used one long finger to right the same spectacles and explained, "It's about Hephaestus. The food, as representative of the whole town is good, but it will soon appear to him as—well, as-as bad as it could be." And then, looking directly to his Baron, said, "His feast has spoiled, sir, and he believes *you* have spoilt it."

(Hephaestus—if asked point blank—would claim he believed nothing of the sort. To admit that the Baron could so taint his otherwise divine meal would be in the same to admit that the Baron had power over him, which the venerable *lord* of merchants could not do. But—silly me—I am getting ahead of myself once again, and, as mother always says, "One thing at a time." I'll deal with him after I've finished this scene.)

Luckily, my brief aside gave our characters a chance to process this, which was a good thing, because Julian was entering and they couldn't very well continue on this subject anyway. Julian, aware on some level that he had interrupted a solemn or at least intellectual moment for his guests, took care to close the door gingerly, as if any sudden movements should trouble the eggs he carried.

"Ah! You're back then, lad," said the Baron, springing to his feet and clapping Julian about the shoulder, "with breakfast, I presume."

The short man—though he did not have much range for extension—craned his neck to see around the Baron and examine the entryway before the door was shut once again. "…aaaaaand without Ten ha. I presume."

"Hmm?" came Julian, setting the basket on the table, "Oh, yes, the blue girl—" but Julian was so startled by their reactions that he forgot what he was going to say.

As Geru coughed, Pigby snorted, Oswald choked, and Fletcher brought a hand to his mouth to pinch his lips shut, the Baron surmised that, given her purple eyes, silvery hair, and nearly reflective skin, 'blue' could indeed be the happiest medium available. It is in this moment that the reader should be glad that Pigby was so large, lest the people of the Isle use *his* skin to define his appearance and call him simply 'the black man'; *I* find 'the giant man' far more charming, don't you?

On the hand, Julian—bless his naïve heart—hadn't put a second thought to it: the simple fact was that if he were to say 'blue girl' to any person in the whole of the Isle, they too should think of Ten ha.

Once the Baron had his full composure he continued straight-faced, "Yes, is *Ten ha* coming?"

"Um… no," said Julian, wondering for a second if her absence was considered his fault. He decided against it. "But Mum's already gone and boiled the eggs, so—"

"Ooh!" exclaimed Geru, "I've a lemon-pepper for just that sort of thing." And started promptly toward the door to fetch it from the cart.

"Lemon? Are you mad?" boomed Pigby, likewise making his way to the exit, in attempt to beat Geru no less. "Clearly such eggs demand dill!"

"No-no-no-no no, none of your grass clippings, you dumb brute! This calls for quality cuisine."

They fought for a moment over the handle of the door, then—once it was open—squeezed through simultaneously while Pigby barked back, "You couldn't spell cuisine with a dictionary open on your lap."

And again the door slammed shut, the Baron cringed, and Julian smiled smugly for reasons he could not discern.

"What were they arguing about?" asked the young man.

"Oh, spices. Seasoning really. For the eggs," explained the Baron, wondering if that was any kind of explanation at all. "See, I would have said cayenne pepper."

"Cumin," said Oswald, from behind his propped-up ankle.

"Salt," finished the thin man.

"At any rate," the Baron began again, "where did you say—or did you say where our lady was?"

Julian—forgive his ease of distraction—thought first of Samantha at the mention of anyone's lady, was then immediately jealous that the Baron laid any claim to her, and finally, when he realized that the Baron did not mean anything of the sort, felt somewhat sheepish at possibly betraying the object of his affections to some stranger, even if he was a houseguest.

"Our lady, the-the-the—"

"Blue girl," offered Fletcher. (Oswald shot a questioning gaze, to which Fletcher shrugged.)

"Thank you," resumed Julian, "Mum said she already left. Got up with the cock and said she had to tend to the horny beast."

"What?" came the Baron

"What?" sputtered Fletcher

"What-what!" stammered Oswald

What? thought the reader.

As Fletcher was already laughing, Julian found himself chuckling nervously as he explained, "She went to the barn. It's where we put the cows and sheep and goats, and she—well, they said to put up your animals there too."

"Oh, the yaks!" said a relieved Oswald, adjusting his glasses for no particular reason.

"Yaks." Julian chewed on the word. It tasted sour. "Well, she said she'd feed them." The young man made sure to catch the Baron's eye. "You're not upset, are you, Sir Baron?"

Oswald smiled at this last, mouthing a gracious, "Bless you" in Julian's direction.

"Not at all," the Baron replied, though he was a bit irked to be the last of his crew to wake up this morning, but did not sound the least bitter when he said, "It seems she's adjusting already."

"She is at that," said Julian. He plucked an egg from the basket and—tossing it between his palms—fell back into the couch beside the old man. "She even went and took the snap-pea with her." As he started his work at the shell, raised his eyes once more and clarified, "Mum'n Manuel's girl, Miriam. Should be exciting for her: beasts like that and all."

XXII – A Bit Of String

Miriam was unimpressed.

For someone as small as Miriam—smaller than Geru, that is—to whom everything was simply 'bigger than her,' the yaks didn't seem much larger than the old bulls, and certainly no bigger than Hephaestus' oxen. They looked to her like overly shaggy cows, who mooed out their noses instead of their mouths, appeared to be growing moss, and retained the most god-awful smell imaginable.

To this end, Ten ha had named the beasts Po and Perry. As she was the only female in the Baron's crew, and logically the only one to know what potpourri was[46], the simple wordplay served as a very satisfying personal pun. She liked crafting puns for herself, and, as some spanned three or four languages, it was a good thing that her humor needed no other audience.

And though she could not give reason, she sang in Mandarin to Po and Portuguese to Perry while feeding each animal individually. Now *this* fascinated Miriam and kept the snap-pea contentedly sitting on a hay-bale, swinging her tiny feet in time with the lullaby.

The foreign strains also caught the ear of a young man entering opposite end of the stable, brush in hand for the eight able oxen. Lance lifted his bangs away from his eyes and held them in his palm as he gazed steadily at the young woman's back.

Ten ha must have sensed this because she stopped cooing to bring a hand to her neck where little goosebumps were raised. She spun abruptly, the hand still behind her head, like some modern anime

---

[46] Though he would never admit it, Pigby too knew sight, scent, and function of potpourri, and would oft smirk at the irony his fellow had created.

promotional still, and blushed. For Ten ha, a blush actually made her skin more peach than it had been before.

Lance near dropped the brush as he realized, with embarrassment, that he had possibly embarrassed the young woman before him. Thus began a fluttering series of "I'm sorry"s from Lance, during which he actually did fumble the brush several times.

Ten ha, somewhat flustered herself, tried to reassure Lance that everything was quite alright, but had gotten so boggled by the tongues that she started in Portuguese, sidled into Mandarin, then—in trying to clear herself of the debris—stumbled somewhere in between the two. In this case, geographically, it took the form of Yiddish, a hodgepodge language all its own which only further confused the poor girl.

Miriam, unable to understand this exchange, resigned to chew on a bit of string.

Ten ha, somewhat aware of the swirling room as she tried to sift through languages, saw that the young man perceived his presence not wanted, and had started to leave, still apologizing. Struggling to find English, she caught herself on a support beam with one hand and stretched the other toward Lance when she bid, "Odottaa!" then, "Подождать! Počkat! 等待!" and, "Aștepta!" Having failed to communicate and seeing the boy back away with his hands forward in defense and brow crooked in shame, she tried desperately with "Vent!" and "انتظر!" and finally, "Wait!"[47]

When Lance stopped, Miriam could not tell if he had actually understood the other girl's request or if it was because the blue girl had finally stopped talking. For her part, after that barrage of alien terms, (probably written in alien writing), Miriam hadn't even deciphered 'wait' from the rest.

Ten ha breathed steadily, though her chest heaved up and down noticeably. Lance gulped once and quickly reestablished contact with her eyes, which—count-your-lucky-stars—were closed. Holding on to the support beam, she tried to wave away her frustration, and said—with as much clarity as she could muster, "Hi."

Lance must have found this a suitable argument for their situation, and so reciprocated with his own brand of, "Hi."

---

[47] To clarify: Finnish, Russian, Czech, Chinese, Romanian, Norwegian, Arabic, and finally English. I apologize if any of these texts read backwards to you natives out there.

Ten ha bit her lower lip; Lance raised his eyebrows; Miriam chewed on the string.

Ten ha—feeling as though she might be drowning in a stream only five feet across but miles deep—realized that, even for all the stirrings shoving their way around inside of her, she had absolutely nothing to say to this man. Sadly, she did what all young women do when they have nothing else to say: she laughed.

"What?" asked Lance.

"Oh!" said Ten ha, as though she had the answer, which of course she did not. She very quickly scanned the room for inspiration, then, realizing that it wasn't a room and was in fact a barn, abandoned the stables to glance at the bored yaks, the oblivious Miriam, and the very sturdy backside of one of the lord of merchants' oxen. "Oh, you know," she said with another chuckle. The narrator cringed.

"I'm afraid I don't know much," confessed Lance. To his credit, this was not a flirtatious line but the honest-Abe's truth[48].

Ten ha laughed again, and, using her prior stumbling as an excuse, explained, "Oh, I—I think I'm a bit light-headed from all that—" And then, as if a light bulb had opened above her head[49], the girl realized that she was trying to regain balance and composure. What a silly course of action this was! A young woman about to fall is a damsel in distress, of course, and a young woman about to fall in the presence of a young man is a young woman who will be caught against his firm and comforting chest, to be cradled by his rippling arms, to gaze up into those lovely eyes (whose color she could not quite distinguish in the low light) and, possibly, perhaps...

There was only one thing to do: placing the back of her free hand against her own forehead, Ten ha exclaimed in the register of a southern belle, "Oh, deary me! I feel a spell comin' on!" and proceeded to collapse.

And to our good fortune, Lance was quick on the draw, for when he heard the young lady declare 'spell' but not knowing what kind of spell she meant, did the only thing that a young man could think to do: he said, "Here let me fetch you some water," and had turned away just

---

[48] For the record, this is not the Honest Abe you're thinking of, seeing as he was not yet born. Coincidence will attest that it probably referred to some old soul from the Isle's past and had been adopted into common usage like Mad Jim or Great Fred.

[49] Light bulbs had not been invented either.

before Ten ha hit the hay—I mean that literally of course, seeing as there was no floor, and instead dirt covered in hay.

Miriam giggled. Lance must have heard the giggle and turned around, for, when Ten had opened her eyes, he was rushing to collect her.

"Are you alright?"

By way of response, Ten ha cursed in Swahili.

"Oh, that sounds bad," replied Lance, "Are you ill?"

And before she could dream up a substitute answer, the most miraculous thing was happening. Afraid that she might faint away again , Lance had scooped her up, placing her own nose within inches of his. Ten ha would admit that fainting occurred to her as a fair course of action when her head came to rest on his shoulder.

Miriam popped herself down from the hay-bale. She took only a few steps closer to Lance, for—even though she was not *afraid* of this foreign man—she was not yet fully comfortable with his stature, speech, or smell[50].

And Lance said, in a way that should make all my female readers tip their heads to one side and go *Awww*, "Well, good morrow to you, little miss."

Miriam brought one hand from behind her back and waved.

"Tell me," said the young man, "where's a good place to get her a drink?" Though Ten ha kept her eyes closed, she knew he had looked down at her when he asked.

Miriam put a finger to her mouth, rolling her eyes up to consider, then turned abruptly and started walking, indicating with a tiny gesture that they follow.

As they strode out of the barn, Lance ventured to ask his ailing charge, "Will you be okay?"

"Yes," she admitted, then, trying to sound innocent about the whole affair, "I think it's all this mountain air. Takes some adjustment."

"Are you able to walk?"

Ten ha took a moment to consider yet again, scrunching one side of her face to indicate so, then said, "Not just yet."

Following Miriam into to open air, neither Lance nor the girl he carried remembered that they had left their respective cattle-brush and oat-bag in the stalls.

---

[50] Lance did not smell bad, mind—leastways, no worse than the barn—but Miriam could still tell that he smelled markedly different.

XXIII – Two Sets of Bloomers

Hephaestus had been ensnared by a one-sided conversation with an uncomfortable kink residing in either the winding sways of his intestines or the folds of his brain. Essentially, the lord of merchants would attempt to will the knot away, and the knot would pointedly ignore him. Salt in the underskin wound, the errant bind would proceed to move elsewhere the moment he discovered and ambushed its hiding place.

For the first time in his somewhat extended life, Hephaestus actually chanced to wonder on the slippage of his wits—if indeed such a horror were possible. This was largely because he could put neither finger nor toe on what it was about the Baron and his crew that seemed so gee-golly familiar. Had he seen them before?—Surely not, or else he would remember their poor manners and general unpleasantness, and yet he knew their shapes, their functions, and possibly even their voices, which—simply because he could not place them—disturbed him.

The set was just far too…perfect, for lack of a better word, covering all necessary range of human extremes: the four men as a group, that is, and the girl as a stand-alone. In his introspective investigation, Hephaestus decided to rule out the blue girl altogether, because attempting to place each portion of her country of origin made his head hurt, a strain which, given the burden of the Baron, was a jot too much. But even the arrangement of the four men, (a giant man, a thin man, an old man, and a short man), struck him as having some special significance, possibly prophetic, as if their presence was a sign of the impending apocalypse. Unless that was with a strong man, a quick man, a… Hephaestus shook his head.

He didn't rightly know why it should bother him so. After all, he had his own servants. Seven to be sure. The childish side of his brain promptly concluded that seven beat five—(the patriarchal side thought that seven beat four and a woman, but that's another story).

Besides that, his servants were all sturdy, bred with broad shoulders, capable of hauling great loads, and of a loyal nature that made many of them seem—even though he was a class or two above—like family. Starting with Trenton, his right-hand-man, a lieutenant (pronounced *left*enant) of sorts and moving on down the line through Cooper, Tanner, Liam, Lionel, and Gus—And Lance!—we mustn't forget Lance—falling in together like a seven-dwarves fairy-tale line-up.

And yet Hephaestus could conclude with certainty that in the judgment of one's servants, he would place second to the marvelous Baron. (If anyone was wondering, Sebastian would place third and last feel honored by the mere comparison.) While Hephaestus had gathered seven sturdy servants, who, in matching uniform, were near indistinguishable from one another, the Baron had plucked five lovely blossoms, each from not only its own classification, but kingdom.

As we all know, especially in the twenty-first century, diversity trumps uniformity, even so finely tailored a uniformity as Hephaestus'. I should think this is because, while the means to perfect uniformity are finite, the means to even just brilliant diversity are infinite. This trend hurt Hephaestus more than he should care to share.

Hephaestus had trained in a great many things; sulking was not among them—neither was skulking for that matter. He could brood, and he could stare through a window looking down on something that he found to be beneath him—(forgive the redundancy)—and did his best to put the two together, but sadly had never figured out how to slouch, stoop, or roll his shoulders forward enough to properly sulk.

As Hephaestus watched the square from the second-story window, Trenton, the eternal watchman, watched Hephaestus, his arms folded about his chest. He was not a big man by any means, but he could fill a doorway like nobody's business, and he refused to let his own master out of the room until he had at least stopped scowling.

"Sir, you say this place is paradise; well, right now, the most likely factor in disrupting that calm is your foul mood—*Not* that interloper, but *you*, sir."

Hephaestus had scoffed at that, though he knew Trenton was right. Of course, he could make a case that his 'foul mood' was a direct product of the Baron's arrival, but Trenton would just roll his eyes. Trenton was an exceptional eye-roller.

Trenton had said that a good night's sleep would make it all seem better. About that he was wrong. Whenever Trenton was wrong, none of the other servants much felt like being in their master's presence. This is why Lance, the newest of the bunch, instinctively excused himself to the stables. The others did not leave the property, but kept degrees of distance between themselves and Hephaestus. Those inside kept a floor between themselves and the master, and any working outside took pains not to cross beneath his High-Honored's window.

You might have assumed that this 'vacation' for Hephaestus and his servants consisted of lounging, relaxing, and otherwise being lazy, but a vacation to a commune *always* includes contribution on part of the guests. In the self-sustained town of Adleship Isle, there was always something to do, whether direct manual labor, middle-management's sorting and allotting of resources, or instruction of younger citizens by the older so that the community would survive for further generations— Hephaestus engaged in this last. This does not mean that the people of the Isle were always slaving and toiling—quite the opposite. A theory of economics will demonstrate that if *all* parties are working to support the collective whole, then no individual would need to work nearly as hard as he would to support just himself[51].

And after their work was done, the townsfolk would become occupied with any of the town's traditional leisure activities. So insightful must have been the founders of this town that many of the games were also productive pursuits. One of their springtime ball games consisted of two teams, each competing to sink a ball into the other's water-trough. Similar to your sports—yes?—except that the troughs were not only full of water but balanced on the goal-tender's shoulders, and as he dodged away from his opponents, would slosh all over the ground, neatly irrigating the field for the ensuing planting.

The children would also engage in clay-packing for the patching and puttying of houses and stone-diving in the pool below the falls, where the smoothest and sturdiest mountain rocks could be gathered. Paper-making from wool pulp and sign-making from tree bark gave way to paper-washing and sign-sanding so that all writing media could be reused for years to come. These last may seem more like jobs, but I imagine if you enjoy company of those working beside you, these tasks would not be particularly taxing. Such was the nature of a workable commune.

---

[51] I say theory because this theory has never been successfully tested.

And at the Libburus' house, there were not only long-term tasks, but everyday chores, like dishes, laundry[52], and wood-chopping. Two of the servants, Lionel and Liam, took turns chopping—more accurately, they tersely argued about whose turn it was, then 'politely' stepped aside when they could no longer deny how long they'd been at it.

The reason for their race to the axe was that the wood-block was positioned under Sabrina's rear-facing window. Why was this significant? Well, after she had reached an appropriate age, every year without fail one of Hephaestus' servants would fall in love with her, and every year without fail she would bed someone else, namely one of the other servants. Because Liam and Lionel were pining after her affections, at least one of them would likely fall for her, and in doing so damn himself to celibacy for the winter. But, then again, winter is long, and young men's minds are easily changed.

Cooper and Tanner, who had each been infatuated with her in years prior, were just aloof enough this season to be potential candidates.

Of course, the reader knows full-well that Sabrina had a taste for someone who was even more exotic than the sublimely conformed servants. If asked about the nature of this curiosity, she would claim that she just wondered if the mustache tickled.

So it's no surprise that when Lionel and Liam showed off their strength and precision, glancing up expectantly toward their lady's window, Sabrina was nowhere to be seen. Point of fact, she wasn't even in her room, making all their furtive glances the more vain. At the moment we arrive upon her, she is seated with a hardy comb in one hand and a healthy chunk of her sister's hair in the other.

"Ow!" exclaimed Samantha.

"Now, now," cooed the older, "it's not ladylike to exclaim. If you are in pain, the best thing to do is faint. But only if a man can see you[53]."

When her sister came across the next knot, Samantha simply gritted her teeth and cleared her throat. Samantha regarded herself in the mirror, trying not to look too obviously at her sister, who was already well-aware that the younger was comparing them. They looked related of course, like sisters from the same parents—(both of them, to be

---

[52] The Libburus' dwelling was one of only two buildings that had a wellspring diverted into it, making it an immediate hotspot for dish duty following feasts and gatherings.

[53] Sabrina was unfortunately not able to appreciate the irony that her advice had tended toward Ten ha.

accurate)—but the manners and attitudes they conveyed were, as you may have guessed, completely different.

Perhaps the simplest distinction was that Sabrina looked far more dominating while Samantha appeared demure. The younger examined the tilt of the head, the shoulders, the hips, and found that her sister's were held in slant, that the bust was pushed higher and that the eyes stayed slitted and smiling, like that python His Highest had brought some years before. Samantha wondered if that was where Sabrina had learned it. She contemplated imitating her sister, wondering if she might be better-served to take the 'angled' look instead of slim, straight, and genuinely genteel. For whose sake, she would not say, though I'm sure you have a few ideas and hopes on that score. Perhaps, Samantha mused, if she played the 'woman' instead of the 'lady' she should win her man.

This narrator finds it ironic that Sabrina was simultaneously considering the inverse. She had never had a Baron before, but she knew—in the same way that a man knows he likes pickles instead of cucumbers—that this man's title and bearing must have been even more regal than Hephaestus'. It was altogether probable that this Baron would prefer a courtly, refined, gentle female specimen over the wantonness that was the young woman's natural state, (not to paint a negative name upon the girl, but she would be the first to admit that she was no stranger to the debauched).

"Sabrina," asked Samantha, gazing into the mirror and wishing that her own eyes were just a little bit brighter, "Have you ever been in love?"

"*That* is not a ladylike question," she promptly responded with authority she may have lacked.

"I just wonder," Samantha went on, clearly not troubled by her sister's reply, "if it's just that feeling in one's stomach, that makes you both want to consume the whole table *and* want to expel it at the same time—" (Sabrina grimaced, having pictured her admittedly smaller sister eating not a table's worth of food, but rather the table itself.) "—or if it's something more."

"Oh, it's definitely more," said the other.

"Then how do you know if you are?"

Sabrina did not answer.

If the Libburus knew his daughters were having this conversation, he would probably send Cletus out to inform all the noble households that they should prepare for a wedding, which would have been a welcome distraction for him in the aftermath of the night before.

See, as far as Sebastian was concerned, the whole affair with the food-fight was his fault, and at that moment was insisting, "It happened on my watch; of course it's my fault!"

Cletus tried to reassure his friend out of this train of thought, but the Libburus was determinedly set on a course of self-scrutiny, which made his mood just as undesirable as that of the man upstairs—(by this, I do not mean 'God,' but rather Hephaestus, who—for the record—is not a god.)

It might occur to the reader that there is a charming symmetry in the way that the two men of power are both being consoled or advised by their respective valets. You may even picture Cletus standing guard at Sebastian's door if you like, so as to mirror the steadfast Trenton, though it would be in image only; Sebastian could not put up much of fight to get past anyone, and Cletus was of both a dignity and cowardice that far overshot a combative response. For that matter, Cletus could never submit to participating in a fight for fear of being punched in the face: Algernon was worried he might get broken, and Ferdinand was terrified of being split[54]. In any case the servants' intentions were exactly identical, the surest of which was to keep any innocent persons from being disrupted by their respective masters.

Though their self-sacrifice was completely noble, this narrator finds it laughable, because it reminds us that the deadliest potential calamity of the Isle was upset[55]. Not war, not poverty, not even loneliness; just the risk of receiving an unfortunate attitude from a fellow citizen.

Luckily for all near bystanders, Hephaestus' steady broiling was stable, contained, and directed—which meant that the only person to whom he might truly be dangerous was the Baron. Trenton did not know how long this mood would last, but he knew that Hephaestus would try to remain painfully polite and keep his pressure-cookery under the surface. It was easy to see of course, but only because he was often in the spotlight and had a habit of being tall. Trenton resolved to simply wait it

---

[54] Algernon=nose, Ferdinand=lips

[55] I have to amend this last in slight. Every now and again, illness affected an individual or two, but the town was so isolated, (and all parties who *did* enter passed through a refrigerator beforehand), that very few strains of disease made their way among the people. Otherwise there was always the potential for routine injury or drowning from the aforementioned activities, but what does one really gain from worrying on such?

out and yawned into one open palm as he settled his broad shoulders into the closed door.

Sebastian's case was a little bit the opposite. See, even in his managerial position, he was very rarely acquainted with such stress or frustration; usually the most taxing problem on his little brain was to choose a pattern among submissions for the given month's quilt square[56]. But in the last twenty-four hours, he had endured more stressors and frustrators than he believed any man—leastways a *leader of men*—should have to endure, and so endured it by wringing his hands and fiddling with his collar and sweating so profusely that he should need to ask for water every few minutes. The way he blustered about his room, spontaneously breaking into fits of sobbing or rueful giggling, reminded the narrator of tales from Bedlam and assured Cletus that his Libburus had the general stability of a loose cannon. Fortunately, Cletus had never seen a cannon, and Sebastian may well have been a loose cannon loaded with marshmallows and stuffed bunnies for all the tangible harm he could do.

Even so, eager to spare bystanders from the horrid upsets that could be caused by such fluffies, Cletus made sure to give fair warning to the daughters to stay away. See, during one of his quests for Sebastian's water, Cletus dropped by Samantha's room and rapped his knuckles twice on the heavy door.

"Misses," he said, using the largely unrecognized plural for 'Miss', "I take it my duty to inform you that your father is liable to combust. I would advise you to make yourselves scarce from the place," to which the girls immediately responded, throwing open the door and squeezing by Cletus.

"Is he alright?" whispered Samantha as she passed.

"He will be, my dear, but if he sees you now, he might implore you for reassurance." Cletus shook his head solemnly. "And you don't want that, miss."

"Come on!" hissed Sabrina already down the hall, tugging on her boots.

Samantha nodded in courteous thanks to Cletus, who in all fairness had been a second father to her all her life, and said, "Take care of him."

"My duty, my dear," announced the other, in a hushed voice of course but puffing up so much about the chest that it made up for the volume tenfold.

---

[56] Yes, the people of the Isle made calendar quilts.

Sabrina took hold of her sister's hand and wrenched her away, down the hall and to the back door. They skitted out of the house, keeping their heads down the trenches of world wars yet to come. When Sabrina saw that Liam and Lionel were not only still at the chopping block but shirtless and steaming, she doubled back the other way. Samantha barely had a chance to see the half-naked men while being whipped around. Bent on escaping and not really looking where she was going, Sabrina collided with a lingering snow-bank about the front of the house, and Samantha, hardly a second behind tumbled in as well.

"What's going on!" yelped Samantha, as she clawed her way out of the snow.

"I'm sorry," replied the flustered Sabrina, thankful that she was wearing two sets of bloomers. As she dusted the snow from her trembling arms and her only moderately dampened dress, she happened to look up in the direction of the well—You remember the well, yes?—where she spotted a small child, head bouncing side to side in rhythm with her skipping steps. Because she neither could call to mind neither the name nor the family of this miniature character, Sabrina simply said, "There's a girl by the well."

Samantha looked up from her dress, from which she continued to scrape errant snowflakes. "Oh, I know her!" she exclaimed, heart catching in her throat for the moment she noticed. Resettling herself, and nearly breathless for reasons which she had not considered, Samantha said, "That's the little girl who came over here with Julian the other day."

At this, Sabrina's ears perked, possibly literally for all the intention behind them. "Julian?" she asked, more with her eyebrows than even her lips, "You mean the young lad who so graciously volunteered to host the Mister Baron and his followers?"

Samantha must have heard the delicious delight in her sister's tone and shot her a look of warning—not a threat, good heavens, but warning. Sabrina, immediately locating the distrust from her younger sister returned the gaze questioningly. The birds had been chirping about the Libburus' house all morning, and both sisters had noted inklings toward the romantic, but since they had never given names to their objects of curiosity, there was no way for Sabrina to know that her sister had not also been awakened by a vision of the Baron that she meant to claim for herself. For the first time in her life, Sabrina was forced to consider that she may yet have competition for the man she desired.

The hair-pulling match that may have ensued was prevented by the sight of two additional persons who fell between neither girl's crosshairs and were emerging over the hill in Miriam's wake. One was obviously the blue girl and the other—given the coat he wore—must have been one of Hephaestus' servants.

XXIV – The Long Ladle

Lance—unyieldingly dutiful—was still carrying Ten ha, who, if it is not too much to say, looked just as pleased as punch. And they followed Miriam who strolled just a little bit faster than they, which meant that she had to stop, turn around and walk back to recollect them.

Miriam had a hunch that the man was slowing down on purpose, and that maybe the grown-ups were talking about things that they didn't want her to hear. For the record, it was perfectly innocent—for that matter, mostly silent. Ten ha, afraid that her time in Lance's arms should be shortened if she seemed too coherent, took great care to appear woozy, though not nauseated, because that rarely seems playful. Lance, afraid that he had initially said something offensive that caused this sudden 'spell' tried to refrain from speaking at all.

Let us be clear on something, Lance had never been outside of Europe, more accurately, had never been anywhere other than her southern and western coastal ports. He had only ever been on one tour, tending a fisherman's haul, and had rarely gotten off the boat in Spain, Italy, or Greece for all the work he had to do. Granted, he had seen some strange and interesting things—interesting compared to his boyhood in Cardiff—but none that nearly compared to the girl he now held.

He had determined two things about her during their last exchange: the first, that she was a witch, what with the foreign incantations and all; and the second, that she was either not a very good witch or simply not harmful to him, seeing as *she* was the one who collapsed from the ordeal. Lance had even wondered whether the English language itself was a counterspell, as he was pretty sure that the magic had reflected when he had spoken back. Considering that she may have tried to hex him, backfiring though it was, he did not rightly know why he still felt a need to both carry and care for her—apparently the male mind is also inscrutable. One thing that he knew for certain was that he was happy she had not turned him into a newt.

"Where's the water, Miss'm?" asked Lance when Miriam ran back to them once again. The snap-pea pointed at an empty hill. Lance decided to assume that a well lay on the other side.

"Lead the way," he said, and Miriam disappeared quickly over the hill's crest, which brings us back to the young women who were noticing Miriam for the first time. They were likewise climbing out of the snow-bank when both Lance with a girl in his arms emerged into view.

Both sisters immediately recognized the blue girl and remembered just as suddenly her ties to the Baron. Oddly enough, and sadly for the young man, they thought nothing on Lance's account. Of course at that moment, Lance was too occupied to notice that he was not being noticed. In fact, the sisters helped this unnoticeability by ducking farther behind the snow-bank, hiding (oddly enough) from two persons that they had never met.

Unaware that they were being watched, Lance looked around to make sure they were not being watched. Yes, the well appeared to be for public use, and Miriam was waving them over welcomingly, but Lance could not tell whether it was his place to use the water within. He had been mightily turned around in their little stroll across the town, but he could tell that this was the house where he and his cohorts slept, pressed like sardines, on ungodly cots under heavenly blankets.

Miriam, the local, who probably had a better sense of proper protocol, was already rushing back to them with a sloshing ladleful of cool, clear water, which she offered to Ten ha.

Ten ha drank and then smiled at Miriam, offering a quiet, "Thank you," to which Miriam beamed. And, feeling Lance's still-concerned gaze upon her, said, "Well, that is *much* better."

"Can you stand, Miss," he asked.

"I cannot tell a lie," came the reply.

"What?"

Resigning that the moment had to end, Ten ha consented with an honest, "Yes. I can."

Lance gingerly let her down, clasping his hands behind his back once she was stably standing to demonstrate that he would never again touch her without her permission. He waited a moment for her permission.

Ten ha, seeing the mansion[57], thought aloud, "Isn't that the boss' house?"

"Well, he stays here," said Lance, trying to be helpful and not sound skittish, "but only for the winter, I'm told."

"Hmm?" then realizing that Lance had assumed Hephaestus and not Sebastian clarified, "No, no, the leader. The lord, the mayor."

"Oh! You mean Sebastian," exclaimed Lance, not noticing that I'd already clarified the point, "Yes, the Liver-man."

"Libburus," came the voice of Miriam from several feet below him. She had already run to the well, refilled the ladle and was holding it aloft for Lance.

"Yes, Libburus," he said, taking the offering with two hands, "Thank you, little miss."

Miriam took a second to beam again while Lance drank. She then snatched the ladle from his hands and returned to the well.

Ten ha watched the small and often silent child excitedly lean into the well reaching with the long ladle and her short arms for yet another drink. "Her name's Miriam," she informed Lance, who nodded toward the well. "And I'm Ten ha."

"I remembered." (He hadn't.)

"And you're Lance," she finished, hoping she might gain his eye contact.

He stole only the smallest glance, accompanied by a miniature blush. Refacing the well, he followed, "I remember that too." (He had.)

"There are two girls staring at us."

"What?" asked Lance.

So Ten ha pointed, and sure enough, there were two young women watching them.

Lance immediately recognized them as the daughters of the Liver-man[58] and startled guiltily for their being at the well. Depending on how long they had been watching, Samantha and Sabrina had caught all three of them red-handed. Or in this case wet-handed, but the notion remains.

Realizing that the jig was up and their spy-game was over, Sabrina pulled herself and her sister out from behind the snow-bank to approach the 'visitors.'

---

[57] Alright, it wasn't a mansion, but it is the biggest house in the town, so I think the term is fair.

[58] Nobody's perfect.

Lance began babbling. Luckily, his tongue was not as dexterous as Ten ha's so even his babbling was slow enough to understand, sounding like, "I'm sorry—we-we—well, the well, we didn't—I—it'll never happen—Oh dear!—I just didn't—I'm sorry, I didn't know—"

But Sabrina, who was much better at taking charge than the fellow called Lance, figured out what he was on about and distilled the situation with, "Oh the well? That's fine. You can use the well; everyone uses the well."

"Sorry we were staring."

To combat Samantha's abject apology, Sabrina quickly elbowed her in the ribs, which not only made Samantha shut up but made her straighten to a posture that was far more becoming for a lady of her esteem.

Sabrina cleared her throat, thus returning all eyes to her. "We were watching you, yes, but that is only because my sister and I wanted to have a word with you, and—well—we didn't want to interrupt your conversation."

"How nice," said Ten ha, trying her best to intercept and keep Sabrina's gaze so that the older would not see Lance. Even without knowing her reputation, Ten ha suspected competition when it approached.

"Is there something wrong?" came Lance.

"No!" Sabrina laughed, "Not at all! Why would you say such a silly thing? No, my sister and I were just hoping to ask you a question."

"What is it?" Ten ha ventured, sounding more suspicious than even she had realized.

"Well…" and Sabrina fell short. The lie had only been thought through so far. For a moment, she wondered if her gifts of misdirection were slipping, but then realized—with relief—that it was the fault of Ten ha and Lance (whose names she did not yet know) for being so quiet. Usually Sabrina would use her target's own words to turn the conversation away from herself and leave her lie cleverly concealed, but she could not dwell on this, seeing as the others were all waiting expectantly for a reply, including Miriam who had returned with the ladle.

The quickest solution took the form of Samantha's shoulders, which Sabrina promptly seized and drew in front of her, leaving the unwitting younger in the line of fire for the yet non-existent question. "My sister was curious about something."

Samantha discovered that her mouth was hanging open. She closed it. "Ummm…" She looked back to glare at Sabrina, but Sabrina was not looking in her direction, so Samantha said the only thing she could think of. "Well, I was wondering about your master, the Mister Baron Sir."

Samantha would have probably continued along that vein, but Sabrina, eyes wide in sudden jealousy, sprang back to her voice and said, "Yes, the Baron. We were thinking that it might be good for us to meet him. After all, there is no reason why young Julian should be the only one to take the mantle of responsibility in taking care of a stranger—"

"Yes, but Julian, as well, we would like to meet," blurted Samantha, losing herself somewhere about the middle of the sentence, "I mean, we've met him, at least—" with another quick glance at Sabrina, "*I* have. But to congratulate him, and—"

"And because my father, and *your* master," Sabrina said pointedly to Lance, "think that Julian would make for an-an-an ambassador—that's the word, yes?—in presenting the Sir Baron, so that he and His Highest Honored can experience a civil…"

"Meal," offered Samantha, finishing the flail with the only word that she felt would fit.

"Meal?" repeated Lance.

"Beg pardon?" came Ten ha.

"Yes, a meal," said Sabrina. "We, that is, our household would like to have your master and the rest of you people join us here for dinner." (Samantha cleared her throat; Sabrina did her best to interpret.) "With Julian, of course." (Samantha bristled.) "Because we want all these bad feelings behind us, yes? I mean, there is no need for…tension, is there?"

Lance scratched at his head, Ten ha pulled at her ear, and Miriam chewed at her string.

"My master wants this?" asked Lance, no longer able to follow whose master was being referred to, quite convinced that Hephaestus would sooner skewer the Baron than sit with him for dinner.

"It wasn't *entirely* his idea," said Samantha, by way of explanation.

Ten ha puzzled over what she had heard, essentially trying to put two and two together to get six. She looked at Lance, who, given his expression, hadn't even gotten to the two. "And you want me to pass along the invitation?" she concluded.

Samantha and Sabrina began nodding. They fought the urge to look at one another, to make sure that they were on the same page or possibly to express a mutual confusion over the situation that they had just invented. Samantha naturally blamed Sabrina for concocting this fine mess simply because she did not want to admit that they were spying.

Lance took this moment to look at his boots; if he studied them intently enough, no one would need ask him to do anything.

Poor Ten ha was already lost in this regard, having been given the task of a messenger. Ten ha was quite convinced that the turn of phrase 'Don't kill the messenger' would not have come into common usage were the messenger not often in great danger. Of course she had been the translator responsible for informing the peace-loving chief of an Incan tribe that war had been declared on him, telling the warmongering Konbaung[59] tyrant Bodawpaya that peace had been declared on him, and even pleading with the high god-king Djowotbu not to use his own foreign son-in-law's skull for a salad bowl on his second daughter's wedding day. For some reason, this new task gave her more cause for fear than any of the others had—or probably ever would.

Even so, a professional to the last, she mustered up the courage and diaphragmatic strength to force out the question, "When?"

"Oh, as soon as you see him," said Sabrina.

Ten ha made a confused face, which is a pity because it is incredibly charming and Lance was not facing her direction. "No, I mean, when is this…" she tried for a moment to say 'dinner,' but it still did not make sense to her.

Lance was gracious enough to finish for her, saying, "Dinner," clearly, as if the affair hardly seemed strange to him. His nonchalance brought Ten ha to the conclusion that he was either far more professional than her—for which he should be applauded—or happened to be very *very* foreign to these kinds of life-threatening discussions.

"Oh!" said Sabrina.

"Oh!" agreed Samantha.

"Oh…" mused Sabrina.

"Oh?" wondered Samantha.

"Oh," muttered Sabrina.

Oh no, thought the reader.

---

[59] A centuries-old dynasty in the location of modern-day Burma, if you must know.

"Well, tonight?" said Samantha, though it was really far more a guess than a statement, so timid that it lifted in inquiry.

"Tonight," repeated Ten ha.

"Well, not exactly tonight. Kind of tonight."

"*Kind of tonight?*" Ten ha looked to Lance to see if the more-foreign man could glean something from this strange regional dialect. Lance looked stumped as well, so Ten ha, with more assurance, turned back to the older sister and inquired, "What is 'kind of tonight'?"

"Well—"

"Well..."

"Well?"

"Tomorrow night!" said Sabrina. "Of course; you haven't been here very long have you?" she asked with a laugh.

Ten ha and Lance looked at one another, trying to confirm that they had both heard the same thing. Lance wasn't quite sure that he had heard anything at all by the end of the exchange, but Ten ha, having dealt with all sorts of people and all sorts of languages could write it off, given that everyone had their own silly little mistranslations. She also took it as clinching proof that the people of Adleship Isle were at some point originally English, for only the English could so bullocks up meaning with their use of slang[60].

Ten ha settled the discussion with a simple, "Very well, then."

Let's regroup, shall we? Without managing to even exchange names so as to properly lay blame when the whole rudding plot goes to hell, the two daughters of the Libburus had set up an event which could only end in blood and tears between the Baron, Hephaestus, and all of their respective compatriots, who would gladly fight on the side of their respective masters. They had, without much thinking, scheduled this battle in the home of their own father who would actually sustain a thirty-eight percent risk of stroke when they told him the news, and burdened Ten ha and Lance, the individuals with the least power among their groups, with the weight of the original information, as well as the probable fault. Finally, to make matters worse, they had posed the engagement only two days after the second largest feast in the Isle's annual cycle[61], when no home, even the Libburus', had enough food

---

[60] Ten ha would have a field day with 20th century America.

[61] The largest being a harvest dedication precisely a fortnight after Saint Norbert's Day.

stores to cover twenty persons[62] in one evening, meaning that they had to—whoever *they* were—go to one of the town food-stores and alert the rest of the citizens to what all was happening. And all this was managed while Sebastian and Hephaestus were hard at work simply getting over the catastrophe that was the previous night.

Sabrina was forced to pull out of this consideration before anyone else, having heard the sound of an axe on lumber and recalling just why she had come around the house this way in the first place. Not only that, but she understood that the longer she remained near the recipients of her deception, the quicker everything might come unraveled. "Well," she said, pulling her sister's arm, "we have to go down to the storehouse and…arrange things." And with that, the girls departed, still trying to collect themselves, while Ten ha and Lance continued to reel.

"So, I guess you have to leave now, don't you?" said Lance as the dust began to settle.

"What?"

"You have to go tell the Baron. I know how it is; you're always on duty, aren't you?"

"Oh…" trailed Ten ha, slowly sinking without an excuse to stay. "I guess," she consented, then looking around herself, "I just need to find… Miriam?"

The little girl popped out from around the back of the house and waved. None had noticed her disappear in the first place; she had simply grown bored by their conversation and left to investigate the same sound of chopping wood behind the house.

"We're heading back home, now, Miriam. Alright?" The little girl nodded and bounced back over to them.

Lance, only briefly distracted by whatever it was that had drawn Miriam away, was trying to draw together suitable parting words, so, by way of stalling for time, knelt and offered a hand to the snap-pea, which she did not take. Still, he said, "Thank you for taking us to the water, Miriam."

Miriam shyly regarded the grass.

Lance straightened again and turned toward Ten ha who stood ready before him, her own right hand presented for him to take.

And when he did, she said only, "Thank you," which was whispered so quietly that only their close proximity made it audible.

---

[62] Yes, exactly twenty including Sebastian's yet unnamed maid-servant.

Lance nodded, tried to swallow, failed, licked his lips, then did so successfully. Without letting go her hand, he asked, "Can you walk home alright?"

Ten ha considered lying further to get him to carry her farther, considered (god forbid!) telling the truth, the whole truth, and nothing but the truth that she had only faked the faint to be close to him; that she didn't want him to leave, much less let her leave; that she never stayed in one place long enough to know what it was like to be in love or even to develop a school-girl's crush; and that she was scared to death of both the way that he looked at her and the very real possibility that he may never look at her like that again. She was convinced that, up until that moment, she had never truly known what it was to be a sixteen-year-old girl, or even a teenager at all, and even more convinced that she did not like it when that sixteen-year-old girl self-refused to say what she needed or wanted, and simply offered a breathy nod.

"Good," said Lance. "Well, goodbye." And he turned and started toward the house.

And she turned and started up the hill, taking Miriam's tiny hand—which was no substitute for Lance's—and cursing her own cowardice. But as she did, she came to remember that time she crossed a jagged ravine on a rotting bridge, or that other time when she braved a lava tube thinner than two feet in width holding nothing more than a jar of fireflies, or an incident hardly a year before in which she quelled a ferocious tiger—who had just mauled two armed gentlemen—simply by standing her ground and speaking in the trainer's native tongue. How was this peril any greater than others she had faced? If she had the guts to inform the Baron of this dog's breakfast of a dinner party, she had no excuse for falling to fear now. And so, with some measure of vicarious confidence, she turned back around and began to say, "Will you be—"

"At the stables tomorrow morning. Same time," he finished from the bottom of the hill, reading her mind exactly the way she hoped he would. Through a nervously excited smile, he promised, "I'll be there."

She rounded again and skitted up the hill, shoulders hunched forward to hide how proud she was, afraid that the bright plum-peach tone of her blush would betray her feelings on their engagement, whether there were any secrets left to betray.

Lance watched her go for as long as he could, then found himself turning back to the house, where he would find further instructions to occupy his time. In his approach to the rear door, Lance discovered two of his fellow servants, and incidentally what had gained Miriam's attention.

Liam wielded the axe while Lionel watched, looking incredibly frustrated and saying, "You're holding it wrong." They were both shirtless.

"Where're your jackets?" asked Lance.

Liam stopped his swing long enough to roll his eyes, and Lionel pointed to where they had piled the garments, concluding the gesture with a snide, "Now, piss off," through the side of his mouth.

"It's freezing out here," observed Lance in wonder.

"We can take it," came Liam, punctuating with a firm *thwack*.

Lance looked to Lionel's arms, spotting the vibrating goosebumps, and remarked, "You're shivering."

"Look it's not for you," said Lionel, "it's for the miss." And Liam pointed with the axe in the direction of the window.

"Who, the daughters?" asked Lance, and it was his turn to feel smug. Prefaced by a laugh, he told the young men who were chilling their rears off, "They just left. Went into town, and you missed 'em."

Liam and Lionel looked to each other in frustration; the first dropped his axe, the second sprang to his feet, and both went to work hurriedly throwing on their matching coats.

Once she was sure that they were out of earshot and eyeshot, Ten ha stopped, knelt, and planted a kiss on Miriam's forehead. She sounded totally breathless, but somehow elated, and so Miriam was not frightened.

Instead, the snap-pea told the blue girl, "You're braver than Julian."

XXV – A Thermometer, a Barometer, and a Journal

"You're a very brave man," the Baron called over the din of wind.

From some twenty feet above on the rock face, Julian shouted back, "Oh, I've been doing this since I was a boy." Feeling his fingers numbing against the stone, he grimaced and muttered to himself, "But not in the winter."

"No, not that." The Baron ground his shoe into its foothold. Once he was certain it was secure, he released one hand from the wall to feel his mustache which had fortunately not iced, then resumed, "I mean the way you so nobly volunteered to take in us strays."

From a ways below, Geru scoffed. This was in part because he took unkindly to the term, but mostly because he was yet too breathless to speak, bringing up the rear as it were.

With no Pigby to haul him, no Fletcher to scout an easier path, and no Oswald to drag down the pace, Geru felt himself the weakest link, a trait which he held in even lower esteem than the word 'stray.'

If you were to zoom out and take a wider scope of the terrain, would see that while, yes, it was a near-vertical incline, it was made up of a series of randomly piled boulders and large sand-papery rocks, which had neither attracted moss nor offered any incentive to slip. Essentially it was like climbing a very uneven ladder. You might be wondering why the insistent yoga practitioner would be the one to be beaten by any rock wall, let alone one so elementary as this. Two things help to answer that question: the first, that Geru would insist to his last that the wall was not beating him; the second, that his legs were simply too short for him to be fairly compared to the others.

I find the most ironic attribute to Geru's lagging pace not his small stature or trained flexibility, but rather the fact that this expedition was on his behest and not the Baron's or Julian's. Why, you might ask? Well, to explore the atmospheric phenomena surrounding the Isle, starting with the source of the falls that did not freeze even in the mountains in mid-December.

So, if you consult the handy little map in the inside cover of your text, you will find that this wall boarders the north end of the town, stretched between a completely insurmountable ridge and that charming falls, which supplied the pool, which fed the river, which ran through the town (that Jack built). See? Just to the northeast of Jonas' little hill, there.

Well, as you can imagine, when Geru said that he needed to examine something, Julian was ready to volunteer to guide him, and the Baron was ready to volunteer to follow young Julian. Remember, he had quite an issue to sort out with our hero, and though we are only on the second day of what will be about a six-week stretch, the Baron was not one to procrastinate, which prompts his next question:

"What exactly inspired you to make such a generous offer?" The Baron tried to speak without panting. He was clearly less experienced with the slopes, and would—like Ten ha—try to blame the mountain air, but he was determined not to show Julian that he was having trouble keeping up. After all, he was a few years younger than Geru yet, and had half a mind to preserve the superhero image that the boy must have had of him—considering that the Baron had traversed the whole of The Big Out There and should have *some* endurance to show for it.

Julian, who had been born, raised, and broken in in this small town, was glad that the Baron could not see his face, seeing as it was beet-red from exertion. He feared that, were he not a ways away, the Baron might question whether Julian was the right native for this job, and if the Baron could question it, then what would Samantha think? I myself do not see the logical progression here either, but I think we can chock it up to love.

So, striving to prove that he was in fact composed, he said, "I can fit more than me in that house, sir."

"Admittedly," admitted the Baron, "but surely there are other houses, some with even more room available than yours. Why were you not afraid when the others were?"

Of course Julian knew the *real* reason, or had at least settled on one that made sense to him, but could not reveal it for fear of the impression it might make. Point of fact, he had never admitted his yearning to any persons, (other than our audience, it seems), and did not know how anyone should take his secret, much less a Baron, who so far outstripped him in class that he was still wary of carrying a conversation. Keep in mind that a few intimate friends, including Miriam, had gleaned what was just past the end of their noses, but they did Julian the courtesy of pretending his secret was still a secret.

Unlike all others though, the Baron seemed to be actively probing, which made the covert Julian more actively evade. So he replied, in a way that most modern readers will understand, "Oh... you know."

This did not help; the Baron *was* hoping to catch Julian in a lie, but only to pinpoint the object or ideal that this young man valued more than the security of his home. He thought it most likely a girl—even assumed that he had seen this girl. Of course he was right, but naturally wanted to know for certain, so that he could skip this inefficient little dance and get right down to business.

As they climbed the wall though—both the Baron and Julian trying to pretend they were more athletic than they really were—the Baron rephrased the question three times and three times Julian batted it away with a slightly different noncommittal phrase.

Once they reached the top, the Baron and the boy had a chance to breathe while they waited for Geru.

"You'd think you could go a little slower," the short man grumbled as Julian pulled him the rest of the way over the cliff and onto what turned out to be a serenely flat shelf. "What's a little common courtesy—after all, I took a bullet in the hip!" Geru declared, proud that he had a better excuse than either of the other two for his breathlessness.

"In his hip?" mouthed Julian to the Baron, while their dwarfish companion dusted off his pants.

"His left buttock," confided the Baron, followed by a brief snork.

"I heard that!" came Geru.

Julian scratched his head; while the foreigners seemed to find this matter perfectly acceptable, it raised the question, "What's a bullet?"

The Baron and Geru looked to one another, neither ready to provide answer to this question. The Baron must have conveyed to his employee that it was his fault for bringing up the word in the first place, because Geru soon responded with, "It's a small piece of metal that can damage flesh if you're not careful, and it's produced by an explosion. You know what an explosion is, yes, lad?"

Julian nodded, he had gathered this from Elke's kitchen on more than one occasion. "Loud noise, big flash, pieces move outsward—duck and cover."

"Very nearly scientific," Geru commended with only a hint of sarcasm, before pulling the pack off his back and withdrawing a thermometer, a barometer, and a journal.

"He's just upset because he was hit by one of those pieces," whispered the Baron, smirking as though it were in jest, though Julian couldn't see anything funny in the matter.

Geru scanned the shelf on which they stood, noting its depth, its elevation, and the basin that the waterfall had carved out, a basin which fueled yet another falls which poured right into the town's river. Mainly, he noted the grass. It was true that there was plenty of grass in the Isle, even with a few snow drifts trying to suffocate it, but to find grass forty or fifty feet above the town's highest settled point, at an elevation where trees hardly grew (outside of this magical mountain pass, that is) was extraordinary enough to prompt a letter to king's own science division— and don't think Geru hadn't considered it.

He took out a small wheeled device from the sack and thrust the pointy end in the dirt. He removed the pin, and the wheel began spinning, the affixed cups catching the wind and pulling with them a knotted string[63]. Stopping it between his thumb and forefinger, Geru brought the specimen close to his face and remarked, "Hmm. Twelve knots."

As the short man scrawled away in his pad, the nib making a *scrrratch*ing sound at the onset of each new line, the Baron strode toward the misted pool. I say 'misted' because the force of the water rushing into it from the falls above created a nice mask of water vapor over the whole of the surface, and probably was a major factor toward Geru's wind. The Baron was fascinated: the upper falls had essentially torn through a mountainside, creating a harsh and unyielding current of what he could only assume was glacial runoff through the most exquisitely curvy canyon—at least so far as he could see. He was half-tempted to try to write a poem, he was so moved.

Julian arrived, and explained that this waterfall dropped into a well that was too deep for any of them to tell, and that the depth gave way to relatively calm water stretching in all directions. Until it drew too far south and turned into yet another waterfall, the same one that fed the

---

[63]Now, admittedly there must be some wires crossed here, seeing as most sources will tell you that this device, the "cup anemometer" was *actually* credited in 1846 to the Dubliner Reverend Doctor John Thomas Romney Robinson, even though we see it used by Geru nearly half a century prior. It is entirely possible, muses your narrator, that Geru was a sometime teacher of the same Rev. Dr. Robinson, but we can never know these things for certain.

pool on the town level. It wasn't highly creative of them, granted, but to distinguish the upper from the lower pools in conversation, called them the big dipper and the little dipper[64] respectively. Of course, young Julian's experience with bodies of water stopped here, with the biggest known pool stretching maybe eighty feet across at the farthest point. He was greatly stirred by the very idea of lakes—with water so big that you couldn't see the other side. Julian imagined that this looked something like the fog at the south end of their town, but more on that later.

"Care to sit with me lad?" asked the Baron, while Geru continued to bustle about with his devices.

"Sure," he said, taking his place beside the mustache man as they overlooked the pools. "Now, I know the hill on the other side of the big dipper is easier to climb, but I think you get a better shot at the falls here."

"And more scope of the town," said the Baron, smiling gently, "This is after all the highest place you could get to, you said."

"Well, maybe not the highest," admitted Julian, and indicated with his head the crags and cliffs that continued to ascend to the north. "But nobody ever bothers to go past here."

"Because this place is perfect?"

Julian shrugged. It may have been for all he knew, but keep in mind that a person cannot judge anything as perfect unless he has seen something *im*perfect in his lifetime, and Julian had never seen anything but the Isle.

The Baron, who had travelled not only all around the world, but by all methods and routes and backwater passages and what you will, had trouble conceiving of any place from which people could not leave— much like Julian's imagination fell short when the Baron tried to describe to him a desert. Julian explained that whenever anyone tried to find a passage away from the Isle, he would either get turned around and wind up right back where he started, or that he would simply never be heard from again, leaving 'missing' and 'dead' to be the most common explanations.

The Baron would have liked to think that maybe those who didn't come back actually reached civilization, but it did not bode well that they never discovered a return route. Otherwise, he deemed it a matter of persistence; after all, Hephaestus had been making the trip in and out for years.

---

[64] Relation to constellations yet to be determined.

"Do you ever think you'll try to leave?" asked the Baron. He squeezed a flat stone against his palm and then slung it into the pool, watching it skip three times before sinking.

Julian pursed his lips. He picked up the first stone he saw, stood and whipped it against the water, where it bounced heartily until the mist obscured it. Some seconds after, they heard a satisfying clink as it presumably came upon another rock at the other end of the pool.

As Julian sat back down, dusting off his palms, he said, "I doubt it."

"And why is that lad?" The Baron adjusted himself closer to the boy, attempting to express some kind of fraternal trust. Given that he had planned for an outing of the expeditious nature, the Baron was dressed no more nicely than Julian, wearing no hat and a plain military regulation jacket—(and Dutch military at that)—and thought he could appear an equal. "If you don't mind my saying: what reason do you have to stay? I understand you have your ties here, but your parents are gone; you've no brothers or sisters to look after. If you wanted to, I could take you with me when I leave. I can always use a man of strong moral fiber." Settling back onto his elbows, the Baron concluded, "You could see the whole world."

Julian seemed to have trouble finding words. In something of bewilderment, asked, "You'd do that?"

The Baron sincerely nodded. "If you want."

Julian chose not to look at the Baron, as if eye contact would force him to accept before he was ready or tip him the other way toward absolute refusal and the inevitable despair at passing up his opportunity. Instead he watched the short man, whose travels were evident, not because of his clothes or devices, but by the fascination with which he took the temperature of the falls, something that could only so intrigue an adventurer.

"Why did you leave, sir?"

"How's that?"

"Well," Julian paused; naturally, he did not want to overstep his station by asking too bold a question, but even more naturally, he was curious. "You left your home, didn't you, sir? What made you leave?"

"Oh, that," returned the Baron, "Let's just say a little book told me to."

Julian, without the faintest idea as to what the Baron referred, nodded in the best understanding he could muster.

XXVI – Some Responsibility

"All I can say is that it's disgraceful!" said Eugene, in such a way that we *know* it was not all he could say. Pacing around a massive table, the one that was used the night prior for the head table, the head of the house just to the south of the Libburus' seethed visibly—first because of his raw fury toward his son's behavior at the Feast-us, second because he could not come up with harsh enough words to express such fury adequately.

"Yes, Father," said Raul, as Eugene continued his shark's circle. The boy of seventeen hunched forward onto his elbows, not in shame or guilt, but annoyance. Clearly, he had heard this lecture, or at least one similar, before. "I under—"

Snapping the fingers of his gloved hand, Eugene likewise snapped, "Don't interrupt me. For shame, son—*for shame!*" Raul rolled his eyes; Eugene was too wrapped up in his own tirade to notice. "Our dear friend Condamine said that you actually doused her in gravy, in a dress that her servants spent the better part of the last two months stitching."

This made Raul smirk, and if you knew Condamine, you would as well. (The sister of yet another noble, she put on more airs than any three of her fellow citizens, wore her hair in an arrangement that looked much akin to the pope's hat, and was delightfully rotund, which made her—forgive the phrase—the butt of many-a-child's jokes.)

The smirk made Eugene scowl. He stopped in his tracks and planted his palms on the wood that unfortunately had not been effectively washed of the stains. "This is no laughing matter! I would think that you might be a respectable citizen, but there you were, hurling potatoes like a common ruffian. To think that this is a boy who will be eligible to act the Libburus by the next election! People look up to you—"

"I know, Father," mumbled Raul.

"Your sisters—*they* look up to you—"

"I know, Father," grumbled Raul.

"And you, my oldest, my only son—*this* is how you treat your family's good name and reputation?"

And Raul repeated the line that he had probably been saying as soon as he learned to speak—Correction!—as soon as he learned to disappoint his father, which was probably not long after. "I'm sorry father."

"Hmph!" humphed Eugene, as he too had trained, "You will be eighteen soon; 'sorry' won't be enough. You need to learn to take some responsibility! Let me ask you," he said, leaning in so close that Raul could smell the faint tooth decay on his father's breath, "Do you want to be a ragamuffin for the rest of your life?"

Raul did not much know what a ragamuffin was, much less if he wanted to be one. He assumed that he did not, so said, "No, sir."

"Good," Eugene returned, straightening, "Then I want you to know that there will be some changes, boy. You will be required to take on a more dignified bearing, you see? You will have to start acting like the noble you are and living like you should. I'll have you know, Raul, that we are going to make some adjustments, that way, by the time you are eighteen, truly an adult and old enough to make your own decisions for yourself, *we* will already have the important ones decided."

Yes, he actually said that, assuming his son's license to run his life—parents, eh? No one knows precisely why eighteen is the proper age for adulthood, but as it stood, the boy would be having his birthday within a week, so there simply wasn't time to quibble about the importance of the event.

What the reader *will* quibble about is what Eugene will say next. If you are astute, you may have already guessed it[65], and even if you have not, you will agree that it places one more degree of tension on our little village during this already-peculiar winter. Eugene took a deep breath, such that the top button of his waistcoat trembled with anticipation. "For starters, I do not want you seeing that ingrate, Julian, anymore!"

---

[65] If you discover that you guessed wrong, don't worry; there is a chance your guess will turn up later.

XXVII – Stones from Slings

What goes up must come down, yes? (Or the other way 'round, given the mood of our last chapter.) Well, barring some spatial or temporal vortex[66], logically, what goes in must come out. Or if not the same thing, then something of equal volume or mass, so as to balance the system. Now, I probably don't need to tell you that the isle was one system that had lasted for decades, if not centuries, so it stands to reason that it must have been kept at least mostly balanced.

I guess we can assume that the self-contained ecosystem existed in something of a Mufasa's Circle of Life pattern[67], such that the cows that were butchered had their unusable remnants re-buried, so as to fertilize the grass that the still-living cows ate in turn which kind of makes the grass a third party to cannibalism—but enough on the conjectural morality of animal recycling! We've heard how the citizens collect wood and stones from the hills in the north and the river that runs through it, and if these items are coming in, then something comparable must be likewise flowing out.

Well, as the river flows north to south, so flows the town's collective digestive tract. And so, at the far south, at the end of the sheep fields, there was a steep drop off, a tipping point to the end of the world, where the waste of the Isle was tossed.

Now, we assume that there was actually a valley below, some crater probably less than a hundred feet down, but we've established that the climate was so bizarre that it will not surprise you to hear that any

---

[66] Actually, studies indicate that Adleship Isle may be located on one such vortex.
[67] To quote *The Lion King*: "…let me explain: when we die, our bodies become the grass, and the antelope eat the grass. And so we are all connected in the great Circle of Life."

theoretical ground below was completely covered by a plateau of fog the whole year 'round—and I mean *completely* covered, stitching along the ridge, clinging to the cliff-face and stretching on to infinity, or at least the next peak, and every bit of it as thick as a New England clam chowder.

Of course the people of the Isle had made every effort to find the bottom, but none of their ropes were ever long enough, and not a soul who tried to venture below the cloud cover ever returned. Additionally, anyone who tried to climb down was accompanied by a scream of sorts, which rapidly faded into faint obscurity. (There was no Loony-Toons mushroom cloud to signify a landing either.) Additionally, the drop claimed one or two citizens who ventured too close every generation or so, so no one really needed to prove anymore that their bottomless pit was in fact bottomless.

To this end, a small fence had been erected a ways from the edge, which straddled the river before it turned into yet another waterfall, to signal that the cliff could give way and pull passersby down with it.

Now here is where we get to disposal of debris—the likes of which I do not need to clarify—but we can assume that with the Feast-us the night before, there were plenty of items that were either unsalvageable or inedible which could serve no purpose other than to be tossed. In this case, *tossed* was literal, right off the edge of the town and through the mashed-potato sheet of clouds.

Every toss began with a large sling. The wielder would gather up whatever refuse he could, wrap it into the sling, and hurl the payload over the fence and off the edge of the world. You may be wondering why they didn't just tip a wheelbarrow or dump it into the river. Well, the answers for this are simple: a wheelbarrow wielder had once arrived on an unsturdy section of cliff and tumbled down, barrow and all, and otherwise, when the citizens dumped in the water, the river had a habit of damming up, which had a habit in turn of flooding the nearby fields, which drowned the grass, which starved the sheep, who lived in the town that Jack built.

Besides, throwing the trash made the whole event more of a game than a chore.

The first thrower of the day was always the person who had thrown the biggest load the last time, which usually meant Clemens, (though Piers, as a strapping young man, could occasionally bump him from his station). This morning Clemens loaded the sling as tightly as he could so that it was probably two feet in diameter, then—after letting the other men admire how tightly he'd packed it—began his arc, whipping it around and around and around.

Every man took his step back, every man that is except for Pigby, who—with his arms sternly folded about his chest—was most intrigued by the process. When Clemens released, he did so with a resolute grunt, which sent his payload out, over the fence, and into the abyss. Immediately, all parties bustled forward, peering over the fence to see it pass into the cloud. It was always a fascination of theirs, how far each sphere had been sent. Additionally, I would postulate that—even though they could never see all the way through the cloud—they hoped that maybe, someday, someone's throw would clear enough of the veil to make the ground below visible. Of course, it never did, but a one-day-maybe hope isn't such a bad thing; it gives you something to strive for[68].

Pigby strove to not embarrass himself. What with his showing at the bread-slapping game, as well as his mammoth size, he had already formed a reputation—as evidenced particularly by the fact that hardly anyone would speak with him—and did not want to fall short of it. Clemens was not afraid, and Manuel was doing his best not to be, but the half-dozen other men were obviously wary. This was not new to Pigby, thankfully, but in the small town of Adleship Isle, he felt more a spectacle than he ever had before, and as he wrapped his first sling tried not to wilt under the pressure of everyone's vigilant stares.

He had thrown stones from slings, but was quite sure that this apparatus was quite a different animal. Being a man, however, he was averse to asking for directions. He took up the sling and warmed it up with a wide steady arc, glancing back to Clemens only once for a nod of approval.

I should note that there is only one truly difficult thing about wielding the trash-sling: see, even though the load is released, the thrower may only let go of one end of the sling, keeping the other secured so as to not lose the sling itself. When Pigby started to release, lo and behold!, he found he did not have a good enough grip on the one and so abandoned his throw halfway through. He lunged forward to try to catch the straps and slipped on the frosted grass, stumbling to land squarely on his behind.

Laughter sounded; seeing as Pigby was a giant of a man, watching him falter and fall was delightfully entertaining to the Isleans. Pigby quickly sat back up, his rear protesting its soon-to-be bruise.

---

[68] Like writing a bestselling novel.

Clemens crouched beside Pigby and asked through his mustache, "Are you hurt?"

"Just my pride," muttered the giant man.

"Don't take it too hard, man," said Piers, arriving at his shoulder.

"Come on, let's get you up," said Manuel, offering him a hand.

Pigby took the generous aid and easily ascending to his feet again.

"It was a fair try," came Clemens, slapping one of his large palms on Pigby's shoulders, which was met with murmurs of agreement and charmed chuckles.

Once the giant man had dusted himself off, he surveyed the crowd and was overwhelmed that not one man stood guarded or distanced from him, and all seemed genuinely good-natured about his failed attempt.

Even so, in guilt and shame, Pigby felt compelled to tell Clemens, "I'm so sorry; I'm afraid I've lost you a sling."

Perhaps the giant man would have apologized more for his faux pas, but for the fact that Clemens was heartily laughing. Clemens tried to sputter something amid chortles, but it must have gotten caught in his mustache because no words actually reached Pigby. Instead, the grocer pointed, and following his finger, Pigby saw the sling, its payload still inside, resting calmly against the fence, which he had not even managed to clear.

Pigby felt an odd sensation in his gut, which moved tremblingly through his chest, and exploded up through his throat and out of his mouth in a deep, booming guffaw, which continued to build as other parties joined in, leaving the cluster of strong working men holding their sides as they hooted over this single failed action which probably made Pigby more a part of the town than any success possibly could have. And that was that.

From there, each man took his turn to throw, until they had all gone, opening the floor for as many throws at a time as there were slings, and Clemens trained Pigby in technique, as a father might a son. As the giant man gradually came to understand the art, the men seemed to see him as more their size and more their color.

They began to converse with Pigby, asking questions and swapping stories as modern-day beer-commercial-buddies do. They learned that yes, he had been all over the world; no, not all people from Pigby's 'town' were as tall or dark as him; and that, yes again, he had eaten the thing that Hephaestus called 'fish.'

Pigby discovered that he could not throw nearly as large of a sling as Clemens, and took such as a promising sign of the lifestyle the Isleans had developed and trained. Because Pigby was still larger and stronger, and Clemens did not want his new friend to feel discouraged, he went out of his way to commend the giant man's evident physical prowess. Pigby seized this opportunity by inviting Clemens to join himself and Geru for their morning warm-ups.

"Is it a kind of exercise?" asked Clemens.

"It's a power-stretching regimen, the school of which is older than this town itself," replied Pigby, "and Geru's a master of it."

The men seemed intrigued, but then, everything about Pigby intrigued them, as everything about the town intrigued the Baron and his crew. The Baron would say that he would naturally hire only persons with a tendency toward adventure and discovery, and as of such, all of his employees sought these traits in others. In this, Pigby found that the men of the Isle did not disappoint, even if they had initially been frightened and reserved.

Now Pigby knew there was still some work to be done where assimilation was concerned, but by the time all of the trash had been tossed, which seemed like hardly any time at all, he felt he'd already made strides sufficient of a week's work. Thanking the men as he said goodbye, Pigby left with Clemens and Manuel, who had work in the storehouse and didn't mind an extra set of hands.

And here is where they are interrupted, for—you see—when I said that Samantha and Sabrina were headed to a storehouse to make arrangements for the dinner, I meant this exact storehouse, and at a time which curiously coincided with this one.

Yes, it gets confusing, considering that so much is happening at once. Tell you what: if you would prefer that more time has passed between the fibbing sisters' last exit and their current reentry, go ahead and assume that they have actually been waiting in the storehouse for quite a while for the men in charge to get back, seeing as almost all parties who worked in the storehouse would have been involved in clean up—like the trash disposal—in the aftermath of the feast-us.

Now that your mental image is set, probably with Sabrina sitting on a crate or bail while Samantha nervously paces, still unsure of what to say to support their lie, you can properly imagine Manuel, Clemens, and Pigby drawing open the door.

Samantha immediately stiffened, her hands held splayed open by her sides as she nodded to the company. All three men stopped—more accurately, Manuel and Clemens halted, and Pigby, following closely, bumped into them but quickly adjusted himself. The tension, he surmised, came from the fact that the young lady looked worried; he did not yet recognize who she was, but he detected that she must have been of some station, lest she would not inspire such a reaction from the other two.

"Hi," she began, and from the one syllable Pigby had an awful premonition that the statement to follow was either about him or would greatly affect him. He was right on both counts.

XXVIII – A Telescope

"See, my first thought was tools," said Fletcher, as he half-supported the hobbling Oswald, gesturing with his free hand, "but then, I thought, is it really fair to give a seventeen-year-old boy something for *work?*"

"The Baron distinctly said that we may not pay young Julian for his services no matter how tempted we are!" protested Oswald, in a manner that suggested he was repeating himself for the third or fourth time.

"Yes, but he didn't say anything about gifts,"

"Oh," came the flabbergasted old man, "well, make sure the Trojan horse can fit through his door!"

"Now, I wanted to give him a book," Fletcher went on, without the slightest consideration for Oswald's sarcasm, "but I can't think of a single story of mine that doesn't mention either money or murder—which is a sad reflection on our culture, wouldn't you say?"

"I say, I think *you're* a sad reflection of our culture," hollered Oswald, with such vigor that a pedestrian coming from the other direction startled, about-faced, and hustled away from them, "so much that I thank God we are not wholly of the same culture."

"For the last time: I wasn't born in Ireland."

Oswald pointed a crooked finger at Fletcher's throat. "I can smell it on you, boy."

"Do you want me to leave you right here? I could. I could just drop you right here, let you crawl back, hmm?"

"Oh, shove off, you blaggard!"

"Blaggard?" repeated Fletcher, incredulous, "How dare you! That is our word and you have no right using it[69]."

"I'll use it if I bloody-well—"

"And what about you? You Tory, you loyalist scum—turn-coat on your own country—"

"That was the rebels!" screeched Oswald, shaking his fist.

"Save it, lumpy—if you were only half the yella-bellied coward you seemed, why I'd—" And Fletcher stopped walking. (Yes, he and the old man had been keeping up a steady pace all through the shouting match.) He looked up and down the street, then regarded the house in front of them, asking with total calm, "Is this the place?"

Oswald adjusted his glasses. "Can't say."

"Here, let me just check." He fished through his pocket for the little map Julian had drawn up for them, and—surveying the street around them—concluded, "This looks about the place."

"Well, c'mon, give it a knock," urged the old man, and Fletcher tentatively tapped his knuckles against the door. He then quickly stepped back and composed himself, like a girl-scout selling cookies door-to-door, so as to make the least-eager-looking first impression as he could.

A voice that he immediately associated with eccentricity hollered from overhead, "Be in a minute!"

Both Fletcher and Oswald tried not to twiddle their thumbs as they waited, but it was hard not to grow antsy when they heard the clatter and clash of what must of have been tumbling cinder blocks[70], which was followed by a woman's voice who hissed something about "Clutter" which gave way to argument.

Only able to catch the occasional word, even then with uncertainty, Fletcher must have thought that they would feel more comfortable if he and Oswald resumed an argument of their own, and so said:

"What about fireworks? I mean, it's something he hasn't seen before, and we've got dozens of the bastards. Don't you think townies would just eat it up?"

"Fletcher," began Oswald, as if he had something more to say, then resigned to, "Let it go."

---

[69] Blaggard, coming from "Blackguard" is slang reputedly of Irish origins. Unlike Fletcher, Oswald would be pleased to claim that no such origin touched his blood.

[70] Not yet in use.

When the door opened before them, and they saw the man that stood behind it, this narrator expected them to gasp, do a double-take, or even start laughing at the image before them. However, both Oswald and Fletcher were so seasoned by their journeys that neither needed to blink at the sight of Dietrich.

This is the first time you've met Dietrich, yes? I'm certain you've heard me mention him before, though not in detail of appearance. Have you seen *Back to the Future*, *Young Frankenstein*, or a stage production of Dürrenmatt's *The Physicists*? Mad scientists are not hard to find in literature in your day, but I must admit, Dietrich was a cut above the curve for the early nineteenth century. He had the exploding grey hair, the thick goggles which seemed to deny any visible access to his eyes, and—though he did not work in a lab—something of a lab-coat, which was no longer white, but had presumably been at some point. My favorite part is that this walking cliché stood in front of two persons who were, in their own right, even more bizarre than he.

He was the resident stargazer, astrologist, palm-reader, salt-licker, and stamp collector. By stamps I don't mean those sticky papery things, but rather reverse engraved templates for pressing into wax seals on envelopes, the likes of which he had so many, he was even considering inventing his own printing press. In fact, such was the only tribute Julian could suggest to show that they meant no ill will, and what better addition to anyone's collection—Oswald thought—than the stamp of the Baron himself; a one-of-a-kind novelty, of which they carried less than a dozen at any given time.

So, before speaking, Oswald reached out his hand and made the offering, which Dietrich took swiftly and curiously. The scientist lifted the goggles from his eyes, and Oswald and Fletcher leaned forward to see that the skin was two or three shades lighter underneath.

"Hmm," grunted Dietrich, shifting his eyes between the strange visitors. Without warning, he tossed the stamp over his shoulder into his dark house, shook his sooty hands from their sleeves, and grabbed one hand of each Fletcher and Oswald, drawing them near to the point of practically falling over—(remember Oswald was still being supported by Fletcher).

He brought the open hands close to his face, squinting and scanning the series of lines, before quickly saying, "Congratulations." He looked up to the men's faces, and, without the tiniest glint of a smile, said, "You will neither drown, nor fall off a cliff, nor be struck by lightning during your stay in the Isle. Goodbye now."

Oswald hardly had time to lift a finger in protest before the door was slammed shut, Dietrich securely behind it.

"I'd say that was informative," said Fletcher, with such undue nonchalance that Oswald could not tell if it was genuinely sarcastic or an acknowledgment that their presence was unwanted.

Oswald felt both guilty for so boorishly intruding on this man's property and time, and frustrated because he truly had no intention of being intrusive—though he was quite keen on asking some questions. See, according to Julian, Dietrich was both the oldest (coherent) man and had the largest wealth of useless knowledge—Julian's words, not Oswald's—making him the best candidate for supplying information on the origins of the Isle. Even so, it seemed Oswald had no choice but to droop and say, "Well, I guess that's—"

But he never finished his despairing remark, as suddenly the same woman's voice started hollering something about "manners" and "etiquette". Before Oswald even had a chance to turn away, the door swung open again to reveal Elke, sporting a well-floured apron and pulling Dietrich by his ear.

She was somewhat out of breath, given the scuffle that must have preceded her emergence, but she smiled as she said, "We would *love* for you to come into our home. Wouldn't we, Diets?"

"Lemmego, woman!" exclaimed Diets through gritted teeth.

"Dietrich Wilhelm[71], invite these nice gentlemen in if you please."

"Fine!" When Dietrich was released he dusted his hands off, cleared his throat and said, "Won't you *please* come in."

Oswald and Fletcher glanced briefly at one another before replying with a markedly British, "Y'Alright," the John-Cleese-esque resonant unison completely overshadowing their respective colonial and Australian origins.

Entering as a unit, the Baron's men were met first with the darkness of the stranger's household—remember there was no electricity in the world, and certainly far less in the Isle, so it was is darker than you might have expected as well. And in the dim light, everything, including the floors beneath their feet, seemed to be coated in a strange grey dust.

"Jesu Christo," remarked Fletcher, "it's flour." And Elke struck up the candles, illuminating one of the most exquisite kitchens the thin

---

[71] To the best I can determine, this was a middle and not a surname, but I still believe that they had such, even if we never hear them.

man had ever before observed. Of course, it wasn't so large, this kitchen, in comparisons to those of lords and sheiks and sultans, but it was so absolute in its assembly of tools and gizmos that Fletcher had to fall backwards. Luckily, Elke was so efficient a host that somehow—almost magically—she had gotten a chair behind him just in time for his collapse.

"Well," said Elke, "as long as you're sitting, you might as well have a muffin, yes?" And before she'd finished the word, it had found its way into Fletcher's hands. He had only a moment to notice he was drooling before his serenity was quite interrupted by a crotchety voice.

"I assume you have some business here—"

"Dietrich! Don't be so frosty; these are our guests."

Fletcher nodded emphatically.

"Yes, and to that end," said Oswald, who had lost his human crutch and found by way of replacement, a wall, "Might I introduce us, Madam—"

"Oh, don't be silly; I know who you are," she said, her smile giving way to the most adorable dimples in her charmingly round cheeks, "You're Oswald, and you're Fletcher," the last making Fletcher beam like a schoolboy being praised for his penmanship.

Keeping a stiff posture that presented him both regally and confidently, Oswald said, "That we are, madam. And we came for some information which I was told you might have—yourself, and Mister Dietrich."

Dietrich *humph*ed. He must not have thought himself stuffy enough to qualify for 'Mister.'

"Yes, of course," said Elke, "Well, Diets, why don't you take Oswald up to the observat'ry and I'll keep the young man company."

"Very well," replied Dietrich, tempted to groan reluctantly if not for his wife's observation, "this way."

And as Dietrich turned away, Elke called, "Oh, get him a crutch, will you dear?"

"Thank you, madam," said Oswald, unsure of how a crutch would help him brave stairs or worse a ladder.

Fletcher didn't have much a chance to see them hobble away, for—remember—he was armed with a muffin. Somewhere between the sugar, the butter, and the crumble-top which reminded him some of Dutch apple pie, the thin man must have wondered aloud, "How do you do this?"

"It's all about portion control and experimentation," she said, fanning the fireplace into a comfortable roar.

Fletcher scanned the walls which were fit with pots, pans, measuring cups and spoons, each set of which looked to have several-dozen graduations apiece. Cocking his head and squinting to better count, asked, "Is that one seventeenth of a cup?"

"You've a good eye," she said casually, "Of course, most people insist there's no difference between the seventeenth and the sixteenth, but I hold that every degree of precision counts."

"It certainly does," mused Fletcher, through flecks of muffin. He almost wished he were having a crisis of faith so this woman's cooking could restore it. And when she approached him, taking a chair for herself and sitting, he could smell on her the same batter and dough and paradise. Such was the delight of this muffin that Fletcher actually achieved a sort of catharsis he hadn't realized he needed.

He was then struck with the most urgent of curiosities which erupted into, "What did you make—last night—the desserts—which one was yours?"

"Guess," replied the other, coyly pursing her lips.

"Um—um—The pudding!" started Fletcher, then knowing that it did not do her justice, rushed ahead with, "The bread pudding! The sticky toffee pudding!" and when Elke began to giggle, Fletcher knew he had to reach further, so started rifling, "Cookies—Cakes—Crumble—Confections—"

"The roll."

Fletcher's heart jumped, then landed on a fluffy pillow. "The roll."

"The roll," she confirmed.

And seeing her soul through her deep-set, wrinkled eyes, Fletcher could picture the roll, could smell it, could feel it against his palm, and even though he had hardly even tasted it, considered this roll the most amazing meal he had ever known, and so observed, "It was heaven."

But it was in that moment, this wonderful, blue-ribbon-at-the-county-fair-winning-moment that Fletcher's foolish brain raised another memory which caused his stomach to plummet through his heels. "I'm so sorry!"

A look of concern came over her face, but before she could try to reassure Fletcher, the man was spouting further apologies: "I didn't mean to—but the food fight—it was all my fault, and your desserts—everyone's desserts, they're gone, and I—"

"Shush, shush now," she cooed, rushing toward Fletcher and putting her hands on his shoulders. Of course, given how quickly the whole affair erupted, it would have been impossible for anyone, including Elke, to place blame on any one person, but even if he was at the core of it—which both Fletcher and Hephaestus believed—Elke clearly did not care. As his head began to sink, Elke moved on from his shoulders and took his face in her hands, saying, "Food is the only art that is created to be destroyed, and it is only in destruction that it is truly enjoyed."

"That's beautiful," said Fletcher, quite certain that Elke had not even intended to rhyme.

"So maybe you started the mess," she began, not actually believing that it could be any one man's fault, "who am I to say that your way isn't just one more to appreciate food?"

Fletcher found her reasoning to be just as delicious as the muffin he had just finished. Her hair completely white under the same flour that smooched about her cheeks and hands, Fletcher could see she was a woman of at least twice his age and infinite times his wisdom, but he was so wanting for more of this precious experience that he may well have fallen in love with her right then and there. He decided he should very much like to kiss her on the mouth and leaned in to do so. Had he never opened his eyes, Fletcher may have assumed he'd achieved his objective, instead of being blocked by a cookie, which quite distracted him from the angel just out of reach.

Luckily for Fletcher, Dietrich was too far away to notice the failed-advance on his wife. (The jury is still out as to whether he would care.)

Now, the house was not terribly big—in fact, each floor was quite petite, but there were three of them, which seemed to give Dietrich and Elke the distance they needed from one another. Basically, the ground floor belonged to her, the penthouse to him, and the second to their bedroom which consequentially housed their fights. And to get between these stations, they had not only two ladders, but a pulley-operated and neatly counterweighted dumbwaiter.

Oswald was rightly tickled by this contraption, such that he longed to lean over the edge to watch the counterweight's movement, even after Dietrich instructed him, "Please keep your hands and arms inside the nest at all times."

Oswald did not know why Dietrich said 'nest,' but he found the nature of the giant thimble in which they stood quite endearing indeed.

Though Dietrich may well have been even older than Oswald, he seemed to draw them on the pulley mostly effortlessly. "So Julian sent you, did he?"

Oswald ruffled about the shoulders. "Let me explain: you see, we are scientists, investigators, and otherwise simple observers of all customs in all lands."

"Hmm," grumbled Dietrich, "that doesn't sound like an explanation to me…"

"Getting to it, my good man," assured Oswald, beginning to realize that he did not much like Dietrich. "You see, in trying to trace out the history of this town and its origins, I asked for the oldest and most learned man—who was still in his wits, that is—and Julian pointed me to you."

"So you're not here for a reading," concluded Dietrich in such a manner that it was impossible to tell whether he was disappointed or relieved. The 'nest' came to a halt, lining them up to the floor of the upper story, which was cluttered in tables which were in turn cluttered in maps and charts and pencils and lenses.

Oswald needed to squint through the dim light to make up much of anything, but then Dietrich yanked a cord, pulling away the drapery to reveal a beautiful open skylight and—sitting beneath it—the most bizarre shaft of wood fitted with pits and pockets and holes and glass.

"Good gravy," whispered Oswald, "is that a telescope?"

Dietrich looked puzzled by the term. He took a moment to check his ears, to be sure they were not at all clogged and mishearing, then informed Oswald, "It's called a stargazer."

"No, this is a telescope," repeated Oswald in wonder. He had seen similar contraptions, but never of this size, and never of this fantastic intricacy, with arrangements that made it more akin to a woodwind instrument than scientific device.

"It's a stargazer. It gazes the stars." And Dietrich proceeded to a table and rummaged through a series of papers, the most of which were documented star-charts, labeled by month and year, and each growing more precise than the last.

"Aren't *you* the stargazer?"

"How's that?" came Dietrich, his head swiveling like a feral animal sensing a new threat.

"*You* are the stargazer; *this* is a stargazer's tool."

Dietrich shrugged. "If I were a decent stargazer, I would have seen your lot coming." He settled upon a paper, pinching it excitedly between his sooty fingers, and proceeded toward Oswald, who still stared in awe at the telescope. "There," he said, shouldering his way in front of Oswald, who, even when stooped over a crutch stood taller. "Is this what you were after?"

Oswald felt a sensation start at the base of his neck and rush out over his limbs like some quick flame running across every hair on his body, extending to the tips of his fingers and toes. He shuddered away this hauntingly exquisite feeling, but when he reopened his eyes, the paper held in front of him was still—without a doubt—a map of England, complete with all its islands, coasts, and nearby countries: somewhat distorted, obviously outdated, but unmistakable in shape. And just to the north of England, at the narrowest part of the isthmus in southern Scotland and drawn in a different ink than the map's contours was a simple black x—an x which, to the best Oswald could figure was within fifty miles of where they now stood. There was no date, but scrawled at the bottom was, by way of signature, *P and A.*

Adjusting his glasses, Oswald asked, "Where—I say, where did you get this?"

Dietrich smiled. "It's always been here. For as long as anyone, or anyone's parents, or anyone's parents' parents, can remember. But this is where we are, isn't it? This is what the stars see?"

Oswald handled the map carefully as Dietrich released his hold, tracing the lines of the paper old enough to not even feel like paper. The edges were faded; there was no date and no notable author with whom to credit the drawing, but it was England—absolutely, undeniably England. And so he asked, "May I take this?"

"No," Dietrich replied, "but you may come back to look at it for as long as you're here."

"Thank you."

Dietrich actually seemed pleased by this; he had Oswald eating out of his blackened palms, and so placed one on Oswald's shoulder to turn him toward another souvenir that hung on his wall: "Then perhaps you can tell me what this is."

The 'this' in question was likewise so shocking that Oswald nearly dropped the map: a wooden wheel, hollowed in the center for a mount, and bearing eight spokes smoothed and rounded like handles.

"It looked like it should attach to a wagon, or a cart, but the shafts extend beyond the rim and so it won't roll; and instead of two or four wheels, there was just this one." Watching Oswald's open-mouthed expression, Dietrich ventured, "But you know what it is, don't you?"

"I'd have to be sure," he whispered. Was he unsure, or just in disbelief? For Oswald, even though logic tried to call him against it, *knew* that it was a ship's steering wheel, though he could not say how such a thing would come to reside in the Isle.

So invested was Oswald in the sheer spookiness of the situation, that when they heard the knock at the front door, he literally sprung up, and had to catch his crutch again on the way down. (I should note that the crutch was not actually a crutch, just a longish pole that Dietrich had lent him for the occasion.)

"Oh, for God's sakes, who could that be?" Dietrich grumbled, with such annoyance that Oswald would have guessed he too was invested in this revelation. He cleared the dust from his scratchy throat with a commanding cough and shouted, "Elke!"

Elke was already up and bustling toward the door, a cloud of flour following her. Fletcher was too occupied by his newest pastry to notice her absence immediately, but when the door squeezed out of its frame, he leaned back in his chair to see.

"Oh!" greeted Elke, "Well, hello girls; what can I do for you?"

"Um," said Samantha.

Sabrina must have decided that 'Um' wasn't good enough, and so followed with, "We were hoping to place an order, for my father's dinner with the Mister-Baron-Sir."

"How's that?" came a surprised voice, which beckoned the sisters peer past Elke to the off-balance Fletcher, who, with his eyebrows arching over his hair line, looked to be having extreme difficulty containing his chin.

Sabrina tried to make a sound, but when she couldn't, her sister assisted with, "Oh…"

Fletcher leaned further back to collect Samantha's statement, and must have passed his balance for the chair slipped out from under him. A credit to Fletcher's grace under pressure, the pastry in his hand remained entirely undamaged.

From two stories above, Oswald's voice responded to the thump with a characteristic, "What—what!?"

XXIX – Two Floorboards and the Back of his Head

Ten ha found Julian's house empty when she arrived to inform the Baron of their engagement, but she kept Miriam at her side—probably as collateral—until Meredith grew worried and took the snappea back with some ruse about learning to pluck a chicken. Miriam was soon disappointed when she discovered that the chicken in question was already dead.

Ten ha fretted in all the normal ways—biting her nails, compulsively checking the clocks which she simply did not trust, plucking out hairs and arranging them by order of shade[72]—until Pigby ducked in through the doorway, looking equally worried. They said in unison, "Where is the Baron?" and each discovered that the other had the same odd and distressing news.

So they tried for a moment to discuss the strange happening, but realized they would much rather burst into tears. Neither could tell precisely why Hephaestus was so frightening—perhaps it was because Fletcher was right, and he really was a wizard. Ten ha ventured that they felt so sullen because neither had any power to prevent a possibly more violent repeat of the night before. Pigby added that, to make matters worse, they had yet a whole day to worry about it.

They spent so much of the afternoon holding their breaths that both grew light-headed, and each had to take a nap while the other stood guard.

When the giant heard persons approaching Julian's door, they took and held hands for moral support, clenching until their knuckles were white, which for Pigby was no mean feat. Unfortunately, it opened

---

[72] To the best of our knowledge, Ten ha's natural hair color contained no fewer than fourteen shades.

to reveal Oswald and Fletcher, locked in debate on whether Dietrich or Elke was *clearly* the more fascinating.

Seeing that their companions appeared somewhere between relieved and frustrated, Oswald took the high road and assumed that they had already been alerted to their prospective dinner-in-hell, and so said, "Oh, have you heard?"

Now, when you stop to think about it, information sharing could probably happen more quickly in the Isle than anywhere else on earth. In a perfect commune, it is understandable that any one person will interact with any number of others over a given day in the execution of his trade, and in that moment the encounter will give way to stories, and the juiciest story will inevitably be carried on until the next encounter, and the next encounter, and so on and so forth.

As far as the rest of the Isle was concerned, there was probably nothing to worry about. See, even though the house of the Libburus was practically wetting itself in anticipation, very few external citizens even suspected begrudging feeling between Hephaestus and the Mustache Man. Individuals had their own reservations against or supporting one man or the other, but they were so unfamiliar with the idea of a feud, that news of a dinner was just one more last-minute event to prepare for, and not grounds to duck and cover. Even if they sensed tension, the people of the Isle wouldn't actually know antagonism if it kicked them in the teeth, and though this gossip made its rounds, it was not exactly the hot-button for the day.

When Manny told Meredith, her response followed, "Oh, isn't that nice—they can have an intimate evening together." For one, she may not have realized that the 'intimate' evening served twenty. For another, she had been hinting to her husband for some time that they needed an evening apart from Miriam and Jonas.

When the Libburus heard, he did in fact faint, disrupting two floorboards and the back of his head. To get him breathing again, one of Hephaestus' servants (Cooper) actually cut loose that day's bowtie, and Cletus insisted it be sent to Hannah for mending before their beflustered leader should wake.

Hephaestus' feelings on the matter were difficult to read. From his corner of the room with his shoulders curled forward all Hephaestus said was, "So...*that's* his game, is it?"

The *he* in question was of course the Baron Pan Bordolo, who was still about the side of a mountain, scouting the town's edges with a boy the more fit and a scientist the more short, and—as the reader can attest—had absolutely nothing to do with the funny business of the day. The two daughters, having seen their father faint at their feet, opted to say nothing and instead shifted uncomfortably.

As this announcement took place in Sebastian's front room, among the general assembly of Hephaestus' seven servants, Lance was afforded the opportunity to be puzzled. He could not rightly place why the Libburus should be so surprised if the whole affair was originally his idea. There were only two viable options: that the daughters had concocted some scheme beyond his ken, or that this fainting was merely a mark of culture and tradition that he did not understand. Lance decided that the latter was far more probable.

The quotation that Jonas was muttering as he passed through Julian's front door seemed very specifically marked for the occasion of the fouled dinner plans. He had undoubtedly been monologuing the whole way home, but the only part the Baron's crew heard, huddled together waiting for their employer's arrival, was, "'Truth lies within a little and certain compass, but error is immense.'"

Jonas closed the door behind him, his stance indicating that he had been walking too often for too many years, possibly under great strain. When he noticed that four near-strangers stood in the room, he actually managed to straighten some in surprise. He paused, then leaned forward, squinting at Fletcher, as if searching for something very enlightening.

Fletcher began to grow uncomfortable, and wanted to swat him away, like he would for a wasp that showed too keen an interest in his dessert; but then Jonas' memory kicked in, and he said, "'A pox upon a pair of pawns,'" as if it were a greeting that people had been using for years. He then patted Fletcher's arm, and—while the others remained frozen—proceeded to the back room and latched the door.

"What in the almighty was that?" asked Pigby.

XXX – A Decent Brick of Chocolate

They kept the same order and general pace in their descent, but the wind had quieted some, and the assistance of gravity, rather than the fight against it, afforded all three smiles and leisurely conversation.

"Um..." thought Julian, "loveliest woman."

"Nepal," shouted Geru from a ways above him.

The Baron took a moment to muse, grinning under his freshly waxed mustache[73]. "That would be a toss-up," he began, "between the Peloponnesian Islands of Lower Greece and the Philippine Islands of Southeast Asia."

"Are those far apart?" asked Julian.

"Half the world away," the Baron called down to him.

Geru took it upon himself to announce, "It's all about the island girls with him."

Julian—though he did not understand this comment entirely— laughed out load. This was the seventeenth in a series of superlative inquiries, and Julian found reason to laugh at most of them. In trekking around the higher ground and falls to the north of Adleship Isle main, Geru had near-filled his journal and Julian had sponged up every ounce of information and nuance about the Big Out There, which—considering how easily the Baron seemed to cover it all—did not seem terribly big at all.

There was something in the satisfaction that he received from this conversation that was unlike anything he could ever remember. See, the most *rewarding* experience was still the mere thought of holding one of Samantha's fair hands, but just anticipation does not offer much in the

---

[73] Yes, he carried a tin of Liverpool Silver on his immediate person for long day trips, in a satchel or breast pocket opposite the book.

way of satisfaction. In fact, Julian was so delighted with his daytrip that he hardly even remembered that he had missed Samantha at the well, an absence that only came with very special circumstance. Even though he didn't understand the Baron's and Geru's jokes about the lost cities of Atlantis, Petra, or Machu Picchu, or what his own home-town had to do with them, elation came from just hearing them—probably because these simple remarks gave him a sense of something greater than himself, to which he might be connected.

Perhaps it was this connectedness which he had been craving most his life, that made him want to open up to the fine gentleman staying at his house, or maybe he had finally arrived upon the appropriate segue. In any case, as they reached the base of the rock wall—(Julian first, who offered a hand to help his guest down)—he was about to tell the Baron that the loveliest woman *he* had ever encountered lived just on the other side of town. The Baron, astute as he was, had thoughts toward the object of Julian's desire, but would not venture the guess so as to not put the young man amiss. But, seeing as they were both on the ground, and Geru—their running commentator—was still struggling to get down the wall, the Baron and Julian concurrently concluded that this was the perfect moment for his confession.

And Julian fully intended to make it, and the Baron to receive it, and Geru to eavesdrop it, and the reader to finally find relief in the unnecessary tension[74], but of course, they were all to be disappointed by the reemergence of a character who had taken quite a break from our story.

"Good-eve, Julian," he said, because the sky above was already beginning to grow dim.

"Junkin!" exclaimed Julian, with forced excitement for the young man who had just interrupted what might have been the most important reveal of his life. "What are you doing out at this time?"

Junkin indicated the wheelbarrow he had set down some fifty feet away. "Deliveries." (Oh, I may have forgotten to mention, Junkin, possessing few specific skills but a decent amount of strength and endurance, was the delivery boy for all of the lower class citizens of the Isle. And, yes, I realize that this cliché plays even more into the notable naughtiness of Sabrina's love-life.) "I saw you comin' down the hill. Wanted to ask if you needed anything." Though he only cooked up the ruse to get a look at the strangers, Junkin would not make eye contact

---

[74] (Sorry.)

Baron or his servant—Geru would have corrected him with 'employee' could he read the other's mind.

"Um... no," said Julian. Then he asked the Baron, "Do you need anything?"

"I'd kill for a decent brick of chocolate," muttered Geru. (The Baron tried not to react to the word 'kill'; Junkin and Julian wondered how slaughtering a sheep or cow could generate a brick.)

"No," said the Baron, "We're quite fine, young sir."

"Right." Junkin could not determine whether he should be frightened, and so skirted the issue by speaking once again to Julian, while attempting not to include the Baron in his periphery. "Will you be going to Raul's birthday?"

"Of course!" Were it not obviously smalltalk, Julian may have been offended that such a question even need be asked.

"Me too," said Junkin, then, as if stalling for time, and having not realized that he could simply walk away if need be, "You know, I've never even seen the inside of Eugene's house."

"Well, I have," boasted the younger, securing his place as a *better* friend of Raul's.

"Yeah, well, you'll be seeing Sebastian's tomorrow. It's like you're practically a noble yourself. Goodnight." And—finally figuring out that he could just turn and go—he turned to leave, giving the others barely enough time to register, let alone accept what had been said.

"Wait, what?" asked Julian.

XXXI – An Open Oat Bag on the Ground

The rock had resolved to no longer be surprised by anything that happened in the town. It assumed that if it kept its composure and simply braced in expectation of the unexpected, then it should not be uncomfortably rattled. After all, the last three chapters have ended with startled questions, and all of the parties delivering these did after all appear somewhat silly in their confusion, and the rock was not going to be party to such silliness.

So, by the third day, when the grandfather character took his seat on said rock, the scratching of his quill waking the hill, all three believed themselves properly prepared for whatever should come. And as sunrise came once again over the mountains, they were faced with the illuminated silhouettes of not only Geru and Pigby but a third party, who, with nothing on his back, was noticeably hairier.

"Tighten the buttocks, Clemens, but don't lock your knees," bid Geru.

Clemens gritted his teeth, shaking some at the newfound strain, but grunted, "This—is—incredible!"

Pigby had said that—in light of the dinner ahead of them— maybe they should forgo the yoga, to which Geru *tsk*ed, insisting that it was all the more necessary in preserving their calm and centering them for the ordeal.

Considering how busy they all became once Julian's household woke up, Geru was probably right.

Fletcher, who was the most acquainted with world fashions, was sent with Julian to get him fitted for a proper dinner suit, accompanied by Clemens, who was a friend of Sherman's and could persuade the man to work double-or-triple-time if need be.

The Baron had decided the night before that they should treat this dinner as a great honor and do their best to bring a dish that would delight all parties. To that end, he sent Ten ha along with her helper, Pigby, to whip up something amazing in Meredith's kitchen. Ten ha protested for a moment that she would not be able to feed the yaks, and when the Baron agreed that it was a good point, designated such as Geru's duty. Thereafter, it was Geru's turn to protest. Seeing as she could not betray her still-premature feelings, Ten ha, said nothing more and only hoped that when Lance showed up, he would understand that she was not absent by choice.

Of course, Lance never managed to show either. Six of the seven sturdy servants were put to strict work making the Libburus' house look new—or at very least only ten years old—with rigorous sanding and vigorous washing which probably damaged some of the structural integrity. The last, Trenton, was up in Hephaestus' room, helping him to compose a speech for the evening.

Hephaestus enjoyed making speeches. Additionally, he enjoyed having speeches to use, and in the Isle, where no one had heard quotations from anyone—except for possibly Jonas, but he's an outlier anyway—Hephaestus could pull from the greatest literature and world leaders without leaving the faintest scent of plagiarism. For you see, no matter how delightful it is, plagiarism loses its entire appeal once the audience has pegged you as an unscrupulous hack.

So here we arrive at a pickle. Then again, pickles are delicious and monstrously appealing on almost any occasion, so I'll change the word to something less pleasant, if that's alright with you. Let us say that Hephaestus was in an asparagus: he had all these wonderful words graciously supplied by famous persons strung together into a beautiful address, but alas, alack, on account of the Baron and his likely knowledge of overused quotations, the lord of merchants had to completely rewrite his speech!

So Hephaestus paced-us as he replaced-us every line which might catch the ear as not his own, while Trenton, dressed in tails, sat on a stool and jotted the dictation in shorthand[75]. Trenton, though he did not often comment, was of the opinion that the more Hephaestus reached, the more he seemed to be accidentally stealing. And though it pained him to

---

[75] I both admire and envy those who can use shorthand. I have this issue of being long-winded, and then unfocused because I am unable to write as fast I think, but more on that later.

do so, he felt compelled to speak up by the time Hephaestus started spouting, "To be a courteous host, or *not to be* a courteous host."

In the same way, Cletus, properly equipped with Algernon and Ferdinand of course, aided his Libburus in preparing for the evening. When Sebastian realized that he was lacking in a bowtie, Cletus could not tell him that it had been snipped the night before upon his fainting, but instead opted to "Go and fetch it, sir" while Sebastian took the opportunity to lie down with a cool towel over his eyes.

So Cletus removed himself of the house and rushed across the river and weaved into the north end of town to the home of the tailor below the falls. He knocked twice before letting himself in—(This was not uncommon in the Isle)—and was about to inform Hannah that her husband had best be finished with the bowtie, when he spotted young Julian, standing on a footstool, with Sherman adjusting a suit of sorts to the boy's shoulders.

That obnoxious thin man sat against the wall, eating what looked to be an apple, but upon closer inspection turned out to be an onion. He crunched another chunk out of the orb and grinned, the juices glistening on his lips and teeth as he waved at Cletus.

Cletus stiffened and bowed, but only so far as to seem polite.

Sherman, his mouth open, froze deer-in-lantern-lights fashion, as if he'd been caught in the act of servicing the enemy. Not knowing the term 'enemy,' so not knowing the concept of 'treason,' Sherman had no good reason for his inability to breathe; even so the visceral reaction was strong enough that he should have to describe it to Piers later that same day.

Trying to quell the situation, Hannah rushed the repaired neck apparel to Cletus once again, thanked him for his request, and bid him and the Libburus best wishes before ushering him out.

Once the door was shut, Cletus breathed a quick, "Insolent."

Which Fletcher paralleled with, "Fop," punctuating the term with another swift bite from the onion.

Julian was somewhat confused, but decided not to dwell on it, seeing as this was the first time he was ever specifically fitted for formal wear and should need to savor the moment.

Of course, the comments through the town about Julian acting as an envoy were all the more spurred by his fitting, but none of them particularly negative. Some were actually jealous, if such an emotion is possible in a commune, saying that perhaps Julian had severely lucked out in getting to host the travelers—and conveniently forgetting that they had been terrified to do so. Either way, the association between Julian and this fresh new Baron brought the boy fame like he had never known, a regard which he only hoped to draw from one person.

As Geru walked toward the stables, his head sitting so low that many people did not notice him approaching, he caught portions of this gossip, and tried not to comment on it as he passed. Of course, Geru is not known for holding back his colorful commentary, and so—though it was not *at all* his intention—added to conversations with things like, "Clearly Hephaestus is no match for my Baron where it comes to wit," or "Well, obviously *we* will be much better dressed than the seven surly servants," or ""Hephaestus circles the world *once* every year? Well, my Baron could do it *three* times."

Now, you might want to fault Geru for stirring the locals, but understand that he was in a bit of a mood for being shunted down to stable detail. His demeanor only grew worse when he discovered, upon arrival that Ten ha had mistakenly left an open oat-bag on the ground, which the animals had gotten into, collectively finished and were awarded with—as you might have guessed, if you are the type to feed oats to beasts of burden—gas. As Geru gagged on the putrid fumes, he noted with regret that he might have to burn his clothing, but then thought the better of it, seeing as the fuel permeating the air might give way to combustion of the uncontainable. At very least, he would need to bathe.

General cleaning and self-sprucing took the forefront of all of Sabrina and Samantha's activities that day. Luckily for them, there was something of a bathhouse in their basement, or else they should have gotten very cold in river main. Now, they did not have an extensive range of product when it came to hair, perfume, make-up, and whatever else it is that women use, but what little they had, they were determined to use. More accurately, each sister was determined to use more product than the other. This gave way to clouds of noxious fumes and cakes of powder, the likes of which should only be reserved for opera sopranos.

Because the sisters spent most of the day in this bathroom, Liam and Lionel kept trying to find excuses to go to the basement, but whenever they did, Clara, the live-in maid-servant, would intercept them and offer to perform whatever duty they used as their ruse. Oh, yes, you haven't met Clara yet, have you? Well, Clara was sweet, but quiet; often annoyed, but rarely begrudging; and though she was probably in her mid-twenties, her grey-blonde hair and the clothes she wore made her appear forty. Most people on the far western end of the town just assumed she was married to Cletus, and so it wasn't until after she went to work for a different noble some years later that she married at all.

The bustling in the Libburus' house was audible to the nearby citizens, but farther than earshot even, the energy and intensity could be felt. Many of the Isleans developed goosebumps for reasons they could not discern just before seeing one of the Baron's crew or Hephaestus' servants, all busily running errands for most of the afternoon. Of course, the sight of Pigby, rushing from door-to-door to collect special ingredients, would have caused reactions regardless, but the determination on his face—as if rushing to collect these food items might save an ailing patient—prompted even greater attention and discussion.

Fueled by Sherman's observations, Geru's snide backhands, and that all citizens had attended the feast two days before, the people of the Isle collectively grew to understand that a competition between the two travelers was to take place. They did not know if this should be a trivia contest or a logic game played on a black and white board—(Hephaestus tried, unsuccessfully, to teach some of them how to play chess a few years before)—but all signs pointed to a face-off, and suddenly the only concern for the masses was the question of who would win.

Over the course of the day, musing turned to debate, turned to argument, and though they had no idea for what His Highest and the Mustache Man were competing, everyone had a need to be right about the victor. Taking sides and rooting was not a terribly new thing in the Isle—remember, there were games and sports year 'round—but suddenly a difference in opinion could lead to more than just a series of jibes between friends. Though this kind of thing was never recorded, the people began whispering that they had never seen a day in the Isle with so many duels[76].

You might assume that the bulk of the citizens were still supportive of their old friend Hephaestus, and you would be right. But there were those who thought the Baron brought a fresh new mood; there were those who appreciated his youth and flair; there were those who had met him or taken a liking to persons in his crew like Clemens, Manuel,

---

[76] I don't mean to alarm you, and, no, this doesn't mean what you think it does— that is if you are thinking what I think you are thinking. Just bear in mind that 'duels' insofar as the Adleship Isleans know them exist in name only, and are purely nonviolent expressions of brute strength and stamina. I give you my word that I will explain them at a later time.

Sherman, and Piers, and (lo and behold!) both Dietrich *and* Elke, who had been successfully disagreeing for near forty years.

And even though Hephaestus would still win a popularity contest, many would wager the success of the Baron in their competition, having assumed—for whatever reason—that he was more resourceful or smarter even than their old friend.

Whether the Baron could feel the confidence that surrounded him, his mannerisms did not show it. While Ten ha cooked in the house down the way, and Fletcher tended to Julian's clothing over at Sherman's, and Geru searched for a good portion of water to take a bath, the Baron had shut himself in the house with his own right-hand-man prepping him for the dinner ahead.

As the Baron's personal pocket-manual proved unhelpful in this event, he and Oswald had settled onto Julian's couch with a stack of books apiece from which they could read all that they dared about traveling merchants, Hephaestus, and outdated Anglo-Saxon traditions. But after several volumes and several hours, the Baron couldn't grasp a single word before him, and may as well have been trying to read the mole on the back of his hand.

Closing the tome with a satisfying *pfhu*, the Baron groaned and resigned with, "That's it. I give up."

Oswald adjusted his glasses. "You're not going, sir?"

"No, I actually meant the books," the Baron explained, staring up at the ceiling, his arms spread open in surrender. "But, sure, that too. I mean, why go? He doesn't actually want me there." (He was right about that.) "No, this is just a scheme to make me sweat, to catch me off-guard so I offend the Libburus by mistake and set the town against me." (About this he was wrong, but were this Hephaestus' aim, he could probably properly execute it.)

At this, Oswald closed his book as well. He rubbed at his eyes with his thumb and forefinger. "God bless Franklin for his bifocals[77]."

Not satisfied with this comment, the Baron stood, strode about a moment, and—his fists against his hips—asked, "But do you agree with me? Do you think maybe I just shouldn't show?"

Oswald thought on this for a moment, or appeared to think on it, because Oswald—bless him—knew the answer in an instant. "No," he said.

---

[77] In my best, I believe this to be a misquotation of our dear Oswald, seeing as the term 'bifocals' was not officially coined until 1824.

"No?"

"No," the old man repeated. "No, you gain nothing by not attending. To not meet him on the field of battle is to surrender, is to give up. And, my good sir," he concluded with a solemn shake of his graying head, "*You* do not give up. Besides that, sir, whatever would your godfather say?"

The Baron smiled, and his mustache seemed to agree. "You know, there are times when I despise you."

"Thank you, sir."

And as the Baron returned to the couch, aware that they had still a few hours before they were expected, he ruefully observed, "He's setting me up for a fall, isn't he?"

"Yes," nodded Oswald, then, indicating with his forefinger, "but pride will lead to his own."

XXXII – Fish-Head Soup!

Cletus twice had to pop outside to tell onlookers and eavesdroppers to "Be on your way, sirs" and finally took to closing every window and corresponding drape in the house. Understand that windows in the Isle were rarely made of glass, seeing as glass was extremely difficult to come by. Geru could not fathom how they had gotten any full panes in the first place.

Sebastian could not fathom the dish in front of him. "I'm sorry," he said, dabbing at the corners of his mouth with his kerchief, "What did you call this again?"

Ten ha swallowed, set down her fork, and repeated slowly, for the fourth time, "Lutefisk."

"Fascinating," muttered Sebastian. "And-and this—um—*cheese* was called—?"

"Gjetost," said Ten ha.

"Brilliant." Sebastian eagerly inhaled another greasy forkful. "So this Ludi-Fisk," he began again, "is it—Would you—Would you say it's an animal, or some kind of fruit?"

From off the Libburus' right shoulder, he could hear someone snort into his hand as he tried not to laugh.

"Um…" Ten ha politely set the fork back down again, cleared her throat and very plainly said, "It's fish."

"Fish!" exclaimed Sebastian, and hooted to himself over this discovery. "Did you hear that, Hephaestus? It's fish! Mmm!" And after he had concluded that bite, told Ten ha, "You know, Hephaestus told me about fish, said they lived *in the water*!" And he giggled at this, as if Ten ha should find it as charming a notion as he did.

"I see," concluded Ten ha, though, to be fair, she did not. She glanced between her fellows, but none of the Baron's crew would catch her eye. With twenty persons crammed around the tables, she didn't understand why she should be given the sole burden of entertaining the Libburus—though apparently everyone else did, seeing as none of them would step in to assist her.

In fact, the only person trying to catch her eye at that moment was Lance, whom Ten ha pointedly avoided, so as to not seem a traitor to her employer. Well, that was the reason she would have given if asked; the real reason was that she was worried she might either melt or faint if she sustained his gaze.

Their little romance aside, Lance wanted her attention primarily because he had the oddest suspicion that there was something misunderstood about the whole dinner party and wished to compare notes, but more on that later.

And whenever Sebastian's mouth was full, the only sound to be heard was chewing from twenty mouths, and cutlery scraping from forty hands.

Well, to be fair, there were only eighteen parties chewing, seeing as neither the Baron nor Hephaestus could abandon the other's steady stare long enough to actually look down at his own plate, a concentration which was aided by their sitting directly across from one another. This orientation had been a poor idea in retrospect, but one that occurred to neither of them when they first sat. Cletus, for his part, regretted not making a seating chart—a *pre*-seating chart, I should say, as I took the liberty of drawing one up for you, after the fact, but still accurate and a good aid in visualizing this scene.

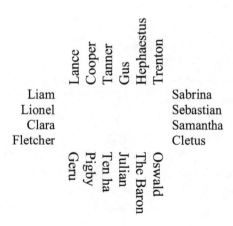

See, they smashed a few large tables together—a couple of which were borrowed from nearby nobles—which allowed for all parties to see each other with reasonable ease. This was Sebastian's idea: he thought that everyone would be much more friendly if none of them felt like they had anything to hide. The clear result was that no one had any*where* to hide.

Sitting down happened in great hubbub, but was accomplished relatively quickly, seeing as everyone had very specific aims. Sebastian wished to be flanked by his lovely daughters, but he kept Cletus on hand if needed. Cletus sent Clara to the other side of the table, so that they could efficiently serve the lot from either end. Both Hephaestus and the Baron wanted to be close to Sebastian, each to show that his will was good, but yet not too close. On Hephaestus' side, Trenton planted himself between his lord and the head of the table so as to not make him look stuffy; and the Baron set Oswald between himself and Cletus because he wanted to look a little more like "just one of the crew."

The Baron naturally had his old friend at one side, and their fine young ambassador at the other, and beyond him, Ten ha sat beside Julian—as she was the translator and he the native. Pigby, who had helped with the entrée of the evening wanted to sit beside Ten ha to bask in some of the glory, and Geru set himself between Pigby and Fletcher so that he could wallop either of them if they spoke particularly amiss at dinner. Fletcher was sent to the foot of the table on the Baron's behest to put as much distance between himself and Hephaestus as possible, which Fletcher appreciated because it sat him beside Clara, who—whether or not either of them was at all interested—seemed about the only eligible woman at the table.

Liam and Lionel, though they both had more seniority and could claim a spot closer to Hephaestus if they had wanted, wished to face the head of the table in order to look Sabrina directly in the—(for the sake of younger readers, let's just say)—eye. As for Sabrina, she wanted to sit closer to the Baron, but Trenton, wise to how she mingled, invited her to take the corner beside him. Samantha did not know where she should sit, or who should judge her for where she sat, or what conclusions they might draw. This is yet again the mark of a sixteen-year-old girl—one who did not grow up too quickly, that is—and so she properly sat beside her daddy, (who would gladly have taken her to a sock-hop, if anyone had bothered to ask).

Now, you may be wondering how the lot came to be so silent for so long. Now, mind, I wasn't there, but to the best I can theorize, neither the Baron nor Hephaestus wanted to speak. See, they each believed the other to have laid a trap—or, worse, more than one—for the evening, and both were so careful not to fall into these non-existent devices that all either could do was wait and see if his rival might tip his hand first. This behavior informed the servants and employees, (semantics, really), who in turn walked stiffly and stoically by one another, nodding with a single grunt as they collectively sat down, as if they were worried that their masters might smite them should they break form and speak to the enemy.

You might also be wondering why Sebastian was speaking at all; I can explain this with certainty, and I'll try not to giggle as I do. Sebastian had two coping mechanisms, and both relied on Cletus. The first was a nap, which he was very nearly incapable of considering until Cletus recommended it, which the man thankfully had done earlier that afternoon. Sebastian, being sensitive to both light and the thought that he might miss something exciting or frightening during a midday nap, required a specific lullaby[78] which Cletus performed.

The second can be attributed to a pep talk, accompanied by a firm faith in karma—maybe not by the same name, I grant you, but a belief that good deed or even just good nature would inspire good treatment from the world, and Cletus enforced the steadfast conviction. Now, understand that the Libburus was not a cruel man, but he certainly was selfish; in fact, even though he put no conscious thought into the matter, he seemed to accept that his being stood at the center of the universe, so why shouldn't its mood be a reflection of his?

So, whenever Cletus helped dress Sebastian in front of that same mirror, he reminded him that, "Positive attitude yields positive results," then patted Sebastian's newly-jacketed shoulder, just like the Libburus' wife had done years before. Therefore, on this night, the Libburus knew that if he washed his face, brushed his hair, and was an open-minded good sport during dinner, he would get to try a scintillating new foreign dish.

And what a dish! Served by Ten ha and carried by a very proud-looking Pigby, the Lutefisk must have been just about the most exciting thing our excited little Libburus had ever seen. Initially, he found the smell offensive, but the taste delightful, a contrast which switched by the second bite. In fact, every new forkful of this curious 'food' offered a

---

[78] If you're lucky, you'll get to hear it.

new opinion and set of sensations, so as to keep Sebastian infinitely pleased by the mere experience of eating.

So, even as the Baron and Hephaestus continued to cast suspicious glances at one-another, Sebastian could remain under the impression that all was well, contained as he was in his own personal 'karma' bubble. Smiling upon finishing this last forkful, he looked up to the sheer multitudes of this 'fish' around the table and expressed his newest curiosity. "I should wonder," he began, pointing at the other fishes on other dishes, "which part is its head."

"Um," Ten ha looked to the others for help, but as none was provided, replied, "There were actually five of them."

"Five heads?" exclaimed the Libburus, "How *glorious*! Hephaestus, you never told me fish had five heads—" Then, turning away from the flabbergasted Hephaestus, he refaced to ask, "What else has five heads?"

"No," she said, slowly, and then deciding it was not slow enough, took a sip of water and said, "No, there were five fish. In all. The Lutefisk—I made it out of five whole fish so it would feed everyone."

Pigby, agitated by the first-person singular which excluded him from the cooking process, and which he corrected with, "We."

And Ten ha, perceiving 'Oui' instead of 'We' nodded.

"Just five?" came Cooper, impressed by the amount of food before him.

"Oh, it's all in the preparation," said Pigby, claiming his authority—(to be fair, he had helped Ten ha a great deal). "*We* can actually serve a great many people with only five fish and two loaves—" and when he finished swallowing, added, "of cheese."

"You're sure it's not the other way around?" asked Fletcher, which earned him a quick slap from Geru. The thin man brought a hand to the back of his head, but didn't voice his discomfort, having been reminded that they were not supposed to speak.

Luckily for Fletcher, Sebastian seemed not to notice and most engrossed in his dinner. When he next looked up, Sebastian repeated, "Then which part is the head?—I should very much like to know what the head looks like."

"There are no heads." This last came from Hephaestus, a perturbed, long-delayed murmur. He hadn't intended to speak, may not have even realized that he had, but it set the Baron on edge nonetheless.

"No heads?" asked the Libburus, trying to conjure the image, "Oh, they don't have them then?"

The Baron's mustache told him to stay cool, but seeing as his rival had gotten the first word in, he felt he too needed to express himself (in some form besides chewing and looking thoughtful). As there was no Geru on hand to smack him, our Baron Pan Bordolo found himself saying, "No, we just didn't cook the heads in this meal," even though he was not involved in the dish-making process, for which Pigby and Ten ha cleared their throats, on which the Baron did not care, "—See, we already made them into soup."

"Fish-head soup!" sputtered Sebastian. "Good lord!"

"It's quite good actually," said Lance, leaning in from his corner of the table to better see the action, and the comment drew a smile from Ten ha. She didn't know whether he meant Lutefisk or fish-head soup. Neither did he.

"Is that your function?" asked Sebastian.

The Baron, who was in mid-sip choked and coughed, "How's that?"

The Libburus cleared his throat, unaware of the semi-scathing looks from Hephaestus, and clarified, "Is that what you do? You know, your duty: you bring fish." Heads began to swivel toward the Baron, as if this were a logical conclusion for his occupation, and the Libburus expanded with, "You're a sort of fish transporter, or fish bringer."

"Or," came Fletcher, somehow forgetting his silence yet again, "fisherman."

"Oh, yes," tittered the Libburus, "that's good. Yes, I rather like that." Then, to the Baron, given an opportunity to use his newfound word, titled him: "Fisherman."

"Oh. Well..." The Baron didn't know how to reply to this, though apparently Hephaestus did. The older merchant looked as though he had just consumed an eel and was realizing—halfway down the esophagus—that it was still alive; do me a favor and try to picture that. This expression, complete with flaring nostrils, bid the Baron admit, "Not exactly."

"Oh," came Sebastian, "And what does that—"

"It means no: he's not," said Hephaestus through gritted teeth, willing the Libburus to let go of the subject, a subject which he blamed the Baron for bringing up, though he'd done nothing of the sort.

And as the Baron looked back down at his plate, somewhat ashamed at having followed the Hephaestus will, he came to wonder why he had had to answer in the negative. On one hand it was not entirely untrue, now, was it? He *did* bring fish to wherever it was he went whenever it was that he carried fish, and though personally the Baron was not a professional fisherman, Pigby probably qualified.

Julian wondered on this too. Might I note that, even though he was invited on the pretense of 'ambassador,' he had not said a single word since entering, and only managed to cough when Samantha curtsied for him. But as the wheels in his head continued to turn, he heard himself ask, much to his own surprise, "Then why do you carry so many fish?"

The Baron suddenly regretted not coming up with signals to effect covert dialogue with the boy; he also noted that Julian had not received Hephaestus' eyebrow memo.

"Yes, well," began the Baron, "that's quite a question, isn't it? Who's got an answer to that? Geru, Fletcher? How about you Oswald?"

"We do eat it," ventured Ten ha.

"You can eat all this!" laughed the Libburus, in shock and excitement. "Why that's incredible! Hephaestus, did you hear that?"

"I most certainly did," glowered the other.

"Mister Sir Baron, tell me why exactly," asked Cletus, his suspicion getting the better of his stoicism, "you would carry such large quantities of fish if you were not a fish-delivery-person."

The Baron did not mean to sound so irked when he returned, "I don't know; why do you suppose your good Hephaestus carries so much cutlery?"

And sure enough, when examining their hands, every person at the table found himself holding a sampling of Hephaestus' cutlery.

But Cletus, somehow offended by the notion that Hephaestus was some sort of cutlery-carrier, (which must have been a frowned-upon profession in the Isle), stiffened and declared, his Adam's apple bobbing in support, "He likes attending dinner parties!"

Now, as you can imagine, half the table descended immediately into snickers, including every servant of Hephaestus (apart from Trenton), and every one of the Baron's crew (excluding Oswald). Though the Baron himself did not laugh, Hephaestus was certain he could see him grinning behind those twinkling eyes, and for a moment was tempted to cast at the man opposite the first thing his hands could reach, which in this case was a spoon heaped in gjetost.

Seething behind his hooked nose, Hephaestus did his best not to react, but noted with chagrin that it was a clear sign that the Baron was winning, that he'd orchestrated such a jibe having only uttered three sentences—the sly devil!

Sebastian, not the least-bit sly or devilish, and so less likely to recognize either, took it upon himself to graciously clarify, "Ah, no, see, Mister Baron, Hephaestus always carries new and interesting things, because he is a travelling merchant." The Libburus seemed quite satisfied with his remark, and took a nod from Trenton to mean that it was the right thing to say.

"Well then, that's precisely why I carry fish," said the Baron, "because I am as well."

Sebastian found himself confused; he had heard the Baron mention such once before, but neither this time nor that did it make any sense. See, Sebastian understood Hephaestus to be a travelling merchant because he always knew his way around, stopped once a year in their little town, and always brought strange and new things to fascinate the folk. So far, the Mustache Man had only qualified for the last, and only by virtue of the fish, which did not equate him to Hephaestus.

As if reading her father's mind, Sabrina put forth her own two— and possibly three—cents, "Excuse me, Sir Baron, but that cannot be all you are, can it now?"

The Baron, having assumed the issue settled and being mid-forkful, was forced to look up and cough when he noticed the slant of the young woman's head, how her tongue curled about the edge of her lower lip, how her eyes held low and slitted. Taking a napkin to tend to the possibility of drool, he asked, "Come again."

"Well, clearly you're not the same as our dear Hephaestus—"

"Hardly," muttered the older merchant.

"—For starters," she went on, "you arrived from the other side, and were unaware of where or what our town was, and I understood that makes not a travelling merchant but—and I believe this was your word," she offered with a nod to Hephaestus, "an explorer."

"Yes, well," went the Baron, careful not to catch too many of the eyes upon him, lest they should make him lose his composure or uncurl his stache, "I suppose I am of sorts. An adventurer, if you must."

The Baron looked to Hephaestus, to see if the other approved of this last, but the older merchant seemed even the more put off by this, but the Baron had no time to qualify this expression because Samantha asked, all in innocence I assure you: "For whom do you adventure?"

What do you say to that when you're in a commune, to the appointed leader in the commune, no less—(which is understandably an oxymoron, but work with me here)—? Even Hephaestus looked baffled by this: obviously—and know that I do not mean this as a negative thing—they travelled for themselves, but 'self' was hardly and understood term let alone ambition in the Isle. And then the Baron did something which will very much appeal to your twenty-first-century sensibilities. He said, "Ummm...[79]"

And the boys likewise took their cues from their boss, each delivering a similarly drawn out "Wellll..." or "Hmmmm..." when stared down by the four persons at the head of the table. Hephaestus pointedly looked away, and each of *his* servants tried to keep from locking eyes with the natives, though they were all eagerly surveying the Baron's crew, to determine what their reactions might be.

Understand this only lasted a few seconds, though they could have been years to the sweating, uncomfortable crew, who hardly even knew why they were so uncomfortable. Finally, it was Geru, prompted by a hungry glance from the Libburus himself, who squeaked, "The King!"

"What?" erupted from too many people to bother to name.

"The King! The King! We are explorers for the King! Please don't eat me!" repeated Geru, so near to hyperventilating by his last that it was (fortunately) indiscernible to Sebastian.

"Oh, good heavens!" came Sebastian, positively overjoyed by this, "The King—did you hear that, Hephaestus?"

"I'm sure I did."

The Baron did not have to look at Hephaestus to know what the expression conveyed, and so stayed locked on the Libburus who exclaimed:

"Well that's marvelous! You are the king's own explorers."

"Well, not the king's own," corrected Pigby.

"Not personally, anyway," added Fletcher.

"But in service of," amended Ten ha, "King and Country that is."

"God save, I say," concluded Oswald.

"Oh! Oh!" chirped the Libburus, calling attention once again back to himself and his lovely realization, "Is this the same King and Country as *this* King and Country, as *my* King and Country too?"

And Hephaestus begrudgingly answered, "Why, yes, sir, it is." Hephaestus shot a glare at the Baron, who—to his dismay—did not burst into flames.

---

[79] Now, I know what you're wondering: why is it "Ummm..." and not "Er" or "Erm"? Well, for one, I guarantee that the Baron Pan Bordolo is actually British, and though he would normally say "Er" or "Erm" needed to extend this particular staller out longer.

"Well, I think a toast is in order," said the Libburus, and the room visibly braced. "To the Mister Baron Sir Bordolo and his service of the King."

"Yes, to a man who is so high in prestige and honors that he has to invite himself to dinners," added Hephaestus.

Samantha and Sabrina gulped; Lance looked at Ten ha; Ten ha looked away from Lance; and the Baron asked "What?"

And the oblivious Libburus proclaimed, "Cheers!" and downed his own glass, while his guests simply stared in wonder.

XXXIII – A Deadly Spatula

Once they had gotten outside and well-enough away from the house, the Baron allowed himself to shout, "For the last time, I did not invite myself!" Though he was wrong about it being the last time, he had every right to hope so, having repeatedly stated such inside during the group argument.

Seeing as the debating sides were mostly distributed on either side of the table, it had a formal tournament look to it, except with Sebastian as the only referee, and not a very good one, given that he was not armed with a whistle and quite in tears once the sparks began to fly.

I would try to go into the substance of the argument, but there were just too many voices and issues raised (most of them irrelevant), for it to make any kind of sense. It largely consisted of Hephaestus and the Baron shouting insults back and forth to one another, being backed by their respective crews. They really had no reason to dislike one another initially—the Baron's crew and Hephaestus' servants, that is—but as they found their higher-ups to be in need of defense, colorful comments came to permeate the already abundant air. Fletcher made a comment on the ridiculous fit of the uniforms, and Gus on Geru's lack of fortitude, and so on. And then someone—I won't name names—called Pigby's color into question wherein his intelligence was concerned, which led to the most heated math-off ever seen[80].

As accusations about who invited whom raised in intensity and volume—giving cause to the Baron's protests of innocence—the sisters continued to inch closer to one another, hoping to work in tandem to keep the fine foundation of their lie from cracking. Don't ask me how, but somehow, they turned the suspicion to Ten ha. (Maybe they would have

---

[80] Though it still pales next to middle-school spelling bees.

named Lance, had they been able to distinguish him from any of the other seven sturdy servants.)

Now Lance, seeing Ten ha shrinking from all of the heavy and potentially violent eyes upon her, took a stand and said, "My lords: It was my fault! I must have misunderstood the young women when they were all speaking very quickly!" And Lance, in keeping with his courageous and manly gesture, took this opportunity to faint.

The Libburus was the first to be excused, escorted by Cletus, seeing as he could not see through his tears and puffy eyelids, but others were soon to follow, like Samantha and Sabrina, who didn't even need to invent ruses for their escape, as their voices were lost the din. Ten ha, the only person who noticed that Lance wasn't getting up, slid under the table, grabbed him by his burly shoulders, and dragged him out of the room. Surely someone would have seen this treachery, but then, Ten ha was quite petite and Lance was so new to the group that his comrades barely knew he existed anyway.

When the last member of the household remaining was Clara— who stood on the Baron's end of the table just to even out the sides— Hephaestus and the Baron observed that they'd reached their time to leave as well. They made eye contact, shortly followed by gestures from Hephaestus' eyebrows and the Baron's mustache, and simply turned and slipped away, knowing full-well that their companions should yammer at one another for quite a while longer.

Which brings us to where we were.

Hephaestus, armed with a long furry cape was careful to swish it out of the way deftly with every strong gesture and stride. His cane also helped emphasize his grandeur.

The Baron did his best to be patiently tolerant of Hephaestus' vanity, and decided to grant this tolerance on the fact that Hephaestus was over twice his age. (This of course was only a guess on the Baron's part, but it happened to be accurate.)

"You turned the place into a circus!" declared Hephaestus, "And no doubt were bloody-well pleased with yourself for it—"

"I told you," replied the other, pointing a quivering finger at the house, "I had nothing to do with that. I didn't orchestrate this! For God's!—why would I want to place myself in such a position? Do you think I'm a glutton for abuse?"

"I think you're a glutton for chaos, Mister Bordolo," came the ready retort.

Sidestepping the remark entirely, the Baron shot back, "Why can't you call me 'Sir Baron'?"

"Well, because I don't believe you are one, Mister Bordolo." Though it wasn't a polite remark by any means, we cannot fault Hephaestus for his honesty.

The Baron noted that if he had a pistol on his person, he should challenge the other to a duel. However, because he was unwilling to produce even the nonviolent evidence, the Baron resigned to cool his next outburst, which would have been—we can only imagine—a masterful barrage of wit. "This is getting us nowhere."

"Agreed," consented Hephaestus after a moment, "Agreed."

"And can you also concede that this Satan's surprise of a dinner party may have been a misunderstanding?" asked the Baron, still counter-circling the other even as he offered this olive-branch.

"I have difficulty conceding that anything involving you could be wholly honest, *Sir Baron*." And with a flourish of his cape, Hephaestus turned and strode away, probably hoping or assuming the Baron would follow him.

Were this a matter of dignity, the Baron would have stubbornly stayed put, so as to not give his rival the satisfaction, but—as far he could tell—there was nothing dignified in the matter at all. On the other end of the spectrum, were he a necessarily cruel human being, the Baron would have surely kicked Hephaestus' cane out from under him when he arrived once again at his side.

"Is this about pride?" the Baron demanded, noticing with regret how much shorter he stood than the markedly older man. "Hmm? Is this all because I have stripped you of some of your precious spotlight, just by standing alongside, or is it something else? Honestly, tell me, because if I am to stay here for the next few weeks I should very much like to know how I should handle you, sir!"

"Maybe by not breaking my rules, Mister Bordolo—"

"Your rules?!"

"*Our* rules!" amended Hephaestus, spinning on a heel to face him, "The seven cardinal rules of *all* travelling merchants; or have you forgotten?"

Though he could not remember all of them in order perhaps, the Baron still said, "I most certainly have not!"

"Then what was that about?" Pointing one long crooked finger at the house, Hephaestus recalled Geru's outburst: "'The King—The

King—Please-don't-eat-me'? What about 'No False Pretense,' Mister
Bordolo?—Or am I to understand that you *do* work for the king?"

"Then why didn't you help me? All you would have had to do is
explain to them that I *am* in fact a travelling merchant, though slightly
different than yourself, and they would have trusted you in it—or does
your stubbornness know so few bounds that it would rather shoot
yourself in the foot than intercede on another's behalf?"

Hephaestus offered no reply. Instead he looked down at his boots
and took hold of his beard in his free hand.

The Baron sighed. He enjoyed having gotten the last word in, but
did not feel so innocent in the matter as he would have liked. So he
placed his own fists against his hips and said, "Look, I know my group is
making more of a footprint in your snow than you'd like. Perhaps it
would be easier if we just left," offered the Baron, "the moment Oswald's
ankle is better, which won't be too—"

"You can't." This assertion was solemn, not angered, and bid the
Baron neither objection nor question. As he waited for further
explanation, Hephaestus came to say in a slow, serious monotone, "There
are only a few weeks out of the year during which it is possible to reach
or leave the Isle, and the blizzards in the dead of winter are unbravable.
Understand, Baron, that I know how to navigate this place because I have
seen and experienced the worst."

The Baron looked to the other with new eyes for a second, then
had to rub them to put them back in their skeptical state. Even so, though
the Baron did not know precisely how or why, he had the distinct
impression that Hephaestus was trying to save his life. To that effect,
Hephaestus was.

The Baron was tempted to ask more on the matter, excepting that
Hephaestus—the cane gripped smartly behind his back like a firm trainer
would his rider's crop—began circling once again. The Baron
instinctively stood at attention, and wondered if Hephaestus should find
this gesture mocking.

Hephaestus turned away from the Baron to regard the town
square and sighed. "I think that perhaps we should effect a zoning
ordinance."

"A zoning ordinance?"

"Yes," and though he sounded plainly sincere and not the least
bit plotting, the Baron had to keep his suspicions alert "That myself
and—to the best, my men—will stay on this side of the river, and you
and yours will stay on the other."

"I don't think that's very much in the spirit of the place."

And Hephaestus, likely drawing on the last string of maturity he had, said, "*You're* not in the spirit of this place, 'Sir Baron!'"

"Oh come now, I'm whimsical and often confusing; if I was anymore in the spirit of the place, I'd be a native."

This gave Hephaestus pause enough to chance to smile. And because it was undoubtedly a sign that they *could* get along, the Baron additionally offered, "And yes."

"Yes?"

"Yes," he repeated, "I can consent to basically keeping away from your zone, assuming that my fellows can get what they need from this side of town, and yours from the other." The Baron swallowed, and it tasted a little of crow. No one—(Yes, not even your narrator)—knows how much this next was bred out of honesty instead of tact, but it came as quite a shock to Hephaestus when the Baron told him, "As you've said, you know these people; I do not, and so will defer."

"To my authority?" finished Hephaestus, hopefully.

"To your experience." The Baron kept firm but respectful eye contact, as might a son who is trying to approach his father as an equal.

"Very well," replied Hephaestus, after he had taken his fair consideration, "but I insist that you take a copy of our rules to hang up at young Julian's. That won't frighten the boy, will it?"

"No. It may not make sense to him," admitted the Baron, "but that shouldn't be anything new."

And as the young Julian, standing with his shoulders against the cold outside wall of the estate, watched the two gentlemen draw up arrangements, he resolved that he should not be nearly so thrown as they might expect. Of course he did not know what these 'rules' were, or why they should pertain to these two if they didn't everyone else, but he elected could count himself as at least somewhat cunning in learning of them at all. After all, he managed to slip out of the argument in the dining room without anyone noticing.

For that matter, so had Samantha. Perceiving that the two travelling merchants were about to return—having concluded their conversation—Julian rounded a corner of the establishment and damn-near ran into Samantha. With the mild frost that had found hold on the ground, she lost her footing, and promptly slipped, and would have collided unceremoniously with the dirt, had Julian not caught her by the waist and aided her in falling forward against his chest.

She slowly looked up, mouth hanging open in something of a gasp, giving the two a silhouette that most definitely inspired several sketches by Walt Disney.

"Sorry!" exclaimed Julian in a sort of furtive whisper, as he helped her back to a posture that was self-sustainable.

"Oh," was the only reply she could give.

Then Julian, feeling somewhat awkward at the prospect of standing beside her without her request said, "Here, I'll go."

Samantha, having been lost in those big brown eyes, behind which resided the truest soul she had ever seen, realized that he was starting to move past her and sputtered, "What? Why?"

"Or-or I could stay," he backpedaled once again. But at that moment, he heard both the Baron and Mister Hephaestus chatting as they approached, and so—before they should round the corner and see Julian in all his awkwardness—he confessed, "But I should go." And with that, Julian brushed past Samantha and into the house, leaving her somewhat breathless and puzzled.

Closing the door quietly behind him, he could hear Hephaestus saying, "Well, Samantha, my dear, what are you doing out here by yourself?"

Julian quickly made his way back into the dining room, and when he arrived found it to be much bigger-looking than he had remembered it. This was owed to two things: one, that every one of Hephaestus' servants had left while Julian had been outside, and secondly, that two of the tables were now overturned.

Two other items that had been overturned were the stout Geru and the chair that was resting on top of him. His little arms flailed, but he made no movement otherwise until Pigby came about and rescued him from the old bit of wood and cushion.

"Confound it all!" squeaked Geru, brandishing a deadly spatula, which could have been why the chair had been turned on him in the first place. "I'd like to see the man stand and face me—*I've* taken bigger!"

Lifting Geru into a standing position and helping the little man right his jacket, Pigby assured him, "I'm sure you have, but no more tonight."

"Why, Julian!" announced Oswald, who was already seated quite comfortably in the corner of the room, "I say, you're alright, son." Oswald stood and with the help of the chair (and soon-after Pigby) made his way toward Julian, explaining, "I'd hoped you retreated, lest we find you a pancake under one of these tables."

"Where is everyone?" asked Julian, scanning the room to conclude that the only remaining men were in fact Pigby, Geru, and Oswald.

"Gone!" declared Geru, "all gone, the bastards. Scarpered when they knew they were no match for us."

"Actually," Pigby modified, "they were called off by their leader—Trent, I think."

Julian, doing his best to calm his general confusion, chanced to clarify, "No, I mean—"

But before he could say what he meant, Pigby caught on. "Oh! No, well, the Baron stepped outside, and Fletcher's down in the kitchen, buttering up the maid so's she has something to tell the Liver-man about why we've gone. But before we do, we should right the room some," noted Pigby, and proceeded to flip one of the downed tables.

Julian made a count in his head and, when he found that one was still missing, asked, "And the girl?"

"Oh, well," Geru shook his head, "we don't know where-in-the-bloody-hell Ten ha is."

Where-in-the-bloody-hell Ten ha was was precisely on the other side of the wall, with one hand pressing a cold towel to an unconscious Lance's forehead, and the other stroking his hair. (It must be noted here that we do not know whether or not Lance was actually unconscious; he may have truly sustained a concussion when his head collided with the floor, or he may have simply been faking so as to receive further treatment from the blue girl. To be fair, she had done the same to him just a day before.) And when she heard her name being called from the dining room, she felt a twinge of perhaps guilt, but probably just fear of being caught with the enemy. Either way, it was her unequivocal call to depart.

Ten ha whispered, "I'll see you tomorrow," and kissed the sleeping boy on the forehead before standing and returning to the dining room. And as the Baron and Fletcher recollected as well, the seven departed toward Julian's house once again, and—though a nearly physical brawl had taken place—not one of them was particularly worse for the wear.

Now, I know what you're thinking: tossed and toppled furniture is a sign of a physical fight, is it not? Well, let me assure you that if there had been an actual fight, Pigby would be the only one left standing... which—by the time Julian entered—he was. Okay, bad example. But understand that when competition takes hold in a heated argument, sometimes the players see fit to toss a chair (or just overturn one onto a dwarf) in order to punctuate a point. Even so, when Julian had come upon the scene in its aftermath, he gleaned a hint of battleground, a concept with which he was entirely unfamiliar.

In truth, the bulk of the evening had been too topsy-turvy for Julian to rightly process, but he thought he had a sense of what Hephaestus and the Baron had been on about, and his suspicions were only confirmed by the large sign, detailing the seven cardinal rules, which the Baron hung up on the wall just beside the front door.

Jonas, who had been asleep in Meredith's house until Ten ha woke him to switch places, took a very long, curious look at the sign when he entered Julian's living room. He leaned in toward it, thumbed at his nose, and with a bit of a wry smile, said, "And when he had opened the seventh seal, there was silence in heaven about the space of half an hour."

Questions

At this point in our story, you might find that you're wondering about some things, and here is where I take a moment out of the busy flow of the narrative to help you sort out your most burning cuiosities.

Having been told the story before (and having had to work my way though it as well), I assembled these four most likely questions:

One – Why is Adleship Isle called Adleship Isle? Don't ask that; it's not relevant. I can assure you if you do keep reading you will receive an answer, though I can't say that it will seem appropriate, logical, or— dare to sound redundant—relevant to you. A name is a name after all, and surely you have not wondered why every city or street in or on which you lived was called what it was called. If you did, good on you for your thirst for knowledge.

Two – How did Hephaestus and the Baron get into the town if no one can leave? Don't ask that; you won't find out for quite some time, so why bother wondering? I suppose you can if you must, and I'm more than certain that characters drop hints from time to time throughout.

Three – How in St. Crispin's name are they going to break rule seven? Don't ask that; first of all, what makes you so certain they do, what makes you so certain you know who 'they' are anyway, and furthermore, I won't even give you an inkling of an answer! And if you can't remember which rule is number seven, I say shame on you, sir or madam. Now, go consult *Chapter XVIII* to refresh your sieve-like memory.

Four – What makes Jonas act the way he does? Keep asking that; though you may not find as full of an answer as you might like. Keep your theories and guesses running and see if you can knock any of them off along the way. I must say, I was excited over this one as well, and I couldn't bear to spoil it for any of you ahead of time.

Now, I of course cannot include questions like Will Julian win his love; Will Julian leave the Isle; or Will anyone of significant note die by the end of this text? These are things that you'll just have to read and figure out for yourselves now, won't you?

Part IV – An Unrefined Feud

Hephaestus swiftly drew his sword from his cane. It was a magnificent specimen—so magnificent in fact that the Baron had not even noticed that the smooth cherrywood had concealed a blade.

XXXIV – A Weathered-Looking Barrel in the Corner

The hill nudged the rock awake when he felt the old man begin his ascent the following morning.

Both hill and rock, though probably more connected to the town than our slowly-slipping Jonas, were anxiously anticipating any words he might have on his recently acquired roommates. The hill could tell that the Libburus' house had created a stir the night before, and the old man, sleeping amongst the catalysts, was the in the nearest position to tell them all about it.

But, much to their chagrin, Jonas said nothing. Leastways nothing of import to the rock or the hill. Instead of explaining this newfound legend that was the Baron Pan Bordolo, he just ranted about the snow on the crests of the horizon and how it looked like mashed potatoes in reverse, with the potato (snow) sitting on top of the gravy (mountain).

As to whether Jonas knew the significance of the past few days, none could rightly say, even his friends the rock and hill, but regardless of how far his sanity had slipped, he was still very aware of the silhouetted men who came into his vision along with the sun, and had to count them twice to assure himself that there were four: Pigby and Geru in sandals, and Clemens and Piers in boots.

And as the morning air began to warm and Jonas trudged once again down the hill, the townspeople began to wake up, and—seeing as there was no ripple of information to tell them otherwise—resumed their lives exactly as they might any other morning. As Julian's household went off to work, so did the harvesters and the cooks and the builders, just as they always had, and by noon, somewhere a child was complaining to his parents, somewhere a noble was lecturing a miscreant, and somewhere two men were taking turns banging their heads against a wall of their choice[81]. See? Normal.

In fact, I'm convinced that the only party who was aware that her duty had changed was the river, who was quite flustered with the assumption that she was meant to divide two men from respective sides of the village. The arrangement was not *binding* mind, but both parties would certainly do their best to uphold it.

As far as their other arrangement, the one concerning the rules, the Baron was sure to remind himself of the sign when he woke, and found it right charming that someone had gone and crossed out rule one[82], so as to remind them all of what a naughty thing they had done. And of course the Baron did classify it as 'they,' because—even though it had been Geru's misstep—the Baron did not exempt himself from responsibility in the least.

And to that end, the Baron was prepared to roll up his sleeves, decide that they were still too long, change his shirt, roll up the new sleeves, and knuckle down with young Julian to aid in the day's carpentry affairs. Julian was glad of this not because he needed an assistant, but because he wanted to listen to the Baron's stories, and sometimes resetting doors and whittling away pointy sticks was dull enough work that it warranted conversation, and lots of it.

Pigby probably felt the same way about Clemens and his potato crates, and was off before any of the others, but not long, mind. The Baron and their gracious host didn't much notice Pigby's comings and goings, what with their own dealings, and Geru—a little medical bag on his little person—had gone to settle some more winter sniffles. We cannot be that surprised that old Oswald followed old Jonas down the way to Meredith's place, and that Ten ha slipped away to hope to find Lance at the stables.

I guess in the hullaballoo of it all, every one of them must have forgotten—or just assumed that "someone else" would take care of it— but in any case, none of the Baron's crew seemed to realize that they had unwittingly left Fletcher unsupervised. Everyone makes mistakes, I

---

[81] This may strike your ear as odd, but rest assured, I'll explain when it's relevant.

[82] If you find you forget which rule is which, consult the back of your book where you will find them laid out in simple form with neither distraction nor dialogue.

suppose; you just hope that everyone doesn't make mistakes simultaneously.

Fletcher initially considered setting up shop. See, he was still pressed to hold to his promise to "Sell twice the loot at twice the price" even without a currency to prove the success of the endeavor. But then again, Fletcher was also charged to act the part of an explorer "for the king," and—as far as he knew—explorers did not set up shop to wait for the buyers to come to them; they took to foot and proactively sought their customers out. Besides, the nature of a stationary shop[83] did engender a certain seller-buyer relationship, which Fletcher believed should best be avoided. Of course, were he really acting in his boss' best interests, he would probably stop the silly contest altogether, because—whether or not he actually made a penny in the process—his efforts were marked to belie a certain older merchant.

Some would say that Fletcher purposefully obeyed the letter of the law and not the spirit, and would snub Hephaestus deliberately. Again. Though I do not doubt that Fletcher found the man entirely lacking in a sense of humor, I should imagine he had no desire to actually hurt his feelings—which we have already learned were more fragile than they first appeared. In any case, I have a theory on the matter that Fletcher simply had a sieve-like memory that only retained the details which resonated harmonically with his fancy, like a competitive boast perhaps or maybe a royal profession. Just to play devil's advocate, a colleague of mine pointed out that Fletcher may have in fact been a genius who merely played the fool so as to not disrupt his preferred lifestyle—a notion to which I do not hold, granted, but which I cannot outright overrule, so, there you are.

Fletcher let himself into their cart to design his pack for the day. Now, I know you've only hardly seen the inside of the cart, and you are probably fascinated as to what crazy knickknacks are on display, but I'll save your imagination the trouble: nothing was on display. Sorry to disappoint, but with such a large load trekking several hundred miles at a time, everything had to be precisely stored in boxes and drawers.

Fletcher began pouring through drawers, and for almost every one he opened, he took whatever was on the bottom, the item that had been there the longest and would not be missed. Scarves and sweaters and cookware and cleanware and a very curious-looking gourde which

---

[83] By that I mean a shop that doesn't move, not a shop that sells parchment and letterhead.

had been hollowed into a horn that did not play, and all stuffed into a backpack, the likes of which might seem strange and interesting and just a little bit terrifying to the people of the Isle.

So, satisfied with his load, Fletcher was just about to leave the cart when he noticed that—though he carried a fair bit of luggage on his back—his hands were entirely empty. What good was a stately peddler of artifacts if he has nothing of note in his hands? So Fletcher reentered the cart, and went straight to a weathered-looking barrel in the corner, which was full to the bursting of even odder whosamawhatsits and thingamajigs—well, maybe not 'odder' per se.

To quote the Baron, "Anything that is a mismatched single from a set, an otherwise functional item missing its key component, or a thing whose origins we cannot prove and so cannot price in full."

To remind them of these classifications, Geru had painted their abbreviations on the front of the barrel:

ATIAMSFAS
AOFIMIKC
ATWOCPACPIF

To save on sanity and time, the crew mostly forgot the long acronyms and called the whole of the lot by the first name, 'Atiamsfas,' or more phonetically accurately, "Adam's fuss." I hold that every person, especially if he or she is a pack rat, should be able to identify when a thing is merely Adam's fuss and—even if it is not promptly gotten rid of—should be moved someplace out of the way so as not to interfere with or clutter that person's life.

But never mind the tangent!

Fletcher, as you must remember, was already packed with oodles, and had arbitrarily decided that he could only take one, one special memento which he could bandy about in his right arm while he tried to pitch the others in his pack, and so passed over the one left shoe worn by King Louis the beloved, the handleless riding crop carried by Archduke Leopold VI, or the single king-piece from the Richard II's chess game which supposedly ceded the bulk of Northern Ireland to the independent Gaelics who thereafter aided in young Henry Bolingbroke's ascension to the throne.

There was a masterfully carved lute that was missing it's lower half, (courtesy of an alligator in the lower colonies); and an elaborate religious scroll which had had its upper half burned away, (courtesy of a small brushfire in the upper Caucasus); but it was a long, slightly bent, expertly preserved ramrod that had been separated from its owner when the Baron's cart rocked too heartily while on a bridge while in a windstorm. See, the musket in full, a stately Revolutionary War keepsake, which had belonged to the backstabber John Huntington—whose original allegiance and subsequent treachery is still unknown—was thrown from the gun-rack of the leaning mobile treasure trove and very nearly disappeared into a river some fifty feet below when the quick-thinking Pigby grabbed hold of the plunger-end of the same ramrod, without remembering that the weapon was free to continue to slide right off into the water.

In any case, holding the stately rod in his right hand, Fletcher had the oddest urge to sing about the seventy-six sackbuts that led the grand procession, and he carried this same sort of grandeur as he made his way into town, gesturing with the nice, long ramrod.

It probably wasn't the ramrod itself that drew the attention of the townsfolk, but Fletcher—as his walking caused literal flocking—felt infinitely pleased with his selection. By mid-morning, he had assembled a following, it seemed, which spread from rumors from the first backyard he stopped by—interrupting a woman at her laundry to talk on a press mechanism for fast-drying which he could show her with relative ease and a simple rolling pin wrapped in unbound wool. In satisfaction and fascination, she told her friends, who told their friends, who gradually came to alert one another of Fletcher's progression and to keep a heads-up as to where he might stop next.

Though they ducked and hid as they followed, follow they did—they being the townsfolk who thought that mayhap this new traveler might have exactly the item they needed for a secret remedy to whatever complaint they had. He was asked about methods of fire-starting, or door-defrosting, or toe-reheating after a long time in the snow. Young children wanted to know about music-making and rock-tossing and the elderly about lower-back support devices for chair-sitting. (Though Fletcher did not *invent* the Lumbar Log, he was certainly a primary agent of its original distribution.)

And as he collected more and more followers—by afternoon willing to follow visibly—Fletcher began to see himself as the Pied Piper, but then realized that this was a problematic metaphor, seeing as he would either be calling the lovely townspeople vermin, or else would be leading them away for vindictive reasons. As an alternative, he quickly considered Jesus, then even more quickly dismissed it, finding the allusion somewhat blasphemous, but more importantly deciding that if he were in fact Jesus, then these people should one day turn on him and nail him to some very finely crafted planks, probably sanded by young Julian himself. Then, in a moment of brilliance, the thin man thought that he should simply be a "Fletcher[84]." Of course!—in fact, why-ever not? In centuries to come, surely people would know *his* name as they did the other two legends, right[85]?

Now, I know that this description makes it seem like Fletcher's agenda was working out swimmingly, but there are two things of which I must remind you: the first, that Fletcher was not dispensing items nearly as often as he was dispensing advice, and the second, that Fletcher had hardly figured on how to *acquire* Adleship Islean specimens.

It was Elke that tipped this relationship. See, even though she hardly could have intended to create a relationship of tradable commodities, she must have discovered over the years that her baking yielded results, because no matter how perfect a commune, any worker would sooner take a beautiful scone than a hard-boiled egg or (worse) no supper at all. When Fletcher was over at Carleigh's, showing her how to mount and operate a double pulley, he heard a heavenly voice say:

"Hello," and a hand waving before Elke continued with, "say there, young man, I've a fresh pan out of the oven, if you should feel like stopping by."

Fletcher nearly dropped the hay bale he was hoisting, and caught it just before it quite flattened a noble old sheep called Cauliflower. If you had tried some of Elke's delicacies, you might as well. Cauliflower didn't seem to mind.

And as Fletcher left to acquire his morsel, the remaining bystanders began chatting amongst themselves, and discussed that perhaps the way to get the traveler—or more important, the traveler's thin man—to pay a visit was to intrigue him with something of their own. Not trade in the strictest sense, but—Voila!—a system of courteous exchange, established for Fletcher's benefit.

As Fletcher emerged from his lovely snack, somewhat flushed and sticky for all his trouble, he was confronted by two women—one boasting a kind of paste which she claimed could hold any wall-dressing to any wall, and the other telling of a long stalk of reed which—if

---

[84] Not to mean the medieval profession.

[85] Well, he may not have been *exactly* right, but then again, you are reading this, aren't you?

properly manipulated—could draw all of the water from a syrup to make the final product all the more thick and rich.

And in return for their time—though he didn't say, "In return for your time"; he more said, "Y'know, I have a very fine iron chisel that could chip away the old dried paste to perfectly flush," or, "Oh, that old pig? If you ask me, he's just constipated, and Geru's got an herb that can—"[86]

Ahem.

And this was how Fletcher made his way from Aubrey to Zelma in just one afternoon.

I don't much believe that he consciously made a point of avoiding the Baron's crew as he wove between the houses and the commoners that surrounded him, and yet whenever he came upon a place where either Julian or Clemens had work for the day, he always seemed to just precede or just miss them. Now, not that they necessarily would have minded—perhaps they would have found Fletcher's little romp perfectly charming, but it is likely that they would have said some things.

See, it was entirely offhand—when a curious chap by the good name of Otto asked Fletcher just what it was he was carrying, to which Fletcher replied in stately regard, "My dear sir, *this* is a regulation British infantry ramrod, who got taken off a gentleman who very fell in battle."

"I see," said Otto, and shuffled off to relate this information to a friend.

---

[86] The editor was quite emphatic that I stop right here, so as to not give my readers unpleasant mental images.

XXXV – Darts

Do you know what day it is in the Isle? You may not remember, seeing as I've only mentioned the date once, and there's been a blizzard and a food fight to confuse you. Well, if you must know, it was the twenty-second of December, which puts us—you guessed it!—just one day before Raul's birthday. Was this important? I should think most definitely yes, and I'll tell you why:

Raul was about to turn eighteen, which was the only really important birthday, because somehow, arbitrarily, it designated the citizen a full-fledged adult in the Isle. Raul was a noble, which, as you already know, makes a person that much more powerful, respected, and likely to write something that wouldn't be either painted over or washed out. And lastly, Raul was just about the only person in the whole of the Isle who was fit to be the next Libburus.

Here's how that works: Eugene, you've met, and of course there's the Libburus, and then there were the houses of Rudolph and Penrod. Rudolph was fairly old, by that we mean fifty-eight, which, as you can imagine, was quite an age in the early nineteenth century, for that matter he had already Libbured for the three consecutive terms before Sebastian, and neither of his sons were eligible. This was because his first son had died in a wood-chopping accident—(not a pleasant story)—and his second had married into a paper-making house across the river and his noblehood was most forgotten. Penrod, though he had three strapping boys, had himself taken a lifelong disease which made him quite weak, sleepy, and unable to control with any regularity his bowels. Besides, the eldest son was hardly eight years old, which wouldn't put any of them in the runnings until at least two more terms—remember, they were only seven years apiece. Penrod did have a younger brother, Geert, who was a fine man indeed in his mid-twenties, but he was most otherwise occupied with a charge more taxing possibly than the whole of the Isle, named Condamine. And nobody faulted either of the charming gentlemen for their sister's state.

Now you may be wondering why Eugene himself was not in the runnings, or maybe you're not, having guessed that—on the whole—the town didn't much like Eugene. As I say, he is not a bad person; I should keep trying to convince you of this, but sadly, very few people in our story, Julian included, agree with me on this sentiment.

But we don't really sympathize with Eugene; we sympathize with his son, Raul, who was—when we find him—throwing darts at a knothole in a tree. Why darts? Well, because they were charming (and Raul found himself charming), they called for precision (and Raul respected precision), and sometimes it felt good to drive something pointy into something sturdy. (As a virgin who had never murdered anyone, understand that this violent phallicism was not conditioned.)

Now, Raul's manner of shooting was quite fascinating, by the way he would line up the shot, squinting one dark eye in line with the first two knuckles on his right hand, and using them to sight his target. What followed was a draw timed with an inhale through the nose, then a swift release and exhale through the lips. So keen was he on his process that he didn't notice the intruder until she was very nearly at arm's reach, but at the same time, so in tune was he that he didn't need to turn around to know who stood off his shoulder.

"Morning, Samantha."

"Don't you mean afternoon?" she returned.

Raul shrugged, then flicked a tiny pin-prick into the bark of the tree.

Samantha shifted uncomfortably, somewhat uncertain of what to say. Let me explain: Samantha knew that there was a pleasantry and formality portion of conversation with any young—or old, for that matter—man, but in most cases, she had the luxury of having the male party do most of the talking, which usually eventually allowed her access to the topic for which she came. She hadn't counted on Raul being laconic.

So, what followed was a series of "Um"s and "So"s and no real progress until Raul, frustrated to begin with, and suddenly out of darts, rounded on his heal to ask—more heatedly than he would have liked, "Look, what are you doing here?"

"I—" Samantha stalled, and considered for a moment having out with it and saying exactly what she had come to say. But upon closing her mouth, recollecting herself, and looking over the boy properly, detected a redness about his eyes and made sympathy the order of the day. Cocking her head in a fashion that would have been quite becoming on a small terrier, Samantha inquired of Raul, "Are you okay?"

Raul looked away suddenly, and—in as many a manner as he could manage—brushed a coarse sleeve across his face, so as to explain, that 'No,' in fact, 'he was *not* crying in the recent hours. Not even a little.' As he strode across the clearing toward the tree, he grunted through his teeth, "My father is a mean, arrogant jerk!" the last of which he emphasized by ripping all of the darts from the bark.

Samantha put her hands on her hips, decided they weren't quite right there, and settled on folding them across her chest. "What happened?"

And from there followed a monologue, the likes of which I'm certain you've heard in coming-of-age films produced during the last three decades. Raul, without any attention whatsoever to the young woman who was listening quite patiently, explained, "It's my birthday tomorrow—*my* birthday!—and all Eugene can think about is how it affects him, what *he* wants from me, but did he ever ask me what *I* wanted? No—What if I don't want to be the next Libburus? Did he ever think about that?"

(The answer to that question is a resounding 'no' as it had never occurred to the father, but to be fair, Raul hadn't managed to think on it either; he merely felt compelled to reject Eugene's wishes, no matter how reasonable they were. But more on that later.)

"And what's more," Raul went on, "he's *so much more important than everyone else*, and thinks everyone else is rubbish—especially if they're from the other side." Turning back to Samantha, who had a rather pained expression on her cold face, Raul tossed his head to one side, and—doing his best to look aloof—said, "Do you know he actually forbade me from bringing Julian?"

As Raul lined himself up with the tree again, he didn't notice Samantha wring out her hands (much like her father did), didn't notice her jerk her head about in all directions as if hoping an explanation should present itself, and hardly paid attention to the quiver in her voice when she asked, almost pleadingly, "So you told Julian he couldn't come?"

But Raul, with a sardonic sort of grunt and another flick of a dart, replied, "No. Not yet anyway. I mean, I know I'll have to tell him, but I don't see why *I* have to deliver his hate-mail for him."

Though her mind was somewhere between trying to quell a fluttering heart and the most assured relief she had ever known, Samantha was so thrown by the last phrase that she had to inquire, "Hate mail?"

"Yeah, it was something Hephaestus said," said Raul with a shrug.

"Well, you're not going to do it, are you?"

And of course Samantha was far more surprised by this outburst than our young gentleman, but even Raul seemed to find it out of character for her and so about-faced once again to ask from beneath a crooked brow, "What? Tell Julian that he's no longer invited? Well, I think I have to, don't I?"

"No," she blurted, then after checking that she hadn't sacrificed her posture to say something so unbefitting, clarified, "It's your party; you can invite who you want to."

Raul scratched his head with the last dart before flicking it once again into the tree. Unable to tell that the young woman was simply grasping at straws, he mused, "That's true. Plus it would be great to see the look on his face... And I guess," he went on, hesitating to make his way to the tree to once again collect his ammunition, "if he did get cross with me, I could always say I simply forgot."

But as Raul made to step forward, he felt the most curious thing: a small hand on his elbow, but with enough resolve to turn him around and face her. She had not properly taken a breath, so when the young woman spoke, it was with assured forward momentum so as to not run out of breath before she'd finished her statement, which went a little like this: "No, here's what you're going to do: you're going to let your friend come to your party, and if your father asks, you will stand tall and tell him that Julian deserves to be there, because after what that young man did, he has shown that he is far more noble in his soul than any of us will ever be in our blood."

And as Samantha took a breath, aware that she was very warm and felt somewhat flushed, she couldn't help but feel awe from the way that Raul looked at her, and was very suddenly self-conscious about how inappropriately assertive she had been. So, clearing her throat, she patted Raul on the chest, and took a step back before saying, "But, as you said, it's your business, not mine. I'm sure you'll do what you think is right. I just..." And with nothing more to offer, Samantha smiled, and excused herself, while Raul watched after her.

XXXVI – Newspaper

"No, no, the coloquintida—the plant—the *Othello*!" insisted Oswald, his hands forward, imploring with the even older man across from him.

Jonas smiled, with his eyes closed and a smug look on his painfully chapped lips, and—recognizing it his turn to speak—said, "Always runs but never walks, often murmurs, never talks, has a bed but never sleeps, has a mouth but never eats."

"My good man," began Oswald, doing his best to make eye contact through the opposite's shut lids, "I mean to speak on the book here, see?" And pointing at the open text on the table, he asked Jonas again, "Do you know what I mean by *Othello*?"

And Jonas, with a little more sternness in his voice, reclaiming that he was in fact the oldest party in the conversation repeated, "Always runs but never walks, often murmurs, never talks, has a bed but never sleeps, has a mouth but never eats."

"He won't stop until you make a guess," said Meredith, presenting each of the men with a steaming mug of what smelled quite a bit like Klaus' coco. Rubbing her father affectionately on the shoulder, the lady of the house added, "He's stubborn that way. But if you don't know, just guess, and he'll move on."

"Well, it's a river, madam," explained Oswald as she went back to the stove, and the simple answer seemed to satisfy Jonas, who laid his hands open-palm in front of Oswald and beckoned with his fingers.

"Turn over a new leaf," said Jonas, then settled back to wait.

Oswald looked at the grandfather incredulously and was busy trying to pinpoint what exactly went on in the other's head, when Meredith interrupted his train of thought with, "He means it's your turn now."

"I know, madam!" exclaimed Oswald, with more frustration than he wanted to show, then, grumbling to himself as he racked his brain, resigned to tell Jonas, "Alright, in the night they come without being called, by day are lost without being stolen—Now, while you think on that, I've some—"

"Stars," replied Jonas promptly, then, holding up one finger to indicate a pause, tried to think on another riddle himself.

"Terrific," muttered Oswald, learning for the first time in his life why Geru and Pigby were so keen on using sarcasm. This distressed him slightly, because—as someone who did not much use sarcasm himself—he had only come to recognize its frequent use on Fletcher. The distress had nothing to do with Fletcher and everything to do with a new and unfortunate musing that perhaps the only reason he had not caught on to more of their sarcasm was that it must have been directed at him.

"Would you like something to eat, Mister Oswald?" asked Meredith.

"No, no, madam," said Oswald, "we're quite alright, thank you." The old man—granted, the *less* old man—then resumed his intent page-turning. See, he had, in anticipating that Jonas may yet be a tough customer, brought his collection of Mister Shakespeare's folios which were loaded with an arsenal of quotability.

"Aha!" exclaimed Jonas, clapping one palm on the table with such fervor that it interrupted Oswald mid-page-turn. "What's black and white and red all over?"

Oswald thumbed at his nose just below the spectacles. "What?"

Jonas swallowed, then repeated slowly, "What's black and white and red all over?"

"I—" began Oswald, then stalling in frustration remarked, "I don't know."

If asked later, Oswald would have defended that, had he had time and patience to properly think on it, he would have muddled through the other's question, but he may not have wanted to in retrospect because this single admission of defeat finally seemed to settle Jonas. To be fair to both parties, Oswald was probably beaten more by Jonas' longevity than his own inability to decipher English riddles. But either way, the single submission seemed to slake the grandfather's thirst for bouts of wit, and prompted him deliver a smug, "Newspaper!" before standing and exiting the household with a broad grin beneath his closed eyes.

Oswald sat in silence and a wee bit of wonder before musing aloud, "Good Mother Mary, the bugger punned me!"

"How's that?" asked Meredith, taking Jonas' place with her own cup of tea.

"Oh!" exclaimed a flustered Oswald, as he came to wonder whether Meredith had heard him say 'bugger,' or, worse, knew what it meant, or—because he was quite fascinated by migratory histories— whether Jonas and in-turn his daughter were at all Bulgarian[87].

"Well it's very simple madam, now that I've heard it, that is," began Oswald, steering the point quite craftily away from his term. "See, he read me a riddle that does more than just obscure semantics, see, but rather loops one into a false sense of security with three very oft-observed colors and then proceeds to de-color one of them."

"Hmmm, I see," she said, though she clearly did not.

Oswald took another proverbial stab at the proverbial pudding: "News is printed in black and white and is *read* everywhere, as in people *read* it. Quite good, I should say."

Stirring the tea with her little finger, Meredith observed, "I'm impressed that you knew so many of them. You know, I should have told you that he wouldn't stop asking you until you missed one, but..."

"But it looked like I was having so much fun, madam?" offered Oswald with so much refinement in his stuffy old tone that it was impossible to tell whether he was being sarcastic.

"No, I was curious how long you could keep up with him. No one else can, so they don't even try anymore. Jonas is a mastermind of the riddles."

Unsure if that last was in reminiscence or annoyance, Oswald took the opportunity to steer the conversation back to his real purpose in visiting Meredith's household. "Yes, and it's a wonder how he learned all of them in the first place."

"*That's* what you were trying to get out of him?" wondered Meredith, and by the way she said it, Oswald had the notion the woman was baffled by why anyone from the Big Out There should care on their tiny little village.

"In a manner of speaking, madam," said Oswald, doing his best to casually wave aside the comment. "Although... you wouldn't happen

---

[87] To get you up to speed, "Bugger" is an English slang term which accuses the accusee of partaking in what was then considered an aberrant and deviant sexual practice, and the ancient derivative of the modern term is of course the Latin ethnic slur "Bulgarus" which irreverently refers to the little-respected Bogomils of Bulgaria.

to know, would you, how he came by such a wealth of knowledge of literary gems, would you?"

Meredith took both hands off the cup of tea, and set them palms-down on the table. "Once more and slower. We've never heard most of the Big Out There's words before."

"Yes, yes, um—what I mean is, madam, that Jonas—your father—says things that he can't rightly have heard before, and yet he speaks them off the cuff as if he's heard them 'round here every day."

"Oh," Meredith finished sipping before speaking again, "Well, you'll never get that out of Jonas. No one can. He doesn't talk about the time before Mother."

"Oh, yes, he is a widower of some years," recalled Oswald, then, catching his possible indiscretion amended, "If this is a sore point for you, madam—"

"Oh, heavens no. It's been more than ten years since. You know, she was a very good to him I remember though. Better than I can be."

"Oh, I'm sure that's not true, madam!"

"Oh, it is," she reassured him, "but I try not to take it too hard. See, Loretta understood him, knew how to reason with him, knew how to manage his oddness."

"His eccentricities?" offered Oswald, as what he believed to be a better term.

"Yes, that too," agreed Meredith. "I think it's that he always acted like he needed Loretta, but now that she's gone, he thinks it means he doesn't need anyone."

"Loretta was your mother?"

"That's right," she said, standing to refill her tea.

"How did she and Jonas come to meet?" asked Oswald, doing his best to sound friendly as opposed to interrogative.

"They didn't exactly," she replied, "My mother grew up knowing Father. He lived with their family, worked with my grandfather, and when he passed away, Jonas just stayed with them and managed the egg farm. Mother said she would wake up to the sound of him singing every morning out in the henhouse when she was a girl—remember he was much older than her—and I guess when she was no longer a little girl, she realized she had always been in love with him, and they set their lives right here in this very house."

"He sings?" asked Oswald, certain that he could use Fletcher's command of music to trace any ditties sung by the grandfather back to a point of origin and maybe some answers. "What does he sing?"

Meredith shrugged. "Who can remember? He stopped after Loretta died. His mind started to fade then too." With a sigh, the lady of the house took her seat once again across from Oswald at the same table that had not only housed her every meal, but her mother's and—to the best Oswald could figure—her mother's mother's before that. "I guess he really did need her," Meredith resigned.

Scooting forward on his elbows so as to bridge the physical distance between himself and Meredith, Oswald timidly conveyed, "If you don't mind my asking, madam, but what was he like? Before she passed... was he—"

"Oh, he'd always been strange." Meredith affirmed, graciously taking the mantle of the conversation from the older party. "No, the references, the jokes, the riddles—that's just his way. He would—I know I have memories of times when he would try to explain or-or even just *remember* something and it wouldn't work, and he'd get frustrated, and Mother would soothe him. No, he's always done that," she repeated, nodding to herself as she reformed old mental images of a younger version of the village grandfather. "Now, he doesn't even try to remember, and not a soul is—or, to best we know, has ever been older than him, so no one will ever know why he says what he says or where he came to know it."

Now, Oswald did have a theory. In fact, he suspected that Meredith had the same theory. The trouble is that in a place that probes the lines that boarder scientific impossibility, it becomes difficult to venture any theory without knowing why or how it works.

Of course, you have some thoughts on why Jonas speaks the way he does in our story, yes? If not, I should guess that you're not paying enough attention, but unfortunately for all of us—astute or not—there will be no answers on this score in this chapter. Oh! But I've nearly forgotten, there is yet one more hint. Would you like to hear it? I should think that you would, but even if you don't, Oswald is sure to lead you into it nonetheless.

Though it actually pained his pride some to say it, Oswald's humane logic bid him ask, "Have you perhaps asked Hephaestus, madam, if he would speak to Jonas?"

"Oh, well," began Meredith, and as she spoke, Oswald could hear not so much resentment but a sad sort of confusion when she informed the old man, "Hephaestus refuses to speak with Father."

XXXVII – An Empty Pack

Oswald found it unfortunate that he left the little house with more new questions than answers but was so fascinated by all of the little Easter Eggs in this town that it was difficult to be too disappointed. Quite the contrary: he was rather elated as he limped back up the hill toward Julian's. His foot, though not quite better was increasingly able to support him as the days went on, and he was becoming so proficient with his crutch—constructed by Julian of course—that he scarcely noticed it as a nuisance anymore. Additionally, he had something exciting to say to the Baron upon seeing him.

"Evening, Oswald," called Julian as the old man approached himself and the Baron.

"Good day, lad," Oswald replied, and proceeded across the clearing to where his employer stood focused intently on the horseshoe in his hand.

"I say, sir," began Oswald, with the kind of giggle in his tone that children have when they are about to say something inappropriate, "I say, what's black and white and read all over?"

"A zebra carcass on the Zambian Savannah," snapped the Baron without looking at his friend, "Now be quiet, Oswald; I'm in the middle of something very important with the boy."

"Sir, you're playing horseshoes," Oswald observed.

"And losing!" announced the Baron, to which Julian and Oswald shared a smirk. The Baron prepared his shot with slow shallow breaths, muttered something (probably in Latin), then threw with such a dramatic exhale that it made the thud against the dirt over ten feet past the post all the more amusing.

"Confound it!" he declared before aggressively dusting off his palms and progressing towards the post. When the Baron lifted Julian's ringing horseshoe, he grumbled, "Beginner's luck."

Without taking his eyes off the Baron in case of eavesdropping, Julian leaned over to Oswald. "He says that a lot to me. Does he say that about everything?"

"Just about," whispered Oswald, then shouted to his Baron, "Beginner's luck indeed, sir!"

The Baron smirked in spite of himself and waved the comment away. "Come now, lad," he called, "We've still a few more rounds to go."

"You said that three rounds ago," returned Julian, with a nod of farewell to Oswald.

The last thing that Oswald heard before he disappeared within the dwelling was the Baron saying, "Yes, well, it's even more true now, isn't it."

When Oswald latched the door behind him, he found Geru on the couch nursing the arch of one foot, which sported a lovely red blister. The short man looked quite well otherwise, which bid Oswald engage with, "Good day, my good fellow."

"Though it seems I can hardly walk, *good fellow*," Geru returned.

"Yes, how thoughtless of me. Perhaps you should like to borrow my crutch." As he proceeded toward what had become his favorite chair, which sat beside an end-table made entirely of stacked books, Oswald allowed himself to feel smug at what he found to be a proper use of sarcasm.

Taking a labored descent onto same chair, Oswald said, "Oh, you know, the grandfather chap challenged me to a bout of riddles."

"Is he not as mad as we first thought, then?"

"Possibly moreso," remarked Oswald, "It's hard to tell; is it Tuesday[88]?"

Geru shrugged. "I think we just need a proper Sunday to anchor us back in. Do they do Sundays here?"

---

[88] This may not make sense to you. Unfortunately, it does not make sense to me either—remember, I'm just quoting here—but I think the nearest bit of evidence you can use to anchor would be the fact that he uses a semi-colon, which means that he relates the ambiguity of Jonas' sanity and his deciphering thereof to the fact that it may or may not be Tuesday. Fascinating.

The easy answer was that, yes, there were Sundays in the Isle, whether or not any ritual heed was paid to them, but then Oswald did not know if the people in this village had any religion besides their support of Hephaestus. This caused him to "Hmm."

"'Hmm' what?"

"Well," began Oswald and went on to explain what I just narrated.

While they mused on a brand of mythology that held not a pantheon of gods, but a single human imposter, Pigby burst through the door, grinning broadly, and looking quite robust in-spite-or-because of the cold outside. "Ah, what a day, what a day!" he exclaimed upon entry, because, yes, Pigby was so endearing that he actually said things like that.

"I love this mountain air," he went on, setting down the pack that no one could even see on his back as his shoulders blocked it out of view, "It makes one feel so alive!"

And, as he went to close and latch the door, he heard a thin man on the other side call, "Hold the door!" to which Pigby consented, graciously revealing Fletcher, whose hands looked quite dirty, whose neck looked quite sweaty, and whose cheeks looked quite red but on either side of a drunkenly satisfied smile, so as to make any aforementioned negative points seem quite moot indeed. I say 'drunken' because Fletcher was not only robust and giddy—(robustly giddy at that)—but actually a little tipsy from the welcoming beverages served him.

"Ladies and gentlemen," he announced with the appropriate swagger, "I give you my day's work!" And with that, he flung the pack from his shoulders, where it landed just beside Geru and his ailing foot, crumpling to reveal its complete lack of contents, and from the way Fletcher regarded this emptiness, his other three fellows were quite aware that this was an accomplishment. This sentiment was reinforced by Fletcher's next comment, which followed, "Nothing says success like an empty pack."

Geru, amused by the turn-of-phrase excitedly asked, "Who said that?"

"Oh, I just made it up!"

"Windbag," grumbled Geru, resuming treatment of his swollen sole.

But Fletcher was too much on a roll to quit even after Geru's frosty rejections, and so informed the lot of his newest endeavor, "Boys, I have decided to become a Fletcher."

"You're going to craft arrows?" came Oswald.

"No, no—a *Fletcher*—*the* Fletcher, the first of my kind—I'm going to be a legend in the art of distribution. Which is why," he conveyed proudly, his hands on his hips like some devilish Peter Pan figure, "I have decided to start coining my own catch-phrases."

"Distributing?" asked Pigby.

"Yes, that's right."

"To the people of the Isle?" inquired Oswald.

"Yeppers," affirmed Fletcher.

"Fletcher!" squeaked Geru, his frustration pitching his voice above even his own range, "We can't sell to them, you nincompoop!" which Oswald confirmed with a stern nod.

"Whoa! *Sell?*" Fletcher held his hands out, palms forward, urging them to please back the carriage up a few paces. "Who said anything about *sell*? I'm talking about *giving* things away. All *I* hoped for in exchange was some kind conversation and the seeds of what I hope to be a wonderful and profitable friendship."

Murmurs of disapproval muttered their ways through Oswald and Geru's lips but remained murmurs because neither had an immediate reason to scold Fletcher. I mean, there *was* the ramrod, but they were not aware of that, so more on it later.

It was Pigby who, because he was much bigger than Fletcher, easily took command of the room by simply stepping into its center and explaining with his sturdy yet soothing voice, "Now, now, I'm certain that—with respect to the inventory, of course—"

"Of course," chimed Fletcher.

"—Fletcher knows what he's doing," resumed a satisfied Pigby, and would have continued with something just as intelligent had he not been interrupted by Oswald, who—though normally a very polite older gentleman—was feeling duly snarky after his day's affairs.

"I say! You know, this is the same man who upset our every good relation with Hephaestus by starting a food fight—say, what[89]!"

Fletcher took a bow.

---

[89] Fun historical footnote: this was the first time in recorded history that competitive tough talk ever included the phrase "Say what?" and in my opinion, it should have stopped there.

"Yes," agreed Geru, scooting forward on the couch to be a few more inches into Pigby's space, "you're trusting the resident cotton-head."

"Yes, and tell me, Geru," began Pigby, "how close are you to solving this little weather phenomenon of ours?"

The short man flustered: "Well, I've made extensive observation—and it's not *little*, mind you—"

"But you haven't reached any conclusion," concluded the giant man.

"Not as such…"

"And you, Oswald," he went on, hands clasped behind his big black back giving an aura of authority, but moreover the calm that comes with knowing one is absolutely spot-on right, "Are you any closer to learning the origins of the town or that grandfather?"

Oswald fumbled: "I'll—I'll have you know, young man, that I've spent most of the day with him!"

"But did you get him to answer a single question directly?"

"Well, no," replied an honest Oswald, and would have felt quite defeated had he not suddenly remembered his latest bread-crumb. "But—I say!—I have been given a hint: the daughter, Missus Meredith, says that Hephaestus refuses to talk to Jonas."

The old man smiled, his wrinkled cheeks creeping up his face to push his eyes near-closed, while the others glanced between themselves, acknowledging that, yes, it was an interesting point.

"In any case," resumed Pigby, careful not to let the lull rob him of his perfect segue, "how can either of you, who can scarcely live up to your own agendas, rail against this man's adventurer's spirit and belittle his accomplishments." (That being said, they were not yet aware of the ramrod incident, but they would be soon enough.)

"Thank you, Pigby," said Fletcher, (most likely not remembering the incident himself), "and I should ask, my good man, how is your endeavor coming along?"

"Splendidly," boomed Pigby, before taking his seat. "I am very much 'one of the guys'—Oh, which reminds me, Geru, we've two more joining us tomorrow: Sherman and Manuel."

"Lovely! Start with one, now on to four, and before you know it, we'll have the whole town in a healthier, more-balanced state." Of course, Geru had no idea of what would happen over just the following week, and looking back, even he would concede that the remark was quite ironic.

As if prompted by the word 'balanced,' the door opened to Julian and the Baron, who were at that moment helping to carry a very dizzy but amiably-smiling Jonas.

"What the devil happened to him?" asked Fletcher.

"He wandered into the middle of our game," said Julian, which alerted the rest of them to the charming raised red lump on the grandfather's forehead.

"We've told you, boss, you've got to watch where you're throwing!" said Pigby, swooping in and scooping Jonas out from the arms of the other two. "I'll get him to bed," he conveyed over his shoulder as he carried what then seemed to be a very light and comfortable figure into the other room.

Jonas, waving an arm over Pigby's shoulder, said, "They who plow the sea do not carry the winds in their hands."

Once they'd left the room, Oswald shook his head at the Baron, saying, "For shame, sir."

The somewhat flabbergasted Baron, standing center of both attention and room, had to ask, "Why do you all assume it was me?"

Geru, Oswald, and Fletcher all looked to Julian and cocked their heads to one side[90], to which Julian dutifully replied, "It was him," before following the giant and grandfather men into the other room.

"So the boy smoked you on the green, eh?" asked Fletcher

"To be fair," said the Baron, before taking a seat to undo his boots, "the ground was rather sloped. And besides, the boy's a master thrower; you should have seen him skipping rocks the other day. I mean," he went on, searching for means to make him relevant to the conversation, "it's not as if he's the superior in juggling or—"

"No," interrupted Geru, "*I* am."

"Fine. But I'm sure I'd be the best musket marksman—"

"Ahem!" *ahem*ed Oswald, "I say, *I* would be, sir."

"Fine! But it's not as though he could best me in fencing—"

"Mm!" exclaimed Fletcher, but with enough food in his mouth that he could not properly vocalize, "No, bo*ffh*, bu*h I* cou*dh*."

"What are you eating?" Geru asked.

Fletcher quickly shoved the last of Elke's cookie into his mouth. "N*uffin*'."

"Well, in any case," the Baron said, "I trust you all had productive days?"

---

[90] To the left, if you must know.

This was followed by an assortment of "You bet!" and "Yes, indeed!" and "I should say so—What!"

"Good," said the Baron, and attempted to reassert himself as leader with, "You know, we are still professionals, and this is no time to become lazy or complacent just because we can't actually sell. Is that understood?"

"Of course!" they replied in such conditioned unison that it was impossible to believe them.

"Right," muttered the Baron, and that was that.

They all went to their respective beds soon after, settling down from their respective hard days' work, with the injured man on the couch, the giant man on the floor, and the other three travelers up in the loft, all chatting about their new findings and theories and swapping Adleship Islean stories until they dozed off into a deep, much-deserved sleep.

They did, however, wake up collectively once more: probably only an hour or so into the group shut-eye, Oswald startled when Ten ha came in the front door, and his exclamation was loud enough to alert the others.

"Sorry," she whispered, as if anyone was still asleep, "Needed my pack," which—to be fair—was at Pigby's feet.

"My dear," called the Baron down from the loft, "Are you just getting back?"

"Where've you been?" asked Fletcher.

"What's the time?" inquired Pigby.

"It's practically midnight!" squeaked Geru, without looking at an hourglass and without actually meaning to answer Pigby.

Finally Oswald finished the barrage with, "Were you out there by yourself, my dear?"

"I just—" Ten ha stopped and squinted through the dark, to see that, yes, all ten eyes were on her. "I got lost coming back," she said, before collecting the smallish bag and excusing herself.

After she was gone, the Baron rolled over onto his back and said, "Well, that's Ten ha for you: can speak a hundred languages, but can't find her way around a one-horse-town."

"Actually," boomed Pigby, in as close to a whisper as he could manage, "come to think on it, I don't think Adleship Isle has any horses."

"Yeah, well," came Fletcher, "it's not really an Island either, so there's not much ground to go on for name confusion."

And the murmurs of "That's true," and "Good point" helped to lull the lot back to sleep.

XXXVIII – A Fresh Sheet of Snow

On the morning of Raul's birthday, there was a fresh sheet of snow, which was odd because snow hardly ever fell over the Isle. Sometimes it got blown in from the east or west gates leading to snow drifts[91], and these drifts occasionally formed large enough masses of ice to make them stick for quite a while, but *new* snow, especially that which fell over the Isle, was infrequent indeed. I happen to mention it because it happens to be very important that there is a nice new bit of snow over the whole of the town, shed by a happy little cloud that found its way where—strangely—few clouds ever did.

Why was this important? Well, I'll get to that, but for now, consider how lovely and festive this circumstance must have been: featuring a potentially annoyed Raul, a possibly uninvited Julian, a positively giddy Samantha, and two precariously-paired English gentlemen who were breaking their loose zoning ordinance for occasion and novelty, which, for English gentlemen was the only good excuse for breaking formally established protocol.

Julian insisted that the Baron accompany him of course, though the rest of the Baron's lot expressed little to no interest in a child's birthday party, except for Fletcher that is, but when he discovered that there would be no piñata, decided that he should rather spend the day pouting in the loft.

Though this text may not show such as often as it should, the boy called Julian was quite a good intercessor between the often clueless Baron and the positively provincial town. In example, that morning he prevented a potential faux pas by simply asking the Baron, "What's that?" when he saw the gift crooked under the man's arm.

---

[91] Like you saw in chapters IV and XXIV.

When the Baron explained that it was a gift, Julian—bless him—apologized, saying that he did not realize it was the Baron's birthday too. You see, in the Isle, it was common practice for the host of a birthday to give items to the guests and not the other way around. I know that this is largely in theory, but here's how I figure it works: you will concede that in a perfect commune, there is no personal property, yes? But of course, for most persons to function within a routine, they need tools and such which, through repeated use and possession, they will gradually come to think of things as 'theirs.' The people of the Isle naturally had items which simply came to live in their homes, whether or not they needed them. Alright, so how is this problem solved in a slighty-less-than-perfect-(but-still-operating-quite-smoothly-thank-you)   commune?   I should imagine that semi-frequent gift-giving in the manner of one giving to many would help redistribute belongings so as to effect a fair and functioning economy. See, though there are very few records of the Isle, some inventories will indicate that on annual occasions, (which we can only surmise are birthdays), large amounts of things will disappear from the noble houses. I think this is poignant because where the nobles will probably invite many more people, (with more items to gift, that is), the common and less property-holding families will probably throw smaller parties. And so it goes[92].

Now, I've gotten ahead of myself, haven't I? Yes, well, if you flip back a ways, you will see we are talking about Julian's aid to the Baron. We might assume that, had Julian been Fletcher's aid the day before, certain complications could have been avoided.

In any case, when the Baron and Julian approached the party, unaccompanied by gift, it was with confidence. Well, maybe that's not true: I don't know if I could say that Julian was *ever* entirely confident when he knew that he was about to see Samantha. Even so, he did look rather stately and dapper in his finest eveningwear, and stood proudly beside the Baron when they greeted Hephaestus.

Hephaestus and the Baron shook hands, both of which Julian noticed were gloved in white, probably so that they wouldn't have to touch each other. Then Hephaestus turned to Julian and remarked, "What a fine ensemble, my boy. Is it two days ago already?"

---

[92] Pigby would later wonder how often they would have to introduce new items into the inventory as old ones became fatigued and unusable, but more on that later.

Julian, not quite knowing how to read the backhand, looked to the Baron, who, smiling, informed him, "It's snide."

"Ah," Julian acknowledged, then refaced Hephaestus to commend him with a nod. "Thank you, sir, for your 'snide.'"

Julian turned and left the two gentlemen so quickly that Hephaestus could not rightly tell whether the boy's comment was truly ignorant or actually a clever rebut. He took his cue from the Baron's smirk.

Sliding beside the Baron to watch the boy make his way into the party, Hephaestus said, "So, you're grooming him up to be just like you, eh?"

"You know, funny thing," began the Baron, a hand to one cheek in admiration, "it really *is* the things they teach themselves which make you the most proud."

"I weep for the future," observed the other.

"Yes, well, I'm surprised to see you here," said the Baron, reasserting eye contact with the much-taller older merchant.

The reply was skeptical at best. "Oh?"

"Yes, now, I would think that you wouldn't attend birthdays—or, of course, *any* annual markers which might remind you of your proximity to death's doormat." And with a smile, added, "Will I see you at New Year's?"

"Charming, Mister Bordolo. Charming."

"As is the way you forget to use my title, but—" The Baron clicked his tongue. "We must make allowances for the senile."

"If this is your way of hustling me along, I'm afraid it won't work."

"No?"

"No. I'm not staying long anyway—Just come to wish Raul well, and then I've an appointment."

"An appointment?" repeated the Baron. "Dear, dear, I hope it isn't serious."

Hephaestus took a deep breath, but otherwise did not disrupt his firm frame. "If you must know, Mister Bordolo, I will be getting a massage."

"A massage?"

"A massage!" Hephaestus confirmed. "Because, Mister Bordolo, I have a certain standing here, and certain duties on which the people of this town depend."

Surely Hephaestus would have continued his explanation, but as the Baron observed him taking a breath, proceeded to jump in with, "Duties like testing massages?"

"No!" snapped Hephaestus, before our mischievous mustache man could speak again, "duties the likes of which are beyond your ken, and the reason I receive positive treatment from these people is because they understand the things I do for them and show the proper respect."

"I think giving massages is a shade or two above the 'proper respect,' old chap."

Hephaestus turned away once again to look to the events of the party. "Just because you've never received it..." he snarled out the edge of his mouth.

"Not from you, at any rate." The Baron Pan Bordolo—or so he chose to call himself—took a deep breath. "I trust the 'zoning ordinance' is faring practically?"

Hephaestus bit back a comment about how the Baron was currently on the wrong side of the river and settled instead for, "Faring fairly. And how are you keeping that band of scoundrels in check?"

"I'll have you know they are professionals," said the Baron, unwittingly defending the unwitting thin man.

But Hephaestus, somehow deciding that the day's mudslinging should be put to an end, resolved with, "Yes... well. Enjoy the party," before making his way down to the man of the hour, who incidentally was, at that hour, a man.

"Your Highestness!" exclaimed Raul as the older merchant approached, throwing his arms around him as if he were the boy's own grandfather.

"Come, come, you're a man now," replied Hephaestus, hoping that the Baron had been out of earshot for the last, (or if he had been within earshot that the continued to be for what the lord of merchants would say next), "When you address me, you may call me Hephaestus."

"Yes, sir!" affirmed Raul with a nod, unaware of the irony.

You may be wondering at this moment, 'Where is Julian?' Or you may be of the astute sort, have concluded to where Julian must have run off, and be going, 'Oh, that Julian...' Well, before you start your *tsk*ing implications that Julian is nothing more than a starry-eyed (if a little obsessive) romantic, may I remind you that Julian had in fact gone the last three days without meeting his lady at his lady's well. This distressed him.

I should think it had something to do with a foot-in-the-door mentality, as if if the young lad didn't keep his usual date, then someone else should jump in on the territory which he had come to hope to think of as his. It wasn't that he had forgotten his engagements, more that the Baron was of such a distracting nature that Julian found himself saying, "Just a little while longer," and the little whiles compounded to a lot whiles at which point the young lady was no longer at the well.

But today would be different: see, Julian knew that Samantha would not be at the well; she would be at the party for a fine young man's ascension into adulthood, which—lo, and behold!—he would be at as well. And to that end, Julian had left the Baron and the older gentleman with the miffed countenance to scout for his lady, with whom he was determined to actually exchange words.

And there, at one of the tables neatly arranged with fine and not-so-fine finger foods, with her back turned to our young hero, was a girl in a green dress. Julian knew the dress; of course he had not memorized the whole of her wardrobe, (though he was coming close), but it was hard to miss what was probably the only purely green item in the Isle that hadn't faded to a milky seafoam. And Julian knew likewise that it was a dress she saved for only the most occasional of occasions; an eighteenth birthday warranted, as did the Hephaestus High-Feast-us just a few days prior.

Julian approached tentatively, thanking whatever higher power that her back was turned as he did, seeing as it gave him time to work on his opening line. He had immediately dismissed 'Hi' as sounding too childish and informal and then quickly steered away from 'Hello' as he considered 'How do you do?' In any case, it was a good thing his feet were consistently moving forward, or he should have reconsidered his way into more and more outlandish ideas had he not arrived by the young lady's side. Though he was somewhere between, 'Nice weather we're having,' and 'Have you tried that brown sauce?' his finger inadvertently made its way to her shoulder and tapped it twice. Julian very nearly startled at his own action, but managed to calm himself just enough to startle when the subject in the green dress turned around.

"Oh!" exclaimed Julian.

"Why hello, Julian!" reciprocated Sabrina.

Julian checked the dress once more in attempt to match it to the face. "I'm sor—I had thought…" and as he trailed, Julian pointed down to the dress.

"Oh, yes," confirmed Sabrina, offering Julian the courtesy of a once-around, accentuating a slanted posture which was very much not Samantha's, "Do you like it?"

"No!" blurted Julian, then quickly corrected himself with, "I mean, yes, I just—I thought you were your sister."

"Oh. Yes, well, I guess I was just in this sort of mood today. Wanted to try on a change. Tell me," she began again as if it were some sort of relevant segue, "is that lovely Baron of yours here today?"

"Yes, he's here," replied Julian with a nod, pointing his thumb generally behind him. "He's sharing some snide with His Well-Traveledness."

"I think I shall go pay my respects. Good day, Julian."

And as she turned to saunter past him, Julian regained himself enough to order, "Wait!" though with more fervor than he had intended. "Um—where is Samantha?"

Sabrina's mouth opened, then closed again. She took two steps closer to Julian, which made the lad instinctively counter back, and she looked at him—as if properly examining him for the first time—with her eyes slitted in what appeared to our hero to be very smug fascination. After some time of causing Julian discomfort, the older sister calmly stated, "She's in the house, if you must know," then swiftly brushed by him without another word.

As Julian made his way to the door of Eugene's house, he felt somewhat confused by the comments of the older sister and yet somewhat elated at how well he had handled the conversation which could have very-well been with the younger. He decided to mark it as a practice, a trial run in preparation for the real thing. In fact, so loaded was he with confidence and gusto that he did not even jump when the door was thrust open just before he reached it.

Eugene did not immediately see Julian, being most loaded with a large box of gifts for Raul to dispense and partially looking over his shoulder as he finished the conversation he had been having indoors.

Maybe it was the fact that the boy blocked his path, or possibly that our young hero was smiling—a gesture which could only be interpreted as a very inappropriate mockery coinciding with the flouting of the other's wishes—which caused Eugene's reaction. The first thing Julian noticed was that the box was promptly dropped, which—as it featured cracking and splintering sounds—struck heavy on his carpenter's soul for all of the broken items within. The first thing Samantha, who stood not far into the same house, noticed was Julian's yelp, more in surprise than pain as Eugene took hold of his left ear. The first thing the Baron and Hephaestus could see or hear were the unmitigated bellows from the unpleasant noble as he forcibly escorted Julian away from his house, with Samantha and the Libburus trailing after them. Raul looked up in time to witness his father dragging Julian just beyond the edge of the crowd.

"I'll teach you not to come 'round here, boy!" yelled Eugene. "The likes of you stirring up trouble—I say, be gone with you! You're not welcome here!" This last delivered with a final thrust sent Julian stumbling forward, just barely regaining his balance on the slick sheet of fresh snow.

He was confused, somewhat hurt, and shaking more than he would have liked, but as he came to straighten himself, Julian knew by some means that he would have thought beyond his sensibilities, that Eugene—no matter his reasons—was wrong. By what he did next, it became clear to even your humble narrator that Julian must have understood *the right thing to do* more than either the Baron or Hephaestus ever had.

As the other guests, silenced from their other conversations, turned toward this spectacle, some drawing nearer in morbid curiosity, everyone wishing to express something but not a one daring to speak, they all saw Julian lift his head, resume a dignified posture, and after tugging his jacket firmly back into place, bid a respectful nod to Eugene. Everyone else, including the Baron and Hephaestus, took a breath of awe as Julian began to walk steadily up the shallow hill toward the main road.

Though her father stopped some ways behind her, Samantha ran until she'd made contact with Sabrina, and, squeezing her sister's hand, pleaded by expression alone for Sabrina to advise her on what to do. Sabrina, likewise too surprised to speak, had the distinct impression that Samantha considered this disagreeable event to be her fault.

To his own credit, Raul believed that the blame was his, and so stepped forward to call out, "Julian!" and as the boy stopped and turned to look at him, entreated him to, "Come back. Please."

Julian wanted to reach to the Baron for advice, wanted to see Eugene's expression, desperately needed to know whether Samantha had witnessed any of this, but something in his gut told him that he should look Raul in the eye and address him alone. "I'm sorry, Raul," he started, and took a steadying breath. "If your father does not want me, I will not invade his home. Happy birthday, Raul. It shall be a shame to miss it."

And Julian, with the same admirable grace, continued his walk up the hill.

Eugene turned on his son, and Raul on his father, and each covered distance to the other, parting whatever crowd lay between.

"How could you?" asked Raul, which was met with:

"How dare you! To deliberately disobey my wishes—"

"It's my party!"

"It's *my* home!"

"It's *our home!*" insisted Raul, unaware of just how poignant of a statement he made for their whole community.

Feeling that the surrounding witnesses were being made uncomfortable by this heated exchange, Eugene stiffened, conveyed a curt, "We'll discuss this later," and withdrew.

Raul's mouth hung open, but no sound came out. He glanced at the Baron and Hephaestus, neither of whom would make eye contact, and scanned the crowd for an answer to just the what the hell was going on, but it wasn't until he saw Samantha, biting her lips closed that he had any idea of what he would do. Checking once more up the hill to see that Julian was not yet out of sight, Raul took a deep breath, and—speaking loudly enough that the young man a ways away was sure to hear—declared, "After everything that Julian's done, he's more noble in his soul than you will ever be in your blood!"

It seemed that time froze for a moment. In the seconds that followed, the not-yet-out-of-sight Julian and departing Eugene needed to stop walking, Samantha and Sabrina stopped breathing, and every single onlooker stood stock still to try to take in what had just occurred. When they began moving again, Eugene continued to his house, his blood piping hot in his veins; Julian continued up the hill, his cheeks burning red beneath closed eyes; and Samantha could only mouth "Thank you" to Raul when she next caught his breathless gaze.

The Baron, with a taste for the absurd, the charming, and of course the melodramatic, started with a smirk which soon became a broad smile. Hephaestus leaned toward him, and, his eyes still on Raul, muttered, "Why do I have the impression, Sir Baron, that this is all your fault?"

"This?" asked the Baron, tickled to his very core by the sheer number of people that this simple series of comments had displaced, "I had absolutely nothing to do with this."

XXXIX – A Cattle Prod

"And I suppose," began Hephaestus, standing in the doorway of Julian's house, "That you had nothing to do with *this* either." In his right hand, he held a slightly worn and irreparably bent Revolutionary War ramrod.

The Baron, who held the door open, didn't even bother to look over his shoulder to call, "Fletcher!"

Fletcher, who had at the moment of Hephaestus' arrival been playing a very riveting game of cribbage, took to the sound of the older merchant's voice like a zebra takes to a bee in her left nostril and up and bolted from the room.

Funny thing is, in a one-bedroom cottage, an escape artist has very little room to escape. It is true that had Fletcher trained more actively under the magicians of Mali—like he always claimed he had—then he should know how to misdirect an audience into thinking that he was little more than a pile of dirt with a small shrub protruding from its top, but alas, he had made no such advances. Instead, he burst into Julian's room, closing the door behind him and diving quite smoothly under the covers. The smoothness of this action was actually quite impressive, seeing as there were three other parties sitting on the same bed at the time of.

Julian, still giddy and still somewhat red-faced from the day's affairs, was relating to Pigby and the grandfather over and over again what Raul had said and how the whole of the village had reacted[93]. He was in the middle of approximately his third-and-a-half retelling when the thin man who was just barely thin enough, forced his way under

---

[93] Granted it was not the *whole* of the village, but a boy can dream, can't he?

young Julian's knees, saying, "Just do what you were doing; I'm *not here.*"

And Fletcher, bless his innocent whimsy, actually believed for a second that that would be the end of it. The door opened, Jonas announced, "A rat! What, ho!" and Pigby grabbed poor Fletcher by his ankles and wrenched him just as swiftly out of the bed.

"Aha! No, wait," began Fletcher, walking rapidly backward on his palms to keep from landing on his face, "I was asleep. 'Tis bad luck to wake a sleeping minstrel—ask anyone!" he protested, aware that he was being lifted quite easily in the air. "Sir, I demand you set me down; I've an inner-ear condition that—" And as he landed in the next second, quite comfortably on the couch, he could only finish that statement with, "Oh."

Stern expressions came from not only the Baron and Hephaestus, but from Geru and Pigby, whose mirrored postures struck a fair chord of humor on account of their drastically disparate dimensions. Fletcher did not mean to laugh, but in retrospect, decided that he should have tried harder not to.

"And what's that supposed to mean?" glowered Hephaestus.

"Well, you have to laugh," explained Fletcher.

But before Hephaestus could speak again, the Baron said, "Fletcher's my man, Hephaestus; *I'll* handle this." He cleared his throat and resumed with, "And what's *that* supposed to mean?"

"Um..." began Fletcher. "Nothing, boss."

Hephaestus and the Baron looked between one another and the thin man, whose only present signal of guilt was how innocent he wished to appear. To be fair, the Baron did not even know of what Fletcher was accused, but he did not wish to be on the wrong side of Hephaestus if indeed Fletcher had given a weapon to a citizen from the Isle. The Baron Pan Bordolo felt slighted by his own reaction.

By this point, Julian and Jonas had followed Pigby out of the room, and Oswald, to the fault of his ankle, was still seated on the floor when he craned to see around the others to ask, "Sir, what's this about?"

"This!" Hephaestus thrust the ramrod forward at Fletcher, who drew back to give it space.

His brows crooked in annoyance, the thin man observed, "It's bent! Why's it bent?"

"Wrong question, Fletcher," said the Baron.

"No, the *right* question," said Hephaestus, tucking the stately rod under his arm, "Is how this same item found its way into the hands of a citizen of the Isle in the first place."

"What is it?" inquired Julian, leaning forward to better peer at it, which Jonas answered before anyone else could by whistling a military ditty for British regulars. He stiffened to the position of attention, stooped though he was, and saluted without dropping a beat. He then about-faced on his heel and proceeded right back into Julian's room and closed the door.

"It is, as our illustrious Jonas pointed out," began Hephaestus, which perked Oswald's ears given what he'd heard about Hephaestus' regard toward the grandfather, "a British musket's ramrod."

"How do you know it's British?" came Fletcher, but Geru—more concerned with the real issue at hand—had to stand on his toes just to wallop[94] him across the face.

"How could you give munitions to civilians?" the short man demanded.

Fletcher opened his mouth to protest, but in an unlucky instant, forgot every word in the English language, which made him quite— what's-the-word—cross.

It was Pigby who rescued his lexicon by reminding him with a counter-clarification, "No, no, I know this one. It came from our Adam's Fuss, didn't it?" To which Fletcher nodded. "This is the ramrod that I rescued, but lost the gun, which belonged to the backstabber John Huntington!" To which Fletcher more vigorously nodded.

Hephaestus turned to the Baron. "Adam's fuss?"

"Oh, it comes from an acronym. Bastardized from Atiamsfas, actually, which abbreviates items unnecessary to inventory, seeing as it is 'Anything that is a mismatched single from—'"

"Yes, yes, that's very touching," interrupted Hephaestus, physically stepping in front of the Baron not only to cut him off, but to hand the damaged rod to Fletcher. "But that doesn't explain how *this* made it into the hands of Lars."

"Oh, yes, Lars! Lars, nice chap; I like Lars," said Fletcher, "How's he doing now: Lars? You know he's a bit slow on the uptake, but pleasant fellow. Did I mention I like Lars?"

---

[94] Alright, if you must know, it was hardly a slap worth noting at all, but I had to include it for Geru's sake, see?

The Baron placed his hands on his hips. "Fletcher." Fletcher stopped talking. "Did you give this to a man named Lars?"

"Oh, well, there were complications to that."

"And we'd love to hear them," finished the Baron. "Come now, Fletcher, we've all got time. Tell us the tale, unless you're suddenly having difficulty remembering."

Fletcher allowed himself to chuckle. "Remember? Boss, I remember it like it happened yesterday."

"It did happen yesterday!" boomed Hephaestus, "Now, sonny, I want some answers, not some pissed-up runaround." And as the Baron was about to object to this order directed at an employee who did not belong to Hephaestus, the older merchant faced his younger rival and with a stern finger bid him, "Mister Bordolo, I trust you can make your man talk, lest I assume that you had some part in this funny business as well."

The Baron Pan Bordolo could tell by Hephaestus' tone that he already suspected him of having part in the 'funny business' of the day. Though he did not truly know what had happened, or even bothered to gather why the rod was bent, he knew that he had to extract the full story of events from the thin man. What he did know was that he did not appreciate being bullied by Hephaestus in front of his own crew, and even less appreciated that he had so little an idea of his own crew's dealings over the past few days that he *had* to defer to the older man for the details. The Baron looked back at the boy, Julian, who was understandably a lot more confused than he was, and acknowledged that he had been too distracted by this same boy to correct the ramrod problem before it became one.

With a silent promise to be more wary—a promise which he later found good reason not to keep, but more on that later—the Baron tilted his head toward the thin man and very solemnly ordered, "The truth, Fletcher. Now."

"Alright." Fletcher glanced between the Baron and Hephaestus, wondering for a moment how much the both of them already knew and were simply testing his moral fiber. Pointing a finger toward Hephaestus, the thin man asserted, "Now it was, to begin, an accident."

As Hephaestus scoffed at this, Fletcher repeated, "It was. See, yesterday, I was making my rounds, and a man came up to me: this man by the name of Otto." And as Fletcher came to grow into his own story, so began, only naturally, his minstrel's trade. Sensing the change in tone, and knowing how thorough the resident dunderhead could be during storytelling, Geru and Pigby naturally took seats on the floor. Only two lines later, the Baron came to follow suit.

"Now Otto, as you may not know, is one of the three brothers who keep the village pig farm, and he—like many others in the town— came to hear of the one called Fletcher, who wandered about with the most marvelous of artifacts that the inhabitants had ever seen."

"'Most marvelous!'" came Hephaestus, where he was quickly interrupted with a collective *Shush* from Oswald, Geru, and Pigby. Hephaestus settled back against the wall, his arms folded about his chest, muttering a complaint about how Fletcher interchanged *village* and *town*[95].

"Now, Otto started following for curiosity alone, and watched as I spoke to his neighbors and his neighbors' neighbors, offering insight and remedy to all of their domestic complaints. And at some point in my walk, Otto came to notice the rod that I carried before me, gesturing as I went, and Otto—in innocent curiosity—chanced to ask about its purpose, saying," and Fletcher curled his shoulders forward and protruded his lower lip slightly to effect Otto's dialect, saying, "'What is that in your hand, sir?'

"And so I said to him, 'My dear sir,' I said, '*this* is a regulation British infantry ramrod, who got taken off a gentleman who very fell in battle.' And that—yes, I say *that* was my single fault to these people, because, you see, in my zeal to broaden the minds and imagination of the men and women who walked in my wake, I said the most clear and accurate thing I could, but Otto it seems—"

"Yes, but this isn't about Otto!" exclaimed Hephaestus. "It's about Lars! Lars, who you lied to; he said you told him it was a cattle prod."

But Hephaestus was once again greeted by group shushes, this time including the Baron *and* Julian.

"Spoilers!" declared an upset Pigby.

"Honestly, you'd think to at least give fair warning," grumbled Geru.

"So inconsiderate!" concluded Oswald, before saying gently to Fletcher, "Go on, son."

Fletcher shuffled his shoulders back into position and, speaking softly, tossed out the comment, "'*To whom* you lied,' but, whatever." The thin man cleared his throat and resumed. "Otto went on back to his own,

---

[95] Personal bias bids me be on Fletcher's side as well.

which happens to be right next to the cow-herding houses, one of which belongs to our gentleman Lars. Now, I don't know precisely how the conversation went, but Otto must have reported something rather exciting, because—sure enough!—along came a Lars, finding me up at Delia's place and near-ready to pack it in for the night, and he said that he wanted to see about my cattle poker.

"Now, grant that in my station at that time, I had consumed some alcohol, some pastries, and a great many good laughs with the citizens, so when Lars asked me so, I said, 'How's that?' which he followed by pointing to the ramrod. 'Oh no,' I said, 'this is a *ram* rod.'

"'Ram, as in male sheep?' he asked me, which confused me of course, seeing as I did not see the overlap in musketmanship and sheep, and so Lars kindly explained that Otto had told him that I carried a *ramrod* which was taken from the owner who died tending cattle. And that's when I realized my slip before; seeing as the people of the Isle know no violence, they could not possibly know of battle, and so our good man Otto heard the word and his brain translated it to the nearest association, which just so happened to be the animal that lived next-door to him.

"So, as you might imagine, I was left with a choice. Either I could correct Lars and in doing so have to raise the attention to the word which no person in this peaceful little village should know, *or*," he said with such emphasis that it demanded a pregnant pause like the one you're reading right now, "I could go along with the mistranslation and send Lars on his way with no need to ever question the use of the new and foreign tool. I, of course, chose the latter.

"Admittedly, I was nervous. I knew not how well this façade would play, but I followed Lars back to his house and demonstrated—as if I had been doing so my whole life—how to properly prod a cow using a ramrod. And, gents, almost to my own amazement..." Fletcher scanned the faces, making certain that everyone was properly leaning in before resolving with, "it worked.

"To think, all this time, we've been carrying the instrument with which to direct a pack animal, with a poke, or a sharp whack, or—if the beast is feeling particularly stubborn—the very motivational sensation of red-hot iron on its backside. And so after a cup of milk with his sweet twin daughters,"—the Baron made a pointed grunting sound—"who are only eight years old, I waved goodbye and went on my way, sure that

Lars would go on to make use of his cattle prod[96]." Fletcher let his hands rest in his lap, his elbows settling at his sides, and the relaxation signaled the end of his story, but still he made certain to put forth one point: "But I have no idea how this lovely thing got bent. That's beyond me; I swear."

"It got bent," Hephaestus said, "when Lars slipped on the fresh snow this morning[97], landing on the rod, and hurting his hip."

"His *hip* will heal," remarked Fletcher, examining the irreparable bow in the once-straight metal, "but this will never work in a musket again. Leastways not a working musket at any rate."

"It's not about the broken ramrod," insisted Hephaestus, snatching the item away from the thin man. "It's about a lie you told, about an item which you distributed, and lying about items is number two."

This comment did not raise hubbub but rather a general cocking of heads to one side, coupled with an assortment of bewildered and sour expressions.

"Well, I'd like to think of it as creative recycling," offered Fletcher.

"It was a lie, and a bold-faced one at that. And to think that if Lars had not slipped on the fresh snow, then I never should have found out about it," mused Hephaestus, seeming to shudder at his hypothetical scenario. "Well, I'll say it's a good thing he did."

"Actually it isn't."

"Excuse me?" asked a very prickly Hephaestus, spinning to face the Baron who had remained polite all this time.

"It's not a good thing," clarified the Baron, "I'd just as soon have had him not slip and you never need know."

"That's outrageous!"

"No, it's not," said Pigby. "If you never knew, you wouldn't be cross with us, and we wouldn't feel obligated to scold Fletcher after you leave."

---

[96] Though Fletcher later decided that cattle prod was indeed a marketable name for a product, he never managed to invent a prototype that he thought functioned to the degree that a 'cattle prod' should. I am of the opinion that had electricity been harnessed more effectively several decades before, Fletcher may have yet been the inventor of the electric device used by modern farmers and prison guards.

[97] Aha! See, I told you the snow was important.

"Not to mention," chimed Geru, "that had Lars not fallen, he should not have gotten hurt, and he'd still have use of a valuable new tool."

"So inconsiderate—say, what!" puffed up Oswald, trying his hand at being belligerent.

The annoyed and flustered Hephaestus waved away the comments with one hand, and turned directly to the Baron, asking, "Do you know why I found out, Mister Bordolo?" and before the Baron could respond, continued with, "It's because they trust me. Lars approached me with this ramrod and said, 'My cattle prod is broken. Can you fix it?' Well, that's who I am to these people, that's how they look up to me, and I will not betray their trust like you have."

"This isn't about trust," returned the Baron, scrambling to his feet. "This is about your ego, your need for control. And my boy—though he's a little misdirected sometimes—did no wrong and hurt no man."

"He broke a rule," said Hephaestus.

"Just barely."

"Mister Bordolo!"

"What?"

"'Just barely,' Mister Bordolo?" repeated an exasperated Hephaestus. "How can we have rules if they don't apply to everyone?" He proceeded with the rod tucked underarm once again to the board with the rules, and after a moment of squinting, observed, "I appreciate that the first rule has been crossed off. I trust the second will be as well."

When there was no response to this, Hephaestus looked the room over, checking the faces of all of the parties whom he had just scolded, and arrived upon Julian's, which was so calmly steadfast compared to his own that it grated on the old merchant's old nerves. "And I suppose you have something to say about this too then?"

Julian blinked twice. "Nope. I'm just watching and listening, Your Most Cheerfulness."

In solidarity, the Baron and every member of his crew bit his lower lip to keep from laughing. This made Hephaestus bristle even more, but in returning Julian's unmoving gaze, he offered a nod and said, "Thank you for your 'snide,'" before excusing himself out the front door.

XL – His Slippers

The sisters returned home soon after the party, which had quickly collapsed around their heads after Eugene disappeared into the house. Sebastian, quite confused by the series of very negative-sounding comments thrown about during what he assumed *should* be a happy occasion, was eager to retreat along with his daughters, but Cletus—as firm a guide as always—took the Libburus by the shoulders, and marched him right back to Eugene's house so that he could have a few words with the ignoble noble.

Without their father present to fuss over them and the 'trauma' they might have experienced, both Sabrina and Samantha were relieved that much of the evening could be spent simply breathing and recollecting.

Samantha's bedroom was located downstairs, by the back door of the house, and had one window that looked out along the hills to the north until they sloped up too high to see over. Because there was no glass in the window, she kept a thick wooden shutter that she simply wedged into its frame in the winter, but whenever Sabrina slept in her room—which was often—the older sister replaced the stiff wood with a heavy drape that was almost as stiff after so many years of use.

The green dress was hung on the wall, and Sabrina had a very hard time taking her eyes away from it, and so drifted off to sleep long after the sister whose cheek rested gently against her shoulder.

Even farther downstairs, Clara, who had withdrawn with the sisters, drew herself a bath which she regarded with one hand before getting in, and once she had, she sat for quite a time. Though there were arrangements of soap and oils, many of which she had used before and quite enjoyed, she did not touch a one of them and so just sat. When her servant's nerves were pricked, she invited a stained slip to join her in the tub, which she scrubbed, then set to dry, then scrubbed again, then set to dry again.

Cletus, somewhat exhausted upon arriving at home himself, found the poor woman on her fifth attempt at cleaning the garment, and helped escort her from the duty, into a heavy robe and into her bed.

Returning to the room of the Libburus, Cletus let himself sigh, which was not commonplace in Sebastian's presence. As he was being helped out of his slippers, Sebastian wondered aloud, "Do you think the boy's alright?"

"He just went out for a walk, sir." Cletus reassured him. "He'll be back."

"Yes, but—" began Sebastian before being interrupted by Cletus' soothing *Shhhh.*

Cletus patted Sebastian on the shoulder, offering a friendly smile which Sebastian accepted with a nod. And as soon as the Libburus had donned his night-shirt, Cletus helped tuck him into bed while his Algernon hummed an intro, which Ferdinand followed with words.

> "The sun's last rays are fleeting
> And daylight is receding
> And the cold night air is rolling in to stay;
> There's still a sight can warm you up
> Even the night can charm you up
> 'Cause nighttime's when the stars come out to play
>
> So lie beneath the starlight
> Whose blanket wraps you up so tight
> And count the blinking twinkling winking eyes
> They'll dance for you forever, dear
> And come to shine year after year
> And even in the saddest nights, you'll come to realize
>
> A star is a star
> So far is so far
> But its light will find you wherever you are"

Whispering "Goodnight" to his Libburus, Cletus gently closed the door behind him and took to his own room. He took off his shoes, set them neatly against the wall, and sat on the edge of his bed to stare at them for several minutes before lying down to sleep.

Hephaestus was certain that no one else was awake by the time he latched the door behind him. Sebastian never stirred, and Cletus didn't say a word, and the daughters never emerged from the younger's room[98]. And in their cramped sardine quarters, he assumed his seven sturdy

---

[98] Hephaestus, like most of the people in the town, forgot about Clara in his mental count.

servants were snoozing. It was only in a passing glance out of his window that he saw a dark figure approaching the house. It was on the second closer glance that he observed the fact that he did not recognize the face of the man who wore one of his uniforms. Hephaestus flared his right nostril, but said nothing. Dowsing the lamp, he resolved to have Trenton speak with Lance.

To credit the Baron's jibes, it was probably the older's age that made him forget this resolution.

XLI – The Sturdy Wooden Wall

When the first thud was heard, the Baron thought nothing of it. In fact, why should he? Strange sounds, especially in an area with a lot of hands and feet performing a lot of tasks were no cause for alarm.

He chose to look about in wonder when he heard the second, seeing as it was accompanied by a grunt, but because he did not see anything worth noting, chose to shrug off any curiosities, and resume listening to Clemens describe the details of meat-packing in the storehouse.

Of course, as it goes in so many fairy tales, the third thud came with such a strong exclamation of pain that it not only startled the Baron Pan Bordolo but bid him ask, "Now what was that?"

Clemens, trying not to show disappointment that his charge for the day happened to be the Baron, and not his new dark giant, looked up from his little scratch-pad and said, "Oh, it's probably a duel—"

"A what?" exclaimed the Baron, before Clemens could clarify.

Clemens blinked twice. "A duel. Gerard and Heller've been arguing; I guess they just decided to have it done with."

The Baron gasped, then hiccupped—because what else could he do? This prompted Clemens to ask, "Are you alright, sir?"

The simple answer was 'No, very much not—in fact, I'm curious as to whether I should panic or simply decide it's an elaborate dream and just let the fantasy ride itself out.' Instead, the Baron leapt to attention—which looked quite amusing, seeing as he was already standing—and announced, "I must see this!"

The Baron did not know what he expected; point of fact, he had never even dreamed that in so safe and simple a village as Adleship Isle that duels existed, but in the few seconds from leaving Clemens' side to running out the door of the storehouse, nothing could have prepared him for what he saw.

The Baron put a hand to his forehead. "Well, blow me down!"

Clemens, not quite sure what prompted the Mustache Man's peculiar demeanor, must have thought that he meant to interrupt the exchange between the conflicting parties, because he hustled out not a moment after to take hold of the Baron Pan Bordolo's arm to keep him from venturing any closer to the two men who were taking turns banging their heads against the outside of the storehouse.

The Baron checked his sleeve to see that it was clean and then rubbed it against his eyes, but when he opened them again he could not deny the vision of the man called Heller, who summoned up a mighty breath before slamming his forehead hard enough against the sturdy wooden wall to knock him cleanly out.

"Clemens," he gasped, "what am I looking at?"

Clemens shuffled his mustache curiously against his lower lip. "Don't you have duels where you come from?"

"Not as such..." trailed a breathless Baron, the synapses of his brain firing incredulously.

"Then how do you tell who's won the argument?"

"Umm." The Baron shook his head, swallowed, and with the hint of a marveling smile, replied, "Slightly differently." The Baron watched as the other man, Gerard helped scoop Heller off of the ground and into a stable sitting position.

"Tell me, Clemens," began the Baron, half-fearful of what the answer might be, "do the men and women here, when challenged to duels, actually bang their skulls on walls to settle disputes?"

"Well, not the women so much," said Clemens, and followed this simple admission with a phrase that would make the Baron infinitely happy: "But, yes."

The Baron, with his supremely curled stache and an unmistakable twinkle in his eyes turned to face Clemens and asked him, "How do I challenge a man to a duel?"

XLII – The First Stone

"I'm sorry, but I still don't understand," said Julian. "Explain it to me again."

Geru and Pigby looked to one another, as if trying to decide silently whose turn it should be to answer. Unfortunately, the short man and giant man had not yet invented rock-paper-scissors. The bigger problem was that the surest reason for why Julian did not yet understand is that Geru and Pigby did not know the reason for the Baron's sudden changing of the guards.

Geru, for his part, figured that the Baron just did it to separate Pigby and Clemens for the day, worried that maybe Pigby's alien influences were corrupting the otherwise provincial townsfolk. Pigby had never managed to draw much from the situation other than the fact that the Baron had stumbled upon all six men dressing behind Julian's house that morning and given the order that Geru and Pigby tend to Julian then and there.

"Perhaps he wanted us to help you with your trade," offered Pigby, following just a few steps behind the boy as they came to the footbridge at the north end of the river.

"No," insisted Julian, toeing the rock for stability. "No, he knows I don't have any work today."

"Well, then it's probably for us," suggested Geru. "I'm sure the Baron Pan Bordolo just wanted Pigby and I to spend some time with you, boy."

"'Pigby and *me*,'" muttered Pigby as he made his way onto the first of the rocks, half-hoping that Geru didn't catch the correction.

"Maybe." Julian hopped from the last of the smooth stones onto the bank of the noble side of the river, and turned around to see how the others were faring. He surely would have laughed at the sight of Pigby trying to balance on a stepping-stone bridge that was quite a bit narrower than him, had he not been so seriously contemplative at that moment. "Do you think he's ashamed of me?"

"What?" came Geru and Pigby both in unison and with such startle that it nearly knocked Pigby into the water. "No!" exclaimed Geru, which was mirrored by Pigby the moment he regained balance.

"Why would you think that, son?" asked Pigby.

And before Julian could answer, Geru supplied the very accurate observation that "The Baron's far more likely to be ashamed of Pigby and I."

"'And *me!*'" corrected Pigby a second time, which Geru must have missed, as he followed it with:

"I just said that."

"Really?" asked Julian, offering Pigby a hand for the last bound, "I'd thought maybe it was because of what I said to his old friend."

"Old friend?" replied Pigby, deciding to not take Julian's offer, seeing as the giant man's weight would probably put the boy in the river. "By that do you mean Hephaestus?"

"And by *friend*," spat Geru, surveying the stones before taking his first leap, "do you mean spineless sea-rat?"

Pigby tried to give a warning eye to Geru, but the short man did not look up as he jumped from stone to stone. Julian chewed at the side of one lip and asked, "Why does the Baron not like Hephaestus?"

"A better question," squeaked Geru, as he landed on the bank with a soft squelch, "is why His Open-Mindedness is so sore 'gainst the Baron. Fact of matter: he fired the first shot!"

"And let he who is without sin cast the first stone," admonished Pigby. Julian didn't have the slightest idea of what any of that meant. "Look, lad, let me explain," explained Pigby. Geru folded his arms across his small chest, and cocked his head to one side to demonstrate his confidence in Pigby's explanation. The giant man swallowed, then began with, "See, the Baron Pan Bordolo and Hephaestus are both very big men. Not like me;" he amended, seeing Julian's eyebrows jump, "they take up a lot of space in people's thoughts and their conversations, and they don't feel well in smaller places."

"Oh, I wouldn't be so sure," interrupted Julian. "His Grandestness has been coming here forever, and the way you say, this is the smallest space in the world."

"That's true," admitted Pigby, trying not to make eye contact with Geru, lest the short man confirm that he was indeed backpedaling, "but they don't know how to share such a small space with someone else as big as they are."

Julian nodded but felt he didn't understand "And that's why the Baron went with Clemens?"

"The Baron went with Clemens," said Geru, "probably because he didn't want Pigby or I to get in any more trouble."

"It's 'Pigby and *me*!'" insisted Pigby with enough volume and fervor to make Julian jump.

"'Pigby and I' is correct!" squeaked Geru.

"As a *subject*, but not in the *objective* case!" Pigby shouted back.

This continued for some time, which could be interesting to some of you—and to those persons in my audience, I apologize—but at that moment, Julian, (the one that this story really follows) had lost track of the conversation entirely. This was not because it didn't make sense to him, (though it actually didn't), but because, once over this footbridge, he was a small field and a wide hill away from the well where he might ordinarily meet his lady. Turning away from the other two men, who shouted over one another, the boy faced the hill and let his imagination take him over top of it, to where Samantha must have stood—Samantha, who may have been terrified at what a terrible thing Julian had done yesterday, or who might applaud his stature and grace. If only he could speak to her...

"Julian?" asked Geru, and the boy turned around, trying not to show that he felt guilty for where his mind had gone, though he did not rightly know why.

Both Pigby and Geru, though appropriately occupied on one another, were suddenly surveying him with concern, so Julian did what any seventeen-year-old boy might do. "Oh, it's nothing," he said, shaking his head rapidly and thereby ridding of his inability to focus. "What was it you wanted to see, Mister Geru?"

"The waterfall!" Geru pointed and began toward the lower falls, and Julian was relieved to think that the focus had been successfully averted from his brief fantasy.

"Haven't you already seen it?" asked Pigby, following after him, and leaving Julian to take the rear.

"Not from this side, no," answered Geru, "which is a shame because you can get much closer on this side of the river than the other. See, I noticed that the pool down here wasn't as large as the one above, and it seems like more water is coming from the falls than ever makes it in the river."

"How do you figure?" asked Pigby.

"Just eyeballed it," explained Geru, "which could mean that it's a question of depth and simple distortions of perspective. However," he said, reaching the rock wall and crouching at the edge of the river to peer into the falls, "it is also possible that some of the water is running underground."

Geru ran his hands along the ground, along the stones at the base of the wall, as if it were some secret form of brail that only he could translate. Upon finding a small, loose rock, he wound it back behind him and hurled the payload through the water where it disappeared. Were it not for the roaring water, he was certain he would have heard a clink on an inner wall behind the falls.

"There was one more reason I came back here," he informed them, straightening and brushing off his hands. "I had to see it to be sure, but gents, look up there."

Where Geru indicated, some five or six feet above their heads (and three above Pigby's) at a slight gap between the near edge of the waterfall and the rock wall, billowed a small, streaming wisp of a cloud. "That's not mist, my friends," said Geru, "that's steam."

"Steam?" wondered Pigby, "But that water's too cold. It's pure glacial."

"You know," came Julian, "Elke gets really cold cream to steam just by pouring it over top of hot berries." And without knowing just how pertinent that relation was, our hero unwittingly imparted an even more crucial piece of knowledge. "She makes it every year for Christmas."

Geru and Pigby both scrunched their noses.

"Christmas?" inquired Pigby.

"You have Christmas here?" chimed Geru.

Julian also scrunched. "What do you mean 'have Christmas?' It's the twenty-fifth of December; doesn't everyone have that?"

"Well, of course," returned the other two, worried that any further hint might tip the boy about something which he would much rather not be tipped.

"That's good," resolved Julian. "I mean, it would seem pretty silly to have a twenty-sixth of December if you didn't have a twenty-fifth."

And as a thought occurred to Pigby, he asked the young man, "Julian, what day is it today?"

"Why the twenty-fourth," replied Julian. "It's Christmas Eve."

XLIII – His Skull

Hephaestus had decided that morning that he was going to have a good day. He hated being proven wrong.

The lord of merchants had let himself sleep for much longer than he would have on a normal day, but today—god bless Christmas Eve—he stayed against his pillow until he could look at the events of the past day as nothing more than a dream. And when he made his way downstairs, both Trenton and Cletus greeted him with respect and decency and the kind of calm that could only come on as bright a morning as this. He put on a long coat which he often rejected as more suitable for a younger fellow, possibly of the scouting or seafaring sort, but on that morning—with the cuffs creased smartly up along his forearms, the old lord of merchants felt it looked quite fitting on him.

When he took his first breath of the crisp outdoor air, he felt compelled to close his eyes, so that his nose could better bask in the glory around him. Some traces of yesterday's snow were still about, but their runoff that melted into the river gave the whole of the village a cool, fresh sort of smell which, in those days, could only happen in the most rural of locations. Hephaestus did not think much of taking his cane with him, or of wearing weathered traveling boots for that matter. These things, as they say, just sort of happened.

There are some other things which don't just happen though; there are some things which—whether or not you know for whom the blame is dealt—can only be the product of design. And Hephaestus happened upon one of these things at just about ten in the morning, on December the twenty-fourth, in the year of our lord that the Baron Pan Bordolo made it to Adleship Isle.

Hephaestus, unaccompanied by Trenton or Sebastian, decided first that he should go take a look at the view of the town from the bell-tower near the bridge, but reconcluded that he should rather go north and up the hill on his side of the falls to see even farther. However, both destinations were turned by a curious sensation which scientists still do not entirely understand[99]: Hephaestus craved a bagel.

Now he knew, having been in the town every winter for as long as anyone could remember, that the best bagels in the town were made by Elke, but he didn't go to Elke's. No, Hephaestus also knew that Elke would not be making a new batch of bagels until a whole two days after Christmas, and that this was a time for holiday treats, particularly sweetbreads and little meat-pies very similar to piroshkies. Elke's last bread of a hardy nature would be in the food storehouse to the south of the Libburus', and that's where he went.

Now, when he saw the crowd, he sensed excitement, anticipation, and even wonder for what they must have been watching. Hephaestus, far from being the least bit affronted that the spotlight was stolen from him, was suddenly swept into vicarious exhilaration by the other onlookers. As he approached the crowd, they easily parted for him, and when he heard a heavy knock on the wall, followed by an audible reaction from the closest row, a little smile in his eyes marked his suspicions. The smile disappeared the moment he recognized the Baron Pan Bordolo, stepping away from the wall. Of course, the Baron's back was to him, and Hephaestus could not see his face, but he couldn't see how or why anyone else in the Isle would be wearing what looked to be a French diplomat's uniform, royal blue with paisley embroidering, complete with honor-cords and a decorative scabbard. The Baron shook his head, undoubtedly shaking away any residual anguish from its impact upon the wall, and offered the same wall to his opponent, who looked far worse for the wear than he.

This stranger whom Hephaestus did not recognize had a red and somewhat scuffed forehead and, when given turn to hit the wall, held up his hands in protest, saying, "No more, sir. You win."

"Oh, it's alright, chap," he heard the Baron say. "Here, let me shake your hand." And as he watched the two men shakes hands

---

[99] Records indicate that Geru may have had some theories. Unfortunately, records about which the records were written were lost, leaving us only the reference and not the context.

politely—friendlily[100] even—Hephaestus was near-ready to commend the Baron for demonstrating such gracious winnership.

It was when the Baron turned around and faced the crowd, arms raised, to declare, "Does anyone *else* want to challenge me?" that Hephaestus began to suspect tomfoolery[101]. It was not the comment itself, or even how the townsfolk seemed to titter in admiration that set Hephaestus off; it was the Baron's smile, which on its own could have been quite pleasant, but accompanied by the twinkling eyes had just enough of a touch of insanity to keep even Hephaestus from speaking.

When another man, Klaus[102] approached, the Baron stepped out of his way and said, "Give it your best, man."

Hephaestus would later tell Trenton that he did not immediately intervene out of horror—complete revulsion for what was happening before him. Even Trenton knew that was a lie. Hephaestus, knowing the rules, and having seen many 'duels,' leaned toward a young boy consumed by the spectacle and touched his shoulder. "Oy, boy!"

The boy exclaimed, "Mister Your Fantasticness!"

But Hephaestus quickly shushed him with a whisper, asking, "What have they wagered for?"

"Nothing," said the boy.

"Then why are they dueling?"

The boy pointed at the Mustache Man, who lined up for yet another hit. "All they wager is if they can beat him. He stakes his champion title against their challenge."

"How long has this been going on?" asked an appalled Hephaestus.

"Since Clemens," said another boy, slightly older and with teeth that looked less attended to, moving in toward Hephaestus. "The Mustache Man told Clemens he could beat him, even after his first duel of the day, and since then, people've just been lining up."

Hephaestus, having some trouble putting the scenario together anyway, had to literally scratch his head as he asked, "Wait, wait, the Baron beat Clemens?"

---

[100] Which, by the by, is one of the silliest-sounding functional words in the English language.

[101] Just for the record, Mister Thomas J. Foolery, who lived just down the street from me and used to carve model ships is one of the most respectable gentlemen I know.

[102] Yes, the one with the cocoa.

As Hephaestus raised his head above the crowd, he heard the younger boy reply, "He's beaten everyone." And there, mouth already agape as he saw the Baron Pan Bordolo wind up to collide with more resonance than Klaus had, Hephaestus noticed the tiniest flash of the Baron's hand beside his head. It was the smallest note of prestidigitation, but to anyone who had studied jugglers, dealers, or magicians—which he had—it was immediately apparent that the Baron didn't hit his forehead with any kind of force against the wall and instead made all of the noise with his well-timed palm.

"Did anyone else—?" Hephaestus began, then closed his mouth again as Klaus, somewhat woozy from his last hit readied himself to follow the Baron. Hephaestus wanted to shout 'Wait!' like some melodramatic intruder come to object to a perfectly reasonable marriage between two very unreasonable people in so many modern romantic comedies. Instead he himself waited and watched as Klaus took another hit, fairly, with all of the impact on his own head.

But even then, Hephaestus couldn't speak; he had to see it a second time to know for certain. The Baron Pan Bordolo planted two feet squarely in the dirt before the wall, reeled back, and—placing his own hand between his chest and the storehouse—slapped the wood for all it was worth, his long, wavy hair helping to mask the daylight that glimpsed between his face and the wall.

The Baron staggered slightly, and the crowd held its breath. Even Hephaestus—who counted himself more observant than the others—leaned forward to see whether this grand gentleman in blue might indeed collapse. But after a moment's pause, the Baron lifted his head and spread his arms to indicate, amidst the applause, that he had not yet been defeated. In fact, he was grinning as he took a bow.

Hephaestus *humph*ed, partially in condescension, but partially in amusement at the Baron's showmanship. As the people whispered excitedly between themselves, and Klaus debated on whether or not he wanted to take another rattle to his skull, Hephaestus swallowed his intrigue and stepped forward.

Klaus looked relieved, immediately the chatter stopped, and the Baron smiled up at his adversary. "Good morning, Hephaestus!"

"I suppose you think you're all sorts of clever, don't you?" the old merchant said softly to the Baron before clapping a reassuring hand on Klaus' shoulder. "That's enough for now, man."

"Oh, thank you, sir," nodded Klaus, then—retaining some traces of his pride—stepped back into the crowd before he began to feel dizzy.

"I believe I was in the middle of a gentlemen's engagement," protested the Baron, doing his best to sound good natured.

Hephaestus scoffed at the term *gentle* but did his best to pay no attention to the Baron as he addressed the crowd. "My friends," he began, "though I hate to interrupt the festivities, it seems our guest the Baron Pan Bordolo has forgotten himself."

"How's that?" asked the Baron, in a tone that mirrored the expression of just about every observer.

Hephaestus clicked his tongue against the roof of his mouth a few times. To anyone not a citizen of the Isle, it would seem clear that Hephaestus was stalling for time. "Yes, barons from the Big Out There don't like to duel on Christmas Eve!"

"It's Christmas Eve?" asked the Baron, and a few dozen townsfolk collectively went:

"*O*-oh."

"And you see, the Baron has simply lost track of the days, because he has been traveling away from his home."

"I didn't know they had Christmas Eve here," admitted the Baron.

Hephaestus tapped his cane against the ground, trying to call attention back to himself. "Yes, so, now that that's sorted, I think you should all be on your ways, alright?"

This was an odd suggestion to receive, but ordinarily, when Hephaestus offered a course of action, the people in the Isle simply accepted it as something that was probably a very agreeable thing to do. They slowly, uneasily began to back away, though not a one of them wanted to. The Baron must have agreed with that sentiment, because as they were looking to part, he stepped forward and said, "If you don't mind, I do have a winner's streak to attend to," which paused their retreat once again.

Hephaestus didn't have any idea of how many duels the Baron had won, but he was certain that it was more than anyone else had in one go. He was also certain that the Baron must have cheated for every victory. "Really, Mister Bordolo," whispered Hephaestus, "I think we'd better stop now and not make this any more of a spectacle than it already is."

"Stop?" exclaimed the Baron, without paying the slightest heed to mute his tone, "Hephaestus, have you any idea what I've just discovered?"

"Discovered?" repeated the other, "You're not interested in discovery. You're just conning them—"

"I'm not taking anything from them!" the Baron protested, and even though Hephaestus was not likely to trust his intentions, he felt that his rival wasn't lying about this. "I just wanted to see how long it would go; now where's the harm in that?"

"The *harm*?!? You have been cheating these people!" announced Hephaestus, speaking deliberately over the Baron, but realizing as he did that the slowly retreating townsfolk had not in fact finished retreating. Hephaestus and the Baron Pan Bordolo halted their argument to slowly survey the townsfolk, the bulk of which seemed—thankfully—far more confused than hurt.

"Ahem," *ahem*ed Hephaestus.

"Yes, well," agreed the Baron. "Should we—"

"No, no, we can do it here," said Hephaestus, "just tactfully."

"Right." The Baron nodded. "Latin or Greek then?"

"Latin," Hephaestus responded, and in a moment of madness informed the Baron of why: "I don't speak Greek."

The Baron would have been quite alright with Latin—in fact, he would have even agreed to French if necessary—but found the comment so surprising that it bid him demand, "What? You mean you don't, or you can't?" As he searched for what the older man must have been hiding, the Baron seem to forget about the crowd which was still intently watching the exchange.

"Leave it be, Baron," Hephaestus shot back.

"You can't, can you?" he exclaimed, and as Hephaestus furtively and frantically glanced about to see who had heard this damning accusation, the Baron's delight increased. He did not know on whose account Hephaestus was embarrassed—other than his own, that is; the Adleship Isleans around them, none of which the Baron knew, had any idea of what they spoke, and not a man (or woman) from either merchant's crew happened to be in spitting range. "Raised in the eighteenth century and never taught Greek! My God, man, how can you possibly call yourself Hephaestus if you don't even speak his language?"

"Be quiet!" hissed Hephaestus, "That's enough of you—"

"Or what? You'll *scold* me again, will you?" The Baron puffed up his chest to look intimidating, but sadly it did not make him any taller.

Hephaestus' right hand squeezed around the handle of his cane until his knuckles went about as pale as the remaining snow drifts. He leaned toward the Baron Pan Bordolo's face just enough to seem intrusive and began with, "Now listen, *sonny*, I—"

"Are you going to duel him, Your Grandestness?"

This comment came from somewhere in the crowd, and happened so abruptly that Hephaestus completely forgot about the threat he was going to make. Even as the lord of merchants demanded, "Who said that?" the instigator did not show himself. Instead the crowd collectively began clapping. We don't know why exactly; perhaps it was to encourage Hephaestus, or just a delayed reaction commending the character who had asked so convenient a question.

"Now just a moment," he protested, but no one seemed to want to hear the protest and so kept right on clapping.

The Baron, who prided himself in his ability to play ringleader to most any circus he stumbled across announced to the applauding viewers, "I don't think he thinks he can beat me!"

"Now, see here—" began the other again, but an enthusiastic young man in the crowd, leaping to see over the heads in front of him called:

"You can do it, Your Marvelousness!"

And as the clapping grew into cheering, Hephaestus moved close enough to the Baron's ear to entreat him, "That's enough, now stop this."

"It's not on me to stop anymore."

Hephaestus tried again, desperately almost, and though it humbled him to do so, truthfully pleaded, "Mister Bordolo, you have completely misconstrued what these duels mean!"

"Then I suppose it's on you to teach me," said the other, smiling.

"I'm sure," came Hephaestus, raising his head to see the excitedly smiling audience, "that the Baron does not want to duel me on Christmas Eve."

But our dear Baron Pan Bordolo was prepared for this and countered with, "I'm sure the Baron can make an exception for the Lord of Merchants!" to which the cheers became a roar.

Hephaestus was about to protest again, but when he saw how smug his adversary appeared, felt that he had a duty to pick up the proverbial gauntlet. Trenton would later accuse his master of confusing duty with pride. "Very well," said Hephaestus and began to roll up his sleeves. To the Baron he said, "You know, I know what you've been doing, and two can play at that game, Mister Bordolo."

"Oh, well, then you step up and demonstrate," offered the Baron.

"Gladly." Hephaestus planted his feet before the wall and raised a finger to the crowd behind him, declaring, "Know this: this Mustache Man is not so impervious as he'd like you to think he is!" And Hephaestus threw the first hit, moving a palm between himself and the wall just as the Baron had. However, unlike the Baron, Hephaestus did not time the hit of his palm for the moment just before his head would have made contact and instead matched it simultaneously with the impressive *puhk* of his own forehead.

"Bloody hell!" grumbled Hephaestus, stumbling backward, accompanied by a hand to the head and the sound of the Baron laughing.

"Well done!" he said, chortling giddily to himself. "Don't worry on it, old man; you'll catch on eventually."

The Baron readied himself before the wall, aware of the buzz of anticipation around him. He took a deep breath, and prepared his strike, picturing how silly Hephaestus must have looked standing behind him holding his head. The Baron wound up, determined to make this collision look more daunting than any before, but just as he was about to pitch forward, he felt a swift impact upon his right arm, which bid him clutch and turn about, saying, "Ow!"

But as the Baron came to face the older merchant, he saw the most infuriated expression below the raised cane just before it came crashing down on his head.

"Ow!" repeated the Baron, but must not have made his point, as Hephaestus came to strike him again.

The Baron gasped and barely stepped out of the way of this swing. As another was readied, the Baron instinctually tugged at the scabbard on his belt, but so securely tied was the long sheath that all that came out was the sword. The song which emanated from the Baron's draw was echoed in an instant by Hephaestus, who let drop the rest of his cane to engage his foe. And for the first time in the history of the Isle, steel met steel.

XLIV – The Rapier

If anyone were to ask it—which of course no one did—the rapier would say that it was invented to sing. Being somewhat insecure of its body, as are all things of an elegant nature, it would not be the first to mention dance as a talent, though it was quite adept at that as well. In both cases, it is quite a lovely and fluid instrument, meant to flit about the air and resonate the subtlest and eeriest of pitches in perfect unison with its movement, and this very nature is betrayed by how it is actually used. Not that it is inherently against violence—(the rapier would concede that it has its time and place, like everything unpleasant)—moreover that whenever it is shoved into a soft bag of flesh, both the movement and accompanying hum are cut short and replaced by an immobile squelch. (Additionally, I should note that rapiers as a group *hate* blood, which rather boorishly stains everything it touches.)

So how, you might ask, did a thing designed with such unbearable precision and grace ever get reduced to so unrefined an end goal as to be stuffed in a sound-dampening ribcage? *I* would venture, though I am by no means an authority on this subject, that pride was the bastard catalyst that started the whole affair. Let me explain: for as long as there has been culture in Western Europe, there has been a rivalry between the French and the Italians who both claim, in retrospect, that they are responsible for inventing every bit of it. I should imagine that at one point—coincidentally and by no fault of their own—both a Frenchman and an Italian perfected the marvelous singing wand separately, and that, when each learned that the other was trying to steal the credit, assaulted one another, each man using the blade itself to prove by his talent that it was *his* discovery.

Well, as you might assume, once one or both of the men were killed, the cost soon compiled with revenges—much in the fashion of

Tybalt slew Mercutio, so Romeo slew Tybalt, so Paris tried to slew Romeo, Juliet missed and accidentally slew herself, which ended with a whole slew of bodies and everyone in the audience (including me) crying. And we don't want that, or else the pages in your hands might get soggy and become difficult to read[103].

Now, we can take some consolation in the fact that not *all* duels end in violent bloody death. There may be those of you who have already decided such extreme dislike of either the Baron or Hephaestus to wish that this duel may yet be final. However, I offer two simple observations which should change your mind: one, I can almost guarantee that both men have a sure shot at redemption by the end of the text; and two, that you will notice that you are not yet at the end of the book, and so would guarantee yourself a much less entertaining read if you were to eliminate the main conflict so far from the close.

As for the Baron and Hephaestus, I cannot say for certain whether either man was actually trying to eliminate the other. Both were very ardently bent on *winning*, but as to whether victory could only be achieved by running the opponent through, no one—not even the dueling parties—knew.

I want you to do me a favor—can you do that? I want you to picture yourself not as one of the men thrusting and parrying about in the little dusty space they had cleared for their endeavors, but rather as an observer, as a citizen of Adleship Isle. Imagine, if you can, that you have never seen an act of intentional violence. Maybe you've seen a friend playfully shove someone into the river on a warm summer evening, or perhaps your mother once swiftly tapped the back of your hand as you reached for another cookie before having finished your all of your beans. But say you weren't raised on the classics of John Wayne, in which men settle conflict by shooting at one another until at least one of them is dead. How would you interpret what you now saw?

I think a lot of people would like to criticize or even dismiss my account right here by saying that violence is innate in humans, but I hold—especially since I know the events I relate to be true—that physical confrontation with the intention of pain or death is a learned behavior. So what might you think when you see the Baron Pan Bordolo making a jab toward Hephaestus' gut, or Hephaestus attempting to swing his blade into the Baron's shoulder? Now, granted you might step back, either of your

---

[103] Before those of you reading from personal devices scoff at this, may I remind you that water is not good for electronics either.

own initiative because you were scared of the swinging metal, or because the persons in front of or beside you did. Let's just say you would *know* that you are uncomfortable with this spectacle, but you wouldn't know why.

And then, in the middle of all the sweating and grunting and contesting for the better opening, how would you react to a thin man racing through the crowd, taking off his jacket amidst rapid-fire orders to excuse him, and bursting between the warring gentlemen before you?

Fletcher did not hesitate to time out his assault. He swung his jacket at the swords as he ran between them, parting the path protected by his fast-flinging weathered leather, and emerged on the other side holding the handle of the Baron's sword. Dropping the jacket, he slid the Baron's blade alongside Hephaestus' and, in turning the handle like an old brass doorknob, twisted the older merchant's sword out of his hand and onto the ground.

The Baron must have realized that he didn't have a sword in hand before Hephaestus did, because the instant after Fletcher disarmed him, he made to leap at his foe once more and was stopped only by Pigby's forearms, which had conveniently clasped around his chest. "Sir!" exclaimed the booming voice, "Have you lost your mind?"

"Give me my sword back, boy!" shouted Hephaestus, to which Fletcher, standing on the hilt, shook his head. Hephaestus took the one menacing step to close the distance between himself and the thin man, and was stopped from doing anything further when he heard a familiar voice call out:

"Hephaestus!" Just making his way through the crowd, the much shorter Trenton planted himself before them and folded his arms about his own chest. Sternly. Apparently this gesture was as powerful as Pigby's had been to the Baron.

Though he could not move, the lord of merchants had every right to glare, and glare he did at the Baron Pan Bordolo. "This is your fault!" he shouted.

"Oh? And who drew first?" retorted the Baron from behind Pigby's arms, and Pigby countered with:

"You should be ashamed, boss!"

"My dear Pigby, it was all in good fun," explained the Baron, but at that moment, he caught the eye of another man who had found his way to the edge of the onlookers. Clemens, probably the largest man in their audience, wore an expression like a child who had just lost his favorite teddy bear.

"Alright, everyone," began Trenton, waving the crowd away, "we're done here. The Baron and Hephaestus are going to go settle this in private."

"What were they doing?" someone asked, and Trenton, because he knew he could not answer turned to Hephaestus.

Hephaestus cleared his throat, straightened his coat, and took one pace forward. "This is how *we* duel."

An apprehensive silence hung in the air for a moment. The citizens of the Isle did not quite know what they had witnessed; both the Baron and Hephaestus were reeling from the sudden and unexpected intervention they'd experienced; and Trenton, Pigby, and Fletcher were trying to figure out what kind of damage control was in order.

The silence was broken by a panting short man, who was shoving bystanders out of his way and saying, "Confound it, Pigby!" as he went. "So inconsiderate! You—" and another moment to breathe, before "You would think you'd accommodate a gentleman whose legs are not so long as yours—a little courtesy, perhaps?"

And as burst through the front row of spectators, Geru observed Pigby behind the Baron, Fletcher holding one sword and standing on another whose tip indicated Hephaestus, and a mediating Trenton who appeared less stoic and assured than he usually did. Geru contorted his face to the point of pain, then just as suddenly released, throwing his arms in the air and exclaiming, "Dagnabbit, Pigby! You see? Now I've gone and missed the whole thing!"

XLV – The Chair at the Head of the Table

He had of course snuck out of his father's house before. Indeed, what growing boy hasn't when his chums want to go for a swim or a climb after the parent-proposed bedtime hour? As a result, Raul had learned how to sneak back into his house in the wee hours of the morning as well, without alerting his father or sisters who slept in the adjacent rooms.

On this particular morning, however, Raul made no effort to be silent or to arrive before his father woke up. This time, when he returned to his house, it was not through a window, not through either of the back entryways, but through the front door. Wearing the same clothes he had had on the day before, and looking a little less brushed up and a little more dirty than he would normally, Raul stood squarely before his father's table, his hands clasped behind his back like a soldier calmly waiting for briefing.

Eugene sat just off the head of the table, his chin resting on his knuckles. "Where have you been?"

"I walked," he replied, fixating on a visible knot in the grain of the table. "I spent the night at Herman's."

"I don't like that boy," came an offhand Eugene.

Raul rolled his eyes. "He's your second cousin, Father."

"Very well," Eugene consented, knowing that his son didn't accept his half-hearted agreement. "I wanted to talk to you last night."

"I know."

"But you didn't come home." Eugene explained.

"I know, Father," repeated Raul.

"Why not?"

"I didn't care to. I needed to do some thinking, and I needed to do it without you."

Eugene bristled but tried not to show it. He was dismayed that his son had left during his own birthday, but at that moment, he was most disturbed by the fact that Raul wouldn't sit down at any of the readily available chairs. In an effort to bridge this distance and help welcome his son to join him at the table, Eugene began to stand, but before he had even risen from his chair, Raul turned his back on him.

"You're right, Father," said Raul, while the older man resumed his seat, "I should be thinking more about my future, possibly even as a one-day Libburus. But I am also a man now, and I will start behaving more like one."

Eugene shifted uncomfortably. Looking up at the back of Raul's head, he hesitantly said, "And what does that mean exactly?"

"It means that you can no longer tell me who I can and cannot see, what I can and cannot do, and where I can and cannot go." Raul let out a sharp exhale, evidencing that he had most likely practiced this particular speech before. He turned about again, and planted his palms upon the table, and looked his own father directly in the eye. "In return, I will do my best to take on a more 'dignified bearing.' I will learn my responsibility, and I will be a good example to my sisters."

Eugene raised an inquisitive eyebrow and asked, "How do you mean to accomplish all of that, son?"

Raul pulled out the chair at the head of the table and sat. "I have a proposition for you."

XLVI – A Hole in his Coat

The Baron Pan Bordolo did his best to explain himself. Though he admitted he had taken things a step or two over the appropriate line, he wanted everyone to know that the curiosities which led to the infractions were perfectly valid. But after a time of the Baron repeating things like, "I just wanted to see if it worked," all that he could get from Hephaestus were snorts and scoffs.

"You misconstrued the point!" Hephaestus had said, when they left the storehouse. "The duel is not a measure of which man's more the imbecile, or who *can* beat another; it's a challenge to see which man wants the prize more!" Hephaestus kept both hands on his cane for most of the afternoon, having been quite disgruntled when Fletcher had taken it in the first place, but used it presently to gesture at the ground when he said, "If two men are fighting over an item in a place where everyone shares everything, then obviously it should go to whichever of them is willing to put himself through more pain for its sake."

"Then why were all the lemmings so eager to challenge me?"

"Because many would rather render themselves dumb[104] than admit that you are more powerful than the whole of their town!"

Though Hephaestus may have spoken accurately that time, that he had so exaggerated previous comments made our dear Baron disregard many of Hephaestus' statements as hooey, humbug, hogwash, or at the very least hot air.

The Baron would however trust the opinion of the large companion whose viewpoint was loftier and more objective than his. It was not Pigby's anger that softened the Baron—if physically applied, it

---

[104] We can only assume that this comment was in line with whatever scientific theory of the day said was the cause of muteness.

certainly could. Rather it was Pigby's cold reason, his frosty tone, and his purely reprimanding gaze. Even before he knew how he had wronged Clemens, the Baron trusted his giant man that the grocer with the walrusy stache deserved a most abject apology.

Of course, immediately following the duel, the Baron had more confusions to address than simply Clemens' feelings. He had no idea for the life of him how Fletcher had known to intercede when he did, and why the others were coincidentally in tow.

To explain that, I'll back up, as it actually starts with the Baron's first duel. You may be wondering about how the Baron had managed to engage in a duel in the Isle at all. The Baron wondered that same for a good while.

See, obviously, in order for his experiment to work at all, he had to get into a frivolous bout with a citizen which grew heated enough to demand they select a wall. Clemens had explained the rules, which will make a lot more logical sense now than they did a few chapters prior. They go like so:

First, one man challenges another to a duel over some disputed matter which implies that if the other backs down, then he must indeed be wrong. Second, the challenged man has the right to select a wall or patch of ground, provided it is not made of stone. Third, the initiator of the challenge must make first strike. And fourth—this one is important— they take turns until one of them cannot or will not take the next hit.

There is a silly caveat, which does not often come into play, but it was related to the Baron even so. If one party feels his opponent's hit was much quieter than his, he can demand that this opponent strike again, but this ruling was rare as it was considered petty. This told the Baron two things: that sound was the only respected measure of impact, and that the people of the Isle were largely bound to the 'honor system.' Though he knew the implications of this system, the Baron conveniently forgot to remember the term 'honor.'

His biggest challenge was finding someone to accept a challenge. Having learned that the duel he witnessed was over use a certain tool, he tried to argue over tools, then food, then information—simple trivia and the like—but anytime he mentioned a duel, the other man would immediately concede. Even then, he very rarely got to ask for a duel or antagonize anyone anyway; the people of the Isle were simply more partial and accustomed to giving things away without dispute.

The Baron met his first significant break with a man named Peter, who was—as the polite euphemism goes—an utter dumbass. The successful bait was a thing which fortunately couldn't be proven: opinion. The Baron casually insisted that the best cakes in the world were made by his mother. Having a mother of his own, an arthritic widow who would die two years after our story takes place, Peter felt a need to defend his family and insisted that *his* mother's cakes were far better, and bid the Baron come with him to his mother's house to taste the delicacies. When the Baron pointed out that that was unfair, seeing as Peter couldn't meet the Baron's mother in return, the duel seemed well enough in order.

After winning his first duel, the Baron obviously wondered—as did any good scientist—whether the experiment was repeatable. Clemens was just the easiest target. Now, the Baron did not know that Clemens was the reigning champion of duels, but having seen how he had taken to Pigby in the bread competition, the Baron concocted the cleverest sideways approach any dueling man had ever considered.

The challenge went something like, "My, my, Clemens, I've just had a duel, and I feel grand. I bet you couldn't feel so after you'd won a duel." As they say, it was all downhill from there.

When Clemens was beaten, much to his own surprise, he skulked away from the ring, and was wandering home to impart the bad news to Rosa when he ran into the blue girl near the stables. Not wanting to go directly home, but hoping for a friend with whom to commiserate, Clemens asked where Pigby might be, which Ten ha—bless her recollection—was happy to impart.

Clemens found Pigby with Geru and Julian, and when Clemens told his friend what had just happened, Pigby near exploded. Respecting the sanctity of one-on-one sportsmanship, Pigby said that the Baron had lied, that he had cheated, and that they needed to confront him.

Julian would have arrived with them, but for the fact that first, he did not understand much of what was going on, and secondly, that on the way, he ran into a young man that he recognized from the night of the Hephaestus High-Feast-us: this was the gentleman who rescued his lady, and from whom he had received such lovely sentiments as "Don't worry; she'll be alright; I know what she means to you, and I will deliver her securely back to her father's care. And by the way, good on you for hosting the visitors when no one else would."

Julian found himself sidetracked by Lance because once again, he was in danger of missing a well date, and the anxiousness of competition was so in the air anyway that he needed to ask Lance's observation on the state of the young lady, so as to prove that the new servant was not trying to horn in on Julian's poorly and illegally secured territory. Additionally, Lance seemed somewhat nervous when they first ran into him, giving Julian even more reason to suspect foul play.

In any case, as the troupe continued, they stumbled across Fletcher and Trenton, who had also happened upon one another, and were exchanging a few unpleasant words on the morality of giving items which had the possibility of rusting in a town where there was so little metal to be found. Fletcher could tell that Pigby was angry, Pigby explained about the Baron's attempts at Islean duels, and Trenton— knowing that his own lord was in the mood for bagels—suspected...

Alright, so even I don't know what he suspected, but he must have concluded that the Baron and Hephaestus would be in the same place at the same time and so took off running, with Fletcher soon to pass him, and Pigby right behind. You already know what became of Geru.

Though neither admitted it immediately, both the Baron and Hephaestus were greatly relieved that Fletcher had come between them. Each man feared that the other would win.

To be fair, the Baron had more reason to warrant this fear, seeing as there was a hole in his coat by the close of the bout, which—after checking that the book in his nearby pocket was safely unblemished—the Baron was delighted to find and present as damning evidence. "Obviously the man was trying to kill me!"

Looking around to see that no Adleship Isleans were in earshot, Hephaestus returned, "I most certainly was not!"

"Oh yes? Well then why is there a hole in my coat just in front of where my liver should be?"

Geru, disgruntled at having missed the sword-play, corrected with, "Your liver's lower, boss."

But the Baron amended this with an even more damning, "Aha! You were aiming for my heart!"

"I did no such thing—I was trying to prove a point."

"'To prove upon thy *heart*[105]'?" asked the Baron, but Hephaestus, knowing something of the bard himself finished the line in perfect cadence:

"'Whereto I speak, thou liest,' Mister Bordolo! '*This* sword, *this* arm, and *my* best spirits are bent—'"

---

[105] A clever retort, wouldn't you say? This particular selection was borrowed from William Shakespeare's *King Lear*, a very iconic speech by the heroic Edgar, who reclaims his right from his bastard brother, and alongside Kent, the moral center of the piece, helps to redeem the dignity of Lear in the final scene.

"Wait, you can't be Edgar," exclaimed Fletcher, "*I*'m the one who interceded heroically and won the day. If anything, I'm Edgar!"

This caused the lot, (excluding Clemens who was trailing behind them in confused silence), to erupt in another glorious shouting match. It was very difficult for anyone present to hear anything that anyone else said. After so many years, I had an even more difficult time of piecing the conversation—much like Humpty Dumpty—back together again.

I did catch one particularly chuckle-worthy comment, which occurred just after Trenton tried to quell the superior gentlemen. The moment he'd spoken, both Hephaestus and the Baron Pan Bordolo—teasing their own obstinance and absurdity—turned to him to say, "Shut up, Kent!"

This was a moment when the cliché, 'This town's not big enough for the two of us' is proven true, for in the middle of their hubbub, who should approach them but Jonas? Though he may have been simply ranting for the fun of it, the grandfather overpowered all other speakers with the pure power of Shakespeare's words spoken well.

The lot had fallen completely silent by the time Jonas reached "'And, from the extremest upward of thy head to the descent and dust below thy foot, a most toad-spotted traitor.'"

Jonas smiled behind closed eyes, folded his hands beneath long sleeves, and continued his walk back home.

After a moment, Fletcher resumed the conversation by observing, "He would be Lear."

But the Baron was not listening to Fletcher. Instead, he was looking to Hephaestus, who did not look uncomfortable until he noticed that the Baron was tracking his reaction to Jonas, after which the older merchant snorted harshly through one nostril. He stiffly tucked his cane underarm as he had the ramrod and bidding a curt nod to the Baron, said, "Mister Bordolo," and split off towards the Libburus' house, hoping that Sebastian would never hear how he had made an ass of himself.

Unfortunately for Hephaestus, both of Sebastian's daughters had been at that morning's duels. Unfortunately for Julian too, who missed yet another opportunity to see Samantha. It was Sabrina who caught the excitement in the air, and, not wanting to go through the crowd, coaxed her sister climb up the far side of the building and onto the roof of the storehouse where they could peer over the edge and admire the Baron as he plied his trade against the other townsfolk.

Samantha did not know why she joined Sabrina, or why her sister looked so smug about their vantage point. She did know however that the shiny wands the two world-weathered men wielded made her uncomfortable.

Though the Baron didn't notice when Hephaestus' blade caught the loose draping of his coat, Sabrina gasped severely and rushed down the roof, arriving safely on the ground with Samantha just as the shouting started. Holding the younger to the wall so that they not betray their position, she listened. The statement, "This is how we duel," occurred to her as one of the most profoundly dangerous animals to ever poke its head into the Isle.

Hephaestus on the other hand hadn't thought much on this explanation. In fact, he totally dismissed it.

Instead, when Hephaestus arrived in his room, and after Trenton had latched it behind him, the older merchant continued to protest the Baron's manners. "It isn't right! After what he did—" Hephaestus grunted something indiscernible and knew without looking that Trenton didn't react.

"Sir, it's not your call," Trenton said, easing his shoulders comfortably into the door.

"Oh, it isn't, is it?" asked Hephaestus. "I think I have a right to choose who I will and won't be nice to."

"Not as a Christian man, and not tomorrow. You owe it to him to set aside your pride. Even if it's only for one day."

"Why pay such courtesy for a shameless libertine who would never do the same for me?"

Trenton shook his head. "You have a duty; so does he. If he decides to piss it away, let it be on him. At least you know that you've done right."

Hephaestus scoffed, clearly trying to put off his unflappable aide. "What satisfaction is there in that?"

"It's never about satisfaction, my lord; it's about peace on earth, good will to men. No matter who they are, or what they've done, sir, Christmas is for everyone."

XLVII – Quite a Fine Gift

When Geru and Pigby woke up, once again before the rest of the crew, and as they gathered their bamboo mats, grey robes, and surprisingly clean wooden sandals, they had no reason to suspect that anything should be different. Of course, Julian had told them that it was Christmas, but seeing as they hadn't spotted a single cross or flag erected anywhere in the village, they found it hard to believe that the people should recognize either a national or religious pastime[106].

The first hint came when they discovered that no one was waiting to meet them outside Julian's. By this time they could expect a tough Clemens, an eager Piers, a tightly-wound Sherman, and a stout Manuel from just down the hill. As no new friends were present, the giant and short man did their best to start without. Pigby had to twice remind Geru that he needed not give instruction. When they finished and remained the only two on the hillside, Geru looked up to his giant friend and said, "I guess they really do have Christmas morning."

He probably didn't mean for the statement to sound depressed. He certainly didn't intend begrudging either, but Pigby found reason to find the comment glum. If Christmas is a time for families to gather, what does it mean to a band of travelers, likely lost or stranded somewhere in the snow possibly with no knowledge of day, night, or whether Christmas had come and gone? Point of fact, not knowing was less lonely.

"You know, it's been eighteen years since I've seen my father."

Geru patted his back as he could not reach his shoulder. "I know, Pigby."

Unlatching the door and entering Julian's house, they found Oswald stirring, their Baron yawning, and Fletcher stretching.

---

[106] In England, it remains both.

"Mornin'," groaned Fletcher sounding very much like the configuration of his right arm: strained, contorted, and thankfully pulling in all the right places.

"Morning yourself," returned Pigby, without the slightest bit of energy or excitement in his words.

The Baron took a break from his mustache wax to observe, "My dear Pigby, there's not the slightest bit of excitement or energy in your words. Could something be wrong?"

"No one came for yoga this morning," explained Geru, and the giant man did not correct him.

The Baron teased the bit of stache in his fingers and nodded. "Well, that's not surprising. It is Christmas after all."

"Christmas?" asked Fletcher.

"What—Say, what was that?" came Oswald, his little finger fishing in his ear to better prepare for the answer.

"I didn't know they did Christmas here," said the thin man before popping down from the loft.

"Oswald!" shouted the Baron, "What's your take on Christmas being here?"

Oswald raised a finger to indicate a pause, then assumed his spectacles before speaking. "English and possibly Germanic or French people; they're in England; Anglo-Saxon through and through in names, culture, architecture, sir; suppose the day and culture and holiday survived without necessarily the religion."

"Charming." The Baron chewed on his lower lip before consenting that Oswald's best guess was in fact the best guess. "Well, then, happy Christmas, all."

Pigby, with his very large back turned from the rest, scoffed, "Happy! This is a day for family. Who's to be happy among us?"

"Well, we're a family!" The Baron descended from the loft and with open arms announced, "We've a standing friendship and traditions all our own, so we've our own little traveling family, and I'm the father." At a very curious look from Oswald, he amended with, "The metaphorical father."

"Who—in leading by example—teaches us to play with swords?" asked Fletcher, which the Baron tastefully ignored.

"At any rate, this Christmas shouldn't be about us; should it? It should be about a real orphan, who's sleeping in the next room who will find family with us as well. Now, come on!"

He waved the lot to follow after him, like a high-school-basketball team's captain in a charming and only-slightly-mocking film about nineteen-fifties America. As he approached the door, the Baron was feeling inspiringly altruistic; after he opened it, he stood scratching his head.

"That's a fine howdy-do," said the Baron to the empty room.

"He must have gone down the hill already," piped Geru.

"Well, you know who else is down the hill?" offered Fletcher, "Ten ha."

The Baron put a palm to his forehead, no doubt to shake the disappointment of a non-Julian in the room. "Of course! Ten ha—I feel like I haven't seen her in days and near-forgot about her[107]."

"Then let's off down the hill!" exclaimed Oswald. He hoisted his crutch from beside the couch, though he did not use it to stand up and put full weight on the ailed ankle.

Pigby looked as though he should wish to grumble, but as the others were assembling shoes for the fifty-foot trek, he decided it best to just follow suit and hope that throwing himself into what seemed to be mock merriment would improve his mood.

Fletcher was at the door before any of his fellows, and opened it ready to bolt out—but instead revealed Julian on the other side, smiling and carrying a large, covered tray, from which steam was visibly escaping. "Good morning and Happy Christmas, my friends!"

And as Julian made his way inside, so followed Meredith, Manuel, Ten ha holding the snap-pea's hand, and in about thirty seconds more, Clemens, with Rosa and the children in tow, apologizing for 'being late.'

Once Clemens had set down a basket of what the crew was convinced was gratin dauphinois[108], Pigby threw his arms around his walrusy friend and failed to resist picking him up off the ground.

Clemens, not used to being picked up or regarded as small in any way, laughed, and only a fraction of the laugh was in embarrassment. Clemens' children were likewise ticked by the image, and once he was set down, Clemens changed the subject by saying, "Ah, Pigby! I want you to meet the little ones," who happened to be four boys and one girl ranging between three and twelve years old, and who had by then learned

---

[107] I'm hoping that you, on the other hand, did not.

[108] A French-accredited potato dish, which is nearly identical to the modern side scalloped potatoes.

to organize themselves by age. "That's our oldest, Charlie, then Carol, Norbert, Egbert, and little Dagobert."

After shaking his hand, both Norbert and Egbert checked their own palms to see if any of the giant's color had rubbed off onto them. Rosa was far more delighted than intimidated by the giant man of whom her husband had so fondly spoken.

Julian and Manuel began to set up on the floor. Overjoyed by the smell and a sudden realization that they must have been hungry, Fletcher and Geru moved the couch out of the way so that the whole lot could share the tiny cottage for Christmas brunch.

When she realized that Oswald still had a hurt leg to worry on, Meredith insisted that she go home and fetch a stool for the old man. Before she could get to the door, though, Oswald stopped her with a gentle palm on her shoulder and the kind insistence, "Madam, I would be honored to sit on the floor beside you."

The crew and two families took their seats and would have started eating immediately, had Miriam not spoken up, exclaiming, "Wait for Jonas!" who fortuitously stumbled through the door soon after.

"Oh, Father! Do you have something to say before we eat?"

Jonas surveyed the group, then the food, then opened his mouth and raised his index finger. However, to dash all expectation, he closed his mouth and sat down between Fletcher and Charlie, Clemens' oldest son. He must have thought what he didn't say was a good speech though, because he appeared quite self-satisfied while reaching for the first potato.

There were not many plates, or much cutlery for that matter, but the serving platters were large enough that everyone could reach them and eat with his hands. And though there was not much variety before them, everyone seemed quite pleased with the arrangement of potatoes, eggs, and chicken.

"I must say, I'm touched," said the Baron. "It says a lot to your character that you would put this together, son."

Julian did his best to shrug it off. "Clemens helped arrange it too."

"Clemens, whom I offended terribly only a day ago, and here he is: smiling, laughing, sitting beside my man like he's his brother, and by extension family to me as well." The Baron never found out whether Clemens heard the comment. As he spoke, the walrusy man looked up and bid a friendly nod to the Baron, which the Baron graciously accepted.

"This town amazes me, Julian. Everyone here is so quick to forgive. Doesn't anyone ever hold grudges?"

Julian shook his head and swallowed his eggs before speaking. "Not when you only know a hundred people. I know what a grudge is, Sir Baron—and that's not just because I've watched you and His Long-Beardedness. Remember, my best friend's father is Eugene. A grudge is just the opposite of a crush, right?" Julian took another bite here, no doubt giving the Baron a chance to process his hint.

"See, I think people are more likely to hold grudges where you come from," Julian explained, tapping one hand on the air as he processed. "I think you've met maybe a *hundred*-hundred people, and if you don't like one of them—Y'know, if one does something that's so bad or even just annoying enough that you can't stand to listen to him, you can hold your grudge and simply avoid him. If the Big Out There's as big as they say, then you don't have to see anyone you don't want to. But here, in our village, in Adleship Isle, just by living and working and eating and keeping friendships, you see everyone—almost every day. So it's so much easier to be nice than mean."

The Baron gave a quick survey of the other faces to see if anyone else had caught this boy's pearls of wisdom. "That's mighty astute of you Julian," observed the Baron, doing his best to recall what the boy had said so he could later relate it to his fellows.

"See, what you and Hephaestus are doing—I don't know a word for it, but you two are both so used to being in your Big Out There that you don't know how to deal with someone you don't like if you have to see him, and work with him, right?"

"The word is 'feud,' Julian. And not a very refined one at that, I'll admit."

"Feud... Alright. Can you win a feud?"

The Baron bit his lower lip because he could not literally chew on the question. "How's that?"

"Well, when does it end?" Julian clarified.

The Baron laughed somewhere between self-mocking and rue. "That's a good question. I don't rightly know."

"Well, will an apology do it?"

Though Julian meant the both of them, the Baron Pan Bordolo skewed the question to relate to only Hephaestus and so asked, "And what would he apologize for?"

"For insulting you," Julian replied, as if it were the most obvious answer in the world. "He treated you like weren't a noble. He treated you like a commoner. You know, even commoners don't like it when people look down on them."

Even though the rest of the dinner party was engaged in conversations their own, and not one of them *seemed* to be listening to Julian's pointed commentary, Oswald had caught almost every word of their exchange. The old man's ears were often scoffed at, seeing as he was frequently demanding 'What, what?' of just about everyone around him, but that morning, he must have yawned just right to unplug his agéd ear canals for a pivotal conversation in our story.

There were of course half a dozen other topics for discussion, but the only other comment of interest to which Oswald tuned in came from Rosa, who inquired of Pigby with far more excitement than she had rightly intended, "Do the men in this yo-guh really not wear anything?"

"Alright, it's getting to be about that time," Manuel announced when the food supplies were dwindling. He quickly cleaned the corners of his mouth and stood. "Come on: let's get shoes on and down to the square."

"Why? Wha's happ'ning?" asked Fletcher, flecks of potato trickling down his lips.

"Christmas!" was Miriam's answer, as if there needed be no other explanation.

In a minute or so, the lot was shoed, coated, and walking down the path to the town square.

"What do you suppose this is all about?" whispered Pigby to the others.

"Probably another feast!" replied Geru, his hands on his own belly for everything that he had eaten already.

Ten ha shook her head. "I don't know, but Miriam was so excited about it—she's been tittering all morning. She's like—" Ten ha was about to say 'kid at Christmas' but since both were already true, amended it to, "like a pig at a truffle farm."

"Bad form, dear!" proclaimed Oswald, which Fletcher followed with:

"Why would you say such a sweet little girl is like a pig?"

Ten ha quickly put a hand to her mouth and scanned the family ahead to see if Miriam had heard. Of course even if the snap-pea did, she continued to skip jovially along the path, head bobbing back and forth as if in a sing-song lilt.

Now as you may remember from earlier in our story[109], Julian's house was on the far west end of town, northwest actually, which put him farther from the square than anyone else, except from maybe the sheep farmers on the southwest side. As they reached the main road, the Baron's crew found that other families were emerging from their houses as well and following the same path. And when they crossed the bridge, they saw little clusters gathered together and chatting amongst themselves.

Remembering the last time he had seen such a gathering, Fletcher shuddered involuntarily.

When the Baron asked Julian what they were gathered for, Julian replied, "I think you'll just have to see it yourself, sir."

Standing between the Clemens and Manuel households, the Baron's crew felt somewhat out of place, but then again, everyone looked so happy and excited that it was difficult to find anything too amiss. Even Geru didn't express his fear that the townsfolk might indeed try to eat them, though he did wonder it to himself.

After having gotten no information from either Julian or Manuel, the Baron rejoined his crew and told them, "I guess we wait, then."

More and more families filled the square, most of them led by their youngest children, and gradually the donut of citizens filled in again, once more leaving an opening to the east gate. On account of looking for Lance, Ten ha was the first to notice that neither Hephaestus nor any of his servants were present.

Julian felt a hand on his shoulder and turned to see Raul. "Happy Christmas, Julian," said the now-not-quite-so-young man.

"Raul!" exclaimed Julian, remarking more at Raul's excited smile than the man himself, "Are you alright? After your birthday—"

"Julian, I talked to my father. For all I know, your being at my birthday was the best thing that ever could have happened to me." And because Julian looked shocked by this, Raul had to nod and assure him, "Yeah. See, afterwards, I did some thinking, and—"

"Raul," came Manuel, pausing the boy's revelation to indicate that the Libburus and his family were arriving in the circle in the square.

"Oh, right." Raul nodded to Julian, and as he began to slip back through the crowd, said, "Look, I'll tell you all about it later, okay? Happy Christmas!"

"Happy Christmas!" Julian called after him.

---

[109] If you don't, you can always consult your map.

As people began to notice Sebastian's arrival, a hush fell over the crowd[110]. The Baron and his crew noticed everyone else noticing him and expected him to launch into a speech, but all that Sebastian did was smile to the crowd, before turning to face the east gate himself.

The bell, sounding from the tower behind them, startled the crew, each of whom turned to see it, though the rest of the town continued to face forward. Oswald remained watching the bell much longer than the others, as he observed for the first time its natural bronze tone which glinted and glanced.

The Baron quietly said to the others, "I think that means it's starting."

"Yes," came Geru. "If only we knew what *it* was."

The it came first in the sound of hooves. The moment they could be heard, pelting along stones just out of view, the children began whispering excitedly, and many of the younger mothers giddily clung to their husbands, their eyes reflecting wonderful memories of Christmases past.

The crack of a whip echoed between the houses, and the first of the beasts emerged. Even the oxen looked eager as they drew the large wagon into the square, and from the wagon's helm, a powerful voice called out, "Ho-ho-ho! Merry Christmas!"

The citizens began to cheer, and even though they recognized the man beneath the fur coat, the Baron's crew applauded as well. The eight oxen were drawn to a halt, and seven large men in brown and green suits leapt off and out of the wagon. Four put stops at the wheels; two hauled out a large crate filled with bags filled with boxes; and the last one, Trenton in a long, pointed cap and reading spectacles, climbed upon the driver's bench beside Hephaestus, brandishing what looked to be a long scroll. After setting down the crate, Lance shot a charmingly sloppy smile at Ten ha, who beamed right back.

Hephaestus, with his hair braided into his beard, and the locks hanging in elaborate beads over the most lustrous emerald coat anyone had ever seen, stood triumphantly, and declared, "The house of the Libburus: Sebastian, daughters, and servants."

Following the cue, Sebastian and family rushed toward the wagon where they were greeted with a box from the crate, which featured

---

[110] Forgive the cliché, but it seemed the most fitting turn of phrase, and we have to consider that this is after all a Christmas story.

two dresses for the girls, new shoes for the servants, and the most ridiculous hat ever to grace the Libburus' wardrobe.

The Baron knew that he wanted to mock Hephaestus, wanted to call him out for the worst in pandering that he could possibly do in a town like the Isle, but all he could do in good conscience was smile and shake his head. As he watched Hephaestus call household names off a scroll and give out gifts, the Baron was duly impressed by the charm and whimsy of his rival's charitable endeavor, regardless of how painstakingly planned-out this tradition must have been. A part of him still saw the gesture as a popularity grab, but it warmed his heart to see just how many people were happy to receive gifts from the lord of merchants.

I find it ironic that even in the most serene community ever thought to have been known, we are all reminded of one of the lifeblood events of the capitalistic modern world market. I will say this though: after learning of Hephaestus' tradition, department store Santas look awfully pale by comparison.

Pigby, a man of inventories and accounts, was stunned by the sheer magnitude of presents and their allocations, each set of which was distributed using a different box. Of course, once Hephaestus had finished giving to the noble houses, the recipients stopped showing the rest of the crowd what they had gotten, so Pigby had less room for concrete conclusions, but he could only assume that Hephaestus' servants had worked on nearly nothing other than the Christmas celebration since their arrival. For that matter he was amazed that the Baron's crew missed the preparation of this operation—in fact, you may be surprised as well that it slipped your notice, but I'm sure if you think on it long enough you'll realize that that's my fault. The giant man turned to Ten ha and asked her, "Did you know about this?"

Ten ha, who had been watching a certain man's arms as they relayed crates from a wagon and boxes and bags from the crates, startled, sputtered, then stammered, "I? Why—What makes you think I'd know anything about this?"

"I missed it too," agreed Fletcher.

"And me," admitted Geru.

"I must say, I never heard a word on this event!" confirmed Oswald.

"No surprise there," said Fletcher, without ever looking behind him to see the old man's appalled reaction.

"Julian, why didn't you tell us?" asked the Baron.

"Well," Julian stalled, not sure if he committed some social foul by not being more forthcoming with this information, "um—I guess I forgot for the most part. I've done this all my life, and so I didn't really think of you *not* doing it. Well, until yesterday: it occurred to me when I ran into Lance and he told me he was working on Christmas."

"You talked to Lance?" blurted Ten ha, before she considered how her question must have sounded.

"Who's Lance?" asked Pigby and Fletcher in unison.

"One of Hephaestus' servants," Julian replied, pointing. "He's the new one."

After the crew, catching sight of the youngest of seven sturdy servants, said a collective *Ahhhh*, Julian resumed with, "After talking to Lance though, I decided to just leave it a surprise."

Of course the biggest surprise of that day's gift-giving turned out to be a shock to Julian as well. As Hephaestus went through his list, drifting farther and farther west along the town, giving clothes, tools, sweets and toys, Julian fully expected to be included in Manuel and Meredith's house as he had for the last few years. However, when Hephaestus called, "The household of Manuel," before Julian could make his way to the center of the square, the lord of merchants followed it with only, "his wife Meredith, Mister Jonas, and young Miriam."

Meredith and Manuel hardly had opportunity to look to Julian before Miriam went running ahead of them, pulling the grandfather by one of his bony hands. When the mother and father consented forward for the sake of following tradition, Julian stood just ahead of the Baron's crew, his mouth contorted in an expression that was teetering between hurt and anger.

"Were you supposed to go with them?" Geru asked him, not noticing that the Baron was trying to non-verbally hush him.

"I guess not," said Julian, and was about to step back again when Hephaestus cleared his throat and announced the next names:

"I would like to call the household of the citizen, Julian, and his houseguests: the Baron Pan Bordolo and crew."

In truth they hardly hesitated, and to everyone else watching, it looked as though the Baron's crew was simply politely waiting for 'household Manuel' to step back into the crowd with their gifts. To the crew, it seemed like a gratingly prolonged awkwardness, during which Fletcher realized and said, "Oh, Christ, that's us," before following the slightly stunned Julian toward their arch-nemesis. The Baron followed Fletcher, a thousand and one explanations racing through his head, each more ridiculous than the last as to why Hephaestus should call them forward. Pigby considered that if Hephaestus ever wanted to give them a bomb, now was the time. Geru pondered a similar scenario, only with poison.

Lastly, Oswald offered Ten ha an arm and asked, "Shall we?" before following.

"Ah, yes, young Julian," said Hephaestus once our hero had reached him, and with a smile, bid, "Happy Christmas."

"Happy Christmas, sir," replied Julian. He looked to Trenton, confirming from the professional nod that he had heard Hephaestus correctly.

"Oy, Julian!"

Julian turned to see Lance holding a box for him, the likes of which was little more than a cubic foot. The box itself was very simple-looking, an unassuming amalgamation of five boards, but on the side it read, 'NW – Julian,' scrawled in near-illegible chicken scratch. Though he did not know the gift within, the mere fact that he had been recognized as a household ensured that this was perhaps the most important Christmas Julian would ever know.

Sidling up to the driver's bench and leaning casually against the cart, the Baron asked the gentleman who sat above him, "Armistice?"

"Christmas," replied Hephaestus.

The Baron pinched his lips together and gave an acknowledging grunt. "Good form."

"Might want to move it," said one of the servants, who—if you recognize him from several chapters before—is called Gus, "There's still a many names to call."

"Yes. Right." Without looking into his new treasure trove, Julian tucked the box under one arm and started back to his spot in the crowd. He wondered if Samantha had witnessed this, wondered if she too recognized that this act treated Julian as an adult. From the other end of the donut, she had, and she did.

The Baron was at Julian's shoulder by the time Hephaestus called the next name. Geru didn't understand why they all had to approach Hephaestus if Julian was the only one who would receive something and grumbled his complaint to Pigby as they retreated once again. Ten ha stalled to look toward Hephaestus' servants, but as she could think of no valid excuse for her behavior, pulled away and joined the others.

"What'dja get?" asked Miriam.

"Well, let's see here," said Julian, and set down the box so the crew could gather around. Granted there wasn't much to be seen from the top view; a man who is charged with giving to hundreds of people can't rightly send a cow to each of them, but he can get them a glass of milk. Milk took the form of chocolates, which were in a sack about the consistency of cheesecloth, large enough to block off anything that might find its way underneath, and on which was written the letters 'OPGFTh.'

"OPGFTh?" asked Pigby in his best to sound it out. "Strange acronym if I've ever heard it."

"O-P-G..." mused Fletcher before concluding, "It's us. Oswald, Pigby, Geru, Fletcher, Ten ha. Practically in order of age."

Geru, who was older than Pigby *hmph*ed at this.

Oswald adjusted his glasses. "I say! Why's it our names?"

"Well, it's your Christmas present, silly," said Meredith.

Her husband, whose lips showed evidence of his own chocolate gift, explained, "His Jolliest always gives out cho-ko-lits on Christmas."

Noticing that his own name was not on the bag, the Baron added his own *hmph*.

Fletcher quickly removed the bag from the box revealing an altogether more-desirable present, which, though it was not labeled seemed obviously to belong to Julian. It was a device he had never seen before, a sleek, white tube with a flattened base, and a slit along the side to see within. Both ends were stopped by some sort of dried mortar, and most curious of all, a miniature ball bearing rolled about inside it. Lifting it up for everyone else to take a good look, Julian chanced to ask, "What is it?"

"It's a level," the Baron informed him. "If you want to know if something's relatively flush, if it's hanging straight, that ball will tell you if it's leaning to the left, to the right, or not at all."

"That's quite a fine gift," decided the young man, which made Manuel feel like his new frying pan was somewhat less special.

"Now, what's all this?" Geru snatched out a set of papers and after a quick glance, announced, "It's a concerto," before handing it to Fletcher.

Beneath that sat a recipe for sugar dumplings for Ten ha, a brief history of the Puritan exodus of Europe for Oswald, an inventory and summary of exchange written by James Cook's personal trade-representative for Pigby, and a journal notating weather patterns in the Scottish Highlands for Geru.

"Has he been following us?" squeaked the short man upon seeing the last.

Having not been looking at the box himself, the Baron was about to conclude b*ad form* on account of his apparent exclusion, excepting that Pigby asked, "Boss, isn't that your coat?"

You remember the blue jacket, yes? That French noble number for which the Baron had very nearly lost hope on account of a rather telling hole about the left side of his abdomen. Well, upon lifting Hephaestus' gift from the box, the Baron first attempted to doubt his own eyes, but for the life of him he could find neither hole nor evidence that one had been patched. "Bugger."

"Did he steal your coat to fix it?" asked Fletcher.

"No, he found me a nearly identical replacement." The Baron held the jacket up so that everyone could inspect and admire how close a match it was; of course he would need to compare it directly later, but even a discerning seamstress would conclude that both coats were made by the same hand, or at least for the same purpose.

"So what's that mean, sir?" asked Ten ha.

"Well, my dear, it means he's won the day."

Looking up from his level, Julian said, "Well, Sir Baron, you may congratulate him once he's done Christmas-giving."

His thumbs still taking in the texture of the marvelous coat, the Baron Pan Bordolo raised his head to see Hephaestus and the mostly-dignified band of servants beside him. And Hephaestus' face, even while shadowed between hood and beard was obviously grinning at each mother, father, and child who approached him. Most of the gifts were small; in fact, a quick look around the circle would reveal that many of the townsfolk were receiving socks among whatever novelties and toys Hephaestus had packed up for them. Questions about how he had arranged this grand gift-giving gesture ricocheted about the Baron's baffled brain, but what he could not question was how happy the haughty Hephaestus had made the people of the Isle.

So when Hephaestus next happened to glance in the Baron's direction, the Baron paid him his due in the form of a gentlemanly salute.

After the last of the boxes had been distributed, Hephaestus called his helpers to remove the stops, to get back on the wagon, and then stood to announce, "Merry Christmas to all, and have a lovely afternoon!" With a crack of the whip, Trenton forced the eight obedient oxen to about-face and steer their way right out of the square again, with several children running after them until they had faded out of sight[111].

"I say, sir," commended Oswald, "Wasn't that a charming performance? A charming performance indeed."

"I would change the exit line," said Fletcher, and when the others looked at him quizzically, defended with, "What? All I'm saying is after all that, you'd think you'd leave on a line with more—I dunno—*oomph*."

"What's *umph*?" came Geru.

"Impact. Bravado. Chutzpah."

"That's not a word!" chimed the shorter.

"It just made sense; it's onomatopoeia," protested the thinner.

"Is onomatopoeia Greek?" asked Pigby.

"Yes!" arrived the shouted reply from Geru, Fletcher, and—because she fancied herself the linguist—Ten ha in unison.

"Quite," concluded the Baron.

Since the major obstruction was gone, the donut began to fill in, beginning with the children of course: those who were either too old or too young to go chasing a cart but who still needed to show their friends their new toys, most which were simply dolls, balls, and miniature games. Soon the adults found their closest friends and were brandishing new rolling pins, washboards, hoes, and—for the very lucky—shoes.

When Hephaestus, still wearing his big green robe and flanked by Trenton reemerged, the people applauded him. Sebastian, practically bubbling over, shook his hand, congratulating him on his lovely Christmas.

Hephaestus' answer to this kind of comment was delivered as though it had been rehearsed for literally decades. "My good man, it was my pleasure, as always."

The Baron didn't know whether he should be hesitant in approaching Hephaestus, but took courage in Julian's seeming assurance that the old merchant would be only a beacon of good will on this delightful, once-in-a-yeartime day. Luckily for the Baron, he did not even

---

[111] Of course, the exit was for the purpose of drama alone, seeing as they only got as far as the east gate before stopping, rounding, and returning to the Libburus' house where they parked. During the following celebration, carousing, and chattering, the servants changed out of their silly green jumpsuits, unhooked the oxen, and quickly escorted them to back to the stable without crossing the main thoroughfare, so as not to break up the merriment by reminding them that the Christmas gifts were carefully planned as opposed to magical and spontaneous.

have to make this decision, because before he could reach Hephaestus, the thin man popped in front of him and seized the older's hand.

"What a wonderful holiday tradition, Santa Claus!"

Now, I don't think that he meant this mockingly, but Hephaestus quickly withdrew his hand and corrected him. "I'm 'Father Christmas.' I'm not a colonist, and we do not use that term here."

Fletcher's eyebrows arched in tandem with his question, "Don't we?"

"Mister Hephaestus," began the Baron, suddenly charged with a sense of duty to prevent his minstrel from speaking with Father Christmas, "I found what you did today a virtuous and honorable thing."

Hephaestus nodded kindly. "You see, Mister Bordolo, I do care greatly about this place."

"It shows."

The older had to recoil some in surprise at the graciousness of this comment. He was still fairly certain that he loathed the man that claimed to be an English baron, and yet he was grateful for the humble compliment.

He would have said so had the very large and very dark specimen not bouldered ahead to say: "Sir! How did you manage to—Ow!"

The last directed toward Geru, who had struck him with his cane. "Manners!" he insisted.

"You just hit me!"

"And that's no need to forget what your mummy taught you." Geru planted himself between Pigby and Hephaestus, while the giant man sputtered, trying to figure out how to respond to this comment[112]. "Hephaestus, thank you for the courtesy of the gifts. Now, I must ask: have you been spying—"

But before he could finish, Pigby lifted Geru off the ground and passed him behind himself to the nearest bystander, who happened to be Julian, coming up to pay his own thanks. Julian nearly fell over while righting a rather red-faced Geru.

"What was that?" asked Hephaestus, but before he could take offense, Pigby continued.

"Sir, this is fascinating to me. How did you know how to give presents to everyone here—to *know* what to give and to whom—I'm stunned, sir."

---

[112] In fact, Pigby's own mummy had been crushed by an unruly hippopotamus when he was too young to quibble about it. Or seek revenge for that matter.

"Well, see, most of the work was already done," Hephaestus began, but interrupted his own explanation when he saw the boy. "Oh, excuse me. Hello, young Julian!"

"Hello, sir. I wanted to thank you for the tool."

"Yes, isn't it lovely?" asked Hephaestus, laying a fatherly hand on Julian's upper arm. The Baron Pan Bordolo was certain that Hephaestus wanted him to see that. "I ran across it on my last tour through Africa and thought it perfect for a skilled carpenter." And as someone else was approaching to thank Hephaestus for his gift, the older merchant, turned to the giant man and artfully segued with, "Oh, and speaking of the lower continent, Pigby, I'll be occupied here; why don't you take that up with my man Trenton."

Holding a smile that tried desperately to crack his cheeks, the Baron collected Julian and escorted him away from Hephaestus, while Trenton went on to explain that most of the work was done by the Libburus himself—(by which we mean his servants and other hands-for-hire in the Isle.) See, they would compile all of the names, genders, and ages of every citizen in the Isle on a list, which Hephaestus would very diligently check, (twice), to make certain he could provide at least a box of chocolates or pair of long underwear to everyone present.

Largely, it became a subject of year-long preparation, or so Trenton told it, over which Hephaestus would keep in mind certain key citizens of the Isle and fetch for them gifts well-enough in advance to need only worry about the ones that he hadn't remembered once he arrived. From there, it was just a question of getting the servants to stuff everything into boxes.

"Why didn't you tell me you were doing this?" Ten ha asked Lance, slapping him on the arm.

Lance, who had just arrived from taking two beasts of excessive burden to the stables, glanced about to make sure no one had seen that telltale gesture. "Well, they never told me. They just called me back from the stables early yesterday; said I needed to write some names and 'rehearse' something. I had no idea this is what the others'd been working on all week."

"I'll bet that was a pleasant surprise."

Lance rubbed at the back of his neck. "Actually not really. Had to wake up really early to move the bulls without anyone noticing."

"Oxen," Ten ha corrected him.

"Right. Did your—um—your boss, the Baron: did he like the coat?"

"Enough that he'll be put out about it for days," said Ten ha.

But the Baron had something else to be put out about at that moment, which showed in how he hustled the lad he was determined to repay.

"Excuse me, sir," began Julian, "but where are we going?"

"Why, my boy! We are going to pay our respects to our dear Sebastian," which made sense, seeing as Sebastian was almost squarely in their heading.

"I want to compliment you, sir," said the Baron once he had reached the sunny Libburus, "on your fine town."

"Oh! I say, Cletus, did you hear that?"

Which was followed by the driest, "Yes sir; I did," imaginable.

"Poor soul's been up all night," Sebastian explained as if Cletus stood more than two feet away from him. "The way he worked every moment 'til dawn, you'd think he was delivering presents to the whole Big Out There instead of just our town. Is that possible, mister Baron?"

"Not that I know of, and not in a single night either."

"Ah! Young Julian, good to see you again," said the Libburus, seizing the boy's hand. "Did you like that you were your own house? Oh, how silly of me, of course you did! Yes, that was my idea," he announced proudly before amending with, "Well actually—to remember it right—I think it was Hephaestus' idea, but he told me that it was mine. Hmm. Have you—Say, Julian, have you any idea of why he might tell me something like that?"

Trying not to giggle, our hero replied, "Not that I know of, sir."

"Ah, very well then." Sebastian wrang out his hands, more to dispel excitement than anxiousness, but the tic stands. Then, seeing the sisters just a few townspeople away, Sebastian waved over his daughters, saying, "Mister Baron, you remember my girls, yes? Samantha, and my oldest, Sabrina."

"Happy Christmas, sir," said Samantha bowing her head modestly.

"Charmed, I'm sure." Sabrina sidled her way between her sister and the Baron Pan Bordolo and offered her hand.

And while Julian gawked somewhat awkwardly and the delightfully sweet powder blue number Samantha was wearing, the Baron was so distracted by his predicament that he up and shook the other lady's hand instead of kissing it.

"Miss Samantha," commended Julian.

"Mister Julian," she replied, unable to meet his eyes, so unaware that he couldn't hold contact either. To that end they remained bowed to each other far longer than social convention mandated. Here's what the bow allowed for though: Sebastian had a moment to beam proudly and largely incredulously about his daughters' manners; Sabrina decided to take offense that the Baron was so distant to her attempt at physical contact; and the Baron's heart leapt somewhere close to his chin as he watched the younger man and woman. Call it a simple reminder; call it a stroke of genius. Either way, the Baron suddenly knew how not to come in second to Hephaestus' only-nearly-perfect gift.

"Yes, well, we best go," suggested the Baron, tapping Julian on the arm and giving him permission to straighten.

"So soon?" asked the miffed Sabrina. "You know, we did just get new dresses, mister Baron, and I would be most flattered if a gentleman of your esteem were to render his opinion on the garment."

"I think His All-Knowingness would like that," replied the Baron. "Come, Julian."

"Yes, sir," said the boy. He shook the Libburus' hand and did his best not to blush while smiling at the young lady. He wondered if the redness in her face was simply a reflection of his, and so hastened to turn about and follow the Baron.

"Sir Baron," he began, jogging to catch up to the gentlemanly brisk pace, "Sir," he said with only the tiniest catch in his throat, "I have something I'm ready to tell you."

"Save your breath, young Julian." The Baron stopped his stride and spun on a heal, causing Julian to nearly run into him. "I know what you're going to say. And I know what I'm going to do for you for Christmas."

"Sir?" asked Julian.

Now, perhaps the Baron would have explained, but at that moment, Raul rushed toward them, saying, "Oy, Julian! Take a look at these boots! They're wonderful; Hephaestus says they're made for 'highwaymen,'" then to the Baron, "Do you know what that means."

"That I do," replied the Baron, teasing one end of his mustache around his thumb.

When the Baron didn't clarify the statement, Raul shifted uncomfortably—he didn't fancy being awkward or unpleasant on a day when everything was so joyful. "Um, well, Julian, I'll see you later. Happy Christmas."

"Happy Christmas back," and as Raul tried to dart past him, Julian reached out with, "Wait, didn't—Didn't you say you have something important to tell me?"

Raul emphatically shook his head, but was smiling too broadly for Julian to worry. "Nah, m'dad and I are gonna announce it tomorrow. At the general post-cleanup assembly, right?"

"Alright," Julian called after, seeing as Raul had already turned to bolt away again.

"Abrupt lad, that one," observed the Baron.

"I guess," replied Julian.

From where he was busily receiving good favor and good wishes, Hephaestus looked up to see the Baron collect his crew, gather the gifts, and start the trek back to the northwest end of town, and did his very best not to be suspicious. Chock it up to Christmas whimsy.

XLVIII – Warm Milk

Samantha pressed her palms to her sides, smoothing the fabric against her skin to better examine her silhouette in the not-quite-large-enough wall mirror. "Are you sure this is right?"

"Of course it is," said Sabrina, fussing with her own sash. "It's the newest fashion."

"Hmm." Doing her best not to be disturbed by the way the chemise dress failed to collect just above her hips, Samantha effected the most regal posture she could and asked, "Do you think it's the same empire as the British Empire?"

"What?"

"You know: what they say about England belonging to so many other little places all over the world—"

"No, no." Sabrina shook her head and approached her sister, wrapping her fingers along the younger's ribcage and incidentally the garment's waistline. "It's Om-peer. So called for the waistline: Om-peer."

Samantha assumed a puzzled expression, and the mirror was just barely high enough to reflect her crinkling nose. "Are you sure?"

"Positive. Hephaestus called the dress 'Om-peer.'"

"How do you suppose it's spelled?"

Sabrina shrugged. "Probably just how it sounds. See?" Indicating her own sash, explained, "You do a sash like so, and everything below can simply drape, that way, all attention is directed to your neck and face."

Samantha knew that her sister enjoyed sounding authoritative, even when she had hardly a notion of what she spoke. Though the directed gaze sounded accurate, she couldn't help but feel like the neckline and the waistline were too close together. Far be it for her to want to call a Christmas gift inappropriate, but in trying to adjust herself to better take in her own reflection, Samantha wondered aloud, "Do these look sheer?"

"What?" Because there was only one mirror in the room, and hardly three feet tall at that, Sabrina had been watching her own shadow against the wall, and when she heard this, lifted the skirt enough to examine it against her fingers. "No," came the response before she'd actually assessed it.

With only the slightest hint of panic in her voice, "I think they are."

"No, they're not."

"Yes, they are!"

"No, they're not," Sabrina repeated, tugging tighter on the sash to better punctuate the exchange.

But seeing as Adleship Islean education did not cover an abundance of punctuation rules, the younger sister misconstrued and so continued with, "Well, maybe not in this light, but, Sabrina, there are only three candles in here. What'll happen when we go out in the sun?"

Sabrina, frustrated, snatched one of the candles and held it before Samantha, insisting, "Hephaestus would not have given us sheer dresses."

"Well, supposing we're meant to wear something underneath."

"No petticoats," replied Sabrina, "it's not meant for layering; look at the hang!"

"How do you know?"

"I just do, that's all," Sabrina explained, and would have continued were there not a knock on the exterior wall of Samantha's room.

Both sisters fell silent, and—because there was suddenly some question as to the opacity of their dresses—covered themselves accordingly. Of course, the heavy drape which blocked off the wind also blocked... Well, to be fair, they didn't know if it even was a person, that is, until he knocked a second time.

The sisters' eyes darted to one another for a moment. And though Samantha's seemed to insist 'No!' Sabrina was closer to the window than her sister and so leaned against the wall to call through the heavy drape, "Who is it?"

"What are you doing?" interrupted Samantha with a whisper, though she was likewise interrupted by the stranger's reply.

"Merely a humble messenger," he called through the drape, (and Samantha instinctively gasped at the voice), "charged to bring a word of truth to the young lady that lives under this house."

"Under this house?" asked Sabrina, though the young man must have thought the comment directed at him and so corrected:

"Under this roof! And I—" he seemed to hesitate. "I've—um—I've come to deliver a message."

"Well, who is it out there?" asked Sabrina and reached to pull the drape aside, but Samantha slapped the back of her hand.

The messenger must have agreed with the younger sister, because he was suddenly sputtering, "No, no, no, don't open the window; I'm only here to speak, and I—um—if you saw my face you might not hear my words!"

"Well, why not?" asked Sabrina, but as her hand ventured forward a second time, so did Samantha's issuing an "Ow!" followed by:

"Would you be quiet!" from the younger sister.

"Samantha?" asked the messenger. "Are you—Is there someone else in there with you?"

"Yes," they replied together.

This seemed to strike him, as it took a moment for him to respond again. "Ah." Pause. "Um." Another pause. "Could you? Um—Sabrina, could you leave?"

A sinfully coquettish grin travelled from Sabrina lips to her eyes, giving them the slant that even in that moment Samantha envied. "Very well," she responded, and got up to leave.

"Wait!" Samantha stood, hurried after her sister, and stopped her as she reached the door. "Wait," she whispered, "what am I supposed to do?"

"You know who it is, don't you?"

"Yes, but—"

"Um—Samantha," called Julian through the drape, "Are you...?"

Sabrina spoke up before Samantha could figure out what to say. "Oh, don't worry, young man, I'll be going soon."

"Oh. Alright." Julian cleared his throat, decided it wasn't clear enough and so tried again.

Outside the window, The Baron continued to pace behind him. "You needn't be so worried, son."

Julian did his best to worry that someone had heard the Baron. "I don't know if I can remember everything you told me to say."

"You'll do fine," insisted the Baron. "I'll be right here." And to assure young Julian of his presence, the Baron Pan Bordolo set a steady hand on his shoulder. Hearing rustling just inside, the Baron readied his mouth by Julian's left ear. "Here we go."

"Okay: I'm back," said Samantha, her forehead resting gently against the drape, her cold fingers intertwining.

"Good. Are you alone?" asked Julian.

Seeing her sister nod, Samantha couldn't help but feel the tiniest twinge of guilt when she replied, "Yes."

"Good." Julian let himself breathe audibly enough for Samantha to glean that he had been nervous, and the thought made her blush. "I've come to say something," he said. Of course the longer he waited, the more curious Samantha became, such that by the time Julian uttered a sound, Samantha attempted to speak as well.

"What?" she asked, then realizing that she must have interrupted him, said, "Oh, sorry!"

But at the same time, Julian was saying, "What?" and then his own "Oh, sorry!" and so on.

"Um," began Julian because he was the first to regain his composure. "My lady…the reason of the unreason with which my reason is affected—*afflicted!*—so weakens my reason that with reason I murmur at your beauty."

The Baron patted Julian's back; Julian breathed a sigh of relief; and after only ten seconds or so, Samantha asked, "What?"

"Um," said Julian, but must have realized that that offered no conclusion and so tried again with the next line the Baron fed him: "The high heavens, that of your divinity divinely fortify you with the stars, render you deserving of the dessert your greatness deserves."

Samantha turned to her sister, who looked just as confused as she must have, then called through the window, "I don't know what that means."

"Oh." Julian hesitated. "Do you want me to say it again?"

Sabrina promptly shook her head. "No. Thank you," said Samantha.

She heard the young man clear his throat again, and wondered if he had caught a sniffle out in the cold before she heard him say, "All the world stand, unless all the world confess that in all the world there is no maiden fairer than the Empress Samantha, the peerless—what?"

Thinking that he had thought she interrupted him, Samantha stammered, "I—I didn't say anything."

"What?" asked Julian, and Samantha very nearly repeated, but for Julian saying, "Oh, yes, exactly." He shot a perturbed and slightly exasperated glance at the Baron, who mouthed 'sorry' for having whispered so unintelligible a phrase.

Samantha looked to her sister who wore a shrug across her eyebrows. "Julian?" she ventured, reaching once more for the drape, but was suddenly startled into withdrawing when Julian shouted, in something of a panic:

"Don't say my name!"

"Oh, sorry!" she gasped in return. Sabrina, also admonishing the younger for her inappropriate question, swatted her shoulder.

Julian resumed, "Um—It's just my name that's your enemy; I am myself, and not just Julian. I—um—What's in a name? A nose by any other name would smell as sweet."

Samantha crinkled her own nose at this, not offended per se but more confused and quizzical than she should like.

Sabrina took an opposite approach. "That's lovely," she whispered with a hand to her heart.

"I guess it would. Er... Julian," began Samantha, unsure of how exactly she should tell him she didn't understand him.

Sabrina seized her sister's arm and insisted through a fierce whisper, "Tell him you think it's lovely!"

Samantha's first instinct was to reject this order, but how could she dismiss the advice of someone who had had more success with men than Samantha could ever want? With only the faintest hint of trepidation, Samantha told Julian, "That's lovely."

The Baron commended the jubilant Julian with, "Well done, lad," in a hushed voice. "Now, here's what you say next:"

"I say," said Julian, "only—um—hamburger and civet in cotton; nor is she one-eyed or humpbacked, but straighter than a grandmamma dimple: but you must pay for the blas...thing you have uttered against beauty like that of my lady."

To be fair, he wasn't that far off[113]. Though the Baron's Quixotic quotation only made sense to him, he still cringed at the missed words.

---

[113] The missed words being ambergris for hamburger, a Guadarrama spindle in place of a grandmamma's dimple, and—as you might have already assumed—blasphemy. The full quotation goes, "I say, only ambergris and civet in cotton; nor is she one-eyed or humpbacked, but straighter than a Guadarrama spindle: but ye must pay for the blasphemy ye have uttered against beauty like that of my lady."

Samantha was stunned. Not only was it perhaps the prettiest thing she had ever heard, it made her fairly certain that she had not in fact heard anything at all. So, incredulously, she turned to her sister.

Sabrina obeyed her first instinct. "What's hamburger?" she whispered to the younger, and though she must not have intended so, Samantha took that as advice and confidently repeated it to Julian.

"What's hamburger?" she asked, while her sister was trying to convey that that was not in fact the right thing to say, so Julian looked to the Baron.

"What's hamburger?" he whispered, which the Baron answered promptly as well.

"A person from Hamburg[114]."

"A person—" began Julian, then realizing that it must have been some obscure 'Big Out There' reference, settled for, "Never mind."

"What's wrong with you?" Sabrina hissed, feeling that Samantha must have ruined the mood.

Samantha responded to Sabrina with, "What?"

So Julian repeated, "Never mind," a little louder;

And Sabrina repeated, "What's wrong with you?" with a little more fervor, which of course confused Samantha, because though Julian's heightened volume was understandable, the sister was directly at her ear.

"Wait!" she told Sabrina.

"Okay," said Julian.

"No, not you," clarified Samantha.

"Oh," said Julian.

"Is she still in there?" asked the Baron, possibly referring to Sabrina.

"'Course—I'm still talking to her," explained Julian obviously talking about Samantha.

"He thinks you've gone away!" whispered Sabrina.

"Oh! I'm still here," said Samantha.

---

[114] Now, I know what you're thinking: A hamburger is a delicious grilled or fried beef sandwich, which has nothing at all to do with ham. However, the delicacy that you now know did not claim that name until the early 20th century as a derivative of the last century's Hamburg minced beef steak. I must admit here that I'm baffled that every food type considered 'All American' is in fact either German or Irish or at least vastly foreign. In fact, the only truly American fare that I can note is the French fry, which the falsely accredited inventors want absolutely nothing to do with, but I digress.

"I thought so," said the Baron, while Julian interrupted with:

"Well, now she's heard you!"

Sabrina's eyebrows arched, and joined her whispering, "She?"

"Is there a woman out there?" Samantha asked, sounding a little hotter of the tone than she would have liked.

"Beg pardon!" came the Baron, puffing up his offended chest like a great owl.

"No!" replied Julian.

And while Samantha was feeling relieved, the Baron asserted back to Julian, louder than he would have liked, "Why not?"

Sabrina recognized this and asked out loud, "Mister Baron?"

"Sabrina?" asked Julian.

The older sister clapped two hands over her mouth and shook her head 'no.'

"No," relayed Samantha, and attempted to salvage the situation by pretending to be her sister and so asked, "Mister Baron, was that you?"

"No," insisted Julian.

"Julian?" she said.

Julian swallowed. "Yes?"

Samantha did her best to pause, but understand that it is difficult to drop that kind of conversational momentum. "What was it you came here to say?"

"I..." Julian fumbled slightly, then up and dropped the football altogether. Of course, the Baron was there to pick it up again for him, but he was held silent by what happened at that moment.

Let us first note that Samantha's door had no latch. So when Cletus, coming down the hall to deliver some warm milk knocked, the door chanced to budge out of the frame, which caused the most unruly of gasps from both sisters.

"Sorry!" exclaimed Cletus, dropping his head in shame and doing his best to close the door again.

"What?" came Julian.

"Shh!" shushed Samantha.

"Just a minute," called Sabrina.

"Who's that?" asked the Baron.

"Cletus!" hissed Samantha.

"Yes, miss?" asked Cletus.

"Not you!" insisted Sabrina.

"Samantha?" asked Julian.

"Sabrina," explained Samantha.

"Julian," began the Baron, but was interrupted by Julian, who pointed at the drape, saying:

"Sabrina."

"Miss?" asked Cletus.

"Go away!" said Samantha.

"Why?" asked Cletus.

"Let's go," said the Baron before starting off.

"Samantha?" asked Julian.

"Go!" she replied, drawing the drape aside and thrusting he hand through. She had reached out to wave him away but was met with the oddest sensation: though it was bitterly cold out that night, the warmest palm had come to rest against her own.

Her heart skipped a beat, she neglected to breathe, and for an instant every nerve in her body seemed to shout something so clearly toward her brain. Unfortunately the message—though quite strong and uttered in flabbergasting unison—must not have been in English, and the synapses didn't decode the foreign sounds quickly enough for her to know what it meant before Julian's fingers slipped away.

Samantha reclaimed her own hand, holding it close to her chest, as if to keep Julian's warmth from escaping it. Staring at the drape, she did not notice Cletus entering and growing quite embarrassed by the gowns worn by the daughters, (which fortunately provided reason why they should not want him to enter). The older of the daughters rushed out of the bedroom, nearly causing the poor gentleman's gentleman to disrupt his tray and milk.

Sabrina didn't pay much heed to the dress' material, (which wasn't nearly as sheer as Samantha had thought), but rather that it would have been long enough to trip over were she not bundling it in her forearms as she bounded up the stairs. A single jump sent her scrambling over the bed and up to the window, on the other side of which sat a cool blue night and two gorgeous male silhouettes walking up the hill. Of course Sabrina thought only one of the two was gorgeous, but occasionally your narrator likes to weigh in as well.

She wasn't the least surprised when the Baron, having obviously honed a keen sense for following eyes, turned back to look at her. When she blew a kiss in his direction, the Baron merely paid a nod in return; Sabrina decided to find it charming.

What she didn't know was that on the other side of her wall, just one room south, stood a wary Hephaestus, who watched the same two disappear from view. Though by now, his memory had quite slipped Lance's midnight gallivanting, he would well-remember Julian's.

Julian didn't notice any of the tracking eyes, nor did he speak until he and the Baron had reached the river that split the village. He did his best to keep the remark from sounding like a complaint. "I don't feel like I've managed to say anything tonight," he said.

"And yet," said the Baron, examining the stones for his first jump, "I think she heard a hell of a lot."

"Did any of it have to do with how I feel about her, Sir Baron?"

Landing on the other side with only the politest of grunts, the Baron replied, "Another night, Julian. Another night."

XLIX – The Small Fence

This is Miss Condamine. *Lady Condamine to you*, she might say, before cackling at her own little joke. She was, for the most part, the only person who laughed at her jokes, mostly because—in the opinion of this narrator—they weren't jokes. Regardless of their content, their delivery was spat through very pointy teeth, accompanied by devilishly beady eyes, and often followed by a cackle, the likes of which no one could find charming.

Condamine lived her life oblivious to this general opinion, but such was often given as the reason she was well-over twenty and not yet married. This did happen on occasion in the Isle, but only when the women in question were very devoted professionals, having no time for a family to distract them from their craft—Julian's Great Aunt Ivy, a carpentress herself who passed away several years before, was one such case. Condamine, however, had no craft and no devotion whatsoever to occupy her time, other than perhaps food.

It is not the most artful segue, granted, but I find it necessary to point out that Condamine certainly ate more than any other resident of the Isle, and—because nothing was paid for or privately owned—was only cut off by her older brother's understanding that the community of Adleship Isle had finite resources and could not simple shower them upon one individual. This would place Condamine in a surly mood, which she remedied either through intensive make-up and hair rituals, or through jaunts across the town to observe the locals.

Where we meet Miss Condamine presently, she is on one such jaunt—after having been denied a third breakfast and poutingly applying enough rouge to make a clown feel self-conscious. Watch as she tries to skip along the stone path, and with what little grace she bends down to strangle a daisy growing between two stones. Placing the daisy in her beehive of hair, she'll continue to frolic this way until she has found some children with whom to interact. Don't worry, she will not eat them, but she will trudge through their murals drawn in the dirt, or knock over their miniature snow villages, offering only a giggling, "Whoops!" as apology.

She was not cruel or vindictive, just bored and completely unaware that anyone else's feelings existed, let alone mattered. This was why she could not, as the other nobles did, teach the young people how to read, write, count, and behave. This—(along with the other obvious reason)—was also why no one trusted her to work in the food storage or any other inventory in the town. The village idiot was not a long-lived profession in the Isle, but Condamine took up its mantle swimmingly.

So when I said a few chapters before that the children liked to poke fun of her, you probably felt the urge to feel bad for her, and I suppose maybe some pity is in order, but if you met Condamine yourself, you would not in good conscience fault the children for their honesty.

You may be wondering why I have waited until now to introduce to you so vivid a personality as Condamine. Not to sound biased, but frankly I don't like her.

You may then be wondering why—if I find her so distasteful—I should bother to include her at all. Several of my readers are probably thinking right now, 'This unseemly lady puts an unnecessary bump in the road of what is otherwise a flawless story!' but I assure you, you will see my reasons just in a few short pages.

Here is why: at the moment you are being introduced to Condamine, one of your favorite characters was engaging in what he believed to be the most exciting tradition of the Adleship Islean feasts— the last of which had occurred after the Christmas supper.

Pigby was not obsessive about cleanliness. He would grow rather testy if presented with a poorly-arranged chart or misaligned spreadsheet, but where tidying was concerned, he had the good sense to see 'good enough' in a simple sweeping or dusting. Still, he was excited to no end about the cleanup days in the Isle, which he had predicted must have followed every large feast day. As luck would have it, he was right.

Basking in the happiness of the previous day, Pigby rose from his cot with a ready smile on his full dark lips. He snatched Geru from a discussion over Oswald's notes on the Isle's origins, and urged him outside to enjoy what was sure to be a fine morning.

Six friends convened on the hill for their morning exercises, and when Manuel complained that two spectators had set up a blanket on the hill above them, Clemens blamed his wife's insistent curiosity.

"Yes, well, far be it for Meredith to be left out if Rosa's coming to watch," grumbled Manuel.

They did their best to ignore their audience, though Pigby was quite convinced he heard giggling (amiably, not mockingly) on more than one occasion. Geru did his best to make himself look taller and pitch his voice lower, and Piers and Sherman did their best not to make eye contact with either the other men or their wives.

Point of fact, the person most affronted by the location of the women was the grandfather, who remembered how alone he used to feel on his rock. As he descended the hill that morning, he was muttering a proverb about solitude.

After concluding their exercises, Geru followed Piers to his end of the town so the short man could assess the health of a newborn sheep, while Pigby accompanied Clemens and Manuel to the storehouse. They gathered the trash of the day before, loaded it up in three wheelbarrows, and carted it towards the sheep fields on the south end of town, where the whole lot would reconvene to throw it off the edge of the world.

At this time, Condamine was becoming bored, seeing as there were very few children up and about. Those outside were busied by their new Christmas gadgets, busy enough to effectively ignore the round annoying woman who had no concept of personal bubbles.

Perhaps you've heard a duck call or used a bear call—though I can't imagine why—and if you have, I want you to think of how quickly those ducks and bears came running. Now, for my part, I've never seen that animals are particularly intrigued by man-made sounds, excepting cats and can openers. Essentially, Condamine was the cat, and the boisterous laughter of others her can opener.

It was hard not to laugh though, watching Geru give a go at the sling. He didn't take nearly as well to falling over as the giant man had, and had to be reassured repeatedly that no one meant to hurt his feelings by laughing.

Clemens had once again started the session, with Manuel right behind him, and so on down the line—including Geru's attempt—until they finally came to Pigby. Perhaps it was the morale from Piers' encouragement or the intimidation of Sherman's keen throw just moments before that bid Pigby load the sling as large as he did that morning. Because of the way he regarded Clemens when he packed it though, I'm quite convinced that it was his friend's silence that egged him take on such a powerful load so new to the game.

As tingling anticipation pervaded the comments and hearty laughs of the men in the field, Condamine decided that she wanted to get closer and have in on the fun. As the giant man stood with his impressively-packed sling, Condamine tittered in excitement. She had come down along the river, and watched from just far enough off that no one had noticed her yet—or perhaps they were trying to ignore her. Condamine herself was quite keen on gaining Pigby's attention.

Pigby's attention was on three things though: the straps in his right hand, the smug half-smile on Clemens' face, and a curiosity on the David and Goliath metaphor which caused him wonder that if he were the little boy with the sling, then how large should the giant be? And as he hoisted the sling, beginning a slow but quickly-accelerating arc, he did his best to distance himself from the chants of the other men that fell into the rhythm of his revolution.

Pigby took two slow, deliberate steps forward, and tuned out Condamine's call of "Yoo-hoo."

Drawing a deep breath, stable against the payload revolving about his head, Pigby neglected to intuit the direction of the oversweet voice which said again, "Yoo-hoo?"

Planting his feet firmly in the ground, ready to push off with his back leg like Clemens had showed him, Pigby was ready to throw when the third "Yoo-hoo!" interrupted not only his ears but his eyes.

As he came to see in the left of his vision a large animal waving a hanky and displaying the most frightening smile he had ever considered, Pigby yelped, released, and sent the large wad of garbage straight into Condamine.

The lady who had crept not quite into the line of fire (but close enough for the odd mistake) looked more shocked than angry or hurt— but then again, there was only a moment for the men of the Isle to take in her expression before the ball of garbage sent her tumbling backwards, through the small fence, and over the edge of the world.

It was the first time anyone had ever heard something hit the bottom.

L – The Dust in the Attic

The Baron would have assumed that Hephaestus' beard got in the way during such tasks as leaning over one's shoulder and whispering into one's ear. He was surprised that when he first heard the older's voice—at close enough proximity to warrant warmth of breath—he was not tickled by any errant grey wires. When he discovered that Hephaestus had braided the long whiskers together and clipped the tail end to his shirtfront as you might a tie, the Baron Pan Bordolo further supposed the older had planned the outfit according to his whispering needs.

Whether the beard was considered or simply coincidence, Hephaestus had certainly chosen his seat for the occasion, taking the bench behind the illustrious Baron and off his left shoulder so as to not be in earshot of any companions. Of course, as Pigby tended to bellow whenever he blubbered, such precautions may not have been necessary.

Pigby sat in the second row, two up from his boss and on either side sat Clemens and Piers, conveniently consoling him for what was hardly his fault. Geru—I suppose for the sake of irony—sat directly behind Pigby and insisted that he couldn't see the funeral proceedings. The rest of both crews were scattered about, as everyone had arrived at different times. The nobles sat up front, Penrod and Geert closest to the Libburus, who—in robes that were a little too long in the arms—presided over the impromptu event, held in the second storehouse, which in mid-winter was almost entirely bare.

Given everything else they had seen in the Isle, the Baron's crew neglected to be amazed that the funeral was thrown together within two hours of Condamine's death. They noted that there was no coffin, but once they heard *how* she had died, they noted no coffin necessary. The address sounded rehearsed and the proceedings procedural, and so the Baron—who had only briefly met Condamine for a brief moment before telling her that a sudden stomach cramp bid him "stand over there for a little while"—neglected to feel guilty for how little he paid attention.

Instead, he focused most of his energies on quietly issuing scathing retorts at Hephaestus, who—considering that he had just given away hundreds of little knickknacks to the people—could not fairly make a case about the footprint that the Baron's crew was obviously leaving.

"Well, in either case," Hephaestus resigned, "You agree that that makes three."

Ashamed that he couldn't stand up for Pigby, who obviously felt terrible for what was obviously an accident, the Baron consented, "Yes."

"And you'll let your man know?"

As if he had heard the last comment, Pigby let out a great sob.

"Trust me," said the Baron, "He knows."

"Good." Hephaestus sidled closer to the Baron, a gesture which pricked the man's personal bubble in a very agitating fashion. "Now, there is the business of rule six."

"Rule six?" asked the Baron, turning around to face him, "I thought 'No killing' was number three."

"It is, but we need to talk about rule six."

The Baron furrowed his brow hard enough that his mustache began to uncurl, and tried not to look in Sabrina's direction when he asked, "Is that the 'No sex' clause?"

"No, Mister Bordolo—"

"'Sir Baron!' Please."

"*Sir Baron*, six isn't sex, six is station."

"Station? Oh, social structure—yes, so it is. What of it?"

"I saw you and Julian leave the Libburus' last night," Hephaestus said, as if that explained the whole of his case.

"And I saw you seeing me," the Baron replied. "Can't say I approve of the spying."

"I've seen the way that boy looks at her." And both the Baron and the lord of merchants shifted their gazes Julian, who—another row up and several seats away—was obviously staring at Samantha.

The Baron inhaled fiercely through his nose before repeating through gritted teeth, "What of it?"

"She is noble, Sir Baron. He is not."

The Baron, more aware of class distinction than most, scoffed at this. "I've heard of nobles marrying down in this town."

"Yes, but it's frowned upon," which the Baron could assume on his own, "It only ever happens when a man wants to dismiss his station and marry a lower woman," which the Baron had likewise observed, "and it is absolutely, expressly forbidden for a Libbur to marry a non-noble!" which should have knocked the Baron's protest flat.

"That girl's not a Libburus!" he exclaimed, clearly missing my last.

"No, not the Libburus—*a* Libbur! Libburus and immediate family, Libbur household—Honestly, mister Bordolo!" returned the exasperated Hephaestus, then, (realizing that he had finished his last few sentences with exclamation points), took a beat to relax. "And as long as we're at it, I should reinforce rule five—that one is the 'to lie with' clause. After all *she* is of a particular social class as well."

"Why would you assume—"

"Oh, it's not what I assume, dear Baron," interrupted Hephaestus, who assumed a great deal about the older daughter, "It's what I would prevent."

Having found the slanted shoulders of the sister in the front row, the Baron sighed and informed Hephaestus of what he'd already resolved, "You'll be happy to know I plan on keeping the proper distance between myself and the—ahem!—other Libbur-girl. And where in God's name does that ridiculous word come from?" he asked.

"It doesn't matter," insisted Hephaestus. "Either way, those girls are not eligible to those your side of the river, and however you may like the boy, however pure his intentions..." As Hephaestus watched Julian, his voice chanced to quiver. "No matter how true his soul, Sir Baron, he cannot break rank and status. Not here, not anywhere."

Of course the Baron's brain was racing to find some way around this decree before Hephaestus had even finished. And of course Hephaestus, without even having to see the glint in his rival's eye, was well-aware of the thought process he had initiated. The Baron started to turn around, started to say, "Well, what if we were to *change*—"

"Mister Bordolo, I know you like to poke fun at me, and you've probably arrived with a little speech already prepared." (Point of fact, the Baron had arrived with no such thing; rule six had not even occurred to him the night before. Though he did mean to initiate the romance without either the girl's father or His Highest's knowledge, he in no way expected this kind of confrontation. Still, he felt it served him to seem one step ahead of Hephaestus and so said nothing.)

Hephaestus on the other hand *had* prepared a speech. "I need you to make me a solemn promise," he said, with every air of sincerity his otherwise-pompous voice might support, "that you will not interfere further on this matter."

"You don't mean—"

"Oh, I mean, mister Bordolo. I mean that I need from you a strict pledge to not concoct any kind of grand scheme which ends with the young lady marrying the young man," and the Baron was still convinced that he could still see his way around this mandate, until Hephaestus next spoke. "If you are indeed a baron, sir—if you happen to be the Baron Pan Bordolo, then I know you would not spit in the face of our God-given hierarchy, because no man who is *truly* an English noble would dare besmirch the entire noble line by breaking these rules."

Hephaestus had won the duel. In fact, he had secured such a swift and effective victory that the Baron would not have had time to curse his enemy before he fell dead on the blade. His mustache drooped in dismay.

"Very well," consented the Baron, but did so so quietly that Hephaestus had to bid him repeat it again.

"Very well," he said, a seal on his honor and duty, which he heartily hoped not to need address again. And if he should wish to falter, the Baron knew one man who would hold him to these promises, his oldest friend and surest compass.

Oswald sat in the far back corner of the room, Jonas by his side and his pen-hand working furiously on a long scroll. (I would say 'tirelessly,' but the cramps in his thumb were evidence to the contrary.)

Jonas seemed miffed when Oswald stole his writing supplies the night before, but warmed up to watching the less-old man scribble so much without cease. Oswald figured that it was because Jonas recognized a crazed fixation in someone else that he only often observed in himself, and was offended by his own assumption.

Though Jonas had turned in at a reasonable hour on Christmas night, Oswald had remained writing at the couch, and must not have slept because he had spent two candles and was a fair way into the third by the time Jonas woke up to visit his friend the rock. In just one night, yards and yards of scroll lay newly riddled with lines and notes and diagrams, detailing a mountain, a steering wheel, and a large bell.

When he was called for the funeral, Oswald was just descending the bell-tower, having taken an impression of the name cast on the town's bell. While it ordinarily would have charmed him that the town was woken on holidays by a bell called Lucky, his brow was too occupied with clenching to let him smile. And because he could not stop writing long enough for facial expression, he certainly couldn't sit through a funeral for someone he was quite convinced he had never met without jotting down more notes.

Of course merely entering the converted storehouse further fueled his rampaging pen. Now, you may find it untoward that someone might be very distracted during a funeral which all members of a village are expected to attend, but it was common for the citizens to make allowances for the very young and old. Oswald was happy to bank in on such a favor.

Oswald watched the Libburus intently, particularly the long staff he carried for the funeral and what Oswald could only assume were 'priestly' duties. Additionally, while everyone else saw that the long rod had had its flat head carved into the profile of a bird of prey, Oswald would wager he had been the only one who recognized that the staff was obviously oil-treated to withstand salt-water.

Though he could see no cross and no Bible, many of the sentiments expressed resonated in his very clogged Anglican ears. And on the old rusted chest that served as a kind of altar, he was certain he could make out an engraving of a rose.

After a final word on the deceased, everyone stood, and a train began toward the altar, on which was placed a very poorly painted likeness of Lady Condamine. Perhaps the artist had decided that rendering her well might reject any sympathies that the so-called grievers would have had. As each individual paid a moment's respect at the altar, the townsfolk gradually began to filter out.

The Baron had made it to the door when Hephaestus' hand took his shoulder and insisted knowingly, "Ah, but Mister Bordolo, you *must* join us for the town procession."

To be fair, not everyone went on the town processions during funerals. Most people usually just followed the Libburus to the square before breaking off for their own homes or work while the Libburus led a very, *very* boring romp around the town with the close friends, the blood relatives, and the obligated nobles, stopping for a moment of silent regards whenever anyone pointed out a spot in the town the recently deceased had enjoyed. The Baron, seeing the nobles line up behind the Libburus and knowing that Hephaestus was challenging his status, consented to follow the lot without really knowing what he was getting himself in for.

He did notice that Julian slipped out of the group before they could make it to the square.

For that matter, so did Oswald. With a fascinated Jonas two steps behind him, he trotted out the door of the storehouse and nearly ran into Geru whom he'd indicated to wait for him.

"Aha," began Oswald, which must have been a greeting in another language, "Have you brought the maps?"

Looking down at his friend's feet, Geru said, "You're limping. Where's your crutch?"

"It's fine, it's fine: I can't write while walking if I'm carrying a crutch—Now, the maps."

"Oh yes." Geru opened the satchel at his side and revealed a stack of papers. He made to hand them to Oswald but was cut off with:

"Keep those. You're coming with me."

"Why?" inquired Geru.

"I need a second set of eyes."

"Why not use him?" Geru indicated Jonas, whose smile pleasantly suggested that he was missing a few important screws.

"Eyes and a fully functioning mouth," amended Oswald. "Now, come on."

Oswald's ankle had gotten considerably better over the last week. Though Geru, a doctor in his own right, had noticed immediately, Oswald barely paid attention to the straggling stride of his lesser foot as they made their way up the hill and over the bridge, just barely beating the procession out of the square, and on toward the three-story house near the top of the river.

Though he had not actually met them, Geru had heard tell of Dietrich and Elke, largely from Fletcher and Oswald, and had decided ahead of time that since they were so well-liked by his colleagues, there must be some terrible fault with them. Even so, when they arrived at the house and Oswald knocked on the door, Geru still took off his hat[115], as was polite. After they had stood waiting for at least a minute—five by Geru's guess—Oswald suggested, "I say: maybe they've not gotten home from the funeral."

"Brilliant! So you rush me here to beat the procession and we're early?"

"There's no need to get angry," said Oswald in his best to sound soothing.

In truth, there wasn't; it was a fine morning, but for Pigby having accidentally killed someone, and even then Geru and Oswald had mostly

---

[115] Akin to a fez, though not as tall.

forgotten about such a trivial detail. The few birds that lived in the Isle were chirping as though it was already springtime, and they could hear the faint sounds of playing children not far off into the meadow. Their laughter captured Jonas' attention immediately.

Jonas had followed the other two, and seeing as the man seemed to be running out of quotations with which to surprise them, he hadn't said a word since the funeral and so gave neither Geru nor Oswald a reason to shoo him away during their scintillating investigation. With his back turned toward them as they waited for Dietrich and Elke, he was clearly a force to be ignored.

"You know the door doesn't have a lock. We could just let ourselves in." Geru reached for the handle and Oswald valiantly popped between the short man and the door.

"Geru!"

"Look, it's not as though we're going to steal anything—"

"Have you no manners?" asked an appalled Oswald.

"Why would they have locks if no one steals anything?"

"They don't need locks; they have manners!"

When they heard the grandfather chuckle, both Geru and Oswald assumed it was directed at their argument. As neither of them liked being mocked, both instinctively turned to regard the chuckle. As they found that Jonas was still facing away from them and into the sliver of meadow visible between houses, they decided not to take offense.

Instead, they regarded five children, none of them over the age of ten, each with a stick or two on their person. The sticks were nearly straight, between two and three feet long, and rid of excess twigs so that when any two children crossed sticks, they could do so with acceptable precision. Oswald and Geru each took a few steps forward, heads cocked to one side[116], flanking Jonas as he observed, "Without a sign, his sword the brave man draws, and asks no omen but his country's cause."

If they had been closer, they might have heard the children discussing whose turn it was to play His Highest and who would be The Mustache Man for each bout, or that they believed the object of this game was to point the stick at the opponent's chest.

Neither Oswald nor Geru knew why they gasped when the door was opened behind them. Elke, looking more than a little surprised to see them as well, apologized for taking so long to answer the door.

---

[116] To the left, if you must know.

"It's quite alright, madam," replied Oswald, having had already assumed that they weren't home. "I spoke to your husband yesterday about the maps."

"Yes, yes, of course. Come on in then," she offered, and as the door was opened far enough to let light in, the old and short men observed that the lady of the house was looking quite flushed.

Standing on his toes to better reach the old man's ear, Geru whispered, "You said they didn't like each other."

Dietrich was waiting at the top of the elevator, goggles at the top of his head, and just as twitchy as ever. He did clear his throat a few times more than usual; in gentlemanly fashion, Oswald decided to credit it to the dust in the attic. The first and only comment he made before delivering them to the maps was to himself, noting, "This's the first I've seen Jonas here in years."

As the cloth had been pulled from the skylight, there were no candles needed to see not only the map that Dietrich had laid out, but the steering wheel hung on the wall.

Geru's dexterous fingers frantically drew unfolded map after map from his satchel as Oswald took care to match them to the one on the table. Jonas and Dietrich leaned over the specimens from the other side, appearing so intrigued that it's a wonder neither man drooled on the documents. Oswald immediately rejected every single map as not a close enough rendering, and was dangerously near the bottom of Geru's pile when he declared, "There! Stop!"

Geru's rhythm ceased, and all four men leaned forward to inspect a document whose contours appeared thrillingly close to the one on the table. Oswald's gaze jerked from one map to the next, checking every consistency to the best of his ability, and finally asking Geru, "Concur?"

Geru nodded. "Match," he affirmed before lifting their map from the table.

Because almost every sample looked the same to his untrained eyes, Dietrich asked the very excited men across from him, "What does that mean?"

"It means, Mister Dietrich, that the way our country was documented when you settled here was the same way it was being drawn in…" His thumb by the date and signature, Geru read, "1642—apparently by P and A."

"That means you've been here not for forever—I say," explained Oswald, "but less than two hundred years."

LI – Torments

Julian didn't know why he ran. After all, it wasn't going to move away if he didn't get there fast enough, and yet some superficial urgency fueled his feet.

As he ran south, past the noble houses, over the bridge, and on down the field, he experienced a rush of exhilaration and worry, akin to vertigo, as if he believed that running too quickly might cause him to slip and slide right off the edge of the world. He halted well before the broken fence, his pounding heels turning up clumps of grass from the muddy field, and gazed along the similar scuffs where Condamine had taken her last frantic steps.

Julian brought a hand to his forehead, feeling the cool sweat which seemed to pulse in time with his collecting breathing. Letting the same hand run back through his hair before dropping to his side, the boy regarded the best glimpse of the Big Out There he thought that he should ever find.

He had never tried to look through the floor of fog as hard as he did that day, wondering what lay below and what lay beyond.

Staring into that most brilliant winter sun, whose rays glanced off the snowy cliffs peaking over the clouds, Julian couldn't help but wonder if it was curiosity and not clumsiness that had claimed the last person who slipped over the edge, or the man who broke through the southern bridge years before. Maybe he and his cart made for too much weight; maybe the river had eroded the supports too far; or maybe it was something else entirely.

The most fascinating thing about that occurrence was that the man's son had been riding in the cart when the bridge began to crumble, but the man shoved the cart the remainder of the way across the bridge, saving his son before the river persuaded him over the waterfall. Not knowing whether it was his own weight that tipped the scales, and not being able to begrudge the unfortunate deceased, the son found it hard not to blame himself, much like Pigby did for Condamine.

Now, I know what you're thinking, and you'd be wrong:

See, if you think about it, logically, it couldn't've been Julian's father that died during the bridge-breaking, seeing as Julian's parents died at close to the same time. Not that it's relevant to our story, but the man whose death prompted the overdue rebuilding of the southernmost bridge was Manuel's grandfather, and young boy who made it to the opposite bank Manuel's father.

Julian's parents died from an unassuming illness, which first invaded Julian's father. Then, as his mother inherited it, Julian was relocated to Meredith's until they were cured. Of course, they didn't emerge from the house, but neither did the illness, and because it happened during the summer, there was no lord of merchants to diagnose their killing condition, and so they may well have saved the town by locking themselves indoors. Not many people thought of it that way though; it was just another disease and another pair of headstones to the people of the Isle.

As Julian watched across the river, he could faintly make out the procession party arriving at the little plot of grave-stones wherein they might set Lady Condamine's[117]. He wondered how closely her marker sat to his parents'. He wondered how long he had been standing there looking out into the wild foggy yonder[118].

Sometimes it is not the actions but the accidents which define a person's life, and sometimes it is these same accidents which define his or her death. It happened somewhere between the Libburus' patting the headstone 'goodbye' and the few remaining followers of the procession—(including the Baron, his rival, and his giant)—conveying

---

[117] I apologize if the following offends your sensibilities, but it may have occurred to you that it would be a very poor use of Adleship Isle's limited space if they buried all of their deceased and left them there eternally. Thankfully, they do not dig up dead bodies from their graves; there were no graves and the 'headstones' marked no heads whatsoever as the heads went over the falls with the rest of the corpses.
As for overcrowding of the stones, every five years or so, the oldest people in town collected and sanded down the oldest stones to make room for the next people to die. You might have thought that the nobles were given priority in these cases, but efficiency of space trumped even noblehood, for all bodies were equal bodies after death.
[118] At least as long as the previous chapter, for the sake of certain simultaneities.

their respects, that Julian came to a momentous decision and started walking north once again.

Perhaps it was Condamine's untimely death that tipped him off, or maybe just a fleeting scent on the wind, but Julian knew that he could not wait for such an accident to define his life.

As he heard the funeral proceedings wrapping up, he stepped into a light jog. As he saw the townsfolk beginning to gather in the square for the post-cleanup assembly, he broke into a run. And as he bounded across the same river, Julian knew what he would see just past the field and over the hill—well, not the kids playing with sticks; he had had no idea that that kind of activity lay in wait anywhere, but he pushed it out of his mind and did his best not to slip as he descended the last few steps before the well.

Julian was met with trepidation when he approached Samantha, not because he was dwelling on any of the rules of class, but because both his pulse and blood pressure rose in relation to his proximity to the lady. Were he to speak with Geru on the matter, the little scientist would have informed him of hormone triggers and pupil dilations and a series of causes to sweat, less than half of which were superstition.

However, had Julian been told of these signals, he may have been able to read them in the young lady whose hands were folded so tightly around one another that both of her elbows had to turn forward to accommodate the gesture.

"Hi," he said, more than a little out of breath, but sounding spontaneous enough to be charming. This made him smile.

"Hi," she replied, and. as if feeling that she had said too much, bit her lower lip to retract whatever other silly things might fall out of her mouth if left unattended. But as she did, she found that Julian was smiling, and so blushed in return.

"Um," began Julian, and because she nodded, he continued, "I was hoping I'd find you here."

"I didn't know if you'd be coming," Samantha returned.

"I've been absent lately."

"I noticed."

"Yeah, but I," began Julian, fully intending to give the best excuse he could, and then stopped short as he realized the lovely gift his lady had given him. "You did?"

She tried not to giggle, seeing as giggling was silly and far too young a gesture for a lady of her standing, but some slipped out. Cupping her hands over her mouth, she collected the excess giggle and resolved to simply nod.

Julian tried not to laugh, but—you know where this is going, don't you?

Neither had any idea of why they were laughing, but it kept on for quite a while. In fact, the laugh was severe enough that it affected Julian's legs and forced him to stagger forward and brace himself against the side of the well. The laugh started in Samantha's throat, but crept skillfully down into her belly, causing her to clutch at her sides and slump into the grass, doubling over as she chortled and guffawed with Julian.

As the young boy wiped the tears from his eyes, the girl tried to catch her breath. As Julian came to rest his chest on the soothing cool stones of the well, Samantha came to rest her back against its circular frame, and there, where his arm hung limply down toward the ground, her hand found his and they stopped.

Keeping the one soft hand in Julian's, Samantha brought the other to her heart to check if it was still beating, and dared not blink, for staring back at her through those big brown eyes was indeed the truest soul she had ever seen.

"I have something to say," began Julian.

Keeping his slow, uneven pace, she asked, "Like you did last night?"

Julian screwed up his lips in contemplating this. "Did you understand any of that?"

She shook her head. "Not a word."

"Good!" he breathed a sigh of relief, "Neither did I." He leaned closer to her face, and she continued to look up at him, and as he tilted his head ever so slightly to the right[119], he whispered, "I still have something to say to you."

"No, wait."

It was soft, gentle—so soft and gentle that it managed to not be the most terrible thing Julian had ever heard, and he fought the urge to suddenly withdraw—successfully!—(thankfully)—because Samantha answered the "Why?" that his expression asked her.

"Not now. Not today," she said, giving him back his hand and helping him back to a standing position. Standing with him, both her

---

[119] Clinching proof that right-tilting on a first kiss is a natural human impulse which need not be learned by commercial television.

346   STOUMBOS

palms at his shoulders, Samantha delivered her request: "On a day that no one has died, no after Christmas clean-up, no Baron and Hephaestus, just us. Then tell me."

Julian meant to say "Okay" in reply, but the blood was thundering so much in his ears that he was quite certain he had failed to hear it. She seemed to have caught the affirmative, as well as the ringing of the town's bell and so said, "Come on," before leading him back to the square for the post-cleanup assembly.

The town chamber had waited for the Libburus and the other processing grievers to arrive before commencing. Geru and Oswald had gathered with Dietrich and Elke with more than time enough to see the bell being rung. By the time the Baron and Hephaestus showed, with a cried-dry Pigby in tow, the speakers were about prepared to speak.

Julian and Samantha were just arriving during the first remarks and hardly heard any of the preliminary announcements, but to be fair, not many other people of note were paying attention either. The Libburus was rehearsing his speech to himself while Cletus went to locate the second daughter. Sabrina, put out that her father had held her arm instead of letting her go to the Baron for comfort during the procession, was trying to weave out of Cletus' line of sight or sense of smell[120] so as to reach the mustache man.

The Baron was obviously arguing with Hephaestus. Well, maybe arguing is a bit strong; more accurately, they were sharing a healthy plate of snide and getting crumbs everywhere[121]! I'll get you up to speed; this is what they were on about as they filtered into the throng.

"That was the dullest experience of my life!" the Baron whispered, knowing that the assertion was absurd hyperbole, "I should have known you just roped me along to get the best of me."

"Oh, so you think I enjoy your company now, do you?"

"I can't see how anything other than bitterness could have motivated you dragging me on that utterly pointless procession."

"Well, how about duty?" offered Hephaestus. "After all, it was your man who felled that dizzy cow—"

---

[120] Algernon could pinpoint the precise angular direction of any member of his household within fifty yards, the second highest nose-direction sense ever to be claimed by an English butler—P. G. Wodehouse's Mister Jeeves, (not yet born), being his only better.

[121] See, I found that terribly funny, but my editor insists that it makes no sense. I suppose I'll leave it to you to form your own opinion.

"And from the way everyone's paying respects, it seems as though they should be thanking him for the service!"

"Ah, yes, thanks! That's something you never hear these days what with the manners of the younger generation."

"My generation is doing just fine thank you, and yours should be well-past extinct by now."

"Then why haven't I heard a jot of gratitude for the gifts I gave your people yesterday?"

"I should imagine it's because you've been spying on them," the Baron replied.

"Well forgive me for having eyes, Mister Bordolo."

"Unfortunately I can't forgive you for having a tongue."

"If I hadn't, you never would have survived the winter."

"Mayhap it's better to die, *sir*, than to be shown such disrespect!"

"And impersonating a baron is not disrespect?"

"Oh! You wouldn't know nobility if it kicked you in the teeth."

"Perhaps you would care to demonstrate!"

"Maybe I will!" announced the Baron, quite loudly enough to receive a shushing from the rest of the group, many of whom were paying attention to the review on the winter food stores.

"Honestly though," resumed the Baron in a whisper, "What were you trying to tell them with those gifts? For God's sakes, you sent Oswald on some kind of sacred mission with those history notes." The Baron Pan Bordolo did not know that it was in fact the bell that acted the catalyst for Oswald's not having slept, but the observation was not far off.

"I gave them each what I thought to be in line with their interests," defended Hephaestus, "That's all!"

"You deny that you were hinting at something about this place?"

"I deny nothing," returned Hephaestus, "I would just like to be given a little bit of credit for so catering to the particular passions of your people."

"Well, I should imagine you did!" the Baron said, with more hostility than he had intended.

"And what of the coat?"

"The coat that I'm wearing right now?" Indeed the Baron was wearing the same blue coat that Hephaestus had given him.

"Yes, that coat!" Hephaestus shot back.

"It's very nice!"

"Does it fit well?" spat Hephaestus.

"It's a little big in the shoulders, but otherwise quite well, thank you!"

"Good!"

"Fine!"

They paused to catch their breaths and try to avert with nods the scathing glances of the other persons in town who were irked by their argument.

The Baron grumbled, "Anyway, thanks for the coat."

"Glad you like it," grunted the other.

"How did you manage to find one?" asked the Baron, but Hephaestus stopped him with a finger to his own lips before indicating the speaker in the center of the square.

By this time, Sabrina had made her way to the Baron's side and attempted to initiate conversation. "Mister Baron, sir."

"Hmm? Oh, I'm sorry dear, but we were listening to the announcement," said the Baron before resolutely facing the center and trying to follow Piers' updates on animal and food rationing.

From across the donut, Julian was also doing his best to pay attention, or as least pretend to pay attention. Once Samantha had gotten them both in the circle she told Julian that she had to go see her father and so left Julian's side while the boy considered his conflicting urges to chase after her against her firmly-worded wishes.

Fletcher made the decision easier. Having been left alone all day and somewhat confused as to why no one had taken him along on their important affairs, the thin man took it upon himself to tend to the snap-pea while her mother and father worked on the after-Christmas cleanup with the other citizens. And from on Fletcher's shoulders, Miriam spotted Julian in the crowd and called his name.

"Well then Julian!" said Fletcher with such gregarious volume that it's odd he was not shushed, "Where've you been, boy?"

Gladly taking the distraction from his stifling decision, Julian asked, "Have you been looking for me?"

"I should say so! I asked Miss Miriam here what she would usually do on a day like today, and she said she would follow Julian—isn't that right, Miss'm?"

"Yep!"

"Ah," came Julian knowingly. "So you can't find anything to do?"

"Not a task in the world," admitted the thin man. "Everyone is so wrapped up in tidying the town that the only people interested in seeing my gadgets are the children, but even they seem like they'd rather play 'duel.' It's quite disheartening; I mean, how can I expect to be '*the* Fletcher' if I can't find an audience to pitch to?"

"It's a problem," Julian agreed.

"Use conundrum[122]," offered Fletcher, "it's a better word."

"How's that?" asked Julian.

"Conundrum!" chimed Miriam from Fletcher's shoulders.

"It's a better word," Fletcher repeated with a smile.

Julian nodded. He thought the word sounded more funny than good, but then again who was he to question a literature expert from the Big Out There? He had a suspicion that Jonas would also use a word like conundrum if given a choice.

Coincidentally, Jonas was at that moment looking for Julian. Unfortunately, he was not as fleety of foot as the thin man and did not have his luck, seeing as he ended up on the opposite side of the square. He was most out of breath and seemed to have inherited Oswald's limp, evidencing that he had been walking very quickly or at least for a much longer time than he was used to.

Sweat on his cheeks and saliva on his lips, he muttered as he went, half in riddle and half in direct repetition of what Piers was announcing. In what could only be described as desperation, the grandfather reached out and grabbed the first person he came upon, who happened to be Hephaestus. He had barely begun speaking when Hephaestus jerked roughly away.

"Unhand me, sir!"

"Hephaestus!" came the Baron, appalled at his rival's inconsideration, and strode past Hephaestus to hold the grandfather up, supporting him by the elbows. "Are you alright, sir?"

Jonas closed his eyes tight and shook his head. "It happens as with cages," he explained so rapidly that even if the Baron were familiar with the quotation, he could not have registered it, "the birds without despair to get in and those within of getting out."

Sabrina rushed to the Baron's side. "What's wrong?"

"Just give him some space, dear," said the Baron, assured that since the grandfather showed no intention of collapsing there was no cause for alarm. Glancing about him, the Baron noted concern among the

---

[122] Now, to be fair, at that time, Fletcher probably would have spelled it quonundrum, but who am I to split hairs?

crowd but was more intent on the fact that Hephaestus had already taken care to give the ailing man plenty of space.

Hephaestus righted himself and—without making eye contact with the Baron—faced the center where Piers was just wrapping up.

With confidence but not the same rehearsed cadence as most of the other things he had said, Piers announced, "And now we have an address from our man, Raul."

Raul on the other hand did look confident, and Hephaestus was tall enough to acknowledge it. Granted the confidence was apparent even to Julian, who faced his friend's back as the young man strode into the center of the square. The Baron Pan Bordolo, being occupied with Jonas did not even notice the new player in the post-Christmas post-cleanup assembly.

When he reached Piers, Raul actually shook the man's hand, which was not even a common custom in the Isle at that time, but it made him look even more assured and—though it had only been a couple of days since—more adult than he ever had while he was seventeen.

"Ladies and gentlemen," he began, "I've learned a lot in the last few days, from my friends, my family, and our visitors from the Big Out There." Julian, Eugene, and every man (and Ten ha) from both crews beamed. "I think it's fitting that the lesson in responsibility came on the day that I turned eighteen, and as you see me now, I am no longer a boy, but a man, possibly to be your next Libburus once our good friend finishes his term."

Taking a break from Jonas, who was rubbing a frustrated wrist against his forehead as he tried to remember what it was he had come to say, the Baron turned to Hephaestus and asked, "Did you help him write that?"

"Not at all," replied the older.

Though the Baron initially wanted to call it cliché, having dismissed the insufferable curmudgeon as author, had to admit, "It's quite good."

"Perhaps there is a lesson in the death of our dear Condamine," Raul went on, "to not wait on life's events to come to us, but rather—like Mister Baron and His Well-Traveledness—to go out and seize them."

Julian swelled with pride at this, for a part of him felt as though the young man was commending his efforts. From the other end of the circle in the square, Jonas knew otherwise. He took a deep breath and grabbed the Baron's arm and struggled to wheeze.

"Careful, there, old man," advised the Baron, but Jonas shook his head and puffed his chest again. The Baron was quite worried that the grandfather should burst a necessary bit of brain, given the strain evident in his face. Hephaestus looked concerned that any burst of brain might get on his clothes, seeing as he was backing away.

At the same moment, Raul was calling two parties in the crowd forward, saying, "If you will join me—"

And as he announced the last, the Baron was deafened by Jonas' sputter of "Oh, how many torments lie in the small circle of a wedding-ring!"

"Wedding ring?" asked the Baron, who, in looking back to the center, spotted the two persons approaching to be Sebastian and his younger daughter Samantha. "Wedding ring!" the Baron gasped, losing track of his throat enough that the exclamation made sound to him alone.

He considered crying out: yelling 'Stop' like that frightened individual on the tracks who thinks—in a moment of madness—that trains can understand English. Sadly, he didn't manage to make another sound. And in this paralyzed state, the Baron coincidentally caught young Julian's eye just in time to shake his head before Raul made his promised announcement.

"I am here today to ask the lady Samantha to marry me!"

Sometimes the accidents which define men's lives are merely thoughtless actions of others.

LII – A Very Simple Proclamation

Miriam had been hushed by Fletcher, who could see his host's distress, and then later by Meredith, when she was handed off shortly after. Following the arm of the person in front of her as they scurried home, the snap-pea did not know for how long she was to remain silent. Taking her cue from Julian, she may have assumed forever.

She did not however understand why the strange assortment that followed the mustache man should rail between one another, especially when their leader—who strode only a few steps behind young Julian—kept shushing them. Miriam eventually decided to take it as a point of pride that she could keep her mouth shut better than grown men (and Ten ha).

Even so, the moment Meredith had gotten the door shut behind her, Miriam asked, "Momma, what happened?"

"An outrage!" exclaimed Geru from just up the way at Julian's house. They had all come pouring in through the door after the boy and were busy trying to assort themselves about the room at any station that looked appropriate for properly consoling Julian, who, though he paced very abruptly and exhaled with extreme ardor, had not uttered a word since the mass stampede out of the square.

In fact, he'd hardly made a sound other than to gulp after Raul's question, which made Fletcher bid him, "Alright then, sit down," while Pigby gingerly but very swiftly escorted the lad onto the couch.

Setting himself, Oswald waved Ten ha away, telling her to "Get him some water."

"Yes," breathed Ten ha before rushing across the room to Julian's jug[123].

"Lad, I am so sorry," said the Baron, "I had no idea he planned to do this." He clearly did not count the grandfather's last-minute warning for much.

"None of us did," Pigby assured him.

"The nerve of the boy!" came Geru.

"I think it's terrible," said Oswald.

"And to think, now you've only got the rest of your life to wonder what you missed out on." Fletcher didn't have time to react before Oswald, Geru, Pigby, *and* the Baron slapped him.

Ten ha arrived to hand a sloshing mug to Julian. "It's not as bad as all that."

"What?" asked Julian before drinking.

"There's no reason to despair yet," explained Ten ha. "She didn't say 'yes.'"

"And why not?" asked Raul, more to himself than his father, sisters, and servants who watched him pacing behind the table. Had his hair been a little less sturdily attached to his scalp, the young man surely would have pulled out a handful during his next emphatic gesture. "I mean, how can I—how can I—how can I—"

This third exclamation of the same might assure readers that he had absolutely no idea of what he was trying to say. To try to prove contrary, Raul raised a finger and, indicating the point to his father, observed, "I move to assert my responsibility, but how can I show that I'm ready to be a man and a leader if she doesn't say 'yes'?"

And as the fuming noble spun about to resume pacing, Eugene held out his palms and slowly stepped forward to subdue his son. "Now, Raul—"

"I mean," began Raul whipping around and forcing his father a step backwards, "does it—does it occur to her what this—what this—" He flailed his hands and wrists in frustration as if to indicate his thought process. "What this says about *me*? I mean, the—everyone saw me—and

---

[123] You may have wondered on this, seeing as I haven't mentioned it. Truth be told, no record of water-storage protocol in the Isle has been found, but I should imagine that most households kept large jugs about which they carried to the river frequently to gather water. After all, what filtering is needed for glaciers, especially in the days before the toxic emissions of industrial factories? Tangent, granted, but sometimes I do so envy the lifestyles of the people in the Isle.

how are they supposed to place faith in me—as a Libburus—when she won't—publicly!"

And because Raul faced his father pleadingly, Eugene concluded that he must have thought he had finished his question.

"Now, it's not so bad," he said, "It's not as if she said 'no.'"

"But-but-but she didn't say anything[124]!" The Libburus wrang out his sweaty hands frantically and turned to Hephaestus to beg for wisdom on the subject, then—resolving that His Grandestness knew nothing of these matters—something he only very-rarely resolved—confronted Cletus and entreated, "Why wouldn't she say something?"

"Now, now, sir," soothed Cletus, "Let's get you into your slippers and help you relax."

"But-but, Cletus! I—My—We—" Surely if someone had invented inhalers at that time, Sebastian would have taken a heavy drag from one. Instead, Hephaestus offered him a pipe. "Thank you," said Sebastian before quickly sucking on the end and coughing to steady his nerves.

The other three waited for him to speak again: those being Cletus, Hephaestus, and Trenton, who once again stood against the door with his arms folded across his chest. "Thank you," he said again, handing the pipe back.

"Now, Sebastian, keep in mind that she may have just been shy," Hephaestus ventured.

Sebastian nodded. "That's true. Oh, now, I feel such the fool! Last night, when Eugene told me what would happen, I was simply overjoyed, but-but I never suspected that Samantha might object."

"You never asked her how she felt?" asked Trenton form across the room.

"Well, the boy wanted to tell her himself. Said that he'd watched her grow up and realized that she was a fine young woman—which I was happy to hear." Sebastian shuddered, not from cold, but that overwhelming nervous energy that builds up in leaders who may or may not be scarcely fit to lead. Looking to Hephaestus, Sebastian explained with a comical sort of smile, "Apparently she said something to him. About being strong and standing up to his father and respecting good deeds more than good blood and that…" Tickled by this, though not quite

---

[124] Seeing as our Libburus was having yet another cannon moment, I truly cannot attach enough exclamation points to this comment, so I'll just stick with one.

enough to fully dispel the dismay, he chanced a sigh of admiration. "What a fine young woman indeed."

"You know, sir, you've no reason to feel embarrassed," assured Cletus. "She did have a very good reason for delaying her answer."

"Yes," Hephaestus cut in, "except it wasn't her who *gave* the reason."

"How could you do that?" Samantha demanded of her sister.

"I should think you would thank me!" protested the older, once they'd gotten into the younger's room with the door shut behind them.

"Thank you! You completely stole everyone's attention—"

"Well, forgive me, but you didn't look like you wanted any attention." And as Samantha tried to speak again Sabrina cut her off with, "No, you will not pretend that you aren't grateful just because you're frustrated. Admit it: you needed to be saved, and my response was the best one available, or would you have rathered stand in silence for another few minutes waiting for someone else to chime in?"

Samantha bit her lip; clearly her sister was right, whether she wanted to acknowledge it. Of course Sabrina's objection to the proposal brought all kinds of pressure on Raul, and the ensuing awkwardness caused a mass migration of the people from the square like cockroaches from the light, but it effectively took the assumptive pressure off of the young girl who should *obviously* wish to marry the first delightful and at-least-mostly-handsome man that comes around regardless of other circumstances like—oh, just for example—love.

For my part, I think her idea was brilliant, if a little bit plagiaristic, but then again, if Miss Sabrina had never had any exposure to outside literature, she might as well be given credit for coming up with the solution—albeit temporary—to everyone's problems.

See, when they were all in the square, just after Raul had asked and just before the Libburus would be giving his proud father speech, during the most uncomfortable conversation lull of any of their lifetimes, Sabrina strode forward and made a very simple proclamation:

"Now, young man," she had said, "I'm sure that our dear father and Libburus could not condone the marrying of his youngest daughter before his oldest has been wed." Though she was fairly certain her father would have already approved any marrying of his daughters, the point was met with a massive murmur of agreement.

Hephaestus, careful not to be completely cut out of this tastefully-dramatic moment, made his way forward and declared,

"Clearly in the wake of such important events, the families of Condamine and the young man and the young lady should be left in peace in their homes to…" And the older merchant stalled because he couldn't think of anything so say, and so retreated in some humiliation. This is probably why Sebastian subconsciously turned away from the man's seemingly slipping reason not an hour later.

But even for his lacking linguistic capability, the townspeople opted to trust their old sage and so complied with his unfinished wishes. Which brings us to where we are now: Samantha's bedroom in which Sabrina is defending her excuse.

"After all, it's not as if he's going to propose to me," she concluded, "So you're off the hook. At least for a few more years."

"Maybe for marriage, but that doesn't solve everything." Samantha sat down on the bed and folded her hands in her lap. As Sabrina joined her, she explained, "I'm still going to see him every day, and he'll still want to court me, and I can't tell him why I don't want to marry him, because if I do, he'll tell father, and I don't think he can take that."

Sabrina nodded, though by the end of it, she'd lost track of which 'he' her sister meant. She watched Samantha rubbing at her own palm, tenderly, as if trying to simulate a hand that belonged to someone else. Offering the younger one of her own, she asked, "So what are you going to do?"

After a moment, Samantha shook her head and replied, "I don't know. I just want to see Julian."

Of course, she never did get to see Julian. Not that night at any rate. See, while Julian was likewise consumed by worry and thought of nothing but seeing his lady, he remembered her mandate that he not profess his love that day. Now, it should have only meant *that* day, but given that she had stalled his confession not an hour before she received a proposal, Julian could not know whether she had ever wanted to hear what he had to say. You may find this frustrating—I know I did—but remember, Julian is seventeen, and teenagers often let insecurities rule the day even when logic fiercely dictates elsewhere. You probably remember a time when you felt so, and if indeed you are under seventeen, good on you for picking up this book, and I am truly sorry if I unduly give away anything important about the passage of life and love you're soon to find.

THE BARON WOULD BE PROUD

You might indeed be thinking that young Julian just needed a push in the right direction by an older, wiser, possibly mustache-waxing gentleman. Unfortunately the Baron remembered his promise too.

And when Jonas returned, looking slightly more lost than usual, Julian tended to the grandfather, and the Baron tended to Pigby, who took very little solace in the reassurance, that "No one really liked her anyway."

Fletcher, having been bored all day, discovered that Oswald needed help on a project, and though Ten ha seemed to try to escape, Geru explained that there was still daylight, and that she should bundle up and come with him. By the time they closed the door on the way out of Julian's cottage, it seemed the door had been closed on the whole issue.

Part V – An Insurmountable Obstacle

*Pigby took two slow, deliberate steps forward, and tuned out
Condamine's call of "Yoo-hoo."*

LIII – So Shameful a Strikethrough

The old rooster who claimed the top of the highest coop waited politely until the even older grandfather had climbed the hill and rock to sound its morning alarm.

Now the rooster made sure to shout at the same time every morning, which meant it was still mostly dark when the cock crew during the winter months, but no one would fault him his consistency, especially Geru who was so tuned to the call that he was off the loft and into his robe and sandals before the second crow came.

When he attempted to rouse Pigby though, he found his giant to be less compliant than normal. Apparently knocking a woman off a cliff is bad for one's back, or so Pigby's posture would suggest. But coerced by Geru's screechy whisper, Pigby sighed and grumbled his way into his attire and collected his mat before heading for the door. He was not prepared for what he saw on the wall.

"Wha—" came the initial startle, then snatching the poster of rules from the wall, demanded, "Who did this?"

Scurrying toward his unnaturally loud companion, Geru saw that the third rule, "Do not kill unless first attacked," had been crossed off. He immediately readied himself to contend with Pigby's rage, but abandoned his fighter's stance when he saw Pigby slump against the wall and slide down to the floor, landing with a dejected *thud*.

As the others were stirring from their big black comrade's initial outburst, Geru decided it was best to persuade Pigby straight into their routine, seeing as finding out whatever inconsiderate prig etched so shameful a strikethrough would just upset him further. "Don't think on it," he said, "Don't you think on it. Come on." Trying to hoist Pigby by use of his own shoulder, Geru urged the giant out the door with only a rebuking look to his fellows for so sorely reminding his friend of the unfortunate happenstance.

"I don't know, Geru," he said once the smaller had closed the door. "I don't feel up to it this morning."

"Oh, piffle!" returned Geru, "You will feel a hundred times better after a few relaxing exercises and time with your friends."

Though it sounded quite comforting in his head, Geru was forced to wonder if his comment had been the worst possible thing to say, because as they rounded Julian's house, they came upon an open hillside and not a soul to be found. Geru expected his giant to bellow, and braced for the shockwave, but turned to find that Pigby merely sank, dropping almost a foot in his posture until he was nearly as short as Hephaestus.

"Now, Pigby," began Geru.

"I should have known," muttered the other.

"Just give it a day to blow over; I'm sure they'll come 'round." But even after he spoke, he saw Pigby turn around and begin trudging back to the house.

Without looking over his shoulder, he mumbled, "Course they'd stay in—I knew they were scared of me—can't hide it—why, the moment I threw that sling I revealed—I did—just a big dumb brute."

"But, Pigby!" said the short one, jogging to keep up, "How could you be an international tradesman's bookkeeper if you were stupid?"

Unfortunately, Pigby's depression had far more inertia than Geru's reassuring comment could. "I'll just have to notify the Baron of his mistake in hiring me, and he'll rectify it."

As Pigby reached for the door handle, Geru tried to swat his hand away, saying, "Pigby!"

"No, Geru! No more. Really, who's going to come spend their morning with a murderer?"

And to answer his question, a familiar voice from beneath a walrusy mustache asked, "Are we too late?" Sure enough: coming up the path toward Julian's door were not only Clemens, but Piers, Sherman, Manuel, and two others. Eyebrows arched in concern, Clemens explained, "Sorry we're so late. Since Klaus and Peter wanted to give it a try, had to round them up too, y'know."

"Had to reason with the wives too," remarked Manuel, which Piers clarified with:

"Well, once Lilli heard that Rosa and Meredith came to watch, I couldn't keep her at home either."

"But we're here," Clemens resumed hopefully.

The walrusy grocer heard the giant man gulp, saw him shudder once, blink twice, and finally turn away. Just as Clemens was about to wonder aloud on Pigby's actions, he was intercepted by Geru, who stepped between them to explain:

"Don't mind Pigby. He's having some trouble with his allergies." Then to his companion, "Why don't you go inside and blow your nose, Pigby, and we'll meet you out back again."

Pigby frantically nodded. Though his wrists had to tend to his eyes and nose to keep them from dripping, his lips were broadly grinning.

LIV – An After-Christmas-Tradition
(or Some Other Innocent Pastime)

Hephaestus had an affinity for symmetry. He tended to wear only clothing with a center seam; he enjoyed eating things more when they came in twos or had an obvious centerpiece; and he found that he far more admired works of art that could be folded or rotated upon themselves in some fashion and produce mostly the same image.

This tendency was not a compulsion per se, but after so many years of tending to his own particular fondness, the lord of merchants' quirk had evolved into a near-immitigable habit. As far as he was concerned, everything should and could have its proper place, and be arranged in delightful harmony. This was why he carried seven sturdy servants, which—though it at first appeared to be a prime number, nearly always leveled off to a precise formation.

If you think about Hephaestus' well-worn wagon, which had two handles on each side and a bar in the back, you will observe that there could be a man for each handle, two across the back, and the last man, Trenton, typically at the helm, guiding the beasts. If one man was needed inside—other than Hephaestus himself that is—he would be pulled from the back of the cart, his partner would slide to the middle of the bracer bar, and all would be balanced again.

Not only was this arrangement nearly-always symmetrical, but it also nearly-always consisted of even numbers, seeing as in any discrepancy, Hephaestus could insert himself as the eighth—often by Trenton's side and never performing the 'manual labor' portion. Additionally, with eight able oxen, there could be a man for each animal, making their total number sixteen, which was divisible by eight, four, and two, each of which was one of his favorite numbers.

Hephaestus also believed that if he had seven men and himself, then none should want for duty, and no duty should be wanted for, and every task was finished promptly and well. This was of course until his man Thurgood had stepped out of office and his boy Lance stepped in.

Now, Hephaestus did not have any particular dislike of the boy; he found him amiable enough and strong enough for their purposes, but Lance provided no necessary skills, and more importantly, no new languages. Hephaestus could have forgiven his coming back to the house late so often and being disappeared early in the morning, had the boy simply been able to understand Greek.

To say that everything needed a function to exist in his world is not to say that Hephaestus did away with décor. Two factors prevented this: the first, that Hephaestus was vain, and the second, that he believed décor *was* a function all its own for presenting the best first impression and receiving the best reception.

The wagon itself was not ornate, but if you ever went inside, (which some of our heroes would one day do), you would see that even the boxes were laid out with pristine accuracy, fine finish, and a sheen that softly illuminated the whole room via merely candlelight. Probably the most expensive ornamental objects that Hephaestus possessed were his own clothes, many of which had come from bishops, sheikhs, and bahitawis[125].

And where appearance items were concerned, he was immensely proud of the cane that happened to also be a rapier, despite the very small hilt. The fact that he could only wield one sword at a time, was a sore-point for the symmetry-stricken merchant, and was only amended when he realized that the symmetry of a duel came from the fact that two parties were needed—one sword apiece—to properly fence. He had initially had the same beef with left-handed swordsmen, then settled his angered nerves by reminding himself of their vertical symmetry, even if not rotational.

But even with every complaint for symmetry he had ever found, Hephaestus had never been so upset by the sight of crossed swords than he was that morning. Even Trenton, who stood off his shoulder could not console him when they arrived in the town square to find several men, teenage boys, and the odd girl, taking turns 'pointing' with the straightest of sticks and rods they could find.

---

[125] An Ethiopian term for 'Holy Man,' translated to 'One who wanders in the desert,' which strikes readers as delightfully exotic and pagan, despite the fact that since the 4th century AD, the staggering majority of bahitawis were Christian ascetics.

Now, Hephaestus looked to his right-hand man for advice, which he fully expected to receive—and not knowing that Trenton had resolved not to give it. See, having witnessed the end of his master's duel with the Baron just a few mornings before, Trenton observed that the sword-fighting Isleans were a natural byproduct of Hephaestus' pigheadedness. Luckily for Trenton, he never needed to divulge this opinion, seeing as someone in the dueling circles spotted Hephaestus and beckoned him over before there would have been time for a comment, let alone a damage control plan.

"Your Well-Knownness!" came a voice, and a boy who must have been about fourteen jogged toward Hephaestus, followed shortly by three others who appeared just as eager. The first boy held his stick aloft and asked, "Can you show us, sir?"

Hephaestus shook his head and brushed by him, leaving the incredulous lad to look to Trenton, who informed him:

"A magician never reveals his secrets." The answer, though not thorough, clearly satisfied the boys who had seen Hephaestus prestidigitize[126] in earlier years. Trenton clasped his forearms together behind his back, and strode after his lord, not quite knowing if these new students of the stick wanted point-by-point instructions or simply to see Hephaestus' sword.

Trenton soon saw Hephaestus' trajectory, which pointed at the only other man in the square who wore the formal servant uniform and who happened to be Lance.

"Good morning, sir," said lance, touching a knuckle to his forehead by way of salute.

"Do you know how long this has been going on?" Hephaestus asked.

"What: the fencing?" came Lance, responding as casually as he assumed the master's question to be. "Only been a couple hours this morning."

"*This morning!?*"

"Well, I saw some doing it yesterday too," Lance explained, then nodded to Trenton whose shoulders arrived to close off their conversation triangle.

Hephaestus came dangerously close to spontaneously combusting. "You saw this yesterday, and you didn't tell me?"

---

[126] *I* think that's a fair shot at the verb form of prestidigitation, but my editor insists that it's prestidigitate, which frankly sounds ridiculous.

"Sir," said Trenton, trying to calm him, but not showing very much support for Lance, who sputtered before speaking.

"Oh," he began, and was about to protest that he was busy, then switched his argument to the *other* truth, which might sound a lot more acceptable. "Well, I—I didn't know this was new; I just thought they were really bad at it."

Hephaestus' hand got as far as Lance's shoulder before he realized that Lance was being quite honest; indeed, how could anyone, especially a man of Lance's stellar wit, know that the people of the Isle were just experiencing swordplay for the first time unless he had been told? Perhaps he thought it an after-Christmas tradition, or some other innocent pastime. It was this innocence that stayed the servant's master from lifting him off the ground by his shirtfront[127].

Instead, he turned back to the square, and watched with hideous wonder the shoddy attempts at thrusts and parries from the people that had been peaceful for all the time he had known them. And then he was forced to correct his brain before it made so grievous an assumption— they still *were* peaceful! Sure, there appeared to be the odd accident where one man was scraped during an attempt to point at his opponent, but of the one to two dozen people taking turns to duel with their sticks, there were one to two dozen smiles, meaning that the Big Out There's dueling style was merely a game to the good folks of the Isle.

Hephaestus chanced to sigh in relief once he'd more thoroughly examined the citizens. "Well," he thought aloud, "at least the Baron isn't here trying to teach them."

---

[127] Perhaps Hephaestus could not have lifted Lance, but then again, adrenaline can give all sorts of people sudden and amazing strength.

LV – The Better Duelist

The Baron and young Julian stood opposite one another in the clearing. Each held a rapier. Julian was convinced his didn't fit.

"They're so sharp," he observed after finishing the salute the Baron had taught him.

"Yes, well, that's why you won't be using these ones," the Baron assured him. "You'll be using blunted sticks. Maybe some metal posts," and then as the unpleasant thought occurred to him, "like Fletcher's cattle prod…"

Julian examined the shimmering edge of the sword in his hand, which didn't seem anything like the bent rod that Lars had tripped on a few days prior. Granted, the tips were sheathed in little bits of rubber, which Fletcher had called contraceptives[128], but Julian had the impression that if he were to trip on this particular device, he might end up with more than a bruised tailbone. What he didn't want to tell the Baron Pan Bordolo was that he was scared of trying this new practice with this shiny wand. Instead, he said this: "I don't understand. If we'll never use ones this sharp, why do you want me to learn to use it?"

"Because it's always better to learn on the real thing than a knockoff. Do you know what I mean?"

"I think so…" Julian had heard Junkin say something similar about women. "Is this what you use in the Big Out There?"

"Um… Yes."

"But if it's sharp, when you win, won't you hurt someone?" Julian asked.

---

[128] This is one more example of how our dear Fletcher was ahead of his time, seeing as though both rubber and condoms had been put to good use by the start of the 19th century, they had not yet combined.

"Well, see, Julian, in the Big Out There, as you call it, sometimes that's just the point. Hold it underhand, boy, so the tip stays on me; you're not a lumberjack."

"Why?" Julian wondered.

"It's posturing for the lunge," the Baron explained, before realizing, "Oh, you meant— Oh, well, sometimes men will draw on one another as a testament of honor, to demonstrate that a man should not be allowed to say or do whatever transgression offended the other."

"Do they die?"

The Baron attempted to shrug, but his brilliant fencing posture prevented it. "Sometimes."

"Over honor?"

"Honor can be a very important thing, Julian," said the Baron.

"Would you die over honor?"

"Well, I'd hope not to," the Baron answered honestly, "but I think I would stand up for my family and their memory if that were to be questioned."

"How about your godfather's book?"

The Baron paused. "How did you—"

"Of all the things you've tried to explain to me, sir, two things you haven't are the book and your godfather, and whenever he's mentioned, you put your hand over your book—like you're doing now, sir." And indeed the Baron hadn't even noticed he'd instinctively protected his breast pocket. "I thought you were defending your heart at first—but you treasure it, and you won't let people talk about it. Is that like honor?"

"It's similar…" The Baron didn't know how to field this question; naturally he wanted to change the subject. "See, in the Big Out There, the more people you know, and the more houses you influence, the more you must defend your reputation. And if the offense is enough, sometimes the only way to make it right is to be rid of the person who committed it." The Baron tested his lunge legs, while making absolutely certain that he was at least two sword-lengths from the novice opposite him[129]. "Does that make sense?"

---

[129] Yes, just in case you were wondering, there were about ten feet between the lad and his Baron, which was more to the older's safety than Julian's; see, if you have ever had a go at classical fencing, you might know that while the expert can stay his hand and keep his opponent entirely unblemished, the most arrogant beginner can award the most errant of welts, bruises, and—if you are working without a tip—skewerings to his teacher.

Julian did his best to mirror the lunge. Once he'd resumed his feet, he replied, "I can't say it does. I mean, if I were to rid of Stephen, who mixes the mortar, because I were upset with him for the state of the mortar and how it neglected to hold a doorframe—which has happened before—but I had 'rid of him,' then I've paid offense not only to him, but the whole town. Because if there's no Stephen to mix mortar, it hurts me, and it hurts anyone who might need something of mine installed, or those who repair the road in the spring, or anyone who relies on any of Stephen's other duties—of which I don't fully know. I don't understand who it helps."

The Baron smiled. "Well, then think of it as proof, lad."

"Proof?"

"Yes. The rest of the world thinks my way, so if everyone here thinks your way then it really must be the best place in the world. Now, like I showed you, the lunge again."

And the Baron and Julian, with some degree of unison, both took their lunges, and both were satisfied that the tips of the swords did not even touch.

"One day, lad, you may find that there's something you care about and want to defend so preciously that you'll bristle anytime anyone mentions it, for fear that they might misrepresent or discredit it."

It was then Julian's turn to change the subject. "You know, Sir Baron, I've never even been in duel."

"How's that?" the Baron asked, before indicating they lunge again, with, "Again."

"I've never dueled—I mean, our kind—I guess I never thought I would," he clarified, coming up from his lunge. "So why should I need to learn *your* duel if I'd never do mine?"

"Well, Julian," came the Baron, doing his best not to sound offended, "You don't *need* to do anything; I just thought it would be a delightful way to spend an afternoon. And if this kind of duel does come into fashion here, wouldn't it be nice to know you could hold secure title against any opponent."

"I suppose."

"Besides, I should think the best way to win is to never be challenged at all. Why, who would want to challenge the boy who had been educated by the best swordsman in the Isle!"

"Will Fletcher be teaching me too then?" asked Julian, with so straight a face that the Baron could not tell how much the boy was making fun of him.

Of course, the Baron decided not to take umbrage at the comment; instead, he chanced to take the high road and feel proud. After all, he was the one who had taught the boy the snide he now used.

Without addressing that the thin man was in fact the better duelist, the Baron Pan Bordolo said, "I'm sure he'd be here now, but Oswald has got him wrapped up in some 'special project.' Tell you the truth, Julian, I don't know what in the blazes they're up to."

LVI – The Large Boat

What in the blazes Oswald and Fletcher were up to would not be revealed until later that night. I say 'revealed' because the relatively-old scholar and the relatively-young bard were working on so spectacular a project that they actually draped a curtain over it to keep their audience from prematurely seeing it, when they filtered into the pews the crew had borrowed from the second storehouse. They waited for night solely for use of Manuel and Meredith's firepit.

Very few had been invited for the evening's performance, and even fewer had any idea of what they were about to witness. As Oswald settled the Baron, his men, his woman, his host, Dietrich, Elke, Clemens, and the household Manuel—making sure that every man, woman, and Miriam could see—Fletcher continued to dart into and out of the large covered crate which stood securely between the audience and the fire.

"I say—I suppose everyone is comfortable then, yes?" Oswald asked, one hand gripping at the other wrist.

"Other than a bit cold?" piped the shivering Geru.

Oswald waved him away and turned over his shoulder to check in with Fletcher, who—though he was completely concealed by the boxy setup and its draping—reached his hand over top and cued the old man 'go.'

"Yes, well! Without further ado," began Oswald, "myself and Fletcher, with the help of our own Geru and Ten ha—" He indicated the two parties who had been deemed short enough to sit in the front row. "—would like to thank your attending our little evening's presentation— Which, if indeed it gets too fright'ning for the young miss, we... humbly apologize."

"I'm not scared," insisted Miriam, folding her arms resolutely about her tiny chest, but given Oswald's last, was forced to regard the six-foot-tall rectangular box which wore a black cloak and was silhouetted against her father's bon-fire with a little more trepidation. She snuggled deeper into the oversized blanket, which—though it seemed purposed just for the nippy night air—could now be drawn over her eyes at a moment's notice.

Oswald, who had always fancied himself more of a student than a teacher, did not check in with all of his audience, but he did wait for his Baron's nod before beginning.

"Right. Once upon a time there was—" began Oswald and would have continued if not for Pigby, who, in order to satisfy his own imagination's frame of reference asked:

"What time?"

"*Tssh!*" came a general hiss from the rest of the crowd.

Pigby attempted to clarify and pointed to his own head, saying, "I just wanted to complete my mental picture."

"Well, see we don't know exactly, but we suspect that it was about a century and a half before we set foot on Adleship Isle," Oswald said.

Fletcher popped his head over the crate again and hissed, "You're breaking the fourth wall!"

"Oh, yes, right, well," blurted the older. He ahemed twice. "Our story begins right here!" And with a dramatic flourish, he yanked the shroud from the crate to reveal that it was not a full box, but rather a frame. And in the frame resided a screen and behind the screen, projecting its shadow, was a map of England on a stick.

"Oh, it's puppets!" exclaimed Meredith, excitedly clapping to herself.

"This," said Oswald, pointing, "is our beloved England. And this," as another large silhouette came to reside next to it, "is the coast of Europe. And we," he indicated with one weathered finger, "are here." He tapped the screen on the little blob that was the merry little island they all called home, at just about the thinnest point of the narrowest isthmus.

Fletcher withdrew the shapes and suddenly, there appeared a collection of people and a large cross.

"Our story begins with a small band of honest Anglicans, who lived in England, and were happy for many years, until their beloved ruler passed away."

A figure wearing a crown quickly appeared and just as quickly tipped over and retreated from the screen.

"The good king—Um, leader—I say—the rightful leader, was succeeded by a twisted little demagogue who put an iron-grip on our great country, and tried to strip these once-free people of their right to practice their God-given religion!"

Murmurs were passed among the crew, because even they didn't quite understand. The Baron took it upon himself to mutter, "It's a Cromwell reference," after which Pigby, Ten ha, and Geru collectively went *O-oh!*

The little figure with devil-horns seemed to nod before he was pulled off the screen.

"Yes, well, the people decided that they wanted to leave England and go to a place where they would be free to practice their religion without persecution: America. So, a selfless band of men and women from mainland Europe—most likely—I say—probably French and German prepared a ship, and arranged to meet the men and women on— Fletcher, England, I need the map of England again!"

When England emerged, Oswald pointed to its east coast and said, "Here! Right here, they were going to meet, secretly, and the whole lot—families and everything—cows, chickens, sheep!—would go together to America. But unfortunately, boats of the little fake tyrant king patrolled the waters of England, making it difficult—nay!—impossible for the respectable persons to escape undetected[130]."

Little and large boats began bobbing along the south and northeast of England and did their very best not to let their sticks get tangled.

"There was one option for our people on their ship as they met— just to the north of Newcastle, there. Go too far south and be intercepted by a patrol at the channel, go too far north and be caught by the hired Scots. On the other side of the island lay freedom, but not necessarily another boat, so the men and women set to take their ship, the Lucky, and drag it across the island."

---

[130] I actually have no idea of how accurate this suspicion of 'patrols' was. The important thing is that Oswald believed it to be true, or I suppose the more important thing is that the people in Oswald's story believed it to be true. I mean, they must have, or else they wouldn't have done what they did.

When Fletcher took the large boat and placed it on the heads of the little crowd of shadow-people, the majority of his audience audibly reacted.

The crew emerged with a dumbfounded "What?" while the townsfolk—who were unfamiliar with what precisely a boat was but decided it must be akin to a floating house—congratulated the men on the screen with an intrigued "Ooh!"

And Oswald felt a need to backpedal. "Yes, well, see—what we think is—See, boats can be carried to sea on rolling logs, and it was the narrowest part of the island, and—"

Fletcher cleared his throat loudly, because nobody could hear him roll his eyes.

"Yes, well, the travelers pulled the Lucky across the island, which—braving the terrible winter and the rolling hills—was no mean feat!"

A mountain was pressed into place, and the shadowy people climbed, still holding the boat.

The Baron thumbed at his mustache, his mouth hanging open somewhat incredulously.

"They were following a trail, looking for a passage through the mountains, on the other side of which resided sweet freedom. And the trail—I say—was shown by a map." Oswald produced the map, that document with which Dietrich had only parted because he was asked to attend.

"It was a map drawn by the explorer-cartographer duo, who signed their maps 'P and A.' Now, I—I say 'I,' sir, found the P who labeled the mountain pass a little ways to the north, in Scotland. Fletcher, England! See, this," he said, pointing to Dietrich's map, "is where I found Perchwick's Pass, and the duo went by Perchwick and Adleship."

"Mommy, that's us," whispered Miriam, and her mother, who was busy biting her nails, hushed the child.

"But they were not looking for Perchwick's Pass—no, our travellers hoped to make a more southern passage." The image of the boat-carriers climbing a mountain resumed. "But it was winter, and they became lost in a storm!"

Suddenly flurries shot into motion all around the shadows, accompanied by roars and pops. The Baron grinned with satisfaction at the timing with which his charming minstrel had instigated the fire behind him.

"A blizzard set them off course! And though the snowy ground made it easier for the boat to slide, the men and women could hardly see their surroundings, until a break in the clouds…"

Oswald paused to wait for the flurries of ash to die down. The shadow people lost their mountain and found themselves instead in a valley.

"As if from God, their saving grace came in the form of an oasis. A crater at the top of a mountain, undoubtedly that had been formed from a long-ago eruption leaving ash-rich soil, with grass and trees and glacial water, and so they put down the boat and resolved to settle down, right here."

The large boat, which had been held by three sticks, was ripped apart, and in its place, Fletcher put up houses.

"The new settlers used the boat and the rolling logs and built their town, keeping the name of the explorer as their namesake— probably to indicate to fellow travelers that they had come to the right place, to a pass called Adleship Aisle. However, they did not know that the real Adleship Aisle lay some twenty miles south, and a couple hundred feet lower."

You may not have realized that the *Aisle* of which Oswald now spoke was spelt with an *A*, as in a theatre or grocery store aisle. The people in the audience had no idea. Fletcher helped them.

Every figure and image was pulled from the shadowy screen, and a sign rose into view, reading ADLESHIP AISLE. It took everyone a moment or two to realize the town's great typo, and if they hadn't by a certain point, they would when Fletcher yanked the A off of Isle.

"We can only surmise," explained Oswald, "that when they first put up the sign at the west gate, it read as it was intended, and that possibly wind or shoddy craftsmanship took the A one day, and since there was no other sign, and it sounded the same—I say—the *Aisle* became the *Isle*."

Oswald hesitated, then committed to bowing, signaling the end of the show. Geru, having provided the notes on the mountain climate, began the applause, which the others soon followed[131]. Fletcher emerged from the screen to give his "Thank you"s—mainly to Clemens and Pigby, whom he fancied the most likely intrigued by what had been performed.

---

[131] Had Geru not contributed, he probably would have criticized how short the presentation was.

Dietrich quickly snatched his map back, and Meredith saw fit to start Miriam on her "Goodnight"'s so she could get to bed. Elke, Manuel, Clemens, and Pigby all circled together with Fletcher in the center and asked after how he had set up the puppets. Geru and Oswald went to their boss, which was lucky, because they were exactly the ones he wanted to talk to, particularly Oswald, who seemed to have left out a great many gaps on the subject of the peoples' religion.

"Well, I couldn't include everything, sir," Oswald replied, no doubt referring to the unwitting Isleans. "But see, I recognized, sir—there was a Lutheran rose on the altar yesterday, but no crosses."

"Yes, but we're talking about a people who forgot their entire history in less than two hundred years!" Though the Baron exclaimed that last, he made sure to keep his voice hushed and that the others were occupied with the shadow-puppet man.

"It's the climate!" came Geru, before Oswald could answer. "It keeps out all other influences."

"See, sir, they didn't want to remember—I say," Oswald resumed, "that's why they have no books and no records. They believe in God; they have Christmas; but no crosses, no Bibles. This town was built by people who had to run from a religiously controlling tyrant, so why restrict people with the things they had fought to free themselves from?"

"That is very philosophical of you, Oswald."

"Yes, and even though they spoke English, I have a theory that the settlers wanted to seem foreign, just in case there was any kind of war and they were discovered, which is why they named everyone Germanic names—Oh!—and a few French."

"Yes, but what about the volcano?" chimed Geru. "I've concluded the warmth of this place; I know why the glaciers melt here, and how the spring comes up. It's a dormant volcano. Erupted—probably for the last time—hundreds of years ago." And though Oswald meant to interrupt again, Geru continued with, "But the thing is, I wouldn't have found that nearly as quickly had His Snobbishness not given me that climatological journal."

"Actually, yes, sir," said Oswald, "I've been meaning to talk to you about that as well. What I said there, about the name of the town and the settling, that was all my best guess, but in the notes that Mister Hephaestus gave me, I found a mention of Adleship and Perchwick's trails as escape routes and a registry for a supply boat that communicated with France called 'Lucky.' Now, these marks matched not only the bell but the '*P and A*' on the maps, and the wheel, but this was what he wanted us to find, sir. Was it not?"

"Well, if you mean to say that he already knew all this, why wouldn't he just tell us?" asked the Baron. "And what about the old man?" He pointed not to Oswald but to the grandfather, who continued to sit at the pew, hands on his knees, rocking back and forth as if waiting for more of the story. "If they've gone and destroyed all of their books, then how does he know what he knows?"

Oswald and Geru looked over to Jonas, and were looking for so long that the grandfather must have felt their gaze because he turned toward them and waved amiably.

"I suppose that one will stay a mystery then," said Geru with a shrug.

Speaking of mystery[132], you may be wondering about one party that I've hardly mentioned; in fact, you might be thinking, 'Where is Julian? I mean, wasn't he at the presentation? Then why has he not reacted?' or worse, 'I thought Julian was supposed to be the hero of the story; has our narrator forgotten about him?'

Well now, I am offended by this sentiment! How dare you think that I should forget about someone so crucial and so dear as young Julian? I'll have you know that I have been keeping a close eye on Julian, and it would be far more fair to say that he has forgotten himself by this point in our story. Yes, of course, the young lad was a sponge for knowledge, and any other night he would have been the first to jump up with questions—so forgive him for featuring a pensive and somewhat depressed side. After all, with everything that had happened in the last few days, wouldn't you?

As the puppet screen was torn down, and the Adleship Isleans made their ways back to their homes, Julian continued to stare at the fire. Perhaps he hoped to commune with his lady via the flames.

Pigby didn't find it his place to confront the boy on his wallowings, but he certainly deemed it the Baron's duty. Especially with Manuel and Meredith having gone inside for the night, the Baron was probably the most guiding grown-up force Julian could have.

"I've made a promise, Pigby," the Baron reminded him.

"Yes, but you've a friendship to the boy, which is more than a promise," rebutted the giant.

"Not against my good name, Pigby."

---

[132] The editor firmly suggested that I strike that segue as being too cliché.

"Shame on you, boss. If you mean for his best, you've an obligation to help him in any way you can—no matter the wager you've struck with a rival."

"Confound it, Pigby! Do you mean to tell *me* what to do—as your employer?"

"No, sir. Respectfully, I mean to tell you what to do as *his friend*. And it's a privilege you shouldn't scoff at."

The Baron looked to the boy, who, though he did not appear quite disconsolate, seemed certainly in need of some friendly optimistic advice. Though he could not bat away Pigby's keen argument, he could not bring himself to break so substantial a promise either, which would—in Hephaestus' eyes—strip away any title of nobility he had.

Hephaestus himself was actually the savior of the moment, seeing as just then, the Baron Pan Bordolo noticed him lurking about the corner of the next house over with his man Trenton, and obviously spying on the Baron and his crew.

"What's he doing there?" asked Pigby pointing to the merchant who unsuccessfully tried to disappear into the shadows.

The Baron bid Pigby excuse him and marched over to the other gentleman, saying as he arrived, "I suppose you've been watching the whole time, have you?"

By way of reply, Hephaestus said, "I can't say I got a very good view of the puppet show."

"Isn't it enough that you own the good favor of every scrap of this town without intruding on my man's private event?"

"What bid me come, Mister Bordolo, was that it *was* private—"

"And you couldn't stand that to which you were not invited," and then looking to the silent Trenton, added, "or you either."

"I resent that, Mister Bordolo; I followed a suspicious trail!"

"Oh, poppycock! You heard about the event somehow, so you must have known what we were doing." The Baron popped his fists onto his hips and did his best to look like a disciplinary parent. "So let's have it, then."

"What?" asked the older innocently.

Trenton chanced to look annoyed—whether to himself or his rival, the Baron was not sure, and so said, "Don't try to wind me up, old man. You gave my men the notes they needed to put that show on; now, what—might I wonder—was the point if you knew all along?"

"Fine!" Hephaestus flourished his cape so over-dramatically that he nearly tripped over it when he strode forward to confide, "I needed a second opinion."

The Baron matched Hephaestus' lean-in. "Meaning?"

"Well, Mister Bordolo, what I gave them is what I used when I concluded how Adleship Isle happened, but I've never been able to compare notes."

Though Hephaestus didn't look to be lying necessarily, the Baron was inclined not to trust so simple an explanation. "Bullocks."

"It is not! Look, I wanted to know if you'd come to the same conclusion I did—which, by the way, you did."

"You mean to tell me that all of this manipulative runaround was just to find out if we'd concur with your hypothesis?"

"Yes!" nodded Hephaestus, his knotted beard frantically bouncing to keep up. "I don't carry historians or meteorologists with me, so I've never been able to check before."

The Baron Pan Bordolo would have liked to have been impressed by this; subtle as it was, Hephaestus had complimented his crew, and intentions of information were—to the Baron—always pure, but too many questions remained unanswered, and the scent of trickery was stronger than trust. With enough volume to not only call the attention of the others but possibly wake the neighbors, the Baron demanded, "Then what else aren't you telling us? What do you know about the weather and the location that you haven't let spill? Hmm? Or are you waiting on another hint?"

Hephaestus, worried heads would turn his direction tried to silence the other with, "Mister Bordolo, please!"

"And what about the old man—that grandfather! What do you know about him?"

"Nothing!" protested Hephaestus.

As the crew began to look over, appearing as though they should soon approach, Trenton went to his master's side and bid him, "Come on, sir."

But the Baron said again, "What is it? I mean, if you've been coming for years, you must have known Jonas most of his life. My God, man, you'd think you were the one who drove him senile!" And as Hephaestus tried to turn, the Baron—wanting more answers than he'd been given—reached out and took the older man's arm.

"Unhand me, Mister Bordolo!" howled Hephaestus, with so much force that the nearby snow-drifts shivered and contemplated falling from their roofs.

"Come on, sir," Trenton repeated, and Hephaestus turned and strode away with him, leaving the scene just as Fletcher and Pigby arrived behind their Baron, and just before the nearest households started opening their shutters.

"What was all that?" Fletcher asked.

The Baron shook his head as he watched after Hephaestus and Trenton. He would have liked to have a snappy line to deliver, but, unfortunately, nothing came to mind.

LVII – His Spot on the Page

I feel a need to clarify something: Hephaestus had not been spying on them. Actually, that's not true— Here, I'll try again.

Yes, though Hephaestus was obviously eavesdropping on the puppet show, it was not any kind of surreptitious behavior that had made him aware of its existence. Though he told his servants to keep him informed on any interesting day-to-day affairs in any town or country in which they stayed, in the Isle, he did not post spies for the simple reason that he did not need them.

To the best I can assume, when Clemens told Rosa where he was going for the night, Rosa may have casually passed that information on to Lilli or Hannah, who—proper gossips in their own right—inevitably started the grapevine about the secretive presentation in their friend Manuel's backyard. Eventually, any grapevines in the town reached the house of the Libburus, which had, for every winter in available memory, housed Hephaestus.

It also housed a forlorn young woman, who had spent the last day not in her own room, but at her older sister's window which could more effectively look out to the well and which—sadly—produced no Julian. Because she said very little and had the faintest hint of redness in her eyes, her nervous father promptly declared her ill, and turned away all visitors, which—the day after the day after Christmas—included Raul.

Thankfully for the feelings of both Samantha and her charming gentleman caller, Sebastian was quite good at making excuses for inattendance. Somewhere between, "Oh, she's gone and caught a bug, the poor dear," and "She's probably just a bit startled with all of this new 'grown woman' and 'proposal' talk around her," Raul stopped trying to generate reasons to invite himself in. And as the boy turned to leave,

Sebastian patted him on the back, saying, "Don't you worry on it; she'll come 'round on her own time."

Sebastian could not understand why his oldest daughter appeared so cross with him for saying that.

In either case, the 'give it time' adage persuaded Raul to not go immediately home to be productive, but rather to the square where he figured he might kill time pointing sticks with the others, arriving just as Hephaestus was leaving.

Coincidentally, Julian was being taught the proper grip for his rapier precisely when Hephaestus turned down Raul's request to teach him.

I should clarify something else: Julian had difficulty not thinking of Samantha normally, and had a much harder time of it when in crisis. Lengthy denial not being one of his strong-suits, our hero actually consented to learning to duel on the sole assumption that the Baron might have some advice on his present predicament.

The Baron, delightfully witty as he was, was not the most observant of chaps, and was also particularly good at denial. No matter what reason Julian gave to stop learning to fence so that they may instead talk about the lady, who—to the best of his knowledge had recently become not his—the Baron simply waved it away with a flick of his sword and a chipper, "Nonsense, my boy!"

Not eager to voice his own issues if not attended to by the man he had decided to trust, Julian withdrew into himself for the remainder of that day and for the majority of the next.

Morning brought more yoga with more intrigued followers and more titillating watchers. It came with eggs and the odd quotation by Jonas. And because Julian refused to go to work that day without giving a reason, this morning and afternoon gave way to each and every member of the Baron's crew making an attempt at encouraging the boy and lecturing their boss.

Now, it's not as though the crew lined up behind one another to recite memorized speeches; in fact, for much of the day, these attempts at rousing conversation were well-spaced apart and as casual as possible. Granted the crew had their own duties to attend to throughout the day, but before they left or as they arrived back home, each got his (or her) two cents in to whatever party was not presently occupied.

But no matter how they reasoned, the Baron continued to hide behind his promise, and Julian to grumble defeatist one-liners like

"What's the use?" (Remember, he is a teenager when this story takes place.)

So in the several hours between breakfast and dinner, Pigby grew progressively angrier with the Baron, Ten ha more and more frustrated with Julian, Geru unimpressed by either's reasons, and Oswald somewhat confused on the whole situation.

Fletcher tried to appeal to both parties' sense of optimism. However, when his opening line to Julian read, "Say there, Julian, there are plenty of fish in the sea," he quickly realized that Julian didn't understand the metaphor, and that he was probably not the right man for the job. The minstrel had only gotten as far as giving a warm smile and saying, "Y'know boss—" before the Baron cut him off with,

"Shut up, Fletcher."

The dinnertime assault was not planned. To be fair, only the Baron and Julian found it to be an assault, and though the others may have been firm to the point of abrasion, they were quite well-meant. And while the rest of the day's interventions defended both parties' dignity by addressing them privately, the seven-person dinner[133] in the smallish cottage left no room for subtlety.

Comment turned to criticism, discussion turned to argument, and it wasn't long before two chairs had been overturned and a plate knocked on the floor. Pigby picked up a spoon with which to gesture heatedly, but the Baron reacted on the defensive, perceiving it as a weapon, and swatted it away.

This made Pigby jab one massive finger at the Baron's chest, triggering a, "Hey, hey, hey! Wash those hands before you touch me!" After all, Pigby had been eating chicken.

Geru tried to yell over both the Baron and the giant and must have hit an ultrasonic frequency, because even though they didn't catch a word of his tirade, it certainly hurt their ears.

To soothe the mood, Fletcher fetched a fiddle, but once he decided the calming strums weren't working, stirred up a mean ditty to accompany the growing chaos.

With each protest made by the young Julian, the younger Ten ha called him another insult—for which she later apologized, but only after insisting that she did it to motivate him. There came a moment when Ten ha actually seized Julian by the shoulders, shook him, and ordered him to "Go see Samantha this instant!"

---

[133] No one knew where Jonas was.

Oswald said mainly, "I say," and "What—what!" before realizing that he had the perfect argument to end all arguments and disappeared to find the proper passage in the proper book.

After about the seventh question to which Julian gave no response, Ten ha turned to her Baron and implored him, "Talk some sense into him, sir; you know he'll listen to you."

"That does it!" The Baron stood. "I would love to help the boy, but you know why I can't! I'm sorry; my hands are tied."

"Then try using your feet, boss."

The Baron shot back at the thin man, saying, "No puns!"

"No, Fletcher's right," came Pigby, "you've got to be more resourceful."

"We've seen you get around bigger obstacles," added Geru.

"Not against my title." Looking to Julian, the Baron nodded solemnly and told him, "I'm sorry, son, but you're on your own."

With that, the Baron plucked his hat from off the hook, popped it on his head and exited the cottage, leaving the lot in defeated silence.

Where the Baron went then is not relevant to this story; what is relevant is who he ran into.

You see, there was one other person of note staying in the Libburus' house, and without an older brother, she had come to consider herself the man of the family—somehow her own father didn't much factor into that decision. With her sister barricaded inside, Sabrina opted to slip out through Samantha's window[134] in order to speak to the orphaned homeowner across the river.

Her thoughts were so determinedly occupied that she did not even notice the exclamations inside the house as she approached. That being said, there were no thoughts so powerful as to completely prevent her from seeing the Baron Pan Bordolo latching the door behind him.

"Oh, hello," she said.

The Baron flourished the hat away from his head and bowed so that the plume brushed the ground. "Good evening, Madame Sabrina; I didn't know we'd be expecting you."

"You're not," she replied. "I needed a word with... Are you just leaving?"

The Baron tipped his head forward and hummed in the affirmative. "I need to clear my head, get some air. So I'm going for a

---

[134] Her rendezvous would have been a lot more secretive had Samantha not been scanning the skyline from her older sister's bedroom.

walk—a nice winter walk." And then after a pause, added, "Would you like to join me?"

Sabrina's eyes widened as she tried to convey by expression alone the irony. "Oh, of all the rotten times…" she observed. "Um…no. No. I have to—" A regretful sigh, and then without losing momentum, "I need to talk to him."

"Oh, well then." The Baron resumed his hat, and with a touch of the brim bid her, "Good luck."

"Believe me, sir, I've been asking for that for days." Without pausing to see his reaction, Sabrina let herself in the front door.

"Aha!" Pigby stood and was saying, "To think you would just abandon—" before he noticed who it was, which caused immediate backpedalling and a bowed head, accompanied by, "Evening, Mum."

"Evening," she replied. "How old are you?"

Pigby checked behind him to see that—yes, indeed—the others were watching. "T-Twenty-eight."

"Mmm. Then don't call me Mum."

Sabrina stepped around the assenting giant man and into the center of the space where all eyes remained upon her, including Julian's. As she approached, Fletcher immediately gave up his seat so she could sit closer to the boy.

"Alright, Julian, out with it," began Sabrina, and because Julian's expression did not change, she added, "Why haven't you said anything to my sister since the proposal?"

Julian blinked twice.

Sabrina had no way of knowing that this had been precisely their topic of conversation before she arrived, but she could tell that they were astonished by her opening question. She chose not to let this baffle her. "Julian, she's been waiting for you. She hasn't answered Raul, but she needs something from you if she's ever going to know what to do here."

"Why?"

"Because you need to talk to her!" exclaimed Sabrina, while Ten ha nodded rapidly in agreement. "Look, do you want her to marry Raul?"

"No," came Julian, after a moment's hesitation.

"Well, have to you talked to Raul about it?" And before Julian could say no, Sabrina followed with, "Well why not? If he's your friend, you tell him! He'll listen."

"Really…" began Julian, and settled on his favorite line for the day: "What's the use?"

Sabrina stared incredulously at the boy before exploding into, "Love! Happiness—marriage—sex[135]!—I don't know—"

"But we can't do any of that!" protested Julian.

"Why not?"

"Because I'm not one of you!"

Sabrina wanted to comment on her disbelief to a third party, but seeing as she did not know any of the Baron's crew particularly well, simply looked away from Julian at an imaginary audience—the reader perhaps, like how the twentieth-century American hero Ferris Bueller might look at the camera—before demanding, "You're going to let *that* stop you?"

"What if your father won't let me marry her?"

"What if he does? Julian, who in God's name ever said it was a rule?"

"I don't know," admitted Julian, "but Raul or Eugene—"

"To hell with them!" proclaimed Sabrina, causing Oswald to gasp at the blasphemy, which made him quite lose his spot on the page. "Look, Julian, it's very simple: do you love her?"

Julian opened his mouth then closed it. He had never been asked that before. A part of him knew that he should have said 'yes,' but instead he shrugged a single shoulder.

Luckily for everyone, Sabrina had recently been Julian's age and knew how to translate such a gesture. "Then why can't you tell her?"

"Because she told me not to."

"What?" sounded the response, but not just from Sabrina; every single person in the room gave the one-word question in near-perfect synch, excluding Oswald, who—still looking through his books for the perfect line—lost his place again.

Julian took a deep breath, so deep that it pulled his shoulders back to their proper posture and made him taller than Sabrina from where he sat. "Just before Raul's announcement, two days ago, by the well, she told me not to say what I was going to say, which was going to be 'I love you,'" but because Julian was an honest boy, he had to amend the last, "I think. And I don't know why she stopped me. Maybe it's because she'd rather marry Raul anyway."

---

[135] In fairness, she probably would have said 'congress' or even something more colloquial seeing as sex to refer to intercourse didn't occur until the latter part of the 18th century which was well-after the genesis of the Isle.

The crew waited tensely for Sabrina to respond to this, but since she merely sat, mouth agape, shaking her head, Pigby had to butt in.

"Julian," he said, "what makes you think that?"

Julian shrugged the same shoulder more slowly. "I don't know. I suppose because he's more right for her."

Now, I don't want you to take the crew's silence as apathy. In truth, all of them wanted to protest this, but not knowing Raul that well, and knowing Adleship Isle's traditions even less, they could hardly think of something to say to dissuade the boy from so terrible a mode of thought. So they said nothing.

Sabrina watched Julian droop once again, and tried to speak quickly enough to keep him from sinking. "You don't think that, do you?"

"Maybe," came the partial reply.

"If you do," said Sabrina, getting to her feet, "I should tell her that that's how you feel and save her from waiting anymore—"

"No, don't!" Julian reached out for one of the hands of the girl who stood before him, but stopped suddenly short of touching her and withdrew. "Don't tell her that. Just... Give me some time."

"Alright. I'll go talk to her." Sabrina gathered her skirts in her fists and started for the door, saying, "Don't give up, Julian—I'll never forgive you if you do." When the older sister coursed out the door, she didn't even bother to latch it behind her.

After she had gone, Julian curled forward until his forehead rested securely on his palms.

Ten ha looked from Julian to Pigby, who looked to Geru, who looked to Fletcher, who looked at his fiddle. Because none of the others could think to comment, it was Oswald—who had looked for his passage—that broke the silence.

"Confound it!" declared the old man, slamming yet another book shut in frustration, "I can't find it."

LVIII – A Perfectly Packed Pipe

The Baron Pan Bordolo believed that there was a certain art to properly stuffing a pipe, and as of such, he could spend nearly an hour doing so before taking the first puff. Though the Baron was quite well-versed in cutting corners, taking those shortcuts available and making others all his own, he reserved the due tedium for certain special tasks like painting a sign, stirring pudding, or stuffing a pipe.

Now these things may not seem important to you, but keep in mind that in the early nineteenth century, very little comfort could be found when wandering out in the world, and the most successful adventurers probably only were so because they knew how to soothe themselves in times of crisis. Why, only a week before, when they were climbing about the Scottish highlands and lowlands, Pigby took to counting stones, Fletcher to matching pitches of the wind with whistles, and Geru to committing individual clouds to memory.

The Baron Pan Bordolo continued to wax his mustache. But, seeing as even a neatly curled stache did not alleviate feelings of anxiety on that particular night, the Baron went out for a pipe. The mustache hated the smoke, and tried to inform the Baron so by drooping, which made the Baron tend to the ringlets, which made the mustache quite happy again.

Were it able to speak, the pipe would have pointed out—quite jealously, I might add—that while the stache was lucky enough to be waxed every day, the pipe was only ever pulled out when the Baron was feeling frustrated or somber. Perhaps this resentment motivated the pipe to irritate the stache.

Though Julian had never before smoked, he graciously took a pull when the Baron offered.

"Easy there, lad," said the Baron as Julian coughed. "All good things in time."

"And they find this soothing?" asked the lad, wiping at his freshly watering eyes.

"Only the disciplined and the masochistic." The Baron retrieved the pipe from young Julian and drew heartily, and with the release came three perfect smoke rings in descending size, shot with such precision that the smallest of the lot passed through the centers of the other two.

"Great Fred," expressed a breathless Julian, which made the Baron chuckle.

They both watched the rings until they faded into obscurity against the darkening sky. The Baron blew two more sets, then relaxed his posture and settled back against the wall of Julian's house, where he had joined the boy only about a minute before.

"So, did the young lady have anything to say?" resumed the Baron.

Julian shook his head. "Just more of the same. I must say, I don't know what to do, sir."

"Hmm." The Baron chewed at his lower lip before saying, "Let me ask you something, son: if it weren't for the status difference, would you let anything stop you from marrying her?"

"Other than herself? I don't know, sir."

"Well, you'd better know. If you want to fight for something, you have to know what it means to you, what you'd be willing to sacrifice. By God!—if you needed to you could run away with her—"

"Oh, I couldn't do that, sir."

"Why?" came an incredulous Baron, "Afraid someone would stop you?"

"No, it's not that. You can't leave the Isle. No one can; in the winter the weather out there keeps us in, and in the warmer months, there's nothing but cliffs on either side of us."

"What about to the north?" offered the Baron, for—though he knew that his crew had come from the west—was sure there could be a source for the waterfall.

"I don't think so, sir. No one's ever managed an in-and-out safe enough for us to hear about it." He paused to shake his head again. "Besides, I'd never want to take her away from here. I'm not sure I'd want to take me away from here. This is my home, sir."

"You know, let's—Here, we're friends, so let's not have any of this 'Sir,' alright? Why not call me Pan?"

"Pan…"

The Baron could tell that Julian was not quite comfortable with the title, and so assured him, "Don't worry, lad. It'll grow on you." The Baron let out a sigh as he turned away from the boy to pick out constellations. Of course, the stars were merely a ruse to shadow his guilt, and so he said, "I hope you understand why I can't help you here."

"Sir?"

"Um, I wish I could help—and I will. I truly will where any part of this is concerned, except for your status, son." The Baron caught Julian's nod in periphery and wondered how sincere it was. "I can't against my name."

"The name Pan?"

"No, the title. My Baron-hood, son."

"The title that you're telling me not to use?"

"Yes, but—It's different. I'm still the Baron, and you still acknowledge that, but if I break your status, I'll discredit mine. More than that—I'll dissolve it." The Baron turned to the boy and, pleading for forgiveness through his eyes, said, "And I can't do that, even for you."

Julian nodded, though he seemed unable to match the other's gaze. "I understand it's important to you—I don't know what it all means—but I know it's not fair for you to give something you need so that I can have something I…"

The Baron raised a quizzical eyebrow as he waited for Julian to finish, but the boy said nothing.

"I'll tell you one thing: if I knew I was doing right by her father, and my friends and neighbors, nothing could stop me from telling her how I feel," resolved Julian. "I guess the rest would be up to Samantha."

"I'm sorry I can't be of more help to you," said the Baron.

"Yes." Julian pushed off of the wall to stand freely. "I hope you do find a way though, sir. To help. I don't know anything about your world, and I'm finding out that I don't even know enough about mine, and I could really use a friend to guide me."

"I see," the Baron acknowledge, but offered no more at that time.

Julian nodded, then made his way back toward the front door, stopping only once to say over his shoulder, "Even if there's nothing you can do for me this time, you'll still be my friend, Pan."

And he shut the door, leaving the Baron with a perfectly packed pipe, a curled mustache, and his own stubborn pride.

LIX – Sabrina's Appalled Expression

"Did he say that he'll come talk to me?" asked Samantha.

"Not exactly, but—"

"Then what—might I ask—was the point of you going there, without my asking you too, without you even telling me?"

"Well, excuse me!" exclaimed Sabrina. "I didn't realize you had the situation so under control; tell me when is the happy day?"

"Oh, shove off." Samantha firmly crossed her arms and stomped her way to the bed, which was not as soft and comfy as your twenty-first-century sensibilities might hope it is. The nightgown falling gently as she dropped to a sitting position, Samantha tried not to grimace at her upset tailbone.

"Look, I'm sorry, and I'll try to help," said Sabrina, unaware of what the Baron had expressed just minutes before, "but I don't really understand how you've gotten yourself into this. If you didn't care about marrying him, what's to stop you my grabbing the boy by his stout shoulders and dragging him through your window?"

"Sabrina!" whispered a shocked, slightly offended, and more than a little titillated Samantha.

"And if you *do* want to marry," Sabrina went on, walking around the bed to face her sister once again, "why in all heaven would you stop him from saying he loved you?"

"He may not have been saying that," protested the younger, with an indicative finger raised.

"Even if he wasn't, what's to stop you from saying it first?" Sabrina took a moment to breathe, then sat down softly on the bed and lay a gentle hand on Samantha's shoulder, "You have to say something. Whether it's yes to Julian, no to Raul, or letting Father know what it is you want—because sooner or later someone's going to get around my little older-sister-marries-first arrangement."

"Why, are you going to marry anyone?"

Had Samantha said such with any less sarcasm the foundations of the house my yet have been surprised enough to crumble. Fortunately, all of the surprise seemed to have been absorbed by Sabrina's appalled expression.

"No," she fiercely returned, then after a moment postulated, "Would it help things?"

"What? How?"

"Well, think of it: I could marry Raul. He'd be shocked by the notion long enough that he probably couldn't come up with an excuse out of it by the wedding day, and that'll clear you until—Well, at least until the next man tries to court you."

Samantha didn't find the occasion funny at all, and so wished to remain frosty about what she assumed could only be a comical suggestion. Even so, it must have tickled her ribs somewhat because a genuine laugh swelled out as she said, "No! Why would you want to do a thing like that?"

"Well, it solves the problem. I mean it will spare you, and I don't know how long it might take me to get married otherwise. Anyway, he's not a bad sort—well-bred, well-kept, just a little shortsighted, and I *like* that in my men."

"You're insane!" insisted Samantha, though it hardly came out between the giggles. And as her sister found this new line of humane torture fun, the younger did her best to scramble up the bed and away from her.

This only made Sabrina crawl after, explaining with dramatics and gesticulations, "It's a good idea! That way, when he becomes Libburus, I wouldn't even need to move out of this house—if only we could arrange the wedding on the same day of his swearing in."

"And what if you find you don't want to be his wife?"

"Aha! I've a plan for that already. See, I'll run him simply ragged. I'll make the most absolute shrew of a wife and keep the stresses so unbearable that he dies a nervous man at an early age. If I wanted could be married again by the time I'm thirty."

"That's sweet, but no. No." Samantha did her best to wipe the foolish smile from her face completely, turning it instead to rue. "What am I to do, Sabrina?"

"Oh, I don't know." Sabrina scooped the blankets out from under her body and swiftly tucked herself in. Propping one elbow on the pillow, she said, "You know, for all my success with men, I've never really understood them. Tell the truth, I don't think anyone does—even themselves."

"So how do you keep them away?"

"Well, it's like Hephaestus' men: if I told Liam or Lionel no outright, I'm sure that one or both of them would spend the next few weeks actively trying to convince me, and ignoring as many *No*s as possible. So instead, I just stall."

"Stall?"

"Stall," confirmed Sabrina. "Just kind of appear stand-off-ish but give them the impression that you'll come to them when you're ready."

"Does that work?"

"Not every time. But it should with Raul. If you don't know what to say the next time he confronts you, just tell him that you'll have an answer by—oh, New Year's Day."

Snuggling under the older sister's arm, Samantha asked, "And what if I don't have an answer."

"Then pick a different date or a different excuse. The more intangible the excuse, the less he can break it down. And if you give yourself long enough, you'll eventually know what to do."

"Hmm," resolved the younger, and nodded as if to plant her signature on the imaginary contract they'd drawn. "Sabrina, you are wise beyond your years."

"No, I'm not," said the other, "everyone else here is just dumber than theirs. Could you get the light?"

Samantha released her sister, licked her thumb and forefinger, then reached over the end-table to snuff out the candle.

LX – Closed but Not Clenched Fists

Julian wasn't sure what he had expected, but it certainly wasn't for Raul to laugh at him.

Julian made every effort to plant his feet more firmly into the ground, and with closed but not clenched fists, he swallowed and repeated, "I don't want you to marry Samantha."

Raul's hands were about his sides, keeping him from doubling over as he laughed, but he brought one up to his head and smoothed out his hair, as if that should rally his composure before speaking. "Oh, but Julian, you're not serious."

"Yes, I am serious."

A brief squawk emanated before Raul said, "Now, Julian, *Julian!* Whatever could you mean by that? I mean, it's preposterous. Whyever would you say such a thing?"

"Because I don't want you to marry her."

Raul stood in stunned silence for a moment, obviously on the cusp of giggles yet again, but when he next made a sound, he implored the boy, "Why would you care?"

Julian swallowed and tried not to grimace at the hard, dry taste. "Because I want to marry her."

Raul stared at his friend, leaning in to get a better view, and once he was convinced the boy's comment was earnest, resumed his laughing. Raul turned to walk away, going to the tree to retrieve his darts and chortling to himself, "Oh, Julian, that is just too charming!"

"So will you take back your proposal?" Julian called after.

"No!" came the incredulous reply. "Why would I ever do that?"

Julian didn't want to stammer, but found himself just so flabbergasted that he couldn't not. "I just told you! I— I—"

"You what, Julian?" said Raul returning with the darts. "You can't even marry the girl. She's the type to be married to the next Libburus, I'm the type to *be* the next Libburus, and you're—well—not."

"But we're friends!" he protested. "Why can't you respect my—"

"You know, I think we should be talking about respect the other way around, here. Alright? You're on my side of the river—For that, *I'm* on my side of the river. What makes you think you've any call to tell *me* what to do?"

"I'm not telling; I'm asking."

"Oh, well, then your answer is no." Raul faced the tree for his next throw and in the same sing-song cadence added, "Sorry."

This might be the point where you expect one party to hit the other, to sock 'im in the jaw like the bar brawl scene in any John Wayne picture, but remember, they are in Adleship Isle. Perhaps more importantly, they're English, so Julian's appalled response sounded like so: "How could you be so discourteous?"

"Discourteous? Now remind me, which one of us is of higher birth."

"So that's it then?" asked Julian. "All this time we've been friends, and you just think I'm beneath you?"

"No, you're not beneath me, Julian," said Raul, sudden concern in his brow as he tried to reassure the lad he still called friend. "I'm just above you—Or—No, I'm explaining this wrong—"

"You've explained enough, Raul; you've shown me that the only reason you can't listen to me is because of my status."

"Oh, sod off," said Raul, turning back to his tree.

"You're sounding just like your father."

Raul spun toward Julian, pointing the dart in his hand at the boy's face and ordering him to, "Retract that."

"Or what? You'll poke me?"

"You'd better listen here, Julian. It's all been settled—I'll have the lady for my wife, and you can be happy for your friend."

"She hasn't said yes yet."

The brows hardened fiercely. "Do you doubt she will?"

Julian did not speak, but he tried to make his shrug look as resolute as possible.

Raul must have noticed that he was standing very close to Julian, and so exhaled, withdrew, and resumed a regal posture before flicking a dart into the tree. "You know what, Julian. I think I'll forbid you from seeing her. Just until things go back to normal, that is."

"You'll *forbid me*?" repeated the incredulous Julian.

"Yes, why not?"

"You can't do that."

"Yes, I can."

"How?"

"It's— I'm—" Raul gestured to the space between them. "Status!"

"Yeah, but you can't order me."

"Why not?"

"Well, who says you can?"

"Who says I can't?" countered Raul.

"This is unbelievable! You may as well order people to sacrifice sheep in your honor or throw themselves off the edge of the world."

"Oh, don't be so dramatic, Julian."

"No, I thought you were better than this," said Julian, "I thought you understood—"

"I *do* understand—now better than ever." Reaching out in friendship he added hopefully, "Maybe when you're my age, you'll understand."

"I am your age! Or I will be soon. But a few months and a few furlongs makes all the difference in the world to you now, doesn't it?" Julian shook his head and began to back away from the man who was yet a boy.

"Julian, come back!" called Raul. "Look, I'm sorry, but I— There's a certain responsibility I have to—"

"No. There really isn't. It's just unfortunate that I'd have to be on *your* level for you to hear me." And he turned and started for home, trying not to react when he heard the next comment called after him.

"If you were on my level, we wouldn't be having this conversation!"

As he refaced the tree to take another shot, even Raul couldn't quite say what he'd meant by that.

LXI – A Veritable Library

You may have expected this from Fletcher, or even Pigby, but—
now that his ankle had properly healed—it was Oswald who bounded up
the front path and in through Julian's door, declaring, "It's up to us!"

"What?"

"What?"

And "What?" from Fletcher, Pigby, and Ten ha respectively.

Oswald continued to bustle into the room, shedding his satchel,
overcoat, and second coat[136] as he went. "It's up to us. *We* are going to
make things right for young Julian."

Fletcher pursed his lips, Ten ha raised an eyebrow, and Pigby
popped his spectacles onto his forehead, all awaiting the context behind
this great declaration Oswald had made. Convinced that he'd seen the
messenger clearly, Pigby adjusted his reading glasses once more over his
eyes and asked, "And how do you propose we do that?"

"Isn't it obvious?" came an excited Fletcher, closing his book
and jumping down from the loft. "We stow away the boy and the girl,
and take them with us—No! First, we fake their deaths, and—"

"That's absurd, Fletcher," Ten ha butted in, "she'd never want to
leave this place."

"It's true, Oswald," chimed Pigby, engrossed in his inventory log
and clearly most missing the point as he added, "It wouldn't work."

Oswald looked a little disoriented[137] but regained his footing.
"Um—No, I say—" Oswald scanned the room to make sure it was only
the four of them. "Is the Baron...?"

---

[136] Just because they're wintering on the Isle doesn't mean it can't get chilly,
especially for an old man.

[137] Were trains in use, I would have said 'derailed.'

"No, he's out with Geru," explained Fletcher. "Went to look at the volcano signs."

"Yes, as I thought. See, I've a thought," began Oswald bringing himself to the center of the room. "The Baron's not able to help Julian on account of a promise against his name, but we—I say we are free to do what we want."

Oswald waited once more for a response, looking as though he thought his comment the most astounding thing ever uttered. But the others merely looked between themselves, puzzling over whether or not they should ask the disheartening question which Ten ha eventually worked up the courage to ask, "How?"

"Ah, yes," came Oswald, and after a big smile and an inappropriately long pause, concluded, "We change his status!"

Though this may seem like a delightful idea to you, the reader, the crew was entirely unimpressed, because Oswald's inconclusive conclusion still begged the very necessary question, "How?"—this time from all three.

"It's—" resumed Oswald, but Pigby's quizzical gaze halted him briefly. After faltering, he began again with, "I—" but was startled by Fletcher's skeptical stare. And as Ten ha's incredulous expression put him off his last "We just—" Oswald resolved, "I don't know." And before the others could sigh too heavily, tried again with, "But-but-but we've all done far more in our time. Why, Pigby here has officiated marriages; Fletcher has blessed temples; I've taken judges' oaths; and Ten ha even healed that paraplegic!"

"He healed on his own," clarified Ten ha with a clarifying finger.

"Yeah, after touching your ankle," added Fletcher.

"It was just a little extra motivation," explained Ten ha.

"It's really indisputable," nodded Pigby.

"The man was convinced I was an angel," protested Ten ha, "and if I informed him otherwise, he might have refused to walk again!"

"Yes, very well," came Oswald, reassuming the mantle of conversation, "but if we can do all of that, I say, what is to stop us from coming up with a way to help the boy. After all, we owe it to him for what he's done this winter."

Pigby furrowed his brow, which shoved the little half-moon spectacles down his nose further. He pushed them back up to their proper resting point before saying, "Except for one problem: none of us is a noble."

"What about Geru?" asked Fletcher. "Wasn't his family some kind of crat[138] in India?"

"His parents were British con artists," corrected Pigby.

"Well, do we have to *be* noble to make someone noble?" asked Ten ha. "After all, Pigby didn't have to be wed to marry people."

"Yes, but what about the Baron?" asked Pigby. "Surely he wouldn't approve of this if he knew."

"Well, then that's precisely why he won't know!" announced Fletcher which led him to stride about the room, gloriously launching into one of his more dramatic speeches. "Pigby, my friend, our dear Baron is bound by his honor not to personally change the boy's place, but he's also bound by his conscience to hope for the best for this same virtuous lad. The Baron Pan Bordolo would not order us to help in his stead, but would he really oppose us? Nay, I daresay, he would hope that we would execute just this plan, properly behind his back, so as to keep him out of any blame. And if that ludicrous popinjay from 'cross the creek should take issue with it, I say, damn his sensibilities—full speed ahead! Why, we've broken three of His High-Horsed Hooey's rules; what's a one more?"

Oswald applauded as Fletcher stuck the landing. "Bravo, I say. And hear, hear!"

"Yes, but if we do it, it has to be solid," said Ten ha. "If we're going to go over Hephe's head—and our Baron's—we need a real noblehood-granting ceremony, or at least one that's very close."

Fletcher shrugged at this. "Why can't we just make one up?"

"Because they'd know," said Pigby. "She's right. Whatever we do, we won't help the lad for it if His Spoilsportness can overturn it upon our finishing."

"Well, then, what are we waiting for?" asked Oswald, a triumphant fist shaking in the air. "We've a veritable library out in the wagon. There's got to be some procedure which fits into some accolade one of us has won—hasn't there?"

"By golly, let's do it!" came Fletcher.

"Well, I've got to run to the stables for about an hour," said Ten ha, "but after that I'm all yours."

"What say you, Pigby?" asked Oswald.

---

[138] To the best I can interpret, 'crat' is short for 'aristocrat' in Fletcher. I'm also going to assume it's a slur.

"I say, let's get cracking. If we want to even the playing field for Julian, we've got a long way to go and a short time to do it."

With the troops effectively rallied to a sturdy morale, not a one of them even bothered to jump when the front door was opened, this time by Julian himself. They all turned to face him, and he nodded to each individually before settling his gaze upon the old man. Licking his lips in preparation, he took the three or four steps to cross the room then cleared his somewhat-raspy throat.

"Mister Oswald," he began.

"Just Oswald—I say, what is it, boy?"

Julian glanced at Fletcher, who—though he didn't know what young Julian was about to say—nodded in encouragement. "Oswald, I need you to make me a noble."

A hand to her chest, Ten ha took in a hopeful sniff, and beside her the giant man pinched back proud tears.

Oswald seized Julian's face, kissed him roughly on the cheek, and exclaimed, "Bless you, boy. God bless you!"

LXII – A Snag

You've heard the phrase "hit a snag," yes? Well, I am of the view that it is not you hitting the snag, but rather the snag that hits you. Not to give the snag too much agency, mind, but if you ever find yourself on a pleasant walk in the woods only to have your clothing caught by an errant branch, would you not rather blame the branch which rudely could not keep its twigs to itself than your own two feet for bringing you there?

Well, as you might expect from any good analogic segue, such a snag hit Oswald's plan. In fact, had it been a physical snag, it would have gone and sprained his other ankle.

The issue was not in hiding the endeavor from the Baron— heavens, no! In fact, when the Baron walked in on the lot researching later that same afternoon and was met with stunned silence, he asked only, "What have we here?" then resolved to leave once he saw the book on Oswald's lap. The Baron Pan Bordolo, indeed more hopeful than suspicious, awkwardly backed away and said, "Yes, well, carry on with your reading," before shutting the door of the small cottage behind him.

Geru was in fact the bigger problem, first because he had not been present when the lot had their profound pep rally, which—had he been there—he may have mocked for its immature melodrama; and secondly, because of how they later decided to make use of him for the ennobling of Julian—but that's another chapter entirely.

To be fair, even Hephaestus wasn't much a problem. The crew had resolved that the lord of merchants would be most suspicious if they spent the remainder of the day indoors, so they drew up a rotating schedule of outside-doings which would show that they were simply acting as normal within the little village of Adleship Isle. Of course, they never needed to fill a single shift beyond Ten ha's trip to the stables, because when she returned, she informed the lot that "Hephaestus has taken to bed with a headache and will not be following much of anyone's activities today."

When asked how she found out about this, Ten ha shrugged and replied, "Grapevine."

When Jonas came back home, with the snap-pea leading him by the wrist, he too spied the volumes open on their laps, one of which happened to be the Magna Carta, and seemed to find it necessary to try to out-quote Oswald, which made Oswald frustrated and Miriam very intrigued.

Julian, particularly well-versed in how quickly the gossip loop in the Isle could explode into every single household, decided that every question little Miriam asked made their plan that much less secretive, and so hustled out both the snap-pea and her grandfather, saying, "I'll be down the way at Meredith's."

With their Baron decidedly out for the evening—at Sherman the tailor's if you must know, both sharing a lovely family supper and seeing if he could get the hole in his original blue jacket patched—and no interruptions from any of the other Isleans, a thin man, an old man, a giant man, a short man, and a woman labored over text after test. But even for all the thin man's whimsy, the old man's wisdom, the giant man's work ethic, the short man's wiliness, and the woman's willingness to translate when the others got lost, they came up with bupkis.

Fletcher, from where he lay atop the loft, let the tome drop open on his chest and groaned loudly.

"Negative energy never got anything done, Fletcher," advised Pigby.

"I'll have you know that I have given up quite successfully—several times—armed with nothing but a defeatist attitude," replied their minstrel, who seemed to be most failing at the merry-making for which he was hired.

"Perseverance, m'boy," offered Oswald, without looking up for fear he might lose his line, "perseverance always pays off."

With a sigh much larger than himself, Geru shut his book resolutely and said, "Well, unless one of us is a Sheikh, we won't make any headway in this one, and Pigby isn't even a Muslim."

"Me?" came the giant man, "If anything, Ten ha's the more likely."

"I was properly baptized," she muttered, her finger furiously following her text from top-to-bottom instead of the others' customary left-to-right.

"Are any of you shamans or medicine men?" asked Oswald, "Because we could make Julian a—Oh! Oh, no—I say—Excuse me, that one's for a ritual sacrifice." And Oswald gave an awkward laugh.

"Couldn't we just make up a title?" came Fletcher.

"For the boy or for us?" asked Pigby.

"Sure," answered the thin man, sitting up in the loft, which was a comical look on him because he had to hunch forward quite a bit to keep from hitting his head. "Either one. I mean, why not? This whole thing is going to be bogus anyway."

"No!" declared Oswald, his metaphoric foot most-definitely down, "We do no good for Julian if someone calls our bluff. It must be real."

"Well, real or not, I think we've killed off this stack." Geru pushed himself off of his chair and set his volume on a pillar of discards, one of six, each of which were just a head shorter than he. "Pigby, care to join me in collecting the next set of books."

"Hmm?" The giant man looked up. "There aren't anymore."

"What do you mean, there aren't anymore?" asked Geru.

"I mean, we're out," Pigby insisted.

"What do you mean, we're o—"

"I mean, we've spent the Baron's supply. There's not a walking library in that cart, Geru. We were bound to hit empty," said Pigby while the others tried to digest the news.

"I say! I-I remember there being more books," stammered a worried Oswald.

Fletcher nodded with him. "Yeah, there's gotta be two more drawers[139] at least!"

"Well, sure, there are some books in there," Pigby conceded, "but I don't think collections of poetry or anyone's personal diaries will help the boy."

"I'm sure it could," said Fletcher, "I've written some great ones!"

"And they'll cheer him up," assured Ten ha, "but they won't grant him title, now will they?"

Oswald closed his book and kneaded his forehead with one palm. "It's hopeless then, isn't it?"

"Whatever happened to 'perseverance'?"

---

[139] Most items in the Baron's cart were measured in barrels, crates, or drawers, rather than by standard denominations of weight and size. The only person who tracked ounces was Pigby.

"Shut up, Fletcher," snapped Pigby.

But even as Fletcher fell silent, no one else bothered to pipe up, signaling that they all—though they hoped not to—agreed with the old man's last. And now that Oswald had been struck by the snag, it seemed there would be no helping the boy.

With a small grunt of acceptance, Pigby said, "I'll start hauling these back," and he went to the first of the book towers and hoisted it up against his chest.

Ten ha gasped—not in reaction to Pigby. No, this was something else entirely. In fact, it was enough to make her suddenly stand and proclaim, "Wait!"

And as Pigby was not exceedingly committed to giving up, he consented with, "Okay," and set down the books.

She took a settling breath, afraid that without it, she might squeak in excitement instead of speak. "There's still one library we haven't checked."

Oswald began to light up again. "Really?"

"Where?" demanded Geru. "The people here haven't even kept Bibles; in fact, the only reason we have any texts at all is because we carried them over the mountain!"

"Oh," realized Fletcher, soon to be followed by Pigby's:

"Ah," which was followed by Oswald's:

"I say!"

Geru looked between them and announced, "That's got to be the most idiotic idea I've ever heard."

And that was what persuaded the lot to break into Hephaestus' wagon not an hour later.

LXIII - A Reflective Wood Finish
and Strategically-Placed Mirrors

All five were astounded to discover that it looked even grander on the inside than it did on the out—(to be fair, only four of them made the initial entrance, but when the fifth came about, he would feel the same way.)

They were actually somewhat hesitant to open it in the first place, because—even though there were no guards standing outside of it with their arms crossed—they half-expected guard dogs waiting inside to feast on them once they cracked the door. But as they heard no alarm when Geru picked the lock, Ten ha, Pigby, and Oswald all chanced to relax—not enough to unhood their lanterns, mind, but certainly enough to venture inside.

All four crammed into the standing-room quarters, sardined so only because of Pigby, and shut the door behind them before they allowed their lights to fully shine. As if by some magic, (more accurately a reflective wood finish and small strategically-placed mirrors) the two lanterns alone lit up the whole space right before their eyes.

"By Jove!" praised Oswald.

"My goodness," breathed Ten ha.

"Well, I'll be," muttered Pigby.

And "Hmph!" humphed Geru.

But Oswald promptly bookended the admiring with, "Alright—best get to work. No telling how long we have."

"Before the Baron gets suspicious or one of the goons catches us?" asked Pigby, trying to survey the room for available books.

"Don't worry about the goons!" said Geru, his voice clanging unpleasantly around the close walls. "I've got the brush-bomb[140]."

"And let's hope we don't have to use it," said Ten ha. "Have you found his books?"

But Pigby was too engrossed in the layout of the inventory to have even opened a single cupboard. "Even the boxes are laid out with pristine accuracy! No wonder he calls himself the lord of merchants," Pigby observed—in innocent awe but apparently without enough tact.

Because he could not reach his head, Geru slapped Pigby's arm. "That's treasonous!"

"Shush—the both of you!" insisted Oswald. "We're here for one thing: his library. Now, where do you think he'd store the books?"

So the four went hunting for that hopefully special game-changing book, the title and origin of which they did not know, shifting little boxes and barrels as they made way for themselves and turning the place even more into a maze than it already was. Geru took the rear, between a curious arrangement of hanging parasols and a box of esteemed oriental fireworks, and Pigby the helm, shouldering up against some kind of novelty birdcage that was affixed to the ceiling. And from that vantage point, the giant man saw something odd, and so remarked:

"Here's something odd?"

Unfortunately, no one was presently able to turn around enough to see what Pigby was looking at, so three whispers of "What?" issued toward his back.

"Well, it's a plaque, fixed on the wall just at the front—engraved in says, '*the wondrous wares of S. and J. Tiegs*,'" turning back to look over one broad shoulder, he added, "looks over fifty years old."

"What do you suppose that means?" asked Ten ha.

"Obviously, it's the original owners of this trav'ling treasure trove," squeaked Geru.

"Either that or Hephaestus' real name," said Pigby.

But before they could consider that further, Oswald declared, "Here, I've found them," and began passing small armloads behind him.

---

[140] Now before you laugh at Geru's taking on any sturdy servants, consider this: Geru in his time had studied everything then known about biology and chemistry, with a particular fondness for botany, which led him to perfect a grade-A chloroform-type mixture which could make bull elephants most forget themselves—no mean feat when you consider than an elephant never forgets—and pass out cold on the hot, hot sand. As it was assembled from about eight different kinds of properly fermented grains and grass, he called it a brush-bomb.

Each took a selection, trying his (or her) best not to disrupt any texts or wall decorations while finding a standing spot to pour through the pages, and everyone but Oswald wanting to discuss this clue on the possibility of the man's real name.

Then the door handle suddenly jiggled and unlatched, signaling that Geru ready his herb for the strike, but the door was opened to reveal a somewhat breathless Fletcher. "Evening, all," he said, stepping into the wagon.

"Fletcher!" grumbled Geru, "I nearly wasted the brush-bomb on you."

"What's the word?" asked Pigby.

"Clear's the word," said Fletcher, his elbows knocking against the wooden crates on either side of him as he took off his coat. "Not a servant in sight—I scouted the whole perimeter. The Baron's gone to bed without a question and Julian gave me this." Fletcher demonstrated a 'thumbs up' to the others before explaining, "Apparently he doesn't want me to lop off my opponent's head."

"Charming," mumbled Oswald.

Dropping the coat to the floor, Fletcher took a moment to survey the walls and ceiling. He whistled once in appreciation. "It looks even grander on the inside than the out. Apparently the fop's as stuffy privately as he tries to make himself look in public."

And Oswald, as if cued by the word 'stuffy' let out a frustrated, "If you don't mind, I've set out a stack of books for you."

"I see that; thank you," replied the amiable thin man, and promptly went to work.

As Fletcher took up the space of wall closest Ten ha, she informed him of the plaque and the names, and was sternly scolded once more by Oswald, who insisted, "As intriguing as this mystery may be in the long term, I say, it is not quite so pertinent as our present charge!" And with grumbles, the nearly excited crew turned back to their dreary reading.

Every fifteen minutes or so, one or more of the crew would ask if they were sure they wouldn't get caught for this. Ten ha continued to reply that Hephaestus' servants were already well in for the night. After the third time she answered so authoritatively, Pigby asked her how she knew this, to which she also replied, "Grapevine."

Through stack after stack, though, no matter how close they came, they never found a title for the boy that was entirely legitimate. Either he would not be qualified enough to receive it or none of them to grant it—usually both. A quick survey concluded that none of them was a king to grant dukedom or earlhood; and even if one of them *had* been a bishop, Ten ha pointed out that ordaining Julian a priest came with a certain vow of celibacy that simply did not permit marriage.

After nearly three hours of browsing, scouring, suggesting, and rejecting, Fletcher saw fit to raise his idea once again. "I think we should just lie about it."

"We can't," said Oswald.

"Well, I can't see us getting anywhere with the truth," returned Fletcher, setting the book down on the spent stack. "Other than Hephe's Kama Sutra manual, I haven't found a single thing of interest in this whole library. And, honestly, I'd rather we wrote a noblehood ceremony ourselves than pick one that only almost works."

"But he'd know," said Pigby, "Hephaestus'd call us on it and stop it before we began."

"You know," came Ten ha, "I hate to say it, but he'd stop us anyway even if it were legitimate."

"Well, then we'll get him out of the way!" offered Geru, "Create some sort of diversion that's so enticing he can't possibly be present for the ceremony."

"But even afterwards," insisted Pigby, "there's no way to keep him from knowing it was all a sham."

"Unless we were to do it in a language he couldn't understand." Oswald slowly stepped into the center of the wagon, and presented a copy of Homer's *Iliad*, written completely in ancient Greek.

Once the seed was planted, the rest of the idea grew sprawlingly, much faster than vine or weed, and cuing the most animated of arguments as the crew grasped at whatever miniature ideas might help their cause. As they left the wagon, having put it all back together in its original layout, no one noticed the other book that Pigby had stolen underarm, which he found of pivotal importance. Of course Pigby agreed with Oswald that this revelation would have to wait until after they had successfully up-ranked the boy. Luckily, there was hardly any time for the giant man's patience to grow thin.

LXIV – The Little Chimney-Ladder

Hephaestus was not used to being shaken awake, but apparently he was off too deeply to be reached by voice alone. Not that he was a naturally begrudging creature—this story not representative—but had it been Trenton who so rudely roused him, the old and trusted friend probably would have been forgiven. Gus was a different story.

The first thing he heard before his eyes willed themselves open was, "Come on, sir. You have to get up and put on your boots."

Hephaestus grumbled something, and must have scowled quite severely—seeing as the broad Gus stepped out of arm's reach—before grunting, "What in the name of heaven have you woken me up for?"

"It's outside, sir," replied Gus without really answering the question, "You need to get up, and I've your boots right here."

Now, Hephaestus loathed taking orders, especially when they came from his servants, even Trenton—but of course, Trenton could fold his arms more fiercely than any man Hephaestus had ever known and thereby must be listened to. The lord of merchants only complied with Gus for two reasons: the first, that his servants only ever ordered him during emergency situations, and the second, that he was simply too groggy to come up with a good excuse not to.

In just a couple of minutes, Hephaestus found himself striding down the hall and out the door of the Libburus' house, giving the ever-vigilant Cletus time only to say, "Mister Hephaestus…" as he passed him.

Once outside the house, armed with lovely boots and his personalized cane, he found three more of his servants—Cooper, Trenton, and Lance—all in proper winter garb, fit with a length of rope, two ice picks between them, and one long staff. Trenton, the leading party, put back his hood and said, "Sir, we've got to go quickly."

"What in the devil is this?" exclaimed Hephaestus. "You're going out into the snow?"

"No, sir," began Trenton, and then amended, "well, yes, sir, but it's after the Baron. They say he's going over the waterfall—that his miniature man found a passage out to the north. They'll be nearly to the falls already."

Hephaestus squeezed his eyes tight and shook his head hard, the wispy braids slapping at his neck. He put his fingers to the bridge of his nose and pressed until he saw little black spots in the corners of his closed eyes. Though he felt he knew why his men were supposed to inform him of such an action, Hephaestus had difficulty committing to the appropriate response.

"What?" he began, "Without me?" and then, "He'll freeze to death! Doesn't he know there's a blizzard out there?" which led to, "That jackal! He'll just pretend there's a passage out there and then come back to trick me, send me off a cliff or to be buried in a glacier!" However, even for the potentially fatal threat of deception, Hephaestus settled on credit and vanity: "He'll cheat me out of discovering the pass up there. We have to go!"

Whether or not it was a fair conclusion, the servants seemed to accept it. "Your coat, sir," said Cooper, handing Hephaestus the elaborate, triple-insolated, top-of-Everest-esque number which must have weighed a good twenty-five pounds. But once it was on his back, the man moved swiftly, leading the charge through Sebastian's backyard, beyond the well, and up among the trees at the lower end of the hill, toward the eastern bank of the waterfall and its little pool, on the other side of which stood the Baron Pan Bordolo and the short man.

"Mister Bordolo!" howled Hephaestus, over the humming undertone of the upper falls, pointing a crooked incriminating finger at the other man's perturbed expression.

"By all damnation!" replied the Baron, only it was said to Geru, and not Hephaestus. "Why'd you have to go run your mouth about the passage?"

"Sorry, sir," muttered Geru without looking at his Baron and showing only the slightest sign that he may have been disappointed in himself. Were the Baron not so distracted by Hephaestus at that moment, Geru's shame alone would have been a dead giveaway.

"I mean, honestly," the Baron went on, "I told you not to tell so many people—didn't I?—but you just had to brag—didn't you?—to every Islean and his brother that we passed, 'We're going to find a north pass out of town!'" And the Baron ended this (stellar) imitation of his resident squeaky scientist with a frustrated grunt of his own.

Surely, Geru would have apologized again were it not for Hephaestus calling to them, "Stay right there! We're going to come up to your side of the river, and we will discover this so-called passage together."

The Baron sneered, which the mustache did not like, by the by— the mustache rightly believed that sneers looked bad on both parties and diminished the twinkliness of the Baron's eyes. With all of the proper poison he could muster, the Baron Pan Bordolo shot back, "With all due respect, sir, kindly bugger off!"

"Oh! Well, I never," began Hephaestus, but as the Baron turned away from him to start climbing the rock face, the lord of merchants never managed to tell him what it was 'he never' did.

Correctly convinced that the Baron was keen on ditching him, Hephaestus resolved that they hadn't a moment to lose to get down the hill, across the river, and up the other side—seeing as there was no feasible way to cross the pool without getting entirely drenched from where they stood. He turned to his men and said, "Well, what are you waiting for? Back down the hill."

Even though the others started without so much as a wink, Lance held ground long enough to suggest, "Wouldn't we be better off climbing the wall on our side? There's bound to be a way to cross up top."

Hephaestus whipped around to face the boy, his eyes narrowing as he leaned in uncomfortably close to his most recent servant's face. "Oh really? And I suppose you know what's *actually* up top, there, do you? I suppose you think you're right clever about all this—Well, I've noticed all your shifting and slipping away, boy, and I've had a mind to talk to you for some days."

"Y-you have?" he stammered, stepping back.

"You know, I don't think I'd like so green a character to come with us today, to lead us off the trail. No, I've decided I've no room for amateurs." Hephaestus' heart pounded rigorously, offsetting him more than he would have liked, but committed to his strange foundless accusation, he abruptly handed Lance his cane and ordered him to "See that this gets back to my room and be ready for a word when we get back."

Lance stood open-mouthed, almost afraid to breathe again in the lord's presence, and holding the near-sacred cane with two hands against his chest. He watched as Hephaestus snatched the long staff away from

Cooper and led his three more-professional servants down the hill. Trenton, taking the rear, calmly gestured... something to Lance. To lance it could have been anywhere from 'It's okay,' to 'Stay calm,' to 'Don't follow him or he'll kill you.' Lance decided to believe all three and promptly trekked back to the Libburus' house.

Once he'd gotten back by his master's side, Trenton asked in a hushed voice, "Why'd you unload on the boy?"

Hephaestus may have at some other point taken the high road, but today he was inclined to reply, through clenched teeth, I might add, "Don't poke me, Trenton. I'm in no condition to accept criticism."

His proverbial stick just inches from the proverbial hornet's nest, Trenton ventured, "Is this because they're finding a north passage?"

"Of course it's because they're finding a passage!" Hephaestus shot back, with all the tenderness of a rabid rhinoceros. "By God, there was a time—just two short weeks ago, mind—when I was the *only* man who could successfully navigate *any* passage into or out of the Isle, and this pirate, this scoundrel, this cheat comes along to find another route that I couldn't locate in years! Well, I'll be damned if I let him think he can do it without me." And over his shoulder, Hephaestus concluded his resolute rant with a harsh, "Keep up, Gus; I've thirty years on you, and I can hike faster than that."

So they came to the bottom, and over the river, and once more up—this time a steeper wall of large boulders—and then along the little chimney-ladder fissured in the wall to the west of the upper falls, to find the Baron and Geru scouting in the distance across even rougher terrain, which none of the Isleans had tried to traverse in quite a few years.

It wasn't until well-after he'd caught up to the Baron, past their collective discovering that there was in fact no viable passage, and actually near the end of their return trip that Hephaestus even bothered to acknowledge that Lance had been right, and that the river-turned-stream was indeed very easy to cross once above the upper falls.

Though it remained a frustrating outing, Hephaestus would have felt much better—crisis of fortuitous discovery-not-his having been assuredly averted—by the time he descended into town once again. I can only say 'would have' though, because their time away had given certain other events opportunity to transpire.

LXV – A Proper Byzantine Censer

Though they by no means considered themselves experts, and certainly had no intention of challenging their yogi, Clemens and the others agreed that Geru seemed to speed through that morning's exercises. But as each man had to disperse to his own doings that day, this particular group consensus wasn't acknowledged until sometime later when the yoga-affiliated Isleans individually found their way into the town square to see something which was even more worthy of head-scratching.

To be fair, no one really meant to stop and watch the spectacle. The first few that formed the initial crowd were merely unwitting bystanders who simply happened to be working within the square at the time, but once they collected together to whisper about what it was they were seeing, any other parties who attempted to pass would see the throng, follow their gazes toward the performance of sorts, and be likewise ensnared by curiosity.

Pigby had supposed that in a town of no currency and therefore no assigned value, no man should need worry on being taken advantage of and would therefore not hesitate to stop and watch their little show. Fletcher determined that if they gave no announcement and just launched into it, then they wouldn't run into nearly so much danger of prematurely revealing their end-goals. Oswald said that nobody who watched it needed to stay for the whole thing, just that there needed to be enough witnesses at any given point to prove to Hephaestus that they had actually done it and thereby making whatever title they gave Julian that much more difficult to overturn.

Julian was informed over and over again that the only thing he had to worry about was standing up straight and looking proud of himself. He managed one out of two for the entire process. When he asked whether the Baron would be okay with what they were doing, Pigby fervently replied, "The Baron would be proud."

It was Ten ha who suggested he wear the Baron's jacket, which looked quite impressive on him, even though he was of slightly less stout frame than the original owner. The pure shade of blue made him look formal to the point of foreign, and the sword-in-scabbard about the waist gave him a proper place to put his left hand, effecting a posture which even the lad found stately. And as the townsfolk began to gather and gawk at the strange goings-on which were being executed in—as far as they were concerned—pure gibberish, Julian continued to silently assure himself that any awkwardness and humiliation he should face this day was for a certain special lady.

It was not to be a long ceremony, and every member of the Baron's crew just hoped that the lady in question bothered to show up before the end. You see, the most they'd managed from Geru was a promise of "Oh, fine! I'll keep him away an hour, but goodness knows, I can't support a lie longer than that." As Geru was already quite upset about being designated a decoy, they decided not to push the matter and be grateful for the little window they had.

Between Oswald (the expert), Ten ha (the translator), and Fletcher (the showman), they'd worked a nice little ceremony running twenty-one minutes, give or take any missed lines. With Pigby and Julian playing trained statues and the grandfather watching the whole affair from the bell-tower, they were about as prepared as they could possibly be.

I shall set the scene for you, if that's alright:

Imagine, if you will, that you are an Islean, armed with possibly a wheelbarrow or a heavy sack slung over one shoulder by his time in your workday, and that your duties naturally find you passing near the town square. And of course, when you hear the sound of a man singing something in a low rolling bellow as you draw close, you would have no choice but to want to peek in—even if just for a moment.

Julian would be the first character to come into view, for he stood over even the crowd that had gathered, thanks to an over-turned barrel. He was dressed neck to ankle in Baron-clothes, and did his best not to tremble. Next you will notice Pigby, whose frame was large enough that all of the Isleans could place him at a glance. Standing at the cusp of the crowd and the open square and looking the very epitome of a bouncer, Pigby was clad in a thick wool jacket, which—huge and red as it was— made him look even bigger. (Whether it was` an *authentic* British royal guard's coat on his back, no one could possibly disprove, but this validity meant nothing to the Isleans, so I'll move on.)

Now, if you were a citizen, you would find a friend or two in the crowd and promptly ask them what in the devil was going on here. But when asked this question, any men or women who had been there much longer would authoritatively respond, "I don't know."

So you might stand on tiptoe, looking over the heads of your friends, or snake your way to an opening, craning to see what is making that noise, and here is what you will find:

Two men, one with long white hair and tiny spectacles trying to look as upright as possible and the other obviously younger and with such keenly set dimples that he couldn't possibly look entirely somber, had dressed in long white robes—not entirely white, mind, but you would have to squint to make out the bits of silvery and gold thread woven into the overly-elaborate and poorly-preserved holy vestments. The man called Oswald possessed a large book and some sort of pole or staff. The thinner man, the lungs of the outfit, swung something that looks like a miniaturized sling, which both smoked and jingled at whomever he shook it.

(Fletcher had always said that a proper Byzantine censer adds class and at least a little bit of mystery to every holy-looking ceremony, and would do so "Even to the shut-ins of Adleship Isle.")

The two men in nearly matching robes were also draped in strange amounts of feathers, bone-shards, and even the rare vegetable in jewelry and pungent poultice form, and sang back and forth to one another, chanting a bizarre tune out of that dusty red-bound book in the old man's hands.

And on the ground, seated cross legged and banging a small drum as she monotonously repeated the other priests' lines sat the blue girl, veiled from head to toe in a deep red fabric that covered her forehead and—if you were looking from too high up an angle—her eyes.

Finally, in the backdrop stood a quickly-erected tent, which might have not seemed a pertinent detail to the audience, but certainly gave the performers a place to duck into to retrieve a prop or quick drink of water.

Whether you would gasp as a member of the Islean audience is dependent on your awe and surprise at the whole spectacle. Whether you, as a reader of this novel, chuckle mildly and shake your head at the characters you have come to find so amusing is your own go-ahead. Knowing them as you do by this point in our little tale, you are surely not surprised to hear that not a man (or woman) in the crew was one to slack when it came to audience interaction and reception. Though none could dance, sing, or recite sonnets like Fletcher, they all knew the sanctity of a powerfully-performed image.

So after enough people had arrived, and there was a fidgeting crowd of onlookers, all at once the drumming and chanting stopped. The whole crew held its collective breath, cuing the fascinated-if-a-bit-edgy onlookers to do the same. And Fletcher waddled out—yes, he had out-turned his feet and effected a deep stoop for the occasion—spread his arms over the crowd, and said... something.

Without removing the hood that blocked her vision, the disciplined translator called over the square, "Whenever he speaks, say back—

"Kyrie eleison!"

Men, women, and the odd child jumped because Pigby, Oswald and Fletcher spoke this last along with Ten ha.

And before any of the Isleans could question it, Fletcher made a statement, and when he reached a humming end, the crew resonated "Kyrie eleison" back with such determination that a few of the citizens had to try it out themselves. By the third or fourth time through this rhythm, most of the audience was at least stumbling through the two alien words.

And once she'd gotten the crowd to say these two consistently, Ten ha changed the assignment. She told them that the good gentleman— which either meant Oswald or Fletcher, but no one was sure—wished to thank young Julian for his work as an ambassador, after which, they would all issue a collective, "Amen."

Fletcher chanted something with a lot of Ss and Ns: "Amen."

Oswald mumbled something under his breath: "Amen."

Fletcher began again, this time in a low voice and Ten ha spoke over him, addressing the crowd: "Now it is Julian's turn. He wishes to be a good citizen, and to help keep this town green and great," explained Ten ha, clearly repeating the intentions of the holy thin man, "and to lead a shining example as he becomes a man!"

Julian tried not to let his eyes betray him, but he couldn't help not to scan the people, looking for Samantha. But where *was* she?

"And because Julian cannot speak the language, our own Oswald will deliver the oath for him." Ten ha bowed her head and placed her hands at rest on the drum.

Oswald took a few steps toward Julian, laid one hand on the boy's foot and the other on a page of the book, adjusted his glasses, and hummed his way into the opening lines of a paragraph or so, which ran with relatively few stumblings. He paused twice, before the words "Julian" and "Hippeis," though I don't know if anyone managed to sort these terms out from the rest of the gobbledygook.

The reason that many might not catch even the boy's name was because they were all buzzing questions between one another: "What oath?" Clemens was heard asking of his wife; "Why does he need to take an oath?" the Libburus chirped in Cletus' ear; "What's he swearing to do?" Raul whispered, having just arrived himself, and was dismayed when the young girl before him couldn't answer.

Now be honest: if all of this was going on in front of you, especially if you had never seen the likes of it before, you wouldn't look away—would you? Good. Neither did anyone in that audience, which is how no one managed to notice what was going on simultaneously.

You see, it just so happened that Lance was returning from the hill when the crew was setting up. Still clutching the cane, which he took as a symbol of his obedience and ability to properly follow orders, he had gotten almost as far as the well when he stopped short at the sight of Ten ha arranging herself in a red cape just down the hill. He moved a few paces closer and onto the next small hilly ridge to get a better view and from there watched the bulk of the ceremony, trying to determine whether it had anything to do with Hephaestus' going over the falls that morning.

So when Lionel woke up, rubbing his eyes as he emerged from the Libburus' house, the first person he saw was Lance. Upon approach, his salutation sounded like so: "What's this then?" voice thick with morning fog.

"Oh—I didn't take it," Lance hastily explained, indicating the cane, "Hephaestus asked me to bring it back for him and—"

"No; not that, you idiot. That!" And he pointed an impressively large, but not impressively clean finger at the square, where there had gathered quite a throng. "Does the master know 'bout this?"

"Um—I don't—He didn't say—"

"Alright then," concluded Lionel and began toward the square, which Lance instinctively blocked.

"What are you doing?" Lance asked, though he could have sorted the answer before it was given.

"I'm going to put a stop to this—whatever it is. At least until Hephaestus gives it an all clear. No big ceremonies are to happen when he's absent. You know that."

Lance didn't know that, but he should have suspected. Still, a loyalty to the young woman in red bid him stand his ground long enough to blurt, "Wait, you can't do that."

Lionel emphasized his next with a shove: "Outta my way!"

"No—um—If we're—Look!" sputtered Lance, his heals chopping at the ground to keep his shoulders squarely in front of Lionel. "We should gather the others first; let's wake up the rest of the boys and have 'em help."

Lionel contorted his face in such a grimace that Lance worried the man might punch him—which would not be beyond Lionel—but the hulking lummox assessed the strength of the crowd surrounding the boy on the barrel and consented with a nod. "Alright then." Turning around toward the Libburus' house, he added, "You know, some of us're gone already—Cooper, Tanner, and Gus—Do you know where they got off to?"

"Um…" and Lance did what any young man might hope to do upon not being able to finish a sentence. He clocked Lionel on the back of his head with the cane which was fortunately still sheathed. Promptly dropping the instrument which would be the source of his worst reprimand ever, Lance watched with horror as his fellow sturdy servant crumpled to his knees and then unceremoniously squashed his face against the chilly dirt.

Lance was sure of two things at that moment: the first that Ten ha would probably not want that bustling affair to be cut short for any reason, and the second that if someone should find the unconscious bloke, interruption was likely to be had. So he locked his arms under his colleague's shoulders and dragged him to the back of the house for the time being, forgetting that he had left Hephaestus' cane on the ground not far south of Sebastian's front door.

At that time, the Libburus was observing, "He really is a fine young man, that Julian. A true soul."

"Now I need help from all of you!" Fletcher told the lot. "What good is a blessing from strangers if the blessing on this boy's adulthood can come from every man, woman, child, sheep, cow, stone, and brick that lays the foundation of this great town?"

This caused a cheer. Where it had started no one knew, but it was quite difficult not to join in. Ten ha's drumming grew louder, which may have been planned or simply a reaction in attempt to be heard over the growing energy in the crowd.

"We celebrate and honor the life and deeds of this *grrrr*eat man!" declared Fletcher, "an orphan who overcame adversity and became the artist and craftsman you know; a selfless warm-hearted soul who offered house and home to strangers; and a thoughtful boy who will surely grow into a wise man! Can I get an 'Amen?'" he asked the crowd.

"Amen!" was shouted back at him, but the minstrel would not be satisfied so easily.

He squatted low, twisting his neck about as though it pained him while clutching one clawed hand at his chest, and yelled in the most gravelly voice his body would support, "I said, can I get an amen!"

"Amen!" this time louder.

So Fletcher jumped back up, bounded the three leaping steps it took to reach the barrel, and placed one palm toward Julian. His eyes closed, the thin man drew in a deep breath then bellowed toward the heavens, "We are here to bless this boy—Now, let me hear you say AMEN!"

On this third and final attempt, the volume was such that Geru, having just begun his return trip toward the falls, wondered if he should fear for avalanche.

"What was that sound?" the Baron wondered aloud.

Thankfully, the lord of merchants, halfway between frustrated and relieved himself, was a little clogged of ear that morning and so said, "I didn't hear anything."

Two people who did hear the last 'Amen' heard it so loudly that they wondered if they should shut the window. Standing in Sabrina's room, craning to see what traces she could of the square, Samantha observed, "See, I still can't tell what they're doing down there."

With her chin on one palm, Sabrina shook her head. "Sweetie, I don't think anyone can." Of course, Sabrina suspected that that was their intent, though she had not yet determined why.

Down at the square, most of the onlookers had swelled with so much excitement that there were very few who suspected anything amiss; one exception was an eighteen-year-old wearing a stern browline and folded arms.

Julian did not see this dissenter; in fact, he was so dizzied by the hubbub in his honor that he had trouble seeing anyone, and was convinced that even if Samantha stood three feet in front of him, he should not know her, but he distinctly heard Fletcher say his name along with some of that foreign babble.

Oswald stood beside Fletcher and conveyed to Julian, or more accurately *at* Julian, "I hereby christen thee, Sir Julian Hippeis[141]."

Fletcher offered a hand to Julian, telling him softly, "It's time to step down now."

Once Julian was firmly on the stone ground, Ten ha pulled her hood back and said to the crowd, "We give you the newly-knighted Julian; a citizen of Adleship Isle and a noble."

There was sudden silence, devoid of even the faintest exhale for a full ten seconds. Julian felt his skin prick with nervous anticipation, for all of the wondering eyes which had recently been congratulatory had turned to pure bafflement.

I, for one, am amazed that everyone heard it, seeing as Ten ha hardly raised her voice to project over the crowd, but as stunned as they were, they must have. Many tried to question this odd new occurrence, but could not find words to ask after it. Some squinted and others cocked their heads, but no one could find any visual difference on the boy.

Even after they had begun breathing (irregularly) again, no one bothered to speak for a time, and the crew quickly started scouring their brains for escape strategies should their noble attempt not a noble make.

But it was the Libburus who rescued the stock-still air by overbrimming with the comment, "Well, that's wonderful! Julian, a noble—why, everyone should congratulate the new noble!" He then turned to Cletus to whisper in excited wonder, "I didn't know we could do that," but most everyone seemed to take his initial cue and with cheers, applause, or at least tentative wonder. Several persons in the audience stepped forward to shake hands with the boy.

Raul turned in a huff and stomped away from the lot, but the happy and confused citizens around him didn't seem to notice.

Julian chanced to sigh and thank the crew, but Fletcher caught him off-guard with a quick, "Don't mention it, lad," before shoving him into the hands of his newfound fans.

The giant man, the old man, the thin man, and the blue girl disappeared into the comfort of their tent, hearing the excited titter outside their protective fabric lining.

---

[141] Hippeis is a Greek term referring to Athenian nobility, the second in the four main class ranks, which was often designated by that person having enough wealth to own a warhorse. The modern translation is simply knight.

"Good God, I'm hot in this thing," said Fletcher, beginning to unstrap himself from the holy vestments.

"Well done, boys!" came Pigby, a satisfied smile on his face. "Oh, and you too—well drummed," he added to Ten ha.

"I didn't know if we'd make it," she admitted.

"Especially with all the ad libbing," said Oswald with a shaking finger.

Fletcher, situated somewhat backwardsly in his robe, effected an innocent and almost hurt expression. "What do you mean?"

"I say—I say, I am talking about that 'can I get an amen' business."

"What are you talking about?" replied the bewildered Fletcher, "That was gold."

"I thought it added some needed spice," agreed Pigby.

Ten ha shrugged her way into tactful neutrality and the middle of the old and thin man, saying, "I think it worked out fine—We ran a bit overtime, yes, but the boss isn't back yet, is he? Well, then we've done what we came for."

It was true; they all took a moment to relax and breathe at this information. Knowing that one of them would eventually be obligated to go out and rescue Julian from his own audience, each member of the crew took it upon his or herself to change as slowly as possible so that he (or she) should not have to do any more work on the affair.

In retrospect, Pigby remarked that he should have just stayed out front to keep watch, but it's those missed opportunities that make for good literature.

It happened much more swiftly than the ceremony itself—in fact so rapidly that most of those who witnessed it firsthand could only put the pieces together after the fact. Julian was in the process of being congratulated by Elke, who tried to inform him what a fine fit he was for the title, when he heard his name called so angrily and loudly that he could not even place the voice.

But when the young man tore through the mass of Isleans, they all backed away to make room for him, creating not so much an aisle as an arena for the coursing youth. "How dare you!" he shrieked, "You can't take her away from me!"

Julian would have reacted more angrily toward his impetuous friend, but for the unmistakable cherrywood cane clutched in his hands. "Now, Raul," began Julian, but it was too late.

Raul drew with a startlingly loud hum the hidden sword and charged our hero.

Some citizens covered their eyes; others tried to step back further, tripping themselves or fellows in the process. Having heard the yelling, the crew tried to force their way out of the tent in a single unit, calling for the boys to stop. And Julian, on little more than instinct and a simple memory of his friend the Baron, drew from the scabbard on the side of the coat he wore, and pointed assuredly at his assailant.

There was one brief clink of metal and Raul emerged on the other side of Julian, with a sword protruding from his middle.

As Raul collapsed and his vision began to fade, he could hear the sound of the town's bell, clanging away overhead.

LXVI – A Snowball or Two

A thick cloud from the south had stepped in front of the sun, shrouding the whole place in grey for the remainder of the day. So even though the mood was twilight, the hour was hardly two o'clock when Geru emerged from the tent, scrubbing at his hands with a steaming rag.

He issued a steady nod to the servant and the two small girls that they could now go inside to join the patient, his father, and mother.

The Baron raised his eyes from his book, but kept to his pipe until the family was securely put away inside that same tent his crew had erected earlier that morning. "So, how is he?"

"He'll carry the scar of humiliation a good while longer than that nick in his side," Geru replied. He went to a dry towel and wrang out his soaked fingers before starting the handwashing process all over again.

"Well done," offered the Baron, though Geru could only *hmph* the compliment away.

"He'll have quite a time if it gets infected, but then again you keep your swords very clean, sir, don't you?"

The Baron accepted the wry hostility from the begrudging surgeon, but only because his short man seemed the only one with a cool enough head to sort through the crisis when it occurred. Though they arrived on the scene after the accidental stabbing had taken place, it wasn't hard to tell what had happened. The Baron and Hephaestus, seeing each other's respective weapons at the site, had to put off their argument for another time.

While Geru gathered his things together for the walk back, the Baron half-read, half-watched the tent-flap for Hephaestus to emerge. Standing somewhat-awkwardly with nothing to lean against, Trenton too awaited the lord of merchants' return.

Eventually the flap parted, and Hephaestus ducked out from under the opening, eyeing the Baron cautiously but addressing Trenton first. The men did their best to whisper so as to not alert the Baron, but he and Geru intently eavesdropped nonetheless.

Trenton's hushed tone was much more effective than the older master's; the Baron only caught snippets about Lance and a cane. Geru would later tell him Trenton's conclusion with more accuracy: that apparently Raul stomped off the moment Julian's title was declared and though he had meant to confront the younger daughter before his newly equal rival had a chance to, saw Hephaestus' cane on the ground and decided to use it. The Baron did however manage to hear that Lance had been shut in the cellar with one of the other servants standing guard, though he would not know for at least another day what this had to do with anything.

Hephaestus' words were quite clear, and though he was obviously upset, there was composure when he bid Trenton, "Thank you, now go tend to the rest of the household."

"Very good, sir," nodded the loyal assistant before excusing himself.

Hephaestus let out a heavy sigh. "Well, I suppose you're immensely proud of yourself, aren't you?"

"Excuse me?" came the Baron.

"Not only have you bumped up the boy—illegally, I might assume—but you've successfully rid of his only competition."

"How dare you!" returned the Baron, standing up and closing the book. "I would never *ever* arrange for that boy to be stabbed, and certainly not by Julian. I had nothing to do with this, as Geru can tell you."

Geru was, at that moment, trying to hustle away before either of them decided to call attention to him, and when his name was mentioned he turned frostily on the two men. "I just expertly patched up that boy; I have had blood on my hands—with no thanks for it from either of you, I might add—and on top of it I missed the ceremony; I will *not* be playing your scapegoat today."

"But whose idea was it?" insisted Hephaestus.

"Yes, tell him it wasn't me," added the Baron.

"No, no, of course not! It was all Oswald—Fletcher ran with it, Ten ha translated it, and Pigby dressed me up as a wild goose for the two of you to chase. Are you happy?"

The Baron apparently was and so turned smugly to Hephaestus, saying, "See? They didn't even involve me enough to let me know that I was luring you away this morning."

"Oh, well aren't they all so clever!" spat Hephaestus.

"Thank you for noticing."

"Mister Bordolo, keep in mind you that you broke a rule—"

"No, it wasn't me—"

"It doesn't matter! Can't you see the consequences of a rule—"

"Fine! So go strike it off my checklist if it's so important to you!"

And though this was shaping up to be the same two-man argument you've already heard, Geru decided that he was fed up with it at that moment and so shouted over both, "Oh, hang the rules! This isn't the result of a rule; this is a result of your pride and your meddling. Need I remind you two that both of the offending instruments of this perfect, *peaceful* town's first honor duel belonged to you—or that stabbing one's friend wouldn't have even occurred to that boy had he not seen you two do it on Christmas Eve?"

The Baron and Hephaestus looked between one another sternly, but said nothing.

"Now, I am going to go home to rest," Geru informed them, "I suggest you both do the same and—the next time you find yourselves in such a situation—ask yourself how important your name is or how important your credit is." Geru offered them one more scoff and turned back home, toting his doctor's pack with him.

The Baron relented and slid the book back into his jacket, signaling that he too would leave. Had Raul not been run nearly through, Hephaestus would surely have committed the next several hours to tearing down Julian's new title, but Geru was right.

It was therefore out of general concern that Hephaestus asked, "What does your man say for infection?"

Though Geru hadn't said exactly, the Baron knew to vouch for his skills and replied, "It'll heal nicely. This is a very clean town—" From about the edge of the square, the short man cleared his throat loudly, indicating that his keen ears had heard the comment and expected the due credit. "And Geru is very skilled with a needle."

"I see." Hephaestus nodded. "It was good work. I'll admit, when he claimed to be a surgeon, I figured him for a con man."

"Oh, everyone does," conceded the Baron, in something of a whisper, "he gets that from his parents, you know."

"Charming," Hephaestus muttered. He wanted to ask something else, but said nothing, only hoping that there was some hint of remorse in the eyes of the man opposite. He screwed up his lips in something of resignation and said, "I will be staying at Eugene's for the moment. I hope there is no more funny business tonight."

"Alright. I'll try to comfort Julian."

"Right." Before the Baron had fully turned away, Hephaestus stopped him to ask, "I suppose there's no way to repeal *Sir* Julian's title, now is there?"

"He's a noble now, and that's that," came the reply.

Hephaestus wanted to contest it, but had no way to do so. Even the Baron didn't know how to unravel something like this: from what he'd heard of the ceremony, it was perfect, foolproof. It gave no evidence in any language Hephaestus could understand that it was fraudulent, (though our Baron was quite convinced it was), but more than that, the blessing of nobility was given more by civilian support than Oswald or Fletcher's chants, which in so a close a community had comparable power to divinity. This did not sit well with the Baron, though he did not know why.

One of Hephaestus' servants had in fact been present for the knighting: Tanner, who had woken up early to find the ceremony (just like any of the Isleans), and watched and participated in fascination. When Trenton arrived back at the Libburus' that afternoon he gave Tanner a stern lecture over his letting the knighting of Julian occur, but really there was no way for him to have known until the affair was over.

Cletus, not knowing that the girls had been watching from the window, was immensely grateful that they had not been present for the terrible act of... well, whatever you might call one boy causing another to bleed in a way that seemed neither like work nor play. But, because he assumed they had not paid witness to the travesty, justly urged his Libburus to stay with Eugene for the evening and night as well.

In fact, more people saw need to tend to Eugene than they did Raul, and this was not because the man was in a rage or even hysteria. Laconia to the suspicion of catatonia had set in, and as much as his wife (whose name I've forgotten, sorry) and his servants tried to console him, all Eugene could offer was a cold, blank stare. Not to discredit the man's moral fiber, but I would assert that his state was not directly tied into fear for his son. Perhaps witnessing a stabbing or the knighting of the boy Julian really had blown a significant fuse in his brain. For my part, I can't understand how more of the citizens did not react like Eugene. After all reality as he knew it had shifted in a way he had not thought possible.

Try to imagine how you felt the first time you experienced sex or chocolate—and if you have never tasted one or either, I shant explain and spoil the sensation—or maybe the first time someone close to you has passed away. How people can face these intense, game-changing instances and not have to sit in wonder for *at least* an evening is beyond me, but then I am exceedingly astute and not very well-versed in denial. It is possible that Eugene actually understood what the precedent of that afternoon's ceremony could mean, unlike all the others who were too wrapped up in their own excitement and fear to properly consider.

But as he would not speak to anyone that day and night, it is impossible to tell exactly what he was thinking.

To be fair, he wasn't the only one who was scared. Many of the parents had ushered their children away, though most of the children present wanted to touch the sword to see how it felt after being dipped into a person. Those persons who had neither parent nor child available either clustered into gossip groups or slowly backed away from the stabbing, and all of them went home soon after when Hephaestus ordered them to. The few who hid among the hills and buildings surrounding the square related to all corners of the town how the boy had been hauled bleeding into the tent, how Julian had been dragged away by the giant, how the daughters of the Libburus came out soon after, looking in vain for the newly-nobled boy, and how they too were sent home but their sputtering father.

And as each group made its way back to work or home, folks began to find themselves in argument—for what can you do with fear of the relatively unknown other than throw it angrily at your best friend?

As the Baron walked back to Julian's, he caught snapshots of these heated debates, and diligently retained every comment he could to discuss at a later time. He was confused that more than even the swordplay the Isleans' biggest collective wonder was whether Julian would relocate to the other side of the river, as if that alone would formally indicate whether or not he had climbed social rank. The Baron had to concede that maybe class was a more pivotal issue than someone's accidentally getting hurt. As it *was* in fact an accident, he was relieved to hear no words of blame cast toward Julian. Similarly, the Baron Pan Bordolo did not expect resentment cast on his own person—in his mind, his not being there should have absolved him of any antagonism.

A snowball or two to the back is not cause for alarm in most cases, but as there was very little snow in the Isle and most of the drifts that remained were largely made up of ice and dirt, the Baron was none too tickled by the dirt-clods that struck him. He was barely beyond the bridge at that point, and there were so many houses about that the children who disappeared with gasps could have come from anywhere. The Baron tugged haughtily on his coat and continued along the path, trying not to think much of the offense.

The glares were harder to ignore, and harder still those persons who backed away or tried to hide their wives or children when he passed. Most damning of all was the man who ordered the Baron, "Hey, get off the yard!" forcing the startled Baron to stumble out into the road once again. Though he had been unwanted and even feared before, the Baron had never suspected that such a thing was possible in the Isle.

So he burrowed his head a little deeper into the collar of his coat and made the last lengths to the boy's house with jogging steps.

Trudging up the little hillside path, the Baron had begun to steady his agitated heart, but to no avail, for when he arrived at the front door it was thrust open before him, causing a gasp, a frustrated grunt, and an exclamation of "Pigby! Maybe someone of lesser stature should keep guard on such a trying day."

"Sorry, sir," replied Pigby. "It's just Geru heard someone coming up the way, and he said—"

"Very well." The Baron waved his giant's comment away and pushed by him, pausing just a moment to inspect the little list on their wall, and observing aloud, "Delightful! It's already crossed off as a reminder." He abruptly tapped the sign, a gesture which was frustratingly between 'I understand' and 'you ninny! I want to rip you off this wall and burn you,' but continued to walk past it. A headcount bid him ask, "Where's Julian?"

A thin man, old man, and woman all started at once with, "Oh, he's—"

But Fletcher was the only one to resolve the statement with, "He's down the way at Meredith's."

"I see." The Baron popped his hands on his hips and strode into the center of the space, surveying their faces as he went. "And the grandfather?"

"There as well," said Pigby, and tried to say, "Actually, sir—"

"Not now, Pigby." The Baron held him off with a hand.

Geru looked perturbed, Fletcher anxious, Ten ha worried, and Pigby waiting on his turn to speak. It was only the old man who appeared somewhat guilty, and so beckoned the Baron ask, "Oswald?"

"Oh, sir, I'm sorry. I'm quite sorry."

"I see," the Baron repeated. "This was your plan, was it?" And when the old man nodded, the Baron met him with a sigh. "Well, I'm not sure if I should be disappointed in or grateful to you."

A muddled Australian-Irish dialect offered from the corner, "Choose gratitude, sir."

"Fletcher!" hushed Ten ha.

"No, it's alright," came the Baron. "Go on. What do you have to say, Fletcher?"

Fletcher checked in with whomever would make eye contact, which unfortunately was only Pigby, but the giant man with his mind on an elsewise detail had nothing for him. Fletcher, being a man who had very little filter between his brain and his mouth said what they were all thinking—or at least what he thought they were all thinking: "We did exactly what you wanted us to do, boss—I mean, didn't we?" Fletcher spread open his arms, both in a gesture of innocent sacrifice and an attempt to commend the geniuses who had worked that morning's plot.

"Now we know you wanted to help the boy," the thin man went on, "you wanted to help him win that lady, but you couldn't step in like that, so we did. Boss, you've got no ground to be upset with us. We just slipped Julian up a notch in the scheme—which's what you'd've done if your hands weren't tied—so's to put him a fair shot against mister-fussy-britches." (It took the crew a second to register that he'd meant Raul and not His Grand Foppery, their usual pin-cushion for verbal barbs.) "I think if we'd've done it and not had that spoiled dandy turn mister-angry-britches, the whole thing would've been a victory without a hitch, and we'd be drinking hero wine instead of glum juice[142]!"

The Baron thumbed his mustache, which—though it didn't like to sway its master's opinions—heartedly agreed with Fletcher, but then again, curled mustaches throughout history tended to favor the most witty argument delivered, regardless of logic or context. Still, the Baron Pan Bordolo had yet to form a verdict, so Geru took his turn.

To clarify, Geru was not often one to swallow more than a thimbleful of pride in a given year, and so did not humble to plead for

---

[142] Idiomatic aside: *glum juice* was what Fletcher liked to call tea that had no alcohol, opiates, or anything fun.

himself very often; he pleaded for the sake of others even less. But that afternoon, he must have seen Oswald's expression, because the next thing he said was, "Give them a break, sir!" And when the Baron turned toward him with surprise, his expression mirroring every other one in the room, Geru continued, "You know it's wasn't his fault the boy found the sword; that's just bad luck. He did a good job—That's right, Oswald, you pick up your chin and be proud of yourself—and, Sir Baron, you ought to tell him you're proud of him too."

And the Baron received this last; he took every word to heart, for he could see how right his short man was, and just as surely shifted from his speculative stoicism to a warm and accepting smile. And Pigby, lips held patiently shut, resigned to wait just a little longer on presenting the document folded in half under his left arm.

"So tell us the tale, then Oswald," the Baron began anew, "How did you do it?"

Oswald's eyebrows arched into hopeful curiosity. "Do you mean it, sir?"

"Yes," he said, "now I want to know what you did this morning."

"Well—I say!—it took a lot more than just this morning, to be sure..." And from there, Oswald regaled the Baron with the story of Julian's request, their failed studies the prior evening, their breaking into Hephaestus' wagon—during which Pigby kept looking for a place to jump in, but to no avail—and finally with a summation of the morning's ceremonies.

As the story grew, more and more voices were added to it, each giving their own flavor, and each politely stepping back down to return the floor to Oswald. Even Geru was far less miffed about being totted off to lure the merchants once the affair was in retrospect, and told his part of the plan with intense enthusiasm.

Now that it was all behind them, the crew was actually disappointed—given all the preparations they had made—that Hephaestus didn't arrive to question their efforts. Obviously, the lord of merchants couldn't read the book they had used, which turned out to be a copy of the Divine Liturgy of Saint John Chrysostom and from which they had recited the memorial ceremony, which was a holy-sounding and thankfully brief series of chants. And of course if Hephaestus had asked about Oswald's ability to officiate in such a process, they had at-the-ready a certain official document, which was no more than a birth certificate from a time that the old man had acted godfather to a girl in Greece fifteen years prior. The certificate was authentic, old-looking, in

Greek, and as it had Oswald's John Hancock on one of the dotted lines, there would be very little room for argument.

Oswald and Ten ha agreed that the most difficult part of the ceremony was memorizing what the translation was *supposed* to be so that there would be no discrepancy between their stories. Pigby, Geru, and of course Julian did not know any of the mysterious language; Fletcher was a quick study, with a supercomputer's memory for songs, and spoke Greek fluently with an Italian lilt, but could not read a word of it; Oswald and Ten ha, not nearly so fast with their lines agreed on the mistranslated gist of every paragraph used and otherwise just relied on the book.

"You know," the Baron added, with a giggle at his own idea, "I think should Hephaestus have wanted me to personally confirm your translations, I would have told him, 'Oh, I'm sorry; this is *Modern* Greek and I'm only schooled in Ancient!'"

The Baron was also curious as to why he heard the bell ringing just as he and Hephaestus were coming down the falls. Though he had thought it could have been a coincidental end-of-ceremony bit or a call for help over the stabbed boy—both of which happened at very close to the same time—Fletcher assured him otherwise.

"Oh, see, that was the worst part," began the thin man. "See, we couldn't spy after you—lest one of you notice we were spying and have to abort the whole thing, so we tried to arrange for the grandfather to do it for us. I spent two, three hours looking for passages from Shakespeare which I could piece together so I could instruct the chum to go up to his rock and watch the waterfall and not come down until Hephaestus had disappeared over the ridge, thereby signaling us that it was all clear for us to start, right? Well, I'd been at the damned cutting-and-pasting forever when Julian here tells me, 'Oh, you can tell him anything you want and he'll hear it; he just *talks* in rhyme and riddle,' see?" Fletcher, seeing the Baron's crooked expression realized he'd gotten on a tangent and not actually answered the question, and so cleared his throat to recenter, before trying to finish with, "So—um—I told him and he was our signal. Sir."

"I see..." muttered the Baron, then turned to Oswald, who helped.

"Sir, we put the grandfather as lookout—on the rock to say when you left, and in the bell-tower to ring if you came back early."

"Ah, *now* I see!"

As each character walked through his unforgettable experience that morning—often alluding to other excites or grand cock-ups they'd had on previous expeditions—the talk grew relaxed and amiable enough that Fletcher was given the go ahead to break out the hero wine, (which was indeed a labeled cask in the cart). All six were seated in an even circle, cross-legged on the floor, passing a bottle back and forth when the door was next opened.

All heads turned, and such was the shortness of Geru that the little bit of wine had touched his system enough for him to exclaim, "Sir Julian—we've missed you! Pull up a rug, boy!"

But the others could see that Julian was not feeling quite so celebratory. Betrayed by the stinging redness around his eyes, their friend and host did not even know how to begin to speak.

Pigby tried to begin for him by asking, "Julian, what's wrong?"

Julian opened mouth, then closed it again to shake his head. After a swallow, he asked, "Is Raul—"

"He's fine, son," replied the Baron, "he just poked himself a little; you've nothing to worry about."

"What if it gets infected?" Fletcher asked in honest curiosity, without rightly considering that this may not have been the best time.

"Why's everyone so hot about infection?" the Baron demanded perhaps more vehemently than he would have liked. "I tell you, he's fine. This is a very clean town after all—" Geru once again puffed up to await his recognition. "And Geru is very short; I'm sure everything will heal nicely."

Julian nodded to himself. "Good." And the boy began to cross toward his room.

"Julian—stay, boy," beckoned Oswald.

"No, I'm—" Julian glanced down at his arms which were still unfortunately sleeved in the Baron's jacket. "I'll go change back into my clothes. You just—don't worry about me."

But by the time Julian had reached his own door, all parties were on their feet trying to halt him, or offering aid, or asking questions. In the commotion, Ten ha managed to slip past the rest of the crowd and, with an arm about Julian's shoulder, said, "Julian, let's talk about this; just you and I, alright?"

And as the boy nodded, she unlatched the bedroom door and started inside. An inquiring look from the lot bid her remark behind her, "You've all got your expertise; now leave me to mine."

Once she closed the door, the remainder of the crew acknowledged that she was indeed the closest one there to being a teenaged person just discovering love.

"You know, I think this trip has been good for the girl," the Baron eventually said, breaking the silence as they came to sit down again. "She's more assertive than I've ever seen her."

Once the circle was completed again, filling slightly tighter for five than it did for six, Pigby presented the withering document he had been waiting to debut.

"What's this?" asked the Baron, leaning forward.

"I don't recognize it," came Fletcher.

"I say—those names..." muttered Oswald, adjusting his spectacles to better read.

"Who in the devil are Solomon and Jonas Tiegs?" clanged a tipsy Geru.

Skipping all of the comments but the Baron's, Pigby explained, "I took this from Hephaestus' wagon."

There was a quick gasp and then hushed voices—as if they were being spied on—saying, "You stole this?" and "Why'd you take it?" and "How're you going to put it back?" and, from the Baron, "The Greek book wasn't stolen from there too, was it?"

"No, we only stole the idea in his wagon—the Liturgy's yours," Fletcher explained.

"But why—I say—why did you swipe that one?" asked Oswald.

Pigby pointed to the names at the top, in a title which read, *Inventory and Manifest of Solomon and Jonas Tiegs*. "This is a log book of the merchants of that wagon—Sir," he clarified, facing the Baron, "last night, we saw a plaque that read *S and J Tiegs*: the wagon belonged to them. Well, I think *that*," the giant man went on, indicating 'Solomon,' "is Hephaestus' real name, and *that* is our dear grandfather chap."

"Wait—You don't think it's the same Jonas do you?" inquired the Baron.

Pigby shrugged by way of response, but Fletcher jumped right in with, "Do you really think anything's a coincidence in a story like this?" Granted, Fletcher had not seen the manifest until a few seconds prior and was overlooking a great-many ironic coincidences which I've documented thoroughly in this text, but he couldn't see any way around them being the same person. "Isn't it obvious? Hephaestus—tired of joint-owning his wares—knocked his own brother on the back of the head to make him thick, dumped him here, and changed his own name so's he could be a lone travelling merchant."

"Brilliant!" remarked Geru, the neck of the bottle gripped tightly in one stubby hand.

"I don't know; they don't look like brothers to me, and the grandfather's voice has got a fair helping of Welsh[143]," the Baron mused.

"Maybe not brothers, but easily cousins," said Pigby. "The trouble is this is all we have to go on, so it could be anything."

"But it might have something to do with what Hephaestus is trying to hide!" said Fletcher, "About the grandfather, you know?"

And as if summoned, Jonas suddenly emerged through the front door. Pigby instinctively folded the manifest and popped it behind his back, and four other men, mouths open, did not know whether to confront or hide the issue from the man. Jonas eyed the lot and after squinting curiously a moment said, "In nature's infinite book of secrecy, a little I can read," before excusing himself again, out the front door and away.

Realizing they had been holding their collective breath, the crew let out a collective sigh.

"That was disturbing," said Pigby.

"I say—he knew, didn't he? That we were talking about him," whispered Oswald.

Wanting to preserve his own sense of sanity and security, the Baron suggested, "It could have just been another quote."

"Shakespeare?" wondered Geru.

"I'm all goosebumped!" exclaimed Fletcher presenting his forearm. "Feel me!"

The jitters of the grandfather's strange and timely entrance soon died down, and the crew could reflect on Hephaestus and the wares of S and J Tiegs. Mostly the conversation consisted of observations of Hephaestus' behavior since they had been staying in the Isle—all of which you've already read—and offered no new conclusive information, but it certainly kept them occupied for a while longer, such that they had hardly moved by the time the bedroom door finally opened.

Ten ha emerged first, closing softly behind her, and telling the others, "He's getting dressed; he'll be out in a moment." And then the blue girl was gathering her things to leave.

"Where are you going?" the Baron asked her.

---

[143] Oh, yes, I may have neglected to tell you: Jonas sounds like a wispy Welshman.

"Down to Meredith's, for bed," she answered, then pointing at the window above the loft said, "It's getting to be night."

Heads swiveled and craned to see and sure enough, the sky had grown dark in the time they'd been sitting.

Fletcher popped up from the floor and announced, "Well, I haven't slept in a full two days, so that's it for me too." Fletcher was quickly out of shoes and coat and snugly tucked in in the loft.

As Ten ha made to leave, the Baron stood after her to ask, "Wait, what did you say to him?"

"Honestly, sir, it's obvious; it's all about the girl. He's been worried she saw him stab that boy, and other than guilt for that being his biggest worry, *that's* what's keeping him." Because Julian's door was unlatched and opened again, she patted the Baron on the arm and said, "But he'll tell you himself."

The blue girl hadn't even closed the front door behind her by the time Julian was saying, "Alright, Pan, are you ready?"

The Baron rounded to face the boy, feeling somewhat off his bearings for the abrupt emergence. "Ready?" he asked. "Ready for what?"

Julian, no longer in Baron clothes or even slightly formal wear, stood firmly before the Baron Pan Bordolo, and without a trace of quiver, explained, "I'm going to go see the lady."

"Tonight, lad?"

"Tonight. And you're coming with me."

The other parties in the crew seemed obviously tickled by this, but said nothing.

"Me? What for?" asked the Baron.

"Moral support," said Julian, moving past him to put on his boots.

"But-but wait, Julian—"

"No, sir—Pan, listen to me." Julian took one sturdy breath, and with precise cadence told the Baron. "I have waited too long, long enough that I let someone else propose; now I am going to go speak to her, or else my being knighted and Raul's being hurt will have been for nothing. Now Hephaestus and Mister Sebastian are not at the house, so you don't have to worry about them. I need to do this. But I need a friend by my side, sir, someone who will help me get as far as her window. Now are you coming or not?"

The Baron bit his lower lip. There were dozens of things he wanted to say—countless cautions and concerns, but instead, he held his shoulders back, his head aloft, and he opened the front door for Julian and followed after, leaving four traveling experts to marvel at their boss and his boy.

"You know," observed Fletcher, "it's a good thing the boss already had his shoes on or else that wouldn't have been nearly as effective."

LXVII – The Chemise Skirt

Every man in the Baron's crew had his own particular bent when it came to the thing known as love. Of course, Ten ha was not invited to this frequent commentary because obviously she was far too young and not enough 'of the world' to know anything about the subject.

Pigby, Oswald, and Fletcher were separated three-musketeers-style by the age-old philos, agape, and eros[144].

Pigby happened to believe that the purest form of love came from genuine concern and care for another's well-being, and—because he was actually exceptionally shy when it came to actually flirting with women—mostly found such a connection through brothers he adopted over the course of his travels. In other words, Clemens was not so exceptional as you may have thought.

Oswald held that a beautiful rose, accompanied by a beautiful ballad, given to a beautiful woman on a moonlit night constituted romance supreme, but then he was from a different age, and was often mocked for his old-fashion sentiments. Bear in mind that even though it had been the eighteenth century, he was still born in the fifties.

Fletcher would defend to his last that love at first sight occurred when the sway of a barmaid's hips are caught in the reflection of spilt ale, and that proof of said love occurred when said hips were in one's (namely Fletcher's) very enthusiastic hands.

Geru tended to drag down the whole discussion by announcing, "Love! It's just a flood of hormones whose delusions are necessary for the survival of the species." Hormones which Geru found quite obsolete,

---

[144] Mode of argument also partitioned the same three into the camps of ethos, pathos, and logos—though not in the same order, but that's another story and another chapter which will not be appearing in this text. Geru was once again the angry outlier.

seeing as by the turn of the nineteenth century, he felt the world to be quite overcrowded already, thank you very much.

The Baron kept out of this debate for fear that too many people might listen to what he had to say. Not that he had a particular problem with misleading those persons gullible enough to take poor advice; no, the Baron simply knew that were he to make a stab on love, romance, or even that old bugaboo (sex), his words would be remembered, he'd risk them being quoted back at him, and then he could never change his opinion on the matter. And as he was getting on in years, the ripe middle age of thirty, no doubt there was far more expectation for him to drop a pearl of wisdom regarding love. Should his comrades (or anyone else) pick up that pearl, string it on a necklace, and wear it every day, then surely he would never be free of his own testament. First and foremost, the Baron believed that it was the sacred right and duty of every well-read, well-bred young man to change his fancy whenever it so suited him. He liked to call this stance tactful neutrality; no member of his crew used so polite a phrase.

But even for every well-thought-out or carefully avoided testimony, I would put forth that the surest evidence we can find of love was in Julian's eyes when he looked at Samantha that night. For you see, up until then, Julian hadn't fully shown love to the girl, having let things like nervousness or class hold him back. Though it may not always be wise, bravery beyond all reason in the face of one's beloved is a key ingredient in what fairy-tale and musical writers like to call 'true love.'

And Julian was exercising bravery for the whole of the brisk walk from his house to Samantha's. Naturally, both he and the Baron kept to the shadows, knowing that any alert would avert the night's intentions, but as this occasion was shrouded in the twilight of Julian's having been attacked and accidentally stabbing a friend, you have to admit that even sneaking across the river took brass ones[145].

Of course, neither the Baron nor Julian noticed the third figure sneaking along in their wake, seeing as sheer adrenaline often trumps observation.

Down the hill, past the well, and into a small ditch, Julian and the Baron eyed the back of the large house, which had one window in which was wedged a board.

---

[145] Which were stocked in the Baron's cart, and could be swiftly produced if asked for.

Julian exhaled swiftly, and the Baron patted his shoulder. "Well done, lad," whispered the older. "Are you ready?"

"Yes, sir," breathed Julian.

"Alright then—Good luck!" And with a slight shove of encouragement, the Baron ushered Julian toward the building, making the lad jog so as to keep from trembling.

Julian had resolved that on that night everything would change: that he wouldn't fall victim to the same patterns, that he wouldn't hold his tongue for fear of sounding silly, and that he would know what to say upon reaching her. The fact that the last resolution was shattered was not his fault, for the moment he reached the house, glancing back to nod to the Baron, the wooden shutter was forcibly thrust outward, striking him on the back of the head and knocking him over.

The Baron winced on the boy's account, and the young lady responsible, silhouetted against the candlelight of her room, put both hands to her mouth and gasped.

"Oh dear, I'm sorry!" she exclaimed, hushed though her voice was, and climbed out the window to help right Julian from the ground. "I didn't mean—I didn't know you were standing so close."

"It's alright," Julian returned, shifting to a sitting position.

"Here, let me—" Samantha shifted around Julian, placing one hand on his arm, and then using the other to inspect his head. "You're not bleeding, are you?"

The lady seemed so worried and flustered by this that Julian couldn't help but chuckle.

"Oh no, you're delirious!"

"No, I'm not; I'm fine," Julian insisted.

"Here," she said, clearly ignoring what he'd just said and turning back to her room, "Let me get you—"

"No, it's fine. Really—See, it's just a lump. It's not like I haven't had one before."

Believing him this time but not able to shake her embarrassment, Samantha chanced to laugh before telling him, "You need to keep your voice down; Hephaestus' men are keeping watch at the doors because of Lance."

The Baron found it ironic that *he* could hear this warning, but then again he was in very ready eavesdrop range.

A part of Julian wanted to ask about this man called Lance whom he remembered having met, but a greater curiosity prompted, "Did you know I was coming?"

"Oh, well..." Julian did not need light to tell that she was blushing. "Sabrina and I saw you two from her window, and I came down to open my shutter for you, but you were already here, and I—Julian!" she exclaimed, eyes suddenly wide with fright, "I saw what happened today, with Raul!"

Julian felt his mouth suddenly grow dry, and he sputtered, "It was an accident—"

"He tried to hit you with that thing!"

"It just happened so fast that I—"

"I was so worried that you had gotten hurt."

And that was all Julian needed to hear. He had been sick over whether Samantha had seen his ill-begotten duel and how she might react to the stabbing, but knowing that she had and that her first concern was for Julian himself, stirred in his being a joy like he had never known. So he reached up, placed one hand against her face and kissed her.

It was in that moment that the Baron was glad he kept a hanky on his person.

Julian pulled away just long enough to say, "I love you," and wasn't the least surprised when his lady said it back.

Then there was the sound of a somewhat distant grunt, and a kind of knock against wood, which made Samantha stop him and look around, eyes flitting like a wary rabbit. Of course there was some wind that night, so it was difficult to tell what exactly they had heard and from where it had come, but Samantha did not want to take any chances and so said, "Quick, inside."

And as she started back through the window, keeping one of Julian's hands firmly in her own, the boy turned and nodded the Baron away before disappearing himself. The flat of wood was wedged snugly back in place just as the second grunt and thud sounded.

The Baron, not knowing the origin of these sounds and not wanting to be spotted, kept his eyes fixed on the house as he sidled away. When he bumped into something unexpected, he very nearly walloped it on the head.

But instead, the silent spectre reached up and kissed him on the mouth. "Hi," said Sabrina, in a half whisper through a half-smile.

"What are you doing—How did you get down here—Goodness, aren't you cold?" asked the Baron, noticing even in the dark that the young lady seemed to be wearing only a nightgown.

"Yes," she replied, and taking the Baron's hand before he could think to snatch it away, said, "Come with me."

"Wait, wait, wait! We can't go through the doors, I heard your sister say—"

"We're not taking the doors." And even as she said this, the Baron was quite aware that she was pulling him toward the wall just below her window, which answered the questions as to how she'd gotten down so quickly. And though he meant to reprimand her for the surprise kiss, he found himself dutifully following her and awaiting her next request.

As he watched the bare feet ascend the stone wall, the Baron couldn't help but be charmed by the strength and whimsy this particular noblewoman retained. And being a gentleman, he tried to keep his eyes on only the feet, though when she stepped onto the roof, suddenly illuminated by the open window, the Baron's jaw dropped in astonishment and he averted his eyes.

"Is something the matter?" she asked.

"My dear, I think you should put something else on."

Sabrina took in both hands the chemise skirt of the gown and said, "Oh, yes, Hephaestus gave them to us: new gowns from Paris. Do you like them?"

Sneaking another glance, he replied, "That's not really the issue."

"Well, come on up, and I can change it if you'd like."

"No, no, that won't be necessary." The Baron took one step back. "I'll be going home now." He took another. "Goodnight." And almost turned to leave.

"You know it's a strange name, 'Pan'—is it not?" the older sister began again. "Comes from the same line as Hephaestus, but younger, wittier, more in touch with nature. I must confess, I don't know *everything* about those old spirits from his stories, but I remember well-enough that the Pan *I* read about would never leave a maiden helpless and alone on such a cold night."

The Baron attempted not to look as astounded as he felt. "You've read the Greeks?"

Sabrina shrugged one shoulder and said, "Your men aren't the only ones who've snuck into Hephaestus' wagon."

And once again, the Baron was forced to reassess the lady, and had to conclude that she was indeed the most intriguing little devil he had ever met. An equally devilish grin was forming under his knowing mustache.

"So how about it, Sir Baron?" she asked, stepping one foot gracefully into the window. "You be my faun, and I'll be your nymph."

Sabrina slipped the rest of the way into the window and a moment later cast the same gown out through the curtains which caught in the air and gracefully landed in the Baron's open hands.

He meant to depart right then, before any thoughts could convince him stay—after all he'd promised Hephaestus, but then he remembered a much more pivotal promise which he'd made to himself: to change his fancy, especially where it pertained to love, whenever it so suited him. Indeed, this occasion and this change seemed to suit him exceedingly well.

The Baron bit his lip before concluding, "History will forgive me." And he scurried up the wall, faster than he had ever climbed a ladder or any set of stairs in his life.

Even as you shake your head, smirking, 'Oh that silly Baron,' you may be wondering why none of the sturdy guards had seen or heard the Baron or Julian, especially since Sabrina had to abandon her whisper when she spoke down from her window. Additionally, you may have concluded that the grunt-and-thud effect had something to do with this. You may have even begun to surmise who was the cause of these interrupting sounds and indeed the third party following the Baron and the boy through the black cover of night.

Ten ha moved much more silently, and was much smaller and considerably more flexible than either of the two men. And she—having heard whispers about Lance and having not seen him since that morning—had the foresight to steal Geru's brushbomb. Two guards, one at the front door and one at the cellar, both sleepy, both looking in a fixed direction as if they were just waiting to be assaulted by surprise, and enough chemicals to knock out near a dozen. Couple that with Ten ha's wit, and any fight would hardly seem fair

And once two were dropped, the young woman opened the cellar to find—as she expected—Lance tied to a chair with a flimsy blindfold made from one of the Libburus' ties.

"Hello?" he called, head turning about to match the source of the sound. "May I go now?" But any other questions were quashed by Ten ha whose lips were on his in an instant.

"If you're not Ten ha, I'm going to hope this is a dream," said Lance, in more seriousness than you might assume.

"Of course it's me," she said, tearing off the blindfold. "I'm freeing you."

"Oh, I'm sorry I couldn't see you today," said Lance. "Did it all go well?"

Ten ha was certain he was talking about the ceremony, but decided to stick to the task at hand. "Hold still," she said, working the knife with skilled hands which could only have belonged to an international chef.

Once his hands were free, she started on the ankles while he tried explaining to her, "Look, the reason I couldn't get out—Why I got thrown down here today—"

The ankles free, Ten ha stood and seized her man's face, telling him, "Look, whatever you did, it made ol' Heph mad, which means you probably did me a huge favor. So unless you killed someone—"

"No," Lance sputtered quickly.

"Good—then I don't care. But you're coming with me, before your guards are replaced."

"You got through the guards just to get me loose?"

Ten ha slid the knife back into a boot, righted herself, and pulled Lance to his feet. "Now what kind of girl would I be if I didn't come rescue my man? Now, stop stalling and let's get out of here."

"Yes, my lady," said a smiling Lance, and the two bolted from the cellar and out into the night.

LXVIII – Grass Stains and Accidental Bruises

Jonas knew the moment his feet touched the ground that this would not be a day to be outside. Rather he felt it was a day to stay boarded up in one's room with one's head under a convenient pillow seeing as there wasn't any convenient sand in which to bury it.

We shall never know the reasons behind his intuitions, or exactly what it was that went on in his head, but on that particular morning, when he set out through the front door before anyone else had woken up, conveniently forgetting his boots, his skin must have received the oddest toe-quivering sensation from the earth below. All he had to do thereafter was sniff the air to conclude that indeed there was something most out of the ordinary on the wind, in the dirt, and probably running through the river for all he could tell.

As the quotation occurred to him, the grandfather began with, "So foul and f—" but stopped himself to shake his head and reannounce, "No—Foul. So *foul* a day I have not seen." Obeying this assumption, Jonas turned around, and walked right back into Julian's room—after all, the boy had not been in all night and could not be accidentally woken. He latched the door behind him, decidedly content that until the following morning it should not be opened for any circumstance or caller (including Julian himself), excepting that in which they house should suddenly catch fire.

The rock would not begrudge the grandfather his truancy. After all, the rock acknowledged that any meeting could be postponed for days of illness, inclement weather, and the rare case of imminent peril. Besides, we can only conclude that the rock and its hill counterpart were even more aware of the looming disaster than the grandfather could be, seeing as they were even more connected to the trembling ground.

STOUMBOS

Now, Pigby and Geru may have had some suspicion, but both parties were more likely to dismiss it as a byproduct of grogginess were there no further evidence. Seeing the grandfather hastily reenter and slam the bedroom door was apparently not evidence enough.

"He's back early this morning," said Geru, having not been awake enough to notice when he'd left.

Pigby tossed the short man his robe and, picking up both their mats, suggested the alternative, "Or we're just late."

"I can smell the sunrise, Pigby," replied Geru with a shaking finger, "you should know better."

Pigby, knowing better, rolled his eyes as he closed the door behind them.

Even for all his stubbornness, Geru was forced to reconsider Pigby's assertion when they arrived to find that not only were their yogaists already present, but that they had already organized and seemed to be waiting expectantly in a little cluster, at which Sherman was center.

Clemens was the only one who stepped forward initially. He approached Pigby and—despite their staunch height differences—did his best to put his arm around the giant man's shoulders, in a gesture which intended camaraderie but smacked more of secrecy.

"Pigby, I'm glad you're here," he began. "We've something to discuss with you."

"Who's we?" Pigby asked, raising an eyebrow to Geru who looked a lot more skeptical than he.

"Me—We—Well, Sherman in particular..." As he went on, Pigby could feel his walrusy friend leading him gradually away from the short man and closer to the cluster. "See, we think that maybe it's time for someone else to take the leader mat."

"How's that?" came Pigby, his curiosity entirely innocent compared to Geru's outraged:

"What?!"

Sherman took this opportunity to say to Pigby, as opposed to the man he intended to supplant, "Well, I've been doing this for some days now, and I think I've the run of it enough to try leading."

"Out of the question!" snapped Geru.

Without heeding the unproductive short man, the quizzical Pigby inquired, "Why?"

Sherman looked back to the others who seemed to gesture him forward encouragingly. "Well, I've some changes I'd like to implement."

"By heaven, you won't!" Geru announced.

"It's not as drastic as you think," offered Manuel. Piers nodded and Clemens slapped a reassuring hand on the giant's back. The other men, whose names are irrelevant, all seemed to concur with this sentiment.

Geru puffed up so fervently in the chest that it looked as though he would either explode or pass out from the pressure, but in his fury he could find no words. Pigby, though afraid for his dwarf's health could think of no good reason why they shouldn't let Sherman have a go at it; granted, his expertise was less, but as far as Pigby could tell Geru should have no authority which might supersede the residents' and so said, "Alright."

This seemed to relieve the tension in the other men, which they carried for reasons even they did not know. Clemens congratulated Pigby on his good sense; Manuel and Piers commended Sherman, and Sherman proudly assumed the space on the ground from which Geru usually instructed. Not knowing what else to do, Pigby went and set up his mat where he always did, leaving Geru alone and still speechless.

Geru attempted to steam, but unfortunately, none would come out of his ears and so relieved no pressure. He looked between the men— for sympathy undoubtedly—but as no one would make eye contact with him, Geru finally set down his mat beside Pigby's, taking his seat and fearing for the worst.

"It's okay," said Pigby, "Even if it's awful, it probably won't last any longer than just today." Unfortunately, Geru had the horrid premonition that just this day was a day that he would not survive.

"Alright, to begin," began Sherman, speaking as though from a memorized list, "I will be changing the name 'yo-guh' to 'exercise'— because it's really just a morning exercise." And it all went downhill from there.

Pigby did his best to comply with Sherman's slightly off instructions and uncreatively named newly-invented poses, trying not to look at Geru for fear of laughing or crying. Still, he was plagued through the whole of these new 'exercises' by the wonder on why Sherman should have suddenly decided that Geru would not direct their morning's endeavors.

Pigby and Geru were not alone that morning; there was indeed much confusion to go around. For example, the Baron was confused when he arrived back at Julian's house to find that all of the yogaists were fully clothed and actually joining hands in a circle. But the Baron did not much think on this, having two other matters most on his mind, neither of which happened to be his charming little affair of the night before.

For one, the Baron Pan Bordolo had only narrowly escaped Hephaestus' return to the Libburus' house. Luckily, he woke up on his own internal alarm, before the yelling commenced downstairs and was dressed and out the window already when Hephaestus bellowed, "What do you mean you must have fallen asleep?" This inspired a brisk climb down the wall and a quick sprint out the yard, which left him a little short of breath and a little quick of heart by the time he arrived at Julian's cottage.

The second reason was much more simple, but to the Baron far more pressing: the question of whether Julian had beaten him home or was still with the lady. Of course you already know the answer and it may mean less to you, but the Barron found it to be the most pertinent detail of the morning. And when he discovered only the grandfather in the bedroom, with a pillow on his face no less, the Baron was overjoyed by the implied success the boy must have found—overjoyed to the point of forgetting why he had bolted from the house, and why Julian may very well have been in grave danger, but for the moment that was of no nevermind.

Hephaestus was of course confused at the state of his servants, but resolved immediately who was to blame. He could not accept that Liam and Cooper should just happen to both fall asleep on the job while Lance untied and unblindfolded himself—much less by cut away his own restraints. Hephaestus set off to the guest room with Trenton where he might concoct a cunning plan for catching the Baron out in a lie about the escaped servant.

Cletus was confused by that morning's breakfast. He initially prepared a meal large enough to manage the whole of the house, but when he found that neither Hephaestus nor Sebastian would be eating— Hephaestus for purposes of plotting and Sebastian still feeling most appetiteless after seeing Raul's wound firsthand—had Clara send the excess eggs back to the cold house[146]. However, no sooner had Clara left than Samantha approached him to insist that she was most hungry that morning and should need enough to feed three. Cletus, being a refined gentleman's gentleman performed the lady's request, and chose not to interrupt the Libburus' much-needed morning nap or Hephaestus'

---

[146] A storehouse on the edge of town which could in the winter foster a refrigerative environment.

scheming to inquire on the matter. In fact, once he had delivered the oversized breakfast to Samantha—which she took brusquely and without comment—Cletus decided to add Samantha to the do-not-disturb list.

Sabrina was only confused for a moment. However, seeing as she usually woke before her gentlemen callers and had to be the one to kick them out, she actually found it refreshing that the Baron took leave on his own accord.

Eugene was still feeling somewhat sick and somber when he first woke, but he was not confused until a little later that morning, after his overnight guests had left. He went to his son's room, obviously, to check on the state of the boy's bandages and found Raul to be sitting comfortably by the window, watching what appeared to be a throng of other villagers discussing something quite heatedly in Eugene's front yard.

When Eugene inquired as to the sight out the window, Raul shrugged by means of his eyebrows and one cheek and resumed his spectating, clearly not wanting to investigate in-person.

Eugene decided not to trouble his wife or servants with this strange gaggle of gossipers on his grounds, and—thinking it to possibly be a group wishing his son well—had a charmed step as he made his way out of the house and before the collection. Surely Eugene would have made an eloquent address, had one of the women not prompted the crowd to surround him by yelling, "There he is! Let's ask him."

Simeon, the man who brewed the beer, managed to get to the front of the group and abated Eugene's startled nerves when he said, "Alright, look, we wanted you to decide something for us."

Eugene checked his posture to make sure it was regal, and replied, "But of course. That's what I'm here for. What can I help you with?"

"Who gets your house?" someone shouted from the back, and since there were about three rows of people mostly encircling Eugene, individual voices were somewhat hard to extract.

"Excuse me?" sounded, more in surprise than immediate outrage.

"Well see," Simeon began again, taking the helm, "we've been talking, and we think that if any of us should become noble and move to this side of the river—"

"Wait, wait—you'll *become noble*?" asked Eugene, not sure whether he should be angered by this or just confused.

"Like Julian," nodded Simeon. "But if more than one of us did, we can't figure out who would get your house."

"Wha—Why—How—This is preposterous!" Eugene concluded.

"Is that because Julian would get the house?" asked another woman, which sent out a wave of agreeing or protesting outbursts.

"No! No one is getting the house!" Eugene yelled, and for a moment the throng was silenced.

"But if we was all nobles like you, then we'd have an equal say in it," said one.

"And we'd rather one of us living here than you," said another.

"You know, I planted this garden," came a third.

"And Thom and I, we fixed the roof," explained Simeon.

"Most've us have put in more work to this place than you 'ave."

"And I teach too," called one more from the rear, which must have seemed a pertinent comment, seeing as the nobles primarily worked teaching the children.

Eugene managed to not fall over from either fainting fatigue or utter disbelief, but he needed to stop this maelstrom. With each new insertion, they seemed to press in closer or become more ardent, so Eugene summed up his voice and strength to protest, "No! No, stop!" Eugene held out both hands and, courtesy of his volume and the remaining traces of respect for precedent, held the comments long enough to squeeze in, "I live here; my family lives here; even if all of you became noble, we would still keep this house!"

They paused to consider this. Hands went to chins or heads, voices retreated, and Eugene chanced to breathe. When he made eye contact with Simeon, who still appeared the primary aggressor, Eugene ventured a concluding, "Do you see now?"

Simeon chewed on the question for a second, then returned, "No, that can't be right," which resumed the roar from the rest of the folk.

Though they had started with just voices, as Eugene tried to slip away, they began to grab at him, wrestling physically for control in a manner that Eugene had not known since childhood, where it was perfectly appropriate to roll about in the grass with one's chums. But as Eugene hit the ground, he was not in the least prepared for the grappling he experienced and immediately thought that he was not dressed for the occasion.

You might find that grass stains and accidental bruises are trivial when compared to the battering his spirit must have taken, but at that moment, Eugene's spirit was drawn in tightly so it could not be vulnerable to any of the words or thoughts circling about him.

Even in that hullaballoo one voice managed to ring out over the rest, saying, "Get off him! Let go!" And though it pained him to bend over at all, Raul reached into the cluster and found his father's wrist, pulling him up onto his feet and away from the others, who did not pursue and did not persist. This being their first riot, they had no way of knowing whether or not they had been successful and so stood and stared while the boy led his father back into their house.

Yes, it was a day of confusion, and that morning, near-everyone in the Isle found a taste of it, but none so much as the boy Hans.

You may not remember Hans—sadly, I've only mentioned him the once, in reference to his limerick performance before Fletcher's song. Hans was a simple boy, no more than ten at the time, and like all good children had his series of chores in addition to his learning schedule, which he often completed and occasionally begrudged. Between himself and the children of the nearby houses, the parents had divided the chores, particularly that of feeding the livestock in the sables, and this day just happened to be Hans'.

Hans toted a bucket of feed and sleepy half-closed eyes as he entered, but when he saw the two bodies on the haybed, clothed in nothing more than each other's hands, he relinquished both the bucket and his unfocused stare. Ten ha and Lance were nearly as startled as the boy when he let out a yell of alarm which was audible across town—even to Jonas, who at that moment had his head buried in a pillow.

LXVIX – His Cherrywood Cane

Supposedly, it is the final straw that breaks the proverbial camel's back, and though the people of the Isle had never before seen a camel, we can fairly assert that it was the image of the boy Hans running out of the stable with his bucket on his head to cover his eyes, for which he tripped and fell into a pile of straw that broke the town.

Though Hans was the only one to see the two servants of rival merchants in their compromised states, it wasn't hard for parents in the nearby houses to guess what had happened—especially once they saw Ten ha and Lance, somewhat terrified and hand-in-hand, fleeing the scene. A quick conferring with the child and one another assured the neighbors that they had concluded correctly, but few were certain as to how they should react to this incident.

Even in the most innocent of towns, children must experience the awkward excitement of discovery, often firsthand and even more often accidentally, leaving their parents or older siblings with the chore of explanation—which afforded even more awkwardness and none of the excitement. But the people of the Isle must have found something more sinister in this sighting, because their pity and comfort, (first to Hans, then to anyone who had heard of Hans' trauma), sounded more blame for the offenders than reassurance to the victims.

Perhaps they recognized the crime against loyalty and how Lance and Ten ha had defied their superiors by consorting with one another. It may have had something to do with the age or the color of the blue girl, which may have struck an inharmonious chord with the socio-sexual mores of the Isleans, who would have never before seen an interracial couple, seeing as all but one of Hephaestus' esteemed servants had been white, and the majority English to boot. Probably more likely that the parents of Hans and nearby children, (with whom he might one day discuss this happening), only begrudged this accident because the frightening and confusing image was brought by outsiders instead of friends or family.

Due to some combination of these reasons or others we know not, the frustrations were already piping hot before Hephaestus arrived to whip them into a raging boil. As he was personally enraged at Lance, every slightly emphatic person and pack animal within earshot became a little more hot-tempered on his account.

Furthermore, the Isleans were so confused and embarrassed that it took them a good twenty minutes to explain to the fuming lord of merchants, his stalwart right hand man, and his downright horrifying Lionel—who did not wear his bruise of battle very well, for the record—in what state Lance and Ten ha had been found.

Though the lord of merchants had been frustrated by his new servant and the Baron's crew separately for days, that Lance had become preoccupied by a woman had never entered his thoughts. Hephaestus, an old fashioned man's man even for that time period, made great personal advances for gender equality that day when he decided to hate Lance and Ten ha equally.

He began with the obvious, "Where are they?" and "When did you see them?" But in his anger, he was so frightening that no one knew how to respond to him. This only made matters worse; simple questions voiced with an enraged tone turned to general accusations like, "Alright—Out with it! Who's hiding them?" and gradually toward the more direct, "If you've got them, I swear, I'll—"

Thankfully, Trenton was on Hephaestus the moment this statement was accompanied by the grabbing of shirtfront, which forced him first to relinquish the whimpering gentleman who had never before been so accosted, and second to not say what it was he might do should the innocent man not give away Lance and Ten ha's whereabouts. Hephaestus took a step back and readjusted his own coat before declaring in his own defense, "This has been an outrage, and every one of you deserves an abject apology, but not just from me—oh no! We must find the two—those scoundrels who burned the eyes and memory of your innocent child—" (Whose name Hephaestus did not know.) "—and bring them forward to confess. Only then will justice be served!"

If you are picturing torches and pitchforks in the hands of an angry lynch-mob, good on you. These items and terms did not make up the literal audience, but figuratively—especially relative to their prior dealings—your assumption is spot on. If you are picturing Hephaestus red-eyed and practically foaming from the mouth all over his tangled grey beard, good on you; that was exactly how he looked.

And he promptly left them there, charging ahead presumably toward the house of Julian. Lionel followed, while Trenton stayed a moment more to calm their nerves and assure them that Hephaestus was just sore over one of his servants and that they should not be alarmed. However, he couldn't stay for long and soon hustled after the others.

But they people *were* alarmed. Not enough for violent course of action, granted, but they could tell that something was definitely wrong and should need to be changed. They had organized to find missing children before and even the odd adult who had fallen asleep at work or some such, but this this was an entirely different kind of mood and intention—sinister even, as I said before. And even if the Isleans did not know what sinister meant or even the meanings of the words that Hephaestus had harshly delivered, they began to discover more anger at the situation than they had before known. Some turned comments against Hephaestus or the new Mustache Man, or their respective crews knowing that at least one of them had to be to blame for what was going on. Others still wanted to blame their own Libburus or the nobles who let the recent events occur on their watch, but the Libburus was in bed and the rest of the on-that-side-of-the-river lot were already trying to quell their own unrests or behind barred doors. Eventually, with no one else to confront directly, the people of the houses surrounding the stables began to argue with one another.

The Baron's crew had likewise been in argument, in pairs or sets through the whole of the morning starting with Geru and Pigby's disastrous yoga affair. Geru decided to have it out with Sherman, and Clemens immediately tried to persuade Pigby into hauling off the dwarf, which put Clemens and Geru at odds with an unfortunate Pigby in the middle.

Fletcher and Oswald, having discovered that one more rule, the fifth rule which happened to concern sex, had been crossed out, took to half-questioning half-accusing one another of having been the one to break it—clearly by violating a gentleman's pact to not enter into certain relations with certain mutual admirations—which led the Baron to question why it had been etched out in the first place, which turned questions and accusations against him.

Geru and Pigby were still squabbling when they stumbled upon this scene, and soon all five were uproariously bandying who-knows-whats back and forth—in three different languages no less, as to keep from getting distracted by other conversations[147].

By the time Hephaestus entered, without knocking, and without a statement loud enough to quell the present pandemonium, not a member of the crew had a mind to notice him. But he huffed and he puffed nonetheless until Trenton had a chance to catch up, enter just behind Lionel, and pluck Hephaestus' cane out of his surprised hand. He banged it a few good times on the wall, ushering a brief postponement of affairs complete with angry glares from all five men.

Pigby, who had been sitting on the couch, stood, showing how much more powerful he could look than the three intruders put together, and Geru, standing just before the giant man, folded his arms formidably. Fletcher clicked his tongue against the roof of his mouth and announced ominously, "Well, well, well, look what the rhinoceros coughed up[148]."

The Baron pulled at one end of his mustache and shook his head, saying, "I'm sorry," though he wasn't, "but I don't recall inviting you."

"No, I daresay no one should find a friendly invitation in this town after what you've done to it," returned Hephaestus, and the accusation was so vague that the crew couldn't help but question it.

"I say! What does he mean, sir?" came Oswald, adjusting his glasses as if to better hear the affair.

Hephaestus scoffed once, a scoff that was a good bit more intimidating with Lionel standing behind him. "Oh, don't pretend you don't know!"

"Well, supposing we didn't—"

"Shut up, Fletcher!" sounded from too many voices to name, none of which were Pigby's.

"No, supposing we didn't," repeated the giant. "If someone hadn't a handle on what you were accusing them, what would you tell him?"

Hephaestus looked more frustrated than anything, but he was genuinely bewildered as to how so pivotal a happening had escaped their collective notice. Resolving that it probably hadn't, but that he should

---

[147] This system was developed sometime back when the six of them (Ten ha included) realized that they could keep three paired conversations running in tandem by exploring one in English and the two others in whatever language was found common by any two other parties. Within a month or so, it was very easy to adjust for whoever spoke Latin, or Greek, or French, or German. When collectively angered, the group made adjustments much less delicately.

[148] I don't know what it means either.

advance matters regardless, he explained, "Well, obviously the seduction of my boy by your girl!" but this statement held no proverbial water.

"Whose girl?" came Geru.

"I say—You've a son, sir?" asked Oswald.

"Julian's our boy!" protested Fletcher.

"Who's seduced?" inquired Pigby.

But the Baron took the rapidly-moving cake with, "Dear lord, was it Sabrina again?"

"No! Not—" Hephaestus let out a loud exasperated grunt then called his tag-team man, "Trenton."

"Your girl Ten ha's been taking a romp with our mate Lance—worst of all this morning, when they both were spotted by a local child in their amorosity."

"*Our* Ten ha? Blimey, gents! Good for her!"

"Ten ha knows how to seduce someone?"

"How dare you, sir, to speak against that good lady's virtue—what, what!"

"Absolutely disgraceful[149]!" (Though it was not clear as to whether this last was directed at Hephaestus' accusation or Ten ha's actions.)

The Baron, who'd taken the moment to furrow his brow and tap at his nose, could not in fairness determine the appropriate response. He did not know if comments on betrayal were in order, or if he should feel protective of the girl, or if he should even trust the accuracy and significance of his rival's allegations.

"So, you're saying, if I may speak it accurately, that my charge, Miss Ten ha, has joined in…cahoots with one of yours and that they have recently exposed themselves to one of the Adleship urchins, yes?"

"Yes!" came Hephaestus. "Now what are you prepared to do about this?"

"Well, I suppose I'll have to have a word with her—can't say I know exactly what to say. Granted, I was young once, but not a sixteen-year-old international linguist in a perfect winter-wonderland-inspired village—which probably has some bearing on the pertinence of the whole affair to her, but—"

"Not your discussion, Mister Bordolo!"

---

[149] Knowing that the Baron was not involved in this round of commentary, I should hope that you would know by now who said what.

"Seriously? Even now when you are enlisting my help, you refuse to use my given name—And what are you doing, now, sir?"

"Well, clearly," Hephaestus began, striding by him to search up in the loft, "you're only trying to stall me, which is precisely consistent with how you would respond if you were hiding them yourself! Lionel, go check in their wagon!"

"Yessir," said Lionel, but was suddenly slapped by Geru who announced:

"You bloody-well will not!"

But Hephaestus was just as prepared to jump on this. "Then admit you're hiding them!"

"Not on your life," the Baron snapped back. "Pigby, go with him, and make sure the man does not touch anything."

"And what if he tries to disturb the wares, boss?"

"Plant his head in the dirt," offered Fletcher.

"Deep enough so he'll grow into a tree!" added Geru, which Lionel barely heard as he was soon gone and with Pigby on his heels.

"How about the bedroom?" asked Hephaestus, satisfied with the loft.

"You won't find anyone in there," said the Baron, following him in.

"I say—you'll disturb the sleeping—" Oswald tried to say, but Jonas, seeing Hephaestus, interrupted with a yell of fright and a quotation that was so startled it hardly formed syllables.

While Hephaestus and the Baron tried to peaceably retreat from the room, fielding accusations from Oswald about respecting the old, Geru approached the still-professional Trenton, demanding, "What is the meaning of all this?"

"The boss needs to find Lance—"

"No, really," Fletcher joined in, "Why's this all such a big deal?"

"You go outside, and you'll hear why," said Trenton, "The whole town's got—"

"Alright, where is she?" came Hephaestus, interrupting the others' commentaries.

"I honestly don't know—and if I did," the Baron added, "I certainly wouldn't tell you now."

"You don't keep track of your girl?" asked Hephaestus.

"You don't keep track of your boy?"

"Look, we can't know where she is all the time," Fletcher yelled over the others. "Besides that she hasn't even been sleeping here."

Hephaestus furrowed a brow for a moment then seemed to understand just what was implied, for he exited, taking back his cane from Trenton, and began the small descent down to Meredith and Manuel's place. As Trenton followed, all remaining eyes turned to Fletcher.

"Fletcher, you numbskull!" announced the Baron, and they all set after Hephaestus. On the way down, they passed a fun tableau of Pigby holding Lionel by his ankles and shaking him upside down, insisting that he let go of a certain scuffed oil lamp. Unfortunately for them, no genie appeared to make the whole debacle disappear. Lionel must not have been rubbing it properly.

Of course a quick tear into Meredith and Manuel's house demonstrated that only Meredith was home and quite upset at that, with Manny having recently disappeared himself to look for Miriam, who had not been at home when Hans' eyes were violated and therefore needed to be tracked down. So as you can imagine, with Hephaestus and the Baron badgering the bewildered Meredith, it wasn't long before she unloaded on the both of them, saying—in a moment of fury with no real sincerity—that they should never again be admitted to the town.

When the ringleaders about-faced and took their leave, Oswald stayed to calm the usually very warm-hearted woman. On the way back, they passed Pigby who was sitting on the face-down Lionel. With Geru nipping at their heels, Hephaestus and the Baron shouldered their way back into the cottage, while Fletcher and Trenton heatedly continued to confer between one another just what was going on with the rest of the audibly arguing Isleans.

"Where is the boy?" demanded Hephaestus as he began to recircle and search the main room.

"Never you mind where he is!" Geru piped in, entering behind the other two.

"You think Julian's hiding them?" came the Baron.

"If he had, you'd never find them," added Geru. "He's lived here a lot longer than you."

But Hephaestus continued in his efforts, thrashing about more and more with each futile gesture, turning over blankets, clothes, and the few pieces of furniture available.

"Look, he's not here! And he wouldn't know where they are," the Baron went on, "For Christ's sake, man, he wouldn't have even seen them today!"

Doggedly ignoring the Baron, Hephaestus stood panting, searching desperately around the room with his eyes—for his hands had done no good—and that's when he saw the list of rules, for the first time since he'd set foot in Julian's house that day. As luck would have it, his glance landed upon the newest strikethrough, scratched across rule five: DON'T DATE THE DUCHESS. His brow narrowed, his jaw clenched, he looked to the Baron and saw the Baron avoid his glance, which was proof enough. Now, Hephaestus was very clever; he was not always sensible, and he hadn't as happy a knack for remembering details as he did in younger years, but clever he remained. In an instant, Hephaestus had deduced exactly how the Baron would have come to break this rule and as of such where the boy must be.

"Really, Mister Bordolo!" was the only thing he said before yet again taking a swift exit.

"Oh, bugger," muttered the Baron, and left after him.

Hephaestus, caring more about ditching the Baron than retaining his servants, brushed by Trenton and Fletcher, and a little ways down the hill tried to do the same for Pigby and Lionel. However, Pigby, disgruntled and stuck with guarding some idiot whose attitude and smell he did not care for, decided to speak out.

"Hey! You want your man back? Or are you just gonna abandon him like you did Jonas?"

Having nearly gotten Pigby out of sight, Hephaestus involuntarily stopped walking and bristled.

"Oh, that's right! We nearly let him get away with that," Geru could be heard saying from the door.

"I'd plumb forgot about it," mused Fletcher.

Hephaestus found himself locked once again in strict eye contact with the Baron, who called, "Well, 'Hephaestus'? What happened to S and J Tiegs?"

Before he even had a chance to think how to respond, Hephaestus heard Trenton shout, "Walk away from this one, sir. It's not your argument to win."

And Hephaestus did just that; the lord of merchants, with a slight slump of shoulder but no slower of speed, simply walked away. This gesture so shocked the Baron that he could not even follow after him immediately.

"Are you just going to stand there?" prompted Geru, while his Baron watched after.

"Where's he going, boss?" asked Pigby.

"I think he's going to the Libburus'—Oh, I don't know, but I think I set him on a trail to Julian possibly—Pigby, now get up off of him—let the man to his feet," which Pigby obeyed though not with delicacy.

"Well, maybe he's just going to go talk to the Libburus," offered Fletcher, "that way *he* can put a stop to all the hysteria."

"You're joking," returned Trenton. "A man like that? He's about as intimidating as spongecake, and less'n solid. Why do you think he's been hiding in his room the whole day?"

"And it's still morning!" squeaked Geru. (He was wrong; the time was ten-past-noon.) "Just think of how much worse it'll get if they're left to their devices 'til evening."

"I don't know," replied the Baron, "but I'm sure that I need to go after him, don't I?"

"And I need to find the snake what's hiding," Lionel added.

"But you concede he's not in the cart?" asked Pigby. When Lionel shrugged and nodded in response, the giant man accepted enough to relax.

"Look, boss, either way, bottom line, something's gotta be done about the town. The people sound raving!" said Fletcher, and Trenton nodded. "Doesn't it say anything in your book about how to put them happy again?"

The Baron, a hand to his chest to defend the unjustly doubted tome, shouted back, "Of course it does, but we haven't nearly enough fudge for everyone! Look, I don't know what's to be done about them," the Baron said again, "but right now, I have to go after him. Fletcher, I'm sorry, but I'm leaving this to you."

Fletcher looked more shocked than any of the others at this mantle of responsibility—which was a considerable undertaking—but the Baron left nonetheless, set on his march across the town, trying to convince himself to walk with a purpose.

Fletcher let out a long, steadying breath and turned to Trenton. "Truce?"

"Truce," agreed the other, and the remaining five gathered together to determine how best to subdue the townsfolk.

Tunnel-visioned as he was, Hephaestus did not see that as a key problem, much less *his* problem as he trudged his way toward the river. In his mind, whatever issue there was within the town could be abated by bringing forth the criminal catalysts and having everyone hear a speech of his. As far as he was concerned, the people of Adleship Isle obviously still loved him, and any animosity toward travelers would naturally be directed at the mischievous devil, the Baron Pan Bordolo.

In fact, as he was moving through one of the well-kept yards of one of the well-kept houses below the falls, he was most heartwarmed by a small child who ran into his path, calling, "Mister Hephaestus, sir!"

As she seemed scared, in need of comforting, and probably no more than four, Hephaestus scooped her up and said, "What is the matter, my dear?"

But before the little darling could reply, surely to describe all of the frightening things she'd heard down by the stables that morning, her mother was standing at the front door, shouting, "Lisa, get away from him!"

Hephaestus, startled, let go of the child, who found her feet upon landing and scurried right back to her mother.

The mother did not wait for an additional prompt, and scolded Hephaestus with, "What right do you have, comin' round here after what you've done? You should be ashamed of yourself—you all should!" And taking the little girl inside with her, she slammed the door, leaving the stunned Hephaestus unsure of exactly what had been accused, let alone whether the reaction was just.

Incidentally, the Baron was already versed in dodging glances by this time on this day, and tried to barrel past even as someone called his name. However, this individual meant not to reprimand him. Oddly enough, the Baron was only two or three houses away from Hephaestus when he was stopped by the dusty and begoggled Dietrich. "Excuse me, sir," he said again, actually grabbing the Baron's wrist to turn him around.

"Oh, Dietrich, it's you!" exclaimed a relieved Baron.

"Sir, I've information for you."

"Yes, and that's lovely, but I must be on my way."

But even as the Baron tried to progress, Dietrich held tighter on the wrist. When he had the Baron's attention, Dietrich jerked his thumb in the direction of his third-floor observatory, which had a small window facing just that direction onto the street, and which—when the Baron squinted—housed three faces in a row: his own blue girl, her burly boy, and the missing snap-pea named Miriam.

"Of course..." trailed the Baron. He looked back to Dietrich and said quickly, "Call down Miriam; she needs to go back to her mother, but keep the others up there until nightfall or I send for them, alright?"

"What? Why?"

"Matter of life and death," explained the Baron, patting Dietrich's shoulder, and was about to leave, but paused to consider, "You know, usually, I enjoy saying that for exaggeration and effect, but it's not as fun when you worry it might be accurate, now is it?"

And he strode away from the puzzled-looking Dietrich, taking swift steps to hopefully intercept the disgruntled lord before he made contact with the most-likely unaware lad.

At that moment, the lad was aware of the hands holding his, the way she was gazing back at him, the smile on her face, and little more. They kissed goodbye-for-now, each promising to see the other soon, but when he tried to turn away, he still had not let go of her hands, which meant they had to kiss goodbye a second and third time before he could truly depart.

She watched him go for as long as she could then dutifully set the wooden shutter back in place.

Julian had his head held high and a spring in his step, and did not immediately abandon this good cheer when he was confronted by the eerie, slow, single-man applause and the frostiest of voices, speaking behind him.

"Well, well. There goes the conquering hero. Once again, we see that Julian has beaten the town." Hephaestus stepped toward the lad, still clapping, his cherrywood cane tightly clenched underarm. "I suppose now that you've jumped rank, nothing will hold you back, hmm? Not a father's blessing, or a daughter's honor."

Julian considered the older gentleman for a moment, then informed him, "You speak past your bounds and better sense, sir. Good day."

And as he continued walking, he was aware of Hephaestus at his back even before the man said, "Don't walk away from me, boy! How dare you turn your back on me when I'm speaking to you."

With an exasperated sigh, Julian casually tossed back over his shoulder, "I have no need for more of your snide."

And Julian was struck. The first impact took his left shoulder, forcing him to one knee, in pain, yes, but more in disorientation; the second across his back sounded across the river, and sent him trying to scramble away, as if from a predator he had never before needed to fear.

"Get up!" shouted Hephaestus, "The great 'Sir Julian'—does he crawl away from his enemies? Stand, boy, and face me!"

Another two strikes, and Julian, confused, hurt, and frightened, tried to cover himself, but with arms that could be targets as well.

"This was my town!" bellowed the other, "My paradise! Well, what is it now, hmm?"

And as Hephaestus advanced, Julian found his voice to say, "Please, sir!" but the older man, a lord of merchants, someone whom he had known as something a god all his life, beat him again.

Perhaps he truly didn't hear him; perhaps he was losing his hearing as well as his control and his mind in that moment on that grey winter day. "So you think you can con your neighbors and bed women and cross swords without consequence, do you? I'll show you!" As Julian tried to soot away again, Hephaestus kicked him, much harder than Julian would have thought he could. "Get up! Stand, boy! Stand, and I'll show you how a *real* swordsman fights!"

And Hephaestus drew the blade from the cane, raising it above the boy and promising to strike if Julian dared him too.

The arms that wrapped around Hephaestus' were not overly swift, but they were strong enough to upset his aging shoulders, making him drop the sword. Locking the man's securely behind his back, the Baron pulled Hephaestus away from the boy and down onto the ground. He was panting, breathless even from his sprint, but he managed to shout to the struggling lord of merchants, "Hephaestus, remember rule four!"

Hephaestus stopped, eyes open, and regarded the frightened boy, then the sword on the ground, and finally in his mind's eye, what he may have done had Julian consented to standing against him. Whether it was the magnitude of the offense, or that he had been reminded of the seven rules, Hephaestus suddenly saw his crime and trembled. And shook. And wept. And as he clung desperately to the Baron who had saved him from himself, Hephaestus held on to each painful, choking sob for as long as his body would allow him.

With no audience of neighbors or either man's crew to see it, Julian found his way onto his knees and shudderingly shuffled forward to the other two, and when he reached them, laid a hand on Hephaestus' shoulder. He let it rest there until his old friend had stopped crying.

LXX – Glaciers

Tilting the glass to better cradle the neck of the cask, he gingerly poured yet another full helping of Chianti for the other man. After taking a long drag himself, the Baron dabbed at his mustache with his handkerchief, then said, "Alright, your turn."

Hephaestus sucked air over his wine-kissed lips, paying his due consideration before settling and saying, "Very well. Fletcher's song."

"The alliteration number?"

"Yes, the alliteration number." The lord of merchants held one cool pause, complete with steadying eye contact. "Did you put him up to that?"

"Just to spite you?"

Hephaestus nodded languidly. "Just to spite me."

The Baron took another quick sip then steadfastly replied, "No."

"Dammitall," came the other and promptly consumed his glass.

"Were you really so certain I'd play that immediate of a prank?"

"So certain that I now owe Trenton five bob!" Laughing, Hephaestus reached for the bottle, which had not touched ground since its opening.

The Baron shook his head amiably. "I didn't even know you well-enough to not like you then."

"Ah, but your minstrel did."

"Don't mind him. He makes fun of everyone, most of all himself," a quick swig, then, "though usually that's on accident."

"Yes, yes, very well—it's your go now; ask me one."

The Baron rubbed one of his tingling cheeks and asked, "Are we ready for the heavier questions yet?"

"Oh, heavens no!" announced Hephaestus, settling back from his sitting position onto his elbows and without paying any mind to the grass or the dirt from the hillside. "We've only been through one bottle between us. Come on, man, let's get a little *warmer* before we set out the cold hard facts now."

As the Baron eyed the one in Hephaestus' fist, he mentally amended that they were well into their second bottle, and even though it was quite a brisk night, the wine in both of their stomachs made the hill behind house-Julian feel very warm indeed. Even so, the Baron would not reject the suggestion, seeing as the Chianti the other merchant carried was perhaps the most excellent bottle of wine he had ever tasted.

"How about Christmas?" he said eventually.

"How about it?" asked Hephaestus.

"Is that on the cards yet?"

"Oh, I've nothing to hide where that one's concerned." Hephaestus cleared his throat, a difficult feat when one is currently drinking, and handed the bottle back to the Baron so that he could use at least one hand to gesture his story. "You see, it all comes from my friend, Reverend Benjamin Moore, and a story he would tell to his son about the night before Christmas, during which a Saint-Nicholas-type incarnation would appear on the roof and enter homes by way of chimneys, bedroom windows, or some such."

"Sounds frightening," remarked the Baron.

"Oh, not at all!" replied Hephaestus, tugging at his beard, "See this character is a jolly fellow who delivers gifts to the good little boys and girls. Sort of a fairytale parenting adventure—you know the like."

The Baron raised an eyebrow at the other. "Not firsthand. For my own part, my godfather only ever showed me how fairytales could help me better break the rules, and acting as foster parent to miss Ten ha, well—as you might imagine—she knows more tales and cultural anecdotes than I do, so I can't really scare or bribe her with commentary on monsters now, can I?"

"Well, in any event," Hephaestus resumed, waving away the possible Baronian tangent, "Benjamin and particularly his son, Clement, have made it a sort of Christmas fixture, and about twenty years back, I decided to employ it here, in the Isle, in the only place where one could actually pretend to be Father Christmas and hope to get a present to every single resident. Over the years, it's become more and more elaborate, and I've gotten to know the citizens better—though not as many or as well as I should like." Hephaestus looked over the town, which—from that distance and height—did not look nearly as turbulent as it felt from the inside, and he could feel a swell of nostalgic pride, which made him

STOUMBOS

happily sigh. "Do you have any idea how good it feels to finally tell someone else this?"

"You haven't told anyone?" came the Baron, choking some on his drink and his own surprise, "Dear God, man, you're not nearly so vain as I thought you were."

"Well, I—" Hephaestus decided that he should not be offended by the Baron's last, and so agreed, "It's true: I have been known to boast myself, but never about the Isle. I can't. Don't you see that if more people found out about it, it could end up...well—"

"Like this?"

Hephaestus didn't answer that thought directly. "I keep any stories of this place from anyone excepting former servants, and actually, now that I mention it, Benjamin Moore, whom I informed of my Christmas tidings during the most sacred of confidential ceremonies:" he took one more sip, then concluded with, "Confession."

The Baron began to laugh. "You bragged about your good deed during a confession?"

"And then I confessed to the bragging and had it absolved. I know how it sounds, but I had to tell somebody, and Benjamin Moore is one of the few preachers I trust to keep this entirely in confidence and not start sending over missionaries to convert the poor town."

"Wait, Moore?" came the Baron, sitting up the more alert, now that it had registered. "Reverend Benjamin Moore, as in the Bishop of New York?"

"You know him?"

"Well, I've met him a few occasions, actually—before he was named a bishop. Fletcher happens to be a friend of his son's—yes, Clement Clarke Moore—awful poet, if you ask me, but they get on well together, so Fletcher must see some potential in him[150]."

"Well, then, good sir," came Hephaestus, raising his glass, "You and I are not so far apart as we first believed—granted, a generation off—but in my opinion, that is worth drinking to."

And the Baron consented, a step behind the other, which meant that he was still drinking when Hephaestus fired his net question.

---

[150] Incidentally, C.C. Moore is the author of "A Visit from Saint Nicholas," which you know as "'Twas the Night before Christmas," and which was published for the first time about nineteen years after this conversation took place. Even more incidentally, Mister Moore needed every one of those years to refine his rather rudimentary craft.

"Did you inveigle Sabrina?"

The Baron sprayed about half a mouthful of wine, then sputtering and coughing, conveyed a quick, "Excuse me?"

"Well, I am sorry; I meant not to catch you off guard, but it is a present curiosity—and rule was crossed off the list, I don't know if it was you, or her, or—"

"Alright, fine. Yes, yes it was," said the Baron, eager to stop the clumsy commentary before it got too far. "I just—I couldn't stop it! She knew exactly what to say to me, and I was—well, I was quite elated, if you must know—but I was utterly helpless. If anything, she jollied *me* into it and not the other way around." And as Hephaestus shook his head, both in amusement and disapproval, the Baron tried to justify himself with, "Hephaestus, she spoke Greek mythology to me."

Hephaestus straightened both in posture and expression to ask, "How did she—"

"She snuck into your wagon. You never knew, did you?"

"Well, of course!" protested Hephaestus, "I obviously—I had—I know when anyone disturbs my—No, no idea. None whatsoever."

"I see." The Baron considered moving on, but his mild inebriation bid him admit, "So did my men."

"They—"

"Broke into your wagon. I'm afraid so."

"Ah. Were you—"

"No, I wasn't. And I didn't put them up to it either; it was the night before they knighted Julian."

"I see." Hephaestus could not determine whether it was proper to feel violated or grateful for the confession. "Well, now I know," he concluded and resigned to have another drink.

"Why did you give the girls sheer dresses?" the Baron asked suddenly.

"Oh, come now—they weren't *that* sheer, were they?"

The Baron cleared his throat and looked rather pointedly at his own knees.

"Oh dear, they were, weren't they?" to which the Baron did not reply. "That's embarrassing," Hephaestus resolved, with a clearing shake of his head. "I just—It was what everyone was wearing in Paris this summer. And I've sort of gotten used to giving current fashions to Sabrina. I suppose I didn't think they would look quite so inappropriate."

"Clearly," the Baron agreed.

Awkwardness turned to chuckles as they sipped, and the two gentlemen mused over their encounters in the Isle, watching the sun fade as they swapped questions and yet another bottle. Finally third form and voice joined them to say, "Excuse me, sirs."

"Oh, Julian!" exclaimed the Baron. "Have a seat and join us."

Julian tried not to look wary of Hephaestus who welcomingly patted the ground beside him. "No—thank you. It's getting a bit cold and dark out here. I wondered if you might need a blanket or two."

"My God, that is simply grand of you, just grand," said the Baron, then turning to Hephaestus asked, "Isn't the boy a saint?"

"Indeed, he is!" nodded Hephaestus, "So gallant and so humble—Oh! To think that I would ever lay an ill hand on this boy. Julian, I am so, so terribly sorry."

"It's alright, sir: you've said," replied Julian, who had heard this apology through various states of sobbing, sobriety, and now drunken sincerity.

"No, I really do mean it," insisted Hephaestus, meaning to stand, but only getting so far as sitting up. "I had no right to call out against your copulation with the young miss; she is a fine woman and virtue is not something you can steal." Hephaestus smiled, convinced he had been profound, and settled back down onto an elbow again.

Julian, a little blindsided, bid, "Excuse me?"

"What he means, lad, is that he has no quarrel with you, or how you and the lady decide to contort yourselves—"

"Consort," offered Hephaestus.

"Yes, thank you, and though I can only truly speak for myself—given our own indiscretions, we've no right to speak ill of your dealings with the girl," explained the Baron.

"Alright, that's enough!" Julian announced, "I've let you two run your mouths on everything you fancy, but I will not condone your sullying Samantha, especially to say that she would ever engage in that kind of behavior."

The Baron cocked his head to one side, and Hephaestus dug a finger into his clogged ear. "How's that?" asked the older.

"But you spent the night!" protested the Baron, "Wasn't that why we broke you in?"

"I went there to tell her how I felt about her. And as for the rest of the night—not that you've any right to ask on it—we talked, sirs. Just talked." Julian was silhouetted against the daylight to the south, but both drunkards could tell how stern his expression was. "Now, I know you two are used to otherwise, and so are some of the people here, but me and Samantha—Sirs, there's still such a thing as decency and honor and respect, and we're going to keep it, no matter what else happens." And he turned to leave, halting briefly to say, "And the others haven't come back yet, if you were wondering."

They had been wondering, but at that moment, as the two merchants watched Julian walk away with more dignity than either of them felt, they could only think on how remarkable this lad was.

"Well, I'll be," mused the Baron.

Hephaestus finished his glass. "Unbelievable. To think that I raged against the boy for what Lance had done, and he hadn't even committed the admittedly blameless offense I thought he had."

"No. To be sure, I've had more a share of licentiousness than my dear Ten ha; she was just unlucky enough to get caught."

Pouring himself another, Hephaestus asked, "How do you mean?"

"Well, I broke a rule," acknowledged the Baron, "granted, *this* one didn't do so much harm, but I see how it could. And if we're being honest, Ten ha was the only one of my people who didn't break any of your seven." And as Hephaestus' pensiveness could be mistaken for confusion, the Baron explained, "Geru with the lie about our intentions, Fletcher with the ramrod, Pigby with that accidental murder, Oswald with the knighting, and me with the lady Sabrina." The Baron, in courtesy, did not mention Hephaestus' attempt at instigating violence from the relentlessly peaceful Julian.

Hephaestus kept his eye on Julian until he'd reached the little cottage, where there seemed to be an old stooped man waiting for him. Thought the Baron knew this shadow to be Oswald, Hephaestus' older eyes and fuzzy emotions caused him to mistake the specter for Jonas. He sniffed, a sound that placed him somewhere between stopping himself crying and mustering up some incomparable amount of courage. "Alright," he said.

"Alright, what?"

"Alright, I'm ready. Let's take the hard ones." And Hephaestus braced himself for the Baron's next inquiry.

The Baron licked his lips slowly. He did not know why he should be so nervous; after all these questions were the reason for their truce and taking to drink. Perhaps it had something to do with unlocking a legend, for indeed once you unveil the magician's secrets you can no longer be amazed by his illusions. But the mustache would not stand for hesitation and urged the Baron forward, molding his lips to say, "Well, let's start with your name."

Hephaestus quickly poured and took another drink, and was dismayed when it did not immediately affect him. "My name is not really Hephaestus. My name is actually"—He tried not to groan audibly—"Pip Heffer." Hephaestus found himself mildly affronted by the Baron's reaction. "Now, don't laugh, Mister Bordolo!"

"I'm sorry!" sputtered the Baron, "It's the wine—Ahem!—I just—How could anyone take you seriously with a name like Pip!"

"Which is exactly why I had to change it! Honestly, never in history or literature has there ever been a hero named Pip[151]."

"At least tell me it's short for Phillip."

Hephaestus hesitated long enough for the Baron to take it as an answer and once more burst into laughter.

"Alright, alright!" came the annoyed Hephaestus, "Don't get too cocky; it's your turn now. Tell me: what's your given name; what's really behind the title 'Baron Pan Bordolo.'"

Steadying himself, the Baron said, "I don't think you'll like the answer—"

"Oh, come off it, man! I told you mine, now it's your turn. We had an agreement."

"Very well." The Baron sighed, regarded his glass and decided to drink the majority of its contents before saying, "That really is my given name. I was born Baron Pan Bordolo."

That Hephaestus was speechless did not convey belief, so the Baron Pan Bordolo went on. "My mother was the Baroness Emily Boyle and my father the Baron Friedrich Bordolo of Jorger von Tollet."

Hephaestus tried to squint at his own eyebrows while racking his brain for memory. He eventually concluded, "I have no knowledge of that barony."

"Well, no one does; it doesn't exist anymore. The whole line vanished—city too, I think. Was renamed during the Polish partitions and redistributed in seventy-two, not long after they were wed. My father stayed to try to sort it out. Died within a few months—we heard word from my godfather, or I suppose my mother did; I was born in the spring of seventy-three."

---

[151] My apologies to Mister Dickens.

"And your mother was a Boyle," came Hephaestus, knowing a lot more about that name than you do, being a gentleman of that day and age.

"Emily Boyle, sister of Robert Boyle-Walsingham, who, after the death of my father, took their name as well and progressed into the Boyle-Walsingham barony, raising me alongside my cousin Charlotte as if a brother. Now, in fairness, the title was largely nominal," the Baron admitted, "With the Jorger von Tollet land seized to the point that the name no longer stood, I would not inherit any rule, but I was raised as a baron, and my mother had me keep my father's family name, because if I didn't, no one would. In fact, even my mother left the Boyle house— about the time I started my travels—got remarried to a commoner, and cut herself out of that line entirely; I doubt many even remember she was part of that line now." The Baron paused to consider the story to see if he had missed any points. Then looking up at Hephaestus began to say, "You know who Charlotte Boyle-Wals—"

"Of course I know who she is!" protested Hephaestus. "Really, Mister B—" and with a grimace, "*Sir Baron*, do you think I would not recognize the given name of the Lady Henry Fitzgerald?"

"Soon to be Lady Henry Fitzgerald de Ros if our dear King accepts her petition[152]."

"Oh, rub it in, why don't you." Hephaestus huffily folded his arms about his chest and grunted his dissatisfaction.

Feeling somewhat guilty for his victory, the Baron offered, "Sorry. If it helps, the baron title is in memorandum; the land that would have been mine was conquered before I was born."

"Yes, but you're still…" Hephaestus seemed about to say 'noble,' but thought the better of it. "You know, that doesn't explain how you came to call yourself a traveling merchant."

"Oh, well, that," the Baron went on, pointedly ignoring Hephaestus' doubtful backhand, "See, that was inspired by my godfather and his book." The Baron patted his breast-pocket, in which was a worn, leathery, hand-written diary of sorts. As this explanation didn't appear to suffice, the Baron withdrew the book and handed it gently to Hephaestus, who opened it with a gasp.

---

[152] Historical footnote: three years later, the Baroness Charlotte Boyle-Walsingham assumed the Fitzgerald de Ros title, connecting herself, and incidentally our Baron to the oldest and arguably most regal lines of barony in England.

"This is the diary—It says—But how did you—No!" And Hephaestus held it away from his face, for he could not bear to see the document that glorified the Baron so splendidly.

On the open page, partially covered by his thumb read the title, *The Surprising Adventures of the Baron Munchausen*, below which the same man had addressed, 'To my godson, Pan: may your travels be memorable, and your adventures unbelievable.'

To which Hephaestus actually commented, "Unbelievable."

"I'll take my book back now," said the Baron, and safely redeposited his security blanket.

Now, it's fair that you may not have heard of the Boyles, or the Fitzgeralds, or the Barony de Ros (pronounced *de Roos*), but if you have not at least heard of the honorable Baron Karl Friedrich Hieronymus Freiherr von Munchausen, I'm absolutely baffled that you managed to come upon *this* book in the first place. The Baron Munchausen was a world-traveled soldier, adventurer, and tall-tale-made man, whose self-professed exploits were considered too incredible to believe.

"Well, I grew up on those stories," explained our Baron. "See, most people know them from Raspe's adaptation, but I heard them from the man himself[153]. Collected my own crew based on his writing during my initial venture, which took me three—closer to four years actually to get around the world and arrive back at his house to tell him joyfully that there was indeed as much magic and mystery among the strange land-forms, raging seas, and barbaric indigenous cultures as he had described! But he'd died. Earlier that year actually; my godfather—somewhat long-distance, yes, but probably the closest thing to a father I'd ever known—passed away before I could tell him how right he was—that there are fantastic and amazing things to be seen in the world if you bother to go out and seek them." The Baron looked out over the town, which he believed was worthy of the other Baron's memory. "So now, I carry him with me. His book never leaves my person, and it gets to see every grand adventure that he inspired. Which I think he would appreciate."

---

[153] It is difficult to say now after so many years have passed whether the edition he carried was anything like the book that survived to be translated and republished for the centuries to come. After all, there were three major publications of the same collected stories before the Baron Pan Bordolo even departed on his first tour, and it's altogether possible that the version he had was composed by Munchausen himself.

"But after all this," came Hephaestus, "after everything we've been through and everything that could have been averted, why did you wait to show me this proof until now?"

"Well, I was going to produce it before," protested the Baron, "but you were so very critical of any of my origins, naturally, I kept it protected, because I will not have anyone scrutinize this book if I can help it. Understand, Mister Hephaestus, that everyone I've ever talked to about his adventures dismiss them as fantasy, and I would be one sorry ingrate if I opened them up for ridicule from self-important know-it-alls.

"Besides," the Baron went on, "I find the world to be all too obsessed with proof anyway, and few remember that finding proof eliminates all the mystery and intrigue that inspired them to search for the proof to begin with. It's like this place; I count it extremely fortunate that Geru never found out *exactly* what makes the whether the way it is, because the fun is always more in the wondering than the knowing. That's what my godfather taught me, at any rate."

"Actually, now that I mention it, "Karl von Munchausen was responsible for naming me Pan, as my father wasn't present to do so— never gave a reason for the name," before the older had had a chance to ask, "I think he just liked the sound of 'Baron Pan Bordolo' even if Bordolo was a surname and not a region. My mother respected my godfather's wishes I suppose because he knew my father better than she ever had; marriages along landholding lines are always more mercenary than romantic, you know."

And as the Baron grew quietly pensive, the wine magnifying a somber mind now more than a jovial one, Hephaestus sighed and finished his own glass before saying, "Alright, there's one more thing that needs to be sorted: Jonas."

The Baron met his gaze to show that he was paying attention but said nothing.

"And to tell it, I have to go back a ways…" Hephaestus would have hired a harpist for just that moment were they not in the Isle. "It begins when I was fourteen. See, being born a Heffer—"

"Born a cow," translated the Baron.

"No, two *f*s, Mister—*Baron!*" He angrily cleared his throat at the sniggering Baron and informed him, "*I'm* telling this story if you don't mind!" And the Baron held his composure behind a quivering palm, which seemed to be enough for the lord of merchants. "Now, my parents were not poor, but they were assuredly *not* aristocrats, which meant that if I stayed in England, I could climb no further. And I won't lie—I despised that: my status stagnation. So I left. Indeed I was smart, I'd a head for numbers, and I managed to apprentice myself to a navigator on a trans-Atlantic vessel, which was rarer in those times."

Once he'd determined that the Baron was not yet impressed, Hephaestus continued: "After nearly two years of such work, I ran across the most wondrous company of men I had ever before seen—"

"The traveling merchants?"

"I'm sure if you'd listen I'd tell you!" Hephaestus groaned, shook his head, then said, "Yes, the traveling merchants, S and J Tiegs— and yes!" before the Baron had managed to speak, "The J was Jonas, the same Jonas who you know, but not yet know why."

The Baron could not discern whether this last was actually slurred or if it just sounded so when coming through the wine filters over his eyes and ears.

"Solomon Tiegs was a very strong, loud man, who could outbargain anyone he met, because he most-assuredly had something in his wares that his mark would be willing to trade for." Hephaestus took another drink and wiped off his lips with a sleeve. "And when he met me, a skilled, strong, young sailor who could read stars, maps, and inventory logs, he promptly bought my services." Spreading his arms wide to indicate his own self and accomplishments, Hephaestus proudly declared, "I became his numbers man! Me, Pip: a boy of sixteen, an inventory manager for a worldwide traveling merchant. Which I suppose put me in the same line of work as your leviathan—what's his name?"

"Pigby," the Baron replied. "And how does Jonas fit into all this?"

"Jonas was Solomon's younger brother, and he was our minstrel. He had loads of books, and read and recited so many lines from—well, from everything—which he used to entertain the wealthy and respected wherever we would go—"

"Oh, I'm aware of their function; why do you think I have Fletcher?"

"Yes, yes." Hephaestus waved away the man who was in his opinion a lesser bard. "Well, we had two translators, one a culture and customs expert, and one a world-religions scholar, an explorer who knew about trailblazing and such, and Gaston, our muscle, just in case of a tiff—which we had a few.

"Well, about a year later, when we passed through Europe again—and I don't even remember why—we decided to take a different path across our homeland, putting us through the mountains just below

Scotland—maybe Solomon was following a map or something. In any event, we hit a storm." Hephaestus paused to swallow, his throat feeling suddenly dry. "A winter storm the likes of which I'd never seen, bigger than any we had expected in those mountains, one big enough to sway the wagon, even against the might of six beasts of burden and seven men. But Solomon had us push through, and we made it here: to Adleship Isle, a lovely, charming town, yes, but a town that didn't know or want us, and couldn't buy anything from us."

"Were they frightened of you?" asked the Baron.

"Oh, of course! But they were amiable, hospitable, helpful. But Solomon wanted us to leave." Hephaestus, who had been teasing the end of his beard between thumb and forefinger, came to grasp and wrap the strands around his nervous palm. "We tried to go the same way, back down the hill where we'd come, and Solomon—he was so sure he could scout the path, but it was too white, and the wind was too strong, and he got too far ahead..." Hephaestus' voice trailed, but his hand only gripped tighter. "Though we retreated to this town as a base camp, we kept going back to look for him, and in two trips we got separated from both translators. On the third, we nearly lost Jonas; he'd fallen into something of a crevice in the glacier, or drift, or whatever, but the trailblazer—his-his name was Max, I remember—found him, and Gaston carried him back. He'd gone delirious from the cold and when we told him that we couldn't keep going out there to find his brother, he—well, that's when everything went away. Everything save for the books, I suppose."

Seeming to notice that his knuckles were losing feeling, Hephaestus unclenched his hand and withdrew it from the tangled grey hairs. He then tried to comb his beard straight, but the alcohol in his blood muddled his motor skills. The Baron scarcely blinked while he waited for the lord of merchants to continue.

"I didn't mean to leave him," he said eventually. "None of us did, but there was only so much we could do there, and he was in no state to travel; he'd gone practically comatose, rarely looked at or spoke to us. And Max said he could get us down the mountain on the other side. So we loaded up the cart, we readied the animals—Gaston, Max, and I—and we promised to come back for Jonas once the weather was more weatherable.

"But we made it down. It was rough, but the three of us reached stable ground on the other side. And we waited for spring. Dutifully, I might add, which was difficult for all of us who had grown accustomed to moving about, but the wagon, and everything in it belonged to the surviving brother who was still in that odd little town—Or, I suppose *this* odd little town. But when spring came, we couldn't find our way back. Even Max, who was a brilliant scout, and said he was sure we were going in the right direction, was lost as to where the town had gone."

The Baron, not understanding why this should be the case began to say, "Couldn't you just retrace—"

"We did. Now, it's harder when your recollection is snow, but still doable, and we found nothing, consistently. Just a ravine cutting off our attempted heading, and then unrecognizable walls and cliffs along the edges of our scouting zone."

The Baron's fingers traced the embroidering in his own jacket, and he asked, "What happened then?"

Hephaestus only managed to get out "So—" before both men were confronted by a troupe—or perhaps troupe sounds too unified, seeing as this group pulled from both crews, though neither in full. Regardless, Trenton and Fletcher led the rhythmically-marching ranks, with Pigby and Lionel visible behind them.

"Sir," came Trenton, "the citizens are back in their homes."

"Oh, well, that's a good thing," said a hopeful Baron, unable to discern why this news was delivered like that of a dying relative.

"Not exactly, boss," said Fletcher, stepping forward. "See, they've only retreated temporarily. There's a fair assembly of 'em says they're gonna replace the nobles, now that they think they can, and some are resisting those, and the nobles are all mostly scared. We got 'em to agree to talk about it tomorrow, so there'll be a meeting in the square, but it will take more than a meeting to clear this one."

"Well, surely, they can be reasoned with," said Hephaestus.

Lionel shook his head and explained, "They've gone ravin'."

"It's worse than ever before, sir," agreed Trenton.

"How bad?" Hephaestus asked.

"Well, they're more violent, sir; some of them spat at us."

"Well, I don't know if we need to panic over a little spit," said the Baron.

Trenton very seriously turned to the Baron and answered, "Only so long before spit turns to stones, turns to swords."

The Baron, trying to channel some semblance of optimism asked, "Pigby, have you tried any of your pull with the workers?"

"Sir, even they're divided. Some are in favor of replacing the nobles; some want to stop the changes; some are in camp Baron, and others are favoring Hephaestus."

"'Camp Baron?'" scoffed Hephaestus.

"Well obviously," squeaked a voice as its owner shoved his way between the others, "every division they're following is modeled after one of you!"

The Baron and Hephaestus looked between one another, and as each saw a partly inebriated and very exhausted traveling merchant, they decided to gauge from the others whether this was true. That none of their crew members would make eye contact was telling enough.

"Very well," said Hephaestus eventually, "go inform the others of the status, and we'll meet you later to determine a course of action."

"Yes," added the Baron, "we've just a few things to discuss first."

Once the others had turned and left, the Baron said eagerly, "Alright, how'd you find your way back?"

"Is this really the time for that?" Hephaestus returned.

"If not now, then when? If it's already a lost cause, five more minutes won't hurt! Now tell me, how was it a ravine one day and a road to Adleship Isle the next?"

Hephaestus raised one curious eyebrow at the Baron. He sniffed through one nostril, and replied, "Glaciers."

"Glaciers?"

"During the winter, the snow fills in and creates a bridge, which is why you can only get here in the winter, but the snow that fills in the cracks is solidified by a blizzard, apparently the same one every year, which starts the day before we arrive and continues to get worse until January. I didn't find out until the next window; see, Gaston gave up after the first unsuccessful trip—said it would be best to think that the town never existed—and after a few attempts, Max gave up as well, leaving me with the wagon and the promise to Jonas.

"Now, I'm not superstitious." He was lying. "But I thought that if we could make it to the town one time, then surely the best time to try would be on the same day from the same direction. And by the next winter, I'd used the Tiegs goods to rope together a crew, and we ascended the mountain—"

"Wait, you're saying that after losing three men, and stranding one in the Isle that you thought it was a good idea to repeat?" inquired the incredulous Baron.

Hephaestus raised a finger, which swayed more than he noticed. "Fact: on that first trip, we found the town in one day, and no one was worse for the wear until we tried to prematurely descend. Which is why I make the trip to the Isle on the same day every year, because every time I have gone on December the eighteenth, leaving no later than four in the afternoon, I have found it promptly, and every time that I have strayed even a calendar day, I've run the risk of impossible-to-navigate weather, suffered huge delays, and wagon issues." Changing the subject from his own obsessive tic which just so happened to prove true, Hephaestus continued with, "Well, as you might imagine, when I found Jonas—'"

"He didn't recognize you?"

"Oh, no, I wouldn't say that. He was terrified of me. And the wagon, when he was too close to it. He'd experienced true trauma, and I was a reminder of it. But…well, I expected him to recover, someday. So I kept coming back. I worked out how and when to leave and return safely each year, to check on him, but he drifted further and further away. And as I grew into more and more prominence in the world of traveling merchants, I also grew more and more invested in this place." Hephaestus regarded the cottage again, trying to tell if Jonas was inside or what it was that he was thinking. A part of Hephaestus hoped the old man could hear him, but he felt that the relic would be too far gone to understand his confession. So he sighed and resolved, "The rest, as they say, is history."

"What about Lance?" asked the Baron.

"What's the matter? I just picked him up in France barely two weeks ago!"

"No, no, as in the threat—you know 'he's history.'"

Hephaestus shook his head. "I don't follow."

"Oh, never mind," resigned the frustrated Baron. "Regardless they're coming this way." And sure enough, walking up the hill, hand-in-hand were the final strapping servant and the blue girl. The Baron turned to Hephaestus to try to confer over a plan to confront them, but Hephaestus was suddenly on his feet and striding—with few stumbles—to meet them.

"Well! You have returned, I see," he said.

"Sir," said Lance with a nod. "I want to apologize for the disruption we caused yesterday."

"And for your dealings with the young miss here?" Hephaestus prompted, indicating Ten ha with his cane.

Lance looked at Ten ha for a moment then announced, "I won't apologize for that, sir."

Hephaestus' eyes narrowed, his jaw clenched, then he put out his right hand to shake, which surprised Lance, Ten ha, and the Baron standing off his shoulder. "Then you have my blessing, young man. And you're sacked."

"S-sacked, sir?" came Lance as Hephaestus released the handshake and proceeded back to his patch of grass.

"Yes," called the other without looking over his shoulder, "first thing when we get back to civilization."

"You know, that is fair," slurred the Baron in agreement.

Ten ha took a step toward her boss. "And what about me, sir?"

"You?" It took the Baron a moment or two to realize what the question was, but he soon reached forward and pulled his ward into a firm embrace, gently patting her shoulder with the hand that held no wine glass. "You, my dear, are a brave, intelligent, tenacious young woman, and you have a place in my crew for as long as you should like.

"Thank you, sir," she said with a smile.

"Now go, the both of you, inside Julian's, and we'll meet you there. We've some planning to do."

"We're going to stage an intervention!" yelled Hephaestus from up the hill.

"Oh and check on Jonas while you're in," the Baron added as they began to depart, "he's had a trying day."

The Baron resumed his seat beside the lord of merchants, and though he knew they should be talking on the town, he had one more question to ask. "You know, you left out one important detail."

"Did I, Sir Baron?"

"Yes indeed: Where did 'Hephaestus' come from?"

"Ah, yes. Well, it happened rather by accident. See, when we were about to leave Jonas there for the first time, he was hardly coherent, but when he spoke to me, all he had in his brain was literature, so the closest thing to Heffer in his memory must have been Hephaestus. Now, obviously, when I tried to hire my own servants later that same year, I didn't feel very leaderly called Pip, and I just started using the name Jonas had given me, Hephaestus, which became a more grand and famous persona than Pip Heffer every could have."

The Baron furrowed his brow intently. "That's it?"

"What do you mean, 'that's it?'" asked Hephaestus.

"Well, I just expected a more elaborate story, something a little more important that just deciding to inherit someone else's mistake. I was hoping for research, deduction, selection, for the perfect name. Even some delusion of divine-endowment."

Hephaestus, his tone turning to offense shot back, "Well, what about you? You don't even know if you were named Pan after the god or some other stupid reason."

The Baron considered that with a "Hmm." Eyes on the dirt below him, the Baron mused aloud, "Look at us: two little men who've called themselves gods for too long, without ever living up to the title."

"I suppose gods wouldn't have gotten into this squabble," agreed Hephaestus, "setting an entire town into civil war."

"What are you talking about? The Greek gods sent entire nations to wars and fueled them from the inside out so that they'd last for ten years."

Hephaestus rubbed at one tired eye, saying, "Yes, what we'd need is a device to *stop* a war."

"As gods or as ourselves?"

"Hmm? Oh, either." Hephaestus poured himself the last glass he would drink that night. "See, if we were omnipotent, we could set everything right, just the way it was."

The Baron mentally chewed on that phrase: *the way it was.* Meaning that he had never arrived, that Hephaestus hadn't lost a few dozen marbles, and most important, that Julian hadn't stepped too far, giving long-content neighbors reasons to feel restless. He dug his fingers into the dirt around a smooth flat stone, and—looking to the little cottage—remembered how he'd watched Julian skip rocks across the upper pool. The Baron gave the little stone enough momentum to roll down the hill and away from them. "Well," he said, "we've already broken six rules."

Part VI – An Uncommon Solution

...behind it rose a most-startling hooded and cloaked four-armed beast whose shadow was cast on the rock wall.

LXXI – Fireworks

The grandfather chap settled comfortably onto his grandfather rock, and both wondered if indeed it might be for the last time. The hill had heard rumors from the river of course, but the rock could not bear to impart this news to the still potentially innocent ears of Jonas, but the ancient weather-wearied minstrel already knew. When his head was out from under the pillow the day before, he had heard some of the scuffles down the way; moreover, he had felt the clear unrest from his fellow villagers, unrest which he could see this morning, in the forms of barred-off windows and sleepy sentries peppering the hills and homes of the people of Adleship Isle.

The twilight was the same, the breeze was the same, and the thick film of cloud at the edge of the world had not shifted a jot, but not a single villager would follow his standard modus operandi once the cock crew. Even routine that was associated with the now-unwanted guests had been terminated. In fact, this grand change of ceremony was as pointed as a holiday—just with fear and threat of violence rather than togetherness and joy. I should mention, it just so happened to be the first of January, making it the first day of the new year, which everyone had conveniently forgotten, which I suppose is fitting, seeing as this arbitrary calendar-mark holiday is representative of new beginnings.

Or abrupt and cataclysmic endings, according the rather pessimistic rock.

But even for all of the rock's very rational dread, the grandfather didn't tremble in the slightest. Now, he did not know what the coming day would bring, but he had a slight leg-up on the rock. That morning, when Jonas looked down at his scrap of paper, it was not to write but instead to read and reread the instructions he'd been given. Whether or not he understood the plan was not certain, but he was entirely assured of what it was he had to do. A grand final performance perhaps, and he was glad the rock could be so supportive.

He took a deep breath in and sighed it back out again, and as a tribute to the place he now remembered as his only home, Jonas began a simple muttering which gradually turned into a song:

> "There lies a pass between the mountains,
> Amidst the caves and rocks and snow,
> And in that pass there lies our village,
> Where trav'lers never seem to go.
>
> But if those trav'lers should arrive there,
> We hope to God that they might know
> That if they do not mind the rules,
> Then they shall reap just what they sow;
>
> For when six rules up and shatter,
> Then we shall surely drown in woe,
> Unless we all can work together,
> And prideful men start eating crow…"

Jonas planted his bare feet back on the cold ground and patted the rock twice in thanks. He folded the instructions three times and tucked the little rectangle into the rope that was his belt. From the same belt he drew a pen, an old cragged number, sharp and hooked. The tip of this specimen had clearly not seen ink for years, namely forty-seven, which apparently was long enough to fall in love, start a family, raise a daughter, cherish a grandchild, and live a truly blessed—if somewhat forgetful—life.

Timelines and accurate accounts were unimportant to Jonas; the story Hephaestus had told would have meant very little to him, but he knew that the gold-engraved JT had something to do with himself, and even for all he had tried to forget, there were traces of a former life which could not be struck from memory.

So when he arrived back at Julian's cottage that morning, the grandfather paused just after the door, took out the decades-dry pen and scratched a long line through *Rule 7 – DON'T PLAY GOD!* With the list completed, Jonas nodded in satisfaction. It seems that some things are too ingrained in a person to ever be lost. I don't know if his supposition was accurate, but I should point out that if asked fifty years prior, Jonas would have claimed that his brother, Solomon, had had been the original writer of the seven cardinal rules of traveling merchants.

Where the two other merchants were at that moment was anyone's guess. However, as the town began to wake up, collectively groggy from trying to sleep with one eye open, the outsiders were indeed the least of their worries. Dozens of families, armed with ready-on-the-tongue words and much harsher attitudes began to collect, as water droplets forming pools and puddles, and each group began to advance its way to the town square, growing tighter in ranks and more unified in spirit.

With steady streams of citizens crossing all three bridges, walking along or beside the paths, no one bothered to notice or care how the crew and servants were slipping their way among the advancing crowds.

No one saw the flashes from hand mirrors. No one smelled the faint dusty smoke of lit matches. No one heard Fletcher whisper to Trenton, "At least it's cloudy today," from deep within one of the clusters. And finally, once they had gotten to the square, no one knew what to do.

They stood silently, eyeing each other, some of them threateningly, but even the ringleaders had no idea where to start. Whether they had come to protest the nobles, or the travelers, or the witness of the obscenities, or something else altogether, every man, woman, and sleepily-confused child said nothing.

The silence was broken by one young woman, whom nobody had even realized was absent. Samantha, running from the direction of her house with Cletus on her heels, was yelling, "Father! Father!" And it took a good fifteen seconds for people to realize that she was looking for him.

"Where is he?" she shouted at no one in particular. "He's not in the house; does anyone know where he is?"

As her genuine surprise and fear began to register, they murmured amongst themselves, asking, *Where is the Libburus? Why isn't he here? Is he coming?* Soon accusations of *It was you! Where have you taken him? Those ruffians have absconded with our Libburus!* sprang to their tongues. But as there were not enough people to blame and only two individuals who could possibly dream of such a course of action, the townsfolk were about to turn upon the traveling merchants when Hephaestus himself strode into the square.

"Mister Bordolo! You have gone too far; I say stand and show yourself or prove that is was you who—"

"Me?" came the voice of the indignant Baron. He broke through a few rows of villagers and opened his arms to show his innocent self. "I have not done anything of the sort—Why don't you tell us why *you* took him?"

"Oh, really Mister Bordolo?"

"Yes!" The Baron returned, advancing on the lord of merchants and into the nearest available clearing. "After all, you're the one with the agenda!"

And as Hephaestus protested this, Samantha found Sabrina and, trying not to panic, asked where their father was. When Sabrina replied that she didn't know, Samantha said, "Then where's Julian? Have you seen him yet?"

Sabrina was about to point him out, but someone in the crowd screamed loudly, turning all of their heads. Hephaestus was saying, "That's the last straw Mister Bordolo," but the words didn't register nearly as much fear as the sword being drawn from the cane. And as the Baron drew to match, the crowd gasped and recoiled. Raul winced for memory's sake, and Julian, inconspicuously preserved in a crowd across the way, shut his eyes tightly, having been warned of what was coming.

A great *BANG!* seemed to shake the air, and the blinding flash that accompanied it bid several Isleans to cower and cover their eyes. Several screamed, many parents hid their children, and many who perceived the flash as coming from the north tried to run in the opposite direction.

But before anyone had made it three steps, an even more sudden and more blinding flash set up in the air to the south! This one was red and giant and looked as if it should rain fire down on any who might be caught below it. A third and a fourth went off even more quickly, one green, another gold, each more terrifying and sinister than the last, all on the edges of the square, making each Islean force his way toward the center, where Meredith had come upon the two dueling men.

"What are you doing?" she demanded.

Looking more shaken than her, both shook their heads frantically. "It's not us!" insisted the Baron.

"Put away the wands!" Meredith cried. "Or else it'll come back!"

Many of the nearby people began nodding vigorously, and soon an unintelligible mass of confused and scared demands were coming from all sides for the Baron and Hephaestus to relinquish their weapons.

"Alright! Yes, yes," replied a frantic Hephaestus, sheathing his blade. The Baron, apparently scared speechless, followed suit.

But even as they complied, the angry sky lit up again. Cries of "What's happening?" "Who's doing this?" and "What does it want?" rang out.

"Quick, this way!" came another voice. Looking up, they saw Trenton. And he began to run north, and many followed immediately. Some noticed that all of the flashes seemed to be occurring above and around the square and tried to depart as well, but if they went toward the east gate or any of the noble houses to the south, another burst of fire in the sky above would herd them in the opposite direction.

Somewhere in the mad hullabaloo, Samantha found Julian and took his hand, and he led her and a whole slew of people over the river, then up toward the falls as well, avoiding every blast happening around them.

Fletcher, his two horns on straps slung from his shoulders, hung back with the skeptical stragglers who remained in the square, announcing, "These flashes can't hold us back! Here, watch!"

A protest of "Wait! No!" came from a broad man in a Hephaestus suit, but Fletcher continued into the southern boarder nonetheless.

He nearly assuaged the fears of those watching, when he turned back to smile and say, "See?" but a quick burst behind his back silhouetted him and almost looked to scorch him out of existence in its bright light. Fletcher bellowed in something of fear and pain, and suddenly there were no more stragglers. Fletcher followed the lot, chasing after them with flash-bangs popping up around his ankles. Everyone must have either been too blinded or preoccupied to see him pouring powder out of the white bang-horn and onto the steel strikepad he had sewn into his sturdy leather gloves. When he tripped out of blind disorientation, Gus ran back to scoop him up, and the last swarm continued, up over the hills and across the north bridge and the river rocks.

Children were crying and clinging as the crowds came to intercept each other, becoming again a massive herd heading toward the vertical rock wall at the back of the village. The Baron and Hephaestus were near the front of the lot, and when they saw the fire, they promptly put on the brakes. Several people tripped over themselves or each other, but none wanted to go closer to another fire, especially because lying directly between them and the fire was the still body of their Libburus.

There were gasps, and wails of despair, and many people unable to see or too young to understand asking what he was doing there. Some people asked what, others why, and others how, but no answer was given.

Though the Baron and Hephaestus held fast, Trenton and Ten ha rushed out of the crowd and began to examine Sebastian.

"He's still breathing!" Ten ha declared.

"Why won't he wake up?" someone asked.

"What happened to him?" said another.

And as Samantha reached the front of the group, she started to go to her father, but Julian held her back. She tried to fight his grip at first, but he urged, "It's okay. Trust me."

For the few seconds over which they surveyed the body of their leader, not one person thought, "Good riddance," or "We're better off without him." At that moment, the citizens of the Isle just wanted their friend back. Well, that and for the sky to stop setting itself ablaze.

But as more citizens tried to approach, something startling happened: the color of the bonfire changed, the smoke grew greater, and behind it rose a most-startling hooded and cloaked four-armed beast whose shadow was cast on the rock wall. Some screamed and attempted to run, but fireworks blocked their way again. The creature gestured forward, the shadow looming over the Libburus, from which Ten ha and Trenton retreated.

"It was in the stars!" And as people turned to look, many recognized Dietrich saying, "The stars last night said that we would be punished for what we're doing. This beast must be here to claim its due!"

And as people began to realize that Sebastian was the due, the screams became moreso.

The grandfather, shoeless and cold, having worked his way to the center of the throng, took in the deepest breath he could, and with a voice that seemed loud enough to cross oceans, the retired minstrel silenced even the bangs in the sky with one simple quotation. "Heaven is not always angry when he strikes, but most chastises those whom he likes!"

The Baron and Hephaestus, looking at the giant shadow from which the town was cowering, called out in unison, "We're sorry!" and the creature vanished.

There was suddenly dust in the air, and the fire was gone, and most everyone in the front half of the crowd had to cover his or her moth to keep from coughing. In all of the fuss, it was hard to notice the wet rug, filled with dirt that had been sent over the cliff and onto the fire, thrown by the two largest sling-throwers in Adleship Isle. As Pigby and

Clemens ducked out of sight, anyone who did look would be
disappointed. And with all of the dust and smoke flying about on the
ground level, it was even easier to miss Geru jumping off of Lionel's
shoulders, shedding the long hooded cloak, and both plunging into the
lower falls' basin.

On the other hand, it was not difficult to notice the quick glance
that the Baron and Hephaestus shared, accompanied by a nod of relief
and accomplishment.

When someone asked, "What happened?" Oswald was ready:

"I say, isn't it obvious?" he said as he made his way to the front
of his audience. "God has seen how you are changing this town—the two
of you," and his pointing at the Baron and Hephaestus was met with
eager nods, "and everyone else who has been angry, or bitter, or
vengeful, or proud. Clearly God is talking to you. Now will you listen?"

Some people wanted to object to what he was saying, but as the
realization sunk in with greater and greater weight, not one of them could
think of a way to oppose him. Clearly it was god or some divine power,
whether from the stars or that beast—whoever he was supposed to be.
Obviously, no person could create those lights in the sky, and even if they
could, who could it possibly be? Both Hephaestus and the Baron were
accounted for, and the blue girl, and Julian, and even Lance as neighbors
came to recall who had been in the square.

The Isleans looked between one another, but did not know what
to say. Surely there must have been something wrong for them to become
so upset with each other during the past few days, but it was difficult to
figure out exactly what.

And as Oswald stood expectantly, wanting for someone else to
speak, it was Julian who decided to take the proverbial baton.

"You're right, sir." He let go of Samantha's hand to stand before
the others, and even before he began, the Baron, Hephaestus, and anyone
else who had been given assignments glanced between one another to
check whether or not this had been part of their plan. "It's time to
apologize, and to put things right. Which is why I'm going to stay living
in my cottage, I'm going to keep right on being your carpenter, and I
won't be a noble anymore." There were a few gasps and looks of awe,
and Samantha put a hand to her mouth, but it seemed that the biggest
surprises were already over.

After the moment or two it took for his sentiment to take hold,
most of the villagers were nodding. "Now we've a village to run," young
Julian went on, "and sure, it may not be as big or as crowded or even as

interesting at the Big Out There, but it's ours, and we've been doing it well for generations, so why stop now? I mean, take a look around you, everyone." And they did. "You may have come to the square this morning in separate groups, but now that we're here, we're all together, mixed around between the young and the old, the farmers and the herders—" and making sure eye contact with Eugene added, "and east and west sides of the river. Can't you see? We're still the same town we always were; we just needed a reminder of what we were about to let slip away, but this, right here, in how we'll band together again, and ask forgiveness instead of making demands, that's what'll keep this town grand, and that's how we're going to start the new year."

And that morning, fate was on our hero's side, for as soon as he'd finished, before anyone could even begin to clap, the Libburus, still lying on the ground behind him, coughed some of the dust off of his face and stirred himself awake.

"Father!" sounded from both daughters, who rushed forward to collect him, followed by Hephaestus, and soon after by Cletus and Clara.

And as Sebastian began to sit up, with no impairment of movement aside from dizziness, he asked, "Did I miss something?" and "Dear, dear, have I fallen asleep outside again?"

As this was evidence enough for the Isleans, they began to cheer, or hug one another, or simply be flooded in relief. From on the ridge, Clemens patted Pigby heartily on the back, and on the other side of the pool, the dripping Geru and Lionel contentedly shook hands. And Julian caught the eye of his friend the Baron, who smiled broadly at him, more proud than he'd ever been of anyone in his fantastic life, sporting tears in the corners of his eyes which he was not yet ready to wipe away.

"Do you remember what happened, sir?" Cletus asked of his Libburus.

"I remember a bittersweet smell," he admitted, "but no."

Without making eye contact with the others, Sabrina made sure that the brush-bomb was still tucked securely into the bustle of her dress.

"Hephaestus! Hephaestus!" said Sebastian, grabbing the lord of merchants' forearm, "Tell me: am I alright?"

"You're doing quite well, my friend. In fact, you've just made everyone comfortable and happy again."

"Oh, really?" The Libburus had to survey the smiles of the crowd around before he could actually accept this credit. "Well, good for me then!"

STOUMBOS

LXXII – The Tales of His Godfather

To commemorate their achievements that morning and to give a blessing for the new year, the people of Adleship Isle had an impromptu ceremony during which Hephaestus and the Baron Pan Bordolo were required to throw their respective weapons off the edge of the world. Thereafter, they filtered back up to the square to celebrate their newly re-recognized peace and friendship and, of course, the first of January. The few instruments in the Isle were brought forward and stirred into a jovial melody to accompany dancing, relaxation, and—once Simeon could haul the batch over the bridge—beer.

The rivals and the lad remained overlooking the edge of the world, where they had said they'd meet if all went well. (To be fair, they had said they would meet there regardless, but no one had wanted to admit the possibility of defeat.) Of course, once they were there, it seemed that there was very little to say but congratulations and thanks.

However, even with everything that had succeeded, the Baron kept finding one raincloud hanging over Julian's future, for which he profusely apologized.

"It's alright, sir," Julian repeated. "I know how she feels now, and I can wait if I need to, until she's not in the Libbur-house anymore. And what's more, she understands why I chose to."

"Even so," continued the compelled Baron, "you do know that you can always leave with me when I go, and take her with you."

Julian laughed lightly. "Pan, I'm never going to leave this place. It's my home. And I'm going to go have New Year's with my neighbors." He shook the Baron's hand, and then Hephaestus', telling the latter, "You know, I was really glad when you threw away that cane."

"Hmm?" came Hephaestus, "Oh, yes, well for the good of Adleship Isle, you know."

As Julian walked away from the two men, both regarded him, but not to acknowledge how much they had learned from him or how much he had matured in just over a week's time. No, they merely watched and waited for the moment when he was out of earshot so the Baron could turn to Hephaestus and say, "You didn't really chuck your cane, now did you?"

"Oh that, well..." trailed the crafty lord of merchants. "Trenton made the switch. The real one is safely back in my wagon; I carry two fakes just in case of this sort of thing."

The Baron regarded his colleague with more amusement than mockery. "This sort of thing can happen more than once?"

Hephaestus nodded with a wry smirk. "I used to have *three* facsimiles. Ah, and here comes your thin man."

"Ahoy there!" called Fletcher as he approached.

"Good morning, Fletcher," greeted the Baron, "I heard your performance was quite the success."

"Oh, boss, it was thrilling! But see, I've never used the flash-bang that many times that close before—It got me so blind that I actually fell over and had to be rescued."

Hephaestus, the little more stern, cut into the thin man's daring tale with, "And the notes."

"Here." Fletcher pulled the scraps of paper out of his back pocket and handed them one-at-a-time to Hephaestus as he tallied off their agents' assignment cards. "This is Clemens, Meredith, Dietrich, Sabrina, and Jonas. Meredith told me she'd been pretty shaky on her cue, but—"

"I thought she managed marvelously," interrupted the Baron.

"They all did," added Hephaestus. "Have you a match, Sir Baron?"

"That I do." The Baron struck a light and held it under the papers until the corner caught. "That'll do," he breathed as Hephaestus let the pieces fall to an ashy heap.

"And you're sure all of the fireworks have been cleaned up?" asked Hephaestus. "No mounts left lying around?"

"Trenton gave me the good-to-go, boss," Fletcher replied. "Most of your men cleared their launch sites before the Isleans even made it back from the falls."

"Good," said Hephaestus, and as the Baron had nothing more for him, Fletcher opted to excuse himself.

"Well, Happy New Year, sirs," he said with a quick salute before bounding off, likely to catch one of Elke's newly-baked batches of muffins.

"You see, he's very nice if he doesn't feel animosity from you," the Baron said, watching after his favorite fool.

Hephaestus humbly chuckled. "Yes, well, I'll think twice before I talk down to a stranger again. Who knows: he could turn out to be a peer. Or a superior, *Sir Baron*." And though the man had said it playfully, the Baron could tell Hephaestus turned any mockery against himself and his former attitude.

The Baron didn't let himself sigh before saying, "You know, I think I could stand to be called 'Mister Bordolo' for another week or two."

Chancing to light up with hope, the other asked, "Do you mean that?"

"Well, it's been working this long..."

"I must say, I'm not certain what we're going to do with our time if we're being friendly until the blizzard lets up."

The Baron shrugged. "I suppose we'll relax. Are you a chess player by chance?"

"I am actually."

"Well, there you go." As he looked up at the town, where he could hear music and dancing—and assumed that the larger *thump*s must have come from Pigby—the Baron shook his head in frustration. "I don't know what to do about the boy. He can't elope, he wants to stay here, and by all natural laws he should have the right to marry that girl, but he can't. I can't see sitting for weeks and not helping him find some way to get around the rule, but after everything else we've been through?" Hephaestus and the Baron shared raised eyebrows at one another.

"Well, maybe if you didn't outright break the rule..." mused Hephaestus toying with the braid in his beard, "I seem to recall you saying something about Ten ha, and her being your ward."

"I'm her foster parent, yes, but that's neither here nor there."

"No, no, what I'm saying is, you are of English nobility by blood, and Julian—well, he's an orphan." And as he could see the Baron beginning to register, the lord of merchants made one more personal pride play. "And I, Mister Bordolo, unlike your Oswald, can legally officiate and notarize marriage, last rites, and *adoption*."

The Baron blinked three times and considered slapping Hephaestus with the glove in his back pocket. "You, sir, are a beautiful human being. Why didn't you tell me that before?"

"Well, obviously, I had the rules to preach," Hephaestus replied. "And I didn't believe you were of honorable blood in the first place."

The Baron consented to Hephaestus' reasoning. "Do you think the girl's father will go for it?"

"After he hears about the boy's speech, he'll stop at nothing to wed those two; and so long as Julian stays to his own house on his side of the river, I don't think the other citizens will make a peep."

"And Jonas?" wondered the Baron, squinting to see if he could make out the grandfather chap among the indistinguishable specks of Isleans.

"I think Jonas will just continue to do what he's always done, and for that, I won't feel guilty. In fact," he said, righting his posture and throwing his scarf over one shoulder, "I think I'll go join the others. We each deserve a victory muffin; what do you say?"

The Baron appreciated the genuine smile and invitation, but he resolved, "Not just yet. I think I'll stay a little while longer." And as Hephaestus graciously turned away to let him be, the Baron Pan Bordolo suddenly found himself asking, "Hephaestus, do you think we did the right thing? Playing god and all, just to get this place back to the way it was?"

Hephaestus considered the Baron's words, but as he came to look over him, the lord of merchants noticed that his rival's hand was nervously resting on the same breast-pocket that contained the tales of his godfather. And so with a more reassuring and fatherly smile than our Baron Pan Bordolo had seen in quite some time, Hephaestus told him, "The Baron would be proud." With that, he left, his ornamented cape swishing behind him, a testament to the grace and glory he would continue to carry.

Our Baron, smirking, turned his gaze back to the horizon, the peaks just barely sticking out of the shelves of fog, and the sun's timid rays worming their way through the overcast winter sky. And yet the Baron Pan Bordolo felt warm, quite warm indeed. So warm in fact that he did not even bother to apply another coat of Liverpool Silver to his ringed mustache before returning to the square to celebrate New Year's Day.

Epilogue – The Seventh Sturdy Servant

It took twenty-two days for Geru (and Hephaestus' weather-man, Cooper) to agree that the blizzard had gone down enough for them to depart, over which time the town continued to remain peaceful and happy, and in many ways the behavior of the merchants and their fellows needed not change. Pigby continued to develop friendships, Fletcher continued to circulate their wares, and Lance and Ten ha continued their delightful affair, though with a little more discretion by way of a well-insulated tent stationed beside the upper falls. The Baron and Hephaestus continued to get better at chess, so good in fact that they had to have shouting matches about the intricate strategies at least once a day. And the grandfather continued to keep his daily appointment with the rock.

Now neither crew broke any more rules, at least as far as the Baron and Hephaestus were willing to acknowledge, as they had discovered that the rule breach itself was not nearly so damaging as making that breach known to the Isleans.

When Hephaestus agreed with this point in saying, "Ignorance is bliss," the Baron felt a need to postulate further:

"Yes, but only when you remain ignorant of your ignorance."

And most of the Isleans followed this pattern precisely, continuing to believe that some god had felt wronged and stepped in to put things right. After all, once they *were* right again, the townsfolk realized that they'd been happy all along and had no incentive to investigate further with no unrest to prick their curiosities. Even the few who had been given assignments had not known the full scope of the plan and decided to remain a little in the dark for their own sakes.

And Julian, who between Hey-Day and New Year's had observed more than he had ever thought possible, was more content and delighted than any to return to his old life, but for one exception.

Hephaestus had been right that Sebastian and Sabrina would be delighted by the prospect of making Julian a part of their family, and as news of Julian's courtship with the lady Samantha became more commonplace, most of the rest of the town seemed quite pleased with the notion as well. Meredith and Manny were overjoyed by their young friend's new fiancée, and even Raul, a slight limp courtesy of a sore side, came around enough to congratulate Julian before a week had passed.

The Baron's adoption of the boy came without ceremony or hoopla, and, as it smoothed out the final wrinkle in their arrangement, the Baron went immediately into wedding-planning mode—which Julian put a stop to.

"But why not get married right away?" the Baron asked.

"Because we'd be expected to start a family right away," Julian explained. "Maybe to move house, to draw up special plans or documents for Libbursing—I don't rightly know, but we'd like to wait. Besides, with everything that's gone on this year, I'm really not keen on another holiday, birthday, anniversary, or any cause for celebration. Let's talk about it next winter."

Of course, it had become commonly accepted that even though the Baron and Hephaestus would go in opposite directions once they hit the sea, they would reunite the next winter to return to the Isle, which meant that their leaving was not nearly as sad as it could have been. Even Ten ha and Lance, who would likely not be journeying with either merchant beyond England, had promised Miriam that they would come back to visit for Christmas.

Most of the Baron's crew asked at least one person if they should wish to leave their homes and join the ranks of traveling merchants' employees. But Clemens had a family, and Elke had Dietrich, and Dietrich had his house, and most everyone had an inarguable reason for staying. Especially Julian, who was asked by both merchants more than any other Adleship Islean.

The boy continued to say, "Thank you both, sirs, and I'll see you next year." He hugged his new father farewell and stepped back into the crowd, where Samantha was waiting to take his hand.

"Well, I suppose this is it," said the Baron, more to himself and Hephaestus than any of the townsfolk.

"Yes, we best be off while it's still light," added Hephaestus, and they both began to take their formations for the journey home, while their crews bid their final goodbyes to their closest friends.

A harshly-cleared throat bid them pause, and when they turned around to look, they saw one young man stepping out of the crowd, his wound having healed, and his gait once more straight and strong. "Actually, sir," said Raul, "if you wouldn't mind, I'd like to come with you."

Before Hephaestus had given an answer, Eugene shouted, "No!" and rushed forward to stop his son. "No, you will not leave—what about your town?"

And though his father was flustered to the point of provoking a fight, Raul remained serene as he said, "Sir, I'm a man now, and I want to find my place in this world… and I've discovered that it's not here. I'm not your next Libburus; I think you'll find someone who fits the description by the time Sebastian is ready to step down." And he looked to Julian, saying, "Julian, I'm happy for you both; really I am, and you've always done right by this place and by me." Turning back to his father, he concluded, "But I haven't, and it's time for me to go." He patted the hand that was holding his arm, which, to its owner's surprise, released.

Hephaestus watched the new man, and found that he was reminded of the teenaged Pip Heffer who set off to have adventures and live a richer life. So he beckoned Raul to "Come along," and the seventh sturdy servant accompanied them down the mountain. The people of the Isle watched until snow and distance had blurred the travelers completely from view.

Afterword

Hello. Yes, this is your narrator once again. It has come to my attention that *some* readers—not to imply you specifically—might be somewhat pernickety over the historical accuracy of this tale, and in this regard, I should very much like to 'come clean' as the phrase goes. I apologize in that I truly meant not to offend any of you, and took it as the storyteller's prerogative, but since I am simply racked with guilt, I shall come out and say it.

I would like to announce, before there is any more confusion or debate on the subject, that the mustache treatment called "Liverpool Silver" does not in fact exist and never has. Yes, I made it up as a means of accenting a character, belying the true nature of products at the time, and I am terribly, terribly sorry if in this I led any of you astray.

There. Well, I say I feel much better, don't you? Yes, I think I'll have a scone.

About the Author

Mike Jack Stoumbos is a high-school teacher and test-prep tutor from Washington state. In addition to teaching, he often works through his excess creative energy in partner dance, karaoke, and—of course—writing. Although Mike Jack had written and produced several plays, *The Baron Would Be Proud* is his first published novel. In fact, this story was first conceived as a musical, (and perhaps one day an adaptation will find its way to the stage).

He lives with his wife and their parrot in a place that's a little less remote than Adleship Ilse, and he continues to write a variety of fiction and non-fiction. Of everything that he has written *The Baron* is still his favorite to re-read, and he will forever be jealous of the Baron's mustache.

The Seven Cardinal Rules of Traveling Merchants

I - NO FALSE PRETENSE: You may not—upon entering a new town, territory, province, or principality—claim any untrue purpose for your arrival.

II - NO MISLEADING SALES: You may not lie about the functionality or value of items for sale to primitive or modern persons.

III - NO KILLING: You may not kill any native inhabitants unless first attacked.

IV - NO INSTIGATING: You may not purposefully provoke native inhabitants to attack so you may kill them, and thus comply with the self-defense caveat of rule three.

V - DON'T DATE THE DUCHESS: You may not sleep with influential men or women.

VI - DON'T CROWN KINGS: You may not rearrange the political or social structure of any nation or community for your or anyone else's benefit.

VII - DON'T PLAY GOD! You may not—having acquired a greater knowledge of science and superstition—take advantage of any people by pretending to be a god.